# Corambis

*Ace Books by Sarah Monette*

MÉLUSINE

THE VIRTU

THE MIRADOR

CORAMBIS

# Corambis

Sarah Monette

ACE BOOKS, NEW YORK

**THE BERKLEY PUBLISHING GROUP**
**Published by the Penguin Group**
**Penguin Group (USA) Inc.**
**375 Hudson Street, New York, New York 10014, USA**
Penguin Group (Canada), 90 Eglinton Avenue East, Suite 700, Toronto, Ontario M4P 2Y3, Canada
(a division of Pearson Penguin Canada Inc.)
Penguin Books Ltd., 80 Strand, London WC2R 0RL, England
Penguin Group Ireland, 25 St. Stephen's Green, Dublin 2, Ireland (a division of Penguin Books Ltd.)
Penguin Group (Australia), 250 Camberwell Road, Camberwell, Victoria 3124, Australia
(a division of Pearson Australia Group Pty. Ltd.)
Penguin Books India Pvt. Ltd., 11 Community Centre, Panchsheel Park, New Delhi—110 017, India
Penguin Group (NZ), 67 Apollo Drive, Rosedale, North Shore 0632, New Zealand
(a division of Pearson New Zealand Ltd.)
Penguin Books (South Africa) (Pty.) Ltd., 24 Sturdee Avenue, Rosebank, Johannesburg 2196,
South Africa

Penguin Books Ltd., Registered Offices: 80 Strand, London WC2R 0RL, England

This is an original publication of The Berkley Publishing Group.



FIRST EDITION: April 2009

Library of Congress Cataloging-in-Publication Data

Monette, Sarah.
Corambis / Sarah Monette.—Ace hardcover ed.
p. cm.
ISBN 978-0-441-01596-2
1. Wizards—Fiction. I. Title.

PS3613.O5246C67 2009
813'.6—dc22

2008054341

PRINTED IN THE UNITED STATES OF AMERICA

10 9 8 7 6 5 4 3 2 1

For
Joan D. Vinge
and
Ellen Kushner

# Part One

# Chapter 1

## *Kay*

One by one we walked the labyrinth beneath Summerdown, and one by one we came to the engine, dark and cold, at its heart.

We each carried a lantern, and when we reached the central chamber, we hung them on hooks, spreading light into the corners, so that by the time the last man entered—Dennis Rigby, seventeen, and as devoted to Gerrard as any soldier twice his age—the engine was pitilessly illuminated, all its claws and spurs and strange stained gears.

The light also showed Gerrard, looking better than he had for nearly two indictions, the lines of tension that marked him even in sleep finally eased, his eyes bright and clear and untroubled. He stood beneath one of the lanterns, consulting a sheaf of notes, and when the Margrave of Benallery asked him if he was sure he knew what he was doing, he laughed, as brilliant and warm as a summer's day, and said, "I know I do the right thing, Walter. Will that hold thee?"

Benallery smiled back—my friend Benallery, who had not smiled since Beneth Castle fell to the Corambins—and Gerrard called across the chamber to Mark and Robert Easton to bring him the blessed knife and candles they had procured, with some difficulty, from the intended in Howrack.

I knelt beside Gerrard as he began copying a chalk diagram from his notes onto the floor and said, as quietly as I could, "Would be happier an the magician-practitioner had come with us."

He graced me with a smile and said, "I know that, Kay. Didst not tell him so, and loudly?"

"Gerrard—"

"Peace, Kay." He touched my hand where I braced myself against the floor, and his warmth gathered behind my breastbone. "He hath the right to make his own choices. Thou knowst I have never disagreed with the Corambins about that."

"I know," said I. "And I do not begrudge him his—"

Gerrard laughed again, drawing everyone's attention. "Thou liar," he said fondly. "Of course thou begrudg'st him his choice. Wouldst force him to walk the labyrinth at swordspoint an I let thee."

"But thou wilt not," I said, daring the familiarity, and was rewarded by a moment of Gerrard's full attention.

"No. I will not. Thou art a soldier, and I honor thee, but it is no victory to force all men to live by soldier's rules. We must allow others to choose their own lives"—and the twinkle lit his eyes again—"even when we most disdain their impudent folly."

I could not help laughing. "Yes, my prince," I said and stood to direct the others into the places indicated by the magician-practitioner's notes.

Gerrard had discussed his plan with me, with Benallery, with the other men about him whose judgment he trusted as much as their loyalty. Was a desperate undertaking, and so we all said, but Gerrard merely nodded and invited us to propose a better plan, one that would ensure Caloxa's independence without further loss of life.

We could not, and all of us, whether soldiers or courtiers, had been strategists since the cradle. Caloxa was losing the war; Corambis had more men, better supplies, stronger magic. She was not weakened, as my own Rothmarlin was, by generations of fighting bandits and savages in the mountains. She was not contending with forty indictions of subservience, nor with those who had decided they preferred servitude to freedom. If we were to succeed now, it could not be in direct combat.

Thus, the engine.

How, exactly, Gerrard had learned of it, I knew not. His mother's family held margravate over the area; perhaps he had been told nursery tales of the beast beneath the down which would waken and save Caloxa in her hour of greatest need. The labyrinth was common knowledge, though no one would walk it. The intended in Howrack told us that the labyrinth was *verlain*, a word he had most certainly not learned at the Theological College in Wildar. Was an old word, a country word, meaning "forbidden," meaning "sacred" or sometimes "unclean," meaning "that which we do not touch."

Gerrard and I and a magician from Barthas Cross had walked the labyrinth. We had found the beast—the engine. The magician had squeaked and stammered, but in the end he had figured out how to wake it. He had given Gerrard notes, though he was too craven to walk the labyrinth a second time. He professed not to know what the engine would do when woken; Gerrard was not worried. I was, but Gerrard was right that we had no choices left, nothing but this engine between us and despair. Gerrard believed it to be worth the risk, worth the sacrifice that might be asked of him, and I could not doubt him.

We took our positions; Gerrard had allowed me the place at his left hand, to guard him. Dennis Rigby stood to his right, his loyalty and love shining out of him as brightly as any candle flame. Gerrard read the magician's notes one last time, then folded them away and began the ritual that would wake the engine of Summerdown.

It required blood, and Gerrard gave it blood, his brightness joining the other, darker stains. It required fire, and he gave it fire, dripping the wax from the blessed candles carefully in the places the magician had specified. It required breath, and he gave it breath, stepping fearlessly into the center of the engine's splayed glory to breathe upon the small shining plate that alone of the rods, the gears, the wires and armatures, was untouched by the tarnishing force of passing indictions. The engine began to hum, a deep boneaching sound, and Gerrard turned his head to smile at me.

I saw his smile, and I wanted, with the sudden pitiless clarity of a lightning bolt, to drag him away—out of the engine's maw, of the labyrinth's heart, out of the cold and sleepless dark beneath Summerdown. But even as I opened my mouth to shout to him, it was too late. The engine was awake.

It *threshed.*

Gerrard was the first to die, impaled from five different directions at once on the engine's taloned arms; he had no time to scream, not even time to realize the terrible magnitude of his mistake. I would have been the second, except that I was already moving, trying to reach him. A thing like a spider's leg, jointed and clawed, bristling with thorns of metal and bone, lashed out at the place where I had been standing, but I was at that moment just far enough inside its reach to duck the blow that would have taken my head off as clean as a sword cuts a dandelion stem. I might have been screaming; an I was, I could not hear myself.

Dennis Rigby died instantly. So did Peter Varnham and the Easton brothers. Benallery survived the first cut, but he made the mistake of trying to fight the engine, and the arm disemboweled him on the backstroke.

I could not reach Gerrard. The small shining plate was burning brighter and brighter, and I could not look away from Gerrard's body, draped around it like a solstice garland. Brighter and brighter, and the arms, dripping blood, were returning to their original positions. Brighter, and Gerrard's dead eyes were staring at me, all beauty lost in death. Brighter, and I could not reach him.

The light exploded into my head, and the last thing I knew before the darkness was that we had failed.

## *Mildmay*

I knew that river was going to be trouble the moment I laid eyes on it.

The one map we had said it was called the St. Grainne, and if there were any bridges or fords or anything, it didn't mention 'em. Seeing as how there was only sort of a road, I hadn't exactly been hopeful, and, well, maybe there *had* been a bridge once, but there sure as fuck wasn't now.

I looked sideways at Felix before I could stop myself, but I got lucky and he didn't notice. Most of the time these days, he didn't notice nothing, but then sometimes he *did*, and didn't matter what it was, I guarantee you I'd done it wrong. And powers and saints, he could skin a turtle with that tongue of his. Now, I mean, I didn't like that other Felix none, the one that didn't say nothing and didn't notice nothing and didn't care about nothing—he spooked me the fuck out, if you want the truth—but at least he wasn't *trying* to make me mad enough to punch him. But it was all one or the other. I could have a statue or I could have a pissed off wolverine, and until Felix got his head out of his ass, those were all the choices I got.

Before you say anything, I'd *tried* to think of a third choice. I'd laid awake at night trying, going around and around like a grist-mill donkey, and as far as I could see, there just wasn't one. Talking to him wasn't no use, because either he was in that horrible dead place where he didn't see me and didn't hear me, even if he nodded in all the right places and did what he was told, or he was fucking evil and anything I said—*anything*—he'd just use to pick a fight. And I couldn't leave him. Never mind the binding-by-forms, bailing on him would've been the same as killing him. He was tearing himself up inside, and I knew it, even if he'd've set himself on fire before he admitted it to me. But I couldn't help with that, not without he let me, so all I could do was stay with him and try to keep him safe and try to help him get to where he thought he had to go.

Now personally, I was pretty sure Lord Stephen wasn't going to be sending letters or nothing to find out if we'd done what he said and gone to the hocuses in Esmer, and I was furthermore pretty sure that if we just disappeared, he'd be so fucking grateful to be shut of Felix, he wouldn't ever ask. But Felix didn't see things that way. The first really big fight we'd had, in this putrid little armpit of a town called Erbeche, about three days north of Mélusine, had been because I'd been fed up with trying to find somebody who'd even *heard* of Corambis, much less had the first fucking clue about how to get there, and I'd said, why didn't we just tell Lord Stephen to fuck himself and go to Vusantine or something.

Felix hit the fucking roof.

You would've thought—everybody in Erbeche probably *did* think—I'd said, why didn't we go find a sheep and take turns fucking it. I can't even list all the things he said I was accusing him of being, and I really think if he'd thought he could get me to go along with it, he would've challenged me to a duel. But I ain't a gentleman, and duels are just fancy knife fights and just as fucking stupid. It was for sure the last time I made that suggestion, though, even as a joke. He thought he had to go to Esmer, fine. It wasn't like I had anything better to do. It wasn't even like I had some better place in mind.

Small favors: from what I could gather, which wasn't very fucking much, Corambis had been settled, *way* back in the day, by the same sort of people that settled Vusantine and Mélusine and Castabella Myria, and we'd sound weird to them but not, you know, like we'd come up from the wrong side of the world. We'd probably be better off than we'd been in Skaar even, where they speak this crazy-ass dialect that sounds half Tibernian and half Norvenan, and no matter which half you pick, you're wrong.

So we went north, and north some more, and you know, I hadn't even known you could go this far north and not hit the end of the world, but we kept going, and there just kept being more world in front of us. And then there were the mountains. I remembered how back in Ardring, I'd got a mercenary to draw a map for me, along of how the Mirador's maps weren't worth the paper and ink they were made with once you got north of Fiddermark in Skaar, and we didn't have money to get a better one, even if I could've found a mapmaker I trusted farther than a cat could sling a carthorse, which I couldn't. So what I had for a map was what that mercenary with his long braided mustaches had drawn for me on the back of the least awful of the Mirador's maps, and then additions and corrections from anybody else I met who seemed to have half a fucking clue. "Big fucking mountains," he'd said about the Perblanches. "You can't miss 'em."

And, well, he was right about that.

It'd taken me a couple days even to understand how big they were. I mean, you got to understand, I'd never *seen* mountains before, although I knew stories about them, bunches of 'em. But I'd always just sort of thought, okay, big hills. And that was wrong. That was completely fucking wrong. The Perblanches were *not* big hills. They were big fucking mountains, and if I ever met that mercenary again, I was buying him a beer. So we'd got to 'em, and then we'd got over 'em, and now we were coming down the other side, and that was how we'd ended up here with this river and no way across it except the hard way. It wasn't as wide as the Sim, but it was deep, and the rocks that stuck up and made it look like maybe we could get across were all uneven and not nearly big enough for comfort and even from here you could see they were slippery as fuck. Back in Maugery, the last decent-sized town before the mountains smacked you down on your ass and laughed at you, I'd traded both our horses for a mule. I'd been glad of it more than once, and I was glad of it now. She'd already shown as how she was part cat, and I figured I could trust her to get across without breaking a leg if there was any way in the world it could be done at all. Which was more than I was sure I could say about me.

I glanced at Felix again, pushing my luck, but he was staring at the river like he'd never seen one before. He had a thing about deep water, most especially the Sim, and I couldn't tell if the St. Grainne was flipping him out or if he was even seeing it.

Powers and saints, I hated the fuck out of this.

My heart was going too fast, and my mouth was dry. It took me two tries to get my voice working: "Felix?"

Wherever he was, it was a long ways off. I stood there and watched how much it hurt him to come back. "What is it *now*?" he said, kind of snarling, like this wasn't the first time I'd said a word to him all fucking day.

And, you know, all at once I'd had enough. I mean, I was sorry Gideon was dead and I was sorry Felix had gotten exiled and his life had gone to shit, but none of it was my fault. I was doing my best here, even if it wasn't good enough, and my life was also pretty lousy right at the moment, not that he cared or had even fucking noticed.

"Nothing," I said, snarling back. "Absolutely fucking *nothing*. You go on and be as nasty as you like, but I ain't putting up with it no more. Come on, Rosamund." And me and the mule started across the river. I didn't look at Felix because I didn't want to know. I was *done*.

About like I'd figured, the mule didn't have no trouble at all, aside from a couple of rocks that tilted and splashed her, which she didn't care for. Me, I didn't have it nearly so good. I'd been doing a lot better with my leg. I was using Jashuki, the cane Rinaldo'd given me, doing like he'd said and remembering I was lame. And okay, maybe I wasn't going to win no races except against a bunch of other crips, but my leg was stronger. On the other hand, it wasn't what you might call reliable, and this was exactly the sort of thing I shouldn't be trying to do with it. There was a point about two-thirds of the way across where I thought I was going to stick fast and that was going to be it.

"Mildmay!"

Well glory to the powers, he actually remembered my fucking name. "*What?*"

Pause. "Nothing. Just . . . be careful." Which was probably the nicest thing he'd said to me in three months.

"You got it," I said, and powers and saints, I was pathetic. Because it helped. All at once, I saw what to do so I wasn't stuck after all. When I finally made it to the bank and could turn around, Felix had started across. He looked pretty sick about it. I wondered about asking if he needed some help, but then I imagined how he'd say, *And just what do you think* you *can do?* and I kept my mouth shut. I may be slow, but I ain't a martyr going around asking to be kicked.

Felix got stuck at the same place I'd got stuck, and he was looking sicker and sicker. And maybe I was more a martyr than I wanted to think, because I opened my fool mouth and said, "You doing okay?"

I braced myself for him to take my head off, but he didn't. He was quiet a moment and then he said, "Not really. I think the stone under my left foot is working loose."

"And you ain't moved off it because . . ."

"Because I don't see any place to move *to*," he said through his teeth.

"Okay. Just hang on. I'm coming out—"

"Don't be an idiot. There's no point in having both of us drown."

"Yeah, but I can swim," I said, edging back out onto the rocks. "So maybe neither of us has to drown. Which I'd be okay with."

He made a noise that wasn't quite a laugh. "You're damnably pig-headed."

"And you ain't?"

"Point," he said. "Mildmay, please don't come any closer. I don't want to . . . that is, I don't think I can . . ." And then it was too late. I was close enough that I *saw* the rock tilt out from under him, and I saw a couple of ways I could maybe've saved myself if it'd been me, but it wasn't me, it was Felix, and he didn't have a chance. He went into the river with a splash that soaked me clear to the bone.

Which was just as well, because the next second I went in after him, same way I'd done under Klepsydra. Because I knew just exactly how much Felix couldn't swim.

And may Kethe preserve me from ever doing anything so fucking stupid ever again. Because *fuck* the water was cold, and my clothes were pulling me down and my hair was in my eyes and my bad leg was fixing to cramp just based on how *fucking cold* the water was. I thrashed after Felix and got a handful of his shirt collar just in time to drag him off smashing his skull open on a rock the size of a pumpkin. We both went under, and another rock got me hard across the back, hard enough I got a lungful of river water I really didn't want. So it was maybe half a minute before I could get myself sorted out, and that was when I realized Felix wasn't fighting—not me, not the river—and that was so fucking wrong, I thought for a second he had to be dead. I got myself braced somehow, anyhow, I didn't care, and hauled him up, a handful of hair and a handful of shirt. His eyes were closed, but I could see he was breathing, so that was okay, and then he said, not opening his eyes or nothing, "You should let me drown," and I just completely lost my shit.

I don't even know what I said—well, okay, what I yelled, top of my lungs, coughing and getting another breath and yelling some more, too fucking mad to stop, because it was either get the words out—all them horrible ugly words that I didn't even mean—or beat the shit out of him. Which I could do, but it wouldn't fucking help. Not with anything. But powers and saints, I wanted to, wanted to so bad it wasn't just the cold making me shake.

And then he was saying, "Mildmay, stop. Please." And instead of me holding him up, it was the other way around. "Please. I didn't mean it."

"Yes, you fucking did," I said, but I finally calmed down enough to get a real breath. Which hurt like swallowing knives, and after that I just kind of leaned on Felix for a minute, even though I was still pissed at him. Then he sighed, a deep sigh almost like a shudder, and said, "Let's not take root here."

We dragged each other up onto the bank, and then we just lay there awhile until Rosamund the mule found us and came to chew on my hair. "Back off, lady," I said, but I got up to dig through our stuff for dry clothes.

Felix, sitting and watching me, said, "Do you know the legend of St. Grainne?"

"Nope. You?"

"I feel certain she drowned saving the life of something stupid—a small child or possibly a sheep."

I wasn't sure how I was supposed to answer that. I tried, "I don't think they make you a saint for saving a sheep."

And for the first time in forever, it wasn't the wrong thing to say. He kind of grinned and said, "They do if it's stupid enough," and I knew it was his way of saying thanks.

So we changed clothes and got going again, and we didn't say nothing about the fit I'd pitched, and we didn't say nothing about why I'd pitched it, neither. But I thought Felix seemed more *there*, like maybe, ugly as it was, it was something he'd needed to know. That I cared enough to pitch a fit.

## *Kay*

I had fallen into darkness, and into darkness I awoke. I sat up slowly, raised my hand to my face; my fingers were shaking. Although I felt the crusted stickiness of dried blood in my hair and on my face, none of it seemed to be mine; was nothing obstructing my eyes. The lanterns had gone out, then. I was bitterly cold, and the reek of fresh blood was clogging my throat. I shoved my knuckles against my teeth, bit down hard.

I knew not which way I faced, could not remember where the door was. Even if I had, what point was there in moving? The hope of the descent of Hume was dead. We had already lost the war, save for this desperate chance. This desperate failure. Benallery was dead, and Robert Easton. Gerrard had slaughtered all our best generals along with himself.

Except, it seemed, for me. The thought was a bitter mockery. Was I now to raise Gerrard's banner and fight on for the honor of his infant son? Lead Caloxa into more death, more destruction? Would be for naught an I did, except that I could bring more men down with me, and surely that of all things was the one I did not need. An I wished to die, were quicker ways. Quicker and less cruel. I almost reached for my sword in that moment, but another thought stayed me, and I pressed the heels of my hands against my eyes. Blessed Lady, give me strength—someone had to inform the margraves and soldiers waiting in Howrack that Prince Gerrard Hume was dead, that the war was over and we had lost.

And was no one for that task save I.

I groped for my coraline. Did not require light to say the five stations of the meditation for the Lady, and I needed the clarity, the strength, the bulwark against the darkness and the blood.

I had reached the third station—*Lady of the gentle hands, of the patient weaving*—when I heard noises.

My first nightmare was that the engine was waking again, but a moment's breath-held tension reassured me on that head. Were living noises, footsteps and voices; the chink and clatter of metal came from swords and armor, not the engine's deathly arms.

Some of the margraves must have chosen not to wait.

They would have lanterns; although I had no desire to see the chamber of the engine, I could not help straining for the first hint of light. But was nothing and nothing, although the noises got louder, and I remembered the way the light had swelled and flowered with the approach of each of my friends. And then in the darkness, were voices—clear and plain and Corambin.

"Strewth, the smell!" "What did they do, butcher an entire flock?" "Oh." "Oh blessed Lady . . ." Someone was vomiting. And still was no light. I got to my feet, desperately, madly hoping for some change, some lessening of the blackness, some glimmer of light, a flash, a crack.

Nothing. Was nothing.

"Holy fuck! Someone's alive in there!"

Soldiers. Common Corambin soldiers. And I was blind. I remembered the searing light from the heart of the engine. Maybe was but temporary then, a light-dazzlement such as men suffered in a snowfield on bright days.

Even as I tried to comfort myself, I knew I lied.

"You! Who are you?" A commander's voice, high-pitched, a little nasal, but unmistakably upper class. I could not tell where he stood; the echoes of the engine's chamber bewildered me. "Do not draw your sword! Tell me who you are and what in the Lady's blessed name has happened here!"

An I drew my sword, would but be to fall on it. "I am the Margrave of Rothmarlin," said I, my voice harsh, grating almost to nothing on the last word. "And what has happened here is a catastrophe."

"Rothmarlin." Was a muttering among the soldiers that I could not hear clearly and did not try to. "Where is the Recusant?"

"Prince Gerrard is here. He is dead." Appalled, I heard myself continue: "They are all dead."

"All?"

"All save me."

"And how did you survive?" He sounded suspicious, and I could not blame him.

"Ill fortune."

More muttering. Would they kill me now, cut me down where I stood? Certainly was what I deserved.

The commander said, "My lord of Rothmarlin, I must ask you to surrender."

"You think you cannot defeat me?" Perhaps he had not yet realized that I was blind, but was only one exit from this room, and he had at least six men with him. The stories told about me were varied and wild—Gerrard had delighted in them—but not even the most gullible Corambin could possibly believe I was capable of fighting my way out of this killing pen.

"To end the Insurgence," said the commander. "If the Recusant is dead, and you alone of his commanders remain alive, then you must surrender your army."

Lady, blessed Lady, do you see me still? "They must be granted amnesty," I said.

"Amnesty for traitors?"

"They did but follow their margraves. We may be traitors to your Convocation, but they are not. Grant them amnesty and let them go. They will not rise again. I swear it."

"You will surrender your person," the commander said flatly.

I clenched my hands until my nails bit into my palms. "You will grant the pardon?"

"The margraves must present themselves for judgment."

Exculpating the common soldiers indicted the margraves. But we at least deserved it. We had chosen rebellion and commanded our liegemen to serve us. They had been caught between betrayal and betrayal and had chosen as best they could in their loyalty to their margraves and their love of Prince Gerrard.

Who was dead.

"Yes," said I. "We must be judged. I grant this. But the common soldiers will be pardoned?"

"Yes."

"Then I surrender my person to you—I regret I do not know who you are."

"No, since you will not face me. Are we northermen so far beneath your regard, my lord of Rothmarlin?"

"I cry your mercy. I cannot . . . I do not . . ." I heard my own rasping inhale, as a breath wanting to be a scream. "I am blind."

The Corambins were perfectly silent for a moment; I tried not to imagine them staring at me. Then their commander said, "I am the Duke of Glimmering, and I accept your surrender." Curtly, to his men, "Take him."

They came at me from just behind my right shoulder. I held still as best I could, but they were not satisfied until they had borne me to the cold stones of the floor and bound my hands behind me. My sword was wrenched from its scabbard, and hard fingers wrested my signet from my unresisting hand.

I bit a cry back to a grunt as a hand fisted in my hair and dragged my head to the side. Heat near my face, too near, and I tried to pull back but could not.

"He's blind right enough, Your Grace."

"Good," said the Duke of Glimmering. "Then bring him. We have a war to end."

## *Felix*

Before we left the Mirador, I had asked to see Gideon's body and been refused. I still wasn't sure why, whether Stephen had decreed it part of my punishment or whether the body was truly so hideous that someone had wrongly considered it a kindness. My last memory of Gideon was of his cold anger, his voice saying flatly in my head, *You have made your position perfectly clear, thank you.* It was no comfort to know that he might have been willing to forgive me, that he had gone to his death because Isaac Garamond had sent him a message purporting to be from me. I had not killed him, but I could not begin to count the ways in which it was my fault he was dead. Strangled and dead and lost.

I dreamed about his death, terrible dreams, true dreams. There was arguably no room in the Mirador I knew better than Malkar's workroom, the stench of the Sim, the red mosaic pentagram—ruined now, and I was glad of it. In my dreams, the cracked glass of the pentagram was lit by Isaac Garamond's cold, pale blue witchlights as he sat, smiling, in the middle of the room. Waiting.

Gideon comes in, checks as he sees Isaac. He is no fool, and there is a moment when he might escape, when he could simply step back out into the corridor and leave. Every time I dream this—*every* time—I beg him to do it, beg him to change events that have already happened. And every time, just before he makes that choice, Isaac rises and says, *I know I'm not who you were expecting to see. But I do have a message for you.*

Gideon is suspicious, but worse than that, he is jealous. I made him jealous, and I know I thought I had reasons, but now I don't know what they are—now, crying, screaming, desperate to make him hear me.

He can't, of course. I'm not there. I don't know where I was exactly when Gideon died—was I in Mehitabel's sitting room, watching the distrust in Vincent's eyes? was I already on my way to Isaac's room, to let him kiss me, touch me, fuck me?—but I was nowhere near here. Nowhere near.

Gideon raises his eyebrows at Isaac, inviting him to proceed. Suspicious, jealous, curious. I wonder if he suspected Isaac of being the Bastion's spy, but I can't ask. I wasted every chance I had.

*It's not actually from Felix,* Isaac says, as charmingly abashed as a boy caught lying. *But I had to speak to you, and I didn't think you'd come for me.*

Gideon gives him a quirk of a shrug, indicating that he's more right than wrong.

*Shut the door, would you?* Isaac says; probably his nervousness is even real.

And Gideon shuts the door.

If I'm lucky, I can make myself wake up at this point, but mostly I'm not lucky. Mostly, I get what I deserve: a perfect view as Isaac slips his garroting wire out of his pocket. He's telling Gideon some rodomontade, something about the Bastion and Major Goliath and dreams, high-pitched and rambling and he's using it as an excuse to move around the room, as if he were pacing, as if he were too frightened to stay still.

And what he wants—what he *must* want—happens. It becomes clear he's not going to be done anytime soon, and Gideon sits down in that chair so thoughtfully placed in the middle of the floor. I think he means it pointedly—he was very good at letting a gesture, an action, say what he couldn't—but it doesn't matter, because Isaac is ready, and he drops the wire over Gideon's head as neatly as a seamstress embroidering a flower.

I wish I could believe it was over quickly. I wish I could believe Gideon didn't know what was happening. But I watch him die, over and over again, night after night, and I know the truth. It wasn't quick. It wasn't painless. And Gideon knew. Gideon knew, and he fought, and he died. In my dreams he died again and again and again.

And I woke up in the mornings and wished I had died with him.

I moved only because Mildmay would not let me stay still.

Sometimes I hated him for it, for his insistence that I eat and bathe and have opinions about things, that I make decisions. I had savaged him more than once, said horrible, hateful things—because it was easy, because it was the fastest way to make him leave me alone—and how did he repay me? He saved my life again, as he had been doing since the day we met.

*Why do you bother?* I wanted to ask him, but I was afraid of sparking another conflagration. I was afraid of the power I had to make him that angry, angrier than I had ever seen him. And more afraid because it wasn't my own vile temper that had provoked him. He was angry *for* me as much as *at* me, and I didn't know how to deal with that. So I said nothing and despised my own cowardice.

But after we left the St. Grainne, we walked together, and Mildmay told me the story he'd gotten Rosamund's name from. It was long and very complicated; I wasn't at all surprised to find there was a labyrinth in it—along with a queen who was also an evil wizard, a winged lion, a magical sword, an oracular serpent, and a man made of brass. The story took all afternoon to tell, in Mildmay's slow, slurring drawl, and it was nearly dark when we came upon the ruined house.

It could never have been much of a building, one storey, two rooms, but the walls—what remained of them—were stone and had been carefully laid. There was nothing whatsoever left of the roof or floor, and the stones were blackened. "Fire," Mildmay said softly.

"A long time ago," I agreed.

"Yeah." He laughed, a short, harsh, barking noise with no humor in it. "Not like we could've saved anybody if we'd got down here last night."

Neither one of us was happy about fire. The mother whom we both barely remembered had died in a fire, *the* fire, the Fire of 2263—or, I was startled to discover I remembered, 19.7.2, the second indiction of the seventh septad of the nineteenth Great Septad after the Ascension of Tal-Marathat. Half the Lower City had burned. I had been eleven. Mildmay had been . . .

"How old were you?"

He knew exactly what I meant. For all the radical differences between us, all the ways in which we did not understand each other, on this subject, we might have been truly raised as brothers. "Five. The next Trials, Keeper made us all crowns out of trumps. Because we weren't dead."

*And how many Trials after that was it before she seduced you?* But I didn't ask that question, because I didn't want to have that fight again. I said, "This must be thirty years old, at least."

"Yeah," Mildmay said, looking at the trees standing in the middle of what had once been the larger room. He was stone-faced and seemingly uninterested, but he betrayed himself by asking, "What d'you think happened?"

"How should I know?" I said. "Probably the chimney caught on fire—that would happen to a house like this, wouldn't it?"

"Happens to tenements often enough." Pin-scratch frown between his eyebrows, quite visible in my witchlights. Then he shook himself. "Well, there's a stream, and it's flat, and the trees'll keep out the wind."

"And it's dark," I agreed.

"Yeah." We looked at each other, and didn't need to say what we were both thinking.

We did not put our camp within the boundaries of the ruined house; neither one of us would have been able to sleep, and we knew it. Mildmay took care of Rosamund in grim silence, and when he sat down by the fire, I could see he was still frowning.

To distract him, I said, "So why name her Rosamund?"

It took him a moment, but he said, "Well, Rosamund's lover—"

"Arbell," I said to prove to him that I'd been listening, and he gave me one of his sidelong looks that were as close as he allowed himself to get to a smile.

"Yeah. Well, it sounds a lot like Arvelle, which is what the locals call the mountain we just climbed over. And since Rosamund in the story tames Arbell when he's been enchanted into a beast—"

"Maybe our Rosamund will tame the mountain. Clever."

It was hard to tell, but I thought he blushed. Certainly, he waved a hand at me in a dismissive gesture.

"I'm perfectly serious," I said, a little offended. "It's very clever." And then, when he still wouldn't look at me, a horrible thought entered my head. "Mildmay, I've *never* thought you were stupid."

"You've said it a time or two." He was staring at his hands, with their scarred, broad knuckles, where they rested on his knees.

And I'd said it recently. *Get away from me, you stupid little rat.* The memory was abruptly, terribly vivid: standing in the hallway outside my suite, blood on his face, blood on my rings. Black, howling fury eating everything inside me. I'd wanted to hurt him, wanted it so badly I could feel it, the foreknowledge a bitter ache in the bones of my hands, in the tense muscles of my forearms.

And here was proof that I'd succeeded.

Guilt was like the taste of ashes. If I could not deny my own culpability, my own cruelty, I could at least indict a coconspirator: "And Kolkhis said it again and again. Am I right?"

"Let's not talk about her," he said, his voice gone flat, and he did meet my eyes then. Not defensive, not upset: simply telling me plainly and without dramatics to back off.

Six months ago, I probably would have pushed. Pushed until he fought, until one of us was yelling. Or maybe both. But I was desperate tonight to prove I could learn from my mistakes. "All right," I said. "But I *don't* think you're stupid. And Rosamund's a great name. Means 'the world rose' in Midlander."

That got his interest, eased us away from the point where a fight could have started. "Rose like the flower?"

"Yes. It's a conceit I've seen used in old Imperial texts, that the stars are all roses, each with the potential to bloom as our world has."

"So the sky's a rose garden," he said. His eyes had softened; he liked the idea.

I'd made myself think of the Khloïdanikos, of its backward stars. I knew there were roses there, but I'd never paid much attention to them. I wondered if the Troians were familiar with the conceit of the rose of the world.

Mildmay's voice brought me back sharply: "So there could be other . . ." He waved his hand, indicating the ruined house and the trees around us and the mountains looming in the dark. "Other whole worlds? With people and everything?"

"It's a theory," I said. "I don't find it terribly likely myself."

"Oh." He seemed a little disappointed.

"I don't know everything."

"You don't?" Bright, bright mischief in his eyes, and I couldn't keep a straight face well enough to glare at him.

"No, twit." He ducked his head, and although he didn't smile, never smiled, he looked absurdly pleased. "And I'm not an astrologist. Just because I don't think it's likely doesn't mean it isn't true."

"Huh," he said, and then his breath caught, and he slowly eased his right leg straight, bending his head over it so I couldn't see his face.

After a moment, when his shoulders hadn't relaxed from that tight defensive hunch, I said, "Are you all right?"

"Yeah. Fine." He didn't raise his head.

"Just tired, then?" That got his head up, and I smiled at him to let him know he hadn't fooled me.

He gave me a one-shouldered, unhappy shrug. "Little bit of a muscle knot, that's all."

"And you prefer to suffer nobly in silence rather than letting me do something about it?"

"It's no big deal," he said with another unhappy shrug, as if I'd put my hand on his shoulder and he was trying to dislodge it.

"It *will* be a big deal if it turns into a cramp," I said. That had happened a couple of times since we'd left Mélusine, and both times, he'd been sick and sweating with pain by the time he'd confessed to me anything was wrong. I realized now, shamefully, that his reticence had been partly caused by my own deplorable behavior—although I could at least say for myself that, both times, I had helped him, not savaging him when he was already hurt. "Mildmay. Don't be stupid about this. Let me help."

He held my gaze for a moment, though I couldn't tell what he was looking for. Then he sighed and said, "Yeah. You're right," and began carefully maneuvering out of his trousers so that I could massage the scarred mess of his right thigh.

He wouldn't look at me as I worked, his head tilted back as if he were staring at the stars. It irritated me, and I finally said, "What is it, exactly, that you're embarrassed about here?"

He twitched, but didn't move his head. Or give me an answer.

And then I thought I knew. "You know this isn't your fault."

That got a snort.

"*How* is this your fault?" I dug into the knotted, damaged muscles of his thigh harder than I'd meant to—which at least got a reaction out of him, a faint yelp, although he still wouldn't look at me.

"Should've been more careful," he said. "Like Rinaldo said."

"That's a little easier to do when you're not saving your idiot brother from drowning," I said reasonably.

"Well, yeah." And he sighed and relaxed, and I was able to feel as if I was actually doing him some good.

## *Kay*

I was taught as a child that forgetfulness was one of the Lady's darker mercies; I had not understood then, but I came to in the wake of Gerrard's death, for I woke in perfect blackness and had no memory of falling asleep, much less any idea of how I had come to be where I was—wherever that might be.

My first, confused thought was that I had been taken prisoner by the Usara, for their prisons, deep in the caverns beneath the Perblanches, were lightless: oubliettes in truth, for one both forgot and was forgotten while one lay there. I was aching with cold, which I also remembered, but I could not remember rid-ing against the Usara since the summer of four indictions back, and I knew I had returned thence to Rothmarlin, for I had found waiting for me . . .

Ah, Lady, dost hate me so? If forgetfulness was but a dubious blessing, memory was most certainly a curse.

It had been Gerrard's cousin waiting for me, Dominic Hume, who had died in the first battle of the Insurgence, bringing me the summons to Barthas Cross and the start of Gerrard's most ill-fated war.

And now Gerrard was dead. I had surrendered to the Duke of Glimmering, and I was, it seemed, truly blind. And still I remembered nothing of how I had come to be in this place. I remembered nothing after my signet being taken from me in the room of the engine.

For a moment, my heart almost locking immobile in my chest, it occurred to me that I might still be there, but I realized on my next painful, half-panicked inhale that I could not be. There was no scent of blood.

I took stock of myself as best I could; I did not seem to have taken any hurts. I was naked and knew not what had happened to my clothes. I was lying on cloth—burlap, I thought, something coarse—and as I tried to move, I found there was a manacle around my right ankle. I sat up and felt it: Corambin make, for it had a lock, and the chain was padlocked to a ring in the wall. The blood had been cleaned from my hands. And there must surely have been blood on my face, in my hair. I felt that I had drowned in Gerrard's blood.

What else had I lost? What might I have done that I now knew nothing of? What might have been done to me? I shut my eyes—a damned pointless gesture—and strove with the darkness in my mind, a perfect match for the darkness in my eyes. I pressed the heels of my palms against my eyes, hoping even for false colors, but there was nothing.

I began to shiver with cold that had no bodily source. How much time had I lost? What time was it now? Without sight, without knowledge of how much time had passed, how could I hope to know? Anyone I asked—assuming I was even given the chance—could lie to me, and how would I be able to tell?

My hands clenched in my hair, and I was struggling with the urge to rip out a double handful, from frustration and fear and the desire to control something, even if only my own pain, when a voice said, "So this is the Margrave of Rothmarlin."

I reached reflexively, uselessly, for the sword that was not there.

"Oh, I'm sorry," the voice—reedy, nasal, Corambin—said with savagely patent insincerity. I heard footsteps come closer, boot heels against flagstones. "You really can't see me, then, for I've been watching you for five minutes, groping about like a mole. And even Rothmarlin's legendary cunning does not, I think, stretch that far. You are blind."

*A blind beast,* my mother's voice said calmly in my head, and I straightened my spine as a man might flinch from a blow. She had told me the stories of the *usar*, the presiding spirits of the Usara, until the winter I was ten, when Intended Hervey had died and the new intended said my mother's stories were pagan superstitions and were corrupting me; my father, more for the sake of the peace than my morals, had bid her stop. I remembered only bits and pieces of the stories now, but the clearest of those memories were the stories involving the Veddick, who had been beneath the mountains before the usar came and would be there still long after they were gone, blind and hungry and trapped by its own bulk in caverns so deep and dark no man would ever find them. The country people around Rothmarlin called the occasional earth tremors Veddick's footsteps, though none of them had any idea who "Veddick" was or why his footsteps should shake the ground.

I had gone in fear of the Veddick as a small child, but I had left that fear behind, along with other childish things, when I first rode to war. Had not even thought of it for a wheel or more, but now I remembered my mother's voice, with its soft Usaran lilt: *a blind beast, lost in the darkness beneath the world. It calls out as it walks, but there is none to answer it, for all its kind perished long ago.* Blessed Lady, I had *feared* the Veddick. Had never thought what it would be like to *be* the Veddick. But now I knew, and I wished with all the painful, useless fervor of my heart that I did not.

"Who are you?" said I.

"I suppose we weren't properly introduced," said he; I could hear the truth of him, anger and festered grief and raw personal hatred, and for the first time since I assumed the margravate of Rothmarlin, I feared another man. "My name is Thomas Albern. Thanks to you, I am the Duke of Glimmering."

I knew instantly what he meant, for it was thanks to a certain warrior of the Usara that I had become Margrave of Rothmarlin at fifteen, but Glimmering continued regardless, "My brother Geoffrey stood against you at Angersburn, where you cut him down and beheaded him like a dog. I have five oath-sworn Caloxan soldiers to testify it."

Not Corambin. No Corambin soldier who had marched into the Anger River's narrow valley against us had come out of it again, marching, limping, or crawling. We had slaughtered all three hundred of them. I had beheaded their commander, and I remembered the rich satisfaction I had felt, remembered that my arms had been blood-soaked past my elbows. I had not let my men take the head as a trophy.

"An he had beheaded me, would you reproach him thus?"

The blow rocked my head to the side; I tasted blood. Had I not been blind, it would not have touched me.

"You will not speak of him," said Glimmering, his voice rising in pitch and volume. I felt the bone and heat of his fingers against my skin as they clenched on my shoulders, and he dragged me forward so that his breath was hot and foul on my face when he spoke again: "You will keep a civil tongue in your head or I will have it cut out. Do you understand me?" He sounded more than half-mad, and I was not fool enough to believe his threat an idle one. Had myself done worse on provocation no greater.

"I understand," I said and shut my eyes, since I could not judge well enough to lower my gaze. At this moment I wanted to do nothing to cause further offense. Blind was horror enough; blind and mute—I shuddered away from my own imaginings.

Slowly, Glimmering's fingers relaxed. He let me go with a shove so that I fell back on my elbows. "See that you remember," said he, and I knew he used the word 'see' deliberately. "And the proper address for a duke is 'Your Grace.' "

I knew that—was not my brother-in-law a duke of more ancient foundation than Glimmering? But was no place here for my pride. "Yes, Your Grace."

"There," said Glimmering. "Even savages can be taught."

And someone else said, "Yes, Your Grace."

I jerked myself upright again, drawing my legs up as best I could, although the chain kept me from bending my right knee more than halfway. Was an unmistakably Caloxan voice, without even the Corambin veneer that education often gave. It was worse, far worse, to be seen thus—blind, naked, and chained—by a Caloxan. Glimmering and his soldiers were northermen; they mattered not.

Glimmering said, "Intended Marcham has come to hear your confession."

The Intended of Howrack, a sour-faced man, older than myself, a bitter despot as back-country priests often were. He had not opposed Gerrard, too cannily aware of his dominion's views to do anything so unpopular, but I was not surprised to find him bending the knee to Glimmering. Caloxan or Corambin, Eadian or Caddovian, no priest was ever entirely free of his loyalty to the Descent Esmerine, that last withered vestige of the kings of Corambis. Priests now, and they claimed descent through augury and portent, not through blood, a dynasty of celibates: the current Prince Aethereal had no more bloodright to the Corambin throne than I did. But that mattered not, for his power, despite the title, was not the power of princes. He commanded the honor of every priest in our two countries, and if he was loyal to the Convocation, as every Prince Aethereal since Saint Edgar had been, then so were they.

"I have nothing to confess to Intended Marcham," said I.

"No?" said the intended. I had not realized before how much his voice sounded like the raucous cry of a crow. "Thou hast brought death and strife to every corner of Caloxa and thou hast nothing to confess?"

"I did as my lord commanded me, and that has never been counted a sin, either in Caloxa or out of it."

"And what of thy lord?" said Intended Marcham with horrible slyness. "What of his death, most blood-boltered and terrible? Hast nothing to confess there, either?"

"Nothing of evil. Of stupidity, yes, and arrogant folly. Of blindness, and for that I am fitly punished."

Was a silence which I found both frustrating and frightening, for I could imagine in it the duke and the intended conveying much to each other with their eyes. And was in fact the duke who spoke next: "Then you consider yourself innocent of all wrongdoing?"

"Is not what I said. I said I have nothing to confess to Intended Marcham, and that much is truth."

"Would you rather make confession to a different intended? I'll call in my private chaplain, if you'd rather."

"No, I thank you."

"Let me put it to you this way," said Glimmering, and his hands were on me again, pinning me back against the wall. "It wasn't an offer. You may confess to Intended Marcham, to Intended Albern, or even Intended Gye, but you *will* confess. I will have you pronounced a penitent by sundown or I will have you drawn and quartered and fed to the pigs."

I knew a dozen ways to remove his hands from my person, had I not been blind and chained to the wall like a dog. But I was helpless, twisted and pinned and unable to free myself, and a dark little voice, very soft, whispered that he could do to me anything he wished, and I could not stop him.

"Who is Intended Gye?" said I, and my voice was steady, even if hoarse.

Glimmering's grip on me loosened slightly, and part of my mind imagined viciously and hopelessly what I might do to him, while the rest attended to his answer. "He is chaplain to my foot soldiers. He is undominioned and poor." And thus looking for preferment. But if my choices were Marcham, Albern—clearly kin to Glimmering by his name—or a poor foot soldiers' priest . . . "I will make confession to Intended Gye."

"Very well," said Glimmering; he sounded suspicious, as if he thought I mocked him. But my choices were few and wretched, and I did not wish to die at the Duke of Glimmering's pleasure.

Glimmering let go of me. I heard his footsteps crossing the floor again, and then a confused jumble of sounds that had to be him leaving the room, perhaps holding the door for Intended Marcham to precede him? I heard the door close again. I pushed myself away from the wall, moved to a position where the chain would not drag the manacle against my skin. I was shivering, I realized, though for a moment I could not think what that meant nor what to do about it. Then it came to me, as if I read it from a book: I was cold. Awkwardly, groping, I managed to find the edge of the topmost . . . sack. Was a pile of burlap sacks, used for conveying potatoes or the like, and set thriftily by against further need. I wrapped the sack around my shoulders, curling in on myself as best I could, and listened to Glimmering's voice rising in argument with someone outside the room. By the time I heard the creak of door hinges again, I was no longer shivering, although I was not warm.

Glimmering said, his voice cold and tight, "The prisoner, Intended." He shut the door again with a bang. I stayed as I was, huddled and unspeaking. Was not my place to deliver the opening lines of this farce.

"My lord Rothmarlin," a man said after a moment, Corambin vowels, but the diction not as sharp as Glimmering's. "I have come to hear your confession. I am told you asked for me." He sounded young, nervous, and although I heard his footsteps—softer shoes than Glimmering's boots—he came not within arm's reach.

An he feared me, he was even blinder than I. "I dislike Intended Marcham," I said, "and Intended Albern I take to be kin to the duke?"

"His brother."

"Indeed. If I must confess to someone, you seem the least objectionable of my choices."

He stammered, taken aback.

"His Grace of Glimmering made the matter abundantly clear," said I, which made him stammer even more. "May we get this over with, Intended?"

Thus prompted, he stumbled into the ritual of confession. My coraline was lost with the rest of my belongings, but I could count the beads' progress in my mind against Intended Gye's words. If I had doubted he was Caddovian, as most Corambins were, my doubts would have been dismissed by his faltering. No Eadian priest, with indictions of saying the coraline daily before he ever reached the point of hearing confession, would stumble thus. But Intended Gye got through the invocation, however gracelessly, and said, "What would you—I mean, what burthen wouldst thou give to me, child?"

I supposed I should be grateful he knew the Eadian forms, but I was not. I said, "I would tell you a secret, Intended, that I may not face the Lady with it upon my shadow."

"I am listening."

I took a deep breath and said it, the thing I had carried in the darkness of my soul shadow for indictions: "I loved Gerrard Hume."

Intended Gye's silence was bitterly gratifying. "You . . . loved him?"

"I loved him," said I. Was no easier to say the second time. "I loved him as a man is meant to love the woman he takes to wife. The love which only unnatural men, monstrous men, would commit the sin of feeling for another man. That is the love I bore Gerrard Hume, and that is my confession."

"That's *it*?"

"Is not enough?"

"Well, it's hardly the sort of thing . . . I mean . . . it *is* a sin, but not . . ."

"You would prefer I confess to murder and rape and treason? Would wish me to lie, Intended? Is also a sin, you know, to make a false confession."

"You deny you've committed murder?"

"I have committed war. If is murder to kill Corambins in battle, then I suppose I have committed murder. But by that reckoning, I murdered my first man when I was fourteen."

"Fourteen?" His voice squeaked slightly on the second syllable.

"I rode to war against the Usara. And I know not how many of them I killed."

"You were in the army at fourteen?"

"Army?" I could not help laughing, although it was as bitter and painful as choking on a fishbone. "Is no *army* in Caloxa. Have you fought us all this time and not known that? Is but margraves and their armsmen and what common men will answer the call. I rode at my father's side when I was fourteen and two indictions later I rode as margrave. I have been killing men in battle these twenty indictions. Shall I do penance for each of them, unnumbered as they are?"

"Do their deaths burden you?"

It was not the response I was expecting—was the response of a priest, not a nervous boy or a Corambin duke's running dog—and perhaps I did not have it in me to profane confession by lying. "No," said I, "but it burdens me, somewhat, to think that perhaps it should."

"Ah," said Intended Gye. "Is your heart made of gears, Lord Rothmarlin?"

I was surprised that he knew the story of the Automaton of Corybant; I had not thought it favored among the northermen. But he was right to ask, right even to guess that that was how I thought of it, although I tried not to. I tried not to compare myself to the magician of Corybant who made himself a clockwork heart and became a monster. He destroyed the city of Corybant, which once he had loved, for he no longer remembered how to love, nor why. Was but a fable, and yet it haunted me. I knew I had flinched at Intended Gye's question, knew that if he watched me, he had his answer, regardless of what I might say. But I said it aloud, to punish myself, "I fear that it is."

"Do you think that penance will assist you to amend yourself?"

"No, I do not. But you know as well as I do that that is far from being the point of this maneuver."

"I will not commit you to penitence unless I believe it will do good," said he, and I heard a weak kind of stubbornness in his voice. Would not be sufficient for him to withstand Glimmering and Glimmering's brother and crow-voiced Intended Marcham, but he could ruin his career before they browbeat him into backing down.

And what cared I if a Corambin pup destroyed himself on a point of doctrine? Was I not a monster with a clockwork heart? But I could not let him sacrifice himself to no purpose, nor destroy himself for such a curst-yellow cat as me. I drew breath and found words that were not false: "I know not. Perhaps good may come of penance, even to me."

"Very well." I thought from his voice that he knew I spoke more for his benefit than from my own belief, but he did not argue. A rustling noise—did he stand? when had he knelt?—and then his footsteps, retreating. The door opening, closing. An indistinct murmur of voices, and then the door opened again, and many footsteps approached, more than I could count or track. I was hauled to my feet, losing the sack I had wrapped around myself for warmth, and held while someone's hands, unpleasantly hot, unpleasantly sweat-slick, unlocked the shackle around my ankle. I was dragged away from the pile of burlap, out the door, and through a space that made no sense, that might have been as wide as the sky or as narrow as the grave for all I could reckon. Could not even tell if I was being dragged in a straight line; without sight, I could not understand what my other senses told me. Then a hard shove, and I fell, ending on my hands and knees in shallow, frigid water. I recognized the smell, coppery and harsh, of the natural spring that welled out of the rock beneath Our Lady of Marigolds, Howrack's church. This would be the pool, and I shut my eyes uselessly, trying to remember the church's geography. Had been there only once, in Gerrard's train. Had noticed little, except Intended Marcham's sullenness and the breathtaking cold of the water. Already, now, my fingers were starting to go numb.

I knew the ritual of penitence, had witnessed it more than once in Our Lady of Crevasses, the tiny church that served both castle and village of Rothmarlin, and all the farmers and trappers and shy wild men who lived in the valley below and the Perblanches above. Had even seen an involuntary penitence when I was a child, although I'd been too young to understand the nature of Annie Lilleyman's crime.

I knew what came next, and I prayed to the Lady to grant me the strength to bear it.

## Felix

I didn't wake suddenly—no jolt, no gasp, no pounding heart; I had to drag myself out of the dream, like dragging myself out of quicksand, one agonized, clawing hand at a time, and I might not have succeeded before dawn if it hadn't been for a voice in my ear: "Would you just wake the fuck up already, so I can belt you one and go back to sleep?"

Mildmay. I blinked hard, thrashed a little, and then I was awake, staring at the banked-down embers of our fire and feeling Mildmay's hair tickling my neck.

I rolled onto my back and called witchlight—just one, just enough to limn the exasperation on his face.

"D'you ever get a good night's sleep?" he said.

"Sometimes. Not tonight, though."

He was still frowning at me, but the nuances shifted. "What is it? I mean, aside from a bad dream."

"That wasn't—exactly—a dream."

"Okay," he said slowly. "Then what was it?"

"I don't know if there's a word. Memory, maybe. Or haunting."

"You dreamed about ghosts?"

I told him my dream. I told him how I'd dreamed of the house burning, of armored men standing around it, watching, making sure no one escaped. The house burned, horribly beautiful, a great howling rose of a conflagration, and in its center, dark shapes writhed and died.

"People," Mildmay said, his voice barely a whisper.

"Yes."

"But—" He hesitated, eyeing me uncertainly.

"What?"

"Well, I mean, I don't know nothing about this stuff, but how d'you know it wasn't just a dream? You know, a nightmare or something?"

It was a fair question; I said so, and felt him relax slightly. "But I don't have a good answer for that one, either. I can tell the difference, but I don't think I can explain it so that it'll make sense to you."

"That's okay," he said, hastily enough that I knew he was afraid I'd try. "So long as *you*'re sure."

"Yes, I'm sure. I wish I weren't."

"It's a bad way to die," he said, agreeing.

"And they . . . No one buried them or said prayers for their souls. The soldiers watched until they were sure everyone was dead, and they left a man to be sure the fire didn't spread—nice of them, wasn't it?—but they didn't even drag the bodies out. They didn't do *anything*."

A pause, and suddenly he was pushing himself up. "Oh for fuck's sake, is this like your crying people again?"

"I beg your pardon?"

"You know what I mean," he said, almost savagely. "I don't know why I'm surprised. You got a thing about dead people, and there ain't no fucking arguing with it."

For one searing apoplectic moment, I thought he was accusing me of necrophilia, but mercifully, before I could find my tongue, he went on, "So out with it already. What do we got to do to let these poor people rest?" And I realized he was talking about the dead of Nera, and the dead of the Mirador, and most recently Prince Magnus. I could even admit he had a point—but what else could I do when faced with the dead's silent, helpless suffering?

"Well, I don't know," I said crossly. "Oddly enough, I'm not familiar with Corambin funerary rites."

"Saints and powers," Mildmay said. "So, what? We ask the first person we come across? That'll be fun."

I reminded myself that it was the middle of the night and that it was my fault he was awake. "I thought the best thing to do would be to ask the ghosts."

"Ask the . . . Are you just saying that to yank my chain, or do you mean it?"

"Oh, I'm quite serious. After all, I went to a good deal of trouble to learn how to talk to the dead. I might as well get some use out of it." I sat up and called more witchlights.

"What—*now?*" His voice actually rose, and I felt a reprehensible pleasure in having rattled him.

"I'm certainly not going to get back to sleep."

"But shouldn't you—"

"You have some advice to offer? From your vast knowledge of necromancy and thaumaturgical theory?"

He moved back; I wasn't sure whether it was to give me room or to get farther away from me. "Do what you want," he said. "You will anyway."

"Selfish and wayward as always," I agreed furiously, and shifted my sight as I had learned from Vincent Demabrien and from *The Influence of the Moon*, so that I could see the noirant energy around us.

Darker than night, it gathered and eddied and slowly became the shapes of those who had died here. Three of them were indistinct, barely even memories of having once been human, but in the center of the ruin, burning even in death as fiercely as a phoenix, there was a woman. A wizard. One hand was raised either in defiance or salute; the other clutched something against her, a swaddled bundle. Her eyes met mine through the flames, and she spoke a word I could not hear. And the object in her arm twisted, struggled against her grip, and I realized it was a child.

I jerked back, bumping against Mildmay, and broke my concentration.

"Whoa," he said. "Hey—you all right?"

"Yes," I said, although he could surely feel the shudders going through me and thus knew I was lying.

"It must've worked."

"Oh, yes," I said. "It worked very well." I told him what I'd seen.

"Powers," he said. "But you—I mean, nobody threatened you or nothing?"

"They're just ghosts. Patterns. It's not that."

He waited.

I said, "You know Malkar brought me to the Mirador."

"Yeah," Mildmay said cautiously.

"And he didn't . . . he didn't tell the truth. About me."

"Well, he wouldn't."

"No," I said and even managed to laugh, although it wasn't very convincing. "He told everyone I was from Caloxa."

"Caloxa. But ain't that—I mean, some of the maps said—"

"Yes. They were conquered by Corambis about forty years ago. Just the right time for Malkar's story—that I was the child of a noblewoman who had fled persecution when I was an infant—to sound plausible."

"And . . ." He waved at the ruins of the house, visible only as a greater jumbled darkness against the night.

"Yes. His story was almost true."

"Except they caught her."

"Yes."

"And she died in a fire."

"Just like Methony," I said, and I felt the shiver that went through him in the hand he laid, very gently, on my arm.

"So, did you figure out what to do?"

"Oh. Um. No. That is, I don't think the little ghosts need anything more than just being dispersed. They're almost gone already. But the wizard . . . I don't know. I'll have to try again."

"Or we could get off this mountain, find a village, tell a priest. Felix, this ain't your job." His grip on my forearm tightened, as if he was thinking about shaking me.

"Isn't," I said and pulled away.

*"Fuck,"* he said, under his breath but viciously. "Look. I am *not* the fucking bad guy here, okay? So cut it the fuck out."

"I have to help them," I said, and I hated the note of pleading in my voice.

"I ain't saying you shouldn't. Just . . . hocus ghosts are bad news. Even I know that much."

I thought of Loël Fairweather and what had happened to those who had disturbed his rest. And then thought of a half dozen other stories, all equally nasty, if not quite as rife with carnage. And I realized Mildmay was right; he wasn't my enemy. My enemy was something I couldn't even name, much less fight.

Mildmay must have sensed my capitulation; he said, "Just wait 'til morning. It's gotta be better to deal with this shit in daylight. And, I mean, they waited this long, right?"

"Right," I said. "We should get some rest."

He accepted my tacit truce without making me articulate it, and we lay down again. I thought of the nests Joline and I had made with scavenged blankets and stolen pillows, how we'd drawn circles of protection around them—like wizards did in stories—and how we'd pretended that it would be enough to ward off Keeper. And how it never was.

I could draw real circles of protection now. I wondered if they would be enough.

I wondered what I thought I could ward against that I wouldn't bring into the circle with me.

I did not sleep in what remained of the night.

## Kay

Much later, they left me—shivering, bleeding from the seven ritual cuts across each forearm, dressed in nothing but the thin linen of a penitent's shift, my hair still dripping the bitter coppery water of Our Lady of Marigolds. I was not in the room where I had woken; they had dragged me out into the church's rear yard and there chained me to the catafalque on which lay Gerrard Hume's body, already embalmed. Either I had lost a good deal more time than I had thought, or Glimmering had moved very swiftly indeed. Neither possibility offered any consolation.

For this was my penance, pronounced by Intended Gye, Intended Marcham, and Intended Albern: Gerrard's body was to be displayed throughout Caloxa, and I was to be displayed with it, chained to him in death as—Intended Gye had said somberly—I had chained myself to him in life. *Whither thou goest, I will go* was the burden of the old song, and it was to be my burden, too. I had always been caricatured in the newspapers as Gerrard's tame cougar—drawn as a stunted, ill-favored creature, blood dripping from its muzzle—and I was sure it amused and pleased Glimmering (in the proxy of his equally thin-voiced brother) to treat me as such.

Was one comfort to be had. As I was outside, I knew that it was night. No heat of the sun, no sounds of men or animals. And they had not left anyone to guard me; I knew this for I had heard the argument over whether a guard was needed. I was alone, and they had left no lights, for I neither heard nor smelled anything burning. If someone was watching, there was little for them to see but shadows. Even so, even with the best assurance of privacy I could give myself, was painful to force myself to examine the catafalque with my hands. It felt like another surrender.

They had put a metal collar around my neck; it would doubtless begin to rub welts before dawn. A chain ran from a loop on the collar to another loop bolted to the frame of the cart on which the catafalque had been erected. On the collar end, everything was soldered together, and staying still for that had been yet another test of my nerve. I had small stinging burns at the nape of my neck and down my spine. At the cart end, I found, unsurprisingly, a Corambin padlock, compact and heavy in my palm. I could not free myself, though indeed I knew not what I would do an I could. Was not as if I would be able to find my way out of this yard unaided.

Was not as if I had anywhere to go.

The chain was a long one, long enough that I did not fear strangling at the end of it, long enough that I could make my slow, groping way along one side of the cart, feeling the coarse cloth that bedecked it, could then stand to my full height and move my hands slowly, cautiously, in from the side of the cart, following the drape of the cloth, until my fingers found the soft dullness of dead flesh.

Was his shoulder. Another quarter inch and I found the material of the sleeveless burial robe traditional for Caloxan kings and margraves. I remembered the feel of the velvet from my father's funeral rites, and I wondered who had dared to do Gerrard this last honor. I felt down his arm, then followed the bend of his elbow inward to find his hands folded together over his breast. His sword should have lain beneath them, but of course it did not. Glimmering would recognize that mark of respect.

I moved my hands up his chest and neck, trying not to feel the line of coarse stitches where the practitioners had sewn his body back together. Trying not to think about the other repairs they must have had to make.

Be grateful, I told myself. Be grateful they didn't leave him where he fell or dump him in the nearest midden like so much offal. I wondered what they had done with Benallery and the others. Hoped at least they had buried them decently, but there was no one I could ask, and nothing I could do about the matter even an I knew.

I touched Gerrard's face. Memory told me what I was feeling: the strong line of his jaw, the high bridge of his nose, his broad forehead and his short dense hair, the color of honey. His eyes were only a shade or two darker, and when he was happy, they lightened until they were exactly the same color. I traced the arch of his eyebrow with one finger. I had never told him I loved him; I hoped he had never guessed. Eadian to his bones, he would have been horrified, guilty. He had had enough burdens to bear without that.

The heat of tears on my face told me that I was crying. I rubbed them away out of an old, old reflex. My father had called me a violet-boy, told me tears were only for those not strong enough to fight.

My sister, Isobel, his favorite child, never cried.

"Thou wert right about me, Father," I said aloud, rubbing my face with both hands, hearing my voice waver and hitch as it were a stranger's. Was not strong enough to fight. Was in truth a violet-boy, for if Gerrard had asked it of me, I would have . . .

Mindful of the chain, I pulled myself up onto the catafalque. I could feel and hear myself sobbing, but as if from a great distance. It mattered not. I touched Gerrard's face, forehead, nose, the cool molding of his lips. "Am sorry," I whispered. "Am so sorry." I kissed him once, chastely, like the oath-binding kiss I would have given him when he was crowned king, and then I lay with my head on his shoulder and cried myself to sleep like the girl-child I had never been.

# Chapter 2

## *Felix*

Mildmay woke up coughing.

"It's just the mountains," he said. "Air's too thin."

He kept coughing, though, and I thought guiltily of the frigid water of the St. Grainne. But Mildmay waved that idea off. "I'm *fine*, Felix," he said, glowering. "Do whatever it is you're gonna do with your ghosts and let's get moving."

"No, you were right," I said, and he squinted at me in a way that was partly incredulity and partly (I suspected) a headache he wouldn't admit he had. "The proper thing to do is tell a priest. That's just never been an option before."

He thought about that and decided to accept my excuse at face value. "Okay, yeah," he said, and I shouldn't have been so grateful to avoid another argument, but I was.

Our way grew steadily easier as we descended the mountain. The road became first better defined, then wider, and finally settled into a series of switchbacks with logs set crossways at regular intervals to give people and animals alike something to brace their feet against. By then it was nearly evening, and I insisted we stop, there being a level place beside the road which had plainly been used for that purpose many times before. Mildmay put up much less of a fight than I'd expected, which was also worrisome. I'd become accustomed to his being indefatigable. Sleep did not come easily.

I dreamed of fire again, a dream in which everything I touched burst into flame. I died burning again and again and again, until I was so weary of it that there was no horror left. Half-waking at some point, knowing I was just going to fall back into the fire as soon as I slept, I thought of Iosephinus Pompey and the tricks he had taught me; I didn't have to surrender to this choking, filthy agony. And this time as I sank into dreaming, I summoned my construct-Mélusine, summoned my control over my dreams.

And instead of fire, I fell into thorns.

There was a fairy tale Belinda had told us, about a lady enchanted to sleep for a thousand years and how the briars grew in knots and mysteries around her tower and the only man who could reach her and wake her and love her was an embroiderer who'd gone blind over the white-on-white embroidery of the wedding gown of the Empress of Comets. My construct-Mélusine had become that tower, only the briars were on the inside, hemming me in so that I could not reach the gates. Even if I could have reached them, I couldn't go through them, for the briars bound them shut—even Horn Gate, which once had been held open by wisteria vines. The only opening was the Septad-Gate, where there was a low, ragged gap for the silted, filthy, oily trickle of the Sim to ooze out.

I was trapped.

And as I stood there, trying to make sense of what I saw, the briars began to writhe; I realized just too late that they were reacting to my presence. A long strand like a whip lashed out and wrapped around my neck, dragging me closer so that other, shorter strands could catch my hands, my feet, could twine themselves through my hair. And the thorns dug with tender cruelty into my throat, so that I couldn't fight. Trapped, trapped, and it was almost a relief to catch the scent of smoke. But then it was much worse, because the briars burned slowly, far more slowly than wood and cloth and old dried moss. By the end, I couldn't help fighting, even though it was worse than futile, though it did nothing but coat the thorns in my blood. I struggled as mindlessly as any animal in a trap, wrenching at my wrists, screaming and screaming although I had no voice left to scream with, dying by brutal inches while the briars wove traceries of flame around me.

I jerked awake and was still trying to calm my breathing back to normal when Mildmay woke up, coughing again. He'd told me about his susceptibility to the Winter Fever, and I'd seen it for myself, the winter before this last one. He'd been sick for most of a month, coughing and fevered and unable to take a breath deep enough to carry his voice. And yet, when Gideon and I had tried to express our concern, he'd waved it off. "Ain't that bad," he'd said in that terrible rasping wheeze. "Ain't out of my head or coughing up blood or nothing."

"Well, thank goodness you have *standards*," I'd said, and he'd cursed at me for making him laugh.

But now, remembering that, I wondered what we'd do if things got to a point that would be deemed "bad" in Mildmay's lexicon.

By late afternoon, we were starting to see signs of habitation; I wondered if I should try to persuade him to stop at a farmhouse, but I couldn't face the argument. And that at least turned out all right, because by sunset we'd found an actual town with an actual hotel: the Five Dancing Frogs of Arbalest.

The hotel was run by a woman named Agatha Fawn and her seemingly endless supply of daughters. She was the first person I'd seen who wasn't Mildmay since . . . since we'd passed a woodcutter as we started up to St. Ulo's Pass. For a moment, I couldn't even remember how to talk to a stranger, and then I pulled myself together and asked her about traveling to Esmer.

"Esmer?" said Mrs. Fawn, rather as though I'd asked for directions to the moon. "Well, the best thing would be to take the stagecoach to Bernatha. You can get the train there."

"They keep saying they're going to run a line out here," said one of her daughters, who was leaning on the desk and giving Mildmay a frank and lascivious appraisal. "But am not holding my breath."

"I beg your pardon," I said. "Train?"

"The railroad," Mrs. Fawn said, which enlightened me not at all. And that must have shown on my face, for she said, "I know you're foreign, but where are you *from*?"

"Um," I said. "Mélusine."

And Mildmay and I watched in alarm as Mrs. Fawn became transfigured.

"Mélusine," she breathed, and then her gaze jerked down to my hands, where they were folded on the desk. I wasn't wearing my rings; even if I had felt I deserved them after what I did to Isaac Garamond, they were exactly the sort of thing a traveler in a strange country should *not* go flashing about to all and sundry. But my tattoos twisted and twined across the backs of my hands, gold and scarlet, emerald and azure. "And you're a . . . not a magician, I know they don't use that word. A wizard!"

"Yes," I said, even more alarmed.

"I never thought I'd *meet* one," Mrs. Fawn said. "Have read all the novels from Esmer, you know."

"You have?" I said weakly.

"Oh has she," said her daughter, with emphasis.

"Mama and her romances," agreed another daughter, who'd been brought out of the back by the sound of new voices. They were looking at me with interest, but not the way Mrs. Fawn was, which put me uncomfortably in mind of the way Shannon Teverius's coterie looked at him, moths positively yearning to fling themselves into the candle flame.

"Well, are exciting," Mrs. Fawn said; this was obviously a defense she'd mounted many times before. "And much better than those silly things about places that don't exist. A real wizard!"

"I didn't know anyone was writing novels about . . ."

"Has been kind of a craze," Mrs. Fawn admitted. "Since Challoner published his travel book, oh it must be nearly ten indictions ago now, because I remember I was pregnant with Norinna and my-husband-may-the-Lady-rest-his-soul brought me that and the first of the novels to cheer me up. Mr. Challoner wrote all about Mélusine, you see, and your Mirador"—which she mispronounced horribly—"and the six gates of the city and the Catacombes des Arcanes"—which she also mispronounced horribly—"and it's all just so . . ."

"I see," I said hastily, since I didn't want to know what adjective she might eventually light upon. "I, um . . . That's very interesting. Maybe later we could—"

"Do you have the tattoos on your palms, too?"

Lacking any helpful alternative, I turned my hands palms-up and endured her little "oh" of wonder, endured the way her daughters leaned forward to see better. I was, I told myself firmly, going to draw the line at taking off my coat to let them see my forearms.

Before it came to that, though—before Mrs. Fawn had quite gotten up the nerve to ask me if she could touch the eye tattooed in the center of my left palm—Mildmay said, "We *still* don't know what a train is."

"Oh!" said Mrs. Fawn as if he'd jabbed her with a straight pin. "Of course. I cry your mercy. Is like a stagecoach, but much faster. And it doesn't need horses."

"It runs on rails," one daughter supplied.

"I really don't understand," I said, and felt myself blushing with the admission.

"Well, I know not how it works. Is magic." Mrs. Fawn's expression was almost accusing, as if I should have understood instantly.

"It doesn't matter," I said hastily. "The first step is the, er, stagecoach to Bernatha, right?"

"Prob'ly like a diligence," Mildmay said. "We'll need tickets."

"Yes," said Mrs. Fawn, clearly latching onto the word "tickets." "Will be a banshee for the both of you."

I didn't manage to nod quite quickly enough, and one of her daughters said, "Will not know our money, Mama. Had better explain."

"And thou hadst better get back to the kitchen," Mrs. Fawn said. "Or do the potatoes scrub themselves now?"

The young woman made a face at her mother and disappeared; Mrs. Fawn said, "Just a moment," and dug around in the drawers on her side of the desk. "Here." She laid five coins out on the desk and named them for me: "Obol, penny, hermit, banshee, saint, angel. Two obols to the penny, ten pennies to the hermit. Twenty hermits in a banshee, seven banshees to a saint. And seven saints make an angel, but will probably never see one." Which explained why she'd named six coins but only laid out five. She read my face correctly and said, "No one in Arbalest has angels. Oh, and is a five-penny coin called a thrustle, but you probably won't see that, either."

"Stop!" I said, laughing, although it was hard to make it sound natural, and held up both hands in surrender—a tactic which did not merely stop Mrs. Fawn's lesson, but completely distracted her. Her expression was that of a child presented with a fairy-tale knight, winged horse and all. I was, I reflected grimly, going to have to find some of these Mélusinien novels and see just what it was they were saying about Cabaline wizards.

"Okay," said Mildmay. "You know anybody who might want to buy a mule? She's a good mule."

Mrs. Fawn and her daughter traded a look. Mrs. Fawn said thoughtfully, "Unc' Elmeric would probably give you a good price. Lord Seaward requisitioned both his mules last indiction, and he figures will never see them again."

"Will show you the way," her daughter said with enthusiasm, and I was left alone with Mrs. Fawn. We conducted an exquisitely polite verbal duel: Mrs. Fawn wanted to know everything about Mélusine and did not want to talk about why Lord Seaward had been requisitioning people's mules; I found talking about Mélusine rather akin to having my fingernails pulled out one at a time, and I was exceedingly interested in those mules and what Lord Seaward had been requisitioning them for. When Mildmay returned and I was able to retire from the lists, I thought the honors were about equal. I had certainly told her more than I wanted to about Mélusine, although I'd managed to keep from being cornered into talking much about myself, and I had learned rather more about the current state of affairs in Corambis than Mrs. Fawn was comfortable explaining.

We had come to Corambis, it seemed, at the tail end of a war; we'd only missed the war itself by a matter of days. News of one side's surrender had reached Arbalest only the day before we'd arrived, and that explained a good deal of Mrs. Fawn's discomfiture: the defeat was still raw.

The war had been fought between the northern half of Corambis and the southern—or, rather, as Mrs. Fawn said with a mulish glint in her eye, between Corambis and Caloxa. Any wizard knew the importance of using the proper names of things, and I understood immediately that one of the issues at stake was whether *Caloxa* was the proper name for the southern half of Corambis. Forty years was not enough to settle that question, and I doubted this Insurgence, or its defeat, had done the job, either.

The Corambins of forty years ago had not been as thorough as Michael Teverius. When he came to power in the Wizards' Coup, he had personally murdered every last scion of the house of Cordelius, including the infant prince Daniel. I'd never quite believed the stories of Michael throwing Daniel from the Crown of Nails, but the murders were real enough: one night in a grisly mood, Shannon had shown me the axe, rusting away beneath the blood that had never been cleaned off.

The Corambin generals, however, had been content with executing the king, James Hume. They had left *his* infant son, Gerrard, alive, and that mistake had now cost them, and everyone else involved, dearly. Gerrard, whom Mrs. Fawn called variously Prince Gerrard and the Recusant—another disputed piece of nomenclature—had raised his army against the Corambins, and although Mrs. Fawn said reluctantly that he never had a hope of winning, it had taken the Corambins three years to defeat him. And in the end, he seemed to have defeated himself, for the news brought was definite. Gerrard Hume was dead, and had been dead before the surrender had been given by someone called the Margrave of Rothmarlin.

Before I could dig further, and before Mrs. Fawn could trap me into describing the circumstances of my exile, Mildmay came back. He looked dreadful, almost gray and sweating and leaning on his cane more heavily than he normally allowed himself. And the cough was definitely worse, no matter how he tried to suppress it.

"Is a nasty cough," said Mrs. Fawn. "Pleuriny?"

At a guess, "pleuriny" was what Corambins called the Winter Fever. "I hope not," I said. "We'd like the room for two nights."

Mildmay opened his mouth to protest, then closed it again, but he was still frowning when we reached our room, which was only marginally large enough for two grown men. I closed the door and said, "What?"

He shrugged. "Nothing. Game they play here ain't one I like."

"So? You can manage one extra night in a hotel without playing cards, can't you?"

"Not if we want to pay the bill."

"I thought you just sold our mule."

"That's for the diligence or stagecoach or whatever the fuck they call it."

"And what? You couldn't be bothered to get *enough* money for her? You forgot what you were doing in the middle?"

"Maybe I didn't feel like taking the poor bastard for everything he had, okay?" he said, nearly shouting, and then went scarlet.

"You pick the oddest times to have an attack of morality," I said, which only made him go redder.

But then he said, "Maybe since I'm the one has to deal with it, it ain't no business of yours."

"In other words, I should shut up and be thankful, is that it?"

"You could try it."

"Yes, because I have so much to be thankful for in the delight of your company," I said bitterly.

That hit home; he turned stiffly and went out without answering me. I followed him, and we ate dinner in uncompromising silence before Mildmay, without a glance in my direction, insinuated himself into a card game. I went to bed early. He barely twitched an eyebrow. From his face and his lazy posture, no one could have guessed that he was playing for the money to pay our bill—or that he was sick. I hated myself for my selfishness as I climbed the stairs. This was *my* exile he was funding, after all, Mildmay dragged along only because of the obligation d'âme, and when he'd asked me to cast it, he surely couldn't have been expected to be agreeing to be taken away from everything he'd ever known.

But he'd done that for me before we were bound together by magic. He'd walked across Kekropia for me, for no good reason. It occurred to me that I'd never even asked him why he'd done it, and I shuddered; right now I didn't even want to know.

Maybe when we reached Esmer, I would feel brave enough for that conversation. Maybe, if I was lucky, I would get distracted and forget to ask.

## Mildmay

I'd been playing cards for money since we hit Clerval, along of not having had the balls to ask Lord Giancarlo for what Felix was due on his stipend before we left. So our money'd run out, and Felix wasn't good for nothing, and even if he hadn't been wrapped in that black cloud, I wasn't sure I could've talked him into reading the Sibylline for money the way Mavortian von Heber'd used to. And, you know, I'm a good pickpocket and everything, but that ain't no reliable way to earn a living, especially not traveling. Besides which, I'd only have to fuck up once, and, well, depending on where we were, I might end up in jail for Kethe knows how long, or missing a hand, or dead. And I hated the fuck out of the first two options, thanks all the same, and if I got my stupid self killed, I wasn't kidding myself about how long it'd be before Felix followed. I was mostly working on trying to keep him from leading, if you get me.

I'd been a cardsharp on and off since I had a septad and three, so it wasn't like this was no new thing. And hating it wasn't no new thing, either. So I gritted my teeth and played nice and careful and no cheating, because again that's a good way to end up dead, and mostly I was the best player at the table by a septad-mile or so, and I never bet much and I never bet hard and I never pushed people to keep playing when they decided to fold, and so far nobody'd got pissed at me and so far I'd been able to keep a step ahead of the hotel bills.

So far.

In Arbalest, the game they liked was Horned Menelan, insane fucking thing with rules up one side and down the other, like where you sat and what *color* you were, for fuck's sake. I could play it, but I didn't like it none.

Don't have to like it, Milly-Fox. Just have to win.

## *Felix*

If I squinted at them, the cracks in the ceiling of our room made the shape of a tree, blasted by lightning—and certainly dead, for it was nothing but cracks in dry and ancient plaster. The Dead Tree, the eighteenth trump of the Sibylline, that which offered neither shelter nor pity. The aftermath of betrayal, the cold and merciless light of truth: the full moon rose behind the Dead Tree and flooded the world with its heatless light.

So what does the moon show you, Felix Harrowgate, thief, murderer, traitor, whore?

Nothing I want to see.

I rolled over, but after a moment, I flopped onto my back again. Having the Dead Tree behind me was worse than staring at it. The moon was the governor of dreams, and I had carefully avoided thinking about my dreams all day long. But I couldn't deny something was wrong, and with the Dead Tree glaring down at me, I couldn't deny I needed to figure out what it was.

And I couldn't deny, much as I might want to, that I knew where to start.

I sat up long enough to take my shoes off, then lay down again, making myself as comfortable as I could given the lumps in the mattress and the knots of tension in my shoulders. It took a significant effort of will to close my eyes and several minutes before I was able to find the discipline and concentration necessary to summon my construct-Mélusine.

The briars were still there, exactly as I had dreamed them. I stayed carefully to the center of the clear space; I didn't want to know if their ability to move, their aggression were real, too.

Insofar as any of this was "real," of course, a question that was so far from having a satisfactory answer that I wasn't even sure it had a satisfactory *question*.

But looking at them now, I thought I recognized these briars. They were nothing native to the swamps and farmlands surrounding Mélusine, and for a moment I couldn't place them, beyond that nagging sense of familiarity. But then I leaned, very cautiously, just close enough to see the red cast to the vines, and I knew where I'd seen them before: in the Khloïdanikos, in a ring around an enormous and ancient oak, where I'd put Malkar's rubies for reasons that . . . had seemed compelling at the time. And although Horn Gate, the doorway between this construct and the Khloïdanikos, was closed, the briars were here, shutting me in as effectively as would walls of brick. Yes, something was definitely wrong, and why was I not surprised to find Malkar at the root of it? So to speak.

I thought I saw a wisp of smoke rising lazily from the briars around Chalcedony Gate, but when I turned my head, there was nothing there.

I realized my heart was hammering against my ribs; I'd spooked myself, and given the nature of oneiromancy and dream-constructs, there was every chance that if I stayed, I would start a fire simply by being afraid of one.

I broke my trance with no little relief and sat up. I wasn't going to find an answer that way; the allegories of dreaming were too overwhelming—like trying to solve a maze from inside it and while being pursued by wild alligators to boot. "Wild allegories," I said under my breath and almost managed to smile at the conceit. On the other hand, I had no objection to allegories as long as I had some control over them. I stood up and got the Sibylline out of the box in my coat pocket.

I settled myself cross-legged on the bed and shuffled the cards until their energy cleared, then cut the deck and laid out a proper nine-card spread on the quilt. I mostly didn't bother, not caring for the divinatory properties Mavortian von Heber had so greatly valued, but tonight the ritual might be as much help as the cards themselves. Asking what was wrong with my dreams was essentially the same as asking what was wrong with me, and I knew more answers to that than I wanted to. I hoped structuring the reading might give some structure to what it told me.

Nine cards in a spiral, working widdershins out from the center, all facedown. That last wasn't part of Mavortian's teaching, but something I'd picked up from reading about the diviners of Imar Elchevar, who used bone tablets engraved with runes.

I was staring at the backs of the Sibylline cards, half laughing at myself for being so afraid of them and half just trying to work up the courage to turn over the center card, when the door opened and Mildmay came in.

"Oh, it's you. Much luck?"

He shrugged. "Enough."

"Do you cheat?"

"Don't have to."

He tugged the black hair ribbon free; unraveling from its braid, his hair hung in kinked russet strands to the middle of his back. My fingers yearned to touch it, but I kept them still. He took off his coat, his waistcoat, his cravat, placing them neatly over mine. He sat down on the other side of the bed and took off his boots and socks, then lay down on his back, his hands laced behind his head. "So," he said, "you got Mavortian's cards out."

An unnecessary observation: Mildmay's way of saying he forgave me for our altercation.

He turned his head and raised an eyebrow at me. "You gonna do anything with 'em, or just stare at 'em all night?"

"I hadn't decided," I said. And then, defiantly, I reached out and turned over the center card.

The Spire.

"Shit," Mildmay said, coming up on his elbow to look. "That ain't a good card, right?"

"Not particularly, no." It was the card of the scapegoat; of a fall from a great height—whether literal or metaphorical; the card of betrayal. I did not need an instructor to hold my hand through the myriad parallels to my current situation.

Grimly, because I'd started this and it would be both folly and cowardice to stop, I turned over the second card. That within myself which blocked me. The Three of Staves, reversed, and my fingers flinched back as if I'd been burned. Conceit was the meaning of that card. Third, the past, was the Nine of Swords, despair and madness and martyrdom, and I could feel the blush heating my face. Mildmay was watching solemnly; for all his professed disdain for "hocus stuff," he didn't seem remotely inclined to mock the cards.

Fourth was what supported me, and that was the Sibyl of Swords, a card which Mavortian and I had agreed represented me, but now, looking at all the aspects of myself I saw in the Spire and the reversed Three of Staves and the Nine of Swords, I realized that the Sibyl had to be my magic, my intellect—the things which gave me power even now. Malkar had taken them from me once, but the Sibyl following the Nine of Swords was a cogent reminder that he had not been able to keep them.

I hauled in a breath and met Mildmay's eyes. "Are you following any of this?"

"D'you care if I am?"

"If you want to learn to read the cards, I'd be happy to teach you."

I was surprised when he broke eye contact, more surprised when he muttered, "Reading *cards* ain't no use to me."

"Mildmay?"

He'd gone beautifully, painfully red, and said nothing.

"Mildmay? What do you want me to teach you to read?" Even as I said it, though, I knew, and was ashamed of myself.

"You're just gonna make fun of me," he muttered, lowering his head so that his hair obscured his face.

"I swear to you I won't." It was suddenly vital that I make him believe me. "I *swear* it. On anything you like."

Cold green flicked at me and away. "I don't know anything you care about enough for making promises on."

That brought me up short. We were silent for some moments while I thought about what he'd said. "Do you believe that I . . . care about you?" I didn't have any right to use the word "love."

His turn to think, and I tried not to make lists of all the reasons he could give me why he believed no such thing. Finally, he said tiredly, "Yeah. I know you care. In your own way."

The rider stung, as I was sure he meant it to, but I persevered: "You know I care about the . . . oh, the life of the intellect, for lack of a better term?"

"Book learning," Mildmay suggested gravely, but I saw the faintest glimmer of laughter in the depths of his eyes.

"Yes," I said, grinning back. "Book learning."

"Yeah," he said. "I got that part."

"So if there's one thing in the world I'd never make fun of *anybody* for, it'd be for wanting to learn to read. Does that make sense?"

He thought about that, and I didn't try to rush him, knowing that it wasn't that he was stupid—far from it—but that there were certain kinds of thinking he'd never had the chance to practice. And when he'd considered the idea carefully, he shook his hair out of his face and said, "Yeah. Yeah, I can see that."

"So I won't make fun of you. Q.E.D."

That got me an eyebrow, severely skeptical. "*Quod erat demonstrandum*," I said. "Kekropian mathematicians use it to signal that they've proved what they set out to. The philosophers have picked it up, and you know wizards. Where philosophers and mathematicians lead, how can we possibly resist following?"

"Y'all are batfuck," he said, but I saw the unscarred corner of his mouth twitch. "Finish with your cards, and we can go to sleep."

It was a withdrawal, and I honored it, reaching to turn over the fifth card: the Hermaphrodite. The fifth card was the future, or the solution to the problem, and what the Hermaphrodite had to do with any of it, I had no idea.

Of course, if I knew the answers, I wouldn't be trying to read the cards.

I glowered at the Hermaphrodite and moved on to the outer circle, external influences and forces. The sixth card was that which blocked, and I was unhappy, but not surprised, to see the Unreal City. The Khloïdanikos. The briars. The seventh card was Death, and I was surprised into laughing when Mildmay muttered, "Tell us something we don't know." The past was full of death, death upon death upon grief and guilt and regret, and death, too, was Malkar, who was dead and who had brought death to everything he touched.

The eighth card, support and anchor, was the Two of Wands. Alliance. The cooperation of complementary powers. Mildmay. Tell me something I don't know, I thought, and flipped over the ninth and last card.

The Dog. Loyalty, savagery, the dark beast brooding in the depths of every civilized soul. I'd done readings where the Dog was associated with Mildmay, but Mildmay was the Two of Wands, and in any event, I understood that I had asked Mildmay to solve enough of my problems already. This was not Mildmay's problem, neither cause nor solution. It was mine. Mine and . . . My eyes went back to Death, to the Spire, to the Nine of Swords. Mine and Malkar's, insofar as what I was came from what Malkar had made of me, and if ever there was a dark beast in human form, Malkar was that beast. He wasn't a solution. He was a quite literal dead end.

"Well, that was of remarkably little use," I said, gathering the nine cards back into the deck and shuffling to disperse the pattern.

"I never saw as how the cards did Mavortian much good," Mildmay said, watching as I returned the cards to their box and the box to my coat. "I mean, unless he was actually doing magic with 'em. And that ain't what you were doing, right?"

The possibility clearly made him nervous. "No magic," I said. "Just looking for patterns." I pulled the covers back. The sheets were old and thin and had childishly straggling darns, but they were clean. I crawled into bed, curling up so my feet wouldn't hang over the end. "Are you ready to sleep?"

Mildmay sighed and tilted his head sharply, first one way, then the other, making at least one vertebra crack. "Gonna go clean up," he said. Except for the muted tapping of his cane, he moved silently as he left the room; I knew he would rather have done without the cane and its awkwardness and noise, but his lame leg was only dubiously reliable.

I lay and thought about the Sibylline, despite my best efforts not to. The Spire, the Three of Staves reversed, the Nine of Swords, the Sibyl of Swords, the Hermaphrodite, the Unreal City, Death, the Two of Wands, the Dog. The Three of Staves reversed, the Unreal City . . . The Hermaphrodite, the Dog . . . The Unreal City, the Dog, the Beehive . . .

I jerked entirely, coldly awake, only realizing as I did so that I'd started to drift into sleep. The Beehive. The rubies. That was what connected the Dog and the Unreal City, that was what brought the briars into my construct-Mélusine. I had done it myself, put them in the Khloïdanikos to keep them from contaminating the Mirador, to keep anyone else from finding them. To keep Isaac Garamond from finding them, although I hadn't known then that it was he. Hadn't known that he was the weasel who'd found Malkar's workroom and was continuing Malkar's work.

And before I'd found out, before I'd done anything more than put the rubies in the Khloïdanikos, I'd lost it, lost my concentration, lost the structure.

Lost it in an argument with Thamuris, and how transparent an excuse had I thought I needed?

I heard Mildmay's cane in the corridor. I rolled over, shut my eyes, and pretended as hard as I could to be asleep. After a very long time, it became true.

I was lost in all my dreams that night, which was symbolism I needed no help to understand. First the Mirador, then the dark beneath Klepsydra, and then I heard a slow, massive ticking, and I knew it was Juggernaut, the Titan Clock of the Bastion. I had heard it once waking, and had not forgotten. And then beneath it, I heard a voice cry out in pain and fear, and it was a voice I knew. My brother's voice.

I follow the voice, follow the sobbing and cursing, follow it down a twisting, tightening spiral until, somewhere far beneath the earth, among the roots of the monstrous clock, I find him.

*Every maze has a monster at its heart.* Is that one of Ephreal Sand's dicta, or one of the mysteries of Heth-Eskaladen? It doesn't matter; it's true, and the monster of this maze is Malkar Gennadion. He stands with his back to the door, but that doesn't matter either. I know him instantly. His attention is fixed on the far corner of the room, where Mildmay is pressed back against the wall. Mildmay is bleeding from a series of cuts on his shoulders and upper arms, too thin and shallow to scar; I know the knife that made them. His face is bruised and terrible. There is a wild creature in his eyes.

*This is foolish, you know,* Malkar says. He sounds amused, and I know his voice so well, there isn't even any shock in hearing it again. It's as if I've been listening for it all along.

Mildmay says nothing. He is clutching a crowbar, and I know immediately that Malkar left it deliberately for him to find. As a game.

*You can't kill me,* Malkar continues. *All it would take is a single word from me, and that bar would burn hot enough to cripple your hands permanently. If it didn't burn them right off.* I don't have to see his face to know he's smiling.

*I killed wizards before,* Mildmay says, his voice slurred and dragging and distorted; I understand him because I can fill in the rest of the sentence around that word "wizards," that word I have never heard Mildmay use.

*What was that?* Malkar says, although I'm quite sure he knows. *It's truly a pity you're illiterate. This would go much faster if you had a little slate to write on.*

Mildmay repeats himself, his voice growling and grinding in his throat. And twice more before Malkar affects to understand and agrees affably, *Of course you have, my child. I saw what you did to Vey, remember? But you won't do that to me. You can't.* He advances a step. *Just think of what will happen to Felix when you fail.*

*Don't care about Felix,* Mildmay says, and it should be true. If there are gods, they can bear witness to that much. Mildmay should not care about me. But he's lying. The bar is shaking in his grip.

*Did anyone ever tell you you're a terrible liar?* Malkar says. *Poor little murderer. Poor little monster.* He's almost crooning.

Mildmay doesn't protest, doesn't do anything but watch Malkar with fear and hate and hopelessness in his eyes.

*I could make you give me your weapon,* Malkar says, with just enough mocking emphasis on the word "weapon" to make it clear he doesn't regard it as a threat. *You know that.*

Mildmay's shaking gets worse.

*I don't know if I could make you hit yourself with it—it depends on your willpower. But it might be fun to find out.* He takes another step closer. *I could make you blind and deaf and helpless and leave you that way. I could take your body away from you again, the way I did in Mélusine. I could make you drop that crowbar and go down on your knees right here.* He pauses, tilts his head, making a show of it. *But I think I'd prefer you do it yourself.*

Mildmay snarls soundless defiance, a ratting terrier cornered by a much larger dog.

*Oh you will, little monster. I wonder, does Felix know what you did? Is that why he keeps you around? It's certainly not for your looks or your conversation. Does it amuse him to have a tame killer on his leash?* His voice is low, intimate, dripping poison. *Does he understand what you are? You hide it well, but I see it. And you'll never be rid of it, you know. Never.* There is a terrible weight to that *never* from Malkar Gennadion, who is also Brinvillier Strych—and who knows how many other names he may have had? Who knows how many lives he may have held and used and discarded, how many other lives he may have left ruined in his wake? I wonder if even Malkar himself knows any longer.

*Knew* any longer. This is a dream. Malkar is dead.

Malkar's hand reaches out, and Mildmay flinches hard, but he's up against the wall. Malkar's purring chuckle, and he reaches again. And Mildmay swings the crowbar. But his strength and speed are gone; he's shaking so hard it's a wonder he doesn't simply drop it. Malkar catches the bar easily, and they are frozen for a moment, staring at each other. Mildmay's face is twisted and inhuman, painfully ugly, but I'm glad I can't see Malkar's.

Malkar twists his wrist, a contemptuous flick of a gesture, and Mildmay crumples, landing hard on his knees, his hands going to cover his face. His sobs rack his body, but make no sound. Malkar stands over him, watching. He says, *You will learn, my child, that it is better to obey me,* and, a cruel parody of kindness, lays his hand on Mildmay's bowed head.

I have to stop this. I don't care that it's a true dream, that this is something that has already happened, something unchangeable, something I am only a witness to. I have to make it stop. I have to make *him* stop. As Malkar's hand fists in Mildmay's hair, I lash out, knowing nothing will come of it but unable to stay still, and the dream changes, a different sliver of the past, no less true, as Malkar burns into greasy ashes before my eyes. Burns and burns, and it isn't Malkar any longer, isn't the Bastion; Juggernaut's relentless ticking becomes the crackle and pop of burning timbers, becomes the faint terrible keening of a person being burned alive, and I am one of the dark men who stand and watch and am satisfied with what I see.

What Malkar did not tell Mildmay is that I am a monster, too. But Mildmay knew; he knew that long before I sent him into Malkar Gennadion's trap. I woke with the taste of ashes in my mouth and did not move for a long time, feeling Mildmay's warmth against my back and thinking about monsters. Thinking about Malkar, and Mildmay. And myself.

Finally it was close enough to dawn that I didn't have to pretend to try to go back to sleep. In fact, I could have claimed, if anyone had asked, that I'd gotten up that early on purpose. I needed to find a priest.

One of the Fawn daughters was on duty at the front desk, and she looked at me oddly but answered my question. The Arbalest priest—whom she called the intended—could be found in Our Lady of Floodwaters. She gave me directions, although Arbalest was almost small enough that I didn't need them.

Intended Mallett, a blue-veiled, barefoot old man, was out in front of his church, pulling weeds. He listened carefully to what I had to say and nodded sadly when I was done. "Is the Gann place you found, where Verena Lesley met her end. I know of it. Is considered a bad place—*verlain*, the mountain people call it—and maybe these ghosts are why." I would have liked to ask him about Verena Lesley and the Ganns and *verlain* places, but I didn't want to leave Mildmay alone—not that he needed my protection. I thought I could trust Intended Mallett to do what was necessary, and that would have to be enough.

As it turned out, Mildmay was still asleep when I returned to the Five

Dancing Frogs, and he slept on and off for a great deal of the day. I reread Ynge and wished—a tired, stupid itch of desire for something I didn't even want—for a teaspoon's worth of phoenix. It would be better than being stuck in this little room with myself. But it would also be worse, and at least I was smart enough to know that.

Around sunset, a knock on the door startled Mildmay awake. It was one of the Fawn daughters with an invitation to join the family for dinner. I didn't want to, and I could see Mildmay didn't want to, but neither of us—we agreed with a glance—wanted to offend the Fawns by refusing. We followed the Fawn daughter downstairs and into the back of the building, where the family lived.

The people of Corambis, as I had observed during my brief foray that morning, were short, square-built, tawny and red, lions and foxes. A group of them like Mrs. Fawn's daughters, sons-in-law, and grandchildren were bewildering simply for the sameness of them. I hadn't ever thought about the variations among Mélusiniens—except for my own freakish coloring, which I had been trained to be aware of from a very early age—but I realized now how accustomed I had become to a range of browns, from the velvet near-black of Islanders like Vida Eoline, through red browns and ocher browns, to the light honey brown of Mehitabel Parr. And certainly there were differences in skin color and hair color among even these closely related Corambins, but if I didn't concentrate carefully, the distinctions blurred into a muddle. I foresaw the potential for getting myself into a great deal of trouble and resolved for this evening to say as little as possible.

At first, that strategy worked admirably, for we walked into the middle of an argument between several of Mrs. Fawn's sons-in-law and grandsons. They were discussing, heatedly, what would happen to Caloxa—and it was very definitely Caloxa, not merely southern Corambis—now that the Insurgence had been defeated.

The principal combatants, I managed to get fixed in my head. One, Peter Finesilver, was the husband of Mrs. Fawn's eldest daughter and the father of at least two of the children swarming about the room. He had the self-satisfied air that came from a combination of prosperity and a certain native thick-headedness. The other, who carried one shoulder in an odd hunch, was another son-in-law, Sholto Ketteller; he was obviously, from the moment he opened his mouth, the fire-eater of the family.

Finesilver's position was that with Gerrard dead, it could be as if the Insurgence had never happened. The Corambin governor could come back to Wildar and everything (he said naïvely) would be fine again.

Ketteller practically hooted with laughter at this statement, but the interesting thing was that the other men disagreed with it, too. They didn't want

Governor Jaggard back, his time in office having been marked by a significant upswing in both taxes and corruption. James Fawn, Mrs. Fawn's dead husband's brother—unlike the other parties—was old enough to remember the Corambin conquest of Caloxa; he merely felt that a new governor should be appointed—"Is not like the margraves will listen to Jaggard now, is it? After the fool the man made of himself." The others seemed to be in favor of a more moderate version of Ketteller's fierce separatism. Let the Moot rule, said one of the grandsons, like the Convocation did. And when Ketteller, and oddly enough, Finesilver, protested this idea, he shrugged and said, "Well, then, let the Humes be governors."

"But Prince Charles is only a baby," one of the younger boys protested.

"Can't do any worse than Jaggard," James Fawn said and finally provoked a laugh.

I was surprised to learn an heir to the house of Hume had been left alive, and more so seeing the enthusiasm with which the teenage children in particular supported his right to rule Caloxa. They were rather vague on his hypothetical government's relationship with Corambis, though they seemed to envision a sort of vassal state, much like Marathat's ostensible relationship with Tibernia. I wondered if they'd gotten the idea from their grandmother's Mélusinien novels.

Ketteller had fallen ominously silent during the discussion of Prince Charles. Finesilver noticed, too, and said with deep scorn, "Yes, and Sholto'll be off to join the Primrose Men in the morning."

"Would be, an they'd have me," Ketteller said, flaring up immediately. "Is the only answer."

And they might have been off again except that one of the women—I thought Ketteller's wife, although I wasn't sure—emerged from the kitchen and said loudly, "May the Lady have mercy on this house and all the brawling numbskulls who live in it." And when everyone was looking at her, she grinned, showing dimples, and said, "Leave the argument and come have dinner instead."

## Mildmay

You got to understand, I went into that dinner expecting Felix to throw me to the wolves. As soon as the questions started—how'd you become a wizard, how old were you, did the tattoos hurt, what was doing magic like, and hey, what're y'all doing in our horse-and-a-half town anyway?—I was braced for it. I mean, I could practically hear him do it. Because he'd done it before and for less reason. But he didn't. He sat there and smiled and told lies instead.

I'd got used to thinking of Felix as a terrible liar, about as bad as me, but that wasn't right. He couldn't lie to me worth shit, but that night he trotted out a pack of lies that weren't even within earshot of the real story, and he didn't turn a hair.

I asked him about it later, and he blinked at me like he didn't even know what I was talking about and then said, "Oh, I can't tell lies for myself." That was all he said, and it took me a while, lying there in the dark trying not to cough, to work through it to what he meant, which was that he could tell lies just fine as long as it was somebody else getting the benefit. Like Strych. Or me.

And if you want something to make you feel as sick as a drunk dog, give that one a try. Powers. And what made me feel especially sick was that I couldn't even pretend I wished he hadn't done it.

Nice, Milly-Fox. Very fucking classy. But I felt too lousy even to be really mad at myself about it. Mrs. Fawn had given me extra pillows and made me drink a tisane that tasted like dead leaves and licorice, and you know, I was better than I had been, but I still felt like somebody'd been beating me with an invisible stick all day long.

Beside me, Felix twitched and muttered in his dreams, and I fell asleep myself hoping that telling all those lies didn't make him dream about Strych.

## *Felix*

Dark and stone and dripping water. I am so tired of dreaming of labyrinths. But I don't dare try to change the dream. Burning is worse. The briars are worse.

I wish I could just sit still, but my dreaming self knows I can't do that, either. The monster is hunting; I have to keep moving so it doesn't find me.

I fall and fall and fall again. There's blood on my palms, slick becoming sticky, and I know I'm never going to get out this way, but I can't stop.

And then I fall over something that cries in protest. I almost scream; for a moment, I can't breathe. But nothing attacks me, and when I can calm myself enough to listen, I hear something whimpering. I can't tell if it's an animal or a person, although there's just enough light to see a bulk of shadows. I reach out carefully, slowly, and my fingers encounter cloth. A person, then, who flinches back with a wordless cry.

"I won't hurt you. I'm . . ." But I don't know what I am, and I finally say, "Lost."

"Lost," echoes the other in a raw thread of a voice.

"Who are you?"

"Lost," and I can't tell if it's echo or answer.

"Where are we?" I ask, for I can't tell any longer what labyrinth this is. But the other says only, "Lost, lost," in its ruined voice and begins to sob.

The desperate need to move is cramping my limbs, but I can't bring myself to abandon this wretched stranger. "Come on," I say as gently as I can. "Come with me." I'm more than a little surprised when it stands up with me, but we link hands like children and I continue on my miserable, groping progress.

I can't tell where the light is coming from; it waxes and wanes with no logic I can follow. I stumble frequently, but mostly manage to keep my feet. My companion sobs drearily; I still can't tell if it's a man or a woman. After a while, I realize that there's a light ahead of us that isn't waning, but growing steadily stronger, the oblong shape of a doorway. I urge my companion to walk faster. It says, "Lost," dolefully, but follows me.

For a moment when we reach the doorway, what I'm seeing makes no sense. A wooden table fitted with straps to hold a human body. And then I do know; this labyrinth is St. Crellifer's, and in that case . . .

I turn, and the mad wretched creature that was once Isaac Garamond raises its head to look at me and begins to scream.

No wonder I couldn't rest. I am the monster I was trying to flee.

I woke with a violent jolt, almost enough to send me off the bed, and lay for more than a minute while my heart slowed, staring unseeingly at the sunlight pooling among the rumpled covers. And then I blinked and focused and thought, Where is Mildmay?

I shot to my feet. He wasn't in the bed, or even in the room. His cane was gone, too—and I wasn't really stupid enough to believe that anyone could have gotten him out of the room without his consent. I wasn't.

This was an overreaction, I told myself, and put my trousers on. Mildmay couldn't be in any kind of trouble, and if he'd gotten worse, either his coughing would have alerted me or, surely, he would have woken me himself, not just crawled off somewhere to die like a wounded animal.

On second thought, that sounded like exactly the sort of stupid thing Mildmay would do. I didn't bother with socks or shoes.

But the Fawn daughter I encountered in the hallway told me that he'd gotten up early and asked about their bathhouse. "Said you might be interested, too," she added and told me how to get there.

He was in one of the bathtubs when I opened the door, the steam rising in faint coils off the water. He glanced at me—making sure I was who he thought I was and not a threat—and closed his eyes again. His hair was unbraided, but he hadn't ducked his head yet, and the oil lamps mellowed the harsh fox-red to auburn.

He was beautiful. He was beautiful, and he did not know it and would have laughed at me if I'd tried to tell him so. I turned away, making sure the door was latched before I began to undress.

"Nobody here'll know what kept-thieves are," Mildmay said, his voice simultaneously lazy and sharp. "It ain't no fucking big deal."

"It's still ugly," I said and hoped he hadn't seen my flinch. "And people will still ask what happened."

"They don't ask about my face," he said.

"You frighten them, the way you scowl."

He snorted, but it was perfectly true. I'd watched hotel maids, shopkeepers, bartenders fold and fail under the unrelenting weight of that scowl. If he recognized flirtation, he never welcomed it, and I thought he mostly didn't recognize it. When I'd been trying to flirt with him, in Klepsydra, I'd had to resort to the broadest and most caricatured version of myself to get him to notice. And then he'd blushed and looked at me as if I terrified him.

I had, eventually, stopped trying.

It was an effort to take my shirt off, even knowing that Mildmay had seen my back dozens of times before and was not bothered by it. I untied my hair, ran my fingers through it. Bent to take off my boots and Mildmay said, "I knew a gal once had scars like yours."

I hadn't thought he knew how to do this, how to wield a conversation like a knife. On the other hand, he'd had all the time he needed to learn from my dreadful example. "What was her name?" I said tiredly.

"Jeanne-Zerline. She worked in the Goosegirl's Palace down in the Arcane. Died of smallpox about a septad back."

I took the rest of my clothes off and climbed gingerly into the second tub. Mildmay wasn't watching me. Of course he wasn't watching me. He wasn't interested, and I knew it. The hot water was blissful; I felt my spine relax by slow degrees, and finally I could say, "I remember her. She was older. Keeper'd sold her on already before the Fire."

He didn't say anything, and I would have let it drop, except that a horrible thought occurred to me: "How did you know about her scars?"

He didn't open his eyes. "How d'you think?"

The water was turning my skin red, but I was achingly cold. "Did you pick her for her scars? Did they excite you?"

"No, fuckwit. And that ain't how I knew."

"But—"

He silenced me with a glare. "The St. Dismas Baths. Remember? Where you decided I didn't get to go no more?"

"Oh," I said stupidly, uselessly.

"Jeanne-Zerline never cared about them fucking scars," he said, grabbing the soap and working up a savage lather. "She had one made her left tit lopsided, and she didn't fucking care."

"It can be a . . . selling point," I said, now as hot as I had been cold only a moment before. It had certainly been a selling point at the Shining Tiger.

"What if it don't matter?"

"I beg your pardon."

"What if. It. Don't. Matter." He rinsed the soap off and ducked his head before starting on his hair. "What if you say, I don't care and fuck anybody who does. What happens then?"

"I don't know what you mean."

He sighed and handed me the soap. "I know you don't. And it ain't like I'm any good at it my own self." He slid down to rinse his hair; numbly, I started washing myself. When he sat up again, he said, "If there was any way in the world you could get rid of them scars, I'd help you do it. You know that, right?"

"Yes," I said. My throat was suddenly tight.

"But there ain't. They're part of you. And, you know, they ain't no nice part, but." He bent his head a little, caught my eyes, and held them. "Pretending they ain't there and hiding them all the time, it don't help."

"You would feel differently if that scar weren't on your face," I said bitterly, viciously, watching the soap lather over my pale skin.

"You think?" His voice was neutral, and I was not about to look at him. He carefully worked his way out of the bathtub. He didn't ask for help, and I didn't offer. He dried off while I quickly washed my hair. I got out of the bathtub while he was still rubbing the towel vigorously over his head.

"You think that scar makes you ugly," I said.

He straightened up, watching me warily. How good we are at this, I thought detachedly. How easily we read each other when we're out for blood. "You think yours make you ugly," he countered.

"No. I think my scars show what I am. But you think that scar makes you ugly. You think *you*'re ugly."

"I am ugly."

"No, you aren't." I stepped closer, painfully aware that we were both naked, aware of the scars on his face and thigh, of the scars on my back. Of my tattoos, which were scars in their own way. "Did Kolkhis tell you that? Did she tell you you were repulsive?"

He backed away from me, but there was nowhere to go, and he jarred his shoulders against the door. "Kolkhis don't have nothing to do with—"

"Oh yes she does. Because I'm right, aren't I? She told you you were hideous. She told you no one would ever want to kiss you."

His tongue touched his upper lip nervously. "Maybe."

"She lied." I was close enough now to feel the damp heat of his body, to see water beading at his hairline. "I can show you just how terribly she lied to you, Mildmay."

"No," he said, flatly, with finality, and—unbearably—with pity.

"You won't . . ."

"No. I ain't molly, and I don't want you. And you promised you wouldn't rape me."

His voice wavered a little, but his eyes didn't, and I hated myself. Again. Still. Just one more reason on top of all the others. My hands clenched, and I burst out, "Hit me."

"What?"

"Hit me. If you won't kiss me, hit me."

"Felix, you don't—"

"Damn you. *Hit me.* You want to. You've wanted to for years. I know it, you know it. So *do* it."

His eyes had clenched shut; I could see the tension radiating upward from his fists, turning his shoulders into a bar of pig iron. I wanted to feel his strength; I wanted to feel *him*. I didn't care how anymore. I just wanted him to touch me.

And I knew how to do it.

*"Hit me,"* I said, pushing the obligation d'âme as hard as I could, and at the same time I swung at him.

It wouldn't have been much of a blow in any event—*You hit like a girl,* some tormentor sneered in the back of my head: Keeper? Lorenzo? Malkar? I couldn't even tell—but Mildmay had the reactions I didn't, and my hand didn't come anywhere near his face before he moved, faster than I could see, and I was on my back on the floor, with my ears ringing.

Mildmay was still standing against the door, hands poised defensively in front of his body, and he said, snarling, "You happy now?"

"Deliriously," I said, not moving.

"Good." His eyes were lurid poison green. "Then get the *fuck* away from me. And if you ever do that again, I will fucking kill you. You hear me?"

"Yes," I said, still not moving.

He wrenched the door open and left, not bothering with his clothes. Some lucky Fawn daughter, I thought remotely, was going to get an eyeful.

It was a good minute and a half before I was able to make myself move.

## Kay

The Pigrin train station was like being trapped in a metal rookery. My hands instinctively went to cover my ears, though it did no good, and when the catafalque lurched forward, I had to stagger and lunge to keep my feet under me. I had learned within minutes of leaving the church's courtyard not to let myself fall, for the ox driver would not halt his beasts on my behalf.

I had walked from Howrack to Pigrin, knowing the destination only because the soldiers spoke of it to one another, complaining bitterly that they had not been given leave to visit Miss Evie's, which I knew to be one of Pigrin's jezebel houses. The catafalque stopped several times; each time I, like the oxen, was given water. My hands had to be guided to the dipper; at the third stop, they had to be supported as well, for I was shaking too badly to get the dipper to my mouth unaided. I expected the soldiers to mock me, but they did not. They spoke to me as little as possible, but they were not cruel; when I stumbled painfully over a road stone as we entered Pigrin proper, someone's hand in my shift collar dragged me back to my feet. I did not understand it, but I was grateful.

I did not know Pigrin well; had come here once to speak to Gerrard when his wife, pregnant with Charles, was taking the waters. I remembered walking with Gerrard through the great, vaulted, rose marble halls of the Pigrin Chalybeate, remembered his laughter echoing and the scandalized expressions of the invalids and ancients. Did not remember what we had spoken of. And I had not taken the train, for I hated them, foul-smelling cacophonous horrors that they were—and ah, Lady, who will keep them out of Rothmarlin now?—so that although I had been able to follow a rough mental map from Howrack to Pigrin, for Pigrin itself I had no map. I could only follow the pressure of the collar around my throat. Was all I had ever been able to do, in truth, but it had been easier to bear when I had had some sense of the direction we traveled. Now I felt as though every step might lead me over the edge of a precipice. It shamed me to admit it, even to myself, but without the catafalque to drag me, I might not have been able to move at all.

I could feel blood sticky on my feet against the smooth stone of the station floor, and I wondered if I was leaving a trail of red footprints like the sea maiden in the story. My neck was bleeding, too, where the soldering had left rough edges, and there was the heat of bruises across my shoulders. Art lucky to have come so far without worse injuries, I told myself, and then, in proof or mockery, my foot came down on something that burned it. I yelped like a kicked dog, my whole body jerking sideways, and had it not been for a hard-callused hand that closed around my upper arm, the combination of my unwise movement and the drag of the chain would have put me on the floor.

"Steady, m'lord. You stepped on a cinder, that's all." A Corambin voice, like Intended Gye's. A soldier—the same one who had saved me before?

"Leave him *be*, Oddlin!" shouted someone else, and I recognized a sergeant's voice when I heard it, even with Corambin vowels.

"Thank you," I said in a whisper as raw as the bleeding places on my neck, and the hand was gone. I followed the pull of the catafalque, limping now, trying to keep my burned instep from touching the floor. Trying not to think about the possibility of more cinders.

Then the pull changed, becoming slower and . . . upward? A ramp beneath my feet, stubbing my toes, and I understood: we—the catafalque, the oxen, and I—were being loaded into a baggage car.

The prospect was actually less unpleasant than the idea of being chained in a passenger car with Glimmering for several hours.

The catafalque halted. I heard the sergeant's voice again, this time ordering one of his men to block the wheels and another to help the driver with the oxen. Someone bumped me in passing; I edged to my right, away from the ramp and the open door. Three cautious, shuffling steps, and my outstretched arm found the wall of the car. It would have to do, for I did not think I could keep on my feet any longer. Whether was grief or blindness or something else that weakened me, I knew not, but a journey that would ordinarily have been a pleasant morning's walk had left me exhausted. I put my back to the wall and sat down, drawing my knees up under my chin so that I might be as little in the way as possible. Did not truly expect that to be enough, and it was not. I barely had time to feel relief at having my weight off my aching feet before the sergeant was shouting, equally at his men and at me; I was dragged upright again and pushed hard enough that I could not brace myself. I staggered forward, my hands coming up reflexively, and collided with the side of the catafalque. A hard boost from someone and I was sprawling across Gerrard's shins. "You'll be out of the way up there," the sergeant said; I bit my tongue and did not ask, *Out of the way of what?*

In another moment, I found out. The noise was unmistakable, even if it made no sense here, clattering hooves and an aggrieved noise somewhere between a moan and a yell: the bawl of a cow who did not want to go where she was being driven.

"Cattle," I said blankly.

"His Grace's gift to the Seven Houses," said someone, most likely Oddlin, who had helped me before.

"*Cattle?*" said I, still not quite able to believe it, but then the first of the cows came up the ramp, and if anyone answered me, I had no hope of hearing it.

The half-wild shaggy Caloxan cattle were small but hardy, and their milk was richer than that of their larger and more placid cousins. Listening to the soldiers and the cowherds cursing each other and the cattle indiscriminately, I realized I ought to be grateful to be up on the catafalque, out of the way of boots and hooves alike. But Gerrard was lumpy and dead underneath me, and one good kick from a cow might have put an end to this wretchedness, even if for only an hour. I was not grateful.

I was, though, exhausted, and willing to risk wrath that I was fairly sure would not be forthcoming. These soldiers had their orders, and they would follow them, but they were not zealots. Was it obvious to them that my penance was a sham, a ploy of the duke's? I shifted carefully, trying to find some measure of comfort without further disturbing Gerrard's body. And then, my head pillowed on a wadded section of the burlap draperies, and despite the appalling noise, I fell instantly and heavily asleep.

I woke once when the train began to move—to which the cattle objected, as they had objected to everything else—but no one seemed to be paying any attention to me, and if nothing else, I thought with grim, half-dreaming humor, I'd learned my lesson about seeking trouble. I fell asleep again.

I woke the second time because the train stopped with a tremendous jerk. I was thrown forward and then back so violently that I ended up lying on the floor of the baggage car, entangled with Gerrard's body in an obscene parody of a lover's embrace, the breath knocked from my body and my head ringing like a full peal of church bells. Around me, the cattle were bawling like outraged virgins, the oxen were bellowing, and the soldiers were cursing with an impressive fluency and variety of expression. I lay still, afraid that if I moved, I would damage the body, and after a few moments, the sergeant interrupted his excoriations of the train, the cattle, and life in general to say, "Ah, strewth, we'd better pick up his lordship. Oddlin—you've a talent that way."

So it had been Oddlin who had helped me the first time. I could not decide if it made me feel better to know that I had a champion, or more like a helpless girl.

It took two of them to lift Gerrard's body back into the catafalque. I stayed still, listening to the sergeant ordering someone to go up the train and find out what had happened, listening to the cowherds settling the cattle. "Art not hurt, thou great daft mop," one of them said, exasperation and affection so mingled that they could not be separated, and I remembered Benallery saying to me, long ago, "Just because Gerrard throws himself down a well, doesn't mean you have to jump after him." Even then I'd known, although I hadn't said so, that that was exactly what it *did* mean.

I felt motion and heat beside me, and recognized Oddlin's voice when he spoke. "Are you hurt, my lord?"

"No," I said, being now fairly sure I told the truth. "What happened?"

"We don't know, my lord, but Lark's gone to find out. Come on, then." He lifted me first to my feet and then onto the catafalque; I realized he was larger even than I had thought. Most men were taller than I—and many women, too—but this one seemed a giant, maybe as tall as Angel Vyell, who was over six feet, the largest man I had ever known. I added to my list of things I ought to be grateful for, even if I wasn't able to be, the fact that Oddlin was inclined to be gentle.

They had made no effort to arrange Gerrard's body—and why should they? Was not *their* failed king. Shouldst be grateful, again, that they do not desecrate the body. I thought of bodies I had found after the Usara had finished with them, and could not help shivering a little, imagining those things done to Gerrard.

Hesitantly at first, expecting to be ordered to stop, I straightened Gerrard's body as best I could. None paid me the least heed; though I knew I did a poor job of it, it gave me some comfort to know that I had tried, and that it was better than nothing. I lay down again, but not to sleep. Not when something had happened that my keepers did not understand. I listened—as I should have been doing from the start—and figured out that there were six of them, counting the absent Lark. They had served in the long, grim, bloody siege of Beneth Castle; this assignment was in the nature of a vacation for them, nursemaiding a dead body, a blind prisoner, and twenty-four cows from Howrack to Bernatha.

With a long, rattling clatter, they opened the side door, and I was genuinely grateful for that; the cows made the air rather too rich to breathe.

"Hey," said one, "ain't that that fucking hill we started out at this morning?"

"Summerdown," said another. "Yeah, we've come in a great big fucking circle. Welcome to the army, Tredell."

"Oh fuck you," Tredell said without any malice. "It's just creepy, that's all. I heard Webber talking about it. What they found, you know. I was glad to get away from there, tell you the truth. And now here we are back again."

"Tredell, you talk too fucking much," the sergeant said.

The soldier named Lark returned then, panting, and said that something had gone wrong with the engine of the train and the enginists were fighting over what exactly, and Major Browne said to sit tight and he'd let them know if there was any need for action.

"Meaning we shouldn't be asking in the first place," the sergeant grumbled. "But if I hadn't sent a man, he'd be all over me wanting to know if we were all asleep back here."

"Welcome to the army, Sarge," said Oddlin, and the sergeant swore at him blisteringly while the other men laughed.

My time sense was gone, lost in foul unending night, but it was not very long before the train jerked and groaned and began moving again. The soldiers raised an ironic cheer, and I fell back asleep as abruptly as falling down a well. Although it was Benallery who had followed Gerrard this time, not I.

## *Mildmay*

Powers and saints, I was mad at him. Not so much about him making a pass at me because, tell you the truth, I'd been expecting that for decads. Who the fuck else did he have? I mean, me, I could find a chambermaid or a barmaid or some gal willing to trade my face for the chance to fuck somebody new, but the further north we got, the less we saw guys who were openly molly, and the more we saw people giving the hairy eyeball to guys who looked like they *might* be. Like Felix. It wasn't safe. I knew it, and he knew it, and he was still pretty fucked up about everything, so I wasn't sure he'd've gone hunting anyway.

But there I was, and I knew how he felt about me even if I didn't understand it and didn't share it, so I wasn't surprised at him coming on to me, and I didn't blame him or nothing. No, what had me too mad to see straight was what he did when I turned him down. It wasn't even the part where he was getting back at me by using the binding-by-forms, it was the part where he was using me to punish himself. I don't even know what he thought he needed to be punished for, but I'd knocked him flat on his ass, and he'd practically said thank you. That wasn't about him wanting to fuck me. Not even a little. That was about him using whatever tool was handy to hurt himself.

I wanted to yell at him—no, more'n that. I wanted to howl at him, scream at him, beat him up for real, make him fucking admit that I wasn't a tool for him to use. I wasn't a knife, and I wasn't a fucking clockwork bear, and if he wanted to hurt himself, he should have the common fucking courtesy not to use me to do it. Of course, I also wanted to pin him down and sit on him until he explained to me just *why* he thought he needed to be hurt, and then sit on him some more until he listened when I told him he'd already been hurt plenty and should just let it the fuck go.

But, you know, that wasn't going to work, so I'd let it go, as best I could—but there was one thing I was hanging onto, and that was that I was not fucking apologizing this time. He wanted things right between us, he was going to have to do the work himself. And he was going to have to come out and say he was sorry. The looks he was giving me, and the awful, meek way he was creeping around like he thought I was going to hit him again and this time without being told to—that was all fine, pretty much standard for him when he knew he'd fucked up. But it wasn't enough, and I was not going to fucking cave. Not this time.

# *Felix*

Mildmay's anger was like a third person sitting between us—which was all the more unfortunate as there was barely room for two. The stagecoach was indeed exactly like a diligence, and apparently the drivers practiced the same abominable custom of overbooking. Either that or the need to reach Bernatha had become an epidemic. We were crammed together, shoulder to shoulder, and I couldn't decide if it made me feel better or worse that he let me have the outside seat, so that my other shoulder was against the side of the coach. Sick with gratitude summed it up, and I applied myself rather desperately to the conversation of the other passengers, preferring even the most tedious of provincial gossip to either my own thoughts or Mildmay's black glower.

The man across from me, stout and gray-haired, was silent all the morning and half the afternoon, but finally, when most of the other passengers had subsided into uncomfortable dozes, I managed to draw him out about his country's recent history. He'd been too young to fight when the Corambins invaded forty years ago: "Was only a boy. But my brother answered Lord Seaward's call. Should be his farm by rights, but he never came back."

That war had been about magic, although he was unclear on the difference between Caloxan warlocks and Corambin magicians. Either he truly didn't know, or he didn't want to discuss it with me—all he said was "Warlocks used bad magic," and I didn't press him.

It hadn't lasted long—not nearly as long as the Insurgence—and in general (he suggested although did not say outright) Caloxans were glad of the Corambin thaumaturgical reforms. The trouble was all political.

Corambis had done away with its kings hundreds of years before, "and I suppose they thought was the only right way of things. But their dukes and such aren't like our margraves, and maybe our king wasn't like their king either. So King James had to go, we all saw that, but a Corambin governor in his place was no good answer. And the Moot—" He snorted. "Have never seen that the Moot does anything but fight amongst themselves like a flock of chickens."

So the margraves agreed on nothing, the governors came and went, corrupt some years, incompetent others, and Gerrard Hume grew up and decided it was his place to do something about it.

"I saw him once," the gray-haired man said as we came into the town where we would spend the night. "My eldest boy was with me, and there was the start of all *that* trouble. But is true. He was . . ." He broke off, groping for a word. "He was *kingly*. And he'd come to places like Arbalest—which has not seen a single governor, not once in forty indictions—and he'd listen when people told him what was wrong." He broke off again, and I waited, understanding that I was watching an inarticulate man trying to say something important.

"He wanted to make things *better*," he said finally. "I don't think he ever had a chance—not once Bernatha cast their lot for the Convocation, that's for sure—but I do wish he had."

And then the coach drew up in the yard of a hotel called the Blue Ox, and we disembarked in a graceless scramble. Rooms and food alike were unappealing and overpriced, but the worst thing about that night was that Mildmay was still not speaking to me. I slept fitfully, poorly, and when the overworked maid came around to bang on everyone's door in the morning, I knew suddenly and completely that I couldn't bear another day like this.

I blurted, "What do you want me to say?"

My voice was louder than I'd meant it to be; I startled myself almost as much as I startled him. There were times when I might have taken a petty pleasure in making him jump, but now it was just another thing I'd gotten wrong. It took him a moment to turn from the window; when he did, he didn't say anything at first, simply looked at me, face unreadable, eyes like stone. Then he sighed, and some indefinable tension seemed to bleed away from his shoulders. He said, "You could start with 'I'm sorry.' "

I stared at him.

"What? You gonna try and tell me you don't know you fucked up?"

I shook my head dumbly.

"Or don't I rate an apology?" he said, and he meant it to be sarcasm, but I heard true bitterness and remembered unbidden a dozen separate occasions of deliberate cruelty, things I'd done or said to hurt him, to make him feel as if I didn't care about him, as if he wasn't worth treating decently.

I stumbled over the words as I said them: "I'm sorry."

And what hurt even more was his obvious surprise.

"Okay," he said. And then he tilted his head a little, eyes not as hard but dangerously thoughtful. "D'you know what it is you're sorry for, or are you just trying to get me to let it go?"

I felt my face flood crimson, and I couldn't meet his eyes any longer. "I'm sorry for making a pass at you," I said.

"But that ain't why I'm mad."

And I was staring at him again. "It isn't?"

"Well, a little," he admitted. "But it ain't that. It's the other thing."

"The other . . . Oh."

"Yeah." And he waited.

"I . . . I'm sorry about that, too."

There was a moment when I thought he was going to tell me that wasn't good enough—*Make me believe you mean it, dearest,* Malkar's voice whispered in the back of my head—but then, all at once, he said, "Okay." He didn't smile, of course, but something changed like the sun coming out from behind a cloud, and I knew he had forgiven me. Again. I wondered if I could manage to deserve it this time.

# Chapter 3

## *Felix*

The stagecoach's likeness to a diligence extended to the extreme discomfort of the journey, and by the time we reached Bernatha, it was obvious that Mildmay was worse again. The stagecoach had not been good for him. When he let me help him down in the stable yard of the Gull and Gringolet, I knew he was in a bad way.

"We'll stay here tonight," I said. It was already past sundown; the last hour of the journey was an experience I would go well out of my way to avoid having ever again.

"Be 'spensive," Mildmay said thickly. He was shivering, and I hoped he wasn't developing an ague.

"Don't worry about it," I said—and nearly stumbled over my own feet when he said, "Okay," and actually leaned on me for support.

We should have stayed in Arbalest, I thought—but he'd been impatient to keep going, and he'd truly seemed better. Even last night in the Blue Ox, I hadn't noticed anything wrong. I wondered now, helping him up the stairs into the long, narrow foyer of the hotel, how much of that had been due to his honestly appalling skill at hiding any sign of illness. I wasn't going to yell at him when he was sick, but I rather badly wanted to.

The clerk demanded money in advance; given their prices—"expensive" was a kind word—I wondered if they'd had a lot of trouble with people skipping out on the bill. Mildmay counted the money out owlishly. It wasn't all we had. Not quite.

The room itself was a grandiose closet. I helped Mildmay take off his shoes, got him as comfortable as I could, and then went down to the bar. We couldn't stay here another night, and I needed local knowledge if we weren't going to end up somewhere just as bad.

The patrons of the bar were an odd mix: stagecoach passengers; local gamblers playing what looked like the game Mildmay had so disliked in Arbalest and probably hoping to lure in some gulls fresh off the coach; and a variety of prostitutes, mostly women but a few men, their shabby-gaudy finery not so different from what they would have been wearing in a Lower City bar, likewise hoping for gulls. The prostitutes were the people I needed to talk to; they would know every cheap hotel in Bernatha. But getting them to talk to me was a different matter.

Oh, they were *interested* in me. They started drifting my direction as soon as I came in; I sat with a glass of the cheapest wine I could stand to drink and watched the almost invisible struggle over who was going to get to approach me first.

A girl won; she was sixteen or seventeen, fine-boned for a Corambin, with curly, pale blond hair and dark eyes. She had a long nose and her jaw wasn't nearly as heavy as the Corambin norm; she was actually quite pretty, although not, as they said in Pharaohlight, my type.

She caught my eye—or, to be more accurate, I allowed her to catch my eye—and said, "You must be a long way from home, wherever home is for you. Want some company?" Her accent, like the clerk's and the bartender's, was quite different from that of the stagecoach passengers and the people in Arbalest, more liquid, musical, with a roll to the *r*'s, and the *s*'s shading into *th*'s.

I waved her to a seat. "What's your name?"

"Whatever you want it to be, gorgeous."

I rolled my eyes. "Oh please."

Indignation straightened her spine. I leaned across the table and said, "I don't do women, and I'm not in the mood for that kind of company tonight anyway, but I'll pay you for information."

I watched emotions flicker across her face; then she settled back in her chair. She sounded much older and harder when she said, "What kind of information and how much?"

"Let's start with what I already asked you: what's your name?"

She gave me a narrow look, then nodded sharply, more to herself than me, and said, "My name's Corbie." And when I raised my eyebrows at her, she added, almost sullenly, "Gartrett Corbie. What's yours?"

"Felix Harrowgate."

"Huh. All right, Mr. Harrowgate. Let's see your money."

I put down a banshee.

"Huh," she said again. But she leaned forward, putting her elbows on the table, and blew a stray strand of hair out of her eyes. "Well, you bought yourself some good answers there. So, hit me. What do you want to know?"

"To start with, the name of a cheap and honest hotel."

That made her laugh. "You're asking *me*?"

"Don't tell me you don't know."

She tilted her head a little, frowning at me. "Well, I do know. But how'd you *know* I'd know?"

"Because," I said tiredly, "I know how prostitution works."

Her eyebrows shot up, and she leaned even closer. "Are you looking to get into the game here?"

She'd heard more than I'd meant her to, but I couldn't deny her inference. She was, after all, perfectly correct. "No."

"You'd probably do all right," she said, and I cringed a little at the assessment in her voice.

"I am *not*—" I caught myself. "We don't intend to be in Bernatha long."

"We?"

"My brother and I. But we'll be here some days, and—"

"And you can't stay here. I hear you. So. A hotel I'd stay at, or a hotel I'd take a fish to?"

"Fish" was clearly the Bernathan word for a prostitute's client—"trick" at home. "A hotel you'd stay at," I said.

I'd gone up a notch or two in her estimation, by the way she nodded, and she went up a notch or two in mine, because she thought about it for several moments before she said, "I'd go with the Fiddler's Fox, if it was me. It's in the House of Chastity, but maybe you won't mind that so much."

"I beg your pardon? It's what?"

"You've never been to Bernatha before," she said, not asking.

"No, I haven't."

"Strewth," she said, but mildly. I supposed newcomers were a part of life for any prostitute who worked the Gull and Gringolet. "All right. I give all my customers value for money." And she winked at me so lewdly I felt myself blush.

Her explanation was swift, succinct, and smooth with long practice, if not as detailed as I would have liked. Bernatha was a free city, divided into eight districts; the one we were in, St. Melior, was apparently not considered a proper part of the city, although it was definitely Bernathan rather than Corambin—or Caloxan, and after only a moment's consideration, I abandoned the thought of asking her to explain the relationship of a "free city" to either government. The rest of Bernatha was on a set of three islands; the main island was accessible, at certain times of day, by a causeway from St. Melior, but otherwise, all traffic was by boat. The three islands were divided into seven Houses—which were something like districts, as I was accustomed to them in Mélusine, and something like guilds. The north island was the House of Honesty, being the home of the judicial system and the city government and also the prison of Stonewater. The south island was the House of Mercy, and was largely taken up, most confusingly, by the House of Mercy, which was, Gartrett Corbie told me proudly, the largest hospital in Corambis. The remaining five houses—Prudence, Patience, Loyalty, Chastity, and Charity—shared the main island and all of them tithed St. Melior, although I couldn't make out from what Corbie said whether it was that they paid St. Melior or St. Melior paid them or possibly, in some labyrinthine fashion, both.

Corbie, like her colleagues, was a member (the word she used was "pledge") of the House of Chastity. She was very proud of this, and I gathered it was something one had to work for. "So are there prostitutes who aren't pledges?"

"Oh sure. Lots of 'em." She jerked her chin at a pair of girls on the other side of the bar, double-teaming one of my fellow passengers from the stagecoach. "But the upright dens won't take you unless you're pledged. So you're on your own. And mostly, you don't last long."

"Upright dens?" I said.

She made an impatient noise behind her teeth and said, "*Respectable brothels,*" in what I felt safe assuming was meant as a parody of my voice. "You know, places where your crib has a *lock* on the door."

"Ah," I said. "Quite."

There were hotels in a number of the Houses, but not all of them were pledged. The Fiddler's Fox was pledged, although—confusingly again—not to the House of Chastity. "Loyalty, I think," Corbie said, as if it wasn't particularly important.

There wasn't much point in asking Corbie most of my other questions, but there was one I couldn't avoid: "How expensive are doctors?"

"Are you sick, Mr. Harrowgate?"

"Not me. But I'm afraid my brother has, um . . ." I remembered the word Mrs. Fawn had used. "Pleuriny."

From the grimace she made, even if pleuriny wasn't exactly the Winter Fever, it was just as serious. "A pledged physician-practitioner will cost you an arm and a leg, you not being pledged yourself. And anybody good won't be cheap. But you want to be careful. Make 'em show you their practitioner's license before you let 'em anywhere near your brother. If you go to the Fiddler's Fox, ask Mrs. Lettice. She'll know who you can trust."

Custom was picking up, and Corbie was starting to fidget. "Thank you," I said and pushed the banshee across the table to her.

She looked nearly shocked. "That's *it*?"

I shrugged. "You answered my questions." There was no need to tell her I was buying her goodwill along with her answers. I had a lowering presentiment we were going to need all the goodwill we could get, and I knew how fast news traveled among prostitutes—nearly as fast as among courtiers.

"Are you sure you don't want anything else?" she said, and I might have been offended except that she sounded more worried than seductive.

"I'm sure," I said, standing up, and smiled at her. "You've been very helpful, Miss Corbie. Thank you." At the door, I glanced back; she was still staring at me, looking baffled.

Mildmay was awake when I came in, and obviously wretched.

"You're sick," I said, mostly because I was curious about whether he would continue to deny it.

"Yeah," he said. "Sorry to be such a pain." Not all of the color in his face was from the fever.

"Don't apologize to me," I said, more sharply than I meant to, and he recoiled a little. Add bullying the sick to my list of virtues. "Anyway, it should be me apologizing to you."

"How d'you figure?"

"I'm the one who dumped you in the St. Grainne."

"You didn't *dump* me," he said. "I jumped." And he even managed to sound indignant, although the effort caused an ugly coughing fit.

When he'd recovered enough that he wasn't actually panting for breath, I said, "And anyway I know you didn't get sick on purpose."

"Damn straight," he said. "Hey, Felix?"

"Yes?"

"Where are we? Did we make it to Bernatha okay?"

"Yes," I said, and swallowed against the sudden knot of panic and pity in my throat. "We're in a hotel called the Gull and Gringolet."

"Okay, good," he said and shut his eyes.

## *Kay*

I had never visited Bernatha. Had never wanted to. It was a crafty city, clever and greedy and always double-dealing. The Seven Houses had had no use for Gerrard's fairy tales, and he had not sought, after that first failure, to woo them. Bernatha did not consider itself part of Caloxa, and Gerrard, his pride stung, had announced himself happy to return the favor.

And we had all paid for it.

Hatefully, pointlessly, I envied Gerrard his death. Would have given my own life to save him, but as it was, at least he was spared the humiliation of being led through the streets of Bernatha, a blind beast on a chain. He did not have to listen to the Bernathans' contempt, the Corambins' gloating. Did not have to hear how parents answered when children asked about the funny cart and the man on a leash. The indignities visited on his corpse could not touch him; in death he was inviolate. I had no such grace.

Glimmering had decided, and the Bernathans had been pleased to concur, that the catafalque and I as its appendage should be displayed in the Hall of the Seven Virtues, in Bernatha's Clock Palace—so named for the Clock of Eclipses, sunk deep into the bones of building and island alike. And mercifully silent, as it had been for wheel upon wheel.

Bernatha had a clockwork heart, but that heart did not run. From all I had heard, it had been a heart as monstrous as that of the Automaton of Corybant . . . as monstrous as the clockwork heart beneath Summerdown. I could remember Gerrard laughing at stories about the Automaton, and he considered the reputation of the Clock of Eclipses mere superstition. He had argued with Practitioner Penny about that. I had not cared at the time, but I wondered now, wondered what Penny had been trying to tell him. Maybe something as simple as *Be careful*, but Gerrard had been so certain of himself, so certain he had found the answer, like a hero in a children's story . . .

The blow across the face took me completely unawares. The Hall of the Seven Virtues was full of echoes and chattering voices as the Bernathans and the Corambins celebrated the end of the Insurgence; I had had no idea there was anyone near me.

I fell, my chains pulling painfully at neck and wrists, and a boot caught me in the ribs. "You coward. You craven crawling cringing *dog*. Did you even wait for Gerrard to die before you betrayed him? Did you sign your surrender in his still flowing blood? You vile maggot, you were never fit to lick his boots. Would that he were alive—alive to see the truth of you."

"Blandamere?" I said, bewildered. Blandamere was middle-aged, bull-necked and bull-headed; his hero-worship of Gerrard had been an open secret, but I had not thought he cared about me sufficiently to feel so obviously, rawly betrayed.

"Don't sound so surprised," said he, his voice thick with loathing. He kicked me again.

Other voices, murmuring, "My lord Blandamere," "Come away, my lord," "Is no point, my lord," and the sounds of Blandamere being led—or pulled—away.

I sat up slowly, half-expecting another blow to strike me out of black nothing. But from what I could hear, no one was paying any attention; Glimmering's grating voice was some distance away, and I thought that his back was turned to me. I was shaking, undone not by the physical violence but by my inability to defend myself, or even to be aware of the blow before it struck me.

I recited the coraline in my head to drown out the rising panic. Could not be changed. Was no point in weeping or screaming or any other hysterical display, and especially not in front of Glimmering and the assembled dignitaries, for whom I was already serving as a macabre sort of party decoration. Link by link, I followed the chain back to the catafalque, and I pressed myself against it, for although I hated it, it was at least some protection.

Or, I thought and curled tightly in upon myself, the illusion of it.

## Felix

I slept very little that night. Mildmay was restless, seeming to have developed twice the usual number of knees and elbows, and even when I did sleep, I was afraid of what I might find in my dreams. Or what might find me. I could bear neither another dream of burning nor another dream of Isaac. I had rarely been so grateful for morning, and I was up and bathed and dressed and trying to convince Mildmay to eat at an hour when I would normally have been calculating how many minutes longer I could stay in bed and still make it to court on time.

The thought was not a pleasant one. I sighed and said to Mildmay's lowered head, "At least drink the tea." Lack of appetite wasn't a good sign, nor was the fact that he didn't argue with me or tell me not to nag him. He drank the tea and looked at me shyly, clearly hoping for approval and not expecting to get it. I wondered how high his fever had risen.

"That's good," I said, although I felt like the worst kind of patronizing fraud. And I felt even worse at the way his face lit up, as if I'd handed him his heart's desire. It's just that he's ill, I told myself, but I suspected darkly that his illness was simply letting me see what had been there all along.

Gideon had once said to me: *You must be the only person in the Mirador who hasn't realized Mildmay would walk on knives for you.* I realized all too well, but I still didn't understand, and I wasn't selfish enough to ask him now, when he would almost certainly tell me the truth. Instead, I stood up, pushing away from the table with perhaps excessive force. Mildmay watched me wide-eyed, and I saw for a moment the half-feral child he had been.

"I'm going to ask how we go about getting to Bernatha proper. Stay there." It had been exhausting enough for him to get out of bed, dress himself, and navigate the stairs. I wasn't going to make him leave that chair before it was strictly necessary.

Corbie had said there was a causeway as well as a number of ferryboats called gondols. I personally would have preferred the causeway, having an abhorrence of boats, but the day clerk explained that the gondols were far cheaper. "Were you wishful of hiring one, sir? I can send the boy down to the moorings for you."

"That would be very helpful, thank you," I said and tipped him as generously as I dared. "And, er, how much does the gondol hire cost?"

"Five hermits," he said. "I'll send the boy now."

"Thank you," I said and retreated gratefully to the dining room, where Mildmay was frowning at vacant space. I moved into his line of sight, since that seemed substantially easier than redirecting his attention, and after several seconds, he blinked and focused on me.

"How are you doing?" I said.

"I'm okay," he said, but it was as automatic and meaningless as a clock chiming the hour.

"You're a liar," I said amiably and sat down.

He looked like he was going to argue, but he started coughing instead, a painful, croupy-sounding cough that left him white-faced and sweating. But he sounded more like himself when he said, "Okay, yeah. I'm a liar."

"Let's try again. How are you doing?"

"I feel like shit, thanks for asking."

"*Is* it the Winter Fever?"

"Fuck," he said, exhausted and disgusted and maybe a little scared. "Yeah. It's the Winter Fever. I ain't gonna be much use for the next decad or so."

And that was an optimistic estimate. "It's all right," I said. "We're going to cross to Bernatha and find a cheap hotel, and we'll stay there 'til you're well again."

He frowned at me, although it looked like it hurt. "Shouldn't we be getting on to Esmer and them hocuses you're s'posed to talk to?"

"When you're better."

"But—"

"They're unlikely to go anywhere. And it's not as if they're expecting me."

He still looked unhappy. I said, "It's not worth you killing yourself over." In truth, I wasn't sure he could make it as far as the front door, never mind a complicated undertaking like trying to get to Esmer when we had only an imperfect understanding of what the Corambin railroad *was*, much less how to use it. And then in Esmer we would be in the same position we were in here: staying at the first hotel we came to, without the slightest idea of where else to go. I'd gotten lucky once in the person of Corbie; I didn't want to gamble on being lucky again.

And there was the darker thought that I didn't know what the Corambin wizards were going to do with me when I presented myself to them, or in consequence what would happen to Mildmay. There were too many possibilities, too many of them nightmarish—Mildmay left alone and helpless while I was shut in the Corambin equivalent of the Verpine. Or of St. Crellifer's. "Trust me," I said. "It's *fine*."

"If you're sure," he said. He was really too ill to care, except that he was worried about me.

"Yes," I said firmly, and that satisfied him.

A gondol turned out to be a long narrow rowboat. The gondolman and I packed Mildmay into one end and I sat at the other; the gondolman and his oars were in the middle. The main island of Bernatha, the Crait, seemed disturbingly far away, but having seen the causeway, I knew I would have disliked it just as much—narrow and completely devoid of railings. At least in the gondol I didn't have to worry about Mildmay fainting and falling into the sea.

Of course, there was always the possibility *I* would faint. I shut my eyes as the gondol moved into open water, letting my grip on the edge of the seat go white-knuckled. The wind cut straight through me and everything reeked of salt and dead fish.

"Beautiful day, sir," the gondolman said, sounding unwholesomely cheerful.

I opened my eyes; he seemed to be sincere. I looked at the sun, half-obscured by clouds, and at the sea, tormented into tiny whitecapped waves by the wind. The gondol lurched across them like a drunken horse trying to waltz.

"Is the weather often worse than this?" I said finally.

It made him laugh. "May the Lady bless you, sir, there's not above two months in the indiction all told that it isn't raining in Bernatha. And we're known for our fogs." He jerked his head in a peculiar gesture, which I realized when he continued was meant to indicate the two tall towers visible on the island behind him. "That's why we've got the Sisters. Best lighthouses in Corambis. They say Grimglass is taller, but it can't match them for beauty."

Clearly bragging about their city is a Bernathan disease, I thought, then reminded myself that I would dislike *any* man who dragged me out in a ridiculously tiny boat and then seemed happy about it. I forced myself to say, "They are very lovely," and he beamed at me like a half-wit.

I shut my eyes again; the gondolman began to sing.

# Kay

There was a sentimental picture of which my sister Serena had been fond. She had cut it carefully out of the *Mirror of Mode* and hung it on the wall of the dressing room she and Isobel shared, despite Isobel's strident protests. The picture was called *Most Loyal Friend* and depicted a hound lying across the foot of a freshly dug grave, clearly spurning all attempts from the black-garbed people around it to lure it away.

Perhaps Glimmering had also been fond of that picture in his childhood, for he kept me chained at the foot of the catafalque in the cold and airless Hall of the Seven Virtues in the Clock Palace of Bernatha day after weary, endless day; I sat and clenched my teeth against the urge to howl as that pining hound had doubtless howled. And the good citizens of Bernatha came and gawked and gossiped. And I learned from their jabbering many things I would not otherwise have known.

I hated them for it.

But I listened. Had no choice, unless I would put my hands over my ears like a child. I learned that Glimmering's cattle had been taken to the House of Mercy, where their milk was being given to wounded Corambin soldiers. I learned that there was still skirmishing in eastern Caloxa, in the foothills of the Gorballants; were rumors that Gormont had thrown his lot in with the Usara. Gormont was old, and his only son had died at Thornycroft. An he preferred death to surrender, who could blame him?

I learned that the Convocation had sent a representative to the Seven Houses, one Roderick Lapwing. I learned that the Seven Houses were trying to use this opportunity to wring more concessions out of Corambis. And I learned, a full day before she came to view her husband's body, that the princess was in Bernatha. The wagging tongues did not tell me if Charles was with her; I hoped he was not.

Princess Clara was the daughter of a Wildar merchant. Although I did not understand it, I believed Gerrard's love for her had been sincere. Certainly he was faithful to her; unlike his father, who had sired half a dozen bastards—and I wondered bleakly how many of them were going to end up imprisoned or dead, now that Gerrard's failure had made them dangerous again—Gerrard had had only Charles. He had wanted more children, but he had been confident that there would be time for such matters once he was king.

I did not need my eyes to tell me when Clara at last deigned to pay her respects. The sound of her progress was clearly audible, and I learned something else: Bernatha loved Clara.

Why, I asked myself bitterly, was I so surprised? Gerrard's emotional appeal had been to Caloxan tradition, Caloxan pride, and Bernatha had never considered itself part of Caloxa. It barely considered itself part of Corambis. But Clara, though enthralled by Gerrard's fairy tales, was mercantile in her bones, born to it, bred to it. She had no more head for politics than a pig, but that didn't matter now. She was young, beautiful, and a widow, and she knew the value of a bolt of Ygressine silk against a bolt of Caloxan wool. I kept my head down and wondered, neither happily nor charitably, what she would find to say to me.

I needn't have worried. She made it, by my best estimation, about three-quarters of the way from the door to the catafalque. Then she stopped, said in a low, husky murmur completely unlike her normal speaking voice, "Oh, Gerrard." There was a slithering rustle of fabric, a thump, and then a general outcry. Clara Hume had fainted, and I would have bet, had there been anyone to bet with me, that she hadn't disturbed so much as a hairpin. She was taken out with much clamor and confusion, and I knew, as surely as I knew the feeling of the collar around my throat, that she would not be back.

In fact, Clara Hume did not return to the Hall of the Seven Virtues, but that did not mean I was rid of her. That night, after the Bernathan guards had been replaced by Corambins—for such was the compromise agreed upon by the interested parties, as if there were any need to keep me under constant guard—Glimmering's boots announced themselves.

I was getting better at deducing movement from sound—I was perforce getting a great deal of practice—and I tracked those boots and their aggressive, swaggering stomp from one end of the hall to the other and back before they came and stopped in front of me. He did not speak, and I had no patience for his games.

"What do you want?" I said and added "Your Grace" before he could rebuke me.

A moment's pause and he said, "Clara Hume."

"What of her?"

"Why did she come here?"

"To cause a sensation. And she succeeded."

He moved not.

"I know nothing of Clara Hume's frippery mind. An you want more information, will have to ask her. Or someone in her counsels, as I assure you I am not and never have been."

And still he moved not.

If I could just have seen him, I could have ignored him, but as it was, my entire attention remained painfully focused, straining desperately to perceive clues that would allow me at least to guess at his intentions. Finally, defeated, I said, "What do you want?" the words grating in my throat like broken machinery.

"Want?" said Glimmering, and blessed Lady, how I had come to loathe the sound of his voice. "What makes you think I want *anything* from you?"

"Your continued presence," said I. "Or do you but gawk at the savage beast?"

"I was thinking of what the princess said," he said with a lightness that deceived me not at all.

Was my turn to stay silent. I had never cared what Clara Hume thought of me. An were to begin, it would not be now.

"She said the collar and lead suited you. And that Gerrard would agree."

Was a lie, petty cruelty on Clara Hume's part—or on Glimmering's, for it seemed even a little fanciful for Clara. But still he persevered. "She said Gerrard always called you the most faithful of his dogs."

There, he touched me on the raw, not because it was a lie, but because it was true. Had been a joke between us, a small one, for *kay*, the Usaran word for a cougar, was the word in Murrey, where Gerrard had grown up, for the heavy-shouldered bear-baiting dogs. Gerrard's favorite dog when he was a child had been a kay. So, yes, was true. He had said that. But I had not known he had said it to *her*.

She was his wife, witling. And he loved her. As he loved not thee.

The sudden drench of grief, as bitter and cold as the water of Our Lady of Marigolds, was not that he had loved her, stupid and unworthy woman though she was. Was not even that he had told her of our joke. Was no secret, and I knew Gerrard had never said it cruelly, no matter how Clara might twist his words now that he was dead. But that he had told her—that he had *shared* it with her—showed me what I had always wished not to know. She had meant more to him than I ever could. And with his death, she owned him whole. She was the widow, I merely and always the faithful dog. And Gerrard might have found that valuation just.

Glimmering was still standing there, gloating. "I may be a beast," I said, my voice thick with mingled savagery and misery, "but at least I do not mock other beasts in their grief."

I heard the huff of his breath, as if I had struck him, as if perhaps my words had reached through his self-righteousness. Then his boot heels stomped away. I buried my face in my hands and did not weep.

## Felix

"Oh hey," Mildmay said. "I got you a book."

"I beg your pardon. You did what?"

"From that guy in Arbalest. He said we'd need it more than he did. Here. Toss me my coat."

I'd only just managed to get him out of the coat and lying down. He had gotten a second wind when we reached the Fiddler's Fox, which had made him weirdly, cheerfully scattered. He wasn't at all combative; it was just that I'd say, "You should lie down," and he'd agree and immediately find five things he had to do first. I gave him the coat in preference to having him get up to fetch it, and then watched as he went through its pockets, of which there were an astonishing number, before coming up with a book which he handed to me.

It was called *A Guidebook of Myriad Wonders in the Convocate of Corambis* and had been written by a gentleman named Thomas Lilion. Its most immediately salient feature was a map folded into the end papers.

"And the man in Arbalest gave this to you?"

"Yeah. I meant to give it to you that night, but . . ." He shrugged, and I mentally completed the sentence: *You pissed me off and I forgot about it.*

I unfolded the map across the bed, treating the aged paper with care, and Mildmay propped himself up so that he could see it as well. I found BERNATHA marked in neat crimson letters in the lower left corner, with its three islands distinctly drawn and even tiny boats with oars between them and the mainland. On the other—western—side of the Crait, a much larger boat had been drawn with extravagantly billowing sails, and an arrow, labeled YGRES, pointed off the edge of the map. On the mainland, St. Melior was merely a dot, but I was pleased to see that the guidebook was not so out-of-date as it might have been, for the railways, as identified by the legend, were marked with doubled and hatched lines, one running east and the other running first northeast, through a black dot marked GRANDERFOLD, and then branching like a spider at a dot marked, with more crimson letters, WILDAR. I followed the line north from Wildar, through smaller black dots marked KILREY and SKIMFAIR, and then into a great sprawling jaggedness: FOREST OF NAULEVERER. On the other side of the forest, the railway found another small black city, FOLLENFANT, and then shot triumphantly straight north into a great black and crimson star labeled ESMER.

"They're not shy about their capital, are they?" I said.

"Where's the pass?" Mildmay said.

I searched and pointed to it. "Here." ST. ULO'S PASS, in red, with a badger, presumably part of St. Ulo's iconography, running toward the bottom edge of the map.

"And we're . . . ?"

"Here."

He leaned over to take a closer look. "Shit. D'you suppose the scale's any good?"

After a moment, I saw what he meant. Whereas the distance from St. Ulo's Pass to Bernatha was barely the length of my thumb, the distance from Bernatha to Esmer was nearly the length of my forearm. "No wonder they invented trains," I said.

"Yeah, and looks like we don't have much choice about using 'em. Least, I'm assuming that thing like an ink blot ain't good news."

"The Forest of Nauleverer," I said. "I'm inclined to agree with you. I suppose, it being a guidebook and all, we should see what Mr. Lilion has to say on the subject." The book was arranged thoughtfully by places of interest, and it was somehow not surprising to find that Nauleverer Forest was one of them.

Lilion wrote disapprovingly, and I read aloud: "*Though there be many foolish and superstitious whisperings about the Forest, in Wildar and surrounding communities, yet it is true that the water there is of the clearest, the air the freshest, and the meat the most succulent and healthful of anywhere in the Convocate.*"

"I don't like the sound of them superstitious whisperings," Mildmay said.

"No," I agreed. "And—oh dear. *It was by decree of the Convocation of the Sixth of the Ninety-second that the forest was made a Convocate Preserve, forbidden to any community of more than fifty souls. Further, the construction of roads was most strictly prohibited. Although, that stricture has been once contravened, when the representatives of the Corambin Railway Company persuaded the Convocation of the Fifth of the One Hundred Forty-second to permit them to run the railway from Skimfair to Follenfant, and this in despite of the many persons who spoke against it.*"

"Train or nothing," Mildmay said.

"It looks that way. And really, just because we don't like the idea doesn't mean there's anything *wrong* with it."

"Yeah," Mildmay said and sighed, sagging back against his pillows.

"*There was once,*" I continued reading—because a distraction was better than continuing an inevitably fruitless not-quite-argument—"*a great city in the heart of Nauleverer, called Corybant, the city of the first Corambin kings. It was lost before the Fiftieth, and fearful tales are still told of the doom that came to Corybant and of its shape. Of the laborers to whom I have spoken of the construction of the railroad through the forest, not one saw any signs of a city, although they told me many other tales unfit for the ears of gentle persons. Such was the magnitude of the destruction of Corybant—or, if you prefer, the magnitude of the imaginations of the country people.*"

"'Unfit for the ears of gentle persons.' Those sound like fun," Mildmay said; his voice was failing, this burst of strength almost spent.

"Yes. Pity he doesn't record any of them." I gave in to an impulse—affection, desire, I didn't even know—and brushed a stray strand of hair off Mildmay's forehead.

He gave me a slightly dubious look, but seemed to decide the gesture was not meant patronizingly, and closed his eyes. "What's he say about Bernatha?"

The book fell open readily to the section on Bernatha, as if its previous owner had consulted it frequently. Opposite the beginning of the text (*The city of Bernatha, unique in its situation and customs, was founded by . . .*) was another map, displaying the islands of Bernatha: the House of Honesty to the north, the House of Mercy to the south, the causeway to St. Melior drawn with neat dotted lines, and on the Crait itself, the five houses of Prudence, Patience, Charity, Chastity, and Loyalty—roughly circular, not entirely contiguous with each other—and in the center, the top of the massive hill that was the Crait, a building, towers and flags lovingly drawn, labeled CLOCK PALACE OF THE SEVEN HOUSES.

"They have something called a Clock Palace," I said.

"What d'you suppose *that* is?"

"Well, let's see." Mr. Lilion obligingly printed the names of objects of particular interest in capital letters, so his remarks on the Clock Palace were easy to find. I read aloud, "*THE CLOCK PALACE OF THE SEVEN HOUSES is the seat of government in Bernatha, having been chosen as neutral ground after the Schismatic Massacres of the Seventh of the Seventy-seventh. The structure itself, however, is much older than that, although it cannot be dated with any certainty, due to the catastrophic loss of the Civil Records Hall in the Honesty Fire of the Fifth of the One Hundred Twelfth. The Bernathans themselves believe that the Clock Palace was built by their founder, Agravain the Lesser, and furthermore that it was in order to build the Clock of Eclipses that Agravain came to the Crait, the founding of the greatest city in the southern half of the Convocate being merely a happy consequence.*"

"The Clock of Eclipses?" Mildmay said. "That ain't no nice thing to name a clock."

In the Lower City, eclipses were the worst of ill omens, being as they were the special providence of the God of the Obscured Sun. "It probably doesn't mean the same thing here as it does at . . ." I trailed off as my eye was caught by something farther down the page. "Oh dear."

"What?"

"*The Clock of Eclipses has been defunct for nearly two hundred indictions. After it tolled the solar eclipse of the Third of the One Hundred Seventeenth—an eclipse during which it is said that all the windows of the Clock Palace were obscured by blood, the blood having no known or determinable source—it fell silent. People of Bernatha still speak of 'counting the clock' instead of the common idiom, 'counting sheep,' in reference to the fact that the Clock of Eclipses could be heard throughout the Crait, and—it is said—on still days could be heard on the northern and southern islands as well."*

"It *is* one of them clocks," Mildmay said, almost accusingly.

"A Titan Clock," I said, scanning the rest of the entry. "It certainly sounds like one. Lilion says the Clock Palace is open to the public. If that's still true, I suppose I could—" I broke off so sharply I almost bit my tongue.

"What?"

"No, never mind. I wasn't thinking."

"You should go."

"Mildmay! I can't leave you when you're—"

"Look," he said, and stopped, breathing carefully to avoid another coughing fit. "There ain't nothing you can do for me, 'cept sit here and *watch*. And don't take this the wrong way or nothing, but I'd really rather you didn't."

I looked at him suspiciously, but he held firm. "I ain't gonna do nothing but lie here. I swear by all the saints and powers. And, you know, even if I *could* get up, I don't fucking *want* to."

"If you're sure."

"Yeah. When you get back, you can tell me about it. Go on."

Insofar as I could tell, he meant it, and it would be more unkind—more unforgivable in his view—to assume he was lying than it would be to take him at his word. And it was what I wanted to do.

I thought he was asleep before I closed the door behind me, Lilion's *Guidebook* in hand.

The city of Bernatha, winding serpentinely up and around the Crait, was built predominantly of a pale grayish-brown stone. It was curiously difficult to decide how tall the buildings were, as they were built into and against the slope in such a way that they could be five or six storeys tall without ever getting more than two or three storeys off the ground. In some places, I was not even sure where I ought to judge that one building ended and the next began. The façades were very plain; I supposed between the wind and the sea, decorations wouldn't last long. There were street lamps at close and regular intervals, and I remembered what the gondolman had said about fog.

The people were mostly of the Corambin type, although there was another type, taller, with pale curly hair like Gartrett Corbie's, and there were others still, even shorter and stockier than the Corambin norm, dark-haired and pale-skinned. Everyone, men and women alike, dressed in dark, plain clothes, severely tailored. I found the effect depressing. There were a few people dressed in brighter colors, almost all of them of the taller, curly-haired type, and I noticed that they stuck together, speaking to each other in a language I didn't recognize.

I took careful notice of my path, for while finding the Clock Palace might be a simple matter of persevering uphill, finding my way back, by the selfsame token, could be a rather difficult job. I was heartened by the discovery that Bernatha, unlike many parts of Mélusine, put signs at intersections. The Fiddler's Fox was on Cattamery Road, and I thought I could remember that, even if my sense of direction deserted me as it almost inevitably would.

It occurred to me that the surest sign of how ill Mildmay was, was his failure to remind me not to get lost.

But, as I had anticipated, the Clock Palace was impossible to miss. Built of the same grayish-brown stone as the rest of the city, it wrapped itself over and around the apex of the Crait. Its towers, unlike those of the Mirador, were identical both in height and in architecture and were placed with neat mathematical precision at the five corners of the outer wall. I found the main entrance by dint of walking around the palace wall until I came to it. Here at last was the sort of decoration I was used to: the doors, standing open, were bronze, engraved with the sun in eclipse on the left and the moon in eclipse on the right, with elaborate designs circling and spiraling over the remaining space. It was lovely, and the craftsmanship superb, but there was nevertheless a shiver of superstition down my spine.

Since there was nothing to prevent me, and no reason not to, I entered the Clock Palace; I found myself presented with a sign. One arrow, pointing to the left, read "THE CLOCK OF ECLIPSES—WORKS." The other arrow, pointing to the right, was "THE HALL OF THE SEVEN VIRTUES." I consulted Lilion, who informed me that the Hall of the Seven Virtues was the largest single room in all of Bernatha and that its floor was the living granite of the Crait itself. He also had several lavish paragraphs about the frescoes and painted ceilings, mentioning artists and architects whose names, naturally, meant nothing to me.

I turned left. Two straight hallways and a short spiral stair brought me to a room labeled "THE CLOCK OF ECLIPSES." There was a young man in brown livery whose duty was clearly to guard the clock, and a pair of elderly ladies pestering him with questions he equally clearly had no idea how to answer. After the first few seconds, I didn't even hear them.

It was, unmistakably, a Titan Clock. I had never seen one before, for Nemesis had been destroyed hundreds of years ago, and while Juggernaut was still operational, and I had heard it, my one entry into the Bastion had not been a suitable opportunity for scholarly inquiries. But I had read about Titan Clocks—Ynge even mentioned them as an example of noirant patterning—and studied the precise and elegant diagrams of Diadumenian Butler, who, if the stories were true, had been one of Nemesis's first victims. I knew what I was looking at.

An enormous iron rod rose in the center of the room, vanishing through holes cut in floor and ceiling. When the clock had been operational, the rod had rotated, for I could see the knobbed arms at varying heights and, in the mass of surrounding machinery, the hinged gold squares those knobs were meant to strike. Beyond that, I had no hope of puzzling out how the clock had once worked, what the tiny bone cogs had had to do with the great silver chains that, like the rod, ran from floor to ceiling, nor what the iron hooks jutting from the walls of the room had been meant to hold.

I could, however, feel the noirance like a layer of dust over everything in the room. Deeper in the clock's works, where there were no visitors, it would be mikkary wound around the springs and pulleys, trailing like ribbons of darkness from the toothed wheels. I both wanted and did not want to touch the nearest protruding spike, and it was a good thing the guard was there, for otherwise I might not have been able to stop myself.

The elderly ladies had stopped pelting him with questions about the clock and had moved on to another topic. My attention was caught by a name I remembered from the political discussions in the Five Dancing Frogs: *Rothmarlin.*

"He didn't look nearly so dreadful in person," one woman said.

"Ah," said the guard, trying to look wise. "He's a broken man, that's what I hear."

"I don't care what he's done," the other woman said. "It's not right, putting a man on display like some sort of *beast*. I shouldn't've gone with you."

"It's his penance," the guard said.

"That's not *penance*, sitting there freezing in the hall. Which of the virtues can it possibly teach?"

"Patience," the guard suggested, so pointedly that I had to swallow a laugh.

"And you do penance for *sins*," the other woman said earnestly. "You can't deny his sins, Meriel."

"I'm not trying to. I'm saying the Hall of the Seven Virtues isn't the place for it."

"What better place could there be?"

"An abbey," Meriel snapped. "A hermitage. Our Lady of Fogs, for that matter. Let him do penance as an anchorite. It'd be more seemly than this . . ." She broke off, waving a hand inexpressively.

The guard saw his chance and said, "Now if you'll excuse me, I think this gentleman—"

But I was not in the mood to rescue him, and if he couldn't answer their questions, he certainly couldn't answer mine. "I was just leaving," I said and suited the action to the word.

I retraced my steps back to the foyer and its sign, and there I stopped, stuck fast between my curiosity and what little sense of compassion I could be said to possess. For surely it was, as Meriel said, cruel to gawk at a man like a carnival beast. On the other hand . . .

I sighed and gave in to my curiosity, taking the right-hand corridor.

There was another young man in brown livery at the door to the Hall of the Seven Virtues. He gave me a highly dubious look, but I must have seemed harmless even if patently foreign, for he nodded me in.

The Hall of the Seven Virtues was nothing compared to the Hall of the Chimeras, into which it would have fit five times over. But for this city, with its steep, cramped architecture, it was very impressive. One side was a series of arched windows looking out west over the sea; opposite were the allegorical frescoes Lilion had spoken of so highly. They were rather stiff and spikily angular, quite unlike, for example, the sign of the Fiddler's Fox, which I had noticed for its elegantly stylized curving lines, at once sly and inviting. The frescoes' colors, though, were rich, deeply saturated, and vibrant, as if in reaction to the monochrome of the city's exterior and her citizens' clothes. The ceiling—I tipped my head back for a quick inspection—was likewise beautifully colored, though I found the subject matter unfortunate.

But perhaps that was due merely to the proximity of the black-draped bier like a blot of ink. The body on the bier, surely the Prince Gerrard of whom Sholto Ketteller had spoken so passionately, looked like wax, its features sunken and ghastly, but the man crouched before it looked almost worse.

He was wearing only a sort of nightshirt—that and chains. His manacled feet were bare, and I could see the raw welts on both wrists and ankles. There was a collar around his neck, and it was that which was fastened by a length of chain to the bier. The guards, two strapping young men, were so clearly unnecessary as to seem almost ludicrous. They gave me a look, dismissed me as their colleague at the door had, and returned to a low-voiced but quite intense conversation the subject of which I did not attempt to discern.

The prisoner did not raise his head at my approach. His tawny skin had gray undertones; his face was stubbled; his hair was lank and becoming matted. Since the guards weren't watching, I knelt down and whispered, "Is there anything I can do for you?"

That brought his head up with a startled jerk. He was square-jawed, snub-nosed, not at all handsome and even less so with lines of fatigue and strain bracketing his generous mouth and deepening the crow's-feet around his eyes. They were odd eyes, pale amber striated with gray, and I realized after a frozen moment that they were sightless.

No one had mentioned that Rothmarlin was blind.

"Is Glimmering reduced to petty tricks now?" he said.

"Tricks?" I said. "No, I'm sorry. I don't even know who Glimmering is. I'm a foreigner."

He frowned as he listened to me. "An you are a foreigner, why would you want to help me?"

"Common decency?" I suggested. He lowered his head, making an awkward, clanking gesture, as if to push my words away. And I supposed it even worked; it attracted the attention of the guards.

I straightened as they approached; I didn't hurry, which seemed to discomfit them. And then I smiled and said, "I wonder if either of you could tell me the way to the nearest bookstore?"

The two strapping young men had been surprisingly helpful; I had ended up with directions to three different bookstores and a quite enlightening difference of opinion as to which of the three was the best. In return, I had had to allow myself to be escorted out into the cobbled plaza—broad for Bernatha—fronting the Clock Palace, so that they could point me in the right direction, but that was better than being arrested and I hoped had distracted them sufficiently that their prisoner would not get in trouble.

Although I had asked about bookstores simply because it was the first and most incongruous thing to come into my head, I was certainly not going to discard the opportunity thus presented. For there was at least one piece of information a bookstore could provide that I very badly wanted.

What was it, exactly, that had started this "craze," as Mrs. Fawn called it, for novels about Mélusine?

The nearest bookstore was called Waddilow & Berowne; I found it easily, though for a moment I was sure I had somehow come to the wrong place. This building was simply too big. But the gilt lettering on the window read, very plainly, "WADDILOW & BEROWNE, BOOKSELLERS," and when I went inside, there were bookshelves everywhere. *Books* everywhere.

I realized after a moment—two seconds? ten seconds? as much as a minute?—there was a clerk standing in front of me, and he'd asked twice if he could help me. And I was gawking like any dowdy provincial. My first impulse was to bolt, but that was silly. I hadn't been put out of countenance by a shop clerk since I was sixteen, and this weedy young man with his bad complexion was not a threat. "Yes," I said briskly. "I'm looking for a book by a man named Challoner. A travelogue of some sort?"

"Oh, yes, sir," the weedy young man said with great enthusiasm. He led me on a circuitous path into the depths of the store, stopping in front of a bookcase against the back wall. "We keep all our travel literature together—it saves time. Now, was there a *particular* Challoner you wanted, or . . . ?"

"Actually, I'd like to browse a bit, if you don't mind."

"Of course!" he said, and very nearly bowed. I couldn't tell if he was merely trying to flirt with me or if he, like Mrs. Fawn, had recognized me for what I was. I found that I didn't want to know.

He did at least leave me alone, and I was able to contemplate the bookcase in peace. Corambins printed titles along the spine rather than abbreviating them across, a habit which made books easier to identify although I foresaw that it would quickly lead to a crick in the neck. Challoner took up most of one shelf; they had several copies of each of his books. Happily, it was immediately apparent which one I wanted: *The Daughters of Cymellune* was an old-fashioned and fanciful way to refer to Tibernia and Marathat, but it did, I supposed grudgingly, make for an eye-catching title.

All the more so, I discovered upon opening the book to the preface, because the Corambïns believed themselves to be descended from Agramant the Navigator.

Sternly, I forbade myself to get sidetracked, although I did rather badly want to know how an entire nation could be descended from a king who was historically without issue. I would have plenty of time for such inquiries later. I turned to the section on Mélusine, and in less than five minutes had to put the book back before I disgraced myself.

This Challoner had self-evidently never been in Mélusine in his life. His "report" was based on Virenque's *L'Histoires des Cités Magnifiques*, which was a great work of scholarship and over a hundred years old. I recognized Virenque's ornate turn of phrase; Challoner had cribbed the entire passage on the Arcane directly. I supposed that meant I would not find Virenque anywhere in Corambis, and that was a pity.

But at least now I knew more or less what Challoner must have said to conjure such enthusiasm. Virenque did talk a great deal about Cabaline wizardry, in pursuit of an argument that the Curia was of far more influence and importance in shaping the city than the Lord Protector's annemer Cabinet. Since Virenque was annemer himself and viewed Cabalines with no little suspicion, he had made much of the tattoos and oaths and the mystery of the Virtu. Virenque had been disparaging; Challoner—or at least his readership—was fascinated.

I did not bury my face in my hands and howl, but it was a near-run thing.

A moment's inward contemplation convinced me that I didn't have the strength to investigate the novels Challoner had inspired, but the sheer size of Waddilow & Berowne prompted me to wonder if they had a thaumatology section analogous to the travel section, and I went looking.

Happily, the bookcases were taller than I—there were step stools scattered here and there about the store for the use of clerks and customers—and I was able to avoid attracting the weedy young man's attention. I found their books on magic between an impressive array of books on natural history and a smaller but quite wide-ranging selection on mathematics.

They had more thaumatology books than I had expected; in Mélusine, if a bookstore didn't specialize in thaumatology—though several did, all run by annemer—it was unlikely they would have more than one or two thaumatological books, and those probably the result of trade rather than intent. But Waddilow & Berowne had half a bookcase worth; I crouched down to examine them.

*Principles of Magical Healing*, *Force and Balance*, a *Magician's Primer*, a number of books on magic and mathematics, a disturbing little volume entitled *Magic for the Mechanist*: their selection told me a good deal about Corambin magic in a very short time, and left me confounded. I had expected, foolishly perhaps, that given the apparent obsession with Cymellune, Corambin magic would not be so different from the magic of the Mirador and the Coeurterre, but nothing, it seemed, could be further from the truth. They were materialists, but not as Cabalines were; they seemed to think magic itself was a material force, an idea which I found as alien as any I'd ever come across, and that included the teachings of the Union of Angels, a Cymellunar sect who had believed firstly that magical energy was generated by sex, and secondly that if one practiced magic—and sex—long enough, one would be invited into the angelic orders and would grow wings as naturally as a tree puts forth flowers. None of them had succeeded by the time they were, all five of them, burned for heresy.

I could see, I supposed a little dubiously, how one might get from Titan Clocks—which were, after all, mechanical objects in their most literal aspect—to this kind of dry, methodical, lifeless magic, but then I remembered the spontaneous manifestation of blood Lilion had mentioned, and I was not so sure.

In any event, it was pointless to try to theorize further on the basis of a random sampling of books in a bookstore. And a sharp stab of guilt reminded me that I needed to get back to Mildmay. No matter what he said, I had left him alone more than long enough. I straightened and thoughtfully went in search of my weedy clerk again. He was in the front of the store and quivered like a hunting dog on point when he saw me. I gave him a carefully judged smile. "As I'm sure you can tell, I'm a foreigner, and I've only recently arrived in Bernatha."

He made an encouraging sort of mumble, and I went on: "I don't even know if you have such things as broadsheets?"

He looked discouragingly blank.

For a moment I was perfectly blank myself, trying to think of a way to explain broadsheets. I'd learned to read from broadsheets; Joline and I had made paper crowns out of broadsheets; the best barbecued mutton in

Simside came wrapped in broadsheets. Finally, I said, "How do people learn about important things in this city? New laws? Demolitions? Play performances?"

"Oh, you mean *newspapers*! We only carry the Bernatha papers, but Emblem's has the Esmer *Times*, if you want that. They'll have today's by now."

"Let's start with Bernatha," I said and hoped my nonchalance was convincing.

Bernatha had three newspapers. They looked reassuringly like Mélusinien broadsheets, though with many more pages, and were correspondingly cheap. I bought one, the *Standard*, for a penny-obol; the other two, the clerk said, were "partisan," and I definitely wasn't in the mood for anything of the sort. I extracted myself from his clutches as gracefully as I could and started off from Waddilow & Berowne as if I had the least idea of where I was going.

I had by this time overreached myself most dreadfully. I might have been able to find my way back to the Fiddler's Fox from the Clock Palace—or, then again, I might not—but from Waddilow & Berowne, I couldn't even hope. I did try to retrace my steps to the Clock Palace, which seemed like a reasonable thing to do, but I went wrong somehow and found myself going downhill without ever having, so far as I could tell, stopped going *uphill*. And while that didn't seem like it should be possible, I was not philosopher enough to argue with my own experience, and my experience said that I was, quite plainly, going downhill on the west side of the Crait, toward the harbor. I wished, unworthily but sincerely, that Mildmay were with me.

The sun was sinking rapidly—I'd spent rather longer in Waddilow & Berowne than I'd meant to—and the streets were nearly deserted. I tried approaching fellow pedestrians, but the first pretended not to hear me, and the second actually recoiled, hissing, "I have no business with violet-boys," as he hurried away. I wasn't sure what "violet-boys" were—did Bernatha have street packs as Mélusine did?—but clearly I looked like one.

I stopped at an intersection and considered my options, meager as they were. I could continue wandering aimlessly, but although that was actually a highly effective strategy in the Mirador, it seemed unlikely to help me here. I could try to retrace my steps to Waddilow & Berowne, but I was suspicious that that would work no better than retracing my steps to the Clock Palace had. I could try to navigate by the sun, while it lasted: I was on the west side of the Crait now, and I knew the Fiddler's Fox was on the south . . .

But that was nonsense, and I knew it even as I thought it. Nonsense and a pathetic attempt to avoid the one recourse I knew would work: the obligation d'âme.

Mildmay had used it to find me, the terrible night of Gideon's death, and since then I had been rawly aware of it, as one is aware of the new skin left behind by a healing burn. I had drawn away from it as much as I could, perversely becoming more and more uncomfortable with it the more Mildmay seemed to accept it. I'd thought that was why my awareness of his dreams had suddenly and sharply fallen off, although now I suspected that had far more to do with the briars enclosing my construct-Mélusine than my strength of will and purity of heart.

But there was one thing the obligation d'âme was genuinely good for—as opposed to all the myriad things it was *bad* for, like my selfishness and arrogance and cruelty—and that was in allowing one party to the bond to find the other. And it was stupid to stand here dithering about it as if it were some sort of injury to Mildmay. I'd used the obligation d'âme to inflict those, too; I damn well knew the difference.

All I had to do was let myself look and he was there, fox-red and jade-green and *that* way. Not quite directly behind me, but a good thirty degrees off from what I would have guessed. I turned, chose the street that most closely approximated the direction I wanted, and started walking again.

The shadows were long and threatening; it was already nearly dark, and the street lamps were lighting themselves with an odd hissing sound and a distinct crack of magic. Some sort of machinery, I guessed, thinking of the book called *Magic for the Mechanist* in Waddilow & Berowne, but I had not the faintest idea of how such a thing could be constructed. I was wondering about that, imagining keeping magic in a box ready to strike, like a lucifer, and so it was some time before I realized I was being followed.

In fairness to myself, it had been fifteen years or more since I'd had to worry about difficulties of that kind. Malkar had taken me away from the particular perils of a city, and when I returned to Mélusine, I had almost immediately gotten the Mirador's tattoos and become, as far as the Lower City and its criminal denizens were concerned, predator instead of prey. In some districts, as I remembered from my childhood, it was considered bad luck even to walk in the same direction as a wizard, and I had never once been accosted, not for any reason.

But Bernathan criminals had no reason to fear me; I was merely a foreigner walking alone: an easy target.

"Oh damn," I said, very softly, because of course they were right. I had been stripped of the Mirador's protections, magical as well as political, and I'd never been any good in a fight, half-blind and clumsy. It had always been Joline who had protected me—and there, I thought bitterly, was another way Mildmay was like her. I had a knack for finding protectors.

But I was now, if possible, even worse equipped for a fight than I'd been as a child. Not as clumsy, no, Malkar had dealt with that. But half-blind, and although the stiffness in my fingers didn't normally bother me much, I couldn't even make a fist comfortably, much less hit someone with it. And there was magic, but that was heresy, and I didn't even know why I cared, but I did.

Maybe I had learned something from my stupid, vicious mistakes, after all.

I was walking fast, still tracking toward Mildmay and the Fiddler's Fox, and given my height and the length of my stride against that of the average Corambin, I thought there was a reasonable chance I'd simply outdistance them. But apparently they'd thought so, too, and utilized their greater knowledge of Bernatha to take a short cut. Three men—two Corambin in type, the third of the taller, paler breed—stepped out of an alley directly in front of me. I took a step back, half turning for unabashed flight, and two more men, both pale-haired, closed the distance from behind.

"Now, guv," said one of the shorter, "this don't have to be ugly."

"No?" I said, trying to get the wall at my back, but they flanked me neatly, and I remembered my earlier notion about predators.

"Naw," said their spokesman. "You just hand over your purse and any other small valuables you might have conveniently to hand, and we'll let you go. Not a scratch on you." He smiled widely, like a parody of the morning's gondolman.

"I really don't have enough to make it worth the bother," I said, knowing perfectly well it was useless.

"Oh, no bother at all," said one of the others. "Leastways not to us." And they all sniggered and moved a step closer.

I was weighing my options despairingly when one of them said from my blind side, "Course, if you wanted to give us something *else*, we might be persuadable. I bet that pretty mouth of yours has persuaded people to do sillier things."

I turned my head to stare at him. "You want me to . . ."

"That's not a bad idea," said one of the others.

"Think of it as a warm-up for tonight's business," said a third, from behind me.

It was actually a less distasteful solution than using magic against them, and certainly better than being beaten and robbed, but I couldn't keep back a ridiculous, bleating protest: "But I'm not—"

*A prostitute,* I would have said; later, it occurred to me that the interruption saved me a good deal of embarrassment along with everything else, for they would never have believed me.

But a voice called out, "Hey! Sunny Pingree! Is that you?" It was a woman's voice, and a group of women approaching us, six of them, wearing clothes quite unlike what I'd seen women wearing during the day. Gaudy colors and alarmingly slit skirts and lace and ribbons.

"Ahhh," said one of the pale-haired men, "what do you jezzies want?"

"To remind you of the deal," said one of the women, front and center of their little pack; from her accent, I guessed she wasn't a native Bernathan.

"Seeing as how you've *apparently* gone and forgotten it. You don't roll our fish, and we don't jack our prices so high you and your boys never get laid again. Right?"

Sullen silence, rather abashed.

*"Right?"*

"Right, Miss Emily," somebody muttered.

"Good," she said. "Now clear out before I call the Honest-men on you for disturbing the peace."

They slunk away down the alley, very like the losing side in a dogfight, and one of the other women said, "Mr. Harrowgate, are you all right?"

"Corbie!" I said. "How—?"

"Going out for dinner before work," she said with a shrug. "Oh, Emily, this is Mr. Harrowgate, the guy I was telling you about."

"Holy shit," somebody said, almost low enough for me not to hear. "You weren't kidding, Corbie."

I didn't even want to imagine what that might be in reference to, and said distinctly to Emily, "Thank you for your very timely intervention."

Emily's eyes, wide and brown and not soft at all, summed me up, and then she snorted and said, "That Sunny Pingree. No more manners than a pig. Won't bother you again, though, or I *will* have the Honest-men on him."

"But what are you doing in this part of town by yourself?" Corbie asked me.

"I, um." I could feel my face heating. "I got lost."

"Oh dear," Emily said, with sufficient lack of surprise that I gathered this was not an uncommon happenstance with strangers to Bernatha. "Corbie, we gotta get going, but you want to see your friend home? Will square it with Honeyball."

"Oh, I'm fine now," I said, too quickly. "You needn't—"

"It's no trouble," Corbie said. "You went to the Fiddler's Fox like I said?"

"Yes, but—"

"All right, then." She said to Emily, "Tell Honeyball I'm giving the Straw Market a whirl." And to me, tucking her arm through mine, "Come on." Further protests seemed foolish as well as futile.

After half a block, when I was sure the other women were out of earshot, I said, "Can you tell me something?"

"I can try."

"Those men, they assumed I was a—" I wasn't going to be able to get the word out without my voice cracking, but mercifully Corbie knew exactly what I meant.

"A jezebel? Well, yeah. You're wearing colors."

I looked down at my coat—bottle-green and much the worse for wear. "Only prostitutes wear color in Corambis?"

"Pretty much. At least in Bernatha. I don't know about anywhere else. And, I mean, most people will figure you're just a stranger, but Sunny Pingree and his boys, they ain't too bright."

"I'll have to get a new coat," I said, although I knew we couldn't afford it.

"Um," she said, was silent for three paces, then burst out with "Can I ask *you* something?"

"Certainly," I said, then hedged: "I don't promise I can answer."

She waved that away with her free hand. "You're a magician, right?"

"I, um."

"No, I mean, you *are*. I know."

"You recognized the tattoos," I said with a sigh.

"Well, yeah, but that ain't—I mean, that wasn't what—I mean—oh fuck it." She stopped, gripping my arm so that I was turned to face her. She looked up and down the street swiftly, but it was perfectly deserted. "Like this," she said, tilting her head to lock gazes with me, and as I watched, something shuttered behind her eyes came open.

She was a wizard.

She pulled away from me almost immediately, breaking eye contact as if it were a dead stick, and her wizardry vanished again completely. She might have been annemer. "I'm trusting you here," she said, and there was a wobble in her voice. "And may the Lady protect me, because I don't know if it's the right thing to do or not, but I just don't know what else to do. I don't know where else to—"

"Corbie," I said. I saw her swallow hard. "What is it exactly you're trusting me with? It's not illegal to be a wizard in Corambis, or I would have been arrested days ago. And you're not—that is, I didn't think the Grevillians prosecuted heretics."

"Heretics?" She sounded like she'd never heard the word before.

"Never mind. What is it you're frightened of?"

"You ain't a warlock, are you?" she said, and then buried her face in her hands. By the street lamps, I could see her ears turning red. "Cry your mercy. Strewth, what a question to ask somebody."

She was mortified; I was bewildered. "I'm sorry, I don't know what a warlock is."

That got her head up; she was all but gaping at me, her eyes round as saucers. "There aren't warlocks where you come from?"

"Not by that name. Look, do we *have* to talk about this in the street?" I realized as the words left my mouth that I could have been more tactful about it. "What I mean is, come up to my room and tell me about warlocks. And you haven't asked your question, you know."

"What?"

"You said you wanted to ask me something."

"Right. Yeah, I do. Your room?" Her look was openly dubious.

"I told you, I don't do women. Besides, my brother has very high moral standards. He'd never let me rape you."

That made her laugh. "All right then. We're almost there anyway."

Another block and a half brought us to the Fiddler's Fox, where Corbie stopped and tugged on my arm. "We don't have to go in together. Just tell me which room."

"I beg your pardon?"

"If you don't want to be seen with a jezebel."

"My dear child, I don't care what the desk clerk thinks of me."

She grinned. "Just checking. Some fish get themselves all bent out of shape." We went up the stairs together.

Mildmay was awake when we reached the room, and inclined to regard Corbie with suspicion. I couldn't tell if it was the fever making him more than usually unfriendly or some ramification of his habitual turtle-like reaction to the advent of any young woman. I refused to believe there were any actual grounds for concern. If Corbie had wanted to do me harm, she'd already had all the chances she needed.

Corbie herself was only slightly taken aback by Mildmay's hostile, glowering silence. Looking at him, I thought he was too obviously ill to need apologizing for. His color was bad again, and his breathing was audible across the room where Corbie and I, lacking chairs, sat on the cot Mrs. Lettice had had her man-of-all-work assemble for me.

I had to prompt her to get her started: "All right. Warlocks."

Her explanation was extremely difficult to follow, for what she could tell me was based entirely on what her grandmother had told her, and over the course of Corbie's tangled narrative, I came to have grave doubts as to that lady's sanity, redoubtable though she clearly had been.

Corbie's "gran" had been a wizard, too, and had received what little training she'd had in the days before the Corambin thaumaturgical reforms. The wizards then had been warlocks, and it had been Corbie's gran's abiding fear that one of them, having survived in hiding for thirty years, would come and enslave her. "It's what warlocks do," Corbie said earnestly, a much younger girl showing through her adult hardness. "It's why you gotta hide. Gran taught me how. She said the Corambins couldn't've found all of them, and they were probably training more."

Like Mélusine's fear of Obscurantists, I thought. And although Corbie's tale wasn't what one might call thaumatologically informative, I knew of other cases of wizards enslaving wizards. That wasn't what the Eusebians called it, of course—just as I was sure the warlocks Corbie was frightened of had had some elegant term—but that was what it amounted to. And it was what Malkar had done to me—though I was sure he, at least, would have been happy to call it slavery.

"Well, I'm not a warlock," I said. "Now, what is this question you're so anxious to ask me?"

"Oh. I, um . . ." She was going red again.

"Spit it out, Corbie," I said, and she did, a rush of syllables which it took me a moment to separate into sense: *I was wondering if you'd teach me.*

*"Me?"* I said. "That is, there must be wizards in Bernatha you know are Grevillian."

"I can't afford the apprentice fees," Corbie said, embarrassed but dogged. "I been saving and saving, but I just can't ever get there."

"So you want me to teach you for free."

She winced. "Not like—I'll give your banshee back. I ain't spent it, and it's gotta be worth a lesson or two anyway. See, with the Grevillians, they got a system. You pay the 'prenticeship or you go to their school up in Esmer. But if you don't got the money . . ." She shrugged comprehensively. "I figured you wouldn't be Grevillian, so you wouldn't mind that part, but then I didn't know you weren't . . . I mean, I'm sure you wouldn't, but I didn't—"

"Shut up, Corbie," I said, and smiled at her to show I didn't mean it unkindly.

And then Mildmay said, "Just like at home."

I startled—I hadn't thought he was listening—and said, "What do you mean?"

"Like them kids you were teaching," he said, his voice slow and slurred and drawling; he sounded half-asleep. "Don't got the money, don't nobody give you the time of day."

He was right. And even at that, those children—"children" I called them, though most of them were Mildmay's age or older—had been better off than Corbie, or any of the Corbies trapped in the Lower City. No prostitute was going to be admitted to the Mirador. Unless, as I had, they lied, and lied convincingly. At home, Corbie would have had no option except to learn from a heretic and spend the rest of her life waiting for the witchfinders. Here, she didn't even seem to have that much.

Mildmay said something else.

"I beg your pardon?"

"You like teaching," he said.

That was true and, I thought, was Mildmay's way of giving me his blessing. I looked at Corbie—hopeful, scared, embarrassed, stubborn. "Bring the banshee tomorrow afternoon," I said, and when her jaw dropped, I deliberately misread her surprise. "Well, we can't start *now*."

Corbie came back to herself with a bump. "Oh, lumme, the *time*." She bounced to her feet, said, "I *will* come tomorrow. Um. Half-past thirteen, probably." She was halfway out the door when she remembered to say thank you. And then she was gone, her heels clattering down the stairs.

"What have I let myself in for?" I said, getting up.

"Good for you," Mildmay said. "Keep you out of trouble."

"Oh *thank* you."

He raised his eyebrows at me. "You wanna tell me you came back after dark with a hooker because you *didn't* get in trouble?" He coughed, a slow, thick, ugly sound.

"You have such a suspicious mind. Let me tell you about the part of my day that didn't involve this hypothetical trouble I may or may not have gotten into."

"Anything interesting?"

"Rather," I said and told him about, first of all, the Clock of Eclipses, and secondly, the Margrave of Rothmarlin. He listened the way he always listened, his attention deep as a well, and when I'd finished, he said, "Y'know, in Aiaia, when we were rescuing Gideon and them, we had to get Bernard out of the stocks. That was ugly. Least the sanguette's quick." After a moment, he added, "Don't like menageries, either. All that *staring*."

"I admit to some fellow feeling. I was . . . after the Virtu was broken, Stephen . . . that is to say, it's a long-standing custom . . ."

"Felix," Mildmay said.

I twitched.

"I know that. I was there."

"You *what*?" My voice skied and cracked.

He met my eyes. "They brought you up the Road of Chalcedony on a rope. People threw rocks. That's where you got that scar over your eyebrow, ain't it?"

I felt naked—worse than naked. Exposed. "You . . . you *saw* me?"

"Not up close," he said, as if that made it better. My face was burning; my hands were clammy. I wanted to run, but there was nowhere I could go. I paced the width of the room, but it didn't help.

"Felix." Mildmay pushed himself into a sitting position. "Calm down, would you? This ain't . . ." He coughed, painfully and long. I sat down next to him on the bed, feeling suddenly, deeply exhausted.

"That was *before*," Mildmay said finally. "It don't matter. It's *never* mattered."

I understood what he was saying, but I couldn't believe him. "I didn't know," I said, although it was a stupid thing to say.

"Hey," he said, and he touched my forearm very lightly. "I know you didn't deserve it."

I wasn't sure I believed that, either. I pressed thumb and forefinger against the corners of my eyes, against a ridiculous, burning prickle of tears. "You need to rest."

"Ain't got much choice," he said wryly. "But, look—you okay?"

"Yes, I'm fine." I raised my head to meet a severely skeptical look. "Really. You're right. It doesn't matter."

"I meant it don't matter to *me*. Not that it don't matter. But it don't change—it can't change because it didn't—oh fuck it." He lay down again, and I could see he was struggling for breath.

"No, I understand," I said. "Truly. I shouldn't have—"

"I shouldn't've laid it on you like that," he said and coughed again.

"It's all right. Don't worry about me."

"Can't help worrying," he said, but he was already fading. I touched his hair gently, and that seemed to reassure him, for I felt the last tension leave him and he was asleep.

Corbie's banshee would keep a roof over our heads for another week, but rest was the only medicine we could afford. I hoped wretchedly that it would be enough.

I realized that night, pacing the width of the room while Mildmay slept, that I was actually afraid to sleep, afraid of finding myself in St. Crellifer's or in the Bastion or in the Caloxan woods watching a cabin burn. It was an insupportable state of affairs. I had to regain control of my dreams, and the oneiromantic symbolism told me as plainly as it could that the only way to do that was to purge my construct-Mélusine of the briars that had invaded and blocked it from the Khloïdanikos.

And to do *that*—I was reminded incongruously of the children's story-game that ended "the stick hit the pan and the pig jumped out the window"—I had to find out what had happened to the Khloïdanikos and find out if, as I both feared and suspected, Malkar's rubies were the cause.

Which meant I had to find a way to reach the Khloïdanikos without the use of my construct. In theory, that should have been only marginally more difficult than reaching it through the construct. I was sure a properly trained oneiromancer would have managed it easily.

Of course, a properly trained oneiromancer wouldn't have dug himself into this hole in the first place.

I decided against lying down; I was tired enough I didn't trust myself not to fall asleep. I sat on the floor and composed myself into a trance. The reflexive urge to call up my construct was strong, but I maintained my discipline and instead went back to the first exercise Iosephinus Pompey had taught me. I visualized a golden egg.

The egg was principally a calming technique, Iosephinus had told me, but calm was all to the good here—if asked, I would have admitted freely I was not at my most serene. I meditated on the egg. When eventually I felt steady and if not calm, then at least calmer, I allowed the egg to hatch.

Iosephinus had taught me there were three animals that could hatch from the golden egg: a lion, a mercy-snake, and a hawk. Each of them had a particular meaning, not unlike a Sibylline trump. I'd always gotten the snake, which had made Iosephinus rather melancholy, and that was what I expected this time, although I was hoping, exactly as I always had, for the lion. But what emerged was a sphinx.

I knew a great deal about sphinxes, in several different traditions. The scholars of Cymellune, long lost beneath the sea, had taught that sphinxes were hermaphrodites, that every sphinx was both mother and father to its offspring, that they spent their lives seeking new riddles and that the only way to kill a sphinx was to propound a riddle it could not solve. It would starve to death trying to reason out the answer.

In the Deep Lands west of Vusantine, sphinxes appeared in the vast and complicated allegorical paintings beloved of the citizens of Elzibat and Shalfer. There, they represented secrets and were always portrayed with a key under one paw. They were also always female; the stories said they caught travelers to mate with, and that the only way to escape a sphinx was to force, cajole, or trick her into telling her secret.

The atheist philosophers of Lunness Point said that sphinxes symbolized the relentless thirst for knowledge. In alchemical writings, the sphinx was glass, the daughter of sand. The mystics of the Iulevin Circle had believed the sphinx was the guardian of the Seventh Unknowable Truth.

It occurred to me to wish that I were not quite so well read.

The sphinx stretched, its wings spreading wide, and yawned, showing me teeth that definitely didn't belong in a human mouth. It padded forward on its great silent lion's paws, its wings, dusty rose and gold, folded neatly along its back. Its eyes were silver, luminous as the moon, and fixed on me; I saw the pupils dilate and braced for the pounce, although there wasn't a thing in the world I could do against those paws or those teeth.

And then it sat back on its haunches, affording me an excellent view of both its breasts—small but distinctly feminine—and its penis and testicles, licked its lips with a long, narrow, pink tongue, and said, "Tell me your secret."

"I beg your pardon?"

"You must have one," said the sphinx. "Tell me your secret, and I'll give you my key."

"Your key?"

"Really, darling, you're awfully thick." It lifted its chin; I saw that it wore a collar, and hanging from the collar was a key, carved out of a yellowish-white material.

"Horn?" I said.

"Oh bravo!" said the sphinx, as scathing as any courtier.

"But the briars," I said, and hated my own stupid, bleating voice as I said it.

"I can't help you with the briars. All I have is this key. Besides, what makes you so sure this key unlocks Horn Gate? . . . Oh, don't gape like a fish. It's very unbecoming. Tell me your secret."

"But I don't have any," I said, at which the sphinx laughed so hard it ended up lying down.

"What a ridiculous lie," it said at last, almost fondly. "You have so many secrets, it's a wonder you haven't stifled. So cough it up, there's a good boy."

"But—"

"It's poisoning you. You need to say it."

And somehow when I opened my mouth, the words fell out like stones: "I did it on purpose."

"What did you do?"

"I didn't lose the Khloïdanikos. I threw it away. To . . . to get rid of Malkar once and for all."

"And?"

"It didn't work."

The click was sharply audible; the collar fell away from the sphinx's neck, landing tidily between its paws.

"That was your secret," the sphinx said. "And that is your key." It stood up, stretched its spine luxuriously, its wings spreading and beating. Powerful muscles bunched and it sprang upward, flinging itself into flight.

Alone again, I bent and picked up the key. It was unexpectedly, unnaturally hot, almost burning my fingers. And I had not the faintest idea what to do with it.

The egg had led me to the sphinx; the sphinx had led me to the key. The sphinx had implied—although certainly not stated outright—that the key was not to Horn Gate, but if that was the case, what *did* it unlock?

I looked around and my heart sank. Stone and creeping darkness and there was the rising stench of the Sim. Mélusine. "I don't want to be here," I said under my breath.

"Where wanting to be?" said a voice out of the darkness. I yelped and startled backwards, but came up hard against a wall.

The darkness blinked great pale eyes somewhere about the level of my knees. I realized I was standing at the edge of a body of water—I had no way of judging its size—and my interlocutor was actually in the water, leaning its elbows on the bank.

"Wh-who are you?" I said, managing at the last possible moment to edit *what* into *who*.

"Calling me the Kalliphorne," it said. "And you, dreamswimming, smelling of . . . smelling of . . ." It hauled itself farther out of the water, sniffing at me in a way that would have been amusing if my head had not suddenly been full of stories I'd heard and only half believed. "The foxlike one!" it said triumphantly, then pushed itself backwards, angling, I realized, to get a look at my face. "You not being him," it said after a very long pause; it sounded, not disappointed, but highly suspicious. "Smelling magic."

"No," I said. "My brother." I knew that Mildmay had met the Kalliphorne, although it was one of the many things, in the aftermath of Malkar, that I had never asked him about.

"Brother," it said, drawing the word out and hissing the *th*: *brosssssssser.* "Littermate."

"Er," I said and decided not to explain all the ways in which the two words were not synonymous. "Yes."

"Not hurting him?" it said, still suspicious, and I wondered if it thought I might be Malkar.

"No," I said; it was at least true that I did not *want* to hurt him.

It hissed thoughtfully, then said, "Okay. Dreamswimming, like ghost. Not being happy. What needing?"

"I don't know," I said and sat down. "Where am I?"

"You not knowing?"

"Well, I know I'm in Mélusine *somewhere*. Am I in your dream?"

At first it seemed not even to understand the question, then it said, "Seeing dreams," which told me nothing. There was a sharp, flat sound like the handclap of a giant. I startled again and told myself to relax. Just because it was a man-eating monster didn't mean it was *necessarily* going to attack me.

"Calling husband," said the Kalliphorne. "He knowing more. Giving better words."

*Husband?* I managed not to say.

In a few moments—frighteningly few—there was another set of pale eyes at the water's edge. I couldn't see much more of them than that—dark, spiky shapes and the gleam of teeth—and thought that was probably for the best. They spoke to each other in a language that seemed to be composed mainly of sibilants and gutturals and an occasional drawn-out, indeterminate vowel, like the cry of a cat. Presently, the Kalliphorne said, "He saying we two-worlds living. Dreaming. Waking." One hand, barbarously clawed, rose and made a back-and-forth motion. "Not own-dreaming. Not needing."

Her husband hissed. She said, "Like wizards and annemer. Being both and neither."

None of which made any sense, but then it sounded like mysticism, which generally didn't. On the other hand, it made asking, "Do you know what this key unlocks?" seem positively rational.

I showed them the key, which they sniffed at like inquisitive cats. Another hissing colloquy, and the Kalliphorne said, "Dreaming key means dreaming door," and she pointed at something behind me. I turned and looked: just behind my right shoulder, a door, made of wood and carved in a pattern I couldn't make out.

"Is that door always there for you?" I said, unable to restrain my curiosity.

That, when translated, got an odd clicking sound from the Kalliphorne's husband, and then a considerable period of back-and-forth between them before she said, clearly doubtful, "He saying in dreaming always and never being same thing."

Definitely mysticism, and it would obviously require learning their language to get a better answer. "Thank you," I said. "For helping me."

"Being rule of dreaming," said the Kalliphorne. "Helping dreamswimmers. Always never." She showed her teeth in a grin that made me press back against the wall, and then she and her husband were gone as smoothly and silently as if they were themselves no more than water.

What did that *mean*? I looked at the key in my hand, looked again at the door behind me. But ultimately, it didn't matter, because there was nowhere else I could go. Except into the water, and that wasn't even a choice. I got up, turned. The lock plate was also made of horn, which was confirmation, though not comfort.

I put the key in the lock, twisted it over. There was enough weight and resistance that it took both hands, and I was afraid the key might simply break. When the lock finally released, I felt the jar in all the bones of my hands and wrists, and those that had been broken and healed poorly began to ache.

I turned the knob; it was as stiff as the lock. I wondered again if this was what I was supposed to do, but looking around showed me that the situation hadn't changed. Right or wrong (always or never), I had no other choice. I forced the knob to turn and then had to pull the door open step by grim, struggling step.

And then, when the door was open and I looked through it, I saw a solitary fox in a country of cruel stones. I could see the bright red blood staining the places where it had stepped.

The fox looked up and saw me; its eyes were green as absinthe and cold and afraid. Then it turned away, dismissing me as neither threat nor salvation, and I heard my own voice, as if from a great distance, crying, "NO!" I leapt through the door, as unthinkingly as I breathed.

Always.

Never.

The world shifted around me and shifted again, breaking and reforming like images in a kaleidoscope.

Malkar's workroom, a man spread-eagled on the floor, another man standing over him and smiling.

A hallway in the Mirador, a man lying on the floor, bleeding, another man standing over him, not smiling, but the white, exultant fury on his face is worse than a smile.

A room in the Arcane, a man curled on the floor, weeping, another man standing over him, his face like a mask.

A room in St. Crellifer's, a man strapped to a table, screaming, another man standing over him, grinning in triumph.

A room in the Mirador, a man falling to the ground, screaming, another man standing, his face like death.

A thousand thousand cruelties. Predator. Prey. Rapist. Victim. Everything. Nothing. Always. Never. I don't want to be here, I don't want to be here, I don't—

And then, as abruptly as a lit lucifer, I was somewhere else.

It was sunny here, and I could have cried with relief. None of my labyrinths could feel the sun. The room was large, pleasant, wide windows and white walls, and the floor was light wood that nearly glowed where the sunbeams struck it. The bed which was the heart of the room was covered with a quilt made of lovely cool blues with brilliant blotches of crimson and emerald and topaz. The pillows were piled high, much as I'd done for Mildmay with the pillows at the Fiddler's Fox, and lying on them, lying beneath the beautiful quilt, thin and pale and fretful with fever, was Thamuris.

"Oh," he said, "it's you." And shut his eyes.

I couldn't say anything, couldn't make a sound.

He opened his eyes again, lion-gold and deep, and said, "I'm dreaming you, aren't I?"

"Yes. I mean no."

"Well, that was helpful."

"You're dreaming," I said, "but I'm here. I mean, I'm not *here*—I mean, I'm not *there*—that is, I, um . . ."

The fretful unhappiness on his face had been replaced by amusement, which was better, even if wounding to my vanity. "I can't imagine you babbling like this. I'm not sure whether that's an argument pro or con."

"I'm dreamwalking," I managed. Finally. "So you're dreaming, but it's really me."

"I didn't know you could do that," he said, but he was interested rather than skeptical or defensive.

"I, um, try not to," I said. "It's not a good habit to get into."

"Ah. Then why . . . ?"

"I. Um." I took a step forward, then another. Thamuris's hair was lying in two thick red plaits against his shoulders. His nightgown was white, open-collared; I could see the points of his collarbones with cruel clarity. "I did something stupid and evil and I . . ."

I'm sorry?

I need your help?

I don't know what to do?

All of them true, and all of them things that stuck in my throat and rendered me mute.

"I won't pretend I don't know what you're talking about," Thamuris said and shifted position with a sigh. "Diokletian and I have been doing the best we can, but—"

*"Diokletian?"*

"Who did you expect me to go to for help? After you disappeared and those briars started spreading. It's not like I had many options."

"I know. I . . ." I remembered Mildmay saying, *Don't I rate an apology?*—remembered the bitterness he had tried not to show. "I'm sorry."

"You should be," Thamuris said. "I think you're killing the Khloïdanikos." My heart lurched nauseatingly, and it was just as well he went on without prompting, for I couldn't find breath to speak. "I know it's not what you meant, but the briars started spreading, and they didn't even do what you *did* mean, because the bees just fly right over them, and every flower they land on dies."

I hadn't thought it through—hadn't *wanted* to think it through. But of course making Malkar's rubies into the Parliament of Bees meant in oneiromantic logic that they were now as much bees as they were rubies. "So the briars thrive and everything else withers," I said.

"Essentially, yes. And the briars are . . . well, botanically speaking, they're very odd. They're extremely tough, and if you do manage to break them or uproot them, they bleed. And scream."

"I didn't do that," I said, although it was splitting hairs, and Thamuris knew it as well as I did.

He said, "No, you only gave them something that would nourish them."

"Noirance," I said, for it made perfect sense.

"I beg your pardon?" Thamuris said, and I wondered in an irrepressible, irrelevant corner of my mind whether he'd picked up that particular inflection from me or I'd picked it up from him.

"It's a thaumaturgical theory I got from reading the Coeurterrenes. It doesn't matter. It's just a fancy way of saying you're right."

He glared at me, unimpressed. "In any event, Diokletian and I can't get through the briars, and even if we could, we're both rather doubtful that we could pick up the beehive, and even if we *could*, what in the name of the blessed Tetrarchs are we supposed to do with it?"

"I know," I said. "I know. I have to take it back. Do you think . . . Is the Khloïdanikos dead?"

"Not yet," Thamuris said, almost grudgingly. "It's very strong. But Diokletian doesn't think it can last much longer."

"Diokletian is an inveterate wet blanket," I said, which was true.

"That doesn't mean he's wrong," Thamuris said, unyielding.

"I didn't say he was," I said and sagged down to sit at the foot of the bed. "But there's another problem."

"Yes?"

"The briars. They . . . that is, I'm not sure how, but—"

The world split open with a tremendous rattling clap of thunder and dumped me back on the floor of the room in the Fiddler's Fox.

It was broad daylight, and someone was knocking on the door.

# Chapter 4

## *Kay*

*Common decency,* the foreigner had said in his light, oddly breathless voice, and it was revealed to me, like a bandage ripped off a festering wound, that this was what I was come to, that strangers, *foreigners*, looked on me and felt pity, felt that *common decency* demanded they do something.

The thought was insupportable, all the more so as there was nothing I could do about it. It was not by choice that I crouched here on the cold marble, chained like a beast to my master's dead body, not by choice that I was filthy and shivering, not by choice that I was blind. As they were not my choices, I could not make different ones. I could not even choose to bear my captivity more nobly, for was not as if I had been mewling or cursing or displaying myself lewdly to the citizenry. I had been cuffed across the back of the head, hard and more than once, for "looking" at my lady visitors. I kept my head down.

And was that pragmatism or broken pride? I knew not, and I had not cared, until I had heard the truth in his voice: he would not treat his enemy's dog as I was being treated.

Day by day, my fate became less certain. Glimmering wanted me paraded around the countryside; the Convocation in the person of their secretary wanted me brought to Esmer for a trial or an excoriation or something they had not yet thought of; the Seven Houses wanted me put in Stonewater, which from all the stories was no more than an excuse to avoid the mess and bother of a public execution. No one could decide if I was a traitor or an enemy or a criminal; no one could decide to whom I belonged. They wrangled over me like a bequest in a disputed will. I was viewed by a succession of parties: Glimmering with other Corambin generals; Glimmering with the representatives of the Seven Houses; several different configurations of Bernathans, most of which I could not puzzle out; and finally a group of Bernathans escorting Roderick Lapwing, the Honorable Secretary to the Convocation.

I knew Roderick Lapwing, had met him twelve indictions ago, during the negotiations over Isobel's marriage. He had not been Secretary to the Convocation then, merely secretary to His Grace the Duke of Murtagh. I remembered his hands, soft and unworked and beautifully kept, and his voice, which was the epitome of the Corambin voice that I had been taught to mock as a child.

Here in Bernatha, he did not speak to me any more than any of the others did; an I had been able, I would not have listened as they spoke to each other, but was another choice I did not have. And I could not deny my curiosity. I would have expected the Duke of Glimmering and his staff to be very much about Mr. Lapwing, and yet here he was and I heard nothing but Bernathan voices around him.

They were speaking of the action Corambis would have to take to reestablish governance of Caloxa. The Bernathans were angling openly for concessions, seeking as always to increase their separation from and independence of Caloxa. It was not so much that they wished to be dependent on Corambis as that they considered the Convocation, being farther away, easier to ignore. The Corambins had yet to understand this; thus the Seven Houses were likely to get what they wanted. And later, someday, the Corambins would learn that Bernatha had no loyalty to be bought.

In the meantime, however, it seemed that the governorship of Caloxa was up for grabs, and Lapwing was trying to sound out the Bernathans, to discover whom they favored. Would not have been surprised to find Bernatha giving her support to the corrupt and ineffectual former governor, Miles Jaggard, but perhaps they had not cared for his taxation schemes, or perhaps they were playing a deeper game. All I could extract from the portion of the conversation to which I was an audience was that they objected to the idea that Glimmering, as the person who had ended the Insurgence—merely, as the Bernathans delicately pointed out, by virtue of being the person to whom I had surrendered—should have any say in the matter at all. The cows had clearly not been as effective a gift as he had hoped, and I was pettily pleased.

I was no longer a margrave; I had the bitter, hateful luxury of being petty, and nothing in the long cold hours of my existence to provide better thoughts. I was fed twice a day, escorted shuffling and chained to the lavatory twice a day. Sometimes my guards, and they were never the same men, would allow me to drink from the sink faucet; mostly they would not. At night I slept, still chained, at the foot of Gerrard's catafalque. Sometimes the guards remembered to give me a blanket before they left; sometimes they did not.

I learned to gauge the passing of time by the temperature of the hall, for it was cold in the mornings, and grew steadily warmer through the afternoons. In what I reckoned had to be late afternoon, I even felt the direct heat of a sunbeam; thus I deduced that the hall faced west. And thus also the residual heat which made the nights less horrible than they might have been.

The day after my encounter with the foreigner, I had endured the morning and reached the moment when the warmth began to grow, when a voice said, "My lord Rothmarlin, I must speak to you."

I did not raise my head. "I am no lord."

"Then what am I to call you?"

"Why need you call me anything? Who are you?"

"My name is Edwin Beckett. I was a correspondent of the late Prince Gerrard."

The late Prince Gerrard whose body was no more than three feet from us. But I remembered the name. "Are the man who wants to start the Clock of Eclipses again."

"Yes! And that is why I must speak to you."

"I know nothing about the Clock," said I, perplexed.

"No, not that. I need you to tell me what went wrong."

"What went *wrong*?"

"Prince Gerrard wrote to me because he wished advice about starting a Cymellunar engine he said he knew to exist under Summerdown. I advised him as best I could and told him much about my own efforts. But he did not write me again. And so I must know why he failed."

"Is not obvious enough? He failed because it killed him."

"Surely it's the other way around. It killed him because he failed."

"I cannot help you," said I.

"I have Lord Glimmering's permission to speak to you. He assured me you would be cooperative." His voice was soft and level, but the threat was clear. Glimmering continued to attempt to buy the Bernathans' favor, first with cows, now with me.

"He hired the services of a magician-practitioner in Barthas Cross," I said dully. There was no use in fighting. Was not as if it mattered to anyone save me. And, apparently, this Edwin Beckett. "Anselm Penny was his name. He walked the labyrinth and examined the engine, and he and Gerrard conferred a great deal, but I know not what they said. He sent Gerrard directions, and we followed them. And six men died."

"Tell me what *happened*," said Edwin Beckett, inexorable.

I would liefer have allowed him to set me on fire, but I cooperated as Glimmering had said I would. I described the ritual Gerrard had performed, for indeed I remembered it as clearly as it were engraved in the place inside my skull where my sight had been. Beckett took notes—I heard the scratching of his pen—and peppered me with questions, although at least he was not interested in what had happened when the engine came to life. He wanted the details of where each man had stood and what Gerrard had said and how Penny had determined the sequence in which to complete the ritual's tasks.

With that last, I truly could not help him, for Practitioner Penny and I had not liked each other. Gerrard had been very closemouthed about Penny's letters. He might have told Benallery, but he had not told me, and no, I most certainly had not asked.

"I am no magician," I said. "I did as he told me and did not wish to know more."

"But surely he gave you *some* idea," Beckett began, and then there was a tremendous clattering ruckus at the door, and a voice I recognized said, "Wyatt, remind me never to be accused of a crime in Bernatha."

It was my brother-in-law, the Duke of Murtagh.

His boot heels were sharp and annoyed across the marble floor. He said, "Sir, I don't know who you are, and neither do I care. I need to speak to my brother-in-law, so you are simply going to have to leave."

He might not know who Beckett was, but Beckett, departing in a flurry of apologies, most clearly knew who he was. Ferrand Carey, the Duke of Murtagh, the Dragon of Desperen Field. His was a familiar and distinctive face in the newspapers of Corambis and Caloxa alike. And then Murtagh said in a soft voice, "I'm going to have Glimmering's head on a stick."

"Is my penance," said I.

"Penance," said Murtagh, and I knew the skeptical way his right eyebrow would arch. "I see. Voluntary or involuntary?"

"Involuntary." I could feel my face heating, although I knew not why I was embarrassed.

"Quite," said Murtagh. "And who were the intendeds who pronounced your penance?"

"Albern, Marcham, and Gye."

"Albern. Of course." He raised his voice: "Wyatt, fetch me Intended Albern, would you?"

"What are you going to do?" I asked.

"End this farce."

"You do me no favors if I end in Stonewater."

"You won't. I bring the ruling of the Convocation."

"Which is?"

"You're stripped of land, titles, and property, as I'm sure you expected." His voice was matter-of-fact, and I was grateful to him for not making a fuss. "You are, in fact, a dependent of the Duchy of Murtagh. I am responsible both for your upkeep and your good behavior."

"I assure Your Grace, I have no intention of fomenting rebellion."

"I know you well enough to know that," said he, which was a thought disturbing enough that I said hastily, "What becomes of Rothmarlin?"

"In essence, we're treating the case as if you had died."

"Cecil," I said with loathing.

"He *is* your heir."

"And notable for his lack of participation in the Insurgence."

"That, too," said Murtagh, refusing to be goaded.

"And what will you do with me?"

"Well, I thought I'd find you a wife."

"A *what?*" said I.

"A woman to marry. Surely you've heard the word before."

"I . . . I cry your mercy, Your Grace. I do not contemplate marriage."

"Which shows a becoming modesty in a gentleman of your . . . circumstances." I sank my teeth into my lower lip and did not respond to his baiting as he had not responded to mine. "But there are other considerations." A pause, and I could only imagine him contemplating me, as a tomcat contemplating a broken-winged bird. "You will be well dowered."

"Do not mock me, Murtagh. I may be your dependent at the Convocation's pleasure, but I am not your dog."

"Do all the Brightmores have this monstrous chip on their shoulders, or is it just you and Isobel? I am not mocking you. I am making you a promise, assuring you that you can in fact support a wife and so need not hesitate to enter in upon that state of matrimonial bliss to which, I am informed, all men aspire."

"I assure you, Your Grace, I have no such aspirations." I never had, although I had known I must at some point marry and beget at least one child. Now there was no such duty.

"No? Well, it does not matter. I have them on your behalf."

"You wish me to marry?"

"Very much. And I have a candidate in mind. Her name's Vanessa Pallister; she's the widow of the Warden of Grimglass. It isn't exactly an *exalted* match, but it is not a mésalliance, even for a Brightmore."

"Grimglass?" said I. Now this conversation made a good deal more sense. "Out of sight, out of mind."

"Well, it won't *hurt*. Even the most panicky of my peers will be forced to admit there's very little trouble you can cause out there."

"I told you, I don't—"

"I know. But, Kay, have you not realized? You are a hero of the Insurgence and the last of Gerrard's inner circle. Were you to raise your banner, either for Prince Charles or for yourself, you would draw every malcontent, royalist, and troublemaker in Caloxa."

"Are you *mad*? I'm blind, destitute, a public spectacle, and the man who surrendered to the Corambins. Who's going to follow that?"

"The general consensus," Murtagh said dryly, "seems to be that your surrender is an invention of Glimmering's. And no one believes that any of the rest of it could stop you if you were truly determined."

"Then why am I not in Stonewater already? Why am I not hanged?"

"Oh, for many reasons," he said, his tone light and careless, "including the fact that your sister begged me to protect you."

I jerked as if he had slapped me. He must have seen it, for he said less viciously, "And because I believed—and believe—that your crusading passion died with Prince Gerrard."

I was frozen in that instant, wondering if he had used the word "passion" deliberately as a barb. But there was no way he could know the truth; no one knew the truth except Intended Gye, whom I did trust to honor my secret in the keeping of it. I let my breath out, feeling the weight of my grief settle again over me like a lead-lined mantle. "Yes," I said. "I would not willingly cause more bloodshed."

"That's good," said Murtagh. "And that's why I am getting this nonsensical penance revoked and taking you back to the Althammara, where you can bathe and shave and I'll get a practitioner in to look at you as well."

"You needn't—"

"Oh, I think I do. Raise your head, please."

I did, though I was bewildered. "What?"

"You're staring straight into the sun," Murtagh said, and there was something in his voice that almost sounded like pain.

"Is nothing any practitioner can do," I said, ducking my chin and turning away from his voice. "Blind as stone, is all."

"Yes. That's one of Glimmering's arguments for keeping you on a chain as a sort of object lesson to the people of Caloxa, so you'll understand if I object on principle to taking his word for it." Was always hard to assess Murtagh's moods, for neither his voice nor his face reflected them reliably—and was even worse now, when I had only voice to judge by—but I realized, and was startled to realize, that he was furious, as seethingly, violently angry as I had ever known him. His expressed desire for Glimmering's head on a stick had not been persiflage, but in fact sincere. I had never imagined Murtagh angry on my behalf; it seemed unnatural, unreal, and I was glad when there was another ruckus at the door, for I knew not what to say.

This ruckus was Intended Albern, who was indignant, and also as unhappy as a turtle turned out of its shell at being dragged out from behind his brother. His protests were laced with references to His Grace the Duke of Glimmering and what he would say when he found out about Murtagh's high-handedness, until finally Murtagh said, "If I were you, Intended Albern, I would not be quick to admit my spiritual judgment depends so heavily on the wishes of a carnal prince."

Intended Albern sputtered. "Do you deny that this man bears an intolerable weight of sin on his spirit?"

"So do I," said Murtagh, "but no one is driving me into involuntary penance. And in any event, I find insufficient difference, Intended Albern, between your definition of penance and my definition of torture. And I think the Prince Aethereal will agree with me."

"Murtagh," I said. "Is not—"

"*You* hold your tongue. Well, Intended Albern?"

A pause, uncomfortably long, and Intended Albern said, "Very well." I heard him approach and was prepared for the weight of his hand on my head. He spoke the formulas quickly, pulling his hand away as soon as he could, and he left without responding to Murtagh's pointed "*Thank* you, Intended."

Then Murtagh's boot heels tocked away and returned in company with the duller tread of one of the guards and the rattle of keys. The cuffs around my wrists were unlocked, and then those around my ankles, and then the guard leaned over me in a wash of onions and old sweat and unlocked the end of the chain from the catafalque.

There was a pause, and Murtagh said, "What am I supposed to do with this?"

"I'm sorry, my lord," the guard said, quite audibly nervous. "We don't have the key to the collar."

"Then who does?"

"I don't know, my lord. His Grace of Glimmering, maybe?"

"Of course," said Murtagh, very quietly, and the guard took a jingling step back. "Thank you. You've been very helpful." The guard took that as his opportunity to flee—for which I could not blame him—and Murtagh shouted, "Wyatt!"

"Yes, my lord?"

"I need to talk to Glimmering, and sooner rather than later. Would you kindly induce him to stop by my suite in the Althammara?"

"Yes, my lord," said Wyatt, who was evidently the latest successor to

Roderick Lapwing as Murtagh's secretary and was either stolid by nature or had been with Murtagh long enough to grow accustomed.

He, too, left, and Murtagh said, "Kay, can you stand?"

"Am blind, not crippled," said I, and I hoped I sounded convincingly irritated rather than merely pathetically grateful. I stood up, feeling strange and unsteady without the weight of the chains.

"I perceive," said Murtagh, "that I must keep the other end of this chain so it won't trip you. And then I think . . . will you take my arm?"

"Have I a choice?"

"Well, you can always stay here, though I wouldn't recommend it. Here." He took my hand and guided it to the crook of his elbow. "The Althammara isn't far."

And if I did not accept his help, there was the third option he had politely failed to mention: he could drag me at the end of the chain like a dog. I gripped his arm, and when he moved, I moved with him.

My feet had healed somewhat, but the cobbles of the Bernathan streets still made me limp. Murtagh said, "I could carry you."

"You could try," I said, gritting my teeth. "I don't need to see you to break your arm."

"Your temper has certainly survived intact. Isobel *will* be pleased."

"Sorry."

"No, no. I find it reassuring, actually. Just keep walking."

The Althammara was, as he had promised, only a very short distance from the Clock Palace. Its floors were wood, with lush Ygressine carpets. Murtagh had hired the entire top floor. He handed me over to his manservant Tinder, who was polite and impeccable and made no personal remarks of any kind while he helped me bathe and shave and dress in clothes that were too large but both warm and blessedly clean.

"That's a vast improvement," Murtagh said when Tinder brought me back out into what I guessed to be the sitting room. "You look almost human again, instead of like a particularly ill-conceived waxwork. And—" He broke off. "Hark, I believe I hear the dulcet tones of His Grace of Glimmering in the offing. Tinder, I think Mr. Brightmore would prefer to wait for the physician-practitioner in his bedroom."

"Yes, my lord."

But I stood my ground. "Am not a child, Murtagh. I do not need to be cosseted."

"Who's cosseting? This is going to be a most unpleasant and squalid fight, and I'd rather not have witnesses. Go on, Tinder."

I could not in honesty have said I wanted to face Glimmering again. I let Tinder lead me back in the direction of the bathroom, let him put me in a small room probably meant for a paid companion or a nursery maid or some such, and let him leave me there with the assurance that he would bring the physician-practitioner when he arrived.

I sat on the bed, smelling clean linen and lavender sachet, and willed myself to stop shaking. Was no need to unravel like an old blanket just because Murtagh had unexpectedly come to my rescue. Was all the more reason to be watchful, in fact, for no Corambin duke believed in philanthropy. Any favor Murtagh did, he would expect to be repaid, and I had very little currency left, even of the metaphorical kind.

I heard muffled shouting: Murtagh and Glimmering. I wondered if I could find my way to the door for purposes of eavesdropping. Was a woman's trick, my father had taught me, and I could imagine very clearly his contempt for me. Could imagine my own contempt, the Kay Brightmore of an indiction ago, or a wheel ago, looking at the craven, creeping, spying creature I had become. But it was either eavesdrop or sit in stupid, honorable ignorance, and ignorance seemed worse to me now than the petty dishonor of spying.

I stood up before I could muster arguments against myself. The room was quite small; three steps directly forward brought me to the wall, and from there I moved sideways in an inelegant shuffle to where the texture changed from wallpaper to the wood of the door. It took me what seemed an unreasonable amount of time to find the doorknob, and when I did, I thought, Will serve thee right if Tinder hath locked the door against thee. But he had not; I supposed he had quite sufficient reason to assume that I would not try to escape. I opened the door the width of my hand, and Murtagh's voice floated immediately to my ears, still somewhat muffled, but now intelligible: "I know you grieve for your brother, but revenge is not the answer."

"How dare you assume I would allow personal considerations to dictate my actions?" Glimmering's voice, as strident as iron nails on slate. "Kay Brightmore is a traitor and a murderer and far too dangerous to be allowed to run free."

"Which is why you had him locked in Stonewater as soon as you reached Bernatha."

"I wanted him where I could keep an eye on him. I don't trust the Bernathans."

"You wanted him where you could watch him suffer. Really, Thomas, chained to Hume's bier like a dog?"

"You can't deny it was appropriate."

"No, what I *can't* deny is that it was inhumane."

"Let the punishment suit to the crime."

"That's Usaran law, not Corambin, and not a precedent I care to invoke. It gives the righteous too easy an excuse for behaving like criminals."

"Then you don't deny—"

"When Gerrard Hume raised his banner, Kay Brightmore answered, like six of the other sixteen margraves of Caloxa. His crime is no worse than theirs. And yet I don't see you hunting them out of their castles and subjecting them to this treatment. And that's because you *can't*. Imagine the outcry. No one would stand for it. You took advantage of Kay's peculiar vulnerability to make him your scapegoat, and that, Thomas, is despicable."

"You're only protecting him because he's your brother-in-law."

"Do you think so? I would like to think I'm a man of better principles than that, but perhaps I am indeed no different from you. No matter. I *am* protecting him, and I will continue to protect him, and if you don't give me that key, I will start talking to the newspapers."

"You—"

"He's already an icon. It wouldn't take much to make him a martyr, and you, my dear boy, would not enjoy that at all."

"Are you threatening me?"

"Bravo!" said Murtagh. "I knew you'd figure it out eventually. And honestly, what good does it do you to be petty?"

"He should suffer."

"I think he is, without any help from you."

I found that my hands were clenched so tightly my fingers were starting to ache. Should unclench them, I knew; should get away from the door. But I could not move. Could only stand there, straining to hear.

"How can you pity him? You must know what he is."

"And what is that?"

"A monster."

"Have you ever fought against the Usara?"

"No, of course not. Neither have you."

"No, but I've heard the stories. One of Kay's armsmen showed me his scars once. The Usara, you see, consider war a religious action, and the greater the suffering of their enemies, the greater the glory given to their gods."

"What's your point?"

"If you'd spent your entire adult life fighting the Usara without any assistance from your so-called government, you also might employ tactics that more civilized men condemn."

"Ferrand, he *slaughtered* them! Three hundred men, killed like cattle."

"And your brother Geoffrey among them."

"Yes, and my brother Geoffrey among them. But that isn't my point. My point is that he's a *butcher*."

"Have you read the reports of the siege of Memory-of-Death? Do you know how many Ygressine soldiers General Campton had put to the sword?"

"That's different."

"No, it isn't, and that is precisely what I am trying to tell you. Except of course that, unlike the Caloxans, we're better equipped than our opponent, and better funded, and aren't outnumbered by them at approximately three to one."

"You're making excuses for him."

"No. I'm trying to make you understand him, and I suppose I should stop wasting my time. Just give me the damned key, Thomas, and we can fight about the rest of it later."

The sound of Glimmering slamming the key down on a table was nearly drowned out for me by the sound of a door opening much nearer at hand and Tinder's soft, precise voice saying, "This way, Practitioner."

I jerked away from the door, took a half stumbling step backwards, and . . .

Was as if the world had simply fallen away, leaving me standing over an abyss. I knew it was not true—*knew* I was still standing in the small room in the Althammara that I had walked across in three steps. I knew that nothing had changed, nothing *could* have changed, and yet I could not move, more afraid than I had ever been in my life. I wanted above all else to open my eyes and *look*. But my eyes were already open.

"This would be my patient, then," said a Bernathan voice directly in front of me.

"Yes," said Tinder. "His Grace wishes you to be particularly thorough."

"Yes, I can see why."

There were thick fingers on my face, trying to tilt my head to one side. I knocked the hand away and said, "Never mind His Grace's wishes. Mine are that you either treat me as a man or you leave." And if much of the sharpness in my voice was camouflaged fear, no one needed to know that save I.

"Mr. Brightmore," Tinder began, but the practitioner barked out a startled laugh and said, "No, I deserved that. I beg pardon, m'lord."

"Am no lord," I said. "Just—am no performing dog either."

"Or a medical specimen. I have all the worst habits of my breed. Let's start again. My name is Richard Almond. I'm a physician-practitioner second grade."

"Kay Brightmore," I said, even though he knew that already.

"A pleasure to meet you, Mr. Brightmore," said Practitioner Almond. "Now, if you would allow me to examine your eyes."

I submitted to his examination. Midway through, Murtagh came in and unlocked the collar. I hissed as it came away from my skin, and Almond said, "I think we could do with some hot water here, Your Grace."

"Tinder," said Murtagh, "see to it, would you?"

"Is very bad?" I asked.

"You'll want to avoid open-collared shirts for a while," said Almond. "But I'll give you some salve that will reduce the scarring."

"Glimmering is a thrusting fool," Murtagh said.

"He has made no very good impression on Bernatha," Almond said mildly, "although the House of Mercy is glad of his cows."

"Are you a pledge, Practitioner?"

"I am, although I spend very little time there. I find the House of Mercy rather stifling."

"Insular, you might say," Murtagh murmured, and got another barking laugh out of Almond.

"Yes, you might. I say nothing against my colleagues and fellow pledges, but I was very grateful when I could afford to open a practice on the Crait. And here's your man back with the water. That was quick."

"The Althammara has unusually excellent water systems," said Murtagh. "It's one of the reasons I prefer to stay here."

"I'll remember that. Now, Mr. Brightmore, if you'd remove your shirt."

Much, much later, Practitioner Almond was done with me, and I was able to get into bed and lie back among the clean sheets. Murtagh sent Tinder to get me something to eat, and Almond said, "You're in surprisingly good health, all things considered. You need rest and food and a less exciting life, and I think you'll quickly come to feel yourself again."

"And the other?" I said, and cursed myself for the cowardly circumvention of the words: *mine eyes, my blindness.*

Almond sighed. "I am sorry, although I think you already know the answer. Your eyes don't respond to light. Now, if it were a blockage in the flow of aether, as I admit I thought it might be, that would be one thing, but it isn't. The aether is moving freely both in your head and between your head and your heart. I'm afraid the problem is simply that—if you'll forgive the metaphor—your eyes are burnt out. There's nothing there for the aether to kindle."

"Thank you," I said. As he had surmised, I had expected nothing different. Was Murtagh who asked, "Is there any hope?"

"It seems unlikely," said Almond. "I'm sorry."

"Is hardly your fault," said I. "You do but tell the truth."

"Sometimes," said Practitioner Almond, "that is the cruelest thing you can do."

## Felix

It was Corbie at the door. I had been in that trance—or dreaming—or in some strange state in-between—for nearly twelve hours. I begged her to wait and staggered to the lavatory on feet first numb and then agonized. When I came back, she was sitting on the bed beside Mildmay, looking worried. "Your brother's really sick."

"I know," I said. Mildmay did not stir; if he'd woken while I'd been dreamwalking, it clearly hadn't been for long. I hoped he hadn't; I hated the thought of him trying to call for me and getting no response. "Did you bring that banshee?"

She handed it over and stayed with Mildmay while I went downstairs to present it to Mrs. Lettice, who looked a great deal happier on the instant. She balanced the banshee against our bill thus far, and we came out in the black and even slightly ahead. "That'll see you through to Domenica," she said. Four days. It wouldn't be enough, but I thanked her and went back up to the room.

"Everything all right?" said Corbie.

"Idyllic," I said. "You've bought yourself four days' room and board worth of lessons. And we'd better start with you telling me what you know."

What Corbie knew was painfully little. She had her grandmother's trick for hiding from other wizards, and then she had a hodgepodge of half-understood precepts, some from her grandmother, some from stories about wizards, some from what she'd heard by eavesdropping on magician-practitioners, a few even from her clients. She'd learned how to light a candle from watching the way her magician clients did it. I was surprised to find that she could read—she'd gone to something called a dominioner school until she was eight—but she'd had no further schooling, and certainly not in magic. "Gran said it wasn't right for girls," she told me, and I said tartly, "Well, 'Gran' was wrong."

But that was hardly a matter for a few days. She needed the most basic, brute rudiments of practical magic: essentially, how not to hurt herself or anyone else. That first day, we didn't do much more than get rid of everything she'd learned wrong. She had some very strange ideas about what magic was, as for example that salt water would extinguish it. She told me solemnly that "everyone knew" it took a week for a magician who'd fallen out of a gondol to get his magic back. Half of Corbie's knowledge of magic was nonsense like that, and I had a frightening suspicion that the only thing that had kept her alive this long was the fear her grandmother had drummed into her. She'd been too busy hiding to experiment. I was grateful on one level, for she could indeed very easily have killed herself, but on another, I was furious and afraid that her grandmother's fear might prove to have crippled her.

That, too, was not a matter for a few lessons.

She had to leave at sundown for her night's work; I spent a tiring evening first charming Mrs. Lettice into sending a girl up with some broth and then bullying Mildmay into waking up enough to eat it and then to use the chamber pot. His eyes were dull and glassy, his face slack around the twisting of the scar. As best I could tell, he had no idea who I was. He coughed up several vile wads of mucus, and I hoped that was a promising sign. I had never studied medicine; Malkar had had less than no interest, and the Mirador called it heresy. Hindsight was flawless and did me no good.

I was exhausted by the time I'd got Mildmay settled and at least marginally comfortable again. I crawled into the cot and fell asleep almost before I managed to extinguish the candle. I dreamed all night of fire, sometimes among the buildings of the Lower City, sometimes among the tall trees of the forests of Arvelle; in the flames I saw the faces of the dead: my mother, Joline, Sherbourne, Mavortian, Gideon. And others, children whom Keeper had drowned, children whose names I didn't even remember. Wizards who had died in one of Malkar's attacks. Wizards who, from the testimony of Simon Barrister, we knew had died in the Bastion. The dead of Nera. The dead of the Mirador. I fled from the fire, but again and again I found myself in a dead end, up against a brick wall or a jumble of rocks. And when I turned, there would be a woman standing in front of me, her burning hair lifting from her burning forehead, her eyes like a visitation of the desolation of Hell, her child burning in her arms.

*Revenge,* she said, and held the child out to me.

*I cannot,* I said, and twisted past her to flee again.

I was more tired when I woke up than I had been when I went to sleep. But at least this morning, I had time for a bath.

I might be wretchedly homesick, but I did appreciate the Corambins' mechanical bent as they had applied it to plumbing. Hot water could be produced merely by turning a tap, and I was determined to find someone who could explain to me how, but in the meantime, I luxuriated in it. Hot water was not a substitute for sleep, but it was better than nothing, and I met Corbie that afternoon with a doggedly clear head. She'd brought lunch: a kind of stuffed bread which she told me proudly was a Bernathan specialty. I was to the point of appreciating any food I didn't have to pay for, but I didn't say so.

That day, we started with the one thing Corbie did know: how to light a candle. The first thing I taught her was how to extinguish a candle once she'd lit it. It was counterintuitive, but once she understood the relationship between the two actions, the lighting and the extinguishing, we could work on calling witchlight, which was both useful in a practical sense and an exercise on which a great deal of more advanced work was based. Extinguishing the candle took most of the afternoon. It didn't make sense, Corbie complained, and I finally said, "Yes, that's true, but it isn't *useful.* If you expect the world to be logical . . . well, you're going to have a very unhappy life, for one thing."

She stared at me for a moment, almost outraged, and then laughed. "And if that ain't the truest thing anybody ever said, I don't know what is. All right. It don't make sense. What does it do instead?"

Which was an unexpected way of looking at it, and was the first sign in Corbie I'd seen of the bone-deep inquisitiveness that, far more than power, was the hallmark of the great wizards. Her life had probably taught her to hide that, too.

"You're trying to think of it as the same action as snuffing the candle," I said, "and that's logical, because you figured out how to light it by imagining the same action as striking a lucifer and holding it to the wick. But magic doesn't work like material action. I mean, I suppose you *could* snuff a candle with magic, but you'll give yourself a tremendous headache. Instead, what you're trying to do is to reverse the action of lighting it, to put the flame back in the lucifer."

"But you can't," Corbie said.

"With a real lucifer, no. But this isn't a real lucifer. You put the flame in the wick, Corbie. Now take it out."

She frowned at me, and then her eyes widened. She turned her head to look at the candle, and after a moment, the flame snapped out of existence. Corbie looked back at me, grinning like an urchin.

"Good job," I said, grinning back at her. "You practice that tonight, and tomorrow I'll show you what to do with it."

"Yessir," she said.

But she hesitated at the door. "Mr. Harrowgate?"

"Felix," I corrected her.

"Felix. You said you didn't do women. Did you mean just jezebels or are you a bluet?"

"A bluet?"

"A violet-boy. You know, a man who f—sleeps with other men."

"Ah. Yes. The word we use at home is 'molly.' "

"And are you?"

"Does it matter?"

"Well, I just . . ." She fidgeted with a stray strand of pale hair. "If you *were*, which I ain't saying you are because I don't know, and if you were interested . . . I mean, I know you don't got a lot of money, and with your brother being so sick and all, so if you wanted, I could tell you . . . not that you need me to or anything, I just thought that—"

"Corbie, are you offering to pimp for me?"

She went brick-red. "It's just, you'd do better with a pledged patron. If you were going to, which I know you said you weren't, but if you *were*, I wanted you to know—"

"Corbie," I said, and smiled at her. "Shut up and go to work."

She left in a flurry of skirts and a rattle of heels, and I sat in the darkness of that very small room and tried to pretend I wasn't tempted.

That night, as I realized instantly I should have been expecting, Diokletian came dreamwalking to find me. It was actually something of a relief—which said far more about my state of mind than I wanted to contemplate, but at least I didn't have to worry about fires or labyrinths. Diokletian's disapproval seemed a small price to pay.

I wished—I had always wished—that my relationship with Diokletian were not so fraught with ugliness. But he had chosen certain roles for me at the outset, and they were not roles I was willing to play. I was not willing to be a perfect copy of my mother; I was not willing to be a dutiful son (on the off chance that he was in fact my father); I was not willing to be his damaged protégé. And he had no willingness to deal with me as I was. He found me threatening, outraging, disappointing. I had to be grateful to him, for without his intervention, I would still be helplessly insane, but I could not like him.

He entered into a dream of an argument with Shannon. There had been dozens of those arguments, stupid, stupidly vicious things that had gone on for days. In the dream, we were arguing over what to do with Mildmay. Shannon said, *Drown him like a kitten and have done with it,* and was infuriated by my objections.

*Don't be silly, Felix. It's not like you can keep him.*

In the dream, I knew that if I drowned Mildmay, he would turn into Keeper, and I was still trying to explain this to Shannon when I became aware of Diokletian.

I shoved Shannon into a convenient wardrobe and said to Diokletian, *What do you want?*

*Thamuris said he thought you visited him.*

*I did.*

*So what do* you *want? You must want something.*

*I told Thamuris. I made a mistake, and I want to correct it.*

*Do you really think it's that easy?*

*No, of course not,* I said, irritated. *But I have to try.*

*Then why haven't you?*

The dream had been shifting around us as we talked, and we were now in the Omphalos. Not the Omphalos of the Khloïdanikos, but the Omphalos as it appeared in the waking world of the Gardens of Nephele: dank, dark, and claustrophobic. I walked out immediately onto the portico, and Diokletian followed me. *Yes, well, there's a hitch.*

*What hitch?* he said, frowning out over the distinctly Mélusinien cemetery with which my mind had replaced the Gardens.

*I can't get to the Khloïdanikos,* I said. *The briars have blocked my way in.*

*Have they?* he said; he sounded almost pleased. *You refused my help once.*

*And I'm not asking for it now,* I snapped.

*Aren't you?* He raised his eyebrows in a supercilious manner I found intensely irritating. *You have a better plan?*

Which of course I didn't. *I'll think of something,* I said, but the defensiveness in my voice was clearly audible.

*How like your mother. Determined to cut off your nose to spite your face.*

*Don't flatter yourself, darling,* I said. *It's just that I don't trust you, that's all.*

At least I had the satisfaction of making him mad. He lost his air of detached superiority in an instant and said, *He's dying, you know.*

*I beg your pardon?*

*Thamuris. Is dying.*

*People with consumption usually do.*

*The Khloïdanikos was helping.*

*Yes, he told me.*

*It isn't anymore. Because of what you did. And Thamuris is deteriorating more and more rapidly.*

I could have pretended I was surprised, but it wasn't worth it. *If you're saying this situation needs to be resolved quickly, you're still not telling me anything I didn't already know.*

*So you admit you need my help.*

*No,* I said, and as I said it, I understood what my dreamwalking had been trying to tell me. *I need Thamuris's help.*

❧

In the morning, Mildmay was no better, and I tried rather desperately not to think about what that might mean, keeping myself busy instead with the *Standard* and the old newspapers Mrs. Lettice had given me. I thought she felt it was her duty to help me educate myself about Bernatha.

And the newspapers were telling me a tremendous amount, even if Mrs. Lettice wouldn't have liked some of the conclusions I drew. I learned that Bernatha had escaped the Insurgence largely unscathed, though somewhat inconvenienced, due to the ineffable wisdom of the Seven Houses in choosing to side with Corambis rather than with the Caloxans who were the city's neighbors (much hyperbolous blather here about the superiority of a "free city" to a "margravate city"). I learned that the Duke of Glimmering was an ornament to society whose charm and elegance would be sorely missed when he returned to Esmer. I learned that the men who had defended the railroad line against "the misguided and the savage" were glad to be back with their families. I learned that the Bernatha city council argued over the budget much the same way the Cabinet and Curia did at home.

Not home, I reminded myself. I had lost the right to call the Mirador home, and I would do better to stop thinking of Mélusine as home, too. It wasn't as if I was ever going to be allowed to go back.

A bleak thought, and one I tried not to dwell on.

I noted the air of self-congratulation with which the newspapers reported the profits of aiding the Corambin army; the obsessive lavishness of the discussions of the Houses' annual budgets; the advertisements that framed each page, selling everything from ladies' hand soap to the services of a physician-practitioner third grade who specialized—reading between the lines—in abortions. And then there were the advertisements for livestock and used gondols and tin guttering, which took up pages all by themselves. This was a society in which everything was for sale.

There was a very long essay about relations with Ygres, the country across the sea to the west. Corambis was at war with part of Ygres, and Bernatha deplored it. Bernatha was maintaining trade with the rest of Ygres and was trying to claim neutrality in Corambis's war. "We are only honest merchants!" seemed to be the refrain, and I could not help wondering what the Caloxans made of that.

The discussions of the Insurgence made it very clear that Bernatha did not consider itself Caloxan and probably never had. Bernatha had supported Corambis from the first, meaning that even if the Caloxan forces could have controlled the railways, which apparently they had never entirely managed, they still couldn't have blocked Corambin movement, for Bernatha's was the only decent harbor on the Caloxan coast. There was no Caloxan navy. Why, I wondered, had Gerrard Hume thought he could fight this war at all? But with that question, the Bernathan newspapers could not help me.

Corbie brought lunch again, and while we ate, she told me how she had practiced the night before by lighting and extinguishing the candles in her room after every client. I suspected it had improved her business as well, for even telling me about it put life in her face and made her long nose and dark eyes lovely rather than merely interesting.

She was eager to know what I would teach her today. I called witchlight, and her eyes went wide. She was facing the window, and I saw for the first time that her eyes weren't brown as I had thought but a fantastically deep blue, so deep it was actually more accurate to call it violet. "I can't do that," she said.

"Of course you can. It's no harder than lighting a candle."

"But it's real *magic*."

"I thought that's what I was teaching you," I said.

She went red and said half-angrily, "Don't tease me, Felix, all right?"

"My dear Corbie, I assure you—" I cut myself off, realizing that to her that would sound like I *was* teasing her. "Look. I promise I'm not teasing you. But why would you think I was?"

She got up and stalked over to the window, more to avoid having to meet my eyes, I thought, than because she was truly angry. "I know what I am. I'm a jezebel, not a magician. I figure maybe I can learn enough to get a third-grade practitioner's license, and then, you know, when I'm too old for the fish, I'll have something to fall back on. But I'm not expecting anything more."

I blurted, "Why in the world not?" and startled her into turning to face me.

"What?"

"Corbie, you're . . . How old are you?"

"Twenty-three," she said, her chin going up so defiantly I knew it was a lie. I gave her my most severely skeptical look and waited. She folded fairly quickly: "Oh, all right. Seventeen."

"Better," I said. "Some wizards don't come into their powers at all until they're eighteen or nineteen, you know, and although I don't know the Corambin system, I can't imagine you're starting *ruinously* late; you've certainly got enough power to do whatever you want. And you *know* I was a prostitute. So why would you think you can't . . . ?"

She muttered something at the floor, for a moment uncannily like Mildmay.

"What?"

"I said, you don't sound like it. Even being foreign and all."

"I was taught not to," I said. "I'm sure you could learn likewise." She gave me a look that went beyond skepticism and into outright disbelief. "No, really. It's a matter of learning how to hear yourself more than anything else."

"Could you teach me *that*?"

"Um," I said. Malkar's pedagogical methods had not been ones that I would want to use. And the learning process had been very slow, although possibly Corbie would not be as stupid a student as I had been. "Let me think about that. Right now, let's just work on witchlights."

For all her protests, Corbie listened avidly, and she mastered the trick of witchlights far more quickly than she'd learned to extinguish a candle the day before. The rest of the afternoon was easy, for the color visualization exercises were simple but time-consuming—and more important than they seemed. By the time she left, Corbie had lost the hangdog expression that said she thought she wasn't good enough to learn "real magic," and I was profoundly glad to see it go.

In my dream, I am walking down the hallway in the Mirador that leads from the Hall of the Chimeras to the Lesser Coricopat, a hallway I know as well as I know my own hands. Except, in my dream, the hallway is longer, darker, as if someone has come and taken away half the candles, and I am nervous, walking fast.

There is someone walking ahead of me, a man with long red hair, dressed in black. I think that I know him—certainly, his gait is familiar, that easy, powerful stride like a panther's. But he will not look back, even though I know that he knows I am behind him, and I cannot think of his name. I know—the way one does know things in dreams—that if I can just see his face, I will remember his name, and I lengthen my stride to catch up.

For some reason it disturbs me that I have to work so hard to catch him; I am nearly trotting by the time I come abreast of him. He turns to look at me, his eyes green and cold, and I do know him—he is Mildmay, my brother—but there is no scar on his face.

*Mildmay,* I say, and then falter to a stop. I can't mention the scar and say instead, feebly, *You . . . you aren't limping.*

The look in his eyes is hard impatience, like flint and iron, and he says, *Of course not, you stupid fuck.* Except that he doesn't sound right, not like himself, his consonants as clear and hard as his ice-green eyes. *I'm dead, ain't I?*

I flailed out of bed in a tangle of blankets, my breath coming in hard sobs, and lurched, half-crawling, across the room. For a moment I thought my dream had been a true one; Mildmay's face was waxen and the quilt was not moving with his breath, but then I was near enough to hear the rasp of air in his lungs. I touched his face, my fingers shying away from his scar, remembering despite myself how he had looked in my dream, how different he had seemed without that harsh livid line. His skin was still fever-hot. I found the pulse in his neck; it was labored but still strong.

It had not been a true dream, then. Not yet.

I barely waited for dawn before I was down at the front desk, begging Mrs. Lettice for the name of a doctor.

"You can't afford a pledged practitioner," she said, not as a question.

I couldn't afford a piece of horehound, but I didn't say that. Mrs. Lettice consulted a small black notebook, giving me a thoughtful look, and said, "I'll send Joanna for Practitioner Druce."

Practitioner Druce turned out to be a woman, middle-aged and fierce. She examined Mildmay thoroughly; asked a cogent series of questions, some of which I could not answer due to Mildmay's habit of never talking about himself and especially not to complain; then brought chalk and a straightedge out of her bag and began marking symbols on the floor.

She was a wizard. A magician to Corambins. A heretic back home.

I wavered for a moment between three different kinds of hysterics, and then said, quite reasonably, "Will you explain the theory of what you're doing?"

She gave me a slow, sidelong look. She knew I was a wizard—of course she knew I was a wizard. I realized she suspected me of mocking her, and said more hastily than tactfully, "It's heresy at . . . in Mélusine. So I don't know how it works." And then I held my breath, waiting for her response. If she took offense at being called a heretic, I wasn't sure I'd be able to persuade her to stay. I didn't need anyone to tell me my charm was at low ebb.

But after a moment, her face relaxed into the first real smile she'd shown. "I wondered why you were calling on me, when I'm only a magician-practitioner second grade and you're . . ." She waved a hand. "You've never studied healing at all?"

"No. Is a magician-practitioner different from a physician-practitioner?"

"Many physician-practitioners are annemer. Many magician-practitioners aren't physicians. I happen to be both. Third grade and second grade."

"But not pledged," I said cautiously.

"The House of Mercy and I do not see eye to eye on certain matters," she said, and that was all the answer she was going to give. "As to what I'm doing . . ." Her explanation was lucid and straightforward but more mechanical than theoretical. She knew what she was doing and on a very elementary level, the level of cause and effect, why she was doing it, but not any more than that. I reminded myself that she was here to treat Mildmay, not to satisfy my curiosity, and contented myself with listening and watching and extrapolating privately where I could. I understood why the Coeurterre found the magicians of Corambis so congenial: Practitioner Druce talked a great deal about balance and flow, although the flow she meant was not of magic, but of something else.

She called it *vi* and said it was stagnating in Mildmay's lungs.

"But what *is* it?"

She shrugged and leaned across Mildmay to chalk a series of symbols on the wall. "It's what magic works on. You can't mend bones with magic, but you can use vi to encourage the bone to mend. Or here, with your brother, I can't magically expel the congestion from his lungs or the invaders from his blood, but—"

"Wait, invaders? What invaders?"

She seemed more amused by my alarm than anything else. "The invaders that are making him sick. The invaders that his body is trying to burn out with this fever."

My mouth was probably hanging open in an unbecoming fashion, I realized. "I don't—but how can he have invaders in his *blood*?"

She straightened, dusted the chalk off her hands. "Mr. Harrowgate, have you ever used a minusculium?"

"A what?"

"A magnifying glass?"

"Well, yes, of course."

"A minusculium—think of it as an incredibly powerful magnifying glass. If I had one here, I could take a drop of your brother's blood and show you what I mean."

"He has . . . creatures in his blood? Like parasites?"

"No, no. Like machines. Tiny machines that tell his body to do the wrong things."

The idea was more than a little abhorrent. "But how did they get into his blood in the first place?"

"If I could tell you that," said Practitioner Druce, "I could blackball the House of Mercy instead of the other way 'round."

⁂

Corbie arrived as Practitioner Druce was leaving; she barely waited for the door to close before she hissed at me, "That's *Priscilla Druce*."

"She didn't tell me her given name," I said. "If that's what it is, I see why."

"But—" She broke off and said, "Mildmay must be really bad, huh?"

"Yes," I said and felt myself sag into the truth. "Practitioner Druce was kind enough to allow me to go into debt to her—a practice which I suspect is why Mrs. Lettice recommended her in the first place."

"Oh probably," Corbie said. "It's all right, though. She won't break your shins. But she'll have you up in the House of Honesty if you don't pay her back quick enough."

"I know," I said. "She warned me. And so I . . ." The words knotted and stuck in my throat.

Corbie looked up at me worriedly. "Felix?"

"Corbie, you said . . ." I couldn't get it out that way, either. Corbie was looking even more worried.

"You said you'd be my patron," I ground out finally.

"Oh," said Corbie, her eyes going wide. "Well, yeah, I will, but are you sure? I mean, you seemed like you meant it when you said you weren't going to do that no more, and I know I shouldn't've pushed at it, but I just—"

"Corbie," I said tiredly, "please shut up."

We kept working that afternoon on color visualizations, and if I was distracted, Corbie was tactful enough not to mention it. Practitioner Druce had said the best thing now for Mildmay was sleep, and had reassured me that he could be left for a few hours. So I felt guilt, but no particular concern at going out into the cold evening air with Corbie.

"I guess," Corbie said, "now I got to ask how much you know."

"I lost my virginity when I was eleven," I said, trying to sound matter-of-fact despite the fact that this was history I never talked about. "At auction, actually. I spent the next three years in a brothel that specialized in the tarquin trade."

"Tarquin?"

"Oh, damn it all, of course you don't use the same words. People who, um, enjoy other people's pain."

"Flame," Corbie said; she was now looking at me very dubiously. "You were one of those?"

"No, I was a martyr," I said, omitting my personal preferences from the conversation entirely. "The . . . the other side."

"Shadow."

"Shadow," I echoed, thinking it was uncomfortably appropriate. "So, really, there's very little I don't know about what men will pay to do to other men." My effort at a smile failed abysmally.

"Well," Corbie said, a little skittish around the eyes, but standing her ground, "you don't need to worry about that, because flames and shadows is the Black and White's business, and nobody who ain't pledged has a piece of it. And what we're banking on is your tattoos."

"My tattoos?"

"My friend Georgina reads all those Mélusine novels, and she tells me the plots on slow nights. And I know just how big they are. Everybody knows about the magicians with the tattoos, and even people who don't have a thing about the books will think that's worth paying for."

"Oh," I said weakly. She had it planned out, probably had from the moment she'd recognized me for what I was.

"Hold that thought," said Corbie. "I'll be right back."

I stayed where I was, despite an increasing urge to run, as she ducked into a storefront. An apothecary shop, it looked like, and I wondered what she needed so suddenly.

She came back and said, "Here."

I held my hand out reflexively, and she gave me a small glass bottle filled with pale pink pills. "You should take one now."

"What are they?"

"Hecate," Corbie said, as if it should have been self-evident.

"That didn't help."

"They make it so you can't hex anybody."

"*Hex* anybody?" I said incredulously.

"Not that you would. But. Well. People are a little twitchy about magicians. Like my gran."

Twitchy like her gran, I realized she meant. "Because I might be a warlock," I said.

"Yeah, exactly," said Corbie. "And, I mean, they were worst for other magicians, but they did pretty nasty things to annemer, too."

I thought of Porphyria Levant and the tale of her revenge on Creon Malvinius. "I understand. What exactly does hecate do?"

"It makes it so you can't do magic. It don't last long—you'll be back to normal by tomorrow morning."

"And you know this from personal experience?"

"You mean, have I taken it?"

"In a nutshell."

She rolled her eyes. "Well, no. Seeing as how you're the first person I've ever told I could do magic. But lots of magicians use it."

"*Why?*" I could think of few things I wanted less than to take a drug that would make me annemer, even temporarily.

"Well, people used to take it all the time so the warlocks wouldn't get 'em. Nowadays, magicians mostly take it when they're running for office or petitioning a House. You know, before the vote so there's no funny business. It really is safe."

"Depending on your definition," I muttered, but I didn't need Corbie to tell me I didn't have a choice. I shook one of the pale pink pills out and dry-swallowed it, then stoppered the bottle firmly and put it in one of my inside pockets.

"It'll take about half an hour to work," Corbie said. "C'mon."

Corbie did have a plan, and she explained bits of it to me as we walked.

Prostitution in Bernatha was in some ways very similar to prostitution in Mélusine and in some ways radically different. For one thing, it wasn't merely legal—or mostly ignored, which was a better description of the situation at home—it was a flourishing and vital part of the Bernathan economy. All brothels had to be pledged to the House of Chastity; individual prostitutes might be pledged to Chastity, as Corbie was, or they might be unpledged. You could not—Corbie said and seemed shocked that I had to ask—be a prostitute pledged to a different House, although you might work in, or even for, one of the other six.

As an unpledged prostitute, I couldn't work in a pledged brothel, and therefore not in a brothel at all. There were what Corbie called blacklight brothels, but she said the House of Chastity always caught them, and when it did, it blackballed the clients as well as the prostitutes. "Not worth it," she said emphatically.

So I had to work the streets, which I'd done for Keeper but never since, "except it's better," said Corbie, "if you can work out a deal with a bar."

"Can I?" I said curiously.

She looked up at me and then grinned. "Yeah, you can."

The bar was called Crysolomon's, and the bartender was a close friend of Corbie's—close enough, from the way he greeted her, that if he wasn't one of her clients, he wanted to be. The look he gave me was not entirely friendly, but Corbie whispered something in his ear out of which I only caught the word "violet," and he relaxed considerably, enough to say, "Any friend of Corbie's is welcome here."

Corbie established me at a table in the back, said, "Fish will find you, so don't go trolling," and "don't take less'n five hermits," and left. The rest of it was up to me.

Her bartender brought me a drink—"on the house," he said when I looked alarmed. "If Corbie's right, you're going to be bringing in some custom."

*Fish will find you,* Corbie'd said; I decided not to think about it any further and took a swallow of sweet white wine. I was starting to feel the hecate. The absence of my magic didn't hurt, but I felt a little light-headed, a little dulled, as if I couldn't see or hear properly. And at the same time I felt raw and naked and utterly helpless. It was not a nice sensation.

The first fish found me three-quarters of an hour later, and it was like I'd never left the Shining Tiger. I knew how to do this; there was even a feeling it took me some time to identify as relief. For the first time in twenty years, I wasn't lying.

Crysolomon's had a back room—a storeroom reeking of beer and rats, but the door locked and that was good enough. By the time Corbie came back for me, I had made fifteen hermits and been bought enough drinks to put a buffalo under the table.

Happily, I was not a buffalo.

Corbie sat down across from me and said without preamble, "Are you drunk?"

"Not so's you'd notice," I said and gave her my best smile. "And this way I don't mind the hecate."

"Darren said he'd been watering the drinks, but you look . . ."

"Relaxed?" I suggested. "Happy? Darling, trust me. I am not drunk." I pushed the fifteen hermits across the table to distract her.

"Not bad for the first night," Corbie said and proceeded to subject my poor hermits to some truly alarming mathematics.

Five hermits went to the House of Chastity. Corbie called it the tithe, and it was the price of working in Bernatha without being pledged. "A third?" I said. "Of everything?"

"Believe me," Corbie said, "it's cheap at the price. Jezebels who don't tithe . . . Well, you don't want to know."

That left ten hermits. Five were mine; two and a thrustle went to Darren to keep Crysolomon's sweet, and the rest went to Corbie, although she turned around and gave them straight back, minus two pennies for the hecate.

I walked back to the Fiddler's Fox seven hermits and three pennies richer, with the strange-familiar taste of semen in the back of my throat. I checked on Mildmay—still sleeping, but even I could see the improvement since this morning—washed up carefully, locked the door, extinguished the candle, and lay down. And burst into tears.

It was, truly, like being caught in a cloudburst; it was that violent and that abrupt. I knew part of it was the hecate and this flayed feeling of vulnerability; part of it was the alcohol. And I knew the root of it was the way I'd spent the evening and all the memories that had been stirred up. But what I felt was grief. I missed Gideon so much it felt like I'd been crippled. To say my heart was broken was trite, and in fact it didn't feel broken. It felt *gone*, as if it had been wrenched from my chest, and though it continued to beat, it did so from some great, cold distance, like the moon in eclipse. I rolled over, burying my face in the limp pillow, and as I'd done in the days after Joline's death, I cried myself to sleep.

# Chapter 5

## *Felix*

The next night was easier—also more profitable. Mildmay woke up when I came in, although he didn't stay awake long enough to do any more than mutter, "There you are," before he was asleep again. But it was a good sign, and a reminder that the banshee and seven hermits I now had toward Practitioner Druce's saint were necessary for reasons larger and more important than myself. I slept heavily and woke remembering only vague fragments of my dreams: fire again, and anger. I thought I'd been dreaming about Keeper, although I wasn't entirely sure.

When I came back from the bathroom, Mrs. Lettice was blocking the door.

"Good morning," I said warily.

"Is Lunedy morning," she said. "And I hear you've found a source of income."

"I . . ."

"Charity to the indigent is one thing," she said, "but indigent you are not, from what I hear. A banshee for the week." I opened my mouth to protest, and she said, "And that's at discount, your brother being so ill. I charge Chastity-girls a banshee and twelve, and that's just for the room."

"I'm not seeing clients here," I said.

"And how am I to know that?"

"I just told you?"

"Anyone can tell a lie, Mr. Harrowgate," she said, her eyes bright and hard. "A banshee for the week, if you please. Now."

A banshee and seven hermits became seven hermits on their own, and paying off my debt to Practitioner Druce looked suddenly much farther away. I was glad Mildmay slept through the whole sordid thing.

Practitioner Druce's was not the only debt I needed to pay, and with taking hecate nightly, my opportunities to deal with the Khloïdanikos were limited—especially as I was not about to add oneiromancy to Corbie's lessons.

Now? I thought wearily, but I remembered what Diokletian had said about Thamuris, and I knew I couldn't put it off. I straightened the bedcovers and lay down on top of them, folded my hands carefully, and slowed myself into a trance.

Oneiromantically, it was always easier to find one's way back to a place one had been before. The door with the horn lock led me to Thamuris's room, and I wasn't surprised to find that he was there. Laudanum dreams.

He was standing at the window, looking out at a landscape that I did not recognize and that certainly had nothing to do with the Gardens of Nephele. He turned when he became aware of me. "You're back." He didn't sound surprised, but he also didn't sound particularly pleased.

"I, um . . ."

"No, don't tell me," Thamuris said wearily. "Diokletian has explained to you my tale of woe, and you are *sorry*. You feel *terrible*. You didn't *mean* to."

His imitation of my speech at its most affected was cruelly accurate, and since the things he accused me of feeling were exactly what I felt, he left me with nothing to say.

He came closer. "And I think you *did* mean to. I have had a great deal of time to think about it, Felix, and I think you got exactly what you wanted."

"Thamuris—"

"You wanted to be rid of those rubies. You wanted to be rid of your spirit-ancestor. Did you want to be rid of me as well?"

"No!" I said, horrified. "I swear. I didn't mean—that is, I admit it was stupid and selfish and wrong, but I wasn't trying to . . . I didn't intend to . . . I didn't want to hurt anybody."

"Congratulations," Thamuris said, his voice as scouring and bitter as sea salt.

"Thamuris, please. I don't deny I deserve it, but please. Don't."

He stared at me for a span of time that felt cruelly endless, then said, "Why not?"

"Because I'm going to take the rubies back. Right now. If you'll help me."

He considered that with the deliberation of laudanum and finally said, "Very well. That seems fair. What do you need?"

"I can't get into the Khloïdanikos. The briars are blocking Horn Gate."

"How appropriate," Thamuris said, then held his hands up. "No, I promised. I'm sorry. Then you need me to bring you in."

"Yes. And I may need your help with the briars," I said and added humbly, "Please."

"All right," said Thamuris. "Give me your hands."

It was hard to do, both because I had learned to dislike touching Thamuris for the consumption that burned through him, and because Malkar had trapped me that way once. But I gritted my teeth and extended my hands. His touch was as fever-swampy as I had expected, but he was gentle even though I would have understood if he wasn't. He laced his fingers through mine and squeezed, very slightly, and around us, the dream of his room dissolved into the Dream of the Garden.

I jerked back from Thamuris, and almost immediately tripped over a strand of briars, landing hard and with a yelp. The briars' thorns were as vicious as their vines were tough. I disentangled myself painfully and looked around, my breath coming shorter as I saw the damage I had done.

The briars were the only things flourishing. The flower beds were full of withered petals and broken stalks; the grass was yellowing; the perseïd trees had shed their flowers. Everything looked ill and weak.

"Are you all right?"

I looked up at Thamuris. He looked as yellow and ill as the grass.

"I'm fine," I said, swallowing hard. "Let's get this over with."

Thamuris and I went together to the oak in the circle of briars. Though I did not stop, I glanced in passing at the mostly dead perseïd tree against the ruined orchard wall—the perseïd tree that had been linked to Mildmay by Thamuris's long ago divination—and saw that although it, too, looked sickly, it had not shed its leaves. Perhaps it was unreasonable, but I felt more hopeful after that.

The briars were just as lush and wicked around the oak as they were everywhere else. The oak tree looked mange-ridden, but like the shattered perseïd, it was not yet dead.

It was not too late, no matter how stupid and selfish I had been.

As we stopped in front of the overgrown trellis, first one ruby bee, then another emerged from the depths of the garden to circle hostilely about my head.

"I don't think they can sting," Thamuris said. "Otherwise, they would have stung me when I was trying to reach their hive."

"The briars sting for them," I said without thinking, and we both winced at the truth of it.

Both of us were bleeding by the time I made it into the circle, and the ruby bees were crawling angrily on my face and hands. But they could not sting me, or impede me, and I thought I understood this piece of symbolism as well. They could do harm only to a construct like the Khloïdanikos; they could not touch me if I wasn't stupid enough to let them.

I picked up the hive and watched the bees crawl into it, one by one. The truth of their nature, I thought, and the truth of their nature when I held their hive was that they were ten smoke-stained rubies in a wash-leather bag. That was the truth.

I rested my palm for a moment against the trunk of the oak tree and whispered, "I'm sorry." And then I made my way back out of the circle. This time, it almost seemed as if the briars were fighting me, and Thamuris said in a strained voice, "I'm starting to wonder about these briars."

"Do you think I brought them?"

"No, not that. Hold still." I held still while he very gently removed a trailing whip of thorns from its clawed hold in my hair. "But I don't imagine we're the first wizards to think of, um, storing problematical materials here."

I shut my eyes, only partly to avoid having them ripped out by the vine Thamuris was struggling with. "And like does, in fact, call to like, at least on the thaumaturgic level. So of course this would present itself to me as the perfect place to put these damnable rubies."

"I don't know," Thamuris said. "But these briars—ow!"

We gave up on trying to have a conversation until we were both free of the briars and several feet away. "Hopefully," I said, "they'll quiet down now."

"I expect the Khloïdanikos can tame them, now that they don't have help. What will you do with . . . ?"

"I don't know," I said. "The same way I didn't know before this recklessly stupid experiment." We started walking, a mutual, tacit decision to get away from the center of the damage. "At least I don't have to worry about them interacting with the Mirador any longer."

"You don't?" He sounded alarmed.

Of course, I thought. There was no reason he *would* know. "I'll tell you later," I said. "I'm with Mildmay. We're fine."

"But, Felix—"

"Don't worry. It's all right, really."

"It's not anything good, is it?" he said quietly.

"No," I said and sighed, defeated. "Not really. My lover is dead, and I've been exiled for destroying the mind of the man who murdered him."

Thamuris's breath caught, and I felt even worse; there was no call to be cruel to him, just because I was tired and unhappy and burdened again with this last reminder of Malkar, like a bloodstain that would not wash out of a handkerchief.

"And I've been so mean to you," he said. "I'm sorry."

"No. You were right. The other circumstances don't change that." Thamuris hadn't the least idea of how to go about being mean, but I didn't say so and especially did not remark that I could give him lessons if he wanted.

"Still. I *am* sorry. And I'm sorry for your loss."

Grief howled up, black and choking in my throat, and I fought it back down. "Thank you," I said. "I . . . I appreciate it."

"Are we still . . ."

"Still?"

He stopped walking, and I turned to look at him, raising my eyebrows. "Friends?" he asked.

"I don't think I get to make that decision," I said. "You have every reason to be angry at me."

"I don't like being angry at you," he said, rather plaintively, and I was reminded of how young he was. "Diokletian says I shouldn't be too quick to forgive you, but I don't see *why*."

"Diokletian doesn't trust me."

"I know *that*," Thamuris said, and managed something that was almost a smile. "He says you're trying to corrupt me."

"I'm what?"

"He says that you would never spend this much time with anyone if you didn't want them sexually."

"I'm flattered," I said sourly. "Don't worry, darling. I only want you for your mind." That actually made him laugh, and I felt something unfurling in me, as fragile as a perseïd blossom: hope.

## *Kay*

That tiny bedroom was as a cage, and I was as the captive cougar. I could not leave the room without someone to guide me, and there was no one who would do so. Murtagh was gone much of the time; I gathered from the bits and fragments I overheard that the political situation was not nearly so straightforward as he had tried to convince me to believe. The servants were polite and efficient and unhelpful. Tinder told me that His Grace thought it best if I stayed out of sight. And I even understood. For if I was in truth a "hero of the Insurgence," surely it was to everyone's benefit to keep me out of the public eye, away from the witless bees who would swarm to any rising, whether queen or drone or vicious cannibal wasp. But I was caged, and I did hate it.

Tinder must have spoken to Murtagh, for that evening there was a tap on the door and Murtagh's voice saying, "I hear that you are near-mad with boredom."

"Even an I would, I cannot deny it," I said. I had explored every inch of that tiny, barren bedroom—and certainly I had profited thereby, for I had found a path which I could pace and at least channel some of the energy for which I had no use. But it was not enough.

"Then perhaps you will condescend to talk to me," Murtagh said. I heard him come in and shut the door behind him.

"*Condescend?* Your Grace, I—"

"For the love of the Lady, don't *start*," Murtagh said and startled me so much I nearly bit my tongue. "You are the most arrogant, intolerant, self-righteous son of a bitch I have ever met, but I like that better than when you try to crawl. Humility does not suit you, my lord of Rothmarlin."

"But I am *not* lord of Rothmarlin. Not any longer."

"Does that mean you're no longer yourself?" Murtagh asked; he sounded intrigued. He walked through my pacing as neatly as a girl skipping rope, and I knew by the creak that he'd sat down on the bed.

"Means I must learn to be someone else. Is not fitting for a dependent of the Duke of Murtagh to put on the same airs as the Margrave of Rothmarlin."

"What about the Warden of Grimglass?"

"What?"

"The Warden of Grimglass," he repeated, enunciating distinctly.

"You wish me to marry his widow. I remember. But is no heir?"

"There is a boy of seven. And while he is certainly the previous warden's heir, the question of his guardianship has been ugly and protracted and well-nigh insoluble."

"The previous warden left no will?"

"The previous warden, if you will permit my saying so, was an idiot. His 'will' consists of a letter written to his wife a few days before he died—on campaign in Blandamere, if you were wondering—"

"I wasn't."

"A letter to his wife saying that he trusted she and his three brothers would 'work something out.' "

I considered that from one wall to the opposite. "'Idiot' is perhaps too kind a word?"

"Well, I never met the man, so I try to be generous. But he certainly displayed a complete lack of understanding of either his wife or any of his brothers. One of them is a naval man and has no time for administering the estate, even if he could be reached for consultation more than once or twice an indiction. The other two, however, are ambitious and apparently have been at each other's throats since the cradle, and the widow . . ."

"The one you want me to marry."

"Yes, he has only the one widow," Murtagh said a trifle waspishly. "The widow is a spoilt bitch, but very clever. And of a grasping disposition."

"Your concern for my future happiness unmans me," said I.

"She's a political creature. I don't think she'll give you any trouble, especially if you consent to let her live at least part of the indiction in Esmer. She is much too cosmopolitan for the far west."

"You sound as if you know her?"

"Distant cousin," Murtagh said. "She was Vanessa Carey before her marriage."

"Have not actually answered my question," I observed.

"And now I remember why my chief emotion in the weeks leading up to my wedding was the desire to strangle you," Murtagh said amiably. "Yes, I know Vanessa. My aunt Evelina sponsored her."

"Your aunt Evelina who was at daggers-drawn with Isobel from the moment they laid eyes on each other?"

"That very one."

I paced my circuit twice before I said, "You came up with this plan very quickly. Have you spent many of your leisure moments in the past three indictions contemplating my marriage?"

Silence for another two circuits. Murtagh said, "The night after the news reached Esmer, I got no sleep. Your sister was as near hysterical as I have ever seen her. Every newspaper in the northern duchies was baying for your blood, and we actually gave thanks to the Lady that Thomas Albern is an ambitious, petty-minded, vengeful fool, for it meant that he would not have you hanged out of hand. I knew I could convince the Convocation that with Hume's death, you were no longer a threat, but only if I could tell them what I would do with you—we hear about the Primrose Men in Esmer, you know. I thought very very fast."

"I am rebuked," I said.

"You are a stiff-necked idiot," Murtagh said, and I wondered if I could trust that that was fondness I heard in his voice. "But I actually wanted to ask you about something else."

"I am at Your Grace's disposal."

"Clara Hume."

"Lady give me strength. What about her?"

"Is she as witless as she seems?"

"Very nearly. What has she done?"

"She's cozying up to Glimmering in the most inexplicable way imaginable. The rumor is she's going to make him the prince's guardian. If she's not going to raise his banner and fight on."

"She can't."

"Which?"

"Either. But she can't make anyone Charles's guardian. She has not the power."

"You know this for a fact?"

"Yes. Gerrard's will, which I witnessed, gives Charles's guardianship to Quithenrick."

"Clever. Did Quithenrick agree?"

"Gerrard was fostered in Quithenrick for a couple of indictions. He and the current margrave were very close as boys—Quithenrick's refusal to become *politically* entangled had nothing to do with his personal feelings. And Gerrard knew that if he . . . if something went wrong, Charles was going to need safety more than political vantage."

"And the princess?"

"Knows this perfectly well. Gerrard made no secret of his arrangements, and she agreed to them."

Murtagh made a noise eloquent of frustration, and I couldn't help grinning. "Yes," I said. "Clara is like that."

"Witless little *rabbit*," said he. "Have you any guess where Charles is now?"

"She didn't bring him?"

"Apparently, even Clara Hume isn't *that* stupid. She's being very coy about it, and it's making everyone nervous."

I understood. If Clara had entrusted Charles to someone who intended to use him as a figurehead—which she was certainly pudding-witted enough to do—then the Insurgence might break out again at any time. Would make anyone uneasy. "Is the Margravess of Hornhast in her train still?"

"Hornhast . . . Hornhast . . . No, I don't think so."

"Then I am fair certain that Charles is on his way to Quithenrick, if not already there. Hornhast and his lady were both very much in Gerrard's counsels."

"It would be a tremendous relief if that were true," said Murtagh. "None of us wants to figure in the press as an infanticide, and with the way the princess has been talking, it was beginning to look as if we would have no choice."

I sighed and rubbed my face. "She doesn't understand. Is all a story to her—colored clouds like those witless novels she devours by the hundredweight. She saw herself as Gerrard's true love, and then as the Queen of Caloxa, and now am sure she sees herself as the brave and beautiful widow, tragic but undefeated."

"Oh dear," said Murtagh.
"Precisely," said I.

## *Felix*

When I came up out of my trance, the wash-leather bag was lying on my chest; I had one hand over it as if it were precious. I sat up and shook the rubies out into my palm, just to be sure. All ten of them were there, dark and greasy and loathsome.

A hard shudder ran through me, almost a cramp. I had carried these stones in my pocket for months, worrying—obsessing—about what their influence might do to the Mirador and to the people around me, but I hadn't ever stopped to wonder about what they were doing to *me*.

Now I was wondering. I felt the mikkary clouding around them, and I thought about the terrible, stupid, self-destructive things I'd done over the past two years. I'd worried about Malkar's ghost haunting me, but I hadn't understood that in a way he already was. I'd carried the rubies, and I'd become more and more like the creature Malkar had tried to make me—more and more like Malkar himself.

Cold and sick, I dumped the rubies back in their bag. I had no more idea now than I had ever had of how to get rid of them safely, and I could not bear to look at them any longer. I hid them in the wardrobe, in the toe of one of Mildmay's boots. I would have to come up with somewhere better, but it was foolish to pretend he was going to need those boots anytime soon.

Mildmay was increasingly restless all afternoon, and I was reluctant to leave him to go to Crysolomon's. But I still couldn't see any other choice, much less a better one. I woke him up and told him I was going out, and he seemed to understand me. I hoped.

When I came back, a full banshee richer, he was awake. "Where you been?"

"Out," I said. I didn't want to have this conversation now—or ever, for preference.

He squinted at me. "You ain't been down in the Arcane again, have you? 'Cause you're gonna get yourself killed down there."

It felt like my heart was trying to beat sideways out of my chest. "No," I said, although my voice was thin and much too high. "I haven't been in the Arcane."

"Okay. Good." And while I was still dithering about whether I should try to make him understand we weren't in Mélusine, he closed his eyes and fell asleep.

I slept badly myself; I wanted to go back to the Khloïdanikos, but I couldn't ask Thamuris to bring me in again, and I was afraid of calling up my construct-Mélusine and finding it was still choked with briars. Or burning. Or both. Finally, toward dawn, I fell into a heavier, sodden sleep, from which I awoke with an almost physical jerk to find Mildmay standing at the window.

"What are you doing out of bed?"

He glanced over his shoulder at me and said, "Something's burning."

"Something nearby?"

"Dunno." He looked out the window again. "Could be."

"Are you saying you think we're in danger?" I joined him at the window, but there was nothing to see except the late morning clouds over Cattamery Road.

"Nah. I don't think . . ." He looked up at me, frowning, then looked around the room. "Where's Mavortian?"

Mavortian von Heber was dead and had been for years. I called witch-light to get a better look at Mildmay's face, which made him snarl, an ugly animal expression. But I could see the fever burning in his eyes.

"Mildmay," I said as gently, as firmly as I could, "you'd better go back to bed." I reached for his shoulder, meaning to guide him, but he ducked my hand and, faster than I would have thought someone so sick could move, lunged for the door.

I hadn't locked it, being more afraid of fire than theft. He clawed it open and was out and away, slamming it behind him before I'd even fully realized he was intending to run.

And I had no idea what had spooked him. He wasn't touch-phobic at all, and when he'd been sick before, he'd even seemed grateful when Gideon or I had touched him. I remembered Gideon had rubbed Mildmay's back when he'd started to get muscle cramps from coughing, and Mildmay had relaxed into his touch like a cat.

Well, maybe it was just me. He'd never had to be afraid that Gideon would rape him, after all. I dragged my trousers on, shoved my feet into my boots, grabbed Mildmay's coat, and went in pursuit.

I nearly barreled into Corbie on the landing; she looked badly startled. "Was that . . . ?"

"Yes," I said grimly. "Up or down?"

"Up."

"Thank you. You can go in and wait. It shouldn't take me long to find him."

"Are you kidding? Let me help." She turned to accompany me up the stairs. "Where's he going?"

"I wish I knew. He's delirious. He thinks he's back in Mélusine. What *is* that burning, by the way?"

"Some sort of demonstration in St. Melior. For Rothmarlin. They're burning the Convocation in effigy."

We came out on the roof, where it was drizzling and cold. There was no immediate sign of Mildmay among the chimneys and steep stair steps of the surrounding roofs. I could feel panic rising up like a fist in my chest, and this time I didn't hesitate to use the obligation d'âme. "This way."

"How d'you know?" Corbie said, trotting after me.

"I know how Mildmay thinks," I said, lying through my teeth. I could feel his fever and fear and confusion.

We climbed from one roof to the next. I mentally practiced for encounters with irate roof owners: a lost kitten would make a good story if Corbie played along. Corbie herself continued to talk about Rothmarlin and the Insurgence. I was surprised to find she was both well informed about and distinctly sympathetic to the Caloxan cause. "I don't suppose they ever really had a chance," she said sadly. "It was only because Rothmarlin and Benallery and Hornhast knew what they were doing that they lasted as long as they did. Well, that and Prince Gerrard being able to charm the dead out of their graves. But then Hornhast was killed at Subry two months ago, and Prince Gerrard and Benallery and all the rest of them went off to Howrack, and they all died there. Except Rothmarlin, poor man, and I swear I believe death would have been kinder."

"They all *died*? Just like that? You mean a suicide pact?"

"No, nothing like that." She seemed a little offended on the dead prince's behalf. "The papers didn't have any details. But they tried to work some kind of spell to save Caloxa, and it went wrong somehow."

"Were any of them wizards?"

"No. But for the old magic, you didn't always have to be, my gran said."

"How—" Disturbing, I would have said, but just then I saw him. "Oh, thank goodness. There he is." Mildmay had climbed an old and crumbling collection of chimney stacks and tucked himself in among them very like the lost kitten I had contemplated pretending he was.

"Lumme," Corbie said. "He's shivering something awful. And how'd he get up there?"

"He was trained as a cat burglar when he was your age," I said absently. "Stay here. I'm going to go get a blanket. See if you can get him to talk to you."

"But what do I—Felix!"

I moved as quickly as I could, but I was nevertheless relieved to come back and find Corbie still there, however uncomfortable she looked. "I did like you said and tried to talk to him, but I don't think he even heard me. I didn't get anything out of him."

"You wouldn't anyway," I said. "Did he look at you?"

"Yeah. Watched me the whole time, actually, which was really kind of spooky—meaning no disrespect to your brother, but—"

"Corbie," I said.

"I know, I know. Shut up."

"You kept him here," I said. "That's all I wanted."

Mildmay watched me with an unwavering stare as I approached.

"Mildmay," I said, when I'd come as close as I thought he'd tolerate.

"I ain't going back," he said.

"Going back to what?" I said.

"Oh fuck you. You know what I mean. She'll skin me alive."

I didn't know what he meant, but that *she* gave me a pretty good guess. "You don't have to go back to her," I said.

That made him laugh, but it was a terrible noise, even before it degenerated into a cough. "And what the fuck else am I gonna do?" he said, wiping his mouth with the back of one hand. "Can't fucking go straight no more. Not after—"

"Mildmay," I said sharply, aware of Corbie behind me, listening.

He frowned at me, clearly struggling to make sense of what he was seeing. "Felix?"

"Yes," I said. "You don't have to go back to her. I'll take care of you."

If he'd been himself, he would probably have hurt himself laughing; I knew as well as he did that the pattern of our relationship was markedly the reverse. But he blinked at me, still frowning, and I saw something he usually tried to keep hidden. "Promise?"

"Yes," I said, and I hated Kolkhis of Britomart in that moment almost as much as I hated myself. "I promise."

He thought about it; I could see pain shading into exhaustion as he squeezed his eyes closed. Then he said, "Okay," and climbed down, which he did as if it were as simple and unthinking a matter as going down a flight of stairs. I held my breath, waiting for his lame leg to give way, but it didn't, not until he reached the roof and started toward me. Then he staggered, and for once in my life I moved fast enough. I caught him. He was clammy, hot with fever, and shivering. I tucked the blanket around him as best I could.

"Corbie, will you go for Practitioner Druce, please? Have her meet us back at the Fiddler's Fox?"

"Felix, you can't—" But she saw the look on my face and interrupted herself: "I'm going." She flicked across the roofs as quickly as an alley cat herself. Mildmay and I went much more slowly.

It was three-quarters of an hour before Corbie showed up again. "She's coming," Corbie said as she closed the door behind her, "but she has somebody else she has to see first. I said I thought that was all right."

"Yes," I said. I'd gotten Mildmay back into bed in a dry nightshirt and a towel on the pillow for his hair, and he seemed to be resting more or less comfortably. "That's fine, thank you."

She waved off my thanks and walked over to the window. I stayed where I was by Mildmay; if he was going to try anything like this again, I wanted to know *before* he got out of bed.

"Felix?" said Corbie.

"Yes?"

"I, um. Don't take this the wrong way or nothing, and I'll understand if you say no, I mean, there's a reason I didn't bring it up in the first place, but with having Practitioner Druce in again and everything, I'm thinking maybe you—"

"Corbie."

"Right, right." She nodded sharply, but didn't turn around. "If you want—and like I said, if you don't, it's fine—I can get you more, um, *involved* clients."

The first thing that registered was that she'd said "clients" instead of "fish" as she usually did. "'Involved' meaning what, exactly?"

"Well, remember how I said flames and shadows is the Black and White's business?"

"Vividly. I know it's hard, Corbie, but could you get to the point?"

"I am!" she said indignantly. "Because, see, that's only partly true."

"Which part was a lie, then?"

She turned far enough to glare at me. "If you could stop being an asshole for a second, I'll tell you."

I waved a hand at her. "Pray continue."

She glared at me a moment longer, then went on: "The thing is, it's only true for fish who go to the brothels. If you hire a jezebel to come to a hotel room or a private house or something—not just picking them up in a bar, I mean, but you make an *appointment*—Chastity wants their cut, but that's all, and you can charge more if you do that—like a lot more. But you gotta *do* more."

I quashed a brief, reprehensible desire to catalogue for her just how extensive my repertoire of "more" was. "When you say I can charge more, how *much* more?"

"Minimum for a shadow is a banshee a go. And they say flames tip like mad bastards if you do a good job."

The math was absurdly simple. "I'll do it."

"Felix, are you sure? I mean—"

"Quite sure."

"It's not an every night kind of thing," she said warningly.

"No, I realize that. It's a specialization." In Mélusine, it was also a culture; establishments like the Two-Headed Beast were successful precisely because they offered more than just a safely anonymous place to have sex. Bernatha did not seem to have a similar culture, and I could not decide whether I thought that was fortunate or unfortunate.

"Yeah, all right then." She pinned an escaping curl back into place. "Look, you ain't gonna have time for magic lessons today." She made a face. "Lumme, listen to me. 'Magic lessons.' But what I mean is, why don't I clear out? I can start putting the word out about the shadow thing, and we can just pick up again tomorrow. All right?"

"Corbie," I said, "does Practitioner Druce make you nervous?"

"Nah," she said instantly. I raised an eyebrow at her. "Yeah, fine, you caught me. She scares the ever-living shit out of me, are you satisfied?"

"Go on," I said. "I'll see you tonight." And she went like a firework.

Practitioner Druce was concerned but not, it seemed to me, truly alarmed, which was reassuring. "Pleuriny is a dreadfully tenacious illness," she told me, "and your brother's lungs . . . well, once vi has stagnated in a particular part of the body, it's likely to do so again and more persistently. A kind of metaphysical scarring, if you will." She redirected his vi again and left a series of neat packets of herbs to help with the material congestion. She charged me another half saint, and I gave her the one banshee I had to show good faith.

I hoped Corbie found me a more "involved" client soon.

And I was more than a little surprised when she did.

The next day, she showed up at noon practically crowing with delight. "I got you one," she said, almost before she was in the room. "I got you one, and you can charge the fucking *moon* if you want to."

"Oh?" I said.

"The Duke of Murtagh." She dropped down beside me on the cot.

The Duke of Murtagh featured prominently in the papers these days, having eclipsed the Duke of Glimmering almost immediately upon his arrival. Since his first act had been to remove Kay Brightmore, the former Margrave of Rothmarlin, from the Hall of the Seven Virtues, I was disposed to like him, but Bernathan opinion was decidedly mixed. "He's a flame?"

"Apparently. He's looking for a male shadow, anyway, and he won't go to the Black and White. Too much attention, and he does have a wife. So you're it."

"I won't be, um, stepping on anybody's toes?"

"Nobody's toes to step on. The Black and White recruits pretty hard."

"Okay," I said. I could do this. "When?"

"Tonight, at the Althammara. At the start of the cereus watches: twenty-two o'clock. You'll be staying all night."

"All night?" I looked over at the other bed, where Mildmay was sleeping. "Corbie, I'm not sure I can—"

"I can sit with him. If you want."

"All right." I took a deep breath, released it slowly. "In the meantime, let's talk about color and why I've been making you learn the wheel."

She was a very good student that afternoon, although I had the lowering suspicion that she was being attentive more for my sake than her own. I tried to hide my nervousness, knowing it was both futile and ridiculous. But I hadn't worked formally as a martyr since Malkar bought me—Malkar was a tarquin beyond any possible doubt, but he had no use for the rituals and rules by which Mélusinien tarquins and martyrs played their games. And I hadn't submitted to anyone—not voluntarily anyway—since Shannon. Except for Isaac Garamond, and that had been something else entirely, and uglier.

Corbie's shift at her brothel, the Brocade Mouse, was from six till midnight; I gave her our second room key when she left, then bathed carefully, tying my hair back while it was still wet, and chose the most reputable of my very limited wardrobe.

Corbie had drawn me a map showing the way from the Fiddler's Fox to the Althammara with a little fox to mark the Fiddler's Fox and an elaborate seven-pointed star to mark the Althammara. There was a clock face to show the Clock Palace and enough other landmarks that I thought I'd even be able to find my way back home in the morning.

I left the Fiddler's Fox early, just in case, and I took a dose of hecate before I left. I reached the Althammara at quarter of ten, fifteen minutes before the start of what the Corambins called the cereus watches. I gathered my courage and went up to the desk. "I have an appointment with the Duke of Murtagh."

Clearly I looked more foreign than depraved, for the desk clerk said, "Yes, sir. His Grace said you should go straight up when you arrived. He has the entire top floor."

"Thank you," I said, and climbed the stairs as slowly as I could.

The door at the top was closed. I knocked and was presented with a manservant of a type I recognized from the Mirador: different plumage but the same bird. "I have an appointment with His Grace," I said; it was marginally easier the second time.

"This way, sir," the manservant said and led me into a sitting room appointed in a warm red. "You may wait for His Grace here."

"Thank you," I said. He gave me an infinitesimal nod and departed. I summoned up everything I'd ever learned—from Lorenzo, from Malkar, from Shannon—and picked a spot where the candlelight would catch the streaks of white in my hair. What couldn't be hidden should always be flaunted. And then I did not pace or fidget. I waited.

I didn't have to wait long. I heard a man's voice, rich as brandied cream, saying, "Good *night*, Kay," and then the swift clatter of boot heels, and the Duke of Murtagh entered the room almost before I realized that he had been talking to Kay Brightmore.

The duke was Mildmay's height, slightly on the tall side for a Corambin, with thick, sleek, wheat-colored hair, a few shades paler than his skin. His eyes, deep-set and surrounded by a network of fine lines, were dark golden amber, and they widened appreciably on seeing me. "Goodness gracious. Am I expecting you?"

"I have an appointment," I said and was gratified when my voice came out neither uneven nor shrill. "For twenty-two o'clock."

"Then I was expecting you. But I wasn't expecting *you*. Hold still." I lifted my chin in an old, old reflex and held still while he circled me. "I will have to commend my secretary," he said finally. "The bedroom's this way."

"You have your secretary—" I began and then bit my tongue, but he glanced back as he led me down the hallway opposite the one he'd emerged from, and his face was alight with humor.

"I know. Shocking, isn't it? But a duke can't negotiate these matters personally—one more reason, should you need one, to avoid becoming a duke at all costs—and Wyatt actually seems to enjoy fulfilling my more outrageous requests. Here we are."

The bedroom was exactly what I expected of a duke's bedroom in a lavish hotel. Murtagh closed and locked the door behind us and said, "Now. Tell me your name."

"Felix, Your Grace."

"And you are neither Corambin, Usaran, nor Ygressine. Where are you from?"

"Mélusine, Your Grace." And I raised my hands to show him my palms.

His eyebrows shot up.

"I've taken hecate," I said and could not quite keep the bitterness out of my voice when I added, "I'm perfectly safe."

"I'm guessing," said Murtagh, "that there's quite a story here. And that you don't want to talk about it."

"Yes, Your Grace."

"Ah," he said. "Not in the bedroom. In here, 'sir' is good enough."

"Yes, sir," I said, and a frisson of cold nostalgia went through me.

"That's good," Murtagh said and stepped closer. "So, Felix from Mélusine, you know that I'm a flame?"

It was only barely a question, but he paused, so I said, "Yes, sir."

"And are you a shadow?"

Well, that was the question, wasn't it? I had been trained as a martyr; my earliest memories of sex were also memories of pain, and that had only been reinforced, first by the clients of the Shining Tiger and then by Malkar. After Malkar, I had tried to renounce the whole game of tarquins and martyrs; I hadn't wanted to want it. But I had failed and failed abysmally. There was something there that I needed, somewhere deeper in my heart than could be rooted out. But I hadn't wanted to be a martyr, hadn't wanted to be that vulnerable, so I had tried the tarquin's role, and it had been as addictive as phoenix. But I couldn't be trusted with it. Whether I wanted to or not, I needed to give that power to someone else.

And there was the truth. There, ugly and humiliating as it was. I could not do without and could not be trusted with it. I could become a monster, could become Malkar. Or I could . . . I could . . .

"Yes, sir," I whispered.

"Good," said Murtagh, who in the eerie way of the best tarquins had somehow divined before asking the question that it would be hard for me to answer. He stepped up to me, utterly unfazed by the difference in our heights, put his hand at the back of my neck, and dragged me down—not brutally, but firmly—for a kiss.

I melted into it helplessly, overwhelmed as much by my own self-realization as by his strength. When he chose to let me go, I was panting, dazed, and my sex was as hard as iron.

"Perhaps I'll give Wyatt a raise," said Murtagh. He crossed the bedroom with his quick, decisive stride, and dropped into the armchair by the window. "Undress for me. Slowly."

I'd been trained to do this, too. I undressed slowly as instructed, out of long and ingrained habit leaving my shirt for last. Murtagh was more lavish with praise and appreciation than any tarquin I'd ever known, and I wondered if that was just how flames and shadows interacted, or if he could see how nervous I was.

For I *was* nervous, and getting more nervous by the second. I might have been trained to do this, as I kept telling myself, but it had been years upon years since I'd done it successfully. Malkar had found my professional skills merely amusing, and I had two ignominious failures, with Ingvard Vilker and with Gideon, to remember. What I had done with Isaac had been to punish myself, and while Isaac was cruel, he was no tarquin. It was not the same.

I finally took my shirt off and stood, trying not to shiver, while Murtagh got up and came over to examine me.

"You've clearly done this before," he said, lifting my left arm to examine my tattoos.

"Yes, sir."

"And yet you're about to shake yourself apart." He moved behind me and stopped. "Ah. Is this why?" And a fingertip ghosted along the topmost of my scars.

"No, sir. Well, not exactly."

He came around in front of me again and said, "Explain."

*Do you have all night?* I nearly said, but bit it back. "The scars make me . . . They don't make me *nervous*. Unless you're going to change your mind."

"Oh, far from it," he said, cupping my genitals with one hand. "But go on. That's only half the question."

I settled on a partial truth. "It's been a very long time since I did this professionally." As if to underscore the point, my wretched body betrayed me. My erection had softened while I took my clothes off, but now it was hardening again with no more encouragement than the still warmth of Murtagh's hand.

"How interesting," murmured Murtagh. He stepped away again, and I barely kept myself from lunging after him like a starving dog after a marrow bone.

Murtagh looked me up and down, his gaze lingering on my straining flesh until my face burned, then smiled a predator's smile and said, "Undress me. Slowly."

I obeyed. He was broad-shouldered, heavy boned, his chest densely furred. Scars on his hands and forearms, and an ugly mess, red and puckered, on his right biceps. "Desperen Field," he said. "I was lucky not to lose the arm." I put my mouth on the scar, very gently, and had the reward of feeling him shiver.

When he was naked, his erection matching mine, he said, "On your knees."

I knelt. My mouth was already opening for him when I felt the ribbon slide out of my hair, felt his fingers against my scalp.

"Don't," I said, jerking back, and then I froze.

Murtagh looked down at me, one eyebrow lifted. "I beg your pardon?"

I realized, belatedly, but very sharply, another reason he made me nervous. He reminded me terribly of Malkar. And the realization was making me harder.

*Slut,* Lorenzo's voice said, half-approving, half-contemptuous, and I groped for words. "I'm sorry. I didn't mean to—"

"Oh, but you did," Murtagh said, as gently as Malkar might have, "and we'll discuss the penalty for that later. For now . . ." He reached, deliberately slow, grabbed a double handful of my hair, and pulled me back to him. But even then, although it stung, he gave me time to follow. He didn't hurt me. And that wasn't like Malkar at all.

# Chapter 6

## *Kay*

Murtagh, having been increasingly vile-tempered for most of a week, was in an almost alarmingly sunny mood on Martedy morning. He came in singing to breakfast and wished me good morning with every audible evidence of sincerity.

"Are very cheerful," I said cautiously.

"I had an excellent night," he said, and I followed the sounds of him sitting down across from me. The table at which Murtagh liked to eat breakfast was east-facing, and I could feel the sun. "And I have come up with five new plans to thwart and discomfit Glimmering, at least three of which should actually be practicable, so, yes, I suppose I do feel rather as if the world is a pearl resting on the palm of my hand."

"I may like you better crabby," said I.

He just laughed and said, "Hush and let me pour you some tea."

Over breakfast, Murtagh told me at great and extravagant length the first of his five new plans. I had nearly finished my tea when Tinder coughed and said, "Your Grace, there is a gentleman wishing to see you."

"Has he provided a name?" said Murtagh

"Edwin Beckett," said Tinder. "He said that you would know him, Mr. Brightmore."

I did, at that. "Will the bloody man not leave me alone?"

"I think perhaps we are not at home, Tinder," Murtagh said. "Kay?"

"Is the man who was there when you came," I said. "Has a maggot about the Clock of Eclipses."

"And wants you to sponsor him? Did he not see it was a bad time?"

He made me laugh despite myself. "No, not that. He corresponded with Gerrard and seems to think I can tell him . . . well, I know not what in sober truth."

"You don't have to speak to him."

"No, I might as well. I fear otherwise I will never be rid of him."

"Well, I shan't leave you alone with him at any rate," Murtagh said. "All right, Tinder, show the gentleman in."

I was grateful for Murtagh's support. Hast become so timid, Kay? So girlish and shy? But I had not liked Edwin Beckett and his politely bullying manner, and, no, I did not want to speak to him alone.

He entered on a profusion of thanks and apologies, directed at Murtagh rather than me. Murtagh noticed, too; I heard it in his voice when he said, "I understand you wish to speak to Mr. Brightmore."

"I do," said Edwin Beckett, "although I would also be very grateful for the chance to speak to Your Grace about my work."

"Ask me your questions, Mr. Beckett," said I. "Let us have done with this."

His questions this time took a quite different turn, and I found myself saying, "No," in increasingly horrified and vehement tones.

"There's nothing to be embarrassed about, Mr. Brightmore," said Beckett. "Sex is an entirely natural part of our lives and the most profound and ancient source of power that we know."

"I assure you," I said, "Gerrard Hume was not having *orgies* with his followers, either under Summerdown or anywhere else!"

"I take it," said Murtagh, "that that is the direction your research has been tending?"

"Oh, not just tending, Your Grace. I'm quite convinced that the great release of power which comes with orgasm is the only possible method of starting the Cymellunar machines. They say it was what gave life to the Automaton of Corybant, which was surely the greatest achievement of the Cymellunar magicians."

"Until it went mad and killed them all," Murtagh said.

"That's a superstitious tale, told by those who don't understand," said Beckett. "And beside the point. Think of the achievement of making such a construct move under its own power!"

"Quite," said Murtagh. "By orgasm."

"Exactly! It's the only way. Although I have had only very limited success as of yet, I am sure it's only a matter of time. So to speak. I am sorry Prince Gerrard did not follow my advice."

"I am not," I said.

"I meant that if he had, he might be alive. And the political situation in Caloxa might be quite different—although in that, of course, I have no interest."

"Because Bernatha isn't part of Caloxa," said Murtagh.

"I have never felt it should be counted as such," Beckett said earnestly. "In all our history, we have never—"

Murtagh's foot nudged mine, and I knew what he meant as clearly as if he'd said it. "Have you other questions, Mr. Beckett?" I said, interrupting him with perhaps more relish than was seemly.

"Ah," he said. "No. It seems clear that Prince Gerrard's tragedy was a result of *not* following my advice, which, while very sad, does mean that I need not curtail my own efforts. Thank you, Mr. Brightmore, you've been very helpful."

"I hate to think so," I said under my breath; Murtagh kicked my ankle and said, "If you have any literature, Mr. Beckett, you would be welcome to send it to my secretary, Mr. Parsifal Wyatt. All of my business goes through him, you see. I find it the best way. Tinder will see you out. Good day!"

And we were rid of Edwin Beckett.

## Felix

It was another two days before Corbie netted me another "involved" client, in which time, with the full saint that the Duke of Murtagh had given me, I succeeded in paying off much of the debt to Practitioner Druce, leaving us four banshees and sixteen hermits still in the red when Corbie came in and said, "I've got another one."

Mildmay still had a high fever, although the steam-tisanes were having a definite effect. He hated them, cursing me weakly and coughing and coughing. But the stuff coming out of his lungs was dreadful colors, and I could not help but feel that getting it *out* of his body had to be better than leaving it to fester. I couldn't tell if he knew where he was, or who I was, but at least he hadn't tried to get out of bed again. Possibly, he couldn't, for in the wake of overexertion, his leg clearly pained him as much or more than his chest.

"Another one of what?" I said absently. I was wondering if it would be helpful or otherwise to introduce Corbie to the concepts of noirance and clairance now. Just because I found them tremendously useful didn't mean they would be of any help to a novice.

"You know," said Corbie.

"Oh. Right." I shook myself out of Ynge. "When?"

"Tonight. All night again. And they've got a list of things they want as long as your arm."

"What kind of things?"

"Well, this, for one." She pulled a black silk blindfold out of the pocket of her skirt.

"Gracious," I said. "What melodrama."

"And they got a specific place they're going to fetch you from, and you're not to know anybody's name—there's gonna be a bunch of 'em—and—"

I cut her off. "Corbie. Do any of their demands involve necrophilia?"

"Nec-what?"

"Having sex with dead people."

"There's a *word* for that? Lumme. No. No sex with dead people."

"There's words for all kinds of things. How about coprophilia or urophilia?"

"Well, I know what the 'philia' is now, but what about the rest?"

"Shit and piss," I said, just to see the look on her face—which was entirely worth it.

"You're making that up," she accused me.

"No, actually, I'm not. But they're things I won't do. Like necrophilia."

"Well, they don't want anything like *that*."

"And I don't do women."

"I told 'em that, too. They didn't seem to care."

"Then they can have as many peculiar demands as they want."

"All right," said Corbie. "I'm gonna take you, and that blindfold, to Our Lady of Fogs at twenty o'clock tonight."

"In the middle of your shift?"

"My night off."

"I didn't know you had nights off."

"I got lucky," she said sourly. "So I'll sit with Mildmay again."

"Corbie, are you—"

"It's fine," she said. "We're gonna make a boatload of money tonight anyway. So it's just fine."

I'd assumed Our Lady of Fogs was a church, but it turned out to be a sanctuary just outside St. Melior.

"A what?" I said.

"A sanctuary," Corbie said.

"I heard you. But what do you mean?"

"What do you mean, what do I mean? A sanctuary. Where you bury dead people."

"You mean a cemetery."

"We're not Caddovians," she said with tremendous dignity. "A *sanctuary*. With an intended and a . . . what's the word?"

"I can truthfully say I have no idea."

She made a face at me. "An anchor? Does that sound right? He lives walled up in the chapel."

"Anchorite."

"I knew it was something like anchor."

"So you bury people there, and there's an anchorite. But why is it a good meeting place?"

"It's *sacred*. No fighting. Nobody can be arrested while they're there. People swear contracts there for all kinds of things. Get wills witnessed. Business deals."

"*Business* deals?"

"What?" she said, frowning.

"That doesn't sound very sacred."

"You break a swear to dead people and we'll talk about sacred. So, you know, nobody asks any questions." And at that point, I didn't feel up to pursuing her logic any further.

Corbie was as broke as I was—her word was "skint"—so we walked from the Fiddler's Fox down the Crait, across the causeway, and through St. Melior, a journey which took us a couple of hours. Corbie pointed out various sights of interest as we passed them, including the railway station, two churches, and the site, she informed me, of the murder of Jessmond Tuvey some fifty years ago.

"And we care about this because . . . ?"

So she sang me the ballad all the rest of the way to Our Lady of Fogs.

It was not at all what I thought of as a cemetery. The burial plots were not marked with headstones or obelisks or the more terrifying statuary of the wealthy Mélusinien tombs. At first, I thought the graves weren't marked at all, but Corbie knelt down and showed me that the brick paths were edged on both sides with granite and bolted to the granite were plates engraved with dates and names. "But how do you know who's buried where?" I said.

"That's the chapel-intended's job. The back wall of the chapel is the map, and he keeps it accurate. He has to, for the prayers."

"Prayers?"

The look she gave me was almost scornful. "That's what he's *for*. He prays for the dead."

"And nobody else sees the map?"

"It's *sacred*," she said again.

"What if you want to find somebody?"

I was half-expecting her to say, *Why would you want to?* but this apparently was a commonality between Corambin and Marathine culture, for she said, "You ask the chapel-intended. There's a slot. And if you can't write it yourself, you ask the sanctuary-intended and he writes it for you."

"The sanctuary-intended?"

"Yeah. You know, he does the funerals and weeds the grass and takes food to the chapel-intended. And he witnesses." She waved an arm generally around us, at the merchants' stalls and food carts and clusters of people talking heatedly or arguing even more heatedly. At intervals there were waist-high slate topped pillars, which I realized were meant for people to write on.

"Everything is for sale," I muttered.

"What?" said Corbie.

"Nothing. What do we do now?"

What we did was pool what little money we had and buy dinner in the form of a stuffed bread and two cups of the most vilely stewed tea I'd ever tasted, which I used to wash down the hecate. When we'd returned the pottery cups to the cart, Corbie insisted on going to put five carefully counted out pennies into the "intended's box," a locked box with a slot in the top where those so minded could make donations toward the upkeep of the anchorite Intended of Fogs. "It's why Charity's trying to get rid of the thrustle, you know," Corbie said.

"I beg your pardon?"

Corbie rolled her eyes, although I wasn't sure whether it was at me or at the House of Charity. "Part of this big argument with Patience that's been going on forever and a day. Everybody knows it's a thrustle for the anchorite, so they get rid of the thrustle. It's just mean, is what it is. But anyway, it's five of twenty, so you'd better put that blindfold on."

"Are we in the right place?"

"This is the chapel," Corbie said, waving her hand at the peaked-roofed little building behind us.

"That's it? And somebody *lives* in there?"

"This intended's only been there four or five indictions. But the old intended, he was in there nearly seven wheels. If he'd made it, they would've made him a saint."

I wondered, stupidly and belatedly, if the intended could hear us. I'd read about anchorites, but I'd never actually imagined it, what it would be like to live in a space smaller than the room Mildmay and I shared at the Fiddler's Fox, knowing that one was trapped there until death. I swallowed hard and didn't ask Corbie if anchorites ever changed their minds.

Instead, I put the blindfold on. I couldn't manage the knot behind my head, my fingers refusing to bend the way I needed. "Here, let me," Corbie said, and I went obediently down on one knee so she could reach it. And tried hard not to think about Corbie as a tarquin.

She was very careful, tying the knot firmly but making sure none of my hair was caught in it. "All right," she said finally, and I stood up again, feeling conspicuous and foolish and as if what I was about to do had to be emblazoned on me, as lurid as the red stained glass shrines in the Arcane, that people burned candles in to ward off plague. Corbie's narrow, chilly hand slipped into mine, and after a moment, recognizing the generosity of her impulse, I squeezed back.

And a man's voice said, "I see he obeys instructions well."

I tensed, wringing a faint yelp out of Corbie before I remembered to release my clutch on her hand. She said, "You the party looking to hire a shadow for tonight?"

"Yes. He is as unmistakable as you said."

"One of a kind," Corbie said, and I was simultaneously mortified and queerly warmed by the pride in her voice. "Banshee up front and you pay him and bring him back here with the catmint tomorrow morning. Right?"

"Right you are," said the man. "Come along, shadow." And a stranger's hand, broad and sweaty and unpleasant, engulfed mine. I was on the verge of balking when Corbie said, just loud enough for me to hear, "We'll be fine tonight, and I'll see you tomorrow morning." And I remembered why I was doing this.

The stranger led me rather more swiftly than I was comfortable with, and I had no concentration to spare to wonder where we were going or even to think—much—about the people who might be watching. I didn't think he led me very far, though, before he said, "Up you get," and guided me impatiently into a closed carriage of some kind, about the size of a hansom, as best I could tell. He climbed in after me and thumped on one of the walls or the roof, and we set off with a clatter of hooves.

I knew that if I tried to speak to him, the man would merely rebuff me, and I had not the slightest desire to speak to him in any event. I folded my hands in my lap and sat perfectly still. Malkar had taught me how to wait.

## *Mildmay*

I'm in the Boneprince. It's the septad-night and black as the inside of a black cat in a mine shaft. I don't want to be here. I know something bad is going down. I can feel it, and besides the wolves are everywhere with their eyes like cinders.

Iron-black Wolves. You can't kill 'em, you can't stop 'em. In the story, the children trick them with a deer's heart and then with a crow's heart and finally the little girl takes her own heart out of her chest and throws it into the river, and the Iron-black Wolves all leap into the river after it, and the water puts out the fire that lights their eyes and makes them go. But they ain't dead, the story says. They're just waiting for somebody to strike a lucifer for 'em. And the little girl don't have a heart no more, which ain't exactly what you'd call a happy ending.

And the wolves are fucking *everywhere*. And they're waiting. I hear footsteps, and I know this is who they're waiting for. Boot heels, a light, fast stride, and then I see the witchlights, green and dancing. It's Felix, and the wolves are waiting for him. I try and call out to him, warn him, but I can't. I can't even move. I'm made of stone. All I can do is watch as he comes in the gate, starts up the Road of Marble, and all the wolves get up to meet him. And the stupid fuck doesn't even run. He just stands there and holds something out to them, and just before the first one gets to him, I realize it's his heart.

## Felix

I could tell when we crossed the causeway again and restrained myself from saying something sarcastic. It was no business of mine how these people chose to manage their affairs, and they were certainly not paying me to have opinions.

Perhaps it was the blindfold making the hecate seem more than usually obtrusive tonight, but I could feel my magic being removed from me, stifling gauze wrapping around me one layer at a time, and the light-headedness I was used to was very near to vertigo. I folded the fingers of my right hand under my left, so that I could dig my nails into my palm without the man seeing. I missed the sharp bite of my rings. But I stayed calm.

When the carriage stopped, I heard the door open; then one set of hands pushed me from one side and two more grabbed me and pulled from the other. Essentially, I fell out of the carriage, and they made only token efforts at catching me. I ended on my knees, with hands bruisingly tight on my shoulders holding me up.

"So," said a new voice, and I was losing track of how many of them there were. "This is our shadow. Take his clothes off, and bring him in so we can see what we're getting."

I realized just barely in time that if I resisted, they would simply tear my clothes off me, and this was my only remaining coat. I cooperated, as much as I could when they seemed actively to want me to fight them, and I was naked and shivering in very short order. We were still outdoors, but from the lack of other sounds, I guessed it was a closed courtyard. The hands hauled me to my feet and dragged me, giving me no chance to walk, and then the surface changed beneath my feet, from cobbles to something slick and cold, marble maybe, and the hands shifted and shoved me forward. I staggered, nearly fell, but managed, just barely, to keep my feet.

Someone said from behind me, "Blessed Lady! Look at this!"

I flinched, exactly as I would have from a blow. Someone touched my back, high on the shoulder where I could still feel it, and their fingers skated down, tracing the scar tissue into the desolation.

"Bring that candlestick over here," someone said, and there was no use in telling myself to hold still. I lurched away from them, turning, trying to find somewhere I could hide myself from their avid eyes and greedy hands. But there was nowhere. No shelter, no cover, no kind darkness, only the darkness I was trapped in.

"Well," said someone. He didn't sound distressed in the slightest. Pleased. A cat finding that its prey has a spark of life left in it after all. "I wasn't expecting to need the shackles so early in the evening."

I forced myself to stop, to straighten. To stand still even as I heard their feet coming toward me and felt the greedy, grasping heat they brought with them. "I'm sorry. I was—"

I was backhanded across the face, staggered, but kept my feet. "You were not given permission to speak, shadow. Now. Hold *still*."

I swallowed hard, braced myself as best I could. Hands patted my back and haunches, ran over my chest and stomach. Someone's fingers caught my jaw, tilted my head. "Almost as pretty as a girl."

"Trust me," said someone, "you won't be disappointed."

Someone pinched my left nipple, hard, and I yelped.

"Responsive," said someone, and a hand tugged gently at my sex, while someone else twisted my right nipple. I flinched, but my sex stirred.

"Let's get him down," someone said. Someone's hand fisted in my hair, dragging me in a new direction. There were hands everywhere, shoving, pinching, pulling, patting. My breath was coming fast and panicky, but there were too many of them. I couldn't fight them. I couldn't escape and—I remembered, desperately clinging to the present, to the rational reasons I had agreed to this—if I didn't do this, they wouldn't pay me, and I couldn't pay Practitioner Druce or Mrs. Lettice, couldn't keep Mildmay safe.

Stairs, and it was only the press of bodies that kept me from falling. Stairs and stairs, slick and shallow, then rougher and deeper, and it was getting colder; I didn't know now whether I was shivering with cold or fear or the twist of arousal in the pit of my stomach.

Then the hands jerked me to a halt. "This is our throne," said someone.

"Lie down on your belly. Spread yourself." I lay down, extended my arms and legs, tried not to flinch at the coldness of metal against my ankles and wrists, at the sound of the shackles closing.

"Bring the candelabra," said someone, and even through the blindfold I saw the dazzlement of light, was flooded with it. I lay still, tried not to feel their bodies near mine, their hands on the parts of my back that were still sensate.

"What happened to you?" someone asked lazily. I remembered, and choked on a laugh that wanted to be a scream, the story I'd told Shannon, the Caloxan disease I'd claimed I'd suffered as a toddler. I'd never imagined, spinning that extravagant lie, that I would be answering that same question *in* Caloxa, never imagined that the recoil could hurt so much.

A hand in my hair, dragging my head back. "You were asked a question, shadow."

"A nun's scourge," I said, my voice thin and tight with the strain.

"A what?"

"It's a kind of small whip."

"A *crop* did this?"

"I was a child," I said and gasped with relief as my head was released. I wouldn't have to tell them about the treatments for adhesions, which gave me freedom of movement but left scars of their own.

"A child?" And someone's fingers were moving lower, tracing across my right buttock and hip. "How old were you, shadow, when you lost your virginity?"

"Eleven," I said, and if I had not been shackled down, I would have curled up, no matter how futile it was.

A murmur. Someone was running a finger slowly, one at a time, down the knobs of my spine. "And what about the tattoos? They mark you as a magician, right?"

"Yes." I wasn't going to insist on proper nomenclature.

Someone reached and wrenched my left hand over, exposing the palm; my fingers curled futilely, but I couldn't protect myself, not even in that smallest of ways.

"Barbaric," someone muttered.

Someone was still tracing my spine; he reached my tailbone. He rested his hand flat and said, "Bring me the oil."

My hips jerked helplessly, and he laughed. "Does that idea frighten you, shadow? Or are you excited?"

Please don't make that a question I have to answer. And he didn't, exactly. His hand slid lower, between my thighs, exploring my sex. I squeezed my eyes shut behind the blindfold, clamped my lower lip between my teeth.

But I had been *trained* for this, by every man who had ever touched me, and my traitorous body responded.

"Oh, this one's a slut," he said triumphantly, and my face burned with humiliation even as my sex hardened against his hand. "Get your hips up, slut. Let the others see what you are."

There was some play in the chains, enough that I could get my knees under me. I kept my head and shoulders down, knowing that it made my position all the more obscene but needing the illusory protection of the padding pressed against my cheekbone.

More hands. My teeth sank farther into my lip as I fought back the urge to scream at them, to tell them to get their fucking hands off me. Laughter, and hands spreading my buttocks, oil dripping, horrible and slimy, and I bucked once because it was either that or fly apart, although it achieved nothing.

"He's very eager," someone said, and I felt the same dark gloating in the hand that cupped my sex as I heard in the voice.

"Well, let's not disappoint him," said someone, and I pulled uselessly against the shackles.

The bulk of a body behind me, pressing against my thighs. Fingers prodding me open. I tried to writhe away, but they just laughed, and there were too many hands—hands on my hips, hands pressing my shoulders down, hands, terrible hands, stroking my sex. Someone behind me pushed forward, and I couldn't relax and accept it the way I knew I needed to, couldn't keep myself from fighting, from trying to throw off all those hateful burning hands.

My struggles were as useless as they'd been against Malkar, against Lorenzo, against Keeper. My body was invaded, pinned and penetrated; the hands caressed me, pinching my nipples gently, squeezing my sex. Hands tightened on my hips, and someone began to fuck me steadily, angling his thrusts with cruel accuracy.

The sob broke free despite everything I did to hold it back. Someone's hand pushed the hair off my face, then gripped, holding my head still. "He's crying," a voice said with cool interest.

A high-pitched voice.

Too high to be a man's.

My eyes spasmed open, though it did me no good, and I went rigidly tense, which hurt even more. Someone laughed; there was the press of a body against my shoulder and something rubbed across my face: silky, yielding skin, and I felt the hard nub of a nipple against my lips. I threw myself backwards against the shackles, making a noise that didn't have enough breath behind it to be a scream. More laughter. Someone fucking me knotted one hand in my hair at the nape of my neck. "Release his hands." Someone did. My ankles were still chained and someone had me scruffed like a kitten; I was keening in protest, but I was dragged upright, forced to straddle someone's thighs, while he continued fucking me with the same relentless steadiness. I was displayed for all of them, my arousal jutting out shamefully, the tear tracks on my face attesting to my weakness.

"Shall I?" said someone, the woman's voice again, and there was a hand, narrow as Corbie's, folded around my sex.

I realized what she intended, but they had caught my wrists and were pinning my hands. "No," I said, "no, you bitch! Don't you dare, don't you fucking *dare*!" But the cock up my ass made it impossible for me to get away from her. I was screaming at her, but there was nothing I could do to stop her. She planted her hands on my hips and went down on me, took me in deep, and I couldn't get away, couldn't fucking make it stop, and someone shoved their tongue in my mouth so I couldn't scream, but I was still trying, still trying with everything that was in me to just get *away*, when those fucking bastards made me come.

❧

I can't breathe, I can't see, the world is burning around me. Fire is pouring out of me, from my cock and my hands and my eyes, and the darkness takes it in greedily. I can't stop it. It's Malkar again, taking my magic from me, and I can't use my magic to fight back. And this is worse, although I didn't think anything could be worse, because it isn't stopping; the darkness is drawing more and more out of me. It could drain me entirely and still want more. And I can't fight it. I don't have anything to fight it with.

*I can fight it.*

At first I think I imagined it, but it speaks again: *An thou wilt let me, I can fight it. Needst but give me permission.*

I drag in a breath to say yes, to give the voice anything it wants, and choke on the scent of rotting lilacs.

Fantôme. All my dreams of fire. The burning woman with her burning child. Revenge and fury and now I know why. Now I know what I crossed in the ruins of that long-gone house.

Now I am screaming, screaming without breath, and the voice is still speaking, promising me darkly, *They will die. They will all die for what they have done to thee. Do thou but let me in, Felix, most beloved, and no one will ever hurt thee again.*

"No!" I howl, and I hear someone laughing, but they don't know; they don't have any idea.

I'm shoved forward, my hands clamped at the small of my back by someone's grip, and someone's body is pinning me down, someone's cock is tearing me apart, the darkness is dragging all the life and truth and strength out of me, and the fantôme is still saying, *Let me in, Felix. Let me in and I will protect thee. Let me in and I will punish them. All of them. All those who have hurt thee. I will kill them for thee, most beloved, wilt thou but let me in.*

Someone's hand is fisted in my hair. Someone is thrusting, hard and harder. Darkness before me and the fantôme behind, and I cannot defend myself from both, not splayed and helpless and devastated as I am. I will fail, fall to one or the other, and there will be nothing but death and destruction, blood and fire and—

Someone stiffens, his grip agonizingly tight on my hair. I feel his climax, feel the throb and pulse; it shakes me like a terrier with a rat. Shakes me hard. And then again. And again. And I realize dimly, painfully, that it isn't a human pulse, that it isn't the body brutalizing mine that shakes me.

The darkness no longer pulls at me; the fantôme, baffled, retreats, although I know it's there now, I know that deep current of fire and malice. Someone pulls away from me; my hands are dragged back to the shackles, but I barely notice, caught in the ratcheting mechanical pulse of the heart that surrounds me.

The Clock of Eclipses is running again.

## *Mildmay*

I woke up coughing. I fucking hate the cough you get with the Winter Fever. What it feels like is that somebody's grabbed your spine, right about the middle of your back, and is using it to shake you like a baby's rattle. It hurts, but what's worse than that is it's scary.

When I could finally catch my breath, I looked for Felix, and found his little hooker friend staring at me like she thought I was going to cough up my liver or something. I said, "Where's Felix?"

"Out."

"Yeah, I can see that. *Where?*"

"I don't know," she said.

I pushed myself into a sitting position, although it hurt like a motherfucker.

"What are you doing?" Corbie said.

"I gotta find him. Something's wrong."

"What? No!" She bounced up off the cot and tried to shove me back down. "You're sick!"

"Don't matter. I gotta find him." And let's not even talk about how much I hated that that little tiny gal could just shove me back down on the bed like I hadn't sat up at all.

"He's fine," she said. "Really."

"No, he fucking isn't. *Where is he?*"

"I don't know."

"You don't *know*? Sacred bleeding scabbed-over fuck, what kind of fuckhead are you? You can't let him out on his own. Powers and saints, he can get lost in a *rain barrel*, and he don't have no common sense at all, and Kethe only knows what he's getting himself into, and fuck it, he's in trouble and I have to help him before the wolves get him!"

And then, wouldn't you know it, I started coughing. And I couldn't stop, and I brought up some stuff in a really putrid shade of green, and I couldn't even try to fight Corbie off when she started rubbing my back.

"Fuck me sideways 'til I cry," I said, but it was kind of a wheeze and really fucking feeble.

"It'll be all right," Corbie said. "Really. You've been really sick and kind of out of your head, and I think maybe you're confused—"

"I am not fucking confused," I said, and this time I did manage to push her away and get up on one elbow.

"Before the *wolves* get him?" she said, and it just figured that the one time I wished somebody wouldn't understand me, she heard me plain as daylight.

"Listen," I said, "and never mind the fucking wolves. I swear by all the powers, I can find him, and I need to, because something seriously bad is happening and I gotta—"

At first, I didn't even know what it was, but then it came again, and I did.

"What the fuck?" said Corbie. "What the fucking fuck?"

"It's that clock," I said, because I remembered what this was like, remembered it from the Bastion where you couldn't get away from the ticking, even when you just wanted to beat your head against the nearest wall, beat it to a pulp, just to make it fucking stop. But nothing helped.

"Clock?" And her eyes went big as bell-wheels. "You mean the Clock of Eclipses? Somebody's started the Clock of Eclipses?"

"That's my guess," I said. It was too late. Too fucking late. Whatever it was, it'd happened, and I hadn't saved Felix from it. I slumped back down on the bed, feeling like shit, my head pounding in time with the tick of the clock. "And what d'you wanna bet, whatever's going on, Felix is right in the fucking middle of it?"

She hadn't known him long, but she'd figured him out. "No takers," said Corbie.

# *Kay*

At first, I knew not what had woken me. I lay and hated my blindness, for noon and midnight looked now the same to me, cereus and passion indistinguishable. But the sound I was hearing—was not a dream, was not my own heartbeat. Was a *clock*. But was no clock in my room. Had there been, I would have heard it before. Would not have been woken by it as a sound I did not know.

Could not believe, no matter how closet-demented I became, that Tinder was sneaking in while I slept to leave clocks in my room.

But that meant this noise came from somewhere outside. I got out of bed, crossed to the door—easy enough now, for I had the room memorized whether I wished it or no—opened it. The ticking was neither louder nor softer in the hallway, and other than the ticking, the hallway was silent, meaning that it was probably closer to midnight than noon. Murtagh's household, I had learned, was rarely still if His Grace was awake.

And the ticking persisted, not tremendously loud, but clearly audible, steady, directionless.

Edwin Beckett had wanted to start the Clock of Eclipses again, the gigantic, unnatural clock that lay beneath and through the Clock Palace. Blessed Lady, had he succeeded? Had his orgies succeeded where Gerrard had failed and died?

I knew the steps from my room to the sitting room, and I knew Murtagh's room lay beyond that. I turned, counted, letting my fingertips brush the wall, for I had learned also how quickly I became disoriented. Found the sitting room. Knew how many steps it took to cross it with Tinder guiding me; knew it should be no different an I guided myself. Took one step, hesitated. Told myself not to run craven, took another step. Stopped dead, the world falling away from me again, with no company save that monstrous ticking.

"Kay?" said Murtagh. "What are you doing out here in the . . . oh never mind."

"The ticking," I blurted. "Dost hear it?"

"I do, yes," Murtagh said. "That's why I'm up, which I would not normally be at two-thirty in the morning, I assure you."

I caught myself, reasserted some self-control. Was neither a child nor a woman to behave thus. "Is the Clock of Eclipses, think you?"

"I'm having trouble thinking of anything else it could be," Murtagh said; his voice came closer as he spoke. "You should go back to bed. You didn't even put your slippers on."

They were, of course, Murtagh's slippers, as everything I wore now belonged to Murtagh in truth.

"Am not cold," I said.

"You're mule-headed, is what you mean," Murtagh said. "Come sit down anyway."

I let him guide me to a chair. "It seems Edwin Beckett succeeded."

"Yes," said Murtagh. "And I would dearly like to know how."

## *Felix*

I lost most of the night. I didn't know how many times I was fucked, or how many of them took their turn. They made me come again and again until I was racked with dry agonizing spasms, until my entire body felt raw. When they let me go, I slid down the wall—and I didn't know how I'd gotten there, when I'd been unshackled, anything—and crawled, shivering wretchedly, until I found a corner, where I curled as tightly as I could and hoped to go unnoticed. I could, at that point, have taken the blindfold off—no one would have stopped me, or even cared—but that thought didn't occur to me until much later.

They were celebrating, for they had started the Clock of Eclipses. I couldn't quite believe what I was hearing, that that had been their *intention*, that they had brought me here and fucked me for the purpose of starting the clock, but since they couldn't stop talking about it, I was eventually forced to accept that it was the truth. They had used me, not for pleasure, but in a thaumaturgical working that made not even the most minimal amount of sense. I remembered the Cymellunar Union of Angels, and wondered if any of these people expected to grow wings.

And then I tucked myself tighter into the corner and bit my lip until it bled to keep from shrieking with laughter.

Sometime later, there were hands. "Come on, morning glory," someone said. "Time to go."

I obeyed them because all I wanted was not to be hurt anymore. We climbed more stairs than I remembered coming down, and then there was a smell of damp and someone pushed a wet cloth into my hand. "Clean yourself up. Quickly now."

I did the best I could blindfolded, and someone helped me with rough impatience, and then they gave me clothes—my clothes—and I dressed in frantic haste, although I couldn't manage the buttons of my shirt. It didn't matter; I dragged my coat on over it, and then there were hands again and more stairs, and then, "Come on, up you get," and I was pushed up into a carriage.

It was probably the same carriage I'd ridden in the night before; I wondered if it was the same man sharing it with me. Then I wondered if he'd fucked me, and how many times, and turned my face toward the window just to be sure he couldn't see it.

And the Clock of Eclipses was still pounding beneath us, the vibrations making me dizzy as the carriage descended the Crait. I'd been dizzy going up, I remembered, and it occurred to me that the hecate should be wearing off by now. I felt for my magic and did find it, but it was low and feeble and sullen, not strong enough to light one of Corbie's candles.

We rattled across the causeway, and I found myself thinking, Please don't let it be much farther because I don't know how much longer I can keep from screaming. I couldn't remember how long it had taken from Our Lady of Fogs to the causeway the night before. It hadn't seemed like long then, but that had been a different world.

And then the carriage stopped; I was groping for the latch before the man touched me, and I managed to get out without falling. He descended, too, and caught my hand; I stiffened, but he said, "You did well," and pressed a coin into my hand. "Your master's on her way over." And then he was gone, the carriage rattling away, vanishing into the early morning sounds and smells of a produce market.

Corbie's voice: "Felix? Sweet merciful Lady, what did they do to you?"

I blurted, "You're not my master."

"No, of course not," she said. "Are you all right? Do you, um, want to take the blindfold off?"

Which was the first time in hours that I remembered that I could. I clawed it off one-handed and dropped it; the sunlight made me squint, but it was worth it. Corbie, when I could make out her face, looked like she hadn't slept at all. "Felix?"

"I'm okay," I said. "And they paid me, at least." I held my hand out, and Corbie's face went slack with shock.

"Holy Lady," she said breathlessly. "I thought I'd die and never see one of those."

I looked down. There, in my palm, high relief on a silver coin, a golden angel saluted me with a golden sword.

# Part Two

# Chapter 7

## *Kay*

After the Clock of Eclipses awoke, Murtagh evidently felt there was no longer any need to hide me, whether for my sake or anyone else's. I was allowed to stay in the sitting room after breakfast, and thus to hear much of Murtagh's concerns and his business in Bernatha.

Principally, his purpose seemed to be to prevent Glimmering's clumsy intrigues from making matters in Caloxa worse than they already were. Glimmering—and his supporters in Corambis—wanted to make Bernatha the seat of Caloxan government; thus he had moved his headquarters here, brought cows, attempted to form an alliance with Clara Hume. Because of the rather peculiar laws pertaining to the Corambin army, Glimmering, as the conquering general, maintained considerable autonomy until the civil government was restored, thus Murtagh could not order Glimmering to move his headquarters to Wildar, nor could he compel him to do any number of other things, including releasing Gerrard's body for burial. And he could not countermand Glimmering's standing order that all matters pertaining to the Insurgence were to be dealt with in Bernatha. The governor would be able to, but the governor hadn't been appointed yet. And thus Murtagh stayed in Bernatha, for he was not willing, he said, to leave the fates of Caloxan soldiers in Glimmering's clumsy hands.

"It's actually a rather delicate legal question," he told me on his return from yet another adjudication. "Because of the nature of Caloxan kingship and the oaths sworn to a king, there's some dispute whether it isn't the *Corambin* oaths of loyalty that constitute treason for Caloxans. In any event, my feeling is that you are defeated enemies rather than suppressed traitors, and Corambis treats her enemies honorably."

"As she treated Caloxa forty indictions ago?"

"*That*," said Murtagh, "is exactly what I'm trying to prevent a recurrence of. The Convocation of the One Hundred Forty-sixth handled the war with Caloxa atrociously from beginning to end, and look where it's gotten us."

"Yes," said I. "Quite."

"Oh, damn. Sorry. But that *is* my point. I don't want Corambis and Caloxa to be doing this again in another forty indictions."

"Then what are you going to do about Charles?" I asked, for the question had been preying on my mind.

"Beg pardon?"

"You heard me. Charles Hume. Not to mention all Gerrard's illegitimate half siblings."

"What do you think we should do?"

"You want my honest opinion?"

"Yes. What would you do?"

"Kill him."

In the ensuing silence, Murtagh pushed his chair back and moved away. "He's only a baby. Two indictions? Three?"

"So was Gerrard forty indictions ago."

"There must be a better way."

"Did not say there wasn't. You asked what I would do."

"And you'd kill him?"

"Yes. He is the last legitimate heir of the Descent of Hume. If you truly do not want Caloxa to revolt ever again, kill him."

"You don't think we can compromise?"

"In forty indictions, with a man raised to believe he's the rightful king?"

"Point taken," said Murtagh and immediately switched ground. "And without Charles, the independence movement falls apart?"

"Did not say that, either. But they will have no *legitimate* candidate for the throne, and without that, they won't be able to unite even as much of Caloxa as Gerrard did."

"You're very cold-blooded about it."

"You've met my mother."

A pause. I hated sitting still, but this room was too hazardous to pace in. Too many people going in and out, moving chairs and footstools, leaving strange objects in my path.

Murtagh said quietly, "Did you ever really care about Caloxan independence, or was it all for Gerrard?"

Now I was grateful for that which I had hated a moment before. As I was sitting still, Murtagh could not tell that I had just frozen.

I said finally, choosing my words, "I followed Gerrard because I believed that he cared for Caloxa and her people, and because I believed—and believe—that Corambis and the Convocation do not. You will always put Corambis first, and I believe Caloxa deserves better than that."

"Yes, of course," said Murtagh, even more quietly. "I'm sorry."

We did not speak of Gerrard again. My grief remained mine alone.

Two days later, Murtagh solicited my opinion about the candidates for the restored governorship of Caloxa. Were four of them, ranging from the corrupt and ineffectual former governor to a mad brainchild of Murtagh's to make the Margrave of Quithenrick governor regent for Prince Charles.

"You're still trying to compromise."

"I have to believe compromise is possible," he said. The heat and weight of his hands suddenly closed over my wrists. "Kay, I *have* to."

"Is no business of mine," I said, pulling my hands away. "Have no stake in the government of Caloxa now."

After an ugly pause, Murtagh turned the conversation to his strategies for overcoming opposition to his plans, and we let the question of Charles Hume go. But I could not keep from showing myself a liar, for the question tore itself out of me that night, when Murtagh stopped by my room, as he often did, on his way to bed: "Do you truly think it will work?"

He might have pretended not to know what I meant; he said, "I think there is hope."

"*Hope,*" said I; the word was bitter.

"Don't discount it. Isn't that the cause of the Insurgence? Hope?"

"And the cause of the catastrophe that ended it?"

"Wasn't that caused by despair?"

"How do we tell the difference?"

"I . . ." Silence while he struggled with it. "I don't know."

"Nor do I. Good night, Murtagh."

I rolled to face the wall and did not turn back when he said, "Kay?" Another silence and then he said, "Good night, Kay," and closed the door.

Grief was like black iron, a collar against my throat that could not be unlocked. I might forget about it for minutes or hours at a time, but it was always there. I could not take a full breath, could not be free of the weight of it.

Was neither reason nor purpose in weeping, I told myself savagely. Could not weep the blindness from my eyes. Was no saint to restore life to the dead with my tears. Was but childish self-indulgence, and had I not had enough of that?

I shoved the blankets back and got up. If I had to pace myself into exhaustion, then I would. Was better than weeping.

⁂

Did not speak to Murtagh again until the morning of Gerrard's funeral. The Convocation appointed Peter Albern, a cousin of Glimmering's, as Governor Regent of Caloxa, a compromise which left Murtagh so lividly furious that he was incapable of civil conversation. Governor Albern was, however, persuadable, and although I thought this trait boded very ill, Murtagh used it unapologetically to get matters in train to move the government back to Wildar. That was the limit of what he could accomplish in Caloxa; we would be going to Esmer soon, and I tried not to think about what that was going to mean for me.

And then Governor Albern released Gerrard's body for burial in Our Lady of Fogs, Bernatha's sanctuary.

"The funeral's today, passion hour," said Murtagh. He was standing in the doorway of my room, as if uncertain I would permit him to come closer. I did not stop pacing; an I paced, I did not have to guess where I ought to be looking. "Do you want to go?"

"*Can* I go?"

"I'm offering to take you," Murtagh said sharply. "You will be neither arrested nor pilloried—you may, in fact, have to save me from the latter fate. It was the Convocation they were burning in effigy in St. Melior, not the most heroic and ill-used Margrave of Rothmarlin."

"Am not—"

"I know, I know. You're very conscientious about reminding everyone you meet."

"What wouldst have me do? Lay claim to what the most heroic and ill-used Convocation hath stripped from me? Raise my banner here in this hotel room?"

"Curb your instinct for melodrama. Will you come to the funeral or not?"

"Yes," I said and stopped in the middle of the room, facing a wall I had never seen. "I will come."

⁂

Tinder dressed me, in a Corambin suit which fit, meaning that Murtagh had had it made for me—another gift I could not refuse and did not want.

Tinder was, as always, patient and silent, and I finally braced myself and said, "Tinder?"

"Yes, sir?"

"Do you think someone in the hotel might have a coraline I could borrow? For the funeral?"

Tinder was of course Caddovian—all respectable Corambins were—but he said, "I don't know, sir, but I will ask." And when he came back to take me to out to the sitting room to join Murtagh, he said, "I am asked, sir, to present this to you as a gift from the kitchen staff of the Althammara." And he took my hand to pour the cool beads of a coraline into it.

"A gift?" I said, even as my fingers closed convulsively around it. "Tinder, I can't—"

"The head cook was most insistent, sir. He is from Benallery originally."

"Ah blessed Lady, I can't . . . All right. All right. Tell him thank you. Tell him I'll . . . I'll treasure it. Is it stone or wood?"

"Stone, sir." Tinder sounded mildly perplexed, but I had not the strength to explain that Benallerine coralines were always made of stone, unlike the tradition in the rest of Caloxa, which was for coralines made of wood. Benallery's own coraline, which I'd seen him telling over more times than I could count, had been fobbed with a stone from the Crawcour where it ran beneath the walls of Beneth Castle.

"Thank you," I said and slid the coraline into my pocket.

"Are you ready, sir?" said Tinder.

"Yes," I said; he helped me on with a greatcoat, and I allowed him to take my arm.

Murtagh and Wyatt were waiting in the sitting room. I was handed from Tinder to Murtagh like a package, and Murtagh told Wyatt to get the door.

"Am not that fragile," said I.

"You only say that because you can't see yourself," said Murtagh. "Truthfully, Kay, are you sleeping at all?"

"I sleep," I said.

"Not enough," said Murtagh and led me out.

I remembered quite distinctly climbing the staircases of the Althammara, so I was baffled when we emerged onto the street without descending a single step. "How . . . ?"

"One of the *other* reasons I like the Althammara," Murtagh said. "The top floor has a private entrance."

"Which you didn't use when you brought me from the Clock Palace because . . . ?"

"I wanted you to suffer," Murtagh said cheerfully. "Here. Wyatt hired a carriage. Mind your head. Actually, from the Clock Palace, it's a much shorter distance to the hotel's main doors. I thought the stairs were better than the streets."

I settled onto the padded leather seat. Murtagh sat next to me; he smelled, not unpleasantly, of limes. From the jostling of knees, Wyatt sat opposite. Murtagh rapped the roof, and we lurched into motion.

We did not speak as we drove to the sanctuary. I kept my head lowered; after a few minutes, I took the coraline out of my pocket and began telling the beads. The fob was intricately carved in a pattern I couldn't make out; the other beads were smooth as water. I said over the stations of the meditation for the Lady in my mind, replacing word by word the memory of the last time I had done so. This would be a memory better only by comparison, but it was a memory I could go on from, unlike the reeking nightmare beneath Summerdown.

The sanctuary of Our Lady of Fogs was windy, a sharp scouring wind that seemed to want to flense the flesh from my bones. And there were people here—too many people, and I clutched at Murtagh's arm before I could stop myself.

He gave no indication of having noticed; a few steps later, however, he checked briefly, then continued walking. " 'Sdeath," said he under his breath. "Some idiot told Clara Hume."

"He *was* her husband," I said, trying to be reasonable.

"She must be wearing Bernatha's entire supply of black crepe. There's *miles* of it. And dear sweet merciful Lady, how did she convince Quithenrick to bring Charles?"

"Charles is here?"

"Unless she's hired some other woman's baby, yes. Poor little sprout looks positively smothered. And Quithenrick looks like he's sat on a porcupine."

"He probably just caught sight of me," I said.

"Do you hate each other that much?"

"I have nothing but respect for Quithenrick. He thinks I am a blood-drinking savage and should be put down like a rabid dog."

"I'll keep that in mind. Oh may the Lady give us strength, Glimmering's here. He either has no sense or no shame, and I've given up trying to decide which. He's talking to Governor Albern in what one can only describe as a pointed fashion."

"His Grace of Glimmering is not a subtle man," I said. I couldn't release my locked grip on Murtagh's arm, but at least my voice was even.

"No," said Murtagh, on an exhalation that sounded half like a laugh and half like a sigh. "Here. We shall stand here opposite Clara Hume, and hopefully she'll be so busy glaring at us she'll forget to faint. She hates you, you know."

"Yes," I said. "I told Gerrard not to marry her. And then he had me stand witness at the wedding."

"Well, that explains a great deal. Oh dear. Wyatt, will you intercept Mr. Beckett, please?"

"Beckett's here? Why?"

"I'm not sure," said Murtagh. He sounded like he was frowning. "That is, I can take a well-educated guess at what he *wants*, but why he thinks this is either the appropriate time *or* the appropriate place . . ."

"Mr. Beckett has not shown himself particularly sensitive to 'appropriate,'" I said dryly.

"Point," said Murtagh. "And he may well be desperate by now."

"Desperate? The last you told me of him, he was being adulated in the newspapers."

"Ah," said Murtagh, almost sheepishly. "Yes. Well, that was before the rash of suicides became quite so obtrusive."

"Suicides?"

"People are killing themselves to get away from the ticking. Or, at least, that's what the notes they're leaving say."

I could sympathize with the impulse. The ticking of the Clock of Eclipses saturated the Crait. There was no way to escape from it; I had tried blocking my ears and had discovered I could still *feel* it. And it was always just some immeasurable fraction of a second too slow, so that one found oneself listening for it, waiting for the next hammer blow to strike. "And Edwin Beckett is to blame," I said softly.

"He claimed responsibility," Murtagh said, and I felt his shrug. "Also, I understand that several of the suicides have been among his coterie, which gives no very good impression. The House of Honesty has sent a letter to the Institution, inviting them to come study the clock—and, the letter strongly suggests, learn how to turn the damn thing off. And that leaves Mr. Beckett distinctly out in the cold." He straightened. "All right, brace yourself. Here comes the intended."

It was part of the ceremony: the sanctuary-intended spoke to every mourner before he began the ritual, asking their name and their relation to the dead person. "Ferrand Carey," said Murtagh. "I never met Gerrard Hume in life, but I mourn his death."

"And thou, my child?"

I blinked hard—against the wind, I told myself. "Kay Brightmore. I was his friend."

The pause was awkward; then the intended recovered and said, "The Lady blesses thee in thy grief," and moved on.

His voice sounded young, and I was confirmed in that supposition by his evident nervousness when he began the ritual of burial. He stumbled over phrases he'd surely pronounced a hundred times before, and when he reached the eulogium, it was painfully clear that he forgot the words he'd prepared. "The poor boy," Murtagh murmured. "He's gone so red I'd be worried about apoplexy if he were older."

In Rothmarlin and Hornhast and Gormont, even in Benallery, the mourners at a funeral took the eulogium after the sanctuary-intended spoke the formal words of grieving. The business of the sanctuary-intended was with the dead; he was not expected to be able to speak about the grief of the living. But the more northern and western parts of Caloxa were being corrupted by Caddovian practices, and clearly Bernatha was following them, at least in this instance. Perhaps someone had come to the honest realization that there was no one who could safely be asked to speak Gerrard's eulogium *except* a sanctuary-intended who had never known him.

Gerrard would have wished to be buried in the sanctuary of Our Lady of Caverns in Barthas Cross, where all the Humes were buried, and I hated the fact that I understood—and agreed with—the decision to bury him here instead. His grave might still become a martyr's shrine, but not on account of the people of Bernatha.

I tried not to listen to the sanctuary-intended; it seemed kinder to let his words escape unheeded. Instead, I did as Intended Joyce had recommended when my father died: I remembered Gerrard as I had known and loved him—the honest love of a man for his friend, of a soldier for his leader, not the sin I had confessed to Intended Gye—and as best I could, I forgave him and said good-bye to him. The wind stung my eyes to tears, and in my heart I whispered the truth, *I am sorry I did not defy thee and in so doing save thee.*

Finally, finally, the sanctuary-intended struggled through to the end of the ceremony, and the mourners were released.

But Murtagh and I had not gone two paces before Clara Hume shrieked like the mother of banshees, "Rothmarlin! This is your fault!"

"Keep walking," Murtagh muttered, but I shook him off and turned, guessing as best I could at her location. "And how wouldst know, Clara? Wert thou with him when he died?"

"How dare you!" cried Clara Hume.

"Kay, for the Lady's sake," Murtagh said, grabbing at my arm.

I shook him off again. "Didst cleave to thy husband, Clara? Didst pledge thy faith to follow him? Or didst wear his ring and bear his child so thou mightst be princess and bowed to and made much of? Thou lovedst him not—thou lovedst him *never*—so speak not to me of *fault*."

Murtagh grabbed my arm again, and someone else grabbed the other. "Overwrought," Murtagh said loudly and distinctly as they turned me bodily about, and Clara Hume went off in strong hysterics. It saved her thinking of a response.

Murtagh and Wyatt all but carried me, and after the first few strides, I quit fighting them. "Next time," said Murtagh, "warn me before you start tearing strips off Clara Hume."

"Will be no next time," I said; I was disgusted with myself. "I cry your mercy, Murtagh. I forgot myself."

"I'm not *blaming* you," Murtagh said. "I'm sure I would have done the same. Just . . . What do you want, Thomas?"

"To offer my respects to the Margrave of Rothmarlin," said the Duke of Glimmering.

"Is not here," said I. "May apply to Rothmarlin Castle, where I am sure he will be most delighted to receive you."

"Don't think I'll forget," said Glimmering. Why had his parents not taught him elocution as a child and rid him of that dreadful nasal whine? Better yet, why had they not drowned him in a bucket?

Murtagh made an exasperated, wordless exclamation. "Forget *what*, Thomas? That there was a war? None of us will forget that, I assure you. Now stand aside. I have much to do today, and so do you."

"It doesn't bother you, Ferrand, that you'll have a murderer in your house?"

"Stand aside or I will move you," said Murtagh, and apparently even Glimmering heard the danger in his voice, for Murtagh jerked me forward and I heard Glimmering call, off to the right now, "Will you protect him forever, Ferrand?"

Murtagh didn't respond until we were in the carriage and well away from Our Lady of Fogs, and what he said then was vile, and obscene enough to make a horse drover blush.

## Mildmay

Powers, I was fucked up. And I knew I was fucked up—I just didn't seem to be able to do nothing about it.

I mean, I knew this wasn't the Anchorite's Knitting and the people arguing weren't Mavortian and Bernard. Some of the time I even remembered Mavortian was dead. But knowing that didn't fucking help. I was still stuck and Felix was still in trouble and sometimes it was Strych and sometimes it was wolves, but all of the time it was bad fucking shit and I couldn't fucking get up off the bed.

My chest hurt and my head hurt and I swear by all the powers every separate bone in my body I'd ever broken hurt like a motherfucker and I was either too hot or too cold and every time I coughed it was like dying all over again. And let's not talk about the shit I was bringing up, neither.

Shouldn't nothing inside a person be that shade of green and I had the taste of it in my mouth all the time, brackish and bitter and just fucking nasty.

And did I mention the part where Felix and Corbie wouldn't shut the fuck up? Seemed like every time I made it up away from the wolves, the two of them would be snarling and snapping like wolves themselves. Sometimes it scared me and sometimes it pissed me off, depending on how high my fever was and whether I knew it was them or not. Sometimes it *was* Mavortian and Bernard, even though I knew Mavortian was dead. Sometimes it was Kolkhis and whatsisface, the boyfriend she'd had when I had a septad and one and got the Winter Fever so bad I still don't know why I didn't die of it. Of course, even when I knew who they were, I couldn't follow what they were saying, and eventually it occurred to me that I had the Winter Fever now and must be running one fuck of a fever, not to mention the green shit in my lungs and the glass in my head.

Oh, I thought. Well, that explains it. And then I fell asleep and didn't dream and when I woke up Felix was sitting next to me with these yellow and green bruises all down one side of his face.

I said, "What the fuck happened to you?" His head jerked up, and I was sorry I'd startled him, but still.

"How are you feeling?" he said, like I hadn't said nothing.

"Like pounded shit. What did you do to your face?"

He went a little red. "Don't worry about me. You need to—"

"I ain't *worried*. Them bruises are a couple days old. But I really do want to know what the fuck you did."

He broke eye contact, jerked his chin up. Said, "Your grammar clearly broke along with your fever. '*Those* bruises' is the correct form."

Oh shit. I glared at him, best I could do, and said, "You know perfectly well I don't give a rat's ass. What. The. Fuck. *Happened?*"

He gave me a nasty look back. "We were out of money, and you were out of your head."

"Money? But you don't . . ." *Know the first thing about making money,* I was about to say, but then I remembered my dream and the wolves and what Felix had been before he'd been a hocus. He *did* know the first thing about making money. "Oh sacred bleeding fuck tell me you didn't."

He looked down at his hands. I followed his gaze, and oh fuck me sideways, more bruises and scabbed over patches, and what the fuck had he gotten himself into while I wasn't around to keep him safe? "It is what I was trained to do."

"*Trained?*" I said, and I would've gone on, but I started coughing. Not out of the woods yet, Milly-Fox. And by the time I could breathe again, I didn't care so much about chewing him out.

But then he went and opened his mouth. "You need to rest. What happened while . . . Well, it doesn't matter."

"The fuck it don't," I said, and I wanted to shake him again. How stupid did he have to be? "How bad are you hurt? Tell me that."

"Mildmay, it doesn't *matter*."

"Why not?"

"What?"

"Why don't it matter if you're hurt? It'd matter if *I* was hurt. So why the fuck don't it matter if *you*'re hurt?"

And he was giving me his crazy-blank stare again, like I wasn't even talking the right language. He didn't have an answer. And, I mean, I knew that, but it hurt, it hurt worse than anything, to see it up close and where he couldn't dance around it or pretend it wasn't there.

"How bad are you hurt?" I said.

"I'm okay," he said. "It's just bruises."

"That ain't bruises," I said and didn't quite touch the nasty scabs on his left wrist.

"It's healing," he said.

"Well, *yeah*. Shit *does*. But that ain't the point."

He got his head up enough to glower at me. "Do you want me to just tell you everything that happened?"

"You could," I said, and the horrified look he gave me, like I'd said he could take one of my kidneys out and barbecue it for dinner, was almost funny. Almost.

"Maybe later," he said, meaning *never*, and bounced up off the bed. "Corbie will be here soon. Let's get you cleaned up."

And I let it go. And I ain't even pretending. It was because I knew it would come back.

## Felix

The fantôme waits for me in my dreams. It tries different shapes to seduce me, taking them from my memories: Murtagh, Gideon, Vincent. It offers me a boy with Corbie's long nose and violet eyes; it offers me Mildmay, and I wake—vilely, achingly hard—and slink away to the lavatory to deal with myself as best I can. I don't want him anymore, not like that, but I cannot control what the fantôme finds in the murk of my dreams.

The fantôme shows me the night in the Clock Palace again and again, and I wake shuddering and sweating, but I don't change my mind. I don't give it what it wants, and it retaliates by dragging out all the worst memories it can find. *This can stop anytime thou wishst,* it tells me, insouciant in the shape of Malkar Gennadion. *It is up to thee, Felix.*

But I know that trick—know it, ironically, from Malkar himself—and I shake my head, unspeaking, fearing that the fantôme will have the same gift for twisting my words that Malkar did.

It drops me into St. Crellifer's; I see myself, all bones and dirt and staring eyes, scrubbing floors, and crouched beside me, weeping, is Isaac Garamond. No matter how hard I work, the floor will never be clean, for his tears track red across his face and make a spreading pool of blood at our feet.

I jerked out of sleep again and again, and by the third morning after Mildmay's fever had broken, I was in no shape to deal with his sharp eyes and sharper mind. He expressed a bone-deep desire for a bath, and so I helped him limp to the bathroom and ran the hot water for him. The plumbing fascinated him, and he had a thousand questions about it, none of which I could answer.

He stripped off his nightshirt, as unconcerned as ever with his nudity; that abhorrent dream came back to me, and I looked down at my hands where the bruises were fading to yellow and brown. He used my shoulder to balance as he got into the tub, and I gritted my teeth and stood still for it. He needed me, not my airs and fancies.

He gave an audible sigh, of relief or pleasure or both, as he sat down, and then said, abruptly, "Why didn't you hock your rings?"

"I beg your pardon?" I said, as breathless suddenly as if he'd hit me.

"Your rings. Remember 'em? Big gold and garnet things I been carrying since we left Mélusine? If we were so fucking hard up for cash, why didn't you hock 'em?"

I stared at him. The words barely even made sense. "You want me to sell my rings?"

"No," he said, as slow as if he were talking to an idiot child. "Pawn them. You do know about pawnshops, don't you?"

"Well, yes, but—"

"Felix, I could've gotten them back for you. Two days, tops." He leaned forward, carefully, and put one wet hand on my wrist. "And I'd rather've done that than have you go out and let yourself get fucked for the money. Okay?"

I felt myself going scarlet, and I pulled away from him. The truth was, it hadn't even occurred to me, and I couldn't help resenting his easy assumption of superiority: *he* could deal with our financial difficulties in two days, unlike his poor stupid brother. It was a relief to find an objection: "It wouldn't have been enough."

"No?" he said skeptically, as if he could hear my wounded pride.

"Doctors are quite phenomenally expensive, darling," I said. "We can do the math later, if you want."

"I ain't trying to—oh fuck it. I'm just saying, I hate that you got hurt because of me."

My face was burning; I turned away from him and said, "If you're going to bathe, you might as well do it."

"Felix—" I didn't turn, and after an excruciating pause, I heard him sigh, this time undoubtedly with exasperation. "All right. Have it your way."

I didn't turn around until I was sure he wouldn't try again.

❧

At least with Mildmay on the mend and alert, the arguments with Corbie stopped. Half the time, I didn't even know what we were arguing about, which was not a situation I was used to being in. But Corbie was like a handful of needles, every angle bringing a different attack.

She thought I should "lay a charge" with the House of Honesty against the people who had hired me for their thaumaturgical orgy; from the newspapers, we knew who they were, and she insisted furiously that they were in breach of contract.

"It's not that simple," I'd said, more than once.

"They fucked you up," she said, glaring up at me balefully, "and I don't care about them fancy words, that wasn't the agreement."

"Corbie, it isn't—" But I didn't know how to explain without betraying my own weaknesses. I didn't want her to know what had been done to me any more than I wanted Mildmay to know.

And when we weren't arguing about that, she was apt to go off like a firecracker, defending herself aggressively against what she called "talking down." She said she wouldn't put up with it, and I certainly believed her, but I couldn't figure out what constituted "talking down," or why she thought I would want to do such a thing in the first place.

Mildmay made her wary and unnaturally quiet; that afternoon, after less than fifteen minutes of the strained atmosphere in our room, she said, "Felix, can we go walking or something? Get some fresh air?" Her eyes cut over at Mildmay, and I knew what she meant.

Of course, so did he. "Yeah, since you can't throw me out."

"It ain't that," Corbie said.

If I'd had the chance, I would have told her it was useless, but Mildmay said, "Sure it is. And I ain't even a hocus, so I don't know what you're so twitchy about. But go on. Least I'll be able to sleep."

"Mildmay," I said, although I didn't know quite what I wanted to say.

"Go *on*," he said, and Corbie gave me an imploring look; I gave in.

We walked downhill, away from the Clock Palace, for reasons neither of us was prepared to discuss. The farther we walked, the more anxious and unhappy she looked, and I finally said, "Corbie, what is it?"

"I, um." She fiddled with the lace on the cuff of her coat. "You're going to Esmer, right?"

"When Mildmay's well enough to travel, yes."

"To go to the Institution?"

"I don't know," I said. "I need to present myself to the governing body of the wizards of Corambis, but I don't actually know what that is."

"The Congress. That's the Institution." She frowned up at me. "Why do you got to 'present' yourself to them?"

I wasn't prepared for that question, even though I should have known it was coming. I nearly tripped over my own feet, and then had to school myself not to jerk away from Corbie when she reached to steady me. "I, um . . ."

"Oh," said Corbie. "It ain't a good reason, is it?"

"Depends what you mean by 'good.' It's certainly a *cogent* reason. But, no, it isn't a very nice one."

"Are you sick?" she said, and the anxiety in her voice was rather embarrassing. "Some kind of magicians' disease?"

"No, nothing like that. I . . ." I couldn't lie to her; I should have told her the truth days ago—should have told her the truth the instant she asked me to teach her. "I'm exiled from Mélusine because I . . ."

I'd said it to Thamuris, but Thamuris knew me and knew what dreadful things I was capable of. And although I had taught him some things, being a far more experienced wizard than he, I had never thought of myself as his teacher.

"I destroyed a man's mind," I said, the words hard and flat and not even half as ugly as they should have been to describe what I had done.

Corbie's eyes were wide and very dark. "Why?" she said.

"Does it matter?"

"Well, yeah, actually. Because if you did it for a reason, that's one thing, but if you did it just for fun, that's something else."

"No, I didn't do it for fun. He murdered—" My throat closed, the words so much harder to say awake than they had been in the Khloïdanikos. "He murdered my lover."

The fantôme stirred hopefully in the back of my mind, and I denied it.

"So you had a reason," Corbie said.

"I don't know," I said wearily. "But you were going to ask me something else."

She gave me a doubtful look, but let the subject go. "Yeah. I was. Because I was wondering . . ."

She was going red. "What?"

"Can I go with you?"

"I beg your pardon?"

Tomato-red now. "When you go to Esmer, can I go with you?"

"Why in the world would you want to?"

And she might be deeply embarrassed, but she got her chin up and answered the question. "Because you're teaching me. Because you don't think it matters that I'm a girl. Or that I'm a jezebel. Because I want to learn *more*."

I felt strange and cold and rather remote. "I'll have to talk it over with Mildmay," I said. "Let's just call today a wash, and I'll see you tomorrow, all right?"

"You ain't mad that I asked, are you?" she said. "Because I know maybe I shouldn't've, and maybe you're sick to death of me, or, you know, you don't—"

"Corbie," I said. "Shut up. I'm not mad. I just . . . I need to think and I need to talk to Mildmay. Tomorrow, all right?"

"All right," she said with a quick, jerky nod, and darted away.

I walked back rather more slowly to the Fiddler's Fox, where I found Mildmay awake, despite what he had said. I told him what Corbie wanted. "That's kind of a mess," he said.

"You have no idea," I said and sat down beside him.

"Well, I kind of do," he said. "Because I know how you feel about taking apprentices."

"This isn't—" But of course it was. That was exactly what it was, and I realized that I was actually shaking, very slightly.

"Felix," Mildmay said. "You ain't him."

"No?" My voice cracked.

"No," he said, steady and patient. "You wouldn't hurt a hair on that little gal's head. I can see that just as well as she can."

"Are you jealous?"

He snorted. "I'm sick, is what I am, and it's making me say stupid shit. No, I ain't jealous. I wouldn't be a hocus if you paid me. And she's a good kid. I knew kids like her at home, and I would've wanted them to take this chance if they had it."

"Which chance?"

"The chance to get out," he said. "To not be so fucking stuck somewhere that you can't even tell if you want to be somewhere else because there *ain't* nowhere else. Ain't a chance I ever had."

"But you got out," I said. "You *are* out."

"Huh," he said. "I s'pose that's true."

"So you don't mind?"

He gave me a slow, assessing look. "I don't mind." And one eyebrow went up. "If you don't."

I wanted, suddenly, to snap at him not to make allowances for me, that I wasn't the damaged, frail creature he obviously thought I was. But he was still sick, and I was morbidly uncertain that if I told him that, I would be telling the truth. So I said, "I don't mind, either," and if it was a lie, at least it was one he didn't call me on.

I could not simply keep running from the fantôme; like the remorseless ticking of the Clock of Eclipses, it could follow me no matter how deep I went into my dreams. I had to fight, even though I had no idea how.

My construct-Mélusine was bare of briars, but also barren, like the stones of a house left standing after a fire, and all the gates were now standing wide, a series of panoramas I did not want to see. I made the circle, grimly dragging them shut, though the effort jolted all the way up to my shoulders and made my hands ache dismally. When I paused in front of Horn Gate, afraid to look through at the Khloïdanikos but equally unwilling to cut myself off from it, the fantôme said from behind me, *Is this thy fortress, Felix? It cannot keep me out.* And all around the circuit, the gates slammed open, one after the other, in the order in which I'd closed them.

If I went into the Khloïdanikos, it would only follow me, and I had already done enough harm there. I turned around, hating each individual motion, and found the fantôme standing on the black glass circle that was all that was left to represent the Mirador. It was wearing Isaac Garamond's face.

*Who are you, truly?* I said.

*I am rachenant,* it said, as if that were an answer.

*Rachenant?*

*The spirit of vengeance,* it said. Its eyes were not Isaac's eyes; they were red as blood and black as slaughter and not even remotely human. And then I jerked back, realizing how close to it I'd come without even noticing.

*Felix,* it said in mock sorrow and spread wide hands that a moment before had been reaching for my wrists. *Dost not trust me? I wish only to serve thee.*

*I do not want your service.*

*Thou canst not lie to me,* it said, and Isaac shifted into Malkar. *I can see the truth of thee. Beloved.*

*I want you,* I said carefully, *to leave me alone. If you can see the truth of me, you can see that I mean it.*

*Dost* think *thou meanst it,* the fantôme agreed with Malkar's worst smile. *But in thy heart, thou dost desire me.*

The idea came to me as sharp and sudden and brilliant as a lightning bolt, and I acted on it in the same instant. Instead of retreating, I charged the fantôme. It could take Malkar's appearance, but it didn't have his mass, and

I drove it backwards, south, into the stagnant black tarn that was both the Sim and my madness. I pinned it, my hands locked in claws around its throat, and I held it under with both my weight and my magic, forcing it to follow the rules of the construct it had chosen to follow me into, forcing it to drown. When at last it lay still and limp, not Malkar any longer, not anyone, I shoved the body out until the undertow caught it and dragged it down.

I slept peacefully and well the rest of the night.

Corbie was prompt the next afternoon, and her anxiety made my throat hurt. "Let's go up to the roof," I said and ignored the look that Mildmay gave me. It was no business of his.

Corbie followed me without complaint, but when we reached the privacy of the roof, she said, "You're gonna say no, aren't you?"

"Corbie, it's not that I don't *want*—"

"Oh fuck you, of course it is. I don't blame you, but don't lie about it, all right?"

"I'm not the right teacher for you," I said desperately. "I don't know anything about Grevillian thaumaturgy. Anything I taught you, you'd just have to unlearn anyway."

"Who fucking cares about thaumaturgy?" she yelled at me. And to my abiding horror, she began to cry.

"Oh fuck it," she said; she was already digging out a handkerchief. "I wasn't going to do this, I swear I wasn't, but I thought I had it right, I thought I . . . I thought you *liked* me."

"I *do* like you. Corbie, it's not about *liking*. It's just . . ."

"Just *what*?" she snarled.

And, horrified, I heard myself say it: "I had a teacher. He abused me. And I don't want . . . I don't trust myself, Corbie. I know I *can't* trust myself. And I don't want to hurt you."

"Too fucking late."

"I know. I did this all wrong. I . . ." *Don't I rate an apology?* "I'm sorry."

She sighed and said, "C'mon and sit down. I can't think with you looming over me like this."

"I don't loom," I protested.

"You're most of a foot taller than me. Of course you loom. C'mon. *Sit.*"

I felt as if I owed it to her; I sat beside her, leaning against one of the chimneys.

She blew her nose and glared at me. "So. Tell me about this teacher of yours."

"Corbie!"

"What?"

"I can't just . . ."

"It ain't that hard. Look, you said you liked me, and Mildmay said you liked teaching. So I really want to know what the problem is here."

"Okay," I said. "You want to know? His name was Malkar Gennadion. Or one of his names. He was a blood-wizard. He was at least a hundred years old, maybe more like two or three. I don't know. He bought me. From the brothel I was working in, when I was fourteen. And he took me to this place called Arabel, which was, oh I don't know, fifty, sixty miles from Mélusine, farther from home than I'd ever been in my life. We stayed on the estate of a friend of his. Insofar as Malkar had friends. And sometimes, every few months, he'd . . ." I'd never told anyone this, and the words were drying up in my throat even as they were forcing themselves out. "He'd give me to his friend for a night. In 'payment.' And then one night he suggested they share me."

She was watching me, her eyes serious but not shocked. I swallowed hard and went on: "I don't mean to imply that this was the first time I'd ever been used by two men together. But Malkar had told me he loved me. He'd told me I was special. He'd told me he 'loaned' me to Hestrand—his friend—because he had to, that he had no money to pay rent. But then that night . . ."

I couldn't go on. I couldn't. But my mouth opened, and I said, "Malkar was fucking me up the ass, and he'd got my hands behind my back, and Hestrand was fucking my mouth, and Malkar says to Hestrand, 'Do you know the story of how I found this treasure?' And Hestrand says, 'No,' and Malkar tells him. He tells him the whole thing, fucking me slow the entire time, and then he says—I remember it word for word—'He's a clever little beast, but his true aptitude is always going to be for being fucked.' And they proved it that night. They did things to me . . ." I managed a jagged sort of noise that might have been a laugh. "And the next day, when I tried to talk to Malkar about it, he just said, 'Don't make a melodrama out of it, dearest. It's not worth it for a molly-toy like you.' And I felt . . . It wasn't about the sex. It was the betrayal, the way he didn't even bother to *lie* to me." I shook my head, trying, again, to shake away the past, and said, "That was my teacher. That was the man who taught me everything I know."

After a moment, she said, "Is that what you sounded like? Before?"

I listened to my own words again in my head and winced at the way my vowels had slid into the Lower City. "Yes. Only worse. Worse than Mildmay."

She nodded, her eyes thoughtful. Still not shocked. She said, "But when I tried to tell you I couldn't learn real magic because I was a jezebel, you got mad at me."

"I . . ." I realized my mouth was hanging open, and closed it.

"So you're not like him," she said, as Mildmay had said. "And we know you're not going to fuck me anyway, because you don't do women. So what's the problem?"

"Corbie, I can't—"

"You keep saying that," she said. "But I think what you mean is, you're scared to. And that ain't the same thing. So, all right. I ain't gonna force myself on you. You decide what you want, and when you do, you let me know. I'll be at the Brocade Mouse."

"Corbie—"

"Shut up, Felix," she said, and then smiled at me, a real smile, though tired and too old for her. "You got some shit to work through. I get that." She patted my knee, very gently, and then was up and away as light on her feet as a butterfly.

I sat shivering for a long time after she was gone.

## *Kay*

The day before we were to leave Esmer, the evening post arrived while we were having tea, and Murtagh, as he generally did, opened his letters in between bites of pound cake. He frequently provided commentary, sometimes scurrilous, sometimes merely informative, and I listened with almost painful attentiveness, knowing that what he was really doing was educating me in the finer points of Corambin—and particularly Esmerine—politics. He was also still negotiating with Vanessa Pallister and her brothers-in-law over a marriage he seemed determined to push through; although it made me deeply uncomfortable to find myself cast as the bride and Murtagh as my father, was not as if I could have done anything about it myself. Even more uncomfortable was the realization that I did not truly have the option of refusing, unless I wished Murtagh to hand me over to either Caloxan or Corambin justice. And in that I found myself following my sister Isobel, who had not had the option of refusing the marriage I had negotiated with Murtagh. She could have entered a convent, as I remembered saying to her more than once, but a woman less suited than Isobel to the life of a contemplative was hard to imagine, and I had known that full well. I was ashamed of myself, both for doing such a reprehensible thing and for never once, in twelve indictions, stopping to consider what I had done. No, not until it happened to me, and then I was all indignation and hurt and anger. *Then* I found it reprehensible.

Would not even be able to apologize to Isobel. An I did, she would box my ears. And I would deserve it.

But this afternoon, Murtagh had mostly notes from Bernathan potentates, expressing their sorrow that he was leaving, their hopes of future good relations, "et cetera et cetera," said Murtagh. And then the brisk sounds of letters being opened and unfolded and stacked to one side ceased. "Hello," said Murtagh. "This is different."

"What is?"

"This," said he, and I heard the faint crinkle of paper being flourished, "is a letter from one Intended Marcham, of Our Lady of Marigolds in Howrack."

"Intended Marcham?" My mouth had gone dry; I found my teacup and burned my tongue on too large a swallow. "What does he want?"

"Interesting that you should ask. His handwriting is nearly illegible and if the man was ever taught to spell, it clearly didn't take. He says he's very concerned because . . . Kay, I can't make this word be anything but *verlain*. Can that possibly be right?"

"Yes," I said, and my voice sounded as hollow as I felt. "He's talking about the engine."

"Which is *verlain*? Whatever *verlain* means?"

"Yes. It's a country word. It means 'forbidden.' "

"Ah. That explains why he's talking about a curse in the next line."

"A *curse*?" I had feared he was writing to protest the dissolution of my penance.

"Yes. He says that's what killed Gerrard and the others and struck you blind, and he says now it's punishing the people of Howrack for not stopping you. Everyone's sickly, he says, and the crops are slow, and he's quite sure it's because of this curse."

"And he thinks what? That you can do something about it?"

"Well, I'm not sure about that, either. I swear his spelling is getting worse as he goes along. He seems to think I *should* do something about it. Either that or he thinks *you* should do something about it. I can't quite tell."

"He's the intended. Why doesn't he do something?"

"You want me to *ask*?" Murtagh said, and he sounded so utterly appalled that I started laughing.

"No," said I. "I wouldn't ask that of you."

"Good. Because I wouldn't do it. You've met the man. Is he actually a lunatic?"

"Did not meet him under the best of circumstances," I said. "But, no, I did not think him mad."

"Then," said Murtagh, "I'm afraid his wits have turned. Happily that problem is neither mine nor yours. It belongs to the unfortunate people of Howrack and, I suppose, to their margrave."

"Murrey."

"Couldn't happen to a nicer fellow," said Murtagh with satisfaction, and I heard him wadding the letter into a ball and pitching it into the fireplace.

## *Felix*

The Brocade Mouse was lavishly appointed but not—I noticed as a skinny not-quite-teenage girl led me back toward Corbie's room—particularly clean. At night, no one would be able to tell, and the customers were the last people in the world to care. Corbie's own room, though not much larger than a pocket handkerchief, was perfectly tidy and smelled pleasantly of rosemary and lavender. She was mending a layered cerise skirt when my guide opened the door and said, "Gentleman for you, Miss Gartrett."

"Call me that again, Nell, and I'll take my hairbrush to your backside," Corbie said without looking up; then she raised her head and squeaked. Then coughed and said, "Felix. How nice to see you. Come in and sit down."

This parody of politeness was far worse than belligerence. But I sat where she directed, on a spindly chair with a patchwork seat cover that was certainly not original, and folded my hands to keep from fidgeting.

After Corbie had stared Nell into closing the door again, she shoved the skirt aside and gave me a sidelong, wary look. "So. You've made up your mind, then?"

"I, um."

"You *haven't* made up your mind?"

"No, I have," I said hastily. "I just . . ."

She waited a moment. "Are you trying to tell me you don't want to teach me, or that you do?"

I couldn't meet her eyes. I stared at the tattoos on the backs of my hands and managed to force the words out: "I do."

"You don't sound like it."

It was what Malkar would have said, merely in order to prolong the agony for another round. But I looked at Corbie, and she didn't look like she was enjoying this any more than I was. "No, I do," I said. "I'm just . . ." The words stuck like fishhooks, but I had to say them: "I'm afraid I'll fail."

I'd been taught never to fail, by the scars on my back, by Malkar's ingenious cruelty that left no mark, by the avid eyes of the Mirador, predators and carrion-eaters waiting to take their comrades down. I had learned never to admit the possibility of failure, to carry everything off with a lofty air of omnipotence and a smirk. But if I didn't want to be Malkar—and I didn't, desperately didn't—I couldn't treat Corbie like that, couldn't close the gates with her on the outside.

"Well, I'm afraid I'll fail, too," Corbie said. "So we're even."

"I guess we are." I stood up. "Unless you have an objection, we're leaving for Esmer tomorrow morning."

"That's awful quick," Corbie said, but she didn't sound upset.

"Is it a problem?"

"No." Her smile was sudden and radiant: still not my type, but she was lovely when she was happy. "I'll be glad to be gone."

## Mildmay

It was a good thing I had Felix, or I would've drowned in that fucking bathtub three times over. And it was a good thing he wouldn't listen when I told him not to come along. Powers.

What was nice, though, and it was the first thing I'd felt really good about in a long time, was that he didn't try nothing. He could've groped me, and he didn't. He didn't stare at me. He didn't even say nothing, and I'd really been expecting he would. Because when he wanted something, he pushed. He pushed until you pushed back, and then he pushed some more. I mean, we'd *had* that conversation about how I didn't want to sleep with him, and that hadn't stopped him bringing it up again.

Maybe this time I'd pushed back hard enough.

Or maybe he was honestly trying not to be a prick about it. The way he did look at me when he looked—little sideways glances and no eye contact—was the way he got when he thought I was right to be mad at him. Because of course he never fucking apologized, even when he knew he ought to. So he'd do that twitchy no eye contact thing like he thought I was going to hit him until I gave up and forgave him for whatever the fuck it was he'd done.

But I wasn't mad at him now, and he wasn't acting like he thought I was, except for the way we just didn't have eye contact no more and especially when I took my clothes off. And, I mean, it wasn't like I could ask, *So why ain't you staring at me while you got the chance?*

And okay, I knew part of it was that he was embarrassed—that ain't the right word because it was worse than embarrassed. He was ashamed that I knew what he'd done, although how he'd thought he was going to hide it I don't fucking know. And he was even more ashamed that I knew he'd done it to punish himself. Because, you know, he's a smart guy. If he'd had his head on straight, he would've seen that wasn't his only option. But he'd *wanted* to make a martyr of himself, and powers and saints, I guess that's a pun.

I didn't figure that if I asked, he'd say anything to the point. He wouldn't undress with me in the room, and leaving aside the scars on his back, he didn't have no more modesty than a tabby cat. So he didn't want me to see, and I got to admit I didn't want to look. And it wasn't like he wasn't *talking* to me, in any of the Great Septad and six ways he had of doing that, including the one where he talked my ear off. No, we were having real conversations, and everything, and he even remembered his promise to help me learn to read better and we were actually working on it. It was just this one thing where he wasn't saying nothing and I wasn't saying nothing and it was like waiting for a thunderstorm to break.

And I'm pretty good at waiting—got a lot of practice, thanks—but I'm a fucking terrible liar, and that's what this felt like, like we were lying to each other by not talking about it.

So the night before we left Bernatha—he'd gone out and bought train tickets and come back all flustered and red in the face because somebody'd been nice to him—laying there in the dark, I said, "Felix?"

I knew he wasn't asleep, but setting out to have a serious conversation with him was kind of like planning a burglary. You did it step by step and you never assumed nothing.

"Yes?" he said. I rolled up on one elbow, and I could just make him out, laying on his back and staring up into the dark like there was something written on the ceiling and he was reading it.

"I'm gonna say this wrong," I said, "because I always do, but—are you okay?"

At least I got his attention. He rolled onto his side, and I knew he was squinting at me. "Of course I'm o—all right. Why wouldn't I be?"

"If you were hurt—I mean, really hurt—you'd tell me, right? You'd let me help?"

"I'm not hurt," he said and sat up. "Are *you* all right? What brought this on?"

"Never mind," I said, and I flopped back down on my back. "I'm glad you're okay."

"Do not *never mind* me in that tone of voice," he said, sharpish but not nasty. "You're worr . . . Oh."

He got it. I was glad it was dark, because neither of us had to try to look at the other. I could just lay there and stare at the ceiling and feel like the world's prize half-wit dog.

After a while, Felix said softly, "What are you really trying to ask?"

Powers and saints, why do I start these things? But he didn't sound like he was getting ready to tear into me, so I said, "I ain't trying to pry or nothing."

"I know that," and I thought maybe he was smiling a little.

"And maybe it's just that I don't know nothing about it. I mean, maybe it ain't no big deal, and I'm just—"

"Mildmay. You're babbling. Which you don't do."

Oh fuck me sideways. I took a breath and just said it: "Whatever thing you got yourself into must've been pretty nasty. I mean, going by the bruises and all. And I just wanted . . . I mean, I figure you ain't hurt too bad 'cause you're moving okay and all and not feverish or nothing, but . . . I mean . . . *inside*, you know, in your *self*, are you okay?"

Felix said, "You're asking about my feelings," like he couldn't quite believe it.

I put my arm over my eyes, because even in the dark I was blushing. "I guess so."

"I'm not going to go crazy again," he said, and I winced, because I'd been hoping he wouldn't figure out I was worried about that. And, you know, I wasn't worried a *lot*. But he'd told me what Strych had done and there was that stupid fucking dream about the wolves that wouldn't leave me alone, and I didn't know. I'd never been into the whole tarquins and martyrs thing, so I didn't know how you could tell when it felt like rape and when it didn't. But with the way he hadn't been looking at me, I'd been afraid that maybe this had felt more like rape than otherwise.

"I know that," I said, even though I'd been worried. "I was just . . ."

"Worried about me," he said, and his voice was kind of funny, light and a little unsteady and even more breathless than usual.

"Felix?" And now I was worried all over again. I sat up, and would've got up and gone over to him, except that I saw the white blotch of his hand come up.

"I'm all right," he said, like what he meant was *Leave me alone*. "I just hadn't . . . well, I suppose I hadn't expected you to care."

My jaw dropped, but before I could figure out what the fuck to say, he went on: "I didn't mean that the way it sounded. I know you care. I meant, I didn't expect you to . . ." I heard him take a deep breath, the same way I had. "Prostitution is a filthy business."

"So's murder for hire," I said, sharper maybe than I should've, but powers and blessed fucking saints, where the fuck was he getting the idea I thought I was better than him?

"I know," he said. "I just meant, the details are . . . sordid and humiliating and I wouldn't blame you if you were repulsed by me."

He sped up as he went, so the last half of the sentence was basically one word. Which told me I'd better go slow and careful and think about what I was saying before I said it.

"This isn't about—"

"No!" he said fiercely, although even if the lamps had been lit, I wouldn't've been able to see his face, because he had his head buried in his hands. "I was . . . I was wrong. I have to respect your choices, and I forgot that."

"You pushed," I said.

"Yes. And I shouldn't have. I wasn't . . . I wasn't thinking clearly."

*You were lonely and scared and hating yourself.* But I didn't say that. "So we're not talking about why I won't sleep with you."

"No," he said, not as fierce now. "Not that."

"We're talking about being friends. About why I'm your friend."

"Are you?"

"Well, I try to be," I said, and that made him laugh a little.

"I know. Sometimes I make it difficult."

"Sometimes you do," I said, not agreeing to be mean, but because it was the truth. "But what I was trying to say was, I *do* want to be your friend. And I'm not gonna change my mind or think less of you or something, just because you've done stuff you ain't proud of. I mean, we can trade if you want. You tell me how much money you made fucking, and I'll tell you how much money I made killing people."

"I don't know. I never saw the money."

"Yeah, well, neither did I."

I don't know which one of us started laughing first, and I'm not sure how long it took us to calm down again. But finally, Felix said, "You know, for depraved and unnatural monsters, we're not very good at it."

"Prob'ly time to try something else," I said and yawned—it's the worst of the Winter Fever, how even when you can breathe again and you don't feel like shit all the fucking time, you can't lift a hairbrush without having to lie down for an hour. "I'm just saying, if you want to talk to me, you can. I'd . . ." And I was sleepy enough that telling the truth wasn't as hard as it'd been. "I'd like to listen. If it's what you want."

"Thank you," Felix said, and I knew for once he'd heard me right.

# Chapter 8

## *Felix*

The schedule by which trains ran in Corambis was so complex that they published it in a book, a neat little sextodecimo volume bound in green leather. It was called *Ottersham's Compendium of the Corambin Railway System* and referred to in conversation as if it were itself a person, as in *Ottersham says the train to Copperton only runs on alternate Venerdies*. I was told by the clerk at Waddilow & Berowne that the Usaran savages consulted Ottersham as an oracle; although I wasn't sure I believed it, I would have liked a detailed explanation of the numerological system of divination they allegedly used.

I purchased Ottersham, and with it, a smaller, paperbound pamphlet entitled *Ottersham's Errata for the Second of the One Hundred Fifty-second*, which was an appendix detailing all the points at which Ottersham was wrong. "It's mostly the Insurgence," said the clerk, "and things will probably get back to normal fairly soon now that we've got a governor again and everything. But for now, you'd better check the *Errata*."

The journey Mildmay, Corbie, and I were facing—and for which Corbie was little better prepared than we were, as she had never been out of Bernatha in her life—was a complicated one. We had to take a train from Bernatha to Wildar, and then take a different train from Wildar to Esmer. Trying to coordinate the schedules of the Bernatha–Wildar and the Wildar–Esmer trains simply in Ottersham was hard enough; adding the *Errata* to the mix made the whole thing so nightmarish I had surrendered and thrown myself on the mercy of the ticket clerks at Clave, Bernatha's train station, where it had turned out the conundrum was even more complicated than I had realized, for Esmer had three train stations, Lily-of-Mar, Fornivant, and Pollidean, and I had no idea which one I wanted.

"I need to go to the Institution," I said helplessly, bracing myself for the inevitable *Which Institution?*

But in fact the clerk, a plump young redheaded woman with tawny, freckled skin, said, "Oh, then you want Lily-of-Mar," and proceeded with perfect aplomb to book three tickets from Clave to Dennifell Station in Wildar, and then from Dennifell to Lily-of-Mar, as if navigating Ottersham and its *Errata* were the simplest thing in the world. "There. The train leaves Clave at nine-thirty-two on Martedy, and you'll reach Lily-of-Mar at twenty-twenty-seven," she said. "If you're going to the Institution, you'll want a hotel in Ingry Dominion, which is cheaper than anything in Mar anyway. Would recommend the Golden Hare, if you don't already have somewhere in mind. Is clean and cheap and the landlady's the widow of a railroad man."

She handed me a folder with the tickets: crimson pasteboard printed with black. "Thank you," I said. "You've been very kind."

Her smile was beautiful. "Is why I like my job."

I'd told Corbie to meet us at Clave, for I suspected Mildmay would be as much as I could manage, if not rather more. Not that he had any wish to be difficult, but it was still as much as he could do to get to the lavatory and back unaided. I wasn't sure we should be making the journey to Esmer so soon, but Mildmay was determined. And I could not help admitting, when he asked me outright, that I wanted desperately to get away from the ticking of the Clock of Eclipses. Every time I tried to go into a trance, the ticking shook me out again. I couldn't ignore it; I couldn't work with it—I'd tried that once. But not a second time. It showed me everything drenched in noirance, showed me the rubies, still hidden in Mildmay's boot, pulsing to the rhythm the clock laid down.

Mildmay said, and his dreams concurred, that the Clock of Eclipses reminded him too much of Juggernaut and the Bastion. "I ain't gonna get better with it ticking at me all the time, so let's just *go*, okay?"

And I'd said yes.

I'd hired a vinagry, paying extra to cross the causeway rather than having to negotiate Mildmay in and out of a gondol—even though I found vinagries both ridiculous and disturbing. I perfectly understood the satirical engraving I saw in one of the newspapers, of a man, in harness and blinkers, pulling a vinagry in which a horse, elegantly dressed, reclined at leisure. But it was an economical mode of transportation, and sensible for Bernatha, and it would get Mildmay to Clave Station without exhausting him.

Getting him down the stairs was disaster enough. We'd known his lame leg was going to be worse after all this time confined to bed, and thought we were prepared. He had the cane Rinaldo of Fiora had given him, and I was right beside him, ready to support him if he needed it. But with the first step down, his knee joint made an ugly popping noise, and his leg simply buckled. I made a frantic grab and caught his coat collar, but if he hadn't had the reflexes and sense to throw his weight backwards, all I would have accomplished was falling down the stairs with him, and while misery might love company, that seemed a bit excessive.

"Fuck," Mildmay said shakily after a moment. "Sorry about that."

"Are you all right?"

"I think so. Powers. Ain't had that happen in a long time."

"It's happened before?"

"Back in Troia," he said, as if it hardly mattered, and Mrs. Lettice appeared at the bottom of the stairs with a cluster of maids behind her, wanting to know if we were all right.

In the end, the vinagry man came inside, and he and I carried Mildmay down the stairs. Mildmay hated it but endured, his face red and his teeth digging into his lower lip in a way that made his scar even uglier. He was delighted, though, by the vinagry, saying, "Wouldn't this make the Handsome Men as sick as dogs?" as we steadied him into it. I had no idea what he meant, but I was glad for anything that made him happy. I noticed when I climbed in after him, though, that all the color had gone from his face, and he leaned back into the cushions and shut his eyes.

"We don't have to leave today," I said guiltily, "If you'd rather—"

"What, go back up all them stairs? No thanks." He opened his eyes and frowned at me. "I'm fine. I mean, all I got to do is sit down all day anyhow, right?"

"Yes, but—"

"Felix," he said, in a particularly long-suffering tone. "Let me make my own choices here, okay?"

"Right," I said, and was glad to be able to turn away and watch the vinagry man strapping our carpetbags onto the back of his cart; I'd hidden the rubies in the bottom of one, bundled into the toe of a sock. Mildmay muttered something under his breath, but I didn't hear it clearly and I didn't ask him to repeat himself.

Mildmay looked eagerly at everything, even if he didn't have the energy to lean forward, and I told him about the things I could—things Corbie had told me and things I had read in Lilion. As we rattled across the causeway, he frowned. "Weren't we in a boat on the way over, or did I just dream that?"

"No, we were in a boat. A gondol." I pointed at one sculling past toward the Crait.

"You must've hated the fuck out of that," he said.

"Oh, don't sound so gleeful about it."

"Well, considering what I had to do to get you in the boat out to the *Morskaiakrov*, I'm thinking this is payback. I'm just sorry I missed it."

"You should be," I said darkly. "Because it will never happen again." And I felt rewarded sevenfold for the misery of that crossing by his laughter.

Clave was a vast brick building, like a tunnel with all the surrounding earth removed, people streaming in and out of it as steadily as ants. "Good thing I left plenty of time," I said, once we were standing on the pavement with our bags and the vinagry man had been hailed by another patron and trotted off.

"Um," said Mildmay. "Yeah." He edged a little closer to me.

"Are you all right?"

He glowered at me. "Ask me that again, and I swear by all the powers I'm gonna break your nose."

"I'll take that as a yes," I said and grinned at him.

He lost hold of his glower, said, "Yeah, okay. I'm good enough to get by on—just ain't looking forward to this none, you know?"

I did know, could imagine what an ordeal this must represent in his fragile state. But we were already beginning to attract stares. I picked up our bags, hesitated a moment—but the worst he'd do was curse at me—and said, "If you want to, er, hold my arm, I won't take it amiss."

"Powers, do I look that bad?" He seemed astonished more than anything else; I winced a little at the evidence that he knew just how much I disliked being touched.

I said, "I don't want to get separated," which was true.

"Okay," Mildmay said, eyeing the crowds. "I can see that." He tucked his free hand neatly under my elbow, and I had to admit I was heartened by the contact, too.

Inside, there were people everywhere, rushing from one unknown place to another, arguing with ticket clerks, haranguing men in crimson and black uniforms with gold trim, exchanging greetings or farewells, standing in clumps and staring at us, which made Mildmay's grip on my arm tighten until I said, "Ouch," and he eased off.

Corbie found us—I was, as Fleur had once remarked, as good as a burning torch in a crowd—and came rushing over. "The Duke of Murtagh's taking our train!" she blurted. "And I think he's got Lord Rothmarlin with him!"

"Good morning, Corbie," I said dryly. "Did you sleep well? And what in the name of the Virgin of Sothen did you do to your hair?" Instead of the untidy curls I was used to, Corbie's hair was slicked flat against her skull and pulled into a smooth and complicated knot at the back of her head. It was also several shades darker. She was wearing a dark coat and a dark sheath skirt, none of the lace or exuberant colors of her normal wardrobe; she looked, in fact, nearly indistinguishable from any other woman in the station.

"Hair pomade," she said, a trifle guiltily. "Didn't want to go off to Esmer looking like a half-breed jezebel."

"Half-breed?" Mildmay said.

"Yeah, you know. Half Ygressine. With the hair and the nose and all." She looked from Mildmay to me very doubtfully. "You guys hadn't noticed?"

Mildmay and I exchanged a glance. "We'd noticed your hair and, er, so on," I said, "but I suppose we didn't know what it meant."

"Means my daddy was a sailor off one of the Ygressine ships that come in and out of Patient Harbor every damn day. It's all I know about him."

"I don't even know that much," Mildmay said matter-of-factly, and from her puzzled look, he turned to me. "Didn't you tell her?"

"It didn't seem relevant."

"Powers," he said. "You mean you didn't want to talk about it." He turned back to Corbie and said, still perfectly matter-of-fact, "Our mother, his and mine, was a whore. I don't know nothing about my father except maybe he had green eyes."

"We should get to the train," I said, knowing it was obvious I was changing the subject and not caring.

But Mildmay said, "Oh powers and saints, with the crowds. Yeah. We'd better."

It was easier than we'd feared. Mildmay and I were such obvious foreigners—even in Corambin clothing—that people's inclination was to stop and stare, thus impeding other travelers, but giving Mildmay, Corbie, and me a clear path. And when someone saw and recognized the tattoos on my hands, people began actively getting out of my way, although I couldn't even guess what they thought I might do. I'd have to ask Corbie about those Mélusinien novels her friend had recounted to her.

"Just like home," Mildmay said, only loud enough for me to hear.

"I beg your pardon?"

"You think people in the Lower City don't scramble to get out of y'all's way? Only difference is, they don't stop and gawk." He was glowering again, this time in disapproval of the Bernathans' bad manners; for no reason I could explain, that cheered me up immensely.

There were signs pointing the way, handsomely painted in crimson and gold: "DEPARTURES FOR WILDAR." They led us to a hall running the length of the station building, open to daylight at both ends. The train, the same brilliant crimson and gold as the signs, was perfectly alarming, a manufactory's dream of Yrob the World Snake. The head of the train was jet-black with crimson and gold trim, long-snouted with a wide-mouthed chimney sprouting like a tree from its middle. I supposed it had to be the engine, the thing which somehow moved without horses to pull it, and which would, in its turn, pull all these carriages after it. It was making terrible noises, as if it had to give birth before it could start and its child had iron claws.

"Sacred bleeding fuck," Mildmay said very softly. I was inclined to agree.

Our good fortune was that the servants of the train were professionally accustomed to people who had never ridden, or seen, a train before. We were handed from one polite gentleman in a crimson and gold uniform to another and ended up eventually in a second-class compartment despite having third-class tickets because the last of the polite gentlemen, alarmed by Mildmay's increasingly grayish pallor, prevailed upon the occupants to share.

The compartment had been booked by two women, and they watched us with—at first—mistrustful gazes. They seemed reassured by Corbie edging into the compartment after me, and Mildmay was clearly not malingering, having gone a dreadful dead-fish-belly-white and needing my support simply to sit down without falling. He managed a nod at the two women, and then did not so much lean back as collapse into the corner, and shut his eyes. After a few minutes, when his breathing had evened out, he said, "I'm okay," without opening his eyes and, as far as I could determine, fell instantly asleep.

I let my own breath out slowly and turned to smile at our audience, feeling Corbie's anxiety beside me. The younger woman blushed and averted her eyes; the elder returned my smile and said, nodding at Mildmay, "Will he be all right?"

"He's recovering from the, er, from pleuriny. He'll be fine. I'm Felix Harrowgate. He's my brother, Mildmay Foxe. And this is"—Corbie's foot connected briskly with my ankle—"Miss Corbie."

"Frances Leverick," said the older woman. "And my traveling companion is Olive Bridger."

The younger woman managed a mumble and a much weaker smile.

Miss Leverick I judged to be forty or so, Miss Bridger probably Mildmay's age or a little younger. Both of them had the heavy-jawed squareness to their faces that I had observed to be typical of Corambins. Miss Bridger was remarkable only for her flax-pale hair, being otherwise indistinguishable from any other young Corambin bourgeoise; I wondered if she, like Corbie, was of Ygressine blood. Miss Leverick's face had considerably more character, laugh and frown lines both; her eyes were light brown, flecked with gold, and very sharp. They were both dressed respectably in dark suits; Corbie had judged her wardrobe well. Miss Bridger wore some unbecoming pearls; Miss Leverick's only jewelry was a ring, amber set in silver, on her right index finger. As far as I had been able to determine, rings had no thaumaturgical meaning in Corambis; I was fairly certain in any event that Miss Leverick was annemer. Miss Bridger, on the other hand . . .

I leaned forward, caught and held her attention. Her eyes widened; she jerked her chin up, breaking eye contact, and I sat back.

"I'm glad," I said, "that you've learned that much." I had not, when Malkar found me. And then my words, my tone, echoed in my mind, and I was chilled by how much like Malkar I sounded, a predator deigning to toy with his prey.

"Everyone learns," Miss Bridger said tightly. "Resisting a warlock is the first thing we're taught."

"Warlock?" Miss Leverick said. "Olive?"

"He ain't!" Corbie said indignantly.

"He tried to enthrall me," Miss Bridger said.

"Oh please," I said. "I did no such thing."

"He wouldn't," Corbie said, still indignant. "He's my teacher."

Miss Bridger turned rather sharply to look at Corbie; they locked stares, reminding me irresistibly of a pair of cats squaring off for a fight. "Ladies," I said, kicking Corbie's ankle in my turn, and they looked away from each other quickly, both flushing.

"I'm sorry," Miss Bridger said, diffident again. "But that's what warlocks do, and that's how it starts. It's why you must never look another magician in the eye for too long." And, faltering, "It's terribly rude."

"I apologize," I said stiffly, well aware that although I had certainly not been trying to enthrall the child, I had been bullying her. As Cabaline wizards habitually did to determine who ought to defer to whom. It was an ugly habit anyway, and in Corambis it looked as if it might get me in more trouble than I could talk myself out of.

"You must be a magician, then," Miss Leverick said, her voice carefully neutral.

"Wizard," I corrected and, bracing myself, showed them my palms.

Miss Bridger actually gasped. Miss Leverick said, "That will teach me to dismiss Una Semmence's novels as nothing but lurid nonsense. Are they really . . . ?"

She started to reach out, then stopped and looked at me. "Go ahead," I said; I owed them this much for being so dramatic about it.

Miss Leverick's touch was very light. "How fascinating," she said. "Is it true they're done with magic?"

"They're done with needles," I said and pulled my hands back, resisting the urge to tuck them against my sides.

"I beg your pardon," said Miss Leverick. "I didn't mean to make you uncomfortable. You must get tired of all the ridiculous notions people have. Have you been in Corambis long?"

"Only a few weeks," I said, returning her smile. "And that mostly confined to a hotel room. My brother fell ill coming over the pass."

"Oh how dreadful," said Miss Leverick. "And traveling is tiring enough without adding illness into the equation."

"Do you travel a great deal?" I asked, hoping to distract her away from my affairs. Corbie was still staring fixedly at the door of the compartment, face and neck an unbecoming blotchy red; there would be no help from her for a while yet.

But my stratagem worked very well, as it turned out Miss Leverick had traveled from one end of Corambis to the other. She had even been south of the Perblanches—once—although she said apologetically that she had found things very uncomfortable and had no particular desire to do so again.

At that point, the train began to move—with an appalling lurch that both Miss Leverick and Miss Bridger assured me was normal. Corbie looked more than a little wild-eyed; Mildmay didn't even twitch.

"Have you not traveled on a train before, Mr. Harrowgate?" Miss Bridger said. Again like a cat, she was now carefully ignoring Corbie.

"I'd never seen a train before this morning," I said, entranced by the rapidly moving view out the window.

"Oh," said Miss Bridger, another little gasp.

"The railways don't extend past the Perblanches," Miss Leverick said, "and as far as I know, no other people have developed steam-powered travel. Am I correct, Mr. Harrowgate?"

"I've certainly never heard of such a thing before," I said.

They left us alone for a while, as Corbie and I watched the buildings and streets of St. Melior gradually give way to countryside: farmland and then, after perhaps an hour, open meadows which then shifted again to farmland and then another city unfurled itself around us.

"Granderfold," said Miss Leverick before I had to ask.

Granderfold was smaller than St. Melior, and not nearly as prosperous. The buildings looked older, and most of them could have used a fresh coat of paint. I took the opportunity of our stop to fetch Lilion out of my pocket and unfold the map. Corbie leaned in, and we read the names of the towns: Bernatha, Granderfold, Wildar, Kilrey, Skimfair, Follenfant, Esmer. And the Forest of Nauleverer in the middle of it all.

Miss Leverick and Miss Bridger returned from a brief promenade along the platform, and Miss Leverick said with immediate interest, "What a fantastic map! That must be Lilion's *Guidebook*. He was a surveyor for the Company, so he actually went to the places he writes about."

I thought of Challoner cribbing from Virenque. "Quite. 'The Company'?"

"The Corambin Railway Company, sorry. My father also worked for them, and I've never entirely lost the habit of thinking of them as a sort of combined god and scapegoat. Whenever anything went wrong in Father's life, it was always the Company to blame. In his old age, he even blamed them for his gout."

The train jerked into motion again. This time Mildmay made a faint sound of protest, but did not stir. Miss Leverick said, "We reach Wildar in half an hour or so. Is that your destination?"

"No," I said, "we're going to Esmer."

"Oh!" said Miss Bridger. "So are we!"

"Three cheers for you," Corbie muttered, but I didn't think either of the women heard her.

"You're welcome to share our compartment on the Esmer train," Miss Leverick said. "It will certainly be more restful for your brother."

"That's very kind of you," I said. "Thank you."

Dennifell Station was even worse than Clave; it was, Miss Leverick informed me, the Company's southern hub and the busiest station in all of Corambis: "Esmer has more traffic, but three stations to sort it through." Mildmay was groggy—not insensible, but truly not capable of managing by himself—and Corbie was showing a distressing tendency to cling, which I diverted by giving her to Mildmay to lean on. Miss Leverick, I decided, was almost certainly a saint, for she led us through the chaos of Dennifell and got us established in a compartment that was the mirror image of the one we'd left, all without turning a hair. I didn't even have a chance to worry about missing the train until after we were all sitting down again and I'd unfolded Lilion's map.

From Wildar to Kilrey was an hour; Corbie and I again watched out the window while Mildmay slept and Miss Leverick and Miss Bridger talked quietly. As we left Kilrey, Miss Leverick said, "We stop for lunch in Skimfair. Would you and your companions care to join us, Mr. Harrowgate?"

"We would be delighted," I said promptly, but couldn't help checking my pocket watch. "Lunch? Isn't it a trifle early?"

"There are no stops in Nauleverer," Miss Leverick said, "and we don't reach Follenfant until seventeen-thirty."

"Ah. I see." I looked at Nauleverer sprawling across the middle of the map. "Lilion says it's all wild?"

"There are some villages," Miss Leverick said, "but all near the edges. No one lives in Nauleverer Deep."

"There are stories," Miss Bridger said.

"Oh, not just stories," said Miss Leverick. "I don't remember the final count of casualties for the laying of the Follenfant–Skimfair line, but it was appalling. More than twice that of the Esmer–Whallan line, which is I don't know how many times as long. One of my students was a spike driver, and he says the forest hated them. When he'll talk about it at all."

"Nobody cuts wood in Nauleverer," Miss Bridger said. "Not deeper than you can see the edge from."

"And this train journey is safe?" I said, half-suspecting that they were merely teasing me.

"The rails are iron," Miss Bridger said, as if that explained everything.

"And . . . ?" I said.

"Iron for warding," Miss Leverick said.

Iron for warding was sheerest nonsense, otherwise every wizard in the Mirador would be wearing iron rings. But I didn't want to start an argument with an annemer and an untrained student; I created a diversion by opening the *Guidebook* to the entry on Nauleverer and reading them what Lilion had written, as I'd read it to Mildmay in our room at the Fiddler's Fox.

"Good old Lilion," Miss Leverick said fondly. "Didn't believe in anything that didn't bite him first. I wonder what stories *he* heard."

"Stories?" said Mildmay, coming suddenly alert. Then, "Powers, where *are* we?"

"Good morning," I said. "I'll remember this in future if I ever need to get your attention in a hurry." He ducked his chin, blushing a little, and I answered his question: "We are somewhere between Kilrey and Skimfair, where we are going to have lunch with Miss Leverick and Miss Bridger." Mildmay looked warily from one to the other; I remembered belatedly how much he disliked having strangers watch him eat and added, "And perhaps we can prevail on them to tell us stories about Nauleverer. Here," and I directed his attention to the map.

He forgot instantly about his self-consciousness, and over his bowed head, I said to Miss Leverick, "You said one of your students was a spike driver. What do you teach?"

The answer to that question brought us into Skimfair; clearly Miss Leverick had been drawn to teaching by a natural propensity to lecture. She was employed by something called the Society for the Advancement of Universal Education, and she gave lectures on Corambin history to chapters of the Society all over the country. When she wasn't traveling, she taught a history class. "In the evenings," she said.

"For people who work during the day," Miss Bridger added, hero-worship naked in her eyes. Miss Bridger was the daughter of the Society's chapter president in St. Melior. The occasion of Miss Leverick giving a lecture in St. Melior had been utilized to provide Miss Bridger a companion for her trip to Esmer and the Institution, where she was starting at the Women's Thaumaturgical College. Beside me, Corbie shifted, but did not speak.

"Our goal is particularly to reach those people who did not have opportunities for conventional schooling," said Miss Leverick. "I teach a great many retired railway workers, house servants—I have one student who began as a chimney sweep and is now a jockey."

"So anybody can come?" Mildmay asked.

I startled; I hadn't realized that he was paying attention, much less that he was interested.

He'd made an effort to speak clearly, and Miss Leverick went up in my estimation, for she made a corresponding effort to understand him, and did not look to me for a translation. "Yes," she said. "There is a minimal fee for the classes—we have to rent a room, and there's the matter of supplies—but the lectures are always free."

Mildmay nodded his thanks and went back to the map. Miss Leverick watched him for a moment, then said to me, "It has been very painful, these past few indictions, giving lectures on the historical schisms between Corambis and Caloxa. I am grateful, of course, that the Insurgence has ended without further bloodshed, but I remain convinced that if the Convocation would pay better attention to its own history, it need not have happened at all."

"Ah," I said weakly, and counted myself fortunate that we were slowing to a halt in Skimfair before Miss Leverick could launch into one of her classroom lectures.

Lunch was at the station; much of Skimfair's economy seemed to be centered around providing food for railway travelers, and Miss Leverick said we would find the same to be true in Follenfant. She was clearly known and liked by the station staff; it was not accidental that we ended up at a secluded corner table with a servitor saying in a confidential murmur, "You don't want the fish today, Miss Frances. Fairlee put too much pepper in again."

We followed the course of wisdom, and let Miss Leverick order for the table. The food—not fish, but a chicken en casserole—arrived promptly, and I reminded Miss Leverick that there were stories about Nauleverer.

"Of course," she said. "There was one I remember, about how you must never go to sleep in the Forest of Nauleverer. That if you lie down for too long, the roots of the trees will reach up and pull you under the earth. Old Mrs. Worthing used to say that all that was ever found of people who slept in Nauleverer were a few well-polished bones."

She went on easily, and we learned about the wolfmen said to live in the forest's heart, the streams whose water was as beautiful as daylight and as lethal as nightshade (which was also said to grow in the forest in vast quantities), the will-o'-the-wisps who tempted unwary travelers off the path, and a dozen other such stories.

"And what about the, um, doom that came to Corybant?" I said, remembering Lilion's dry skepticism.

"Well, that depends very much on whom you ask," said Miss Leverick. "Some don't believe there was ever a city in Nauleverer at all—our records before the reign of Lessander the Archivist are spotty at best, and so there's no conclusive proof that Corybant is more than a cautionary tale."

"Cautioning about what?"

"The dangers of machines," Miss Leverick said, dropping her voice dramatically. "The story is—well, the most common story, for as I said, there are several. The common story is that the people of Corybant built a great machine which could move by itself."

"Like a train?" said Mildmay.

"No," said Miss Leverick. "Well, maybe. But not on rails. The Automaton of Corybant could walk. It was the guardian of the city and walked the streets at night, keeping the people safe."

"But," I said.

"Yes, exactly. But. The story is that the Automaton went mad."

"It went *mad*? How can a machine go mad?"

"They send people mad," Mildmay said. "Like Nemesis."

"Not the same thing. It went mad?"

Miss Leverick spread her hands. "It is the doom that came to Corybant. Their machine that they had built to move and act as people do went mad as people do. It destroyed the city down to its foundation stones, all in one night. And it slew every person who crossed its path. Some say the knocken are the descendants of those who escaped."

"The knocken?" said Mildmay.

"I imagine Olive knows more about the knocken than I do," Miss Leverick said, and Miss Bridger blushed and murmured, but did screw up enough confidence to speak. As we finished our meal, she explained the knocken, gnarled, anthropophagous creatures who lived along the course of the Wildar River. She even related how a childhood friend swore he had once seen a knocken peering at him from a sewer grating in Kilrey. "And a man my father knows who works for the Wildar Water Utility, he says that sometimes when they find bodies in the sewers, there are bite marks on them that don't look like rat teeth. But," Miss Bridger added scrupulously, "he may have just been saying that to scare me."

Miss Leverick and I raised our eyebrows at each other, but held our tongues, letting Miss Bridger tell us how the knocken were supposed to come from the part of the forest that had been logged long ago. "I never heard that about Corybant. It's the spirits of the trees seeking revenge," she said.

We were all silent for a moment, and then Miss Leverick consulted the watch she wore at her lapel and said, "We'd best get back to the train."

Corbie went ahead with Miss Leverick—pointedly *not* with Miss Bridger—while I waited for Mildmay to brace himself up. When I found a way to get letters to the Mirador, I would have to remember to write to Rinaldo and tell him how passionately grateful I was for the cane he had given my brother. "How are you doing?" I said, hoping it would be a more acceptable question than *Are you all right?*

The look Mildmay gave me under his eyebrows told me he knew exactly what I was thinking, but he said amiably enough, "I'm okay. Think I slept better on the train than I did in bed."

He looked better, no longer tinged with gray, but I was careful to let him set the pace as we went back to our compartment. He looked up and down the crimson length of the train with keen interest, said, "Hey, Felix, what runs this thing? Is it magic?"

"Steam power," I said, remembering Miss Leverick's comment, "but I have no idea how they generate it."

"You mean like a laundry boiler? What if it busts?"

He looked genuinely worried; I said, "I doubt that will happen, but we can ask Miss Leverick. She seems to know a great deal about the railways."

"She's a nice lady," he said neutrally.

"I'm sure we can find the money, if you want to attend her class."

"You're sure these hocuses in Esmer won't just throw you in jail or something?" He looked even more worried; I hoped the idea hadn't been preying on him all the way from Mélusine.

"It's not heresy here, remember?"

"Yeah, but—"

"Later," I said, for I did not want to have this discussion in front of an audience.

"Okay," he said and let me steady him into the carriage.

---

There was a forest near Arabel; I had gone there with Malkar to be taught the names and properties of the trees and plants. It had been nothing compared to the Forest of Nauleverer, like a single ragged militiaman beside the massed and shining armies of the Emperor.

Within minutes of entering the forest, the train was wrapped about in darkness as thick and sharp as night, and a polite crimson and gold gentleman came to light the lamps in our compartment. Looking out the window, I could see only the shadowy and massive shapes of the trees, but I felt the mikkary with all the distinctness my eyes could not provide. "And it goes on like this?" I said involuntarily.

"Six hours," said Miss Leverick. "And pray that nothing goes wrong."

# Chapter 9

## *Felix*

But, of course, something did.

It started, so far as any of us knew, with a juddering, screeching, howling halt, so abrupt that we had no chance to brace ourselves—and I was not sure it would have mattered even if we had. Corbie and Mildmay and I were thrown forward onto Miss Leverick and Miss Bridger, and there was nothing I could do about my elbow colliding with Miss Bridger's ribs. There was a yelp from the direction of Miss Leverick, and then the lights went out, and all five of us were jerked off the bench and onto the floor. My back thumped against the opposite seat. Miss Bridger got inadvertent revenge for my elbow when her knee hit my groin an instant before the rest of her weight landed solidly on my solar plexus. I made a painful, keening whine between my teeth, lost under Miss Bridger's scream, and then the train was finally still.

I couldn't find *up*, but I shoved and scrabbled sideways out from under Miss Bridger and called witchlight. I would have liked to have claimed cool-headed pragmatism—if anyone had asked—but it was as much animal panic as getting away from Miss Bridger's weight had been. I discovered I had pressed myself up against the door of the compartment, somehow crawling over Corbie in the process; Corbie and Miss Bridger were a heap of dark cloth and straggling flaxen braids in the middle; and over by the window, Mildmay and Miss Leverick were as entangled as the last king of Cymellune in the coils of the Thalassant Wyrm. Someone was cursing in a steady and very inventive mutter; I realized after a moment's blankness that it was Miss Leverick.

"Miss Leverick?" I said, although I could barely get enough breath to form the words.

Her invective broke off abruptly, and she raised her head. Nothing ever looked quite normal by witchlight, but I did not think that entirely accounted for the sallow cast of her complexion.

"Are you all right?" I said and winced. The question got more inane every time it fell out of my mouth.

Her mouth compressed into a straight line. "I seem," she said thinly, "to have broken my wrist."

❧

Half an hour later, matters were not quite so dire. The lights were back on. Polite crimson and gold gentlemen had come around with complimentary cups of tea, and a practitioner had been found—a shabby, worn-out-looking woman traveling third class—to splint Miss Leverick's wrist and encourage her vi. Remarkably, Miss Leverick was the worst of the casualties, along with a scullery maid in the galley who had been scalded. "Not too badly," the practitioner said reassuringly. "The girl must have reflexes like a cat."

The crimson and gold gentlemen also provided explanations: the train had stopped because of a fallen tree across the tracks. "It may be some time before we can drag it clear," they said apologetically, from which Miss Leverick and I deduced that by "tree" they meant "behemoth."

"Shouldn't we help?" Mildmay said.

"By 'we,' of course, you mean me," I said. "*You* couldn't help lift a teacup at the moment." Since he was holding his cup in both hands, he was hard-pressed to argue with me.

"I'd help," Corbie said, but then looked worried. "But I don't know what I could do."

Miss Leverick said, "If they need help from the passengers, they'll ask. But the engine-practitioner can probably handle it."

"Engine-practitioner?" I asked.

"Every train has two enginists," Miss Leverick said, "the men who actually drive the train. One is annemer. He deals with the throttle and the brake and watches the track for exactly such things as monumental tree trunks. The other is a magician-practitioner who watches over the magic which mediates between the steam boiler and the gears of the train. And, of course, they've found that having a magician along comes in handy more often than you'd think."

"We're like a pocketknife that way," I murmured. Happily, Miss Bridger had at that same moment asked Miss Leverick how long she thought the delay might last, and Mildmay was the only one who heard me. He snorted and bumped my shoulder with his.

"I don't know," Miss Leverick said wearily.

"What if we're stuck here all night?" Corbie asked, even more worriedly.

I said, "I observe that there are people strolling beside the train. Miss Bridger, Miss Corbie, why don't we walk down and examine the situation for ourselves?"

"That's an excellent idea, Mr. Harrowgate," Miss Leverick said gratefully. "Go on, Olive. You can report back."

Miss Bridger acquiesced, frowning. Corbie bounced to her feet. I said to Mildmay, "No, don't even think about getting up. I can take a walk without your supervision."

"Okay, okay," he said, raising his hands in mock surrender. Just as we were leaving the compartment, he added, eyes gleaming wickedly, "Don't get eaten by bears."

## *Kay*

In my dreams, I was still sighted; I dreamed of fighting: blood and the screams of horses and the terrible moans of dying men. And then I dreamed of the Usaran woman who had come to my tent in the middle of the night and offered herself to me if I would release her brother, who was a prince, a *cephar* as the Usara styled such things. In the dream I saw her clearly, although in truth the dark-lantern had shadowed as much as it had illuminated: wide hips, heavy breasts, everything in shades of copper and gold. She pushed her breasts up with her hands, showing me the dark discs of her nipples. She was beautiful, and it cost me nothing to deny her.

In reality, I had told her to put her dress on and go, and she had put her dress on and attacked me with the knife she had concealed in its folds. That night had ended with the cephar keening over his sister's body and me getting seventeen stitches in my right arm. She had almost been fast enough.

But in the dream, she merely turned away for a moment, pushing her fingers through her long, dark hair as she arched her back, and when she turned again to face me, she was Gerrard, smiling at me as I'd seen him a thousand times, but naked and aroused.

I tried to protest, looked around frantically for something to offer him: a cloak, a blanket, anything to cover that rampant nakedness. And when he spoke, it was that Usaran woman's words, though his own voice: "Do I not please you, Cougar-cephar?"

I realized that I was naked, too, and that he would see the truth in my body's response. Was no sin to have a taste for the violet-boys; sin was a matter of the spirit, not the body. Was sinful to deny the body's truth. Was sinful to make a mockery of the sacred love between men and women by confusing the body's needs with the spirit's, and I feared Gerrard would see that sin writ large upon my face.

He stepped forward.

I stepped back.

And the world crashed around me; I woke falling, woke blind, woke cramped on the floor of a train compartment with someone's elbow thumping painfully against my head.

"Ouch," said Murtagh.

"What happens?" I said and winced at the plaintiveness of the question.

"I'm not sure," said Murtagh. "The train has stopped and the lights have gone out. And I'm afraid I've fallen on top of you."

"That part I had observed, thank you."

"Well, it's the best I can do at the moment." He picked himself up, regaining his seat, and I began cautiously to follow suit, knowing it was possible I had injured myself and did not yet feel it. Gerrard had been particularly fond of the story of the Usaran ambush which I fought my way out of, then looked down and said to my sergeant-at-arms, *Is a bloody arrow through my leg. When did that happen?* I still had no memory of being shot, although I remembered with great distinctness having the barbed head pushed the rest of the way through my leg so that it could be drawn out.

"Wyatt!" called Murtagh.

"Yes, Your Grace?" Wyatt called back from the other end of the carriage.

"Are you all right?"

"Yes, Your Grace. Shaken but unharmed. As is Tinder."

"Good, good. Would you go see if you can find out what's going on?"

"Yes, Your Grace."

I managed to get back into my seat; as far as I could tell, I was uninjured.

"As if Nauleverer weren't bad enough," said Murtagh.

"Is that where we are?"

"Oh, of course it is. This sort of thing could hardly happen anywhere else."

"Your Grace has no fondness for the forest?"

"No, My Grace does not. I hate it, to be perfectly frank, and if I'd been part of the Convocation of the One Hundred Forty-second, I would have stonewalled the railways until we *all* died of old age. What's that word your friend Intended Marcham used?"

"*Verlain,*" said I.

"*Verlain*, yes. That's how I feel about Nauleverer. We shouldn't be here."

Was not as if, at that moment, we had anything in the way of a choice. After some time, Wyatt returned and said, "There's a tree down across the line, Your Grace. It's enormous. The enginists aren't quite sure how to move it. But the porters are setting the train to rights, and they're going to bring tea to everyone."

"Because nothing is more suitable in a crisis," Murtagh said, but he was gracious to the deeply apologetic porter, and I at least was grateful for the tea.

Murtagh was, for once, more restless than I, and after we'd drunk our tea he said abruptly, "I want to go look at this monstrous tree. Do you want to come? After all, a promenade in Nauleverer is not something one gets the chance at every day."

"True," said I. "Yes, I would like to come."

I had learned, perforce, to trust Murtagh. He helped me down from the carriage, and I took his arm as if I'd been doing so all my life. The air smelled damp, of trees and rocks, of water and rot; there was only the very slightest of breezes, which after the relentless wind of Bernatha was almost a relief. I smelled the engine, too, as we neared the head of the train: hot metal and soot and a sharp crackling smell that I supposed might be the magic that made it run.

I walked in the direction Murtagh led me, and after a while, he said, "May all the angels preserve us. 'Enormous' does not begin to describe this tree. Lying on its side, it's nearly taller than the engine."

"How will they move it?" I asked.

"I imagine that's going to be the job of the engine-practitioner, poor man. If I were him, I'd put in for—*shit!*"

"What?" I said frantically; he had gone tense as wire beneath my hand, and I had never heard him use an obscenity before.

"Nothing," said Murtagh.

"You cannot actually expect me to believe that."

"I, ah . . . I just saw someone I wasn't expecting to see."

"From your reaction, I would guess it was Clara Hume."

He laughed, but it was shaky and not terribly convincing. "No, nothing like that. It's . . . it's no one you know."

"Murtagh, you sound like you've seen a ghost."

"It's not that bad," he said, and he did sound a little better. "It was just the surprise. And I was afraid he'd see me, but I don't think he has."

"You could just tell me," I said, and he twitched and went tense again. "Or not."

"It's not you. It's . . . I don't want Isobel to know."

"Don't want Isobel to know," I repeated slowly, only half-convinced I'd heard him correctly.

"Ah, damnation, I'm just digging myself in deeper every time I open my mouth. Kay. As a friend, will you forget I said anything?"

It took me a moment to find any reply at all. "Are we friends? Truly?"

"I had hoped we were," said Murtagh, and I was still caught between deriding his unexpected naïveté and asking him why in the world he would seek my friendship when the noise came.

It was like no noise I had ever heard in my life, and I could not, either then or later, find words that would describe it fully. It sounded something like a train engine, something like a rockslide, and something like a vast and vastly rusty hinge. I could not tell how far away it was, nor in what direction.

And then Murtagh was dragging me in the direction from which we'd come, his grip like iron and his voice muttering a hoarse prayer. The noise came again; I could tell that it was much closer, and now, underlying it, I could hear a ticking sound, like the cursed ticking of the Clock of Eclipses.

"Blessed Lady, be kind to us in this the hour of our extremity," Murtagh muttered, and I recognized the Caddovian version of the Canticle of Desperation.

"Murtagh," I said, desperate in my turn, "for the love of the Lady and the saints and the angels, what *is* it?"

"I think," said Murtagh, in a thin and horrifically steady voice, "that it's the Automaton of Corybant."

And a voice cried, "*GET DOWN!*"

Murtagh and I dropped like stones. I felt something pass over us, sharp and hot and indescribable, and then hands were dragging me again—away from the shriek of metal and fury, and I cooperated as best I could—and someone was saying, a light, breathless voice, strangely familiar although I could not think why, "That may distract it, but I doubt it will do more. How do I kill it?"

"I don't know." A woman's voice.

"Not helpful, Corbie. Anyone? It's *your* monster. How does it die?"

"There aren't stories about that," said another man's voice, lower-class Corambin by the accent.

"That's just *stupid*," said the breathless voice, with a wealth of feeling. "Well, what about your train here? If it went mad, how would you kill it?"

The lower-class voice must belong to one of the enginists, the practitioner from the way he said promptly, "Burn out the thaumaturgic converter. But I don't know if that thing—"

"I've got to try *something*," said the breathless voice. The woman made an odd protesting squeak.

There was a noise like the end of the world, howling and banging and a rising steam-whistle shriek, and a terrible stench of burning metal, and then nothing. Even the ticking had stopped.

The breathless voice said, thoughtfully, "I think I burned out more than the converter."

## *Mildmay*

What I *wanted* to say to Felix was more along the lines of *Don't go off and leave me here with this nice lady whose wrist I just broke,* but that was gonna fly like a stonemason's kite, so I didn't. And I could even get behind the idea of giving Miss Leverick a break from Miss Bridger—and giving Corbie something else to think about, which the saints know she needed. I just didn't want to be the one left behind.

But I wasn't feeling up for taking a walk, and I couldn't pretend I was. I sat and looked out at the little blotches of light from the windows. After a minute I saw Felix and Corbie and Miss Bridger go past. Corbie looked up and saw me and nudged Felix, who waved at me. I waved back.

And it figured that Miss Leverick wasn't just going to sit there and let me ignore her. She said, "This is a most unfortunate introduction to railway travel, Mr. Foxe. I assure you, I've never broken a limb before."

There was nothing for it. "Sorry 'bout that," I said. "You probably caught my stick just wrong." And I showed her Jashuki's knobby head.

"Even if I did, it's hardly your fault," she said, and she sounded pretty cheerful about it, for a lady with a broken wrist. "That's an interesting cane. Is it Mélusinien?"

"Nah. It comes from the islands."

"Islands?"

Fuck me sideways, Felix, did you have to go and leave me to give the geography lesson? "South. The Imari."

"Could you draw a map?" She was frowning, but she looked interested, and I figured she was probably after anything that could keep her mind off her wrist.

I thought about it. "Well, I s'pose. I mean, so long as you ain't gonna try and navigate by it or nothing."

She smiled and said, "To pass the time, Mr. Foxe," and I figured I was right about what she wanted.

She had a little notebook, kind of like the ones Felix used back home, and a pen, so I turned to a blank page and drew a square up at the top of the page. "That's Mélusine."

"All right."

I drew another square further down the page. "And you go south and get to St. Millefleur. You go further south and you get to where Cymellune used to be."

"Used to be?"

"Yeah, it, um—"

"Corambis is said, in its earliest histories, to have been settled by those fleeing the foretold destruction of Cymellune. So it was actually destroyed?"

"Oh yeah," I said.

"How?"

I looked out the window, but there was no sign of Felix. Fuck. "It got swallowed up by the sea."

"I'm sorry, I didn't quite follow."

"It sank," I said, and dealt with the *s* as best I could.

"It *sank*? Like a boat sinks?"

"Dunno. Felix might could tell you."

She didn't take the bait. "The city fell into the ocean, then?"

"I don't know," I said, spacing the words out careful. "I just know it ain't there now. So here." I drew a sort of spiral. "That's where it was. And here's the way the coast runs now." Which, okay, I was mostly making up, but I'd seen some maps that showed that part of Tibernia, so I didn't feel too awful about it.

"All right," she said, and thank you, Kethe, she was going to let it go.

"So then you go south some more, if you got a boat to go south in, and you get to the Imari." And I had no fucking idea what the Imari looked like, so I drew some circles and told her the names I knew: "Imar Eolyth, Imar Elchevar, Imar Esthivel. There's others, but I don't know 'em. But that's where Jashuki comes from."

"Jashuki?"

"The, um. The *koh*, Rinaldo said it was."

"The what?"

"The, well, this guy," I said, tapping his friendly, ugly head. "He's a kind of guardian or something. The friend who gave the stick to me said he was a friendship spirit."

"How lovely," said Miss Leverick, and she actually sounded like she meant it. And then she looked up at me. "You must have left a great many friends behind when you came to Corambis."

"Um." *Fewer than you'd think* is what I almost said, but I bit my tongue. I settled for "I wasn't gonna let Felix go wandering off by himself."

She smiled. "Is he so feckless?"

I wasn't quite sure what "feckless" meant, but I didn't want to say so. "No common sense," seemed a safe enough answer.

"He's lucky to have you then," she said, and that was when there was this great big burst of green light from somewhere around the front end of the train.

Powers and saints, I nearly fell off the bench again. Miss Leverick twisted around. "What was that?"

"Felix," I said, because it *was*, and I didn't even know if it was the binding-by-forms saying so or just too much fucking experience.

I was trying to get up and Miss Leverick was saying, "Mr. Foxe, I really don't think you ought to," when there was another big fucking burst of green light and this noise like somebody caught a thunderstorm in a soup tureen and the train jerked once, just hard enough to knock me back down on my ass.

Me and Miss Leverick looked at each other. She said, "*I'*ll go," but she wasn't no steadier on her feet than I was, and I said, "Don't. Somebody'll come tell us if there's something we need to know. And I mean, it ain't like either one of us is gonna be any use."

She sat down again. "I hate to say this, but you're right."

So we sat there, both of us staring out the window although there wasn't nothing to see, just the big dark shapes of the trees, and I really did know better than to let myself think I saw things moving back there in the shadows. And we waited. Because there wasn't nothing else we could do.

After a couple minutes, people started walking back from the front end of the train. They looked excited and maybe a little scared, but not sad and not angry, so I figured whatever Felix'd done, he hadn't got himself or anybody else killed, and that made it a little easier to wait. Not a lot, mind you, but a little.

When Felix and Corbie and Miss Bridger finally showed up, they had a whole flock of guys in those red and gold uniforms with them, and Felix had on his wet cat look. Corbie was talking a mile a minute to one of the uniformed guys. Miss Bridger's eyes were big as bell-wheels, and she was hanging on Felix's arm in a way that maybe explained the wet cat look and maybe didn't.

"Oh dear," said Miss Leverick. "Olive is . . ."

I didn't want to make her find the word she was looking for, so I said, "He don't like being touched." Which was true, and a whole lot easier than any of the rest of it.

"Oh?" said Miss Leverick, but I got lucky and Felix was in the doorway of the compartment by then, so I didn't have to answer her.

The wet cat look was even stronger close-up. Whatever had happened, it hadn't been his idea and he didn't want to talk about it.

Not that he was going to be able to get anybody else to shut up. Miss Leverick hadn't even *asked* before Corbie and Miss Bridger and two of the guys in uniform were falling all over themselves to tell us. I couldn't make much sense of it: "monster" and "smashed the tree to splinters" and "machine" and somebody said "the Automaton of Corybant." "It almost killed Mr. Malley," said one of the uniforms, "and Mr. Rundell's spells just bounced off it."

"And Mr. Harrowgate killed it!" Miss Bridger cut in. "With a lightning bolt! I don't think even a virtuer could have done it."

"But it did clear enough of the tree out of the way," said the other uniform, "so we'll be moving again as soon as everyone's settled and Mr. Malley's had a dr—"

"Restorative cup of tea," the first uniform said loudly. "And we thought maybe you'd like the same."

"That would be very kind of you," Miss Leverick said, smiling at them.

They nodded and sort of bowed and jostled each other out of the doorway. Felix shut the door, locked it, and dropped down beside me, burying his face in his hands. His ear—which was all I could see of him—was bright red. Yeah, he loved attention, except when he really deserved it, and then it embarrassed the fuck out of him. Like it wasn't okay for anybody to say anything nice about him. Ever.

"You did good," I said. "You didn't get eaten by bears."

For a moment, I didn't think it was going to work, but then his shoulders started shaking, and pretty soon he was laughing so hard he couldn't catch his breath. Corbie was good and didn't try to disturb him, and Miss Leverick did her part by dragging Miss Bridger into some sort of real quiet conversation, and by the time the uniforms brought our tea, Felix had his balance back.

He took a sip of tea and pushed his hair out of his face and answered a question I'd decided I wasn't going to ask him. "It never got anywhere near me. Perfectly safe."

If he wanted to get me going, he was going to have to try harder than that. "Good," I said. "*Was* it the whatsit?"

"The Automaton of Corybant? It certainly could have been, from what I saw in the approximately three discontinuous seconds I had for observation while trying to avoid getting my head taken off."

"That's my boy," I said, instead of grinning at him, and he gave me a special version of his wet cat look, like he hadn't blasted a fucking enormous crazy machine to bits just to put up with smart-ass remarks from me. But his lip was twitching.

And then Miss Bridger said, "But how did you *do* it?" and Felix went tight as a knot again.

"Olive," Miss Leverick said warningly.

"But—"

"Even if Mr. Harrowgate wished to discuss it, I doubt you would understand his explanation. You are, after all, not even a student yet at the Institution, and you yourself said you didn't think a virtuer could have achieved what he did."

Miss Bridger went all stiff and outraged, like Miss Leverick had slapped her. Felix rubbed the bridge of his nose and said, "I don't mind," although it was plain as a wart that was only half-true at best.

Miss Bridger said, "No, Miss Leverick is right. I shouldn't pester you. I apologize." She turned and stared at the compartment door, and we all heard her sniff like she was trying not to cry. Miss Leverick made a face at Felix that looked like part apology and part wanting to brain Miss Bridger with her own handbag.

Miss Bridger was about the age of the kids Felix had taught in the Mirador, and he'd had months to work out how to deal with them. He said, "Miss Bridger, how much do you know about light-spells?"

"Um." She gulped, but I gave her credit for trying not to sob all over Felix. "Light-spells?"

"Like this," Corbie said, and she called up a little spinning purple chrysanthemum and then winked it away again.

"Oh," said Miss Bridger. "Yes, I can do that."

"Show me," Felix said, nice and quiet and calm.

She gulped again and nodded, and she was pretty tough for a little bourgeoise gal, because she did it. I mean, it wasn't much—little yellow spark like a lightning bug forgetting to go out—but it was there.

"Good," Felix said. And then he called his witchlights. Three of 'em, each the size of my thumbnail, and each three times as bright as Miss Bridger's—or Corbie's—without even trying. And, you know, green.

Miss Bridger made one of her little gasping noises, and even Miss Leverick looked impressed. Corbie just tried to look like she'd seen it all before. Felix smiled, but it wasn't one of his five-alarmers, or even the smile he got when he was pleased with himself. He just looked tired. "When you can do this," he said, "find me and I'll show you the next step."

"The next *step*?" Miss Leverick said.

"You don't go straight from here to lightning bolts," Felix said, and his witchlights spun in a circle and disappeared.

"When did you start studying magic, Mr. Harrowgate?" Miss Bridger asked.

There wasn't any smile left. "When I was fourteen." And they both got the message that he wasn't going to talk about it.

The train lurched and groaned and started again, and I was leaning back into my corner when somebody tapped on the door.

"*Now* what?" said Felix under his breath, and then louder, "Come in!"

It was a skinny little Corambin guy with big ears, and the way Felix twitched, you would've thought that little guy was a ghoul or a blood-witch or something. But he didn't do nothing scary, just kind of bowed and said, "His Grace the Duke of Murtagh wishes to offer you his hospitality for the remainder of the journey."

I saw the look Felix and Corbie gave each other, but I didn't know what it meant. And then Felix said, smooth as silk, "I would be delighted. Thank you. Are my companions included in this offer?"

"Of course," said the skinny little Corambin, and he offered his arm to Corbie like he was some kind of lord himself.

Just one fucking thing after another, I thought, and reached for Jashuki.

## *Felix*

The dead of Corybant were still screaming.

I was trying not to hear them because I couldn't help them. They weren't even ghosts, just screams, a pattern ingrained so deeply into the noirance of Nauleverer that I could not imagine any way of making it stop. I could push it to the very back of my awareness, but it was a relief when the train started moving, even a relief—although an ironic one—to have an opportunity for physical movement, following Murtagh's manservant down the swaying corridors of the train.

Here was another new experience to add to my ever-growing list. I'd never had to negotiate a social encounter with a former client before, and certainly not one who had seen me . . .

I am not embarrassed, I told myself firmly and knew perfectly well it was a lie.

The Duke of Murtagh was exceedingly gracious, and I admired him for taking the bull promptly by the horns. A single glance between us agreed that this meeting occurred between duke and suddenly notorious wizard, not tarquin and martyr. He also introduced Kay Brightmore without any evidence of uneasiness, although it was another potential social nightmare. Brightmore looked far better than he had the last time I had seen him, both healthier and better groomed; Murtagh was clearly a kinder jailer than the Duke of Glimmering.

Brightmore returned my greeting civilly, but frowned. Then his face cleared. "I remember your voice," he said, sounding surprised. "The foreigner with common decency."

"What's this?" said Murtagh. "You two have met before?"

"I wouldn't go that far," I said. "We encountered each other in the Hall of the Seven Virtues."

"And you are now slaying monsters," said Brightmore, something like bitterness on his face. "I thank you."

"No more than anyone else does, Kay," Murtagh said. "Mr. Foxe, you should sit down, I think."

"Oh, I'm fine," Mildmay said, sounding alarmed at the attention, but he was starting to look a little gray.

"Sit," I said, and he sat obediently next to Brightmore.

At that point we reached some necessary distance from Corybant, and the screaming faded; I tried not to sigh with relief too obviously.

The train carriage suitable for the dignity of a duke was not at all like the second-class compartments. It was divided, not into closed boxes, but into a series of semi-open rooms, with curtains that could be drawn to shut each off from the next. One of the rooms was set up with beds, another with chairs which were bolted to the floor but had some cunning mechanism whereby they could be turned to face either the windows or the center of the carriage. There were two together at one end, then a group of six, and then another two. Mildmay and Brightmore being in one of the paired sets, the rest of us sat in the group of six. I sat at one end, so that my bad side had Mildmay—and Brightmore, who was unlikely to make any sudden dangerous moves. Corbie got the seat next to me, possibly by the expedient of treading on Olive Bridger's toe; Miss Bridger took the third seat. Murtagh took the opposite side, and Miss Leverick sat next to him.

It was inevitable that we would talk about the Automaton of Corybant—less inevitable, but a great relief to me, that Miss Leverick and the Duke of Murtagh would get into a terrifically polite argument about whether the machine I had destroyed was in fact the Automaton of Corybant as described in folklore.

"It was *there*," said Murtagh. "I don't see the need to construct elaborate and, if you will forgive me, implausible explanations when the obvious truth is there in front of us."

"Yes," said Miss Leverick, "but *if* it is the Automaton of Corybant, it's been there for what, eight, nine centuries? Why would it suddenly wake up now? What elaborate and implausible explanation do you have for that?"

Murtagh snorted with sudden laughter. "We should ask Mr. Beckett that, shouldn't we, Kay?" And to the rest of us: "The man who apparently restarted the Clock of Eclipses had some quite remarkable theories about Cymellunar engines."

"Why do you say 'apparently'?" I said. It was a somewhat risky question, but I had been reading the newspapers very carefully, and the explanations given had been both vague and curiously misleading; there had not been so much as a hint of what had truly happened in the deepest basements of the Clock Palace. But none of the newspaper accounts had suggested that Edwin Beckett was not the person responsible.

"Because I've met the man," said Murtagh. "And listened to his theories, which seem to me some of the most arrant nonsense ever dreamed up by a half-educated turnstile-witch."

"You know something about thaumatology?" I said.

"Only what a well-educated annemer can pick up," he said with a shrug and an easy, gleaming smile. "Which I fully admit may be less than the knowledge of a half-educated turnstile-witch. But I do not believe that the great works of Cymellunar magic were achieved in the way that Mr. Beckett suggests."

I hope not, I thought and for a horrible second feared I'd said aloud. But Miss Leverick said, "You must know more about Cymellune than we do, Mr. Harrowgate. Your brother showed me where it was. And he said it sank?"

I turned my head to raise my eyebrows at Mildmay, who gave me a half-exasperated, half-helpless shrug back. "I know some things about Cymellune," I said cautiously. "And 'sank' is perhaps not the best word. The survivors spoke of a wall of water, which rose above Cymellune and crashed down upon it. And when the waters receded, the city was gone. About their magic, I know a fair amount, for my own school of wizardry is descended from the great schools of Cymellune." I remembered, just in time, that the newspapers had not explained Mr. Beckett's theories and instead of denying outright such slipshod practices among Cymellunar wizards, asked, "What is Mr. Beckett's suggestion?"

"Nonsense, as Murtagh says," Kay Brightmore said brusquely, and continued, changing the subject with the ruthlessness of a sanguette blade, "I know you are a foreigner, Mr. Harrowgate, but where are you from?"

"Mélusine," I said.

"And such a tremendously long way from home," said Murtagh. "What brings you to Corambis?"

Wicked amusement in his eyes. I said, "It is a very long story."

"We have nothing but time," Murtagh said amiably.

"I am an exile," I said. Predictably, Miss Bridger gasped.

Murtagh smiled at me, acknowledging his victory, and said, "And what of you, Mr. Foxe? Are you also exiled, or do you accompany your brother out of the goodness of your heart?"

Mildmay, I saw, did not like Murtagh. He said shortly, "Not gonna leave him alone," and I was probably the only one who understood him.

"Mildmay feels," I said lightly, "that I'm not fit to be let out on my own."

Murtagh's eyebrows went up. Miss Leverick, who seemed to be picking up at least some of the undercurrents, said, "He said as much to me. It seems to be common between siblings. Certainly, I am still not convinced that my second-youngest sister can be trusted to boil water, although I would like to say, for the record, that there is considerable experiential evidence to back me up, including the incident of the beef brisket which set my youngest sister's hair on fire. Fortunately, my second-eldest brother has quick reflexes. Unfortunately, what he was holding at the time was a jar of my mother's loganberry syrup, which is, as I and all my sisters can attest, the stickiest substance in the Duchy of Kennerack."

"Miss Leverick, you're making that up!" said Miss Bridger.

"No, no, I assure you," said Frances Leverick, and she told stories about her large and apparently quite accident-prone family all the way out of the forest and into the remains of the daylight.

# Part Three

# Chapter 10

## *Mildmay*

Felix came into our room at the Golden Hare in the Ingry Dominion of Esmer and said, "Dinner's in an hour."

"How'd you manage that?"

"Mrs. Davidge is an exceedingly kind lady. Unlike Mrs. Lettice."

But he wasn't looking at me and his face was going red. "She reads them crazy-ass novels, don't she?"

"*Doesn't*, not *don't*. And I don't have the faintest idea what you're talking about." Red as a bad sunburn. "As I said, we've got an hour. Why don't you read to me?"

"You don't have to," I said. "I know it ain't no fun for you."

"That depends on what you mean by 'fun,'" he said, coming over to sit on the bed beside me. "If you mean, do I find it amusing, no, I don't. But if you mean, isn't there something I'd rather be doing, no, there isn't." He glanced up at me, but then looked down again quick. He was funny about eye contact. "I'm trying to . . . Look. I've been really horrible to you, and I'm trying not to be, all right?"

And I knew he didn't mean just the past few months when he'd been surly and bitchy and hateful about fucking *everything*. He meant the way he'd been when Gideon left him, and the shit he'd pulled over getting Vey Coruscant killed, and all the way back even to having been a prick on the *White Otter* and in the Gardens of Nephele. He'd gone blotchy red, and his hands were tight-clenched in his lap, and I knew he wasn't looking at me now because he hated apologizing and he was really really bad at it.

"It's okay," I said, as gently as I could. "I'll get the book." And it was worth it just for the way he stared at me, eyes big as bell-wheels, like nobody'd ever let him off the hook before in his life.

## *Felix*

The news of my encounter with the Automaton of Corybant spread with a rapidity that would have done the gossip mills of the Mirador proud. By the afternoon of our first full day in Esmer, there was a delegation from the Institution, a virtuer and two adepts first grade, inquiring for me at the desk of the Golden Hare.

I'd sent Corbie out to learn the city; in truth, I couldn't have kept her in if I'd wanted to. Mildmay and I inspected each other before we descended, agreeing ruefully that we looked as well as could possibly be expected.

The Corambin magicians were nervous—obviously so, and I remembered Miss Bridger saying a virtuer wouldn't have been able to deal with the Automaton as I had. I had dismissed that claim as ignorance and excessive enthusiasm, but perhaps I had been wrong to do so.

Virtuer Hutchence was my own age, more or less; he was stocky and cheerful and seemed not terribly impressed with his own rank. The adepts were Lillicrop and Rook, and they were some ten years older. They were professional men where Hutchence was an academic, and were very dignified and dour. I couldn't tell them apart.

They let Hutchence do the talking at first, which suited me very well. I knew how to deal with academic wizards. We exchanged credentials and chatted briefly about the relationship between the Coeurterre, with which the Institution was familiar, and the Mirador, with which it was not.

"What about your companion?" said Virtuer Hutchence.

I smiled. "He isn't a wizard."

And Hutchence simply nodded and said, "Now, about the incident in Nauleverer . . ."

I described what had happened, to the best of my ability—I had no basis on which to speculate about what the monster had been, except that it had been mechanical, twice the size of a man, and clearly hostile. Hutchence nodded and took notes and was settling comfortably into a disquisition on the flora and fauna of the Forest of Nauleverer and its reactions to the railroad when one of the adepts interrupted: "And you killed it with a lightning bolt?"

And, reminded, Hutchence was nervous again.

"Not a lightning bolt, exactly," I said. "The experiments I know of in calling lightning all ended very messily."

"Then what was it?" said the other adept.

"Do you want the entire theoretical framework of Cabaline luxomancy?"

"That hardly seems necessary," the first adept said, sneering.

"What Mr. Lillicrop means," Hutchence said hastily, "is that we don't need a full explanation now. Merely a broad outline."

As a placatory gesture, it was a failure. Lillicrop and Rook looked offended, and I myself resented the implication that I was accountable to the Institution, even though that was exactly why Stephen had sent me here.

"I did this, only amplified." I summoned witchlight, hard and fast and aimed very precisely. The corner of Hutchence's quire glowed briefly, brilliantly green, and caught fire.

He yelped and dropped it; he and the adepts backed away, and I couldn't tell whether they wanted distance from the flame or distance from me. Mildmay nudged me aside and stamped out the fire before it had a chance to really catch.

"Does that answer your questions, gentlemen?" I said.

Hutchence picked up the quire and examined the singed edge. His entire face had become round with astonishment. "Luminiferous aether!" he said. "I had no idea it could do that!"

"I beg your pardon?" I said.

"We can all manipulate aether," he said and called witchlights of his own, very small and not very bright, but a veritable constellation around his head. "But since it is heatless and has no mass, it never occurred to anyone that it could be made to have an effect on material bodies. How very astonishing."

"Aether?" I said. I sorted through five different ways of saying, *I have no idea what you're talking about,* and settled for the most dignified: "I'm not familiar with that term."

"The old term is vi," Lillicrop said, sneering again.

"I thought that was something only people have."

"Oh, no, no, no, not a bit," Hutchence said brightly. "Aether, or vi, is the substance of magic. People have it, animals have it, objects have it. It's just that only magicians can *use* it."

"Manar," I said inadvertently. Ephreal Sand wrote a great deal about manar, the world of the spirit, in *De Doctrina Labyrinthorum*, but it had never occurred to me to connect manar to my witchlights. It had never occurred to me, I realized, to think about my witchlights at all.

"I'm not familiar with that term," Rook said, and I turned quickly enough to catch the mockery on his face.

"You wouldn't be," I said and smiled at him as if I hadn't noticed. "It's Kekropian thaumaturgy."

"How quaint," said Rook.

Lillicrop and Hutchence were muttering together, and Hutchence looked up to say, "I'm quite sure the Circle will want to speak to you in person, Mr. Harrowgate."

"The Circle?" I said. "I understood your governing body was the Congress."

"The Congress is all of us," said Hutchence. "The Circle is like our Convocation. I imagine you'll be asked to appear before the Congress as well, but the Circle first."

"Um," I said. "Mildmay, do you have those letters?"

Of course, he did. Mildmay kept track of everything.

"Letters?" said Hutchence, accepting the oilskin packet. "You didn't say anything about those earlier."

I only wished I thought I could have gotten away with not mentioning them at all. "They're for your Circle," I said, and I was feeling unsettled enough to be deliberately nasty. "Not for their flunkies."

Hutchence took it in perfectly good humor, although I could see him, sharp behind his amiable, slightly naïve façade, noticing I'd been put out of countenance and wondering why. Lillicrop and Rook were simply offended; before they could say so, Hutchence said, "I will be sure Virtuer Ashmead receives them. Mr. Lillicrop, Mr. Rook, I recall your urgency to return to your offices."

He shepherded them out, closing the door behind himself with a politely definite click.

Mildmay gave me one of his unreadable looks and said, "Next time you're gonna set something on fire, you wanna warn me first?"

"It could have been worse," I said. "My first choice of target was Mr. Lillicrop's cravat."

---

I had not sought the Khloïdanikos since the night in Bernatha when I drowned the fantôme, afraid of what I might find there—or what I might bring with me. But that was a wretched way to repay Thamuris for his help and kindness, and so finally, lying that night in the Golden Hare, I gritted my teeth and reached. Horn Gate was, most thankfully, still open; I plunged through it without stopping.

The Khloïdanikos was green again; though it was not as vibrant as it had been before I had brought Malkar's rubies into it, it was clearly repairing itself, returning to its centuries-held equilibrium. Thamuris was there, sitting on the bench we had always favored, and he, too, looked better. He turned his head sharply as he sensed me, and bounded to his feet. "Felix! Where have you been? What *happened* to you?"

"It's very complicated," I said, rather weakly.

"Yes, I can see that," he said. I looked down at myself and saw tatters of noirance whipping about me. "Is there something . . . *with* you?"

"Not any longer, I hope. It's called a fantôme."

"What is that?"

"It's a kind of revenant. The old necromancers used them."

"A spirit-ancestor?"

"A dead wizard. My understanding is that by allowing the ghost to possess them, the caster could make themselves immeasurably more powerful." Certainly that had been the aim of the foolish wizard in Hermione. The murdered Caloxan wizard had simply not been picky about her means of revenge.

I could see Thamuris's revulsion. "And you sought to increase your—"

"Not me!" I cried out, revolted in turn. "I wouldn't . . . I don't . . ."

"I'm sorry," Thamuris said, and was my friend again, not the stone-eyed judge. "I'm sorry, truly. I know you wouldn't. But why did it—"

"Hunt me? I . . . I attracted its attention. Inadvertently. And it is—it is the nature of fantômes to be—hungry."

"Like a fire," Thamuris said.

"Yes," I said. "Like a fire."

"Can I do anything to help?"

"No, it's gone. I just need some time."

"Well, let me show you something that maybe will help. At least, I think it is encouraging." I followed him, and by the ruined orchard wall, the perseïd tree was . . .

"It's budding?" I said; I wasn't sure I dared to believe it.

"I've been watching it for you. Not that I would be able to do anything if—"

"Thank you." I touched one of the tiny white buds, laid my hand gently against the tree's black bark.

"Is Mildmay . . . all right? I know you said he's with you, and if the perseïd really is linked to him somehow . . . I didn't know, but I was hoping."

"I think maybe Mildmay *is* all right," I said, and it occurred to me that this might be the first time in all the years I'd known him that that was true.

ᔕ

At breakfast, as if to refute my hopeful dreaming, Mildmay was frowning and silent—not that he was ever talkative, but there was a weight to this silence that made me uneasy—and finally, I said, "For the love of cats, what is it?"

The green eyes flicked up at me and away. "I had this weird dream last night."

"Oh?"

"Yeah. You were in it. So was Thamuris."

I'd never had any ability to hide things from him, and the evidence indicated I wasn't going to start now. I felt my own guilty flinch, and Mildmay said, "It wasn't just a dream, then." He sounded grimly unsurprised.

"The obligation d'âme," I said. "I did warn you about—"

"And I heard you. That ain't the part I'm interested in. Was it really Thamuris—not just you dreaming him, I mean?"

"Yes, it was really Thamuris," I said dully, braced for the next inevitable question: what was this fantôme we were talking about?

But Mildmay said, "How long you been talking to him in your dreams?"

"Since we left Troia, roughly."

He didn't say anything for a long moment; when he did speak his voice was quiet, almost reflective: "You motherfucking cunt."

"Mildmay, what—"

"I figured he was dead," he continued over me. "I figured he died three fucking indictions ago, and all this time you been talking to him?"

"You didn't say anything about—"

"For fuck's sake, Felix!" He'd never turned that look on me before, impatience, almost contempt, like flint and iron. Like that terrible dream of him dead. "How was I s'posed to know you and him were doing hocus things in your sleep? And does it really take that much to figure I might want to know?"

"You hate 'hocus things.' "

"That he's *alive*!" Mildmay all but howled. Then he caught himself. "No, never mind. No point. If you'd realized, you would've said. Just—is he okay? I mean, aside from the consumption?"

His forgiveness almost hurt more than his anger, especially because I wasn't sure he was right. I *hadn't* realized, but even if I had . . . I'd known I was being selfish, even before Thamuris's indictment, but just how deep had that selfishness run?

I took a deep breath. "I think he's all right. He doesn't like to talk about it."

"Well, he must be sort of okay. I mean, if he's meeting with you regular."

"I think he's surprised the celebrants, that he's doing so well."

"That's good," Mildmay said, and to my great relief he let the subject drop.

I tried all that day to think of a way to tell Mildmay about the fantôme, and I couldn't. It was—well, it was ridiculous, wasn't it? As if my life was nothing but one catastrophe heaped on top of the next, without even the decency of a layer of tissue in between. I remembered Mehitabel comparing my life to a romance, and that was exactly, horribly right.

The fantôme is gone, I told myself. No need to distress him. And I did my best to believe it.

## *Mildmay*

The letter from the Circle came the next morning.

"I expected as much," Felix said, but not like it made him happy or nothing.

I watched him open it and read it—after a moment, his eyebrows went up. "Well, I wasn't expecting *that*."

"What?"

"They say that if the inquiry goes well, they're prepared to offer me a lectureship at the Institution."

"You mean like a job?"

"Yes. Exactly like a job."

I didn't even care he was being snarky at me. Because, you know, I'd been *trying* not to worry about money and us not having none and what Felix might think he had to do about it this time, but I hadn't been doing real well. So all at once it was like I could breathe again, except for the part where Felix was still frowning.

"What's this inquiry thing?"

He made an unhappy kind of coughing noise, and I was right back to not breathing. "They, ah, they've read the letters from Stephen and Giancarlo. They're concerned."

"Yeah?"

He shut his eyes for a second. "Stephen gave them authority over me."

"Okay. And?"

"They are concerned about what they call 'a clear and blatant abuse of power.' I think I'm on trial. Sort of."

"Sort of?" From what I knew, you were either on trial—and most likely going to get yourself hanged—or not. It wasn't a thing you could do "sort of."

"Well, it's not a *real* trial. They're quite careful to explain that neither the Circle nor the Congress is a judicial body. They can't send me to prison or have me executed or anything like that. Although I imagine they could make strong recommendations to whatever 'judicial body' there is here."

"So what *can* they do to you?"

"What Mortimer Clef said. At my real trial." His mouth twisted, and he shoved his fingers through his hair, which was always a sign he was fretful. "They can bind my magic."

"And you're gonna let 'em?"

It was a real question. I meant it, and after a moment where I thought he was going to skin me alive, he saw that I meant it, and his frown went from pissed off to just kind of thoughtful.

"Because," I said, "you don't *have* to."

"We've come all this way," he said, not disagreeing exactly, but like it hadn't occurred to him that he had a choice.

"I know. And I ain't saying we *should* bail. Just . . . well, we don't really know nothing about these hocuses, and I don't know, it seems like maybe you shouldn't be in a big hurry to let them do shit like that to you."

His eyebrows went up. "That was quite the speech."

"Don't do that."

"Do what?"

"Don't try and change the subject by picking on me. It won't help."

He kind of flinched. "Old habits," he said, and I knew what he meant was *I'm sorry.*

"I know that," I said, to both what he said and what he meant. "I'm just saying, don't do it. Because I ain't gonna play, and there just ain't no fucking point, is there?"

"I suppose there isn't," he said. Then, abruptly, "If I didn't . . . if we left, where would we go?"

"Where d'you want to go?"

"Home," he said before he had a chance to catch himself. And then we just both kind of sat there for a while, along of there being nothing anybody could say.

❧

In the end, though, Felix decided to go ahead and let the Circle take their best swing. Because, he said, first of all, if he ever *was* going to get to go home again, it'd be because he'd done what Lord Stephen wanted and had plenty of witnesses to prove it. And besides, he'd been thinking along the same lines as me about money and us not having none. It would be much more comfortable, he said, to be exiled with a steady income than without. And, you know, I really couldn't argue with him.

So I cleaned up his dark green coat as best I could, including darning a rip that Felix swore up down and sideways he hadn't put there, and braided his hair for him, and when we collected Corbie from her little mousehole of a room and went downstairs, there were five more letters waiting at the front desk, and Mrs. Davidge looked kind of like she'd got slapped in the face with a dead fish.

Felix gave the letters the hairy eyeball and said, "I'm sorry to have been such a bother to you, Mrs. Davidge."

"Oh, no bother, Mr. Harrowgate," she said, and she was looking at him funny, but not like she didn't like what she saw. "It's nice to have a guest who brings such distinction to the hotel." And she put a newspaper on top of the desk, with this weird picture of a guy and something like a walking clock, and I could read the letters across the top: "MONSTER MACHINE FELLED BY MAGICIAN HERO."

Felix went tomato-red. I said before he could get his mouth open, "We need to get to the Institution." And of course she didn't understand me, which at least gave Felix something better to do than yell at her.

"Well," she said, "the easiest way is to take the fathom to Greville Station."

"The fathom?" Felix said, and he sounded like he was expecting another monster.

"Oh, I know about that," Corbie said. "I figured 'em all out yesterday. C'mon, I'll show you."

So we followed her outside where we got to find out what being a carny freak was like. Because, I mean, there wasn't no way to hide Felix—too tall and too pale and with the hair. So people stared. And whispered at each other. And I heard at least one kid yelling, "Hey, the foreign magician's come out!"

Felix went stiff, and for a moment I thought he was going to bolt back inside the hotel. But then he said through his teeth, "How quaint," and all at once it was like he didn't even *notice*. He just went where he wanted to go and it was like nobody else even existed. Except that he went slow enough for me to keep up, which was nice of him and I sure as fuck appreciated it.

After he'd got into his stride, he said, "Corbie, what *is* the fathom?"

"Trains underground," Corbie said. "It's the niftiest thing *ever.* And we're right near the station, too."

And sure enough, there at the end of the street was a sign saying "SUNFLOWER STREET STATION" and a big flight of stairs going down right in the middle of the road. Corbie started down, then realized we weren't with her, and turned to look up at us. Me and Felix gave each other this *you go first* look, and I finally said, "At least there won't be the Sim to fall into," and the way he tried not to laugh told me I'd read him right. He went down the stairs, and I went with him.

It was better lit than I would've thought, and not so much like a cave. Brick everywhere, and the floor was done in these little black-and-white chessboard tiles, and they'd plastered a big stretch of wall to put a painting on it. It was pretty, but all I can tell you other than that was that it had to be something important in Corambin history, because everybody was wearing weird clothes with these enormous white ruffs that made them look like a bunch of heads on platters. "Quaint," Felix said at it and paid our pennies to a skinny little gal with a bad complexion in return for three pieces of stiff paper with "EMFR" printed on 'em in smudgy black ink. She read the newspapers, too. You could tell.

And then it was like the station for the other trains, and we followed the signs to a platform, and everybody there gawked like a bunch of half-wit dogs, too. Felix kept his chin up and stared straight across the tracks at the brick wall. Me and Corbie stood one on each side of him, like he was a spider and we were his hired goons. It was just as well we didn't have to wait very long, because I could see somebody was going to get up their nerve to say something, and I didn't have the first idea what Felix was going to do when they did. I was extremely fucking glad to see the train pull in, although it was dark and smoky and something that I otherwise would have thought twice about before I got into.

I herded Felix into the back corner, where I could sit between him and everybody else, and pointed Corbie at the seat opposite where she'd block at least some of the view. Felix let me do it, too, although he looked at me like there were some things he would've said about it if we'd been alone. That was fine. I sat next to him and glared black murder at anybody who looked like they were thinking about saying something. And once the train started up again, it didn't matter nohow, because with the screeching and the rattling and the speed of the thing, everybody was too busy trying not to get knocked off their seat to say anything, and even if somebody had, there wasn't no way we could've heard 'em.

Every station had a sign, and I really was doing better with the reading, because I read "GREVILLE" just as fast as Felix and Corbie did. Hauled myself up, got us off the train and onto the platform, and then we followed the signs that said "OUT" along a weird, square little passageway, and then the world's narrowest staircase, couldn't go more than one at a time even if you wanted to, and then we were out in this big glass birdcage sort of thing, and powers and saints, I hadn't thought glass could *do* that.

"Don't gawk," Felix said in my ear, and it was him herding me now with Corbie trotting along ahead of us, out of the birdcage and across this ironwork bridge over the street and through an arch with words on it that Felix said, when Corbie asked, were in Cymellunar. Past the arch, there were more stairs. These weren't as bad on my leg, but I was still not liking them at all. We came to a landing with a bench, and Felix stopped and fidgeted a little and said, "You don't have to come with me, you know. You could just wait here. It'd be all right."

I stared at him, and he went red and fidgeted some more and wouldn't meet my eyes. Finally, I said, "I'm gonna pretend you didn't say that," and started up the next fucking flight.

At the top of the stairs, where I could look back the way we'd come and see the dome of the glass birdcage and pick out ways I could climb it if I had to, Corbie said, "I got most of this sussed out. Where're you supposed to go?"

"You've been very busy," Felix said in that way he had where you couldn't tell if he thought it was a good thing or a bad thing, and consulted his letter. "Arkwright Hall."

"Yeah," said Corbie. And she pointed at a building that looked to me like the Butchers' Guild in Mélusine. It was also about as far away from us as you could get and still be in pointing range. Which figured.

So we started off, and Corbie told us about looking around the Institution. "The boys here are nice," she said, kind of smirking, and just for proof, a kid going the other way stopped so fast he almost ruptured something and said, "Corbie! Can I help you . . ." And then he registered me and Felix, and his eyes went round and a little glassy

He was my age, so he was probably a student, and he seriously needed to shave because that beard wasn't doing him no favors. But Corbie smiled at him like he was gold-plated and said, "Robin, this is Mr. Harrowgate and Mr. Foxe. We're going to Arkwright Hall."

Which was the opposite direction to where he'd been going, but he turned right around and came with us. And he handled Felix okay, making out like he didn't know just *exactly* who he was, and Felix got him to talk about the classes he took, and his teachers, and how he'd passed his practitioner tests that winter and was starting work for the adept level, and I limped along behind and listened and, honestly, was pretty impressed with how organized these hocuses had got themselves. Nothing like the catch-as-catch-can way things worked in the Mirador, and it didn't sound as mean as the Bastion, where all the hocuses had to be soldiers, too, with kids at their second septad being told they were lieutenants and basically used like fodder for the majors and colonels. Gideon'd talked a little about the Bastion. It gave me the creeping crawling screaming horrors, and I wasn't even a hocus.

So it seemed like the hocuses here were getting taught right and nobody was using them the way Gideon had been used and Mehitabel's sweetheart had been used—and Felix had been used, for that matter. Felix asked a couple kind of delicate questions, and yeah, it turned out they were really careful about that, along of the Caloxan warlocks who they'd only gotten rid of with the war five or six septads ago.

By the time we got to Arkwright Hall, Felix had charmed Robin completely, and that was good. Because when Felix mentioned as how he might be teaching, Robin lit up and said he'd want to take that class, and he was sure his friends would want to, and basically made it sound like they could start the cult of Felix anytime Felix gave the word. And, okay, I ain't no big fan of the cult of Felix, but it was sure as fuck better than that Mr. Lillicrop and Mr. Rook looking at him like he was a wild animal that had been taught to do a trick.

So Robin gave Felix a card with the address of the room he had on campus, and Felix kind of squinted at it and said, "Would you mind showing Corbie? I'm terrible with directions, but if she knows the way . . ."

Corbie opened her mouth, but Robin said, "I'd be delighted," like he'd just been given a present. And I saw her figure out that Felix didn't want her to see what happened with the Circle, and she went from pissed off to hurt to okay with it in about half a second and said, "You want to meet me back at the Golden Hare, then?" She went off with Robin and left me and Felix standing between the big ugly columns on the front of Arkwright Hall—*exactly* like the Butchers' Guild—and both of us nervous and not wanting to say so.

"I hope I didn't just talk him into cutting a class," Felix said.

"He'll just say he met you," I said, and he made a face at me, but it was only for telling him what he knew was the truth anyway.

"You sure you don't want to bail?" I said, and he straightened up and quit looking so dithery.

"I'm quite sure. Come. Let us face the lions."

"Lions?"

"In Cymellune, in the late empire, heretics—who were legion—underwent trial by lion. They shut you in a cage with a certain number of lions—the number was theologically significant and thus varied from heretic to heretic—and if the lions didn't eat you, your heresy would be granted what was called a Lien of Orthodoxy, which meant that the priests and scholars would reassess it and decide if perhaps it wasn't heresy after all."

"How many times did it happen that way, that the lions didn't eat the heretic?"

He gave me a smile that was all teeth and nerves. "Once." And pushed open the door of Arkwright Hall.

## *Felix*

I had always been vain, and I was well served for my vanity with that appalling story in the newspaper and the way the Corambins looked at me now, as if I were a cross between a saint and a medical curiosity preserved in brandy. It had been not merely pleasant, but almost desperately satisfying to get

Corbie's new friend Robin to talk to me, to see him warm from awe to something more like friendly interest. Inside Arkwright Hall, I was alarming and freakish again, and they watched me nervously as they tried to figure out what they ought to do with us. The Circle—as was explained to us by students and magician-practitioners and annemer clerks—was in session, and no one wanted to disturb them. But at the same time, Virtuer Ashmead and Virtuer Hutchence had both apparently mentioned that they were expecting me, and so no one wanted to send us away, either.

It was not comfortable. We ended up in an antechamber which, despite differences in decoration and furniture styles, was spiritually indistinguishable from the antechambers around the Hall of the Chimeras: the Cerise, the Cerulean, and all their cohort. Mildmay sat down with ill-disguised relief, and I dissipated my nervous energy by pacing. Seven steps up and back, which wasn't really enough, but it was better than trying to sit still. Mildmay watched me pace until the door opened and a nervous clerk peered around the edge of it. "Mr. Harrowgate? The virtuers are ready for you."

"Marvelous," I said and smiled at him to make him flinch. I waited deliberately for Mildmay to get up. Waiting games were familiar territory. Mildmay gave me a doubtful look but said nothing. He would follow my lead, and the comfort of knowing that was tremendous, like a bulwark I could rest my weight against. No matter what the Circle said, Mildmay would not turn against me.

The clerk led us through a series of high-ceilinged and commensurately echoing hallways, all very clean, as if they were never used. The doors he brought us to were clearly meant to impress, but next to the bronze doors of the Hall of the Chimeras, they were merely large. I was glad to find something in Corambis that did not make me feel like an ignorant provincial.

The clerk tapped on the door, then opened it to slip inside, closing it again before there was even time to wonder if we were supposed to follow. I looked at Mildmay, who gave me a one-shouldered shrug and said, "We can wait here as easy as there."

"Only without somewhere you can sit."

His gaze went flat and annoyed. "I'm a cripple, not a fucking invalid. I'm fine."

"That isn't actually the point," I said, which made him relax. "I'm merely noting that their hospitality leaves something to be desired."

"Oh, okay," he said and looked around assessingly at the tall, clean, barren hallway. "Yeah. I see what you mean."

"It's information," I said.

"And we need all of that we can get. Yeah."

It was fifteen minutes before the clerk reappeared to beckon us inside. Like the other rooms in Arkwright Hall, this one was large and clean and nearly empty, save for the table around which the virtuers sat. There were ten of them, all men and most of them older than I. They were well dressed by Corambin standards, which made them look like a funeral party to me, even though I knew that the oppressive, somber colors were simply what Corambins considered normal. They watched us in impassive silence as we crossed from the door to the foot of the table.

When I reached the foot of the table, the wizard at its head stood up. "Mr. Harrowgate? I am John Ashmead, Dean of the Institution." He was nothing like Giancarlo to look at, being small and spare and wearing his dun-colored hair cropped very close, but his dark eyes were sharp and intelligent, and he had Giancarlo's air about him, a forthright man professionally accustomed to compromise.

I nodded respectfully and watched with careful attention as he introduced the other men around the table. Next to him was Virtuer Giffen, who was the President of the Institution and thus—I guessed from their behavior—more important than Virtuer Ashmead. He glowered at the air in my vicinity without any direct acknowledgment, as did Virtuers Gotobed, Tandy, Wooller, Pluckrose, and Bullinger, while Hutchence, Simond, and Maycock at least made eye contact. Virtuer Hutchence even offered a smile, and I was glad he wasn't holding his singed quire against me.

"And who is your companion?" Virtuer Ashmead asked.

"My half brother, Mildmay Foxe. I would count it as a great kindness if you would find him a chair." Behind me, Mildmay made a noise of protest, but my attention was on Ashmead. And Ashmead acquitted himself admirably, saying without hesitation, "Yes, of course," and directing one of the clerks lurking along the wall to bring a chair for Mr. Foxe.

Mildmay might be annoyed with me—by the very flatness of the look he gave me, I suspected I would be hearing about this later—but he wasn't obstinate enough to refuse to sit down. And I was standing close enough, and knew him well enough, to see that it was a relief to get his weight off his bad leg. He muttered something that might have been "thank you" to the clerk, and I said, "Thank you," more audibly to Ashmead.

He said, "Yes, well," cleared his throat, and began the inquiry.

The Circle was better at this sort of thing than the Curia had ever been. The Curia could be distracted, embarrassed, turned against itself. The Circle simply kept asking questions until it got answers, and then it asked questions about the answers it got. It could be distracted, but never for long, and Ashmead was always there to be sure the point at issue was not forgotten. I hated him for it before I'd even finished explaining the historical enmity between the Bastion and the Mirador.

Because they wanted to know *everything*. They refused (said Virtuer Ashmead) to make an ill-informed judgment, and I was glad I'd insisted they give Mildmay a chair. They made me explain the politics and the thaumaturgy, and they wanted to know what would have happened to Isaac Garamond if he'd gone to trial, and then Virtuer Simond said, "Then I don't understand. If he would have been executed anyway, why did you do . . . *that*?"

I felt Mildmay's sudden, perfect, unbreathing stillness behind me, but there was nothing in the world that could induce me to lie about this. I said deliberately, "The man he murdered was my lover."

Even Virtuer Ashmead was visibly taken aback. There was a moment of utter silence, and then all the virtuers were talking at once. Virtuer Wooller became quite alarmingly red in the face shouting about sin, but I noticed his opponent was Virtuer Bullinger, who had heretofore looked as if he would be torn apart by wild dogs before he said a word in my defense.

I didn't attempt to make myself heard, but dropped back to crouch by Mildmay's chair. He had his head in his hands, but raised it to say, "You couldn't've eased 'em into it a little?"

"I'm not going to deny what I am," I said, hurt.

"Course not. But you didn't have to do it like that, neither." I heard both exasperation and affection in his voice when he added, "You got all the tact of a bull alligator. A *hungry* bull alligator."

"They asked," I said defensively.

"Hey," he said. "It's okay. I kind of figure they deserve it."

I wanted to tell him I didn't need or want his approval, but that would only be another lie. Virtuer Ashmead called me; I squeezed Mildmay's forearm and stood up, and the inquiry continued.

They did not ask me questions about my sexual habits, although I thought one or two of them wanted to. They did ask about Gideon, and I concentrated on keeping my voice level and my breathing steady as I answered.

And then they swerved to ask about the Virtu and how it had come to be broken. If Mildmay had not been there, I might have tried to lie, or at least not to reveal all of the truth. But Mildmay *was* there, and although I knew he would understand, and possibly even condone, my reasons for lying, I could not bear to let him witness an act of such cowardice. I did not mention the rubies, which were a later development, and one I didn't want to try to explain, but I told the truth about what Malkar had been, about what he had made me, and as they asked questions, as I answered them, I found myself thinking, There's another lie I never have to tell again. There's something else I don't have to pretend not to be. I had expected the truth to feel like the burden it had always been, since Malkar—buried deep, his weight along my back, both hands in my hair pulling my head back so that each breath was a strain—said in my ear, "You must never tell anyone, my darling. Shall I tell you what I'll do to you if you do?" And he told me, adding details in his purring voice until I was crying and struggling to get away, but between his cock and his hands and his smothering weight, I couldn't even move, and he'd sounded satisfied—although he still didn't move, wouldn't move until I lay as limp and helpless as a dead kitten beneath him, and only then did he fuck me—when he said, "You belong to me, Felix. You always will."

Not anymore, I thought savagely, and told the Circle about the obligation de sang, the binding-by-blood.

They recognized the term. Bindings were familiar to them: the binding-by-blood, the binding-by-forms, the binding-by-troth, the binding-by-obedience . . . bindings I'd never even heard of, and I'd thought I knew them all. The inquiry degenerated for a time into its own mirror image, and I discovered that "flame" and "shadow" were also technical terms in Mulkist thaumaturgy, for a warlock and that warlock's slaved wizards. The oldest of the wizards, Virtuer Pluckrose, unbent abruptly and described meeting, in his teens, a warlock who had been hunting for shadows. "I ran from her," he said, "and she laughed and said, 'I'll find you when I want you, little treasure.' I had nightmares about her until the war, until we stopped them."

"And there are no warlocks left now?"

"None," Ashmead said positively.

I was beginning, unwillingly, to believe that Malkar's choice to claim I was from Caloxa had not been random. I knew he had been in the north—in the Norvenas, ruining Mavortian von Heber's life—and now I could not help suspecting that he had met a Caloxan warlock. After all, if one had tried to flee (and died, burning, in the midst of her vengeful magic), others almost certainly had as well. And perhaps they had succeeded. And found a sympathetic ear in Brinvillier Strych.

And that final piece of truth was pressing at me, the truth that proved my likeness to Malkar, that proved I was the mirror he'd tried to make me. I opened my mouth and the words fell out like stones: "I cast the binding-by-forms on my brother."

"Because I asked you to!" Mildmay said, struggling to his feet. His response was so immediate that he must have been expecting my confession.

"The binding-by-forms?" said Ashmead, as if he could possibly have misunderstood me. "The shadowing?" They were now all ten of them looking at Mildmay with appalled pity.

"I asked him to!" he shouted at them. "And he ain't never—" He stopped and said, for the first time in my memory using correct grammar: "He hasn't abused it."

"Yes, I have," I objected.

"Once. And that was . . . You won't do it again."

"No. But, Mildmay—"

"The binding-by-forms is corrupt by its nature," said Ashmead. "Is it still on him?"

We both looked at him blankly. "It can be taken off?" I asked.

Their expressions were mingled pity and contempt, and I hated them. "Your Lord Protector," said Virtuer Giffen, "asked us to curb your powers. I begin to see why." He looked around the table; the other nine wizards were nodding.

I wanted desperately to defend myself, but there was nothing I could say. I couldn't even claim my intentions had been good, because all too often, they hadn't been. "I agreed to submit myself to your judgment," I said, in lieu of excuses, pleas, or justifications. And then I swallowed hard and said, "What must I do?"

There was a brief mute colloquy among the Circle, which seemed to result in Ashmead being saddled with the dirty work. He stood up and came around the table; he was moving slowly, clearly reluctant, but I saw nothing but grimness and resolve on his face. "The binding-by-obedience requires physical contact," he said, "but nothing untoward. Nothing like, for example, the binding-by-troth."

I remembered the kiss I'd forced on Mildmay to seal the binding-by-forms and could imagine what the binding-by-troth might have involved.

The other virtuers rose and formed a circle around Ashmead, Mildmay, and me. "Give me your hands," said Ashmead.

I obeyed him. I'd already made my choice, made it months ago and held fast despite Mildmay's arguments. I wasn't going to back down now.

He said a string of words; I recognized the language as Cymellunar, though none of the words was familiar. The pain was unexpected, quite literally blinding, and my knees buckled.

What happened next I could not quite comprehend; there was a rush of movement, the sounds of collision. Someone yelped. I blinked, forced my eyes to focus, to track. Ashmead was no longer holding my hands. I was on the floor, folded over my own knees like a dropped marionette, and Mildmay was standing over me, clearly prepared to use his walking stick as a weapon. The snarl on his face was inhuman, frightening. I could feel the obligation d'âme jangling in my head, an echo of the clamor it must have been causing in Mildmay's.

"Mildmay," I said. "Mildmay!" I reached up, careful not to jar his lame leg, and put my hand flat on his chest, as high as I could reach. That seemed to break the near-fugue he'd entered into, and he looked down at me, his face relaxing into a frown.

"He was hurting you," he said, as if that explained everything. His eyes were very clear and very cold, the eyes of someone I did not know. He had been an assassin, and it occurred to me that I had been stupid never to realize what that meant. I had used it—had used *him*—but I had never thought about what it meant that my gentle, silent brother, who had saved me from myself over and over again, had been—to be unpleasantly blunt, as he had been when the subject had come up—a murderer for hire.

He's saved you from yourself, but have you ever considered that maybe you should return the favor?

Carefully, carefully, I snaked out from under him, so that I could stand up. Carefully, carefully, I said, "I agreed."

"Yeah, but you—" He stopped himself, but I heard the rest of the sentence as clearly as if he'd said it: *you agreed to what they did in Bernatha, too.*

"Listen," I said. "They're right. I've done some terrible things, and I—"

"Need to be punished," he said sourly.

I recoiled.

"You been punishing yourself for months," he said. "I mean, if you're sure this is right, that's one thing, but don't let 'em do it because it's just another way you can hurt yourself."

The saving grace, I thought with semi-hysterical detachment, was that there was no possibility the virtuers had understood him.

Ashmead, frowning, said, "We can remove the binding-by-forms first."

"Won't change a fucking thing," Mildmay said, and I could tell they'd understood him by the way all of them startled and three of them blushed.

Ashmead now looked frankly perplexed. "Mr. Harrowgate?"

"Mildmay," I said. "Sit down."

He glared at me.

"I *will* use the obligation d'âme if you make me."

"Felix, are you *sure*?" And while he looked merely hostile, he sounded agonized.

"I'm sure I don't want to fight our way out of here," I said unkindly. It jolted him back into self-awareness. He looked at the virtuers, who were clustered against the table watching him warily, then turned a bright, mortified scarlet and sat.

I said to Ashmead, "Are you still willing to allow me to teach?"

Ashmead was nonplused. "Do you *want* to?"

"I need employment." Mildmay shifted, and I said, "No, you won't. Now hush."

Ashmead glanced at the other virtuers, but they seemed to have abdicated responsibility, for he looked back at me almost immediately and said, "Yes. We need teachers. And I think your experience could be very valuable to our students."

*As the closest thing to a practicing warlock they're ever likely to encounter,* I finished, but only in my head. I held out my hands. "Do it."

He did not take them, looking troubled. "It shouldn't have hurt you. I don't—"

"It's most likely Malkar's fault. Think of it as, oh, thaumaturgical scar tissue." Like the scars on my back.

He looked from me to Mildmay and said firmly, "I'm going to undo the binding-by-forms first."

"My brother," I said and glared at Mildmay, who glared right back, "will not interfere."

The virtuers formed their circle again, albeit reluctantly, and Ashmead took my hands.

This time, I was prepared, and the pain did not surprise me.

## *Mildmay*

Felix wouldn't look at me.

The virtuers had done their thing. I'd felt the binding-by-forms go, like a dislocated joint popping back into its socket. I'd still wanted to kill all ten of the sneering bastards, but that was just along of me hating them. The extra thing, the thing like a rat chewing on my heart, that was gone. So I sat and thought about what I wanted to do to them instead of getting up and actually doing it.

I could see that what they were doing hurt Felix like a motherfucker, but he didn't make a sound, and he was still standing when they were done. White and sweating, but still standing. Virtuer Ashmead looked like he wanted to open Felix's head up and rummage around until he found out what was wrong. What made me kind of like him, even though I still wanted his balls on a chain, was that he looked like he wanted to fix it once he'd figured out what it was.

Which is to say, he looked almost as sick as Felix did.

And Felix wouldn't look at me.

I mean, he wasn't making no real eye contact with nobody—and I didn't fucking blame him, either—but even when he looked in my direction, he never got no higher than my knees, and when Virtuer Ashmead said, "We have a contract to discuss," Felix went with him meek as could be and left me with Virtuer Hutchence.

Virtuer Hutchence waited until all the other virtuers had cleared out, and then boosted himself up to sit on the table. Which I was pretty sure virtuers weren't supposed to do.

I raised my eyebrows at him, and he gave me a grin that made him look like he hadn't even reached his second septad yet. "It caused Pluckrose and Wooller physical pain when they offered me a seat in the Circle. But I'm the only enginist here who can teach worth a damn, so they didn't have a choice."

"And now you got stuck with me," I said cautiously.

"I'm sure it's supposed to be a punishment," he said, and he sounded so cheerful about it he made me laugh, even though I was trying not to. Then he sobered up and said, "And someone should keep an eye on you. We don't know very much about the effects of bindings on annemer and, well—you shouldn't be alone."

"I'm fine," I said. "Worry about Felix, not me."

"John's very good. The best medical magician on the faculty. Your brother will be fine." And he didn't even sound like he thought I was crazy for caring, although I knew he was probably thinking it.

"I really did ask him to do it," I said, speaking slowly and doing my best to keep my consonants from going to mush.

And he must have been dying to ask: "But why? Why would you *ask* someone to do that?"

Fuck me sideways. "It's complicated," I said, "but none of it's his fault. *None* of it."

Virtuer Hutchence looked at me funny, like he wasn't sure he should believe me, but I could see him figuring that if I didn't want to tell him, he didn't have no way to make me. He said, "If you want someone to talk to . . . I'll swear silence like intendeds do."

I shook my head.

"I won't judge," he offered. "Neither you nor Mr. Harrowgate."

"Don't like talking," I said. Which was true, and a fuck of a lot simpler than all the other reasons I wasn't going to go spilling my guts to him, no matter how nice he was.

He sort of hesitated, then nodded. "Well, the offer stands if you change your mind."

"Thanks," I said. I knew I wouldn't, and he probably did, too.

The door opened, and a student came in. You could tell them from the clerks because they didn't dress as nice and mostly they looked hungry. At home, I would've assumed they were pack kids.

"Hutch? Jowell said you were in here."

Virtuer Hutchence stayed right where he was and waved the student over. "What is it, Cyriack?"

Cyriack didn't even look at me. He said, "There's another report of a failure on the Barthas Cross line."

Virtuer Hutchence sat up straighter. "*Another* one? That makes, what?"

"Three in the past two weeks," Cyriack said, sort of gloomy and proud all at once. One of those guys that are never happier than when they've got bad news to wallow in, I figured.

"Was it the same thing?" Virtuer Hutchence asked, and I ain't even going to pretend I followed the conversation after that, because I didn't. Something about the trains, and something going wrong with the magic that made them work. At least it didn't sound like nothing was exploding.

They were still going at it like badgers with a hole to dig when Virtuer Ashmead brought Felix back. Felix was still pale, and he still wasn't looking at me, but I could see he'd pulled himself together some. At least enough that Virtuer Ashmead was smiling like he was glad he was giving Felix a job and not just from charity, neither.

"Then I'll see you Lunedy," he said to Felix.

"I have some ideas already," Felix said, "but I'll be glad to get a better understanding of your curriculum." His eyes slid sideways and didn't quite hit me. "Are you ready to go?"

"Sure," I said, and levered myself up. Powers and saints, I hated being a cripple. Before we'd made it to the door, Virtuer Ashmead had got himself dragged into the discussion with Virtuer Hutchence and Cyriack, and I ain't even sure they noticed us go.

Felix didn't say nothing all the way back to the glass birdcage, and the whole trip on the fathom, and then all the way back to the hotel. And sometimes he got like that, when he was mad or when he was thinking about some hocus thing, but this wasn't that. Because he never forgot for a second that I was with him, and he never forgot about letting me keep up with him, and he never looked through me like I wasn't there. I waited, because whatever the fuck was going on in his head, I didn't want to try and get it out with an audience, and especially not an audience that was already staring at us with eyes big as bell-wheels.

But as soon as the door of our room closed behind us, I said, "What's wrong?"

He twitched, but said, "Nothing at all," in a pretty good fake of his normal voice. "I have gainful employment and an entire new system of magic to study. What could possibly be wrong?"

I looked at him a moment, until his nerve broke and he turned his head. "If you want me to believe you," I said, "you might want to work on that smile. You look sick as a lemon. What is it?"

He sat down on the bed and yanked the ribbon out of his braid. "It's nothing."

I waited. And he knew as well as I did how this was going to go, because it wasn't even half a minute before he caved. "If you want to go home, I'll get an advance on my salary from Ashmead."

"If *I* want to go home? What about you?"

He shook his head, tiredly, like he was trying to get rid of something. "What I want isn't your problem any longer."

"What the *fuck*?"

He flinched, lowering his head so that all I could see was his hair like a veil. "It was only the obligation d'âme that forced you . . . I know you never wanted to leave Mélusine."

Kethe love the both of us, here we go again. And I couldn't stand it. Because I knew him, and I knew that if he got his way, we'd be going around and around on this same fucking thing until we either died of old age or I upped and strangled him just to get him to shut the fuck up about it. He was punishing himself again. I said, "Felix."

And I waited until he raised his head, although he was still sort of twisted in on himself so all I could see was the yellow glint of his good eye. It'd have to do. I said, "What I didn't want to leave was the Lower City. Okay? And I can't go back. For the same reasons I couldn't go back in the first place."

He was frowning. "But . . ."

"What the fuck do you think I've got to go back *to*?"

"Oh," he said in this little nothing of a voice.

"Look," I said, and even though I wasn't sure it was the right thing to do, I sat down beside him on the bed. Left side. Always the left side unless he needed somebody guarding on the right. He turned a little so he could still see me, but he didn't startle or flinch or get up again to get away from me, so I figured I was okay.

And then, of course, I couldn't think of a single fucking thing to say to him.

He was twisting his fingers together, still hunched in on himself like he was expecting me to hit him. Which was probably what happened every time things got rocky when he was a kid, and you know, I wasn't laying no bets about Lord Shannon, neither. It would've been easier if I could've just hugged him, but he didn't work like that, and finally I said, "I chose, you know."

"What?"

"When I asked you to do the binding-by-forms. I *chose*."

He muttered something, and for once it was me asking somebody else to repeat themselves. "False choice," he said more distinctly, but not looking up.

"Well, it was a rock and a whirlpool kind of thing," I agreed. "But listen. I ain't sorry."

"You should be," he said darkly.

"No. Felix, for fuck's sake. I love you, okay? And that has absolutely fuck all to do with the binding-by-forms. If you'd get your head out of your ass for a moment, you'd know that."

Well, at least it got him to look at me, even if he was staring like nobody'd ever told him they loved him before, and while I was pretty sure that wasn't true, it did occur to me that he could probably count on the fingers of one hand the times somebody'd said it without there being sex involved. And have fingers left over, too.

I figured I'd better push while I had him silent and listening. I said, "And what that means is I'd take it as a personal favor if you'd quit expecting me to leave. Because I ain't going. And now that the binding-by-forms is gone, you can't make me."

He made a funny choking noise and then he started laughing. I wasn't sure why, but it didn't hurt me none. And when he got himself back together, he didn't look half so tragic as he had.

And when he smiled at me—a real smile, and a pretty good one, even if his eyes were a little too bright—and said, "You were a terrible *esclavin*, you know," I knew we were going to be okay.

# Chapter 11

## *Kay*

Upon reaching Esmer, Murtagh handed me over to my sister and absented himself promptly into the arms of the Convocation, leaving me to Isobel's disposing. I was put in the nursery, away at the top of Carey House where I would not disturb anyone if I screamed or raved or battered myself senseless against the walls. The rooms had not been used since Murtagh himself was a child; I smelled the lingering traces of cedar and lavender under the stronger scents of soap and wood oil and burnt dust from the fireplace.

Seemed like pleasant rooms, insofar as I could tell: ridiculously large for a single person, but were no drafts and the dormer windows, facing east, were each large enough for a window seat. For all that I scorned myself for it, I could not help being drawn to the warmth of the sun.

Isobel allotted me a single servant; his name was Springett, and he was Caloxan-born. His hands were gentle, and his voice polite. He had been, he told me, the body servant of the duke's uncle Guy, who had died the previous winter at the unimaginably ancient age of ninety. Springett was accustomed, in other words, to the service of invalids, and I was pricklingly grateful to him for not putting it so bluntly.

On Domenica morning, I was woken by Springett's polite tap at the door. "What happens?" I said, hastily sitting up—as if that made me in any way less vulnerable. "Have I overslept? Is something wrong?"

"No, sir, not at all." I identified the sounds of Springett setting down the shaving tackle and can of hot water. "But Mr. Julian will be coming in an hour to take you to church, and Her Grace said she thought you'd like breakfast first."

"Mr. Julian? *Church?*"

"Yes, sir. Will you get up, then?"

"Have I any choice?"

"It is His Grace's pleasure," Springett said, so very neutrally that I knew I did not.

"Very well," I said and shoved back my bedcovers to stand.

Julian Carey was the only son of Murtagh's younger brother. The brother and his wife having both died, he in the Insurgence, she in a carriage accident or somesuch, Julian had become the duke's ward. He was sixteen and a student at the University of Esmer. Isobel had told me he was sullen, but since her barrenness made Julian the heir to the duchy, was foolish to imagine she would have any fondness for the boy.

But church? What in the name of all that was holy was Murtagh thinking?

I shaved and dressed myself, but had to trust my necktie to Springett. That at least had naught to do with my eyes—had never had the knack of a four-in-hand.

I said, feigning casualness, "What church enjoys the duke's favor?"

"The Carey family has always attended Our Lady of Mirrors, sir."

"Of course," said I. Our Lady of Mirrors was the largest and most beautiful cathedral in Corambis. The Dragon Duke did nothing by halves.

The breakfast table was between the windows in the outer room. I sat down, found the teacup by its heat. I sipped, letting it scald the dry foulness of dreams out of my mouth. Then, gingerly, I found the rim of the plate, gingerly let my fingers skate toward the center, ready to pull back at the first hint of something sticky. Instead, they encountered dry toast, and I heaved a sigh of relief. That I could handle without fearing for my clothes.

I made the tea last as long as I could, so that I had not too many moments of empty idleness before a knock came, not at all like Springett's polite tap.

"Come in," I said and congratulated myself that my voice was steady; I even sounded as if I had some control over who entered this room.

The hinge squeaked.

I turned my head toward the door. After a moment, there being neither speech nor movement, I said, "Yes?"

A boy's voice, very Corambin, very sulky: "I'm Julian Carey. Uncle Ferrand wants me to take you to church."

"So I have been informed." I stood up, moved away from chair and table, but stopped carefully in the middle of the room.

The boy's breath huffed out. "What must I do?"

"Give me your arm. And warn me about stairs, uneven ground, things of that ilk." I banished the memory of embarrassment in Lily-of-Mar Station on Mercoledy, when I had stumbled over the raised lip of a seating area and gone to my knees.

"All right." He jingled slightly as he approached. Jewelry, or perhaps the mockery of soldier's harness that Isobel said was in fashion now. Broadcloth beneath my fingers, a boy's skinny, awkward arm. He smelt faintly of citrus; he was old enough to shave or he pretended he was. "We'd better go," said he. "Uncle Ferrand will have kittens if we're late."

"Lead on," said I.

Are the same hallway and stairs they were on Mercoledy, I snarled at myself. Thou didst manage then, so is no point in megrims now. My grip tightened on Julian Carey's arm, but I did not clutch the bannister as it were my only hope of salvation. And I did not fall—though it was a near thing at the foot of the stairs, for Julian forgot to warn me.

He muttered apology; had he been a boy fostered to Rothmarlin, had I been Margrave of Rothmarlin still, we would have had words about courtesy and elocution, but he was not and I was not, and I most sincerely did not wish to be late to church.

In fairness, his guidance improved markedly thereafter. And I thought it was clever of Murtagh, the devious weasel, to have sent his nephew as my guide. He had assessed the Brightmore pride to a nicety, doubtless from too much experience: I might fear leaving Carey House to the extent that my heart was beating hard and fast against my ribs, but never to the extent of confessing my weakness to a sullen boy.

Seven steps down from Carey House's front door, and we turned left. I heard horses in the street, the creaking of wagon frames, the stately wooden clatter of the wheels. Were persons on the sidewalk; I caught fragments of conversation as we walked, and was a small child howling in protest, though I could not tell what its grievance was.

Once we were past that disturbance, I dared ask, "Is far to Our Lady of Mirrors?"

"Only a couple of blocks," said Julian, as one to whom this city was neither foreign nor frightening. I reminded myself not to cling to his arm like a shy debutante and straightened my spine. Almost immediately, however, my resolve was destroyed by an ugly, tangled interlude, a bewilderment of glancing blows and scents ranging from perfume to carbolic soap and chattering, indifferent voices and overlying it all a strange hollow howling—if it were a child protesting, the child was monstrous and ancient and most probably mad, and that which it protested was unbearable and irredeemable.

And then, just as suddenly, the throng was gone.

"Mr. Brightmore," Julian said thinly, his voice barely polite, "you are bruising my arm."

I dragged in a breath and forced my fingers to relax. "What . . . what *was* that?"

"What was what? Oh, the fathom station? Uncle Ferrand says Grandfather nearly quit the Convocation over that, having it so close to Carey House."

"Fathom station," I said blankly.

"You know, the fathom. The underground public railways. Don't they have them in Caloxa?"

"Trains underground?" I could think of few things more horrifyingly unnatural—though it did most clearly explain the howling of that monstrous child. The Veddick's child. "No, they do not."

"Oh." He was silent for a few paces, then asked, all a-sudden, "So what happened to your eyes anyway?"

"An accident," I said, truthfully enough.

"You don't look blind," he said, deliberately offensive or naturally tactless. "Was it magic? Did a warlock do it?"

"There are no warlocks," said I.

"Oh." He sounded puzzled. "But that's what the Insurgence was about, wasn't it? Bringing the warlocks back?"

"Blessed Lady, no! We may have been fools, but were not *stupid*."

"I beg your pardon," he said, stiff with affront. Was silent after that until we came to Our Lady of Mirrors, where he warned me brusquely of stairs, a door; and then the damp incense-laden heat of the cathedral struck me in the face. Julian tugged me to the left and hissed in my ear, "Take off your shoes."

Would be senseless squandering of breath to remind Julian that I had been brought up in religious orthodoxy just as much as he had. I knelt and removed my shoes and socks, tucking my socks into the toes of my shoes as I had been taught as a child.

When I stood up again, was no one near me. I could hear other people rustling and shifting. I waited a slow count of five before I said, "Julian?"

"There's cubbies for the shoes," said Julian's voice, somewhere in front of me and about the level of my knees. "I was just putting mine away. I'd better get yours, too."

"Please," I said shortly and reminded myself that I could not be angry at

Julian for not coddling me. He was not my nurse. Did not want one in any event.

Then he was back, citrus and broadcloth. "Let's go."

"Are we late?"

"No. Here's the pool."

The pool was heated, as I had heard the pool of Our Lady of Fallen Leaves in Wildar was. I was glad of the warmth lapping over the tops of my feet, glad this was not Our Lady of Marigolds with its icy, bitter water.

Julian forgot to warn me when we reached the far side of the pool; fortunately I felt the shift in his body and managed the step up without tripping. He was tense now, in a way he had not been either in Carey House or on the sidewalks of Esmer, and although he said we were not late, he was dragging at my arm as were nevertheless a terrible need for haste.

I planted my feet.

"Mr. Brightmore!" he protested.

"An we are not late," I said pleasantly, "is no call for breaking my neck, and I would liefer not."

"It's perfectly safe! No stairs or anything!"

"Is still no reason to go at it like rabbits running downhill. Especially in a holy place."

He was tugging at my arm, but I could not make sense of his desperation until a voice said from my right, "Hello there, Carey. Who's your friend?"

"Oh. Um. Hello, Thrale." Julian's voice squeaked on the last word, rising to a childish treble. He coughed and said, "This is my aunt's brother. I'm just going to find him a seat—I'll be right back."

This time, his jerk at my arm was vicious, and I did not, in sober truth, wish to explain myself to another stripling. I followed Julian's guidance forward on cool, slightly slick flagstones, and only barely managed to bite back a yelp when he stopped and pushed me hard to my left. I staggered, and the hand that reached out for balance found the scrolled back of a bench. "There," said Julian, "you'll be fine."

I reached for him—though what I would have done had I caught him, I knew not—but he was gone. Racing back to his friend Thrale, no doubt.

I took a deep breath and neither screamed nor blasphemed luridly—nor both. Slowly, praying that no one watched, I found the seat of the bench—smooth leather, soft with age—and settled myself on it. I was all right, I said to myself. Nor injured nor truly frighted, though the boy was a feckless mooncalf and should be taught better. I was in a great Corambin cathedral; no harm would come to me here.

Then that thought struck me as almost unbearably funny, and I had to bite my lip to keep from laughing out loud.

Was someone next to me on the bench—probably a row of persons, but I could only hear, feel, smell the one. A lady, smelling of attar of roses, dressed in something that sounded like silk when she moved.

At home, it would have been almost unforgivably rude not to turn and greet her; at home, I would have known her. I wondered if etiquette was the same in Esmer; then I wondered how she would respond to my Caloxan accent. I faced forward, said nothing, and distracted myself by wondering if Julian would return.

He had not by the time the service started. The intended began without censing the points of the compass; I tried not to heave a sigh of relief. I might and did despise the Corambins for their slovenly Caddovian ways, but was no denying it made the worshippers' role simpler and less strenuous—and I did not need to fear becoming disoriented and being unable to find my place on the bench.

I gave the intended but very poor attention. "Let your heart embrace forgiveness," said the intended, but my heart was embracing anger and fear. I found myself hating the crowd of Corambins around me, hating them for having light when I was trapped in darkness, hating them for making me afraid without even having the decency to realize it.

As one would expect from the greatest cathedral of Esmer, the choir was all but unearthly; the countertenor soloist sounded like the voice of the stars. I wanted to stand up, to scream, to tell them they had no right to create such heartbreaking beauty when Gerard was dead, my country doomed to servitude, and myself alone and afraid. Selfish, yes, but so were they. They did not care that this serene harmony was built on blood and death and pain.

I sat, my nails digging into my palms, and said over my coraline in my mind. Intended Frant, Gerrard's chaplain who had died at Subry, had once said to imagine each iteration of the coraline, each syllable of the meditation, as a pebble dropping into a clear pool, the ripples spreading of faith and love and tranquility, for yourself, for those for whom you prayed, for the world which was in such sore need. Did not quite dare to take the beads out of my pocket; I feared to reveal myself as an Eadian. I feared, and no number of prayers would change that.

The service ended; the woman beside me stood up. Awkwardly, stumbling, hunched, I rose, shuffled to the end of the bench, and then stood, clutching the back in both hands as people brushed and jostled past me. The noise caught and echoed, showing me the vastness of the vault, and the press of bodies began to make me dizzy. I felt as if the floor was shifting beneath my feet; my head was too light, too large, my pulse pounding in my temples. I will not faint, I said grimly to myself, biting the inside of my lower lip hard enough that I tasted blood.

The throng thinned out; the echoes died away. Could not unclamp my fingers or straighten out of my ludicrous defensive hunch. One set of footsteps now, a soft slapping of bare feet against marble, echoing and wheeling through the unknowable space of the cathedral; I could not tell whence they came or where they were going, until a male voice said, frighteningly close, "Are you all right?"

Was not Julian's voice, and I cursed him in my heart.

"I am fine, I thank you," said I. But none of my muscles would release their burden of tension, and the words sounded as if they had been ground out between great meshing gears.

"Are you alone? Is there someone I can fetch?" A soft voice, young, either gentle or feigning so.

"No, thank you. Please. Am all right. I just . . ."

"You are white and shaking. And I do not know you. Are you of this dominion?"

Lady of Dark Mercies, do you hate me so much? "Are you the intended?"

"Yes. I . . . Oh. You're blind. I beg your pardon. I did not realize."

Each fresh humiliation was a knife slashing deeper and deeper across the vulnerable veins of the wrist. I only wished my metaphor were real enough to die of.

The intended said, "Please. Let me help you. I cannot have you taking root in the sacristal. The vestry would never let me hear the end of it."

I was grateful for the joke, however nervous and labored. I said, "I have become disoriented. If you will but guide me back to the pool . . ." I shall be not one whit better off than I am now.

"Of course. May I know your name?"

"Kay Brightmore," I said.

There was only the slightest hesitation before he said, "Constant Godolphin," and his voice revealed nothing of his thoughts.

"I am . . . I am a dependent of the Duke of Murtagh." I could barely force the words out; I imagined my life's blood running down the back of the bench, spreading in an ever wider pool across the cold, echoing floor.

"I will send a message to His Grace," said the intended. "Or . . . I could walk with you back to Carey House if you would like."

"You are very kind," I said. "I do not like to bother His Grace unnecessarily."

"Then we will do that," said the intended. "I must fetch a coat. Are you all right to stay here for a moment?"

"Yes, thank you," I said and heard his bare feet pad briskly away.

I stood and said the coraline, trying to imagine my body as the pool, my heart as the stone. Slowly I straightened my cramped shoulders; slowly my fingers released their punishing grip on the back of the bench.

In the stillness, I heard someone wading through the pool, and my heart stopped in my chest.

"Kay," said Murtagh. "You have no idea how gratifying it is to find you here."

"Your Grace," I said through gritted teeth, my fingers digging into the bench back again.

"May I ask," said he, coming closer, "*why* you are here?"

"I told Julian to go on without me," I said savagely.

"Ah." Was a long, chilly pause. "I will have a word with Julian. And I beg your pardon for asking a foolish question. Shall we go home?"

Carey House is not my home. "Yes, but the intended . . ."

"What about the intended?"

"He offered to escort me back to Carey House. He went to fetch his coat."

"How kind of him. Then we will wait to express our gratitude."

I misliked the tone of his voice. "I am sure he would do as much for any in his dominion."

"Assuredly," said Murtagh.

Before the silence between us became unsupportable, the intended returned. "Your Grace," said he.

"My dear Constant," said Murtagh, as affable as a cat smiling at a caged finch. "I do apologize for the bother. A miscommunication, I fear."

"Oh, no bother. But I'm glad it was only a miscommunication."

"Quite," Murtagh said, and were nuances and overtones to their words that I heard without being able to interpret. "Your concern is appreciated."

"It is part of my duties as intended to care for the welfare of my dominion."

"We are fortunate to have an intended who is so scrupulous in his attention to duty."

"Your Grace is too kind."

A silence, thick and jagged-edged. Hating it, hating that I could not see their faces to judge, I said sharply, "Murtagh? We were going?"

"I beg your pardon, Kay. Intended, your indulgence, please. I need to get my brother-in-law home."

"Of course. I shall hope to see you both next Domenica."

"Of course," Murtagh said, and I mumbled something that might have been agreement or denial; I myself did not know which I meant.

Murtagh guided me patiently, fetching my shoes for me, warning me not only of stairs and curbstones, but also of more ambiguous obstacles, such as a pavement artist and an inquisitive brace of dogs. He warned me also of the fathom station, and I said, "Do you use it?"

"The fathom? No, I do not. But Tinder goes to visit his mother in Rhamant Dominion, and he tells me it is crowded and dirty and you must be careful of getting cinders in your eyes."

"Is it worth it?"

"For whom? It obviously is for those who use it, and it brings considerable revenue to the city."

"But it . . ."

"Yes, Kay?" He sounded amused.

"It is unnatural and blasphemous," I said stiffly. Is the child of the Veddick who cries beneath the earth.

"So certain divines have been saying for years." He *was* amused, damn him. I did not answer, knowing I could not do so civilly, and so we returned to Carey House, to my high prison, in silence.

## Mildmay

I don't know where Corbie was Savato or who she was with, and it was no business of mine. But Domenica morning, early, there was a tap on the door. Felix hadn't slept—every time I'd woken up, he'd been laying there on his back staring at the ceiling—and as soon as it was daylight, I'd chased him off to take a hot bath, because it beat all fuck out of him killing me or me killing him, and I wasn't sure which was going to come first.

So I opened the door, and it was Corbie, looking pink and scrubbed, and with her hair all flat again, and I hadn't even got as far as *good morning*, before she blurted out, "You wanna come to church with me?"

"Church?" I said.

"Yeah. Mabel who works in the kitchen, she goes to Our Lady of Enduring Stone, and it's only a couple of blocks. So I thought maybe you'd like to come."

"I, um." I didn't even know what to say. "I mean, I don't worship your Lady. You know that."

"I know," she said. "But you don't have to. The Ygressine sailors go to Our Lady of Tides all the time in Bernatha, and I don't even know what they worship. The Lady won't mind."

And, well, what else was I going to do? Wait around for Felix to pick a fight? "Okay," I said. "Lemme get my coat and tell Felix."

She looked worried. "D'you think he'd want to . . . ?"

"No," I said. Felix didn't have any religion, as far as I could tell, and he didn't care. And when I told him I was going to church with Corbie, he just said, "Have fun," all snarky, and I left before I said something I'd kick myself for later.

Corbie explained everything to me, about taking your shoes off and walking through the sacred pool—which was actually kind of nice, you want to know the truth. The church itself was round and humped, sort of like a Lundy loaf, and we sat in the back row of benches along the south wall. It was where I would've sat anyway, along of being close to the door, but Corbie said it was the visitors' bench. The church was a lot smaller than what I was used to, but then I'd always stuck to the cathedrals in Mélusine when I felt a need for churchgoing. They were so big the priests couldn't even see everybody there, never mind learn their names or anything, and that was the way I'd always wanted it.

So I felt kind of exposed, with this little church and all these people who knew each other by name. The priest was a fat guy wearing this long blue veil, and he actually came over and said hello and had we been in Ingry Dominion long and where did we worship at home and all the rest of it. I let Corbie do the talking, and she managed to make it sound like she was answering for both of us without telling any actual lies, and I could've kissed her for it.

The service was sort of weird and sort of interesting. The Corambins' prayers to their Lady were really pretty, although also creepy. They called her things like Lady of the Dark Waters and Lady of the Patient Hands, and I couldn't quite figure out what it all meant. I liked the singing, though, and then the priest, who was called an intended, talked for a while about charity and being aware of your blessings, and then it was over and we were wading back through the pool again.

Corbie was quiet for a little on the way back to the hotel, but then she said, "So your brother says he doesn't do women."

"Won't touch 'em," I said.

"What about you?"

"Sorry?"

"What about you? Do you do women?"

"Um, yeah," I said. I couldn't see why she wanted to know, but there wasn't no point in lying about it.

"So, do you want to do me?"

I knew I was gaping at her like a goldfish, but I couldn't fucking believe I'd heard her right.

"C'mon," she said. "If I'm not your type, I ain't gonna get mad about it."

"It ain't that. I mean, you're pretty and all. I just . . ."

"*What?*" she said, and she stopped walking so I had to turn and face her.

"Why're you asking?"

Her head jerked back a little. "I ain't gonna charge you, if that's what you mean."

"No. I mean, yes. I mean, sort of. Just . . . you want to fuck me?"

"There some reason I shouldn't?"

I waved my hand, kind of at my face and kind of at my leg and kind of just at me in general. "I ain't no prize."

"I ain't talking *marriage*," she said. "Look. Come on up to my room, 'cause I got the feeling you and Felix weren't real happy with each other this morning. If you don't want to do anything more, you don't want to. It's fine."

"I didn't say I didn't want to," I said, and I felt my face go bright hot red.

"Well, then we do," she said. "Look. It's a quick fuck, that's all. You don't got to think it to death."

So I went with her up to her room, which was this sort of cubbyhole on a half landing. Barely enough room for two people and the bed with the door closed. But Corbie didn't seem to mind.

She sat down on the bed and tilted her head at me. "You still look like you're thinking way too hard."

"I got, um. History."

"You wanna tell me about it?"

Well, I did, and I didn't. And there wasn't no good way to say most of it.

"I know about Felix," she said. "It ain't like that, is it?"

You know *some* about Felix, I thought, but I wasn't going to say it. "No. It ain't like that. I just . . . Look. I've fucked whores, and I'm okay with that. But every time it's more than that, it just . . ." Kolkhis. Ginevra. Mehitabel. "It's bad, okay?"

Corbie thought that over. "So if you don't pay me, it must go bad, is that it?"

"Not like that," I said, because put that way it sounded fucking dumb. "I just don't want to get into nothing big, okay?"

And she grinned. "Only thing I want to get you into is plenty small, believe me."

And there I was blushing again, may Kethe save me from my own damn self.

"Mildmay, c'mon," she said. "You really never fucked for fun before?"

"No," I said slowly. "I guess I never did."

"So let's," she said. And I just didn't have no arguments left.

## Felix

Savato night, I did not sleep. Domenica night, too tired to stay awake, I slept, and I woke up three times from dreams that the Automaton of Corybant was attacking and I had no magic to fight it. Each time, Mildmay woke and got his arms around me and murmured things like "It's okay," and "Just a dream," until I stopped shivering and panting. If he was worried about being that close to me, both of us nearly naked, it didn't show. And all I wanted was for him to stay.

"We never said it," I said into the darkness, for I had no witchlights to call.

"Who?" said Mildmay.

"Joline and I. We never said it. We didn't dare."

"Joline? The little girl you said—"

"You remind me of. Yes." I was surprised, and touched, that he remembered. "We both knew what happened to someone if you loved them. If you *said* it."

"They went away," Mildmay said. He understood, absolutely.

"Or they changed. They hurt you. Or you hurt them." I sat up, wrapping my arms around my knees. "Keeper said he loved us, you know."

"Before or after he drowned you?" Mildmay asked savagely.

"Both. We figured he was lying, but how could we be sure? So we didn't say it. And Joline . . ."

"She went away anyway."

"She died," I said.

"What's the difference if she didn't come back?" he said, with a sort of horrible reasonableness that made me shudder.

"Don't do that."

"Do what?"

"Don't . . . I'm not a child. I know the difference between leaving and dying."

"Yeah. How 'bout the difference between loving somebody and hurting them?"

I shut my eyes hard, tears stinging. "You really think I'm that . . ." There was no other word. "That fucked up?"

I startled him into laughing, a half-pained exhalation. "I think you're seriously fucked up, yeah."

"Do you think that about everyone who plays the martyr? Do you think all tarquins are like Malkar?"

"Whoa," he said, and he sat up beside me. "When'd we start talking about sex?"

"We were talking about love."

"Yeah," he said. "We were talking about you and Joline."

A cold hand crushed my chest, stealing my breath. "I . . . I . . ." But I couldn't say anything. There weren't any words, there wasn't anything except this icy, dragging pain.

"Felix." Mildmay's hand was on my arm. "I *thought* maybe . . . Do you think you have to let people fuck you for them to love you?"

"No, of course not," I gasped. "What a stupid notion."

"Yeah," he said, with such profound sarcasm that I knew he knew he'd caught me. "You got that right."

I rested my burning face on my knees. He sighed and stretched; his breath caught, and I knew his lame leg had given him a twinge.

"Almost dawn," he said. "Might as well get up. You get paid today, right?"

"You say that like you have plans for my money," I said.

"Oh fuck yes," he said cheerfully, and even in the mostly-darkness of our room, I knew the movements of him reaching for his cane and standing up. "First up is the hotel bill, and then I figure we ought to look into finding someplace to live."

"I'm getting an *advance* on my salary, not—"

"I been asking around," he continued over me, " 'cause I figure if we get close enough to the Institution you can walk, you won't have to use that fathom thing all the time. And that's where all the students live, between the Institution and that other thing, the Universal-whatsit, so it's cheap anyway."

"University," I said. "The University of Esmer."

"Yeah, that. Hey, d'you know, was it or the Institution here first? 'Cause I've been wondering if the hocuses followed the professors or the professors followed the hocuses."

"Universities are an ancient and honorable institution," I said, so grateful for a neutral topic I could barely keep my voice steady. "There was one in Cymellune. There's one in Aigisthos. And the Universitat in Igensbeck, of course. Most places that have universities, the wizards are part of the faculty. I don't know why it's separate here."

"Probably something to do with them warlocks. Most everything is, seems like." A scrape as he lit a lucifer and touched flame to the candle. "How come Mélusine don't have one?"

"A university?"

"Yeah. Does Vusantine have one?"

"Not exactly, although I imagine many people would tell you the Library of Arx is the same as a university. Tibernia and Marathat and the western Grasslands follow an even older tradition of scholarship which rejects the idea that learning can be regimented and measured. It's a personal matter, you see, between a scholar and his teacher and his . . ." I laughed, startled. "I suppose Thamuris would call them his spirit-ancestors. The authors of the books he reads."

Mildmay paused in the middle of braiding his hair to make an interrogative grunt around the ribbon he was holding in his mouth. He had exceptionally high standards for decency before he'd even go as far as the lavatory in the morning. I hadn't understood why until I'd realized how many of the maids seemed to loiter in our hallway, or on the landing. I'd asked him, and he'd gone red and muttered something about the things people read in novels.

I did not, however, want to tease Mildmay about it, so I said, "The west tends more toward communities of scholars than schools per se, although naturally a good deal of teaching goes on."

Tying his ribbon, Mildmay said, "Yeah, but Mélusine don't even have that. 'Cept the Mirador, and that's just you hocuses."

"Mélusine has scholars," I protested.

"Yeah, but no *communities*. I mean, even the musicians have a school, but . . ." He said harshly, "It's the witch hunts, ain't it?"

"I beg your pardon?"

"Hard to be a community when people are calling you a heretic every time you open your mouth to tell somebody else what you think. 'Less you're a Cabaline, of course."

The witch hunts were a painfully sensitive issue for him, and I had learned we could not discuss them without arguing viciously. My fault as much or more so than his, and I did not want to have that argument again. Not now. Possibly not ever.

So I took a deep breath and surrendered. "You may be right."

"I *what*?"

"You may be right," I said again, not sure whether I was pleased or hurt by his obvious shock. "It's a plausible theory, in any event."

He stared at me a moment longer, then said abruptly, "I'm gonna clean up," and left the room.

I lay down again, intending only to rest until he returned, and woke up several hours later to a room flooded with sunlight. I had a moment of disoriented panic, and then I remembered. The binding-by-obedience. I felt like I was strangling, but it was only my magic that couldn't breathe. I would become accustomed, in time.

Mildmay was in the chair by the window, frowning over one of the newspapers.

"What time is it?" I said.

"Whose timekeeping you want it in?" he said without looking up. "I'd call it the fourth hour of the day, you'd call it ten o'clock. The people here call it some damn thing with flowers in it."

"They also call it ten o'clock."

"Yeah," he said irritably.

"Anything interesting in the papers?"

"Depends. What's a pestilence?"

He pronounced it slowly, but correctly, although I heard the hesitation as he wondered what to do about the final *e*.

"Plague," I said and sat up. "The newspaper's talking about plague?"

"No. I mean, yeah, but not like you mean. They're talking about sheep."

"Sheep?"

"Yeah, the sheep in, um, Murrey Margravate are all dying, and they're calling it a pestilence. Although, I kind of think that's just because it sounds better than saying nobody knows what the fuck is going on."

"Cynic."

He shrugged. "These newspaper guys get awful excited about stuff." I knew he was thinking of the stories printed about the Automaton of Corybant, and the accompanying shameless speculations about me.

"They're in competition with each other. Whoever tells the most grandiose lies wins the readers."

"So it's just like gossiping, only on paper."

He sounded so disgusted I couldn't help laughing. "It does seem that way. I'm going to go bathe, and then let's go to the Institution and see about that advance."

"You got it," he said. "I'll find more words to bother you with."

He did, in fact, have three more additions to his vocabulary when I returned, and we ended up discussing the word "cleave" all the way to Arkwright Hall. ("They're talking about this woman cleaving her husband like it's a good thing," he said, "and, you know, I guess it could be, but it don't seem like the kind of thing the newspapers would get behind." I bit my lip to keep from laughing and said, "Did they perhaps say, 'cleaving *to*'?" "Oh," said Mildmay. "It makes a difference?") I wondered what the real reason was that Kolkhis hadn't properly taught him to read; it certainly wasn't the reason he always gave, that he was too stupid to learn.

He didn't want to come into Arkwright Hall with me, although he didn't want to tell me why. I finally let him go because I knew from experience that if he was determined to, Mildmay could communicate a bad mood to everyone who came near him like some sort of plague. I found my way to Virtuer Ashmead's office alone.

It was not a large room, and it seemed smaller than its actual dimensions because it was crammed with shelves of books and a hulking monstrosity of a desk, itself nearly invisible beneath stacks of paper. Virtuer Ashmead stood up when I tapped on the half-open door, and beckoned me in.

"How are you doing?" he said.

"Oh, I'm fine," I said.

He looked at me as if he could tell that my smile was fake. "In the old texts, the binding-by-obedience is called the choke-binding. Its effects are not pleasant."

"Unless you're offering to lift it, this conversation is pointless," I said. "Please, let us talk about other things."

# *Mildmay*

So I convinced Felix I was okay to go out on my own while him and Virtuer Ashmead talked about hocus stuff, and I didn't tell him why, along of not wanting to have the fight—*any* of the fights—that would just boil down to Felix having to be the boss of everything. And mostly, you know, I didn't mind, but it sure could get in the way of getting things done. So I picked his pocket for the card the student had given him because I figured if anybody knew where you could hire rooms for cheap, it would be these kids. And that was the thing I most principally wanted. I was *done* with hotels.

The card said *Robin Clayforth, The Mammothium, Room 322.* I wasn't sure I'd read it right, but I flagged down a guy outside of Arkwright Hall, and he told me how to get there, no problems.

The Mammothium looked like it'd started out in the world as a flashie house, and I liked it for not looking so much like the Butchers' Guild. I thumped up onto the porch, and since there wasn't nobody around, and no signs to say otherwise, I went in.

And stopped dead. I knew my mouth was hanging open, but for the longest time I couldn't seem to do a thing about it.

Smack dab in the middle of the front hall, where flashie houses would've had a statue or a fountain or a big fucking vase of flowers, the students had a skeleton. And it was the skeleton of some animal I'd never even seen before.

And it was fucking enormous. I mean, they'd *had* to put it in the front hall, because there was nowhere else it would've fit. And powers and blessed fucking saints, the *tusks* on the thing. I mean, I'd seen wild pigs. But they were nothing—*nothing*—compared to this thing, whatever the fuck it was.

And I was still standing there, gawking at it the way Felix had told me not to gawk at the glass birdcage, when somebody came clattering down the stairs. It was the student who'd come in to talk with Virtuer Hutchence on Savato, and I said, "What the fuck *is* this thing?" before I caught myself. Can't take you anywhere, Milly-Fox.

But he took it in stride. "It's a mammoth. Mr. Foxe, isn't it? Mr. Harrowgate's brother?"

"Yeah," I said. "You were with Virtuer Hutchence. Sorry, but I forget your name."

"Cyriack Thrale," he said. "Is Mr. Harrowgate with you?"

"Nah," I said, and his face fell. "He's with Virtuer Ashmead. But what's a mammoth? I mean, I ain't never seen one."

"Well, you wouldn't," said Mr. Thrale. He came around the mammoth to stand beside me. "Given that the last of them died several thousand years ago."

He didn't look like he was kidding, but— "Several *thousand*? You can't know that."

"That," he said, "is what the magic is for."

And, okay, it was absolutely the answer I deserved for sounding like I didn't think he knew what he was talking about. "Sorry," I said. "None of my business. I just meant to ask—"

"No, honestly," he said. "Sorry. I didn't mean to sound flip. It's why we're the Mammothium." Brown eyes, dog-earnest, and either he really wasn't yanking my chain, or he was the best actor I'd ever seen, including Mehitabel Parr.

"Okay. So how does it work?"

His eyes lit up and he told me. In detail. Now, mind you, I didn't understand more than half of it, but I got enough to be sure it was for real, that this enormous fucking thing in front of me had died so long ago I couldn't even begin to imagine it. Then he stopped and cleared his throat and said, "Of course, I don't really know much about the mammoths."

"You don't?" Because it didn't look that way from where I was standing.

"No. I work on bog people."

"On which people?"

"Bog people?" he said, like he expected me to know what he meant. I guess I looked blank enough to convince him I didn't, because he said, "Oh. Well, there are peat bogs. North of Esmer, mostly, but really all over the western part of the country. And people cutting peat—it burns, you see, and it's quite cheap, cheaper than coal—well, sometimes they find bodies in the bogs."

"Sure," I said. After all, it was what the St. Grandin Swamp was for, only it sounded like these bog things were a fuck of a lot more useful.

Only it wasn't the same, because nobody knew who these dead people were. And somebody got curious, and they asked somebody, who asked somebody else, and it ended up here, where they figured out these bog people were really old—not as old as the mammoth, Mr. Thrale said, but older than Cymellune of the Waters. So the hocuses started studying them, the way hocuses do.

I said, "You don't mean necromancy, right?"

"Blessed Lady, no! That would be . . ." He shuddered and said, "Disrespectful," although I was pretty sure that wasn't the first word he'd thought of.

"Sorry," I said. "I was just worried."

"Are there necromancers in Mélusine?" he asked.

"Yeah. You could say that. But if you ain't doing necromancy, what are you doing?"

And he smiled at me, kind of shy which made him look a lot younger all at once, and said, "Would you like to come see?"

The first thing they'd had to do, Mr. Thrale said as he led me up the stairs, was keep the bodies from decaying. "The bogs preserve them frighteningly well, but once you take them *out* of the bog . . . We had one decay to bits even while we were unpacking it. We have some spells that work all right. But this is where we keep them." He unlocked a door. The sign on it said something about keys.

"You keep it locked all the time?"

"Some people," he said, "have very primitive senses of humor."

"Oh. Right."

"We've actually had to put warding spells on Henry."

"Henry?"

"The mammoth." He called witchlight as he stood aside to let me in. "We named it for the last king of Corambis. Inappropriately, actually, since Adept Gower thinks it's female, but you know how things stick."

The room was long, and it felt narrow, but I thought that was just because of the shelves on either side, which were deep enough to fit a person on and so cluttered with boxes and papers and jars that you couldn't even see the walls. There was a box on the table that ran down the center of the room.

"This is our best specimen," Mr. Thrale said and flipped the catches.

It was a nicer box than the Kennel had put Luther Littleman in, and the guy in it was in better shape than Luther Littleman had been, too. He was a funny color, and he looked a little squashed, but he was all curled up on himself like he was sleeping, and you could almost believe he'd open his eyes and cuss us out for bothering him. His hair was braided up in these fancy knots, and he was wearing sandals that laced up around his calves. There was a blanket covering his middle, but since it was dark blue and everything else was the same sort of rusty orange color, I figured the hocuses had put it over him.

Lined up alongside him, there were a bunch of sticks: three long ones and six shorter ones split into y-shapes. "What're those?"

"Ah," said Mr. Thrale. "We think he was a warlock."

"Okay. And?"

"It's a very old punishment—it was outlawed centuries ago. But if you had to get rid of a warlock, the only way to do it was to drown them in a bog and then stake them down so they couldn't come back."

"It's not like that'd help," I said.

"I beg your pardon?"

"Sorry. Thinking of something else. So this guy was bad news?"

"We think so. Adept Gower has a friend who's spending his winters going around and asking all the old grannies for the oldest stories they know about bogs, and they're fairly conclusive. If you have something—or someone—evil, you throw it into the bog, and the bog swallows it."

"And then it gets dug up later to be somebody else's problem."

I had to say it twice, and then he frowned at me. "If he was evil—there's none of that left now."

"No, course not. Sorry. You were gonna tell me what else you know about this guy."

"Yes," he said, and brightened right back up. A lot of it wasn't even magic, just looking at things. Like his sandals were made out of leather. I asked about his hair, and Mr. Thrale said they weren't sure.

"Adept Gower thinks maybe it has something to do with his magic, but really that's just a guess. This isn't, though." He touched the dead man's face, and I watched the weird orangy color just clear away like spilled water in a circle about the size of my palm. His skin was still darker than Mr. Thrale's, but his hair was a lot lighter, almost white-blond. Mr. Thrale lifted his hand, and the dead guy went back to orange.

"Wow," I said. "So, can you tell by magic that he was a warlock?"

I had to repeat myself, but then he shook his head. "No. What makes someone a magic-user . . . well, no one really knows what that is or where to find it."

"Then how can one—" I stopped myself using the word "hocus." Mr. Thrale wouldn't know what I meant, and it wasn't fair to him. "How can one magic-user use another's magic? And how can the Circle shut somebody's magic down, if they don't know where it is?"

"I'm sorry," he said. "I really didn't catch very much of that."

I'd gotten too worked up for anybody but Felix to be able to understand me. I said it all again, slower. Mr. Thrale listened intently and nodded and said, "With living magicians, it's a matter of aether and controlling its flow. But dead things have no aether."

"What about annemer? Do I have this aether stuff?"

"Of course you do," he said, like he was shocked I could think I didn't. "What magicians can do that annemer can't is *move* aether—take it from one thing and put it in another. That's what necromancy is. Putting aether in something that shouldn't have it."

I wished Felix was here because he'd know what questions to ask and whether this was all as crazy as it sounded like to me.

"So you don't really know this guy was a warlock?"

"It's an educated guess." Mr. Thrale was giving me the hairy eyeball in a really polite way. He knew he'd hit me on the raw somehow that didn't have nothing to do with his dead guy, but I wasn't going to spill my guts.

I mean, it wasn't even my business, really. It was Felix's, and I didn't know how he wanted to handle it. Just because it drove me batfuck insane that he'd let the Circle do that to him, didn't mean I had any right to go around telling the world. But before I'd figured out anything I could say to get past it, Mr. Thrale blinked and actually rocked back on his heels a little. "I'm so sorry. This can't be why you came here. I just—"

"It's your work. You're excited about it. I get it." I would've smiled at him, but that'd just make everything worse. "Actually, I was looking for Robin Clayforth, but maybe you could help me?"

"If I can. With what?"

"I'm looking for a place to live. For me and Felix. Cheap is good."

He was nodding. "Yes, of course. I know of some places." He gave me a considering sort of look. "I was on my way home when I ran into you, so if you wanted to go now, that would be very convenient."

"Okay, yeah. Let's."

"Excellent," said Mr. Thrale and closed that dead and drowned warlock back in his box.

That night, I was woken out of a sound sleep—and one thing I will say about having the binding-by-forms gone, I sure was sleeping better—by Felix saying, "Mildmay. Mildmay, I need you to do something for me."

"What?" I said. I sat up and after a second where I couldn't think why it was so dark if Felix was awake and talking to me, I remembered about the binding-by-obedience and reached for my lucifers to light the bedside candle.

He was crouched on the floor beside the bed, staring at me, and his hair was wet.

"What is it?" I said, and I was thinking fire or machine-monsters or something, but I couldn't figure out why his hair was wet—and not just his hair, but the whole top half of his nightshirt.

And he looked at me with his wide, panicky, spooky eyes and said, "The fantôme."

At which point I started feeling pretty panicky myself.

I knew what a fantôme was. Sort of. Well, no, not really, except what Mavortian von Heber'd said, that it was a ghost that had managed to possess somebody. And I remembered it taking a whole roomful of hocuses to get rid of the one in Hermione. Four indictions ago or more. When Felix had been batfuck crazy, and oh merciful powers, I did *not* want to be dealing with that shit again.

I said, very carefully, "That was a long time ago. D'you think maybe you just had a bad dream or some—"

"Not *that* fantôme," he said. "The one in the ruined house."

"What the *fuck*? What fantôme in the ruined house?"

"I thought it was just a ghost," he said, hugging himself and shivering, and I could see water dripping off his hair onto the floor. "But it tried to . . ."

I saw his throat work and could fill in the rest. No good. No fucking good at all. But seeing as how I wasn't a hocus, there wasn't nothing I could do about that part.

"So what are you doing?" I said. "Why are you all wet?"

"Water," he said, like it was any kind of a useful answer. For all that his eyes were open and he was talking to me, he wasn't really awake. Because if he'd been awake and himself, I would've gotten a fuck of a lot more words, even if not more sense.

"Yeah, okay, never mind. You said you needed me to do something. What is it?"

And he looked at me, wide spooky scared as fuck eyes, and said, "Drown me."

"*What?*" I realized I'd grabbed a double handful of his wringing wet nightshirt and dragged him halfway onto the bed. "What the *fuck* are you talking about?"

"Drown it," he said, cold water dripping down my forearms. "I tried, and it didn't work, so do it this way. Drown me, and it'll be gone."

"We are not drowning you, you stupid fuck!"

"But it found the rubies. We have to get rid of it." His teeth were chattering.

"Fuck this for the Emperor's snotrag," I said. I struggled up, dragging him with me, and started stripping that soaking wet nightshirt off him. He fought me, but not very well.

"People can be revived," he was saying when I got it off over his head, all earnest and patient like he thought it was going to make the least bit of difference to me. "From being drowned. Keeper revived Rhais once. Not twice, though."

I gripped his shoulders, looked him square in the eyes. "We. Are. Not. Doing. That."

"But I can't fight it. It found the rubies, and they took my magic, and there's nothing left. Mildmay, there's *nothing left*."

Powers and saints, I didn't know how to deal with this. He was shivering and he was so fucking skinny I could count every rib, and he was looking at me the way he'd looked at me when he was crazy, like he knew I could make things better, but he wasn't sure I'd *bother*. I fucking hated that look.

But there was one thing I knew. "Yes, there is. *You*'re left."

"Me?"

I looked around, snagged one of the hotel towels, started drying his hair, trying not to be rough, although I was too mad and too scared to be really gentle. "Yeah. You. Felix Harrowgate. *You*." I jabbed a finger at his breastbone. "You're more than just your magic, ain't you?"

"Am I?" He sounded like he really didn't know.

"Powers," I said through my teeth. "Yes. *Yes*, okay? Them hocuses can't take that away from you, and neither can no fucking ghost-hocus, so don't give me this shit about there being nothing left." I flung the towel across the room. "Look at me."

It took him a moment, but he did finally raise his head.

"You see me? Me? Who am I?"

He licked his lips. "Mildmay," he said in a rough whisper.

"Good," I said. "And you trust me?" My hands closed on his cold shoulders, and I shook him once, not hard but sharp. "Do you?"

"Yes," he said, a little stronger. "Yes, I do."

"Okay," I said. "Then you trust me about this. There's *everything* left, and the fantôme can't have you. You hear me?"

"Yes," he said. "Yes, I do." And he shuddered, shuddered hard, his face twisting. When he opened his eyes, they were clear again. He frowned at me. "Mildmay, what—"

"You awake?" I said.

His frown turned into a squint; then he looked down at himself and back up at me, and I think he would have bailed if he hadn't been buck naked and with no place to go. "Did I . . . What did I do?"

"You were trying to talk me into drowning you. Along of this fantôme you apparently got and ain't seen fit to mention before."

"Oh. *Oh*." He turned away from me, went wandering around the room like he was looking for something, only if he'd really been looking for something, he couldn't've helped finding it in about a second and a half, because the room was just not that fucking big. "I, um . . ."

"You gonna try and tell me it was just a bad dream?"

"No," he said, his shoulders hunching a little. His back really was a mess, scars on top of scars and crossing scars and the worst one like this dead gray rope knotted across his left shoulder blade and most of the way down to his hip. Every time I looked at it, I thought it must've laid him open to the bone, and every damn time, I wanted to find his keeper, even though I knew the fucker was dead, and beat him to death with his own fucking whip.

Felix got himself turned around again, although he wasn't even trying to meet my eyes. "I was trying to find a way to tell you."

"Next time, you might try just *saying* it. You know. Instead of waiting 'til you're sleepwalking or whatever the fuck that was. Because that ain't no fun, if you were wondering."

He kind of flinched.

"What?" And then I knew, because it was Felix, and powers and saints, it made too much fucking sense. "There something else you ain't been telling me? About them fucking rubies, maybe?"

"I, um . . ."

"Fuck me sideways, Felix, just spit it out already."

He kind of stuck for a second where he was, and then he started talking. And, you know, most of what he said didn't make no sense to me, but I got enough of it.

And it wasn't like I'd needed telling that anything that had *anything* to do with Brinvillier Strych was bad fucking news.

"So you're stuck with them," I said when he finally ran down.

"Yes," he said, and he went to get his other nightshirt out of the carpetbag.

"And the fantôme?"

"I thought I'd gotten rid of it. But I hadn't."

"You said it found the rubies."

"Did I?" he said, like it didn't matter, but I knew better.

"Yeah. What's that mean exactly?"

"Nothing good."

And, yeah, I'd figured that out already, but he sounded so tired—so fucking *beat*—that I let it go. He didn't need me nagging at him. If there was something I could do, I had to trust he'd tell me.

## *Kay*

I had taken to asking Springett the date every morning. I realized full well that it was an annoying and repetitious habit, as bad as any child demanding to know how many days *now* until his birthday, but I could not break myself of it. I could not deny the fear crawling up inside my chest that, did I but allow it, I would become an invalid, not merely in that my body was not whole, but in that my mind was not, either. Thus, I demanded to know the date, and I demanded to know the color of my clothes, and whatever he might think of me, Springett answered my questions. I tortured myself with the idea that he might lie to me, for indeed, how could I confirm the truth of what he said? But he did not seem the sort of man to do it; though I doubted I knew much of who he was in truth, his hands were always gentle, and I did not think—could not allow myself to think—that his hands could lie to me. I had often seen the truth of a man in the way he handled his horse, or his hounds.

And on the day that he told me was Domenica, Julian Carey came again to take me to Our Lady of Mirrors.

I supposed that in a novel, the situation might be comical, though I did not find it so myself. Julian, standing well away as if he thought I might try to attack him, said, "Uncle Ferrand says I am to apologize. And that I am to take you for a walk after church."

"And thus I am your punishment," I said, and did not try to curb my bitter tongue. "How kind of Uncle Ferrand."

"I *am* sorry," Julian blurted. "I didn't think."

I believed him, for he was nothing but a spoilt child. "You thought of your friend," I said tiredly.

He had no answer to that. I heard him shift his weight uncomfortably, his jewelry clinking. Shallow, spoilt boy, not worth any drama. I said, "We should go, should we not?"

"Yes," he said gratefully, and as I rose from my chair, he crossed the room to give me his arm.

Was easier, this second time, to leave Carey House. I could not brace myself for the fathom station, exactly, but at least I knew what it was and that I had only to let Julian tow me through the press of bodies and the unearthly howling. When we reached Our Lady of Mirrors, he was careful of me, and when he guided me to a seat, he sat down beside me.

I did not want the boy to make himself a martyr. "You don't have to sit with me," I said. "Just come back when the service is over."

"No," Julian said. "Uncle Ferrand would notice. And believe me, he's mad enough at Aunt Isobel for not letting us sit with them."

"Of course." I was, after all, the only blind man in the cathedral. Murtagh would only have to turn his head to see whether Julian was obeying orders.

"You and Aunt Isobel really don't like each other, do you?" Julian said. He sounded curious, a little shocked; I should, I realized, have faked some sort of response to news of Isobel's hostility. But perhaps that was not worth any drama, either.

"We have always hated each other," I said. I folded my hands in my lap and bent my head over them.

"Always?" He sounded even more shocked.

I wondered if had ever been a time when Isobel had not resented me. Had she looked at her newborn half brother with affection?

Before I had to answer Julian's question, the service began. I paid better attention to the intended this time; it made a difference to know that his name was Constant Godolphin, to remember that he had been kind to me. He preached about the necessity of peace, the duty incumbent upon each follower of the Lady to work actively toward harmony (like many intendeds, he had a taste for musical metaphors). "Peace," said the intended, "is not merely the absence of strife. It is the *refusal* of strife."

But what if one cannot refuse strife? I thought. What if one has not the luxury? The people of Rothmarlin might refuse strife; it meant nothing but death if the Usara did not choose likewise. And I had chosen strife again when I chose to follow Gerrard. But so had the Corambins of forty indictions ago chosen strife; if they had not so chosen, the Mulkist warlocks would still hold sway in Caloxa, and that might be peaceful, but I did not think it could in any way be considered right.

Is easy to refuse strife when thou standst in a cathedral in Esmer, when no one in thy life has offered thee harm.

And is easy, I answered myself, to disdain peace when thou hast fought all thy life. Thou art no soldier now, nor margrave, nor anything save an invalid. Perhaps thou shouldst give a little more thought to peace.

And another thought formed before I could stop it: What good has all thy fighting done thee?

None. Gerrard was dead; Cecil held Rothmarlin; I was a duke's dependent whose skills—with sword, with bow, on horseback, on foot—were worse than useless. Thus far, I had spent much of my time sleeping, healing, and when I was alert, I explored my new home, if home it was, determined not to be prisoned in one chair. Every day I could endure for longer, and my mental map of the nursery was complete, though vague in places. What I would do with the long empty hours once I had recovered my full strength, I knew not.

And if I kept thinking along these lines, I would turn Julian's afternoon penance into torture indeed. I recited the coraline in my head, drowning out my own gnawing thoughts, and wondered if there was any difference between the peace the intended preached and the tranquility the coraline brought me. Could I have one without the other?

When the service was over, Julian said, "Let's wait until the crowd has thinned out a little. It'll be easier for you."

And you won't have to worry about encountering your friend Thrale. I bit my tongue against the words, for I was burdened with Julian this afternoon as much as he was burdened with me, and I had no great fancy for braving the crush in any event. I could hear the muted babble of voices, the splash of feet in the pool, a great rustling murmur of cloth and bodies, and I did not want to be among them.

We were still waiting when I heard feet approaching us, and beside me, Julian scrambled to his feet, dragging me up with him. "Intended," he said, nervous enough that his voice cracked. I reached forward and found the back of the bench in front of me. An anchor.

"Julian," said the intended. Constant Godolphin's soft, gracious voice. "I am pleased to see you well. And Mr. Brightmore. I had been afraid you would not return after the mischance last Domenica."

"That was my fault," Julian said, and even a spoilt child could have his own sort of bravery. "It won't happen again."

"I'm glad to hear it," said the intended, and I could not decide if was some sharpness under his habitual softness, or if was merely my imagination.

But, no, Julian heard it, too, for there was diffidence in his voice when he said, "Intended, could I ask a favor?"

"Of course, child," the intended said, though not warmly, and I deduced that whatever the issue was between the intended and the duke, Julian was a part of it.

"Not for me," Julian said. "For Mr. Brightmore. I thought, if you showed him the cathedral, then perhaps coming here wouldn't be so . . ." He trailed off, and I wondered just how much of my fear and unhappiness I had betrayed.

"That's a very good idea," the intended said, his voice warm now with approval, and Julian muttered, "Uncle Ferrand bade me *think*."

*Think how you would feel if you were blind.* I could all but hear Murtagh's voice. Blessed Lady, I had become an object lesson in this silly child's moral education.

On the other hand, I reasoned with myself, fighting a wave of sick humiliation, seems it has done some good. Julian *had* thought, and he had conceived of a notion that might actually make my life more bearable.

"I would be very pleased," said the intended. "Give me a moment, for I must say farewell to Mrs. Chepstow and Mrs. Storridge, but I will return directly."

His footsteps padded away; I wondered if he was like the intended in Barthas Cross who argued all winter with the vestry about the sanctity of socks, or if he enjoyed going barefoot.

Julian said, "Is this all right? I'm sorry I didn't ask you first, but I wasn't expecting the intended to come over, and really he'll be a much better guide than me."

"Perfectly all right," I said, mostly to curtail the flow of his words. "If you'll return in, perhaps two hours?"

"Return?"

"I won't tell your uncle. You need not be tied to me all afternoon."

A silence. He said, sounding hurt, "I *said* I was sorry."

"And I accepted your apology. You needn't stay."

"Oh," he said. "Do you wish me to go? I'm sorry, I didn't think—"

"I care not," I said, and realized too late how harsh it sounded.

He said stiffly, "I think I should stay, thank you."

Then the intended returned, and I was spared the attempt to placate. The intended said, "Where would you like to begin, Mr. Brightmore?"

This was a new thing. Since I had been blinded, I had known only two places properly: the old nursery in Carey House and the tiny hotel room in the Althammara. Both those places I had learned by trial and error, by creeping about with one hand against the wall, or feeling my way from one piece of furniture to the next. I had never entirely learned the hotel room, because I was never sure enough of privacy to be thorough. In Carey House, I seemed to have nothing but privacy; was no one to watch my childish fumblings, nor anyone to ask for help. On Venerdy I had become hopelessly lost—richly deserved comeuppance for reckless overconfidence—and had finally resorted to crawling, hands and knees, until I ran into a wall. And then crawling along the wall, in and out of a corner, until I found the door frame. Then, blessedly, I had known where I was, and had been able to walk, upright as befitted a man, back to the chair by the fireplace. And there I had sat, shaking, my eyes stinging with tears I would not weep, for nearly an hour before I could regain my composure.

Would be none of that here. Not in front of the intended, and not in front of Julian Carey. Carefully keeping my voice calm, light, a little disinterested, I said, "In truth, I know not. I had no familiarity with Our Lady of Mirrors before I was blinded, thus I cannot even hazard a guess as to its . . ." I released the bench back to make a two-handed gesture. "Habiliments."

I was proud of myself, both for saying *before I was blinded* as if it mattered little and for the gesture, which proved I did not fear the unknown space around me.

Yes, with Julian to one side of thee and the intended to the other, thou'rt most brave.

"Well," said the intended, "then let's be methodical and start with the entryway and the pool."

As it turned out, Julian was as methodical as the intended, and both of them were far more patient than I. They spent hours that afternoon showing me the cathedral, the sacred pool, the wall shrines, even the Altar of Mirrors. Was I who finally admitted fatigue and asked Julian to escort me back to Carey House.

Soon enough, I would start to slip and think of it as "home."

## Felix

Mildmay went out Domenica afternoon, on another of his errands he preferred not to discuss. I was too relieved to care, for I did not want an audience for what I had to do. I had thought I had defeated the fantôme, banished it if not destroyed it entirely, but I had been horribly wrong. It had merely been waiting, searching for advantage. And it had found its advantage in the rubies, adding their noirance to its own, weaving a trap of nightmares for me: rape instead of seduction. It had failed, but I knew that was only because Mildmay had been here, because he had woken me. If it tried again, as it certainly would, I had no illusions about my own ability to withstand it.

I had failed in banishing it when I had my magic, and now with the choke-binding on me the idea was merely ludicrous—but there was a difference between magic and will, and it was the will that the fantôme worked on, while it was the magic that it wanted. And dreamwork was not magic, though it could be the basis for thaumaturgical workings.

And I had the Sibylline.

I sat on the bed in the Golden Hare, as I'd sat on the bed in the Five Dancing Frogs, and laid out the Sibylline. This time, I was divining simply for the card that would represent the fantôme. I was expecting the Dead Tree or the Siren, but what came up, over and over, regardless of what method I used, was the Hermaphrodite.

"This makes no sense," I said to the cards. The Hermaphrodite was the card of the union between the male and female aspects of the self; it could symbolize a literal union between man and woman, or close cooperation between wizard and annemer, but more often indicated the need for the waking self to attend to the dreaming self or for rational thought to heed emotional need. *And there are many arguments,* had said Mavortian von Heber dryly, *over which of these is the male and which the female.* It was the card of balance. Also, I thought, the card of the sphinx.

There was no point in using the cards if I wasn't going to trust them—a lesson that Iosephinus Pompey had very nearly beaten into my head when he started teaching me oneiromantic symbolism. I put the other cards away, crossed the Hermaphrodite with the Parliament of Bees, and descended into a trance.

My construct-Mélusine was still barren and desolate, a cold schematic in gray stone. The ruby bees made small stiff flights around my head. As I had before, I made the circle, closing the gates. This time, I shut Horn Gate without hesitating.

*Thou knowst that will not work,* said the fantôme. *Even thy magic could not make thy fortress fast against me.*

*Oh, it depends,* I said. *You see, I'm not trying to keep you out.*

I turned and said to the bees, *Hold.*

The worst thing about Malkar's rubies, the *worst* thing, had always been the knowledge that I could use them. They obeyed me now, circling the fantôme, which wavered from Isaac's shape to Mildmay's and then vanished entirely. But it was still there, for the bees continued to circle. With all my strength of will, I imagined a prison for a ghost, not of rock or of iron, but of glass and blood and dust. I put the Hermaphrodite within the prison, and then, imaginary hands clenched with entirely real effort, I put the fantôme within the Hermaphrodite.

Its shriek of protest went through me like iron nails through paper, but I held fast to my image. The Hermaphrodite within the prison blinked, and when it opened its eyes, they were red with fire and fury, dark with blood and madness.

Fantôme.

The bees landed one by one on the glass and began to circle, just as they had done in the air.

*Why dost prison me?* said the fantôme. *I would serve thee.*

*You would devour me.*

*They are the same,* said the fantôme.

*I do not wish your service.*

*Thou art mine to serve,* it said implacably. *And thou liest. Thou wishst my service with all thy heart. I have seen thy heart, Felix Harrowgate. I know what it holds.*

*You do not. You see only what serves you.*

*I see what is there.*

*No,* I said and twisted into waking.

The construct-prison held. I knew the fantôme's rage, but did not feel it. I was not free of it, but at least I wouldn't wake Mildmay in the middle of the night again because I could not tell the fantôme's urgings from my own thoughts.

And nothing, not an emperor's ransom or the chance to go home again, would make me take the rubies out of their wash-leather bag. For now, I was using them, but I knew in the darkest, twisted corners of my heart how little it would take for them to begin using me.

## Mildmay

Cyriack Thrale led me to a place I wouldn't've found on my own, but that was just fucking perfect for me and Felix. Big old brick apartment building, with a courtyard with a tree in the middle, and an apartment that was twice the size of anything I'd ever had in the Lower City, and if I was doing the math right, it cost about half as much. And it came furnished.

I made the deal with the landlord Domenica afternoon. When I got back, Felix was sleeping like a dead thing. I didn't know if that was okay or not—because he hadn't fucking *talked* to me, the secretive son of a bitch—but I figured finally that his body needed the sleep anyway. So I watched in case something bad happened—well, something bad I could recognize—and when he woke up, he said the fantôme had been "dealt with."

"That a permanent kind of 'dealt with' or the other kind?" I said, and he hunched up a little and said, "I'm working on it," and I left it at that because he still didn't need the extra grief from me and it *still* wasn't like there was anything I could do. I figured my best bet was to give him a distraction, so I told him about the new place, and he chewed me out about not telling him, and we were okay again.

Lunedy morning, we moved ourselves in, us and our carpetbags, and Felix was unpacking our stuff into the closet and the big ugly bureau when he suddenly stopped and said, "You know, this really won't do."

I looked up. He was standing in the middle of the room, holding his dark green coat out in front of him and looking at it like it was a cat he'd just dragged out of the milk jug. And, you know, seeing it in bright mid-morning sunlight, I knew what he meant.

Back in the Mirador, I'd packed two of his coats, the dark green and a dark blue. They were the plainest coats he had. I didn't feel like getting bashed over the head so somebody could pick the bullion out of Felix's sleeves.

The blue coat had lasted until just past Fiddermark, when we hit a patch of the nastiest weather I've ever been out in. We'd both ended up soaking wet and covered in mud. And then we'd gotten in this kind of tangle with the gate of the hotel courtyard and somebody else's nasty-tempered horse, and the coat had ended up with a hole in it you could put your hand through. I'd expected Felix to yell at me or yell at the guy who owned the horse or just plain yell, but he hadn't. He'd stripped out of the coat and given it to the hotel-keeper's wife for her patchwork and hadn't said a word. Two days later, he *had* yelled at me, gone off like a string of firecrackers over Kethe knows what, but I'd known it wasn't about whatever the newest thing I'd done wrong was and it wasn't even about the coat. It was about Gideon and being exiled and the whole fucking mess that he just couldn't talk about.

But anyway, that was the end of the blue coat. The green coat, which Felix didn't like as much for reasons I didn't even try to understand, had made it the rest of the way, across the mountains and everything, and it was still perfectly decent—I mean, any secondhand store in the Cheaps would jump at it—but there was a button missing and the color was going in places and my darns weren't what you might call invisible. "Shabby" I guess is the word I want, and not how you want to look when you're getting ready to stand up in front of a roomful of strange kids and convince them you're worth listening to.

"And you're no better," Felix said, giving me a frown like he'd only just noticed.

"Hey," I said. "No one's gonna expect me to look flash."

His frown got heavier. "You know I have no more social standing here than you do."

"Sure you don't," I said, and I was being snarky for sure. "You're a hocus and you talk right and—"

"You could learn," he said, cutting me off so sharp that I guessed he'd been looking for an excuse to say this for a while. "You're learning to read. You could learn—"

"Don't," I said, cutting him off as sharp as he had me.

He gave me this look, sort of bewildered and a little hurt, like I'd slammed a door in his face he'd thought I was going to hold.

Oh fuck me sideways 'til I cry. But we were going to have to do this sometime. "Say I did. What d'you think it'd change?"

"I don't—"

"It wouldn't make this fucking scar go away, would it? I'd still sound like a half-wit."

"You don't—"

"Felix," I said, and he stopped. "I know how I sound, okay? Kolkhis used to—" I shut my mouth, hard.

"No, go on," Felix said, and now he was watching me instead of the coat, his eyes bright, like he was hunting me. "What did Kolkhis do?"

"Don't matter. Point is, I can't change the way the words come out. And I'd rather . . ." I didn't know how to explain it, something I'd been doing so long I never thought about it anymore.

"You'd rather play to people's expectations than challenge them," Felix said. He sounded sad, like I'd disappointed him. "Well, it is your prerogative. I just wish—"

"Do I embarrass you?" I said, and it came out nastier than I'd meant.

He went red like a sunrise, right up to his hairline. "It isn't that."

"You're a fucking terrible liar," I said, and he went redder. "No matter how flash I talk, I'm still going to embarrass you. You know that."

I could see him wanting to deny it. But he *was* a terrible liar, and we both knew it, and he was smart enough to know that lying to me here wasn't going to help.

And because I'm a mean son of a bitch, I sat there and watched him struggle and didn't do nothing to get him out of it.

Finally, he dropped the coat and said, "Maybe I need to be embarrassed then." He was still red in the face, but his chin was up, and he met my eyes like he was daring me to say he was lying now.

"But you hate . . ."

"Maybe it will be good for me. I told you, a long time ago, that I can't change what I am. And maybe that *is* true. But I want to try."

"You been thinking about this."

He shrugged. "On and off. It's easier, out of the Mirador."

"I thought you were homesick."

"I was. I am. But just because I want something, doesn't mean it's good for me. Rather the reverse, in fact."

It took me a moment, but I thought I knew what he meant. "Phoenix?"

"And Malkar. And Shannon, for that matter. I have a long and inglorious history of wanting what hurts me." He laughed, though not like anything was funny. "I was trained as a martyr. As I think you've already gathered."

"I'd sort of guessed."

"I have preferred the tarquin's role," he said, his voice chilly now, kind of distant. "But that's just vanity."

Which, okay, not the word I would've used. But I didn't say nothing, and he must've been wanting to say this for a while, too, because he kept going. "You see the pattern, don't you? I want to be hurt. And if I can't get it one way, I find another."

"Um," I said, because I wanted to argue with him and couldn't.

"Sometimes," he said, still chilly and real far away, "I think I am very, *very* stupid."

And powers, I had to ask. "Is that what happened in Bernatha? You wanted them to hurt you?"

"No! I didn't want that. I didn't want any of that." But his color was up, and there was something wrong here. I waited, because silence was the one thing Felix just couldn't stand. And sure enough, after a moment he started pacing. "Do you think I wanted it?"

"No," I said, because I knew he hadn't. Except he had. He'd wanted to be hurt. To be punished. But he hadn't wanted what they did to him. I'd known that as soon as he'd tried to distract me from the bruises on his face. And then it hit me, and the words got out before I could stop them: "That's why you let them put that fucking binding on you, isn't it?"

"What?"

"The binding-by-obedience. You *let* them. Because you *didn't* let those fuckers in Bernatha . . ."

It was the look on his face that shut me up. He'd gone paper-white, and his mouth was flat and hard. And his eyes were fucking wild—not angry, the way I was used to. This was something else. "You want to know what they did?" he said, and his voice wasn't much more than a whisper.

I didn't—really fucking didn't—but I would've had to be blind, blind and deaf and fucking dead, not to see that he needed to say it. "Tell me," I said.

He did. He told me the whole thing, flat out, no fancy words, no dancing around things. Started with the hecate and the blindfold and just kept going. He didn't even fucking blush. And I listened to the way his voice changed, the vowels getting longer and darker. I'd heard him slip before, maybe once or twice, but this wasn't the same thing. This was more like him pinned under me at Nera, screaming curses at me. This was what he'd been before Strych got him. This was the part of him that was my brother all the way down to the bone.

He was trying to shock me, too. There was something—I don't even know the right word. But he told me how they'd made him come, and he was watching me with his wild, spooky eyes, and I knew what he was looking for. Good thing I had a lot of practice in not giving it to him. And besides, if there was one thing I'd learned from Kolkhis, it was just how much you couldn't control what set your cock off. Didn't mean fuck all about what you wanted. He finished, still watching me, still waiting for me to scream or puke or run away or whatever the fuck it was he thought I was going to do, and I said, "They hurt you."

Short, choppy nod. Still waiting for the sanguette blade.

I said, "They hurt you, and you didn't control it."

It was more like a flinch than a nod, but it was a nod.

"And you didn't control what your body was doing, neither."

He finally looked away from me, and there was the blush. Some of it was shame, even though he had to know the same thing I did, that what they'd got his body to do didn't mean nothing about nothing. But most of it was . . . I knew the word Felix would use: *fury*.

"So you set it up to happen again."

That got him looking back at me in a hurry, and about half a step away from murder if I was reading him right. "Yes, you did," I said before he could think of the words to tell me I was full of shit. "You showed them hocuses what you could do and you gave 'em Lord Stephen's letters and you went in there and you told them every fucking thing you could think of to make them do what you wanted. They hurt you, but you controlled the whole fucking thing. And you got what you wanted."

"I don't want this," he said, although his voice wasn't much more than a whisper.

"You were right," I said. "I see the pattern."

He turned away, shoulders hunching, hands going up to his face, and I said the only thing I could: "I'm sorry."

He shuddered, and it was a moment before he answered me. But when he did, he'd got his vowels back: "You, of all people, have nothing to be sorry for."

"Yeah, but—"

"I *was* right," he said, and he straightened up and turned back to smile at me. It wasn't a great smile, but I thought it was real. "I am very, *very* stupid."

"You been hurt," I said, because I understood all about how that made a person do stupid shit.

His eyebrows went up, and he stared at me a moment. "You don't have the least taste for tarquinage, do you?"

"I don't—"

Powers and saints, I'd been looked at like that before, but only by brothel madams weighing me up to see what I'd go for and how much it was worth.

"I ain't into pain."

"Pain is only part of it," he said.

I had chills going up and down my spine, and I couldn't keep my voice quite steady enough when I said, "I don't know what you're talking about." Because I knew how this went. I'd seen him hurting, so he turned around and hurt me. Like a clockwork bear. Wind him up and watch him go.

But this time he didn't. He kind of shook himself, and his face changed somehow, some way I didn't have words for, but that dark unhappy thing was gone. "Power, darling," he said, drawling it out to make fun of himself. "It's what everyone wants. Didn't they tell you?" Then he bent and picked up the green coat and said, "I think it's time I became a Corambin gentleman. New clothes, get my hair cropped—"

"Your hair?"

"Don't sound so shocked." His smile twisted a little. "I prefer not to appear before the students of the Institution as some kind of exotic savage. And after all, it's just hair."

"Right. Course."

He paused, fidgeted, gave me a sidelong look. "Do you want to come? I promise not to be dreary anymore."

Yes, of course I went with him. What the fuck else was I gonna do?

And he was right. He wasn't dreary at all.

## Kay

On Mercoledy, Isobel arrived as Springett was clearing away my breakfast and announced that I was coming with them to meet Vanessa Pallister's train.

I descended the stairs on my sister's arm and hoped she was not—as I most excruciatingly was—remembering that other, infamous time we had walked together, her on my arm, when she was given in matrimony to Ferrand Carey. Gerrard had begged the sacrifice, and I had given it, although Isobel had been furiously derisive of my right to do so. And yet it would still have been worthwhile, the wedding together of Murtagh and Rothmarlin, if only Isobel had been fertile. If only there had been a child in the long sere years before the Insurgence. Perhaps the Insurgence would not have happened at all.

Perhaps cats will spread their wings and fly to the moon, I mocked myself.

Isobel did not take me the same way Julian had, and I bestirred myself to ask, "Where are we going?"

"The stables," she said and added condescendingly, "We do not walk to Fornivant, Kay." For a moment, I wished to be sighted again purely for the vicious pleasure of boxing her ears.

Were more stairs down, and then the surface beneath my feet changed, and were echoes, strange ones. I slowed, and Isobel said impatiently, "Is a tunnel. Between the house and the stables."

"It sounds . . ."

"Brick. Is just brick. Now come on, please, or we will be late."

"And Murtagh will be so very vexed."

"Actually, yes, he will, and I would prefer not to spend the day with *both* of you bristling like porcupines."

"I do not—"

She laughed, and the echoes were distressing. "Hast been a porcupine since thou wert but two hours old, Kay my lad."

She knew me too well. We knew each other too well, in sober truth, and it did occur to me, as Isobel led me up the stairs into the stable, that perhaps a wife would be a mercy, for then I would not be in my sister's care.

The stables smelled as clean as it was possible for any stable to smell, and mercifully they did not echo as the tunnel had. Murtagh's carriage smelled of leather mostly, though inevitably also of horses. I felt his presence as Isobel and the footman guided me in, smelled the sharp citrus of his cologne. He waited until I was seated to say, "Good morning, Kay."

"Good morning, Your Grace," I said, as Isobel climbed in and the footman closed the carriage door.

"Have we not had this discussion? We are as brothers. Can you not unbend sufficiently to have done with the 'Your Graces'?"

"As you wish," said I.

"Is Julian joining us?" Isobel asked, her voice too light to be trustworthy.

"Yes," said Murtagh. "He is, of course, late."

Isobel's sigh was deliberately audible.

I said, "Who was it he met at the cathedral on Domenica last? Did he tell you?"

"He did not tell me," Murtagh said, "but I know quite well who it was. Cyriack Thrale, a student-magician at the Institution, whom Julian met somehow through the University. Julian is a trifle foolish about Mr. Thrale."

"If by 'foolish' you mean 'soppy,'" Isobel said.

"My dear," Murtagh said reprovingly. "Julian takes after his mother in the, ah, ferocity of his enthusiasms. He values Mr. Thrale's friendship very highly."

"He behaves like a milkmaid. It's unseemly."

"He is very young. And I believe Mr. Thrale is very kind to him."

"As long as it's nothing more than kindness," said Isobel. I kept my head bent, my hands folded in seeming tranquility.

"Julian may be a mooncalf, but he will not disgrace his name," Murtagh said, and at that dreadfully opportune moment, the carriage door opened again, and the carriage shifted, springs groaning, under Julian's precipitous entrance.

"I'm sorry I'm late," he said, joining me on the bench. I realized that the citrus smell on him was the same as on Murtagh and wondered if Murtagh had given it to him, or if he used it on the sly.

"I've spoken to you before about punctuality," Murtagh said. "Kindly take the lecture as read and do better next time."

"Yes, sir," Julian muttered.

A sharp rapping sound: Murtagh telling the coachman to go. We lurched; I discovered that I was on the backward-facing bench. After a moment, I was able to compel myself to straighten my shoulders, to relax my hands.

*Julian isn't the unnatural one,* I wanted to tell my sister. I bit my tongue, hard enough to sting, and blessedly, Julian launched into some convoluted complaint about his music teacher—unless the complaint was about the piano on which he practiced. I could not tell, and did not exert myself to discern, although I listened carefully and attentively to Julian's diatribe all the way to the railroad station.

I had fought to keep the railway out of Rothmarlin. Even on campaign against the Usara, I had written letters; in the winters, when I could spare time to go to Barthas Cross, I had pled my case to Gerrard. And he had laughed and promised that Rothmarlin should remain unsullied, a promise which he had kept—although was cruelly moot now. I did not know what the Convocation had planned, and I was not going to demean myself by asking. I knew what Cecil's response would be.

"This time, Julian," Murtagh said as the footman steadied me out of the carriage, "you will stay with Mr. Brightmore. I can threaten you with further dire punishments if you think it will help."

"No, Uncle Ferrand," Julian said, as resentful as a smoldering slow-match.

"He was very kind and attentive on Domenica," I said, and in the disbelieving silence, I heard Isobel snort.

But Julian whispered, "Thank you," and gave me his arm; we followed Murtagh and Isobel into Fornivant Station.

Was like being trapped in a sounding belfry with a flock of mad crows. I could make no sense of what I was hearing, could only grip Julian's arm tighter and go where he led. He did remember to warn me of stairs, and when we stopped, he was kind enough to say, "Uncle Ferrand has gone to inquire about the Whallan train. We're to wait here."

Was a wall at my back, and although I could hear the crowd, no one brushed against me. I breathed, carefully, forbidding the flickers of panic that wanted to fan themselves into a fire.

And then a voice said, "My lord? Is that you?" A man's voice, a strong Caloxan accent. "My lord Rothmarlin?"

Oh, no. No. But the voice was already close to me, already saying, "My lord Rothmarlin, do you not know me?"

"I cry thy mercy," I said, "I am blind, and I do not know thy voice to give thee name. Who art thou, I pray thee?"

They were soldier's hands that caught my own, big and square and rough with calluses, missing the tip of one finger. "Ah, my lord," said he. "I had heard, but I prayed I had heard wrongly. I am Lucas Atford. I served with you seven summers in the mountains."

"Seven summers" was only a formula, but I did know the name. And those hands. "Lucas Ironhand, art thou?"

"Yes, my lord," and it hurt to hear the delight in his voice, as if I had granted the dearest wish of his heart merely in remembering him.

I floundered for a moment, drowning in all the questions I did not dare ask: what was he doing here? was he well? did he blame me? Lucas stepped even closer: sweat and soot and the cloying, musty scent of horehound. He said, his voice barely more than a whisper, "My lord, are you all right?"

That question was unanswerable. Lucas said, "We have feared for you, my lord. We would have come to you, had we known how."

Oh Blessed Lady, Murtagh was right; there were people foolish enough to follow me if I tried to wake the Insurgence from its deathly sleep. Were people who would die on what they believed to be my behalf, and the thought was so unbearable that I wanted to scream at Lucas, here in Fornivant Station, a pointed symbol of Corambin wealth, Corambin power, wanted to rip my clothes off so that he could see me for what I was: a man, neither more nor less than himself, scarred, maimed, broken, nothing worth his death, nothing worth *anyone*'s death.

Did not, of course. He would not understand; no matter what I did or said, he would see the Margrave of Rothmarlin when he looked at me, and was as the Margrave of Rothmarlin—and cruelly, I found myself hoping it was for the last time—that I had to answer this challenge.

I said, as carefully as I walked among naked swords, "Is good in thee to worry, Lucas. But thou needst not. I live in my sister's house, and she cares for me." Lady, if you love me, let Isobel not be in earshot, for the sound of her laughing like a dying cat would surely make matters even worse.

"My lord?" Lucas said doubtfully.

*It is over,* I wanted to say. *Half the young men of Caloxa are dead. Gerrard is dead. If thou canst not see that I might as well be dead, then I pity thy blindness even more than thou dost pity mine.* I said, "I am well, Lucas. I hope that thou art well, also."

"Yes, my lord," he said, still puzzled but obedient to the cues I was giving him. "Well enough."

"Good," I said, as heartily as I could. I could not ask him about others who had served with him, lest he take the question as code for something darker. I hesitated for a moment, and then blessed Julian Carey wholeheartedly, for he said, "Uncle Ferrand is waving, Mr. Brightmore. We need to go."

"If you need anything," Lucas Ironhand said in a hoarse whisper, "you just send a message to me."

"I thank thee, Lucas," I said and let Julian drag me away.

He demonstrated unexpected tact: he did not ask. I wondered how much he had overheard. And then my sister's sharp voice was in my ear: "The train's on time, for a wonder. Come, Kay, we don't want to keep Vanessa waiting."

No, of course not.

There were more stairs going up. I fell over them, because Isobel did not warn me. Was Julian who helped me up again, who whispered, "Sorry," in my ear and again sounded like he meant it.

At the top of the stairs—and Julian kept his grip on my arm, remembered to warn me—the racket was even greater and more mechanical. "Is the train here?" I asked, needing information more than my pride.

"Yes. I think Uncle Ferrand's gone in search of . . ."

I had no better idea than he did of what he ought to call the lady. I knew her name, but not her title, since I was uncertain of the rank that accompanied the position of Warden of Grimglass, and I had been too busy pitying myself to ask the correct questions. "Vanessa," I said, because Julian could not, and because I could not force the words *my fiancée* out of my mouth.

"Yes," he said. "And I think—yes, he's found her. He's bringing her this way."

"Splendid," I said faintly. "Where is my sister?"

"She's bull— I mean, she's engaging a porter."

And then there was Murtagh's voice: ". . . and this is Kay Brightmore. Kay, may I introduce Vanessa Pallister?"

Because I had to, I extended my hand. She wore kid gloves, and when I lifted her hand to my lips, as I was constrained to do, she smelled of lilies.

"I'm very pleased to meet you, Kay," she said. She was a soprano, her voice very clear. She was taller than I, but almost everyone was.

"Likewise," I said, untruthful but courteous. "Was the train journey very difficult?"

"Only because the train didn't go fast enough," she said and laughed, a perfect chiming trill that set my teeth on edge. "I've been buried alive out at Grimglass for the past three indictions. I thought I was never going to get to see civilization again."

Not a grieving widow, then. And I reminded myself that was a mercy, since a grieving widow would have had every right to see me as the symbol of her husband's murderers. But I could not keep myself from saying, "It must be hard to be parted from your son, though."

"Richard is a good boy. He'll mind his uncles."

Isobel arrived then, with porters in tow, and the resulting chaos saved me from having to find an answer. By the time we were all returned to the carriage, Vanessa had entirely forgotten what we had been discussing and was eagerly plying Murtagh and Isobel for the three indictions' worth of gossip she had missed.

I had learned, as I learned in my blindness to listen more truly, to hear both what was and what was not said, and I noticed that Vanessa's answer—*Richard is a good boy. He'll mind his uncles*—had little if anything to do with what I had actually said to her. I had asked if she missed him.

Well, clearly, she did not.

My mother had not missed me when I went to war at the age of fourteen. I wondered if I could persuade someone—Springett? Isobel? Julian?—to write a letter for me to the little boy in Grimglass whose mother did not miss him, either.

## *Felix*

I realized as I was climbing the stairs up Caliban Hill on a sharp, windy Mercoledy, trying to think of another way to explain the metaphorical nature of magic to my earnest, industrious, uncomprehending Corambin students, that I wished Gideon were here, not in the guilt- and grief-stricken way I wished I had been able to save him, the way I wished I could speak to him just once more, to tell him how sorry I was, but simply because he would love this challenge, would love discussing it—and arguing about it—with me.

I didn't know how long Gideon had been dead. I had lost track of time somewhere in the rain and mud between Mélusine and Bernatha. Mildmay would know, but I wasn't going to ask him. It was better if I didn't try to keep track of the time. Better not to know how many months Gideon had been dead; better not to know how many days I had lived with the binding-by-obedience like a smothering weight on my chest. I kept myself focused on my teaching, on my reading, on not sliding back into the bad old habit of taking my frustrations out on Mildmay.

As a lecturer at the Institution, I was given an office in a building called, for no reason that I could discern, the House. It was a nice room, large-windowed, and its primary purpose was as a place where the students in my classes could find me if they needed to. Thinking of the hours one could spend in the Mirador trying to track down an errant colleague, I quite saw their point. There was a flaw in the design, however, namely that if the students could find me, so could other people. Letters started arriving before the brass plaque with my name on it had been fastened to the door—mostly invitations to events I did not wish to attend, although some of them were even more bizarre—and later that Mercoledy, I looked up at a knock on the door and found a complete stranger saying, "Mr. Harrowgate?"

He was a middle-aged Corambin, indistinguishable from the multitudes save that his tailoring was better than average, though not as good as, for instance, the Duke of Murtagh's.

"Yes?" I said warily.

He came in, shutting the door behind him, and leaned across my desk to say fervently, "You have to help me!"

"I beg your pardon," I said, leaning away from him.

"You can explain it to them," he said, still fervent. "*You* know that it worked."

"That what worked?" I said. "Who *are* you?"

And he looked at me reproachfully and said, "Edwin Beckett."

I shoved to my feet in a strange mixture of fury and panic and blistering humiliation. "What are you doing here?" I said, my voice a hiss instead of a shout. "What do you want?"

"They're going to take the Clock of Eclipses away from me," he said. "You can't let them."

"Take the . . . It's a Titan Clock! You can't *take* it anywhere."

"The Institution," Beckett said in a thin, precise voice, "is forming a research committee to investigate the Clock of Eclipses. They inform me that no one of lesser rank than an adept second grade will be a member. They *tell* me this is to ensure that only the highest standards of research and thaumaturgy are met. They say they are concerned about amateurs endangering themselves. *Amateurs.*" He snorted. "You can see what they're doing, can't you?"

"Yes," I said, "and I approve."

It almost literally staggered him; he stared at me, mouth agape, as if he had never imagined I might side against him.

"Mr. Beckett," I said, "I don't know why the Clock of Eclipses started again *and neither do you*. What I do know is that you and your friends nearly killed me, or at the very least burned my magic out of me like a spent lucifer. And I furthermore know that no responsible act of magic is predicated on rape. And I know that I want you out of my office. Now."

He stared at me, forehead wrinkling. "Rape? But you're a shadow. You like that sort—"

"If it hadn't been rape, it wouldn't have worked," I said. Abruptly, I could bear the conversation—could bear *him*—no longer. *"OUT."* I strode around the desk, past him. Yanked the door open.

He left the office, then turned. "I'll speak to Virtuer Ashmead. Tell him what sort of person he's—"

"Is that a threat, Mr. Beckett? Funny how it sounds exactly like what you came here to ask me to do." And I slammed the door in his face. Then leaned against the door, feeling myself trembling, and slowly slid down it, for my knees would not support me. I wished Mildmay were here, not least because he would have broken Edwin Beckett's nose. But I had told him not to come with me, knowing that he would be bored, and I was a grown man, wasn't I? I could take care of myself.

"Oh quite," I said in a bare wobbling whisper and swallowed hard against a giggle that I knew would turn hysterical.

I was still sitting there when there was another knock on the door.

"What?" I said; there was a rough edge to my voice that might have been temper or might have been tears, and I myself wasn't sure which.

"Felix?" Not Edwin Beckett. Corbie. I picked myself up in a scrambling hurry and opened the door. She was standing in the hallway half-poised, it looked like, to flee.

"Come in," I said and raked my hair out of my eyes. "I'm sorry. I thought you were someone else."

"I don't want to bother you," she said.

"No, please. Come in."

She did, hesitantly, giving me quick uncertain glances under her pale eyebrows, and perched on the edge of the room's second chair. I made my way back behind my desk and sat down and said, "You were right. I should have brought charges."

"Sorry?"

"Edwin Beckett. He was just here."

"He was *here*?" She looked around as if she expected him to jump out of a corner at her. "What did he want?"

"Nothing I could help him with. But enough of my ridiculous little melodramas. What brings you here?"

Although she attended my class faithfully, I hadn't otherwise seen much of Corbie; the Circle, in the person of Virtuer Ashmead, had insisted that if she was to study magic at the Institution, she had to take classes at the Women's College. It was too late to enroll her for this quarter, so I had argued that it was unfair to charge her tuition, and Ashmead had agreed. I had been sad, but also relieved that she was getting proper instruction, and I had hoped that her failure to seek me out meant that she was happy and learning, but now her chin came up and she announced flatly, "I'm not taking those stupid classes anymore."

I must have looked as if I were going to argue, because she plunged on, "I don't fit in, and they all know I don't fit in, and they're *stupid*, and if this is what learning magic is, I might as well go home. At least at home, I'm just a jezebel. I'm not a performing *dog*."

"Who's making you feel like a performing dog?" I said, grasping for something I might be able to help with. "Is Olive Bridger—"

"Oh for the Lady's sake, Felix, it's all of them! And Bridger ain't the worst—not by a long shot. All the girls can tell I don't have enough education for this, and the teachers are worse. They look at us *all* like that, like girls doing magic is just kind of funny, and they'll pat us on the head and when we get bored, we'll run along home and do our *sewing*."

"Why didn't you say something?" I asked, for this was clearly no new problem.

"You got enough to deal with," she said and added with clear discomfort, "I mean, the choke-binding and everything."

"It's not *that* bad," I said. She looked as if she might argue, so I said quickly, "Look. I'll talk to Ashmead and see if we can come to some sort of accommodation—I want you to be able to qualify as a practitioner if you want to—but they *still* can't prevent you from attending my class. I suppose they *could* forbid me to meet with you here on campus, but they have no control over visitors I choose to entertain in my own home. So you don't need to give up. Unless"—for it suddenly occurred to me that there might be other reasons for her to want to go back to Bernatha—"are you all right for money?"

"Oh yeah," she said, carelessly enough that I thought she was telling the truth. "I got a whatchamacallit—an accommodation with Mrs. Davidge. I do mending, and I got room and board. So I'm all right."

"Good," I said. "I will talk to Ashmead, but in the meantime, keep coming to class. And for goodness' sake, *tell* me next time you have a problem."

She nodded and gave me a relieved smile, and we talked about other things for a while—Corbie was having no significantly greater success in grasping the theory of thaumaturgic architecture than my other students—but as she was getting up to leave, she hesitated. "Are you gonna have more problems with that Mr. Beckett?"

"No," I said and felt the lightness of truth as I said it. "There's nothing he can do to me now."

## *Kay*

On Geovedy I expected no visitors, it having been made clear to me that the negotiations over my marriage were between Murtagh and Vanessa. I was merely a necessary incidental.

I paced the main room of the nursery, wondering if this was what the rest of my life would entail. Murtagh said he intended to make me Warden of Grimglass, but what meant that truly? That I would pace a room on the far western coast of Corambis instead of in the heart of Esmer? No Corambin community would want me as their lord, but perhaps they would accept, were it in name only, were they dependents in truth of—as for instance—His Grace the Duke of Murtagh. He would send Wyatt or another of the young men of Roderick Lapwing's ilk, and I would be prisoned there just as truly as I had been prisoned in Bernatha.

Had reached this stage in my profitless meditations when the door creaked open and Julian Carey said, "Mr. Brightmore?"

"I think," said I, "that you might call me Kay."

"Kay," said he and added shyly, "Thank you. I, um, I was wondering if you might like to go somewhere today."

"'Somewhere'?" said I.

"I thought you might like to choose."

"Is a kind thought, but I know nothing of Esmer. Could not even begin to make such a choice."

"Then would you like . . ." A faint jingling, as if he shifted from foot to foot.

"Yes?"

"Cyriack said if I brought you to the Mammothium, they'd lift the spells so that you could touch the mammoth."

"I cry your mercy. The mammoth?"

Julian explained eagerly and at length, although his explanation made very little sense. "An ancient monster?" I thought of the Veddick.

"You won't believe the tusks," Julian said gleefully.

❧

The Mammothium was part of the campus of the Grevillian Institution, the magicians' university. "We'll take the fathom," Julian said as we started down the front steps of Carey House.

"The fathom?" I said and nearly missed a step.

"I've got enough pennies," Julian said, which had not at all been my concern.

The cursed Brightmore pride rose up again. "Good," said I.

I did not let myself clutch at Julian's arm as we started down the stairs of the fathom station. But then it occurred to me, horribly, that if he had been nursing a grudge, the most perfect revenge he could choose would be to abandon me here, beneath the earth, with the uncaring crowds and the howls of the trains, and my fingers tightened spasmodically.

"Kay?" said Julian. "That—ow!"

My common sense returned to me. Julian Carey couldn't carry a grudge in a bucket. "Sorry," I said, straightening my clawed fingers. "I just . . ." But there was no way to explain without humiliating myself and hurting Julian, who had more than atoned for abandoning me in Our Lady of Mirrors. "Sorry."

"Here's the platform," Julian said. "It won't be long."

The rush and howl of the trains was all around me, directionless. The Veddick called for its brethren and was not answered. Was that better or worse than to hear your kin answer you and yet never find them? Or to find them, and in that finding crash and rend, to kill those you loved even as you were killed by them?

Would be fit for nothing save the lunatic asylum an I did not find some less morbid imaginings. I said to Julian, "How came you to this Mammothium, then, if it belongs to the magicians?"

I attended most carefully—as we boarded the train and rode in rattling, bucketing chaos beneath the city, and disembarked again—to Julian's explanation about his Professor Dombey and an Adept Gower and the mammoth-monster and how once they had learned how old it was, that was apparently not the end of the matter—as I would have thought it, for what more did one need to know about such a creature if one was assured it and its kind were no longer living?—but merely the beginning of all the questions which the professors and the magicians could think to pose. Julian had attended Professor Dombey's lectures on the mammoth and been smitten, whether with the mammoth or the professor I could not quite discern, and had pursued his own questions from the University to the Institution and to the young magicians of the Mammothium. His enthusiasm about Cyriack Thrale was more rather than less deserving of Isobel's word "soppy," and I found myself unworthily hoping that Mr. Thrale would not be in evidence when we reached the Mammothium.

I followed Julian's guidance off the train and out of the station, and followed still, obedient as any dog, across the campus of the Institution, through the strong heat of sunshine and the rising and ebbing babble of young men arguing, and up more steps and into the Mammothium.

Julian was greeted cheerfully by a baritone who said, "Thrale said I should lift the wards on Henry for you, right?"

"If it's not a bother," Julian said, shy again.

"Not a bit," said the baritone. "I wanted to tinker with them anyway. Something Mr. Harrowgate said in lecture made me think I could do a better job with them."

"Mr. Harrowgate?" said I.

"Dean Ashmead hired him to teach," said the baritone. "About how magic works in Mélusine. It's very interesting, and I think there are some applications—"

Had heard someone thump up the stairs outside; now the door opened, and Julian said, "Thrale!"

"Hello, Carey," said a voice I remembered from Our Lady of Mirrors a week and a half ago. "And this must be Kay Brightmore."

I disliked the way he said it. "And you are Cyriack Thrale. Have heard much about you."

"I was just going to take the wards down," said the baritone. "Unless you want to do it?"

"Yes, I'll take care of it, thanks, Clayforth," said Thrale. "You must be busy."

"Oh, a trifle," said Clayforth. "Just let me know when you're ready to put them back up. I've got some ideas."

"All right." A confused noise of footsteps—one set going away to the left, and another circling clockwise in a fashion which told me this room was very large, but otherwise made no sense.

Then Thrale said, "There. The wards are down, so you can do whatever it is you wanted, Carey." And I still disliked his tone.

But Julian said, "Come on, Kay," and led me forward, within the ring of the circle the footsteps—Thrale's footsteps—had paced out. He put my hand on something and said, "This is Henry-the-Mammoth."

It was slick and grainy and hard; I found I could barely close my hand around its circumference. I followed the length of it down as it curved extravagantly and tapered into a point that was blunt but no bigger around than my little finger.

"That's the tusk," said Julian.

I reversed direction and followed the sweep of the tusk back up and up, and up, until finally, well above my head, I found the spread of the skull.

"A monster in truth," I said. I worked my way slowly from what I could reach of the skull, around and down to the shoulder. Followed the massive bones of the leg down to a foot with four strangely delicate toes. Then retraced the leg to find the ribs like the slats of a garden fence.

Thrale broke away from a quiet-voiced conversation with Julian to say, "Some of those we actually had to make—carved them down from whale ribs."

I had begun this mostly to please Julian—and because it was of a certainty more interesting than pacing the nursery floor. But now I found I did wish to *know*, to be able to imagine this beast in its entirety. I went back carefully to its skull. "Julian?"

"Yes, Kay?"

"How much more of its skull is there above my hand?"

"At least two feet," said Julian

Not like the skull of a pig, then. "Has it a neck more like a horse or a cow?"

"Much more like a cow."

"Thank you."

I felt the width of its skull, found its jaw behind and beneath the rack of its tusks. The jaw seemed almost ridiculously small, but with those monstrous tusks—I put my hands out, feeling one tusk to each side of me, here as much around as young trees—perhaps this creature had had no need for impressive teeth.

Julian said, "Kay, if you'd like, Cyriack has offered to show us his bog people."

"His what?"

Another of Julian's explanations more notable for its excitement than its cogency: dead people brought out of peat bogs. "And you *study* them?" I said. "Why not just give them decent burial?"

Thrale and Julian both tried to answer me at once.

I turned around—still between the mammoth's tusks so that I did not need to fear becoming disoriented—and said, "Let us go examine your dead people then." Was *still* better than pacing the nursery of Carey House.

❧

The smell was strong and sour, though not the smell of decay. Thrale could, at least, describe things clearly, and although he was surprised when I was willing to touch his dead warlock, he did not object. I could have spoken of wading in blood at Angersburn, of the charnel house beneath Summerdown, of the night I spent sleeping on my dead beloved's bier, but I held my tongue. Would be mere unkindness, and surely the world had enough of that already.

My fingers encountered hair first, and I was startled into speech: "*Nalattris.*"

"What?" said Thrale.

"Is an old Usaran custom," said I, feeling the tight twisted knots, each secured by its own weight and tension. "When a person is thronged with evils, and particularly when they are sapping his mind—driving him mad, we would say"—although was a poor translation—"the *athen*, the holy man, draws the evils and binds them, each in a knot of hair. And then the knots are cut off, as close to the scalp as possible and without undoing them."

"But no one cut off these knots," Julian said.

"Perhaps," said I, "an he was a madman, he escaped his caretakers and drowned in the bog before that part of the ceremony could be performed."

"No," said Thrale, although he did not sound so superior as he might have. "I hadn't told you yet about the sticks."

"The sticks?"

"To hold him down. His death wasn't an accident."

"Ah," I said. "Must be a most ghastly way to die."

"I should think so," said Thrale.

"Much Usaran magic is built on notions of sacrifice," said I. "The people who pinned this man in a bog to drown, who were they?"

"He died two thousand years ago," said Thrale. "Before the voyage of Agramant the Navigator."

"So is Vedaran," said I. As the Usara were the mountain people, so the Vedara had been the plains people—before the travelers from Cymellune came and slew them to build cities on their land. Were no Vedara left now, and had not been for a thousand indictions or more. "Is likely—or at least plausible—that their magic worked the same way."

"So perhaps it was a sacrifice instead of an execution," Thrale said thoughtfully. "That's very interesting, Mr. Brightmore, thank you."

And Julian said, as I had been waiting for him to say almost since we set out from Carey House, "We'd better get home, Kay."

An there was a difference between the word "home" and the word "prison," I was beginning to forget what it was.

# Chapter 12

## *Felix*

Virtuer Hutchence leaned in at my office door late Martedy afternoon. "What is it, Hutch?" I said without looking up. Beckett had not made good on his threat, as I had been fairly sure he wouldn't—a gamble, but not a risky one—and my relationships with my colleagues were becoming more comfortable. Virtuer Hutchence continued unfailingly friendly and cheerful, and I actually quite liked him. But given the slightest encouragement, he'd grow roots in my office and talk until I wanted to strangle him.

"Got permission from Giffen," he said. "We're going to go out Venerdy and bring the Automaton of Corybant in."

"Bring it *in*?" I said, looking up involuntarily. "Like what, some kind of trophy?"

"To study," said Hutch.

"Are you quite sure that's a good idea?" I said. "It's not as if any of you has been able to come up with an explanation for how it works or why it started running again."

"Well, that's why we have to study it," he said patiently. "And, no, there's no danger. We're going to put it in the Nullity."

He'd mentioned the Experimental Nullity before—I'd gathered that it was his pet project—but always at times when I was trying to escape his conversation. "What, exactly, is the Nullity?" I said.

Hutch beamed at me—I wasn't quite sure whether it was simply because

I'd asked a leading question or whether he knew he'd finally trapped me. "It's a space in which magic doesn't work."

"I beg your pardon?"

"A nullity," he said. "A dead space. No magic. So we'll stick the Automaton in there, and there's nothing to worry about."

"And it's permanent?" I said.

"Until we take it out again. If we do."

"But how in the world do you set something like that up? And how do you keep it going?"

He raised a bushy eyebrow. "Do you really want to know?"

"In this instance, yes, I do."

"It has to do with engines," he warned me.

"So I won't understand it when you explain it. Damn."

"I don't despair of someday teaching you the principles involved," Hutch said. "But at the moment, no. It was my virtuer project, and I sometimes think they passed me just because none of them wanted to admit *they* didn't understand. But it does work. I promise. And anyway, I just wanted to ask if you wanted to come along."

"Come along?"

"On Venerdy. We've worked it all out with the Company—we catch the catmint train out, get there about ten, and then we have a good four or five hours to have lunch and look around and get the Automaton ready for the train from Wildar. They've even agreed to hitch a special car on the end to pack the Automaton into. We'll be back by half past twenty-one at the latest." He cocked his head at me. "Bunch of students going, and me and Bullinger, plus a group from the University. It'd be a good chance for you to meet people more informally. And your brother could come, if he wanted."

Part of me, remembering the screams of the dead of Corybant, thought this was a terrible idea. But my curiosity thought otherwise. "I'd love to come," I said. "And I'm sure Mildmay would love to, as well. And maybe Corbie?"

"That's fine," Hutch said cheerfully, heading out my door with a wave. "The more the merrier."

Hutch, at least, saw nothing wrong with my championing of Corbie; he had been an ally in the long and acrimonious discussion I had had first with Virtuer Ashmead and then with the Dean of the Women's College, a fish-faced adept named Hastings. Aside from a number of questions I was going to ask at a more advantageous moment about women students and how many of them—if any—persevered past practitioner and why it was, when some of the most powerful and intelligent wizards in Mélusine were women, that there were no female virtuers in the Institution at all, the upshot was that they would not accept Corbie as a regular student at the Institution. If she wanted official sanction, it was the Women's College or nothing. But they couldn't prevent me from teaching her, or—said Virtuer Ashmead privately—any other virtuer who felt inspired to follow my example; thus I taught her, and Hutch, and a quiet virtuer named Stone, and she assured me she was happy when I asked. When I told her about the expedition to retrieve the Automaton, her eyes lit up like stars.

I'd make a wizard of her yet.

## *Kay*

Attending church that Domenica had been so sore a penance as to make Glimmering's heart glad, for Vanessa Pallister had been attached to my arm like a leech. Both before and after—and even during—the service, my ears were full of Vanessa's voice, simpering at new acquaintances, gushing at women she had known before her marriage, whispering to Isobel for information about who various persons in the benches around us were. When the intended approached me after the service, the first I knew of it was Vanessa, gushing again, saying how wonderful it was to have an intended who gave proper sermons instead of just telling children's stories. I was astonished that she had noticed.

Intended Godolphin said, "Thank you," uncomfortably, and then, "I just wanted to find out if Mr. Brightmore—"

"*My* intended," Vanessa said, so archly that I was hard-pressed not to grimace or even gag outright.

Intended Godolphin said, "Er. Yes. Um. I'm sure he's in very good hands then." And then either he fled—and I could not fault him if he did—or he was pushed aside by four ghastly, squawking, squealing, gushing women who had apparently been Vanessa's bosom-bows at Miss Flowerdew's.

I was at least spared the ignominy of asking what Miss Flowerdew's was. Serena had dreamed of attending it. Was a Corambin institution, a "finishing school," designed to make girls into gentlewomen. My mother, in one of her rare moments of maternal interest, had told Serena that the things she needed to learn weren't things any school could teach her, and based on the evidence of Vanessa and her friends, my mother had been right.

That afternoon was so ghastly that I found absolute consolation in the silence of the nursery, which in turn had made me fearful that I was becoming in truth an invalid. Thus when Julian came up on Mercoledy and said there was an expedition to retrieve the Automaton of Corybant on Venerdy and Professor Dombey said there was no reason I couldn't come if I had a mind to, I could, in my gratitude and relief, have fallen on his bosom and wept, though I did not.

Rose early on Venerdy. Washed and dressed and breakfasted, and Murtagh had provided his carriage, so that Julian and I traveled to Lily-of-Mar Station in some comfort, rather than in the noise and stench of the fathom. The professors and magicians had hired a private waiting room. Julian found me a chair and said, apologetically, "Kay, I have to go find Professor Dombey, but I think you'll be more comfortable if you wait here, because I don't see him, and—"

"Oh," said a light, breathless voice. "Good morning, Mr. Brightmore."

"Mr. Harrowgate?" I said.

Julian made a slight squeaking noise. Mr. Harrowgate said without any trace of discomfort, "Good morning. I'm Felix Harrowgate, and this is my brother, Mildmay Foxe. You must be a friend of Mr. Brightmore's."

"Julian Carey," Julian said. "Kay's my uncle. Sort of. I'm a student of Professor Dombey's."

"Of course," said Mr. Harrowgate. "Virtuer Hutchence wants me to find your professor, although I told him it was useless since I've never met the man in my life. Perhaps you could point him out to me?"

"Well, I don't see him," said Julian. "I was just going to go look, but I don't like to leave Kay alone."

"Am fine," I started, but Mr. Harrowgate said, "Then we'll leave Mildmay with him. Sit, Mildmay."

His brother's voice, much deeper and slower and slurring, growled something I couldn't make out.

"No, but sometimes I wish I could muzzle you like one," said Mr. Harrowgate. "Just sit and keep Mr. Brightmore company and Mr. Carey and I will be back as soon as we can."

I felt a body drop into the seat next to mine. After a long and very uncomfortable pause, I said, "Good morning."

He answered, and I felt at least cautiously certain that what he said was "Good morning."

He shifted and something tapped against my leg. I startled, and he said, "Sorry," followed by a sentence I could not follow at all.

"I cry your mercy," I said. "What did you say?"

He repeated himself, even more slowly, and this time I understood: "Almost dropped my stick."

"A walking stick?"

"Bad leg," he said. Our chairs were close enough together that I felt his shrug.

"I'm sorry I have such a difficult time understanding you," said I. "Your accent is—"

I startled at his laugh. "Ain't that. C'mere."

He took my hand—his was callused and surprisingly long-fingered—and said, "This is why." He guided my hand to his face.

At first I didn't understand what I was feeling, and then I found his nose, his chin—shockingly smooth for the grown man his deep voice indicated he was—his mouth, and then something wrong, a raised, knotted line that twisted his upper lip and ran from mouth to temple and on into long, coarse hair.

"A scar," I said stupidly and felt him nod. "But how did it—no, that's no business of mine. I cry your mercy." I put my hand back in my lap; touching his face seemed like an unwarranted intrusion, especially as we were surrounded by scholars and magicians, any of whom might be watching.

"Knife fight," he said, and now I could not only hear but also imagine the effort he was expending to make his words clear. "Long time ago."

"A knife fight? A battle, you mean?"

"No. You can get Felix to tell you."

"I know it's difficult for you, but . . . surely my comprehension will improve with practice."

I felt him twitch a little beside me, and he said, "You sure?"

"Unless you have something better to do," I said politely, and that made him laugh again.

"Okay then," he said, and began to talk.

## *Mildmay*

So I told Kay Brightmore the whole stupid story. And he listened, and asked me to repeat myself, and asked me for more information, and it was kind of like the bit in the pantomimes where Jean-the-Wizard makes the statue of King Ming's dead daughter come to life. I mean, nothing could help about his eyes, which were even spookier than Felix's, but his face kind of warmed up around them, and he went from hunched in on himself, to leaning forward and, you know, really *interested*. And he was right. Practice did help. By the time I'd finished explaining to him about kept-thieves, he was only having to ask me to repeat myself on the really hard words, or the words he didn't know. We had a fuck of a time over "Scaffelgreen," and then of course he wanted to know about the public scaffolds and the sanguette and the ketches, and we were doing really well with each other when Felix came back with the kid in tow and said, "The enginists won't hold the train any longer, so we'd better go."

"Did you find the professor-guy?" I said and heaved myself up out of the chair. Mr. Brightmore stood up with me, and the kid came around and took his arm.

"Yes," Felix said. His hair suited him short. Made everything stand out more—his cheekbones and the white in his hair and the rings in his ears and his spooky eyes. People couldn't take their eyes off him. Even here, I could see professors doing double takes, and some of the students were just staring. I mean, *staring*. And I knew Felix knew it, and liked it, but he was real good at pretending he didn't notice. Now, he just rolled his eyes and explained: "He was trying to find some student of his who'd wandered off. Annemer academics are no better than wizards." We started for the train.

"And you thought they would be?" I said.

He laughed, although he sort of turned it into a cough, and said, "Julian, you and Mr. Brightmore are welcome to sit with us if you like. The compartment seats six, and it's only us and Corbie and possibly Virtuer Hutchence if he can be pried out of the enginists' compartment."

"We'd like that," said the kid. "Wouldn't we, Kay?"

"Certainly," said Mr. Brightmore. "Mr. Foxe has been telling me about Mélusine, and I confess I am finding it more interesting than I expected."

Felix shot a look at me. "More of your bedtime stories?" And I was saved having to come up with an answer because we were at the train, and they went on ahead so I could drag myself up the steps in peace.

Corbie was already in our compartment, which was first class along of how we were traveling with Virtuer Hutchence. She was bright-eyed and excited, and I was glad her and Felix had worked out the knot in Felix's tail because he'd go batfuck nuts in a decad if he only had the Institution kids to teach. She flirted with Julian Carey, just a little, and I thought it was funny. She couldn't be much older than him, but she was a grown-up and he was still a kid and kind of awkward with it to boot. So it was Corbie and Julian and Mr. Brightmore on one side, and then Felix and me and Jashuki and Virtuer Hutchence if he showed on the other, but I figured Felix was right and Virtuer Hutchence would stay talking with the enginists all the way to where we got off.

Felix let me have the window along of, he said, me missing all the scenery the first time. And I was glad of it, firstly because I did want to watch and secondly because it meant Corbie could talk to Julian and Felix could talk to Mr. Brightmore and I could sit and look out the window and not have to talk to nobody. So I sat and watched when the train started moving and I watched Esmer come rushing to meet us, and I never seen nothing like it, except maybe in dreams.

## Felix

If nothing else, I decided, this excursion was worth it for the chance to talk to Kay Brightmore. I had never met anyone quite like him, intelligent—sharply so—and not uneducated, but a creature of the physical, rather than the mental. He had campaigned against the Usara since he was fourteen, he said when I asked. When he was fifteen, he became the commander of those annual campaigns, having buried his father the winter in between. He had never had time for formal education

I did not think he had regretted it, for he was clearly not a man much interested in the life of the mind, and a man less suited to the confined life for which he seemed now destined it was hard to imagine: too much physical strength, too much stamina, too little patience, and as far as I could tell, no inner stillness at all. Serenity for Kay Brightmore, I was willing to bet, came in the midst of the maelstrom and nowhere else.

He was interested in my view of the Insurgence and answered quite readily when I asked him about it. About its outcome he was bleakly realistic, and rather savage: "Caloxa is dead," he said. "Long rule to the Convocation and may they choke on their spoils." But when I asked him about causes instead, he proved to have a quite sophisticated grasp of the politics.

The last king of Caloxa, James Hume, had been deposed forty years ago in a war that had been primarily about magic reform. Unlike the Wizards' Coup, however, the reformers were annemer, and what they objected to was the Mulkist school of wizardry, in which one class of wizard was treated by another class of wizard essentially as slaves. "Chattel," said Kay.

"*Ereimos,*" I muttered. The Eusebians' word for a wizard who was prey instead of predator.

"What?" said Kay, and Mildmay nudged me.

I looked up and realized that both Julian and Corbie were listening intently. "Nothing. Go on, please."

For the Mulkists, however, the distinction wasn't about power—well not about magical power. Whether a wizard became a shadow or a warlock depended entirely upon the accidents of birth.

"Is no different," Kay said, perhaps a shade defensively, "than the system of government in *both* countries."

"Is that an exculpation of the wizards or a condemnation of the lords?" I said, amused.

"Is . . . oh, never mind. My point was that it was not, despite the Grevillian rhetoric, inherently evil."

"Open to abuse," I suggested.

"And the Convocation isn't corrupt at all," he said scathingly. "But you're distracting me. The *point* is that the Corambins invaded and defeated us, allegedly on behalf of the magicians, and then very conveniently forgot to go home. I don't deny the sincerity of the reformers, for indeed Grevillian magic has been promulgated throughout Caloxa, but they did not protest the decisions made by other interests which resulted in one injustice taking the place of another."

"How so?"

That got the first spark of real animation I had seen out of him, as he sat up straighter and made a frustrated, impassioned gesture with both hands. "Margraves are not dukes. Our loyalty is not based on the mathematics of power. Is personal, and deeply felt, and you cannot have that kind of loyalty to a committee, even an you *choose* to be ruled by them, which we did not."

"Ah," I said. "And your, er, subjects?"

"They are loyal to their margrave," he said, and I could not tell if it was mere arrogance that made him state it so simply.

"I see."

He heard my skepticism; his head came up, and for a moment it was as if he was actually glaring at me. He must have had a truly arresting gaze when he'd been able to direct it; now it was merely disconcerting. "I know every man, woman, and child in Rothmarlin. I fought the Usara with them. I danced at their weddings and wept at their funerals. I lit candles with them for the Lady. And that is more than our Corambin masters can say of *any* of us."

"And yet you left them for Prince Gerrard."

His shoulders sagged. "I thought it was right," he said, and pressed the heels of his hands against his eyes. I wondered if he had been doing that frequently since . . .

"How were you blinded?"

At once he was as sharply hostile as a porcupine. "*What* did you say?" Every word was edged in glass. Julian made alarmed shushing motions at me, but I ignored him.

"Is it so unreasonable a question?"

"No, not unreasonable at all. Merely uninvited."

"Then you don't have to answer it."

He looked suddenly helpless. "I . . ."

There was a silence; Julian and Corbie were watching us with oddly similar wide-eyed expressions. To all appearances, Mildmay was absorbed in the view out the window, but I knew better than to think he wasn't paying close attention. Kay said abruptly, "There is an engine in the heart of the labyrinth under Summerdown."

"I beg your pardon?"

"How I was blinded. The engine under Summerdown."

"Engine? Like the train engine?"

"No, a thaumaturgic engine. Not, I suppose, unlike the Automaton of Corybant."

I thought of the penultimate trump of the Sibylline, the Two-Handed Engine. "How did it work?"

"Surely you would know better than I. Are not a magician?"

"A wizard," I said, feeling that there might be more than mere nomenclature in the distinction. "I have nothing to do with machines."

"Oh." He was frowning. "Then you're a Mulkist?"

"I most certainly am not. I am a Cabaline, and we do not treat anyone as chattel."

Except Mildmay.

Not. As. Chattel. And not any longer, in any event.

"I cry your mercy," he said. "I meant no insult."

"You can hardly have meant it as a *compliment*."

"No, I didn't . . . I suppose I don't understand magic very well."

"Annemer generally don't," I said cuttingly and was pleased when he ducked his head.

And then I was ashamed of myself. "I'm sorry," I said. "I didn't mean to be so short. But perhaps we should choose a new topic of conversation. It is, I believe, your turn."

And he responded promptly: "How do you come to be a party to this journey? Did they seek you out as the slayer of the machine?"

"I'm teaching at the Institution. And Virtuer Hutchence asked if I wanted to come."

I was half-expecting him to keep needling me about having "slain" the Automaton, but his interest was caught by something else. "Teaching? What do you teach?"

"It's a class on theory, of which Corambin wizards apparently have none."

Kay said, "When you say 'theory,' what exactly do you mean?"

I hesitated.

"Truly," he said. "I would like to know. Unless is something annemer cannot understand."

Touchy pride, and I said quickly, "It isn't that. I'm just not used to annemer being interested."

"Better off not knowing," Mildmay muttered without turning from the window.

Kay's head tilted toward him, but he did not ask, saying instead: "I cannot pretend I have ever been interested before, or that I would be interested if . . . if circumstances were different." His mouth quirked. "My father found curiosity unseemly in a man, and I was cuffed more than once for asking too many questions. But as my father is many indictions dead, and would certainly have disinherited me already were he alive, I pray you indulge me."

"All right," I said. "Just tell me to stop when you've had enough."

"Or when we get to where the thing is," Mildmay said pointedly.

"Whichever comes first," I said.

Kay was smiling, clearly amused by the byplay. In the bright morning light, his face looked unaccustomed to smiling; the lines were all frown lines. He had been a soldier all his life, and he was older than I was.

"All right," I said. "What do you think magic is?"

"I cry your mercy," Kay said. "What do you mean?"

"Magic," I said, and if I'd been able, I would have demonstrated. "What is it?"

"I know not," said Kay, frowning.

I looked at Mildmay, raising my eyebrows, and then remembered that for Kay's benefit, all of this would have to be spoken. "Mildmay?"

"Me?" He looked more than taken aback, very nearly alarmed.

"What do you think magic is?"

"Powers and saints, how should I know?"

"You lived in the Mirador for two years, surrounded by wizards. You've had magic *used* on you. If anyone should know, you should."

Scowling, he said, "Fine. Magic is doing things you don't want to do."

He was obviously thinking of the obligation d'âme, and I remembered, belatedly, the compulsion that had been used on him in the Gardens of Nephele; I might not like his summation, but I couldn't argue. "Julian?"

He looked every bit as alarmed as Mildmay. "I'm annemer. I don't know."

"Guess," I said.

"Power," said Julian.

"All right. Corbie?"

She'd had time to think and said promptly, "The manipulation of aether."

I frowned at her, not entirely teasing. "We just had this discussion in class yesterday. Give me another answer."

"All right," she said with a shrug. "It's the thing inside you that has to come out."

"Better," I said and finished my circle by asking Kay again: "Kay? What is magic?"

"All I know of magic is the engine beneath Summerdown. And if that is magic, then magic is death."

"That was the end result," I agreed, "but how did it work?"

"You want me to describe the deaths of my dearest friends?"

The only possible response was to strike back. "No. I want you to tell me how the *magic* worked. Or what, you walked into the room and everyone died?"

"Felix," Mildmay said, warning.

But Kay didn't seem to mind. "No, there was a ritual." He described it very clearly.

"And none of you were wizards," I said.

"No. The magician would not come with us. He was wiser than we, the little rat."

"I have to admit, I don't know how that could possibly have worked."

"Do you doubt—"

"No, don't be ridiculous. I'm not saying it *didn't* work, just that I don't understand it. So it's not a very good example for my purposes."

"Oh, yes," said Kay. "You were going to explain what magical theory was. I note that you have yet to do so."

"I asked the four of you what magic is, and got five different and unhelpful answers. If I went to the Institution . . . well, actually, what I'm afraid of is that they would tell me *exactly* what magic is, and they'd all agree. But if I went back to the Mirador and walked in on a meeting of the Curia and asked them to tell me what magic is—"

Mildmay started laughing.

"—every wizard in the room would have a different answer. At least two answers would directly contradict each other. And there would be three screaming matches within fifteen minutes."

"Your wizards are a quarrelsome lot," Kay said.

"You don't know the half of it," Mildmay said.

"*But*," I said, before Mildmay could start telling stories in which I would cut a most unattractive figure, "my point is, every one of those answers would be right."

Kay frowned. "Even those that contradicted each other?"

"Yes!" I said, delighted that he understood. "The most important thing about magic is the metaphors we use to understand it, and a metaphor that is wrong is a metaphor that *doesn't work*. No wizard who successfully performs any piece of magic can possibly be using a wrong metaphor. There are *bad* metaphors, dangerous metaphors, destructive metaphors—but no *wrong* metaphors. Thaumaturgical theory, in the broadest sense, is about manipulating our metaphors and, ideally, making sure that the metaphors we use are good ones."

"There must be some sort of consensus," Kay said.

"That's what schools of wizardry are."

"But if it's all whatchamacallits, metaphors . . ." Mildmay was frowning, and he looked up at me suddenly. "Then what *is* magic?"

And all I could do was shrug and tell him the truth: "Nobody knows."

---

At ten-thirty we reached the place where the tree had blocked the railroad line. Corbie took Julian and flitted off to join a group of young magicians I recognized from lecture; they included Robin Clayforth and Cyriack Thrale, whom I observed Julian seemed to know and to be far more comfortable with than he was with Corbie. Kay and Mildmay and I stayed together; the weight of Kay's broad, blunt hand on my arm was not unpleasant, anchoring me against the screams of the dead of Corybant.

I had hoped the pattern in the noirance might have dissipated with the destruction of the Automaton, but if anything, the screams were louder. It was, however, interesting to be back here under less fraught conditions. Hutch had brought an abundance of lanterns and by their light, what was left of Corybant emerged from the shadows of Nauleverer.

There was precious little: a few crumbled stones, the very dim remnant of what—knowing that this had been a city—might have been a road. The trees were moss-grown and gnarled, so vast in circumference that it took three students to join hands around one. Beside the straight lines of the railway, the Automaton lay where it had fallen. Hutch gave me a nod and waved me forward. My impressions of the Automaton had mostly been of a great shadowy bulk with glints of metal here and there and the evil red gleam of its eyes. I had aimed my witchlight at the eyes, reasoning that if there was a thaumaturgic converter or some other central magical device, they would have to be connected to it. It had worked, but that didn't mean the theory was correct. Now, looking at the Automaton in the light of the lantern Mildmay was patiently holding, I saw that it was encrusted with moss and lichen and wound about with vines. "No wonder no one ever noticed it before," I said. "It was busy doing a magnificent impression of a dead tree."

"Then what woke it?" Kay asked. He had knelt down with me, and his hands were delicately traversing the spikes that marked the Automaton's spine.

"I don't know," I said. "I wish I did, or that we could tell how long it was awake before it pushed that tree over." I cleared away the vegetation from the Automaton's head, having to pull to free the vines from what were apparently the thing's . . . horns?

I sat back on my heels. "Mildmay, does this look like a bull's head to you?"

"Maybe," Mildmay said. "If you squint."

"A bull?" said Kay. "Why . . . ?"

"In the religion of Cymellune," I said, "the guardian god—he who watched over and protected his people—was represented as a man with the head of a bull."

"So when they went to build their own guardian," Mildmay said softly.

"Yes. Even if they didn't worship him any longer, they remembered."

"And then," Kay said, "their guardian went mad."

"Do you know any stories that say why?" I asked.

"Corybant was said to be a sinful city. It brought judgment on itself." His tone said he wasn't happy with that answer.

"I don't understand enough about the way these engines work," I said, standing and tugging Kay to stand with me. "Hutch was very kind to let us go first, but I think we'd better get out of the way now."

We retreated to a fallen tree—not nearly such a giant as the one which had blocked the rails and which the Automaton had smashed on its approach to the train—and sat. One group of wizards and annemer scholars had converged on the Automaton; others were moving purposefully if mysteriously about in the sparser woods surrounding the railroad line. The dead of Corybant continued to scream.

Mildmay said suddenly, "Hey, d'you think the stories about the knocken are true?"

"Why?" I said. "Do you see something?"

"Oh very funny. Nah. I just wondered."

"I don't know," I said. "I don't know what happened here. The Automaton is one thing, but the noirance—"

"The what?" said Kay.

"Hocus-talk," Mildmay said.

"Yes, but it's *useful*," I said, and to Kay, "Noirance, and its opposite, clairance, is a way of talking about the feeling of a place, its magic—I suppose, really, its aether. And this place—all of Nauleverer—is *drenched* in noirance, in darkness and confusion and the feeling of being lost."

"Blindness," said Kay.

"Well, yes and no. Noirance isn't about not being able to see. It's about not being able to find your way out of the dark. Being lost in a maze. Or being the creature in the heart of the maze who waits for the lost to come to it, as they always will."

"Felix," Mildmay said sharply, warningly, and I jerked back to myself, shaking away the screams of the dead of Corybant. Without the protection of my magic, I was far too susceptible to noirant patterning, too likely to be dragged into its current, as a poor swimmer—like myself—was likely to be caught by an undertow.

Very abruptly, I understood a part of how my madness had worked.

"In any event," I said quickly, to mask my shiver, "the noirance here is strange. It's almost like the railroad—it runs in lines."

"You ain't making a lick of sense," Mildmay said.

"*Aren't*. And don't tell me you can't feel the mikkary."

"Oh I ain't saying nothing of the sort." And then he frowned. "Are mikkary and noirance the same thing?"

"They're related. Mikkary is—or can be—what happens when noirance is left to stagnate. But mikkary doesn't have to be caused by magic, although magic will make it stronger. Noirance is a kind of magic, and it doesn't *have* to generate mikkary."

"Have lost me again," Kay said, sounding more rueful than irritated. "What is mikkary?"

"The feeling a room gets when there's been murder done in it," Mildmay said.

Kay's face was very still for a moment; then he said slowly, "Yes, I know that feeling well."

"This forest is a room, then," I said, "and something more than murder was done here. And I don't understand . . ." For Mildmay's definition was exactly right. Mikkary belonged to human structures, to *rooms*. With the wholesale destruction of Corybant—with no stone left standing on stone—there should have been nothing left to collect mikkary. "Mildmay, did Nera . . . Was there . . ." I couldn't seem to frame the question.

But Mildmay understood. "Just grass," he said. "Not like this."

"I cry your mercy," said Kay, "for I seem to be perpetually two steps behind your conversation, but—" He broke off, frowning, his head tilting as he tracked something—which I realized as she reached us was Corbie's rapid passage through the site.

She was talking before she'd even reached me. "Felix, have you seen Julian?"

"Julian?" said Kay, coming very sharply alert.

"He kept saying he heard something, so I told him to come ask you about it . . . but he didn't, did he?"

"No. How long ago was this?"

"Not very. Quarter of an hour, maybe?"

Unless Corbie's time sense was far superior to the average, that was anything from ten minutes to half an hour. Either, I thought, looking around at Nauleverer's darkness, was enough to get lost in.

"I'm sorry," Corbie was saying. "I didn't know what he was talking about, and I didn't think he'd—"

"Is not your fault," Kay said with perfect calm authority. "Julian is quite old enough to know not to wander off into the woods by himself. But we—but he must be found."

"Yes," I said, "and the quicker the better. But I'm afraid I don't . . . Mildmay?"

"City boy," he said, raising both hands in an oddly defensive gesture. "But we're fucking surrounded by hocuses. Ain't they good for *anything*?"

"I'll get Cyriack," Corbie said.

"Corbie, d—" But she was already on her way.

"I admit, Mr. Thrale would not have been my first choice," Kay said, "but he does seem to be Julian's friend. Know you anything to his discredit?"

"Merely that I dislike him. But you're right. This is no time to be choosy."

And when Corbie returned with Cyriack, he seemed quite sincerely distressed. He also had a spell, a clever little thing he said he'd learned from an adept visiting the Institution from Sconner, that illuminated a particular person's footsteps. "The window of viability is pretty small," he said, "but we should be—ah!"

The spell showed deep pink smudges on the dead leaves. "Let's go," I said to Cyriack, who looked at me strangely.

"Are you an aethereal, Mr. Harrowgate?" he said when we were away from the others.

"A what?"

His look, when I glanced up from the pink smudges, was even stranger. "A person abnormally sensitive to aether. Generally, no one but the magician who cast it can see the results of this spell. But most aethereals can't do magic."

"At the moment, neither can I." And his reaction, embarrassed rather than surprised, confirmed my suspicion that the Institution as a whole knew about the choke-binding.

After a moment, though, he persevered, and I was reminded of all the reasons I did not like Cyriack Thrale: "They're a bit of a nuisance. Nobody knows what to do with them. You'd think the logical thing would be to train them to assist us, but apparently that's too Mulkist. So mostly these days they go into the church, but that's not really satisfactory either. Some dominions don't want aethereal intendeds, and you can't really blame them."

"Why not?" I said.

"Aethereals aren't reliable," Cyriack said. "I don't mean magicians who have a sensitivity to aether," he added hastily, "but the annemer. They don't have the mental fortitude. They're emotional and easily led—it'd be almost as bad as having a woman as your intended."

"I see." I thought of Vincent Demabrien, who would almost certainly be labeled an aethereal in the Corambin system, thought of Mehitabel Parr, who would stand like iron when young men like Cyriack Thrale crumbled and mewled, and it was probably fortunate—at least for Cyriack—that just then I heard a voice that was not the mindless wailing of the Corybant dead. I broke into a run.

Julian had fallen into a snarled stand of briars woven around and between three of the enormous trees. They had caught him in a dozen different places, and the more he struggled, the more entangled he became.

"Hold still," I said. "Julian! Hold still and let me help you."

He twisted toward me; his light amber eyes were wide in his flushed face and he was bleeding from a long scratch across his forehead. "Mr. Harrowgate! Where are they? I want to help them, but I can't find them! Do you hear them? Who are they?"

"The dead of Corybant," I said, gingerly taking hold of the first strand of briars, "and they are beyond our help."

I looked up as I said it and saw the truth in Cyriack's stiffly judgmental face: Julian Carey was an aethereal, and I hoped, thinking again of Vincent, that his Lady would protect him from the consequences.

❧

It took nearly half an hour to free Julian; I got rid of Cyriack finally by sending him to bring Mildmay, and by the time they made it back, I'd talked Julian through an exercise to quiet the screams—which had the additional benefit of shoring up my own resistance—and was helping him stand up. Mildmay might have grumbled, but didn't, and I thought from the way he was eyeing Cyriack that he'd already figured out my motives.

We returned to the site via a much shorter route, following Mildmay, and found we were just in time for lunch. "I trust," I said to Cyriack, "that you are not a gossip."

"Of course not," he said stiffly and with great offense, and stalked off to join his friends.

"I don't know how much good that'll do," I said to Julian as we crossed the railway line to where Corbie and Kay were waiting. "The more offended a person is by the suggestion, the worse a gossip they generally are, and that goes double for wizards."

I'd hoped for a smile, even a faint one, but Julian said distraitly, "It doesn't matter. I just . . . Mr. Harrowgate, I am so sorry!"

"Good gracious, what for?"

It tumbled out in a disjointed welter of words, and I stopped him where we were, out of earshot of anyone else. Mildmay gave me a nod and went past—I hoped he was going to tell Kay we'd found Julian and he was unharmed.

Julian, I gathered, knew he was an aethereal, had known for years. He'd thought about becoming a priest, but then his parents had died and he'd gone to live with the duke and duchess, and it had been made very clear to him that it was his duty to be the next Duke of Murtagh. "And I'm afraid I wouldn't make a very good intended," he said with naïve honesty.

Murtagh had laid down an iron-clad rule. No one was to know Julian was an aethereal, and he was not to talk about it. It was not an asset for a duke's heir. "Intended Godolphin figured it out somehow, but I swear I didn't tell him. And he wanted me to go to the Esmer Theological College. Uncle Ferrand was *furious*." So Julian had been sent to the University instead, which he loved, and he'd made friends with lots of magicians, and he'd just begun to wonder if maybe he could trust one of them with his secret—his eyes flicked unhappily past me, and I knew he was looking for Cyriack—when this happened and he'd disgraced himself and his descent and Uncle Ferrand would never let him go anywhere again "and what you must think of me I don't know!" he finished, more or less in a wail.

"I think none of this is your fault," I said firmly, wishing I could master Kay's authoritative tone. "And I think we should have lunch."

After lunch, the scholars, both annemer and magician, began preparing the Automaton of Corybant for transport. Corbie, with a mulish set to her jaw, dragged Julian over to help. She had gone very quickly from flirting with him to treating him as a younger brother, and I felt confident she would take care of him. Mildmay, Kay, and I sat on the fallen tree, and, determined to keep my focus on the present and the living, I described Virtuer Hutchence's broadly pantomimed frustration with both his students and his learned colleagues until Kay finally broke down and laughed.

Mildmay said, "He's gonna sock Virtuer Bullinger here in a minute, just you wait and see if he don't." Then he winced. "Sorry, Mr. Brightmore, was that a bad thing to say?"

I wasn't sure how Kay would handle it, but he said, "Only if when he 'socks' him—by which I presume you mean 'punch'—you don't tell me about it."

"Hopefully, gentlemen," I said repressively, "it won't come to that."

"If you mean it," Mildmay said, "you might want to get over there. Because I don't think that professor-guy is helping."

"Damn him for a feckless half-wit," I said, bouncing to my feet. "I'll be right back."

That, as it turned out, was a lie. Hutch and Bullinger really were on the verge of blows by the time I reached them, and I spent the rest of the afternoon, until the arrival of the train from Wildar, mediating, first between Hutch and Bullinger, then between Hutch and Dombey, and finally just telling people what to do. The Automaton was not merely massive, it was heavy and terrifically unwieldy, and it required rather more organized cooperation than came naturally to either wizards or scholars.

But we did get it loaded onto the train, and the party had the same number of members returning it had had starting out, which I counted as a personal triumph.

Julian sat very close beside Kay on the journey back to Esmer, and Kay allowed it. Corbie curled up like a kitten against Mildmay and slept, and

Mildmay put an arm around her and stared out the window. Once we were away from Corybant's noirance and I could relax, Hutch and Kay and I had a long rambling conversation in which I learned a good deal more about Institution politics and also that Hutch was Caloxan by birth.

"You don't sound it," I said.

He winked at me and said in an accent every bit as strong as Kay's, "Have learned the northermen's speech, for they will not take you seriously else. And," he added, dropping back into his usual voice, "I haven't been back to Larrowan since I came to Esmer, and that was when I was Julian's age. It's my childhood speech that sounds strange to me now."

Kay turned his head; he knew where my face was, even if he couldn't see it. I remembered what he'd said that morning: *Caloxa is dead.* And this, too, was what he'd meant.

❧

We reached Lily-of-Mar Station at twenty-two o'clock. Wizards and scholars dispersed. Hutch boarded the carriage with the Automaton, which now faced a farther, complicated journey across and beneath Esmer to reach the Experimental Nullity beneath Venables Hall. Mildmay and Corbie and I saw Kay and Julian into the Duke of Murtagh's carriage and took the fathom home.

Corbie continued to live in that tiny room at the Golden Hare, so she got off at Sunflower Street. Mildmay and I rode two stops farther, to St. Ingry, and then walked to our apartment building under Esmer's hissing streetlights.

He was looking thoughtful, and when we reached home, with the door locked behind us, he said, "D'you suppose this Automaton thing was sort of like the Iron-black Wolves?"

I knew the story, but it didn't help. "I beg your pardon?"

His color heightened a little. "Nothing. Never mind."

"But I do mind," I said. "What do you mean?"

"Nothing," he said again with a shake of his head. "It's stupid."

"That, I doubt."

"No, really, it's just this stupid dream I had. When I was sick. About the Iron-black Wolves. So I'm thinking about them, I guess."

"Well," I said slowly, uncertain how I ought to respond, "given that they're something in a fairy tale and the Automaton is quite real . . . Yes, I suppose there are certain similarities."

"Huh," he said. "They couldn't be stopped."

"Thankfully, that isn't one of the similarities," I said and almost got him to laugh.

But something was bothering him. I sat at our scarred table and watched him limp around the room, checking the lock, then checking the windows, into the kitchen and back out. If I pushed, he'd retreat. I waited, and bit my tongue, and waited some more, and finally he said, "I'm sorry I didn't save you."

"What? From the Automaton? I didn't need saving."

"Not that." He was getting redder. "From the wolves."

"From the *wolves*?"

"Oh fuck me sideways," he moaned to himself, then rubbed the scarred side of his face. "I mean, in Bernatha. The . . . the people who hurt you."

"That was the night you dreamed about the Iron-black Wolves," I said, understanding suddenly.

Red as a tomato now, but he jerked his head in a nod, and then muttered something I didn't catch at all. And that was rare enough these days that it was one more alarm bell added to an already deafening cacophony.

"What was that?"

"I said I didn't save Ginevra either. Not the same wolves, but." He stopped, glaring not at me, but at a crack in the plaster, then said—this quite clearly—"Fuck it, I'm going to bed."

And if he got his way, the subject of Iron-black Wolves would never come up again. I scrambled to my feet, scrambled to keep him, and what came out of my mouth was the truth: "But you *did* save me."

He stopped in the doorway and turned. "The fuck I did," he said, staring at me in frank disbelief.

"Not in Bernatha," I said. "But you couldn't have saved me, just as you couldn't have saved me from any of the other cataclysmically stupid things I've done because I chose to do them. As for example the binding-by-obedience. But you *did* save me. You saved me in Hermione."

"Other way 'round," he said, and I knew he was thinking of the Mirador's curse.

"No, it isn't." I was desperate to make him understand—to make him believe what I was trying to say. "You saved *me*. And you did it again. And again. You *always* save me."

Disbelief had softened into bewilderment, and he said, "I don't understand what you mean." But I thought what he meant was that he did understand and didn't want to.

"You can't save people from themselves. Not Ginevra, not me. But you can give them a place to . . ." I broke off, gesturing in frustration, and tried again. "You're the only one who looks at me and doesn't see the person who made all those stupid decisions. You see somebody who can choose differently. You *let* me be somebody who can choose differently, even when you have no reason to think that I will." His gaze flickered; I didn't need to say Malkar's name. "And that's far more important than being a knight in a story." And finally I found the words I needed. "You help me be someone who can save himself."

His eyes were wide. Probably, no one had ever said anything like that to him in his life. Certainly, I never had. After a moment, he said, "You mean it?"

"Yes," I said, although it was an effort to hold his gaze, to hold still and let him see the truth of me. "I mean it."

"Okay," he said slowly, as if he wasn't sure. And then again, more firmly, "Okay." It was as good as a smile when he said, "Fuck the wolves anyway. You want some tea?"

And I said, "Yes." To all of it.

## *Kay*

Somewhere between Lily-of-Mar Station and Carey House, Julian said explosively out of a dead silence, "Does it bother you that I'm an aethereal?"

"No. Why should it?"

"I'm unstable," Julian said with more bitterness than I had ever heard from him, "emotional, impulsive, easily led."

"You are sixteen," I said dryly.

"I'll probably go mad! Aethereals do, don't they? Or I'll have fits in public or talk to the furniture like Aunt Ella."

"Your mother's sister?"

"Oh yes," he said, still bitter. "There's none of this nonsense in the Carey descent."

"Need not welcome trouble before it comes calling," I said cautiously.

"I heard their voices," he said, and his cold fingers gripped my wrist. "I heard them screaming and screaming, and I couldn't find them. Mr. Harrowgate said there was nothing we could do to help them, but blessed Lady, I *heard* them."

He could add *overwrought* to his list of disparagements. I said, "I think you can trust Mr. Harrowgate," and gently freed my wrist from his cold clutch.

"Oh, I didn't mean—! Mr. Harrowgate was wonderful, and I'm sure he's right. I just . . ." And then he said in a different tone, "We're home. Are you going to tell Uncle Ferrand?"

"Is no business of mine. Is between you and him. But if you think Cyriack Thrale is going to hold his tongue, I fear me you will be disappointed."

Julian did not leap to Thrale's defense as I'd expected, but said, "You think I should tell him first?" Was considerable trepidation in his voice.

"I think," said I, "that no matter how ugly telling him is, will still be better than if he hears of it somewhere else first."

"Oh," said he, and I knew he took my point.

I was grateful, however, to be spared that scene, and did not argue with Springett about going directly to bed. I washed up, donned my nightshirt, bid Springett good night, and walked into the bedroom, shutting the door behind me.

And stopped dead, assailed by the scent of lilies.

"I thought," said Vanessa Pallister, and I heard the creak as she rose from my bed, "that we should talk."

"Did you?" said I. "What about?"

A pause. "You don't like me, do you?"

"Have given me any reason to?"

"And you don't want this marriage."

"Is no matter what I want or don't want," I said tiredly. "But, an you have a point, what I *want* is that you come to it, so that you may leave again and I may go to bed."

"We don't have to be enemies," she said, and the scent of lilies grew stronger. I was braced for the touch of her hand against the open collar of my nightshirt.

"Vanessa." I took her hand and removed it from my person. "What do you want? You know I cannot refuse this marriage, whether I want it or not, so what matters it to you what my feelings are? You've made your own feelings perfectly clear."

She jerked away from me. "Maybe I don't want to marry a man who hates me!"

"You need not marry me," I said. "Will not hinder you an you cry off."

"Damn you, you . . . you *statue*," she said in a vicious whisper. She pushed past me; the door opened and slammed shut again.

Not a statue, I thought. An Automaton, a monster with a clockwork heart. I went carefully to the windows, not knowing what Vanessa might have moved, and opened them wide. By morning, the scent of lilies would be gone.

# Chapter 13

## *Mildmay*

On Lunedy morning, Felix had a plan.

"You want me to *what*?"

"It's perfect," he said. "You need to practice your reading and Kay certainly needs the distraction. And the company."

"But I can't just—"

"Visit a friend?" he said, one eyebrow going up.

"Dammit, don't do that!"

"Do what?"

"Put words in my mouth." I glared at him over the teapot. "I can't go and force him to put up with me."

"He likes you."

"But." I gulped, floundered. "He won't want to hear all that philosophy stuff." Because that's what Felix had, from all the books he'd had in his rooms in the Mirador: seven books on magic and philosophy. I was learning on a book called *A Treatise upon Spirit* by Chattan d'Islay. It'd been Gideon's. I'd been nervous, because I didn't think I was going to understand any of it, even when I could read it, but Felix had just grinned and said that was the point of philosophy books: you read 'em until you *did* understand.

Felix coughed and looked a little embarrassed. "We, ah, have other books."

"We do?" It was news to me.

He looked even more embarrassed. "There are bookstores very near the Institution. Hutch showed me . . ."

"I get the idea," I said. "How much damage did you do?"

"I only bought three," he said, looking hopeful. "And one of them's quite small. I really do need to get a grasp of the basic principles of Grevillian thaumaturgy before I—"

"Felix." Me trying to be stern with him was like a rat terrier trying to be stern with a wolfhound, so you can see why I was surprised as fuck when it worked. He was bright pink in the face, but he got up and opened the closet. He brought three books out and put them on the table in front of me.

I took a minute to read the titles—but it really only did take a minute, and that was pretty fucking amazing. One, like he'd said, was a book about magic: *Introduction to the Grevillian Theorems*. One was called *History of Corambis*. And the third, the little one, was *Common Wildflowers of Central Corambis*.

"None of the wizards here seems to know the first thing about botany," Felix said, and it was weird how nervous he sounded. "And of course I could go over to the University, but honestly I'm afraid they'll just see me as—"

"Felix."

He stopped and looked at me. Hopeful and anxious, and powers and saints this was wrong.

I said, "It's *your* money. You ain't gotta . . . I mean, you ain't, what's the word?"

"Accountable?" he said quietly.

"Yeah, that's it. You ain't accountable to me."

His mouth twitched into something that was maybe a smile and maybe not. "And if I blow our month's budget buying books, you're the one who'll be cardsharping to make up the deficit. Which I think *does* make me accountable to you. Or at least responsible."

"Well, okay," I said. Because that part was reasonable, and I was even glad he was thinking that way. "But you don't got to—I mean, I ain't mad. I ain't gonna be mad." And then I finally found the word I'd been looking for. "You don't got to *justify* it to me."

He'd still been kind of pink, but now he went bright, slow red and then sat down and put his face in his hands. He said, so quiet I almost couldn't hear him, "Malkar gave me spending money, but he always wanted to know what I spent it on. And he would tease me about 'bettering myself' and how all the erudition in the world wouldn't wash off the mud of Pharaohlight. And Shannon teased me, too, about all the time I spent in bookstores and, well, I guess I do get a little overexcited sometimes."

I remembered how happy he'd been, the day he found some book Gideon'd been wanting, how he'd been so bright you could've threaded a needle by the light he was giving off. And I remembered the way Gideon had hugged him, smiling so big it was like his face was going to crack wide open. And I said, "Gideon didn't tease you."

"No," he agreed after a moment, not looking up. "Gideon didn't tease me."

"I gotta say," I said, like I didn't know he was somewhere past embarrassed and just short of tears, "if I was gonna pick one of them for being nice and levelheaded and a guy you'd want to listen to, Gideon'd be it."

That made him laugh. A little choked, but a real laugh. "Mildmay, really. I know you didn't like Shannon, but lumping him in with Malkar is a bit much."

"I'm just saying, if Gideon didn't think you were dumb or embarrassing or whatever it is Malkar and Lord Shannon thought, then you weren't."

"I . . ." And then he sort of sagged. "All right."

"And I ain't gonna tease. You said you wouldn't tease me, I won't tease you. Fair's fair. And you don't got to give me all the whys and wherefores when you buy a book. Okay?"

"Yes," he said. "All right." He took a deep breath and straightened up again. "In any event, I thought you and Kay could read the *History of Corambis*, and Kay would enjoy telling you everything the author got wrong."

"Oh," I said. "Yeah, I can see that." And Felix grinned like the sun coming out.

So he went off to the Institution, and I went off to find Carey House, which I knew was where Kay lived because Julian'd said so.

The thing I liked best about St. Ingry Station was that where the Sunflower Street Station had that snooty mural, St. Ingry Station had this big-ass map of Esmer with all the fathom stations picked out in blue and the train stations in red and everything labeled so I could learn Esmer and practice my reading at the same time. The gals in the ticket booths had got used to seeing me, and sometimes if things weren't busy, they'd come out and show me what dominions they lived in and tell me about things I should be sure to see, like St. Nath's Tower which was all that was left of the kings' palace from back when Corambis had kings, and the Museum of Corambis which was way out in Vander Dominion and had a map of the whole country that was big enough you could walk around on it.

Esmer wasn't laid out as tidy as Mélusine, and no wall, either. So the city just kind of went where it wanted to, and you could imagine the mapmakers running along behind trying to make sense of it and mostly not having much luck.

The Institution was sort of in the middle of the southeast of Esmer, if that makes any sense at all, and I knew all the flash houses were in Nath Dominion because one of the ticket girls had said so. So I found St. Ingry Station—there was a big blue star to mark it—and then worked north and west from Ingry Dominion to Mar to Osper and Phadon and then Nath. One of the stations in Nath Dominion was called Murtagh Station, which I figured was probably a good sign, so I went and asked the ticket girls, and they said as how, yeah, Carey House was just down the block and everybody knew it because of the sphinxes that were one to either side of the door. And I even knew what a sphinx was, so I didn't have to look dumb by asking.

I rode the fathom out and got off at Murtagh Station. I picked a direction that looked flash and started walking, and sure enough, there were the sphinxes, each about the size of a pony, and I walked up between them and knocked on the door.

Servant in livery, and I said, "Is Mr. Brightmore in?" Which, you know, I figured he was, but I could at least try and be polite.

"Beg pardon?"

Oh fuck me sideways. "Bright. More," I said, as distinct as I could.

"Mr. *Brightmore*! Of course. Come in and—" For a second he looked exactly like a fish. "That is to say, if you will wait in the foyer, I will see if Mr. Brightmore is in."

"Thank you," I said. But I liked him for seeming happy that somebody'd come to see Mr. Brightmore, so I didn't give him no trouble. And he came back real quick and said, "This way please," and then he grinned at me and said, kind of low, "Mr. Springett thought I was joking, but he's pleased as a pigeon for his lordship to have a visitor."

"His lordship?" I said.

"Well, he ain't no more," he said, leading me to the stairs. "But he was. And he's a gentleman for sure, and we think it ain't respectful-like to be calling him 'mister,' no matter what them political people say. He's up at the top of the house."

Which figured. I leaned on Jashuki and took my time. I noticed it was the same here as at home—the farther you got from the front door, the more the house looked like people actually lived in it. Things quit being so fucking perfect, and Mr. Brightmore's room when we got there could actually have used a new coat of paint. Of course, that said a whole different set of stuff about how they were treating him, but then it wasn't like he cared. And I kind of thought he wouldn't've cared even if he'd been able to see the walls.

He was all by himself, sitting on one of the window seats with his knees tucked under his chin. He looked real startled at having a visitor, so much that I said, "I don't have to stay if you don't want."

"No, please." He'd uncurled himself as soon as the door opened, and now he actually took a step toward me. "I wasn't expecting . . . but I'm very pleased." Pleased wasn't something he looked like he'd had much practice with, but I thought he meant it.

"I'll tell Cook to send up some tea, shall I, Mr. Brightmore?" said the guy in livery.

"Please," said Mr. Brightmore, although he looked like he'd never had nobody offer to bring him tea in his entire life.

So the servant-guy left, and I said, "This is Felix's idea. He thought you might like it if I read to you."

"I cry you mercy," Mr. Brightmore said, stepping back and sitting down again. "Is not your fault, but I didn't catch a word of what you said."

"Well, we thought you must be pretty bored."

"'Bored' might cover it if spread thinly," he said, which I figured after a moment to work through it was a snarky way of agreeing with me. "But haven't you anything better to do?"

"Me? Powers, no. I mean, what am I gonna do, hang around in the back of the room while Felix teaches?" Which was exactly what I'd done in the Mirador, but that was the binding-by-forms, and I wasn't keen on doing it here any more than I was keen on doing any of the stuff I knew best, that being thieving and cardsharping and murder. I'd been keeping myself busy learning Esmer and especially the little piece of it around our apartment, but Felix was right, even if he hadn't come out and said it. I needed something more. "You mind if I sit down?"

"Please. Of course. I cry you mercy. I am a poor host and have no manners."

I picked the chair nearest him and turned it so we were facing each other. Mr. Brightmore said, "Is hard to imagine him as a teacher."

"He's really good." And, you know, it was nice to say that to somebody who wasn't going to call me a liar just because it was Felix I was talking about.

"Am glad he has fallen on his feet. I cannot imagine what is like for him—for you—to have to put together a new life so far from everything you have known."

"Oh, hey, don't worry about me. The hard one for me was the Mirador."

His head tilted. I'd got him interested. "What do you mean?"

So I did my best to tell him. About the Mirador and the Lower City and what they meant to each other and what it'd been like to try and live in the Mirador after spending my whole life trying to stay away from it.

The tea came somewhere in the middle, while I was trying to make him understand what court was like, and I stopped and poured tea and made him take a sandwich along of him looking like he needed it, and all he said was "Go on." So I did, and that part was nice, too, being able to talk about the Mirador to somebody who *hadn't* grown up with it. Kay hadn't even read the novels. I know, because I asked when I finally got tired of my own damn voice.

"Have never had much time for pleasure reading," he said, almost like he was proud of it. Then his face fell. "And now of course . . ."

"Well, I kind of figure that's what Felix had in mind, sending me over here with this book and all. Now, I mean, you don't got to listen. I ain't exactly good at this whole reading thing, and I wouldn't blame you—"

"You have a book?"

He really hadn't been kidding about not catching a word of what I'd said back when I came in. "Yeah. *History of Corambis.*"

"And you're willing to read? To me?"

"Well, yeah, but like I said—"

"Read," he said, and it was probably the same way he'd told his soldiers to charge.

And that was okay by me.

## *Kay*

That night, as I lay thinking about Mildmay Foxe and his strange brusque shyness, I heard the outer door creak open.

"Who's there?" I called, sitting up.

"For the Lady's sake, hush!"

"Murtagh?" I said, obediently lowering my voice. "What in the world—"

"Isobel thinks it unwise of me to consort with you," he said, shutting the bedroom door behind him.

"Will have stronger words than 'unwise' if she catches you creeping to my bed in the middle of the night."

"I am not," Murtagh said very precisely, "creeping to your bed. There's a perfectly good chair here, and I intend to use it."

Disbelieving, I listened to the sounds of him seating himself. "What do you want?"

"Why do I have to want anything? Can't I just want to talk?"

"To me?"

He sighed. "You really don't think we're friends, do you?"

"It makes no sense," said I.

"Sense? Your experience of friendship must be vastly different than mine if you think it *sensible*."

"You have a point."

"Do you dislike me?" He sounded almost wistful, and I knew not if I could trust that.

But I answered him truthfully. "No, I do not dislike you."

"Well, that's something," he said. "It took your sister most of five indictions before she'd unbend enough to say she found me not displeasing."

"Then was not . . ."

"What?"

"I admit, I have wondered."

"Wondered *what*?"

"If was in truth Isobel's barrenness that has you childless."

Silence, and then Murtagh said, very slowly, "Have I ever given you any reason to believe I mistreated your sister?"

Was danger in his voice, and I said, "I cry your mercy. I meant no such thing. Is just . . . an arranged marriage . . . and I do know Isobel's temperament . . ."

"I assure you, our marriage has been very thoroughly consummated," Murtagh said, but at least his voice had lightened. "And that provides me a very graceful segue to something I did want to speak to you about."

"Vanessa."

"Will you give her a chance, Kay?"

"Matters not what I would give. Is clear enough that the lady is accustomed to take."

"Just try to see past her manner. She is in a difficult position."

"She has all my sympathy," I said bitterly.

"Sometimes I don't know why I bother," he said, and I heard him come to his feet.

"Would be better if you bothered less about me and more about Julian."

"Julian will do as he's told."

"Yes, he will," said I, "even when he should not."

"Good night, Kay," Murtagh said sharply.

"Murtagh!" I said as he opened the door.

"What?" he said, still sharp. But he answered, and was truth in that.

"You were right."

"About what?"

"We must be friends," said I. "Could not infuriate each other so an we were not."

It startled him into laughing, and when he said, "Good night, Kay," a second time, the sharpness was gone.

## *Felix*

I was certain that at least half the students to whom I lectured thought Corbie was my mistress. It was a far more congenial, though senseless, explanation to them than the truth. Corbie, whose sense of humor was reprehensible, did nothing to dissuade them; indeed, if I would have let her do it, she would have draped herself across me like a stole. She was not at all discomfitted by being the only woman in the room, and she had the virtue of asking questions when she was confused, unlike the men, who nodded sagely and tried to look wise.

Things might have been quite different if I had not been her ally—to the rest of the Institution, after all, she wasn't even a student—but that at least I was clear on: Corbie and I were allies.

I gathered up all my courage and told her about the fantôme.

Her eyes got wider and wider, and when I finished, she said, "Is there anything I can do?"

I hadn't even realized I'd been dreading trying to persuade her I was telling the truth—as I would have had to persuade Hutch or any of my orthodox students—until that weight was abruptly gone. "Well, there is, actually. Do you know any stories about spirits of that kind? It called itself a rachenant."

She shook her head.

"Then I'm going to introduce you to one of the great mysteries of wizardry." I grinned at her. "It's called *research*."

The Institution had no library of its own, which I found both deplorable and more than a little disturbing; Corbie and I walked from the House, across the North Quadrangle—past Venables Hall and that which slept in its basements—and climbed the rocky half wilderness of Solstice Hill. Solstice Hill was the point where the University and the Institution met, and there was some considerable dispute about ownership. Thus, in practice, no one owned it, except the students from both sides who used it as a shortcut and a trysting place and probably a great many other things that, as Institution faculty, I didn't want to know about.

We came down Solstice Hill into the University. There were more women students here, and more boys Julian's age or younger. It was louder, more cheerful, and I felt Corbie relax.

"Is it very hard for you?" I asked before I realized I meant to.

"Is what very hard for me?"

"The Institution."

"Well, it would be if I was a student there, but I ain't." She grinned at me. "Don't worry about me, Felix. I got it licked."

"All right," I said. "But tell me if—"

"I ain't going back," she said, and I let the matter go.

Hutch had shown me the University's library, along with all the bookstores in walking distance, and it did make up, at least in part, for the Institution's failure. It was a vast, sprawling building, turreted and gabled and ridiculous. I wasn't surprised that its nickname was the Furbelow. Hutch, who was conscientious, had shown me the side staircase that led directly to the thaumatology collection, and Corbie and I went up that way.

"And all these books are about magic?" Corbie said, frowning. The mere quantity of books didn't awe her; she was familiar with Bernatha's bookstores, even if she hadn't frequented them.

"Yes. And unfortunately, they aren't catalogued."

She looked at me with foreboding. "What does that mean?"

"That nobody actually knows what's up here."

"Oh." Now she looked daunted.

"And this is the only surviving collection of Mulkist writings in the country, or so Hutch tells me."

"Mulkist?" A definite squeak.

"It was a Mulkist warlock who called the thing, and I somehow doubt Grevillian authors are going to have much to say about it. Since as far as I can tell, there *are* no spirits in Grevillian theory." Just as the Mirador didn't believe in ghosts, and it occurred to me, as sudden and sharp and painful as a knife thrust, that even if I was ever allowed to return home, I wasn't a Cabaline anymore. That maybe I never had been.

"Um," said Corbie. "Good point. So, what? I just go look around?"

I shook myself back to the present. "Unfortunately, yes. See what you find."

"That's *it*?"

"In essence." I shrugged at her disgusted look. "It's what research is. You look around, see what you find. Think about it. Do some more looking."

"What about, you know, *magic*?" She called her little purple witchlight, as if to demonstrate.

"That comes at a *much* later point," I said firmly.

"Oh all right," she said, half-grumbling, half-teasing, and I left her there among the books like Eilene among the deathly treasures of Muil.

## *Kay*

Mildmay Foxe was as patient as a stone. He came daily with his book about the history of Corambis and read it to me. We struggled together over the words he didn't know; he confessed early on that he had been only imperfectly taught to read as a child.

"Are no schools in Mélusine?" said I.

"Well, yeah, but for bourgeois kids, flash kids. Not kept-thieves."

"Are no dominioner schools?"

"No dominions," he said.

"But is no one then responsible for the children of the city?"

That made him laugh. "That's the Lower City in a nutshell. Ain't nobody responsible at all."

"But someone taught you something of reading?"

"My keeper," he said, his voice gone dark and curt, not at all as I was accustomed to hearing it. "But I wasn't no good at it, and she found better things to do with me."

I knew I should not ask, and yet I could not keep the words behind my teeth: "Better things?"

"Stealing, cardsharping. Killing people."

"Killing people," I said, merely to be sure I had understood him correctly, but he took it as a sort of reproof.

"Murder for hire," he said and then, although the word clearly vexed him, "assassination."

"I too am a murderer," I said. "I killed my first man at fourteen."

"Huh," he said. "You and me both."

He came each day for a week; we did not speak again of our odd confessional, talking instead of Corambin history and, when I learned how to coax him, the stories of Mélusinien history of which he had an apparently inexhaustible store. On Lunedy afternoon, he was telling me of the gory end to the rule of kings in his city when there was a knock on the door, and before I could say, "Come in," the door opened and Vanessa said, "We have been summoned to—oh! I beg your pardon. I'd no idea you had a visitor."

There was something tight and sharp in her voice that I had not heard before. I said, for I was obliged to, "Vanessa, this is Mildmay Foxe, who is kind enough to come read to me. Mildmay, this is my fiancée"—the word still stuck in my throat like sand—"Vanessa Pallister."

The sounds of Mildmay getting to his feet. "I should go," he said. "I can—"

"No," Vanessa said, sounding almost as alarmed as I felt. "This will only take a moment, and I do beg your pardon for interrupting. Kay, we have been summoned to an audience with my mother. She says we will leave tomorrow, and we may return to Esmer on Geovedy."

"Is your mother always this high-handed?"

"Frequently worse," she said, with that tightness in her voice again. "That's all. I'll have to check Ottersham to find out when the train leaves."

"You will find me here," I said, and she shut the door.

"So," said Mildmay after a long silence, and I heard him sit down again. "That's the lady you're marrying."

"Yes," said I.

"You, um, don't seem real happy about it."

I laughed, though it was bitter. "Is not of my choosing. But, no matter. You were telling me of the mother of Michael Teverius."

There was another pause, in which I knew he was considering pressing the matter. Then he said, easily, "Yeah. Inez Cordelia. Now *she* was a piece of work." And I blessed him silently for letting it go.

Vanessa's parents—cousins of Murtagh in some degree, although I neither knew nor wished the details—lived at Isser Chase, an estate some ten miles out of Isserly, the principal city of the Duchy of Murtagh. The train left from Pollidean Station at noon. Vanessa and Vanessa's maid and Springett and I duly caught it. We did not talk on the train journey north and reached Isserly at half past sixteen.

Vanessa left me with Springett and her maid, Woodlock, in the lobby of the train station while she sallied forth to hire a carriage for the journey to Isser Chase. It should have been my task, but had been made very clear to me that it was not.

I sat where Springett put me and tried with painfully little success to cease thinking. Springett and Woodlock stood nearby, talking quietly. Woodlock was a native of Whallan, hired when Vanessa's Esmer-born maid did what Vanessa could not and quit, and she was clearly very nervous about the new ramifications of her position.

"He's not going to bite you," Springett said, and I realized with horrified amusement that one of the things of which Woodlock was nervous was me.

"We get the papers, you know," she said. "Even all the way out in Whallan."

"I'm not saying he was right, or he didn't do things any decent person would be ashamed to think, but *look* at him. He can't go two feet without someone to hold his hand, and he knows it."

Outwardly, I kept my face blank, as if I didn't even know they were talking; inwardly, I curdled. Truly, Springett had mastered the art of damning with faint praise. And I could not keep from contemplating all that I had done that Springett might think I should be ashamed of.

I considered the course of the Insurgence. Gerrard had raised his banner in Barthas Cross, the ancient city of the kings of Caloxa, and the Margrave of Larrowan, whom I disliked but respected, had been the first to swear fealty to him. I had been the second.

It had been the experience of those of us trained to fight the Usara that had allowed us to last as long as we had. We knew that war wasn't like the colored plates in children's history books; we cured Gerrard of his desire to meet the Corambins head-on. We knew to attack from ambush, to present a moving target, to strike at the most vulnerable target, not the most obvious. If we could have avoided the siege of Beneth, we might still have been fighting. I did not allow myself the fantasy that we would be any closer to winning, but had never been any real hope of that. Our plan had been to outlast the Corambins, not to defeat them.

But Beneth Castle controlled the Crawcour, and the Corambins had already had the overpowering advantage of the railroad. Could not let them have the river as well. It had taken the Corambins three indictions to bring Beneth down, and Benallery's plain little sparrow of a margravess fought them every inch of the way, though it meant her death.

In the aftermath, knowing we were doomed to defeat, watching Benallery struggle against his grief like a man with a mortal wound struggling to stay upright, I had ceased to take prisoners. My men had been as heartsick, as helplessly furious, as I, and although I had ordered the massacre at Angersburn, there had barely been any need. And Angersburn, most likely, was what Springett meant.

As Springett truly said, any decent person would be ashamed. Was I? I discovered that I did not have an answer. My life had been one war after another since I was fourteen, and was not ashamed of that. Had killed far more Usara than the three hundred men of Angersburn, and no one was suggesting I was monstrous for that. I'd waded in blood in a defile of the Perblanches that didn't even have a name. Did it make a difference that it was Usaran blood? It had been just as dark, just as sticky, the reek just as choking. The Usara had been just as dead.

My head ached; I realized I was rubbing my eyes and forced my hands back into my lap.

Springett said, "Are you all right, sir?" He was conscientious, whatever he thought of me.

"Fine," I said, although my voice lacked conviction. "Do you think Mrs. Pallister will be back soon?"

"I'm sure I don't know, sir. Do you want anything?"

"No," I said, because what I wanted was nothing I could articulate, and nothing Springett could give me in any event.

"Some water, maybe?" Springett said, and I realized I was causing him anxiety, most likely because I was sitting with my head down and my shoulders hunched, and my hands were now gripping each other tightly.

"No, thank you," I said. I forced my shoulders straight, forced my head up, forced my face to smooth out of a frown. I turned my head toward Springett. "Truly, am fine. Am sorry to have worried you."

"Yes, sir," he said, although he sounded dubious. I had never wondered about my own skill in lying before. Had never needed it. As a margrave, as a soldier, I had prided myself on my truthfulness. Was one of the reasons Isobel and I struck sparks off each other; neither of us had mastered the art of the politic lie, and we were both proud of it. Foolishly proud? I had never thought so before, but then the truth had never been my enemy before.

I had never been ashamed of what I was.

Now, I was. Ashamed of being blind, of being helpless, of being alive when Gerrard and Benallery were dead. Ashamed of having failed. Ashamed of being a token in the negotiations between Vanessa and Murtagh. Ashamed of . . . blessed Lady, Lady of Dark Mercies, I had not words for what I was now.

I hunched forward again, burying my face in my hands. "Please," I said. "Am fine. Just . . ." Was nothing I could think of to ask Springett to do, except to leave me alone, a child's defiance, a tantrum.

"There's Mrs. Pallister now," said Springett, and some small honest part of me hated him for sounding so relieved.

The smell of lilies reached me first, and then Vanessa's sweet Corambin voice. "Kay? Are you all right, darling?"

"Don't call me that," I said, the words grating in my throat.

"Fine. Are you all right, bonehead?"

She surprised me into laughter. "I am well, I thank you."

"Good," she said briskly. "Then let's get going. I want to reach Isser Chase before full dark."

"Yes'm," said Springett and Woodlock, and I was gathered up with the rest of the impedimenta in Vanessa's wake.

## *Felix*

I'm standing in the courtyard of St. Crellifer's. The doors stand open, and madness is flowing out, dark and corrosive and cruel. Like the Sim. A dead madwoman is standing beside me; her blood is a halo around her head. I don't know why I'm here—don't know if I'm dreaming or if this is true.

*Watch,* says the dead madwoman and points.

And I look up, up past the barred and glaring windows to the roof, where someone has climbed onto the parapet and is standing, peering down. At this distance, I can't make out his features, but I know who it is.

I remember Mildmay telling me once that all the buildings in the Lower City have roof-access doors. *Along of fire,* he'd said and given me one of his solemn sidelong looks that said he knew I knew exactly what he meant. I'd never found that door, but then when I had been in St. Crellifer's, I hadn't known Mildmay.

Then this is a dream. I should be relieved, but I can't feel it.

*What is he doing?* I ask.

*Learning to fly.*

I remember St. Crellifer's. It has three storeys and its steep-pitched attics. I don't know if the drop alone would be enough to kill anyone, but when he jumps—and he does jump, deliberately and hard—he jumps headfirst. The sound of his head hitting the paving stones is sharp and thick, and blood and bone and other things spread across the pavement like flowers.

Or wings.

The dead madwoman touches two bloody fingertips to my forehead and smiles the smile of a saint. *He can fly now,* she says, and I wake up.

## Mildmay

Martedy I couldn't go read to Mr. Brightmore along of him being off meeting Mrs. Pallister's family, and if I've ever seen a guy who would rather've cut his own head off with a butter knife, Mr. Brightmore was that guy.

I was reading the paper to Felix while he ate breakfast, something about a way to make the mines in the eastern mountains safer by using magic to detect bad air earlier, and he just sat there looking sourer and sourer, and I finally said, "What? You got something against mining?"

"Corambins are an ingenious people." I wasn't sure what "ingenious" meant, but Felix didn't sound like he thought it was a good thing. I was trying to decide if it was worth maybe getting my head bitten off to ask, and I guess he knew that look on my face because he said, "It means they're clever. Good at inventing things."

"Yeah, okay," I said, because I could see where they were.

"For example," Felix went on like I hadn't said nothing, "it never occurred to us that the binding-by-forms could be anything but permanent, but the Corambins can undo it in the twinkling of an eye."

He was being a prick on purpose—I knew that look on *his* face. "Okay, I got it," I said.

"Good. I'd hate to have your education interrupted just because Kay's off meeting his future in-laws."

Well, that was just nasty. "You trying to pick a fight because of something I've done, or is it just because you ain't sleeping good?"

"*Aren't sleeping well.* And I'm not trying to pick a fight."

I laughed at him. "The fuck you aren't."

"I'm just explaining a definition. With illustrative examples."

"In case I'm too stupid to get it the first time, yeah, I know." And I wasn't asking him what *illustrative* meant, not if he begged me.

"Past experience has shown . . ." He trailed off meaningfully, and you know, it can't be good to start off first thing in the morning wanting to punch somebody in the nose.

"Yeah, well, past experience also shows you're a fucking prick when you want to be. Guess I should be glad they took the binding-by-forms off after all."

"And why is that?" His horrible purring Strych-voice, and I decided all at once to quit dancing around the fucking thing.

"You know, you sound like Strych when you do that, and I wish you'd cut it the fuck out."

It worked. He went white and said furiously, "No wonder you're glad to be rid of the obligation d'âme. I'm surprised you stay around at all. Or have you changed your mind about that, too?"

"I said I wasn't going, and I ain't."

"Am not."

"I'm *saying*, you get this tone in your voice when you're playing with somebody, and you sound exactly like Brinvillier Strych or Malkar Gennadion or whatever the fuck you want to call him today. Which I get enough of in my dreams already, and don't fucking need from you."

"Then what *do* you need from me?" he said, with a horrible smile, his voice rising. "Food? Lodging? Spending money?"

I looked at him for a long moment before I could say levelly, "I don't need nothing from you, and you might be smart to remember it." And then I left, before one or the other of us came up with something even worse.

I was four blocks away before I could think again, and then I stopped dead in the middle of the sidewalk and tried to figure out whether to laugh or scream.

Powers and blessed *fucking* saints, he'd done it to me again. I could say I didn't want to fight with him—fuck, I could say I *wasn't* going to fight with him—until I was purple and blue in the face, and it didn't make a scrap of difference. He could get me going every fucking time.

"Fuck me sideways 'til I cry," I said, and startled a man passing so bad he almost fell off the sidewalk.

Watch your mouth, Milly-Fox.

I shifted my grip on Jashuki and tried to figure out a plan.

Well, the first thing was, don't go running back, either to slug Felix or to apologize for wanting to slug him. Let him go work that nasty temper out on his students. They didn't deserve it, but neither did I, and they didn't have to live with him.

Right at the moment, that felt like their good luck.

Second thing was, don't go running off and do something stupid like, say, proving to Felix just how much money I could pull down in a day if I wanted to. I'd been looking, because it never hurts to have, you know, options, and I knew where to find a game if I wanted to.

Which I didn't. I wanted to be done playing cards for money. Never fucking mind what Felix thought and how purely satisfying it would be to make his eyes bug out.

I sat down on a bench—that's one thing I'll say for Esmer, they put benches everywhere. I sat down and thought about my breathing for a while, until I was sure I wasn't going to go do something stupid. And then I sat there and tried to figure out what I was going to do instead.

And, okay, I'd got myself calmed down, but Felix's crack about my education was still eating at me. Like I needed Mr. Brightmore around to read a book or something. And that reminded me of Miss Leverick and her Society for the Advancement of Something-or-Other, and I remembered that when we'd finally gotten off the train in Lily-of-Mar Station, she'd given me her card instead of Felix, along of having figured out that Felix would just give her one of his five-alarm smiles and then lose the card.

But I'd kept it, along with Robin Clayforth's card—which Felix *still* hadn't noticed I'd lifted off him—in the little purse I kept money in for fathom tickets and buying flowers from street vendors and shit like that. So I fished it out. *Society for the Advancement of Universal Education, 117 Smiling Angel Street, Tamsen Dominion, Esmer.*

I'd expected not to recognize the street name, and I didn't. I was learning Esmer as fast as I could, but there was a fuck of a lot of it. More than Mélusine, maybe. But I didn't recognize the dominion, either, and I thought I'd been doing pretty well with those.

Well, at least I knew where to find a map.

I hauled myself up. It was easier than it had been for a while, but I figured I was pretty much stuck with Jashuki for the rest of my life. The goons in Gilgamesh had seen to that, which might've made them happy if they'd known. My feeling was, I deserved it for being stupid enough to get within spitting distance of Kolkhis, no matter *what* I thought was at stake, and maybe in the future I could do like Rinaldo had said and remember I was lame.

It was a nice day to be out, sunny and with a breeze. Chillier than it would be at home, but not bad. I paid attention on my way to the fathom station, along of not having been paying none at all on my way to that bench, reading the signs and making mental notes. And if I couldn't quite shut up the part of me pricing everything for a fence—well, old habits die extremely fucking hard.

I planted myself in front of the map in St. Ingry Station and went looking for Tamsen Dominion, figuring it couldn't be near either the Institution or Carey House or I'd know it already.

The dominion names were written bigger than everything else, so they were easy to spot. It only took me a minute to find Tamsen, up north of Nath, a couple dominions out from the center of town. A considerable hike, but not as bad as it could've been. I looked for fathom stations next and got lucky, because there on the south end of Tamsen was Smiling Angel Station.

It was midmorning, and Felix wouldn't go and teach for another three or four hours. I gave the girl a penny and headed down to find a northbound train.

❧

Tamsen was as bourgeois as Breadoven. Everything clean and respectable and flower boxes everywhere, even by the doors of the fathom station, and it turned out the Society for the Advancement of Universal Education was right across the street. Nice big sign over the door, black letters on white and easy to read.

And of course staring it in the face like that, I got cold feet and had to go walk up and down Smiling Angel Street until I'd got over wanting to bail. I found the smiling angel, too, standing right in the middle of the intersection with its hands spread, twice life-size—assuming an angel's the same size as a man—and smiling like it was trying to tell the whole world not to be assholes.

Turned out, at the other end of the block there was a real school: Tamsen Dominion Practicum School, the windows open on account of it being a nice day and a bunch of kids around their second septad all learning arithmetic from a stern-faced lady in a green dress. I thought about what I'd been learning when I was their age, and turned around to head back for the fathom station and home.

You ain't fooling nobody, Milly-Fox, and all the book learning in the world ain't gonna change what you are.

But I stopped by them stupid flower boxes. Felix would know what the flowers were. I didn't. I knew what I was, and what I'd been—what I'd done—but I also remembered Mehitabel telling me that we don't have to stay where the past puts us, even if we can't get rid of it. And me telling Felix the same exact fucking thing.

Yeah, I knew what I'd been. But I had to believe I could be more than that if I tried. I turned around and walked across the street to the Society for the Advancement of Universal Education. Opened the door and went in before I had a chance to talk myself out of it.

It was nice inside. I mean, not fancy or nothing, but all the stuff that could be polished was shining, and there wasn't a speck of dirt anywhere, and the gal behind the desk had a beautiful smile.

"May I help you, sir?" she said, and she even sounded like she meant it.

And of course I'd been working so hard on getting myself through the door, I hadn't stopped to think about what I was going to do once I got there.

"I, um. Is Miss Leverick around?"

"Miss . . . ?"

"Leverick," I said, as slow and clear as I could, and her smile came back.

"Yes, of course. Just a minute—and may I tell her who's asking for her?"

"Mildmay Foxe," I said and hoped her not asking me to repeat it was because she'd got it, and not just because she didn't want to be bothered.

On the other hand, it wasn't like I was hard to describe.

There were chairs, so I sat on one. It was most of a septad-minute before the gal came back, but when she did, she gave me another beautiful smile and said, "Frances says you should come up to her office. Up the stairs, second door on the left. It's open." Then she went back to whatever she'd been doing, and I went out the door and up the stairs and found Miss Leverick's office. Seemed like you weren't nobody in Esmer if you didn't have an office.

Miss Leverick's office wasn't as clean and shiny as the rest of the place. There were stacks of paper everywhere, plus a half-finished quilt in a lapframe draped over the extra chair and a skinny brown cat with blue eyes looking at me like I was everything wrong with the world and then some. Didn't budge off the windowsill though.

Miss Leverick looked up from her papers and smiled like she was glad to see me. We shook hands, and she told me to dump the quilt on the floor, although I was more careful with it than that, and when I was sat down, I said, "I never seen a cat with blue eyes before," along of really not wanting to get into me and what I thought I was doing here yet.

"She's Ygressine," Miss Leverick said. "They're the most fantastic mousers. There was quite the little dustup a few indictions ago, when the newspapers discovered that all the navy's cats are Ygressine instead of honest, hardworking Corambin tabbies. Sailors apparently believe that blue eyes are good luck."

"She's a long way from the sea."

"Many of our students are retired sailors. A Ygressine cat was probably the inevitable solution to our mouse problem. And we've all become very fond of Edmund. She's much friendlier than most of the Corambin cats I've met." She reached back to pet the cat. The cat, obviously knowing a good thing when it saw one, stood up, stretched, and kind of flowed over Miss Leverick's shoulder and down into her lap, where it curled itself up again and, as far as I could tell, went straight to sleep.

"Edmund? You did say 'she,' right?"

"She's named for her ship. The *Edmund Libby*?"

She said it like she expected me to recognize the name, and I shook my head.

"There are ballads about the wreck of the *Edmund Libby* now. It wrecked—oh, it must be a full wheel ago—on Old Sadie's Teeth. The worst storm on record, and in the morning, when the rescue boats could finally put out from Grimglass, there were only three survivors. Two men and the cat."

"*This* cat?"

"This cat. And now her children are populating Esmer. We have a waiting list for her kittens. She's quite famous."

Well, me and Felix had survived the *Morskaiakrov* going down, and I felt all kinds of respect for the cat.

"But you can't have come to talk about either cats or famous shipwrecks," said Miss Leverick. "Or is this just a social visit?"

Powers. "I, um. Well, you said y'all taught classes, and I was just wondering about them."

Oh very eloquent, Milly-Fox. I knew I was blushing, but Miss Leverick just said, "Did you have any particular class in mind?"

"I don't even know. What all do you teach?"

"Let's start from the beginning, then," she said and reached—careful not to disturb the cat—for the top of a stack of paper that turned out to be little booklets. She handed one to me. "These are the classes we're offering next month. I can tell you, of course, about the classes for Illa and Pella, but we haven't gotten those printed up yet."

"Sure," I said, kind of on reflex, and looked at the booklet to keep from saying something really dumb.

Me not knowing nothing about it, that booklet looked pretty good. They had a bunch of different classes. Arithmetic like the kids were learning down the street, grammar and composition and I knew Felix would be after me to take that one. A class on Corambin poetry. A class on Corambin history. And a class on something I had to say to myself twice before I was sure I was reading it right.

"Labyrinths?"

"Oh dear," said Miss Leverick, looking embarrassed. "Mrs. Weatherby has a bit of a hobbyhorse on the subject, and since she and her husband are among our principal donors . . ."

"You can't tell her no." I got that part. "But what does she have to say about 'em? Labyrinths, I mean."

"Ah," said Miss Leverick, looking even more embarrassed. "There are labyrinths all over Corambis, you see, and nobody knows what they're for. And Mrs. Weatherby's theory is—oh dear. Mrs. Weatherby believes that the labyrinths, all of them, were placed at sites of particular spiritual importance by King Edward, the last king of Corambis who could claim direct descent from Agramant the Navigator, and that he knew where to put them because, the people of those days being so much purer and holier than we are, he was in direct communication with at least one and possibly several angels."

"Okay," I said after a moment. "So when you say she has a hobbyhorse, what you mean is she's batfuck crazy?"

Miss Leverick absolutely cracked up. The cat opened her eyes and gave me a disgusted look, then jumped off Miss Leverick's lap and stalked out the door. That just made Miss Leverick laugh harder, but finally she took a deep breath and got herself settled again. She said, "Really, Mrs. Weatherby's class is very popular. She teaches them about the importance of the labyrinth in Cymellunar culture, and the names of all the Cymellunid kings of Corambis, and they take day trips on Domenicas with picnic lunches and such like."

"To look at labyrinths?" Because, why would you want to?

"There are several near enough to Esmer for train excursions. And we convinced the Company to offer a special fare."

"Huh," I said, although I could sort of see the part where getting out of the city for a day might be worth having to listen to a crazy lady yap about labyrinths. "So what *was* the importance of the labyrinth in Cymellunar culture?"

Which I know Miss Leverick only understood because it was her words. "Well, there are several conflicting theories—"

"Figures. But what does Mrs. Weatherby think?"

"Purification. Something about clarifying and channeling one's vi, I think, but honestly I try not to listen to her." She stopped and sort of squinted at me. "You weren't thinking about attending her class, were you?"

"Powers, no," I said. "Just curious."

"Good. Because I couldn't in all honesty *recommend* it." But she looked like she wasn't entirely satisfied. "Are there labyrinths in Mélusine?"

"Um. Well, there's curtain-mazes at the Trials, but—"

"The Trials?"

"Of Heth-Eskaladen. He's the god of . . ." She was eyeing me like she was a hungry dog and I was a side of beef. "What?" I said, although I didn't think I was going to like it.

"A class about Mélusine would be *very* popular."

"Not with me teaching it, it wouldn't," I said. "And Felix is pretty busy."

"It's only one night a week. And I admit our honorarium isn't much, but it's *something*."

"Felix has a job."

"And you?" She added quickly, "Many of our students are from the working classes, and I think they would appreciate having a teacher who was more like them than we well-to-do, well-meaning ladies."

"Powers and saints, lady, I ain't no teacher." I waved a hand at my face, at my ugly fucking scar. "Nobody's gonna pay to come and listen to me when they can't understand half the fucking things I say."

"But how long ago were you injured?" she said. "The physicians of Bernatha can do truly astonishing things—"

"Too fucking long." I shoved myself to my feet. "I been taking up too much of your time anyway. Thanks for the booklet."

"You're welcome," she said, standing up. "I'm sorry I upset you—it wasn't my intent. But do think about it. I don't think it would be nearly as bad as you believe."

"Yeah, sure," I said.

But I was thinking about it all right, thinking about it all the way back to Ingry Dominion. I was thinking about it so hard I went out and did the thing I'd gone over to Smiling Angel Street just exactly so I wouldn't do it. Went out and found the game in the cellar of the Blooming Turtle where I'd been real careful about not looking for it for a decad and a half.

## *Felix*

Corbie appeared in my office with a wad of scribbled-on papers and some unkind things to say about the University librarians. But then, rather than launching into a report on what she had—or hadn't—found, she fidgeted around my office and finally burst out with "Do you think it's wrong for women to be magicians?"

"Could you stop if you tried?"

She went red. "I . . . No."

I nodded. Because that was how it was, for wizards. When I was her age, I would have starved my magic out of my body if I'd been able—anything, if it would make Malkar lose interest in me. But I couldn't deny it, couldn't ignore it. Even now, with the binding-by-obedience wrapped about me as tight and airless as a winding sheet, my magic was still struggling for light and freedom, still struggling to be known. "Then I think, for the sake of every female wizard in the world, we'd better assume it's not wrong. Has someone been giving you grief?"

"Not more than usual, really," she said. Another interval of fidgeting, and she said, "Did you know most of the Mulkist warlocks were women?"

"Were they?"

"Yeah. And people are saying," with a wave of her hand to indicate the general populace of the Institution and University, "that maybe it's a *sign*, that maybe women can't be trusted with power. That it's *unnatural* and *wrong* and—"

"Corbie." She grinned lopsidedly and said it with me, "Shut up."

"I don't think any of that is true," I said gently. "Women who hold power can be good or evil, just exactly as men who hold power can be. So tell me about rachenants instead."

"Well," said Corbie, sitting down finally. "I ain't found much yet. Because it's like people just dumped boxes of books up there. Some of them aren't even on shelves. Although"—and she looked sheepish—"I've been fixing that, a little."

"Good girl," I said, and she blushed like a fire.

"So rachenants are a class of ghost, and lumme, there's more classes of ghost than I would've thought. But they're ghosts of magicians and they're ghosts called up for revenge, and they're ghosts—" She frowned at her notes. "The word the Mulkists use is *vorticant*, which seems to sort of mean unstable and sort of mean hungry and I ain't sure what all else. So it's like a fire that has to be contained by the one who builds it or it'll devour everything it finds."

"Yes," I said; that certainly matched with my experience.

"I ain't found anything about calling 'em up or making 'em go back, although I did find this list of places and times where you should never try to deal with one."

"Unlikely to be helpful," I said.

"Yeah, I know. The books *do* say that you can't ever give in to one and expect to make it out alive. They talk a lot about the Sacrifice of the Caster. That's opposed to other sacrifices, which there's also a list of." She gave me a grimace. "The Mulkists liked lists."

"And with such charming topics, too," I said.

"Yeah. That's all I have so far."

"You've made excellent progress," I said, and because it was true, added, "I'm proud of you."

And the smile she gave me would have lit all Esmer on a moonless night.

# *Mildmay*

In Esmer, they play this game called Caterwaul, which is like a second step-cousin of Long Tiffany—meaning it's pretty much straightforward and not full of girly shit like Horned Menelan is. Or Griffin and Pegasus, for that matter, which I also hate. No, Caterwaul is all about the cards. What you have and what the other guys have and what you can do with it. And some cleverdick things like where you can take a fucking lousy hand and sweep the table with it if the other guys ain't paying attention quite as hard as they should. Or just get that littlest bit unlucky. Lots of bluffing in Caterwaul. And the more you can keep all the cards in your head—who's discarded what and played what and what all that means everybody has to have left—the better you do.

I might've been too stupid for books, but Kolkhis didn't have no trouble at all teaching me cards.

I got to the Blooming Turtle around the ninth hour of the day. Fourteen o'clock, they said here, or pimpernel. I got the hairy eyeball but good, first from the guy at the door, then from the guy at the bottom of the stairs, and then from the guys around the table, but if there's one fucking thing I know how to do, it's how to give the hairy eyeball right back at the fuckers, and since Felix actually had given me spending money—and powers, just the words "spending money" made me want to go puke and then wash my hands 'til my fingernails bled or something—I had a stake when they asked about it. And, you know, probably they figured I didn't know what the fuck I was doing, and they'd fleece me out of my money and that'd be that.

Fat fucking chance.

I laid low the first few hands. Not losing big, not winning big, watching the way everybody else played, how they felt about the guy next to them, shit like that. Don't matter what the game is, you got to know what's going on at the table, or you're fucked. I played real quiet, the way I'd been playing for decads, all the way from Clerval, because we had to be careful and not make anybody mad and still, you know, pay the fucking hotel bill in the morning. And then it just . . . all of a sudden I was done with that. I was done with being careful and polite and not getting in nobody's face.

Just plain *done*.

Maybe I'd make Felix's spooky eyes bug out after all.

## *Kay*

The journey to Isser Chase began in grim silence, but once the sounds of Isserly had died away behind us, Vanessa said, still very brisk, "I feel I should warn you about what you're walking into."

"Had not realized it was an ambush," said I.

"Ambush," said she. "That may be the best description of my mother I've ever heard."

She sounded different away from Esmer, both older and less polished. And far more intelligent. And in truth I was grateful that she was even bothering. I listened intently as Vanessa described her mother's three marriages: first to a naval man who had gone down with the *Fortitude* in the Seventh of the One Hundred Forty-seventh, leaving her a widow with a small child, then to Vanessa's father—there were three children from that marriage, Vanessa being the oldest—and finally to a man named Laurent Shale who was some two indictions younger than Vanessa's elder half brother.

"He is very charming," said she.

"Young men married to older women generally are," said I.

She gave a tiny snort of laughter. "That's certainly been Laurent's strategy. He never crosses Mother about anything."

Vanessa's half brother, a naval man like his father, was currently serving on the *Errant* in the blockade of Alkorazond. His wife and infant daughter resided at Isser Chase, for he could not support them on a lieutenant's pay and his wife had no family in Corambis, being Ygressine.

"Did I mention," Vanessa said bitterly, "that my mother prides herself on being outspoken?"

Vanessa's younger sister was recently married to a lesser lord in Kenneráck, and her brother, to whom Isser Chase technically belonged, was unmarried, "but you will most likely meet his lover."

"His lover?"

"Yes," and she sounded like she was bracing herself. "Ambrose Teller. I like him a good deal better than Oliver, to be honest."

I knew not how to respond. Could hardly decry Oliver Carey for being violet when I knew myself to be the same, but . . .

"Oliver has quarreled with every intended in the dominion," Vanessa said, too brightly. "And with Mother. It's the only thing I've ever known him to stand firm on, so I cannot help but believe he is sincere, even if I don't understand it."

I still could say nothing; I felt as if I had been turned to stone.

"If you're going to denounce him as an unnatural and wicked sinner," Vanessa said, "I really would appreciate a warning."

Was why she had told me about her family in advance. To protect her brother and his . . . his lover.

"No," I said finally. "Will not denounce anyone."

"Rodger was very antique about it. Refused to have Oliver mentioned in his house, that whole 'honor of the descent' nonsense." She sounded as she had in Esmer, bright and hard, but this time I understood that she was defending herself.

I took a deep breath, let it out slowly, steadily. Said, "I am violet myself." Had certainly been no secret in Rothmarlin that the margrave preferred chasing boys, no secret that when I went to Barthas Cross, I sought the jezebels of Clowder Place instead of those of Golden Row, but I had never said the words before, never admitted it might be . . . more. Save in that ugly confession to Intended Gye, and that was a nightmare and wrapped in nightmare and was not the same.

"Oh," said Vanessa in a very small voice.

I knew not what to say to that, either. Am sorry? But sorry for what?

"Is that why you never married?" Vanessa said, as close to timid as I had yet heard her.

"No. Yes. I know not." I sighed. "Is not easy to go courting when you spend the summer months at war and the winter months tending to all the matters you neglected during the summer. And then with the Insurgence . . ."

"Yes," said she. "Did you have someone? Is that why you—"

"No," I said, too sharply.

"All right," she said, and the journey to Isser Chase ended as it had begun, in silence.

⁂

"Oh may the angels love us," Vanessa said as the carriage slowed to a halt. "She's got the whole family out. Ortenzia's been crying. And what in the Lady's name is Amabel doing out of Kennerack? I can see she's increasing from here." She huffed out something that was a laugh or a sigh or possibly both. "Brace yourself."

I heard Springett put the step down from the rumble seat; a moment later, the carriage door opened and someone said, "Welcome back to Isser Chase, Miss Vanessa."

"Thank you, Moss." The carriage jounced as she climbed down, and I heard her say, "Springett will see to Mr. Brightmore."

As someone assuredly must.

But Springett was as tactful about this as he was about everything else, and I was grateful for his support, knowing that Vanessa's entire family was watching.

"Thank you, Springett," said Vanessa, and she took my arm. I let her lead me forward. Whatever quarrels one might have with a fellow soldier, one did not leave his flank unguarded in battle.

"Vanessa, dearest!" I knew immediately where Vanessa had learned her hard, bright voice. "You look so well!"

Vanessa was as stiff as a poker under my hand, and her voice matched her mother's when she said, "Mother, may I present my fiancé, Kay Brightmore. Kay, this is my mother, Paulina Shale."

"Pleased to meet you," I said.

"Likewise," said Mrs. Shale; she made no attempt at sincerity. "This is my husband, Laurent."

"How d'you do?" in a nervous tenor.

"My daughter Amabel, and her husband John, Lord Waring." Amabel's voice was soft, a mumble drowned in shyness; her husband's conveyed infinite disapproval.

"My daughter-in-law, Ortenzia Biddick."

"A pleasure, Mr. Brightmore." Quite deep for a woman's voice, and with a strong foreign accent.

"And I'm Oliver Carey," said another man, deeper voiced than Laurent Shale and without any of Lord Waring's hostility. "Welcome to Isser Chase."

"Thank you," I said.

"Moss will show you to your rooms," said he. "We don't keep fashionable hours—dine with the primroses—so you'll want to change." No, not hostile, but not overly cordial, either.

"How is Ambrose, Oliver?" Vanessa said, warning in her voice.

"He's fine," said Oliver, just as tightly. "You'll see him at dinner." A tiny, awkward pause, but Oliver Carey was clearly not about to apologize to me for anything. "Moss!"

Springett helped me change for dinner—a Corambin custom I found baffling—and took me downstairs again. "The sitting room, sir," he said and established me in a chair before padding away again.

"You must be Kay Brightmore," said a man's voice, young, light, rather nervous. "I'm Ambrose Teller. Vanessa might have mentioned me?"

"Yes. I'm pleased to meet you."

A pause in which he was almost audibly wondering if Vanessa had mentioned *everything*, then he said, "I grieved for the death of Prince Gerrard."

I am still grieving. But I said, "Thank you. I hope now only that Governor Albern will be just."

"Oh you may be sure of that," said a voice behind me, and my grip on the chair arms went white-knuckled.

Thomas Albern, Duke of Glimmering.

"Your Grace," said Ambrose Teller, even more nervously. "I didn't hear you come in."

"You were preoccupied." Glimmering's footsteps came around my chair. "Understandably so. It is not every evening one dines with the architect of a civil war."

"You flatter me," said I.

"Nothing but a simple soldier?" Glimmering asked mockingly. "You don't expect anyone to believe that, do you? Of the Cougar of Rothmarlin?"

"I care not what you believe," said I. I knew that he could see the way my hands were clawed about the chair arms, but I could not relax them.

I heard a door open; Vanessa said, rather breathlessly, "My lord duke! I didn't know you were visiting us!"

"Vanessa," said Glimmering, turning away from me. "As lovely as ever. Yes, I confess I imposed myself on your mother. I wanted to speak to you, and *not* in Murtagh's ambit."

"To me?" she said; she sounded surprised.

"Yes. After dinner perhaps. Unless you want to discuss your future prospects in front of your mother."

"Your Grace's acumen is uncanny," Vanessa said, and I smelled lilies; she had come past him to stand beside me. Perhaps she, too, had learned somehow the difference between a friend and a fellow soldier.

---

That dinner proved that Paulina Shale, as a mother, made my own mother seem positively benevolent. She had not been very interested in me, even less interested in Serena and Isobel, but at least she had never indulged in acts of outright and deliberate sabotage. Listening to Mrs. Shale lecturing Lady Waring on her marital duties, I felt my mother's indifference as a blessing.

Mrs. Shale ignored her son entirely; she spent most of the meal alternating criticisms of Lady Waring and Mrs. Biddick with rather unpleasant adulation of Glimmering. Was very clear that, though it might have been his idea, she had known precisely what she was doing in inviting him to Isser Chase while Vanessa and I were visiting. Over dessert, she turned on Vanessa. She began by inquiring pointedly after Richard, clearly faulting Vanessa, as I had, for leaving her child at Grimglass. "Isn't he lonely, Vanessa? He must miss his father very much—you know, Thomas, that Rodger died at Marrah Ford."

I remembered Marrah Ford; the water had been churned to mud in the first charge, and it became progressively thicker and fouler and redder throughout the long slow torpid afternoon. I remembered the flies buzzing drunkenly, remembered the dead floating away down the Crawcour, remembered washing and washing that night, and being unable to get the vile mud out from beneath my fingernails. I remembered the Crawcour stained red in great clouds that would have been beautiful had one not known their cause.

"Actually," Vanessa said, "Richard barely remembers his father. Rodger spent very little time with him."

"The Warden of Grimglass has so many responsibilities. It must be hard even for a very fit and active man to make time for his family."

"Oh, no," said Vanessa. "Rodger's steward took care of most of that, and his brother Geoffrey the rest. Rodger simply had no interest in children."

That stymied Mrs. Shale only momentarily. She turned to asking about Vanessa's "little school friends," and Vanessa answered, her tone becoming brighter and harder with every syllable as she recounted marriages and children and social successes. I realized that Mrs. Shale knew the answers before she asked the questions. These questions were strategic, designed to emphasize Vanessa's undistinguished first marriage and the positively disgraceful alliance her second marriage would be. It was an ugly performance, and it finally drove me to intervene.

"Was remarking earlier to Vanessa," said I, cutting across Mrs. Shale's next salvo, "how kind it is of your son to share his home with you and your third husband, Paulina. You must be a truly devoted mother to inspire such devotion in return—I myself, I am afraid, am not of nearly so affectionate a disposition."

"And what," said Mrs. Shale, her voice awful with affront, "is that supposed to mean?"

"Mean?" said I. "It means nothing. Was merely an observation."

"I think Kay and I will take our coffee in the library, Mother," Vanessa said, and we withdrew in good order.

Coffee was an upper-class Corambin fad, imported from Ygres Sur; I did not care for it, and Vanessa confessed that evening that she doctored hers with as much cream and sugar as she could get away with. She said, "You don't care what people think of you, do you?"

"An I did, would be but one more misery atop the pile. For truly I have lost that race without the flag ever being dropped."

"How do you mean?"

"One," I said. "Am a Caloxan in Corambis. Two, am—as Glimmering so thoughtfully reminded me—the 'Cougar of Rothmarlin' and half Usaran in the bargain. Mine own countrymen think me a savage as much as you do."

"I don't—"

"Three, am called a butcher by the Corambins and a coward by the Caloxans. Four, have lost my honor and land and power and am now dependent on the charity of my brother-in-law. Five, I have no doubt that this marriage between us will be seen as everything from a reward from the Convocation to—"

"Oh, Grimglass is no reward, believe me," said Vanessa.

"I know you like it not, but—"

"*Like* it? It's not a matter of—"

A knock at the door, which opened before either of us answered. "Am I intruding?" said Glimmering, and I hated how easily I recognized his voice. "Only, your mother is organizing paper games in the drawing room, and you and I should talk. You can send Rothmarlin upstairs."

"Or he can stay where he is," Vanessa said. "What is it you wished to say to me?"

A small pause, and he said, "I don't know what Murtagh has been saying to you, Vanessa, but you need not make this marriage. I realize the connection with the Careys may seem advantageous, but—"

"Have you a better option for me?" Vanessa said coolly. "A more suitable candidate, perhaps, or another way to ensure my son's inheritance against Lord Darne's greed?"

"Well, it's hardly your son's inheritance, is it, if Kay Brightmore is made Warden of Grimglass? Don't think he'll hesitate to sacrifice your son to the interests of his own children."

"That eventuality has been considered," Vanessa said, still cool. "His Grace of Murtagh and I—"

"If you don't know he's got Murtagh wrapped around his little finger, you are a greater fool than I thought possible. There is no agreement made, no promise, that Murtagh will not go back on if it suits him."

"What did he promise you, that the breaking of it rankles so deeply?" said I. "Ownership of me as I were a dog? Caloxa for your own private kingdom?"

"Kay," Vanessa said sharply, "hold your tongue."

"Ah," said Glimmering. "I see. You think you have him broken to bridle."

"I find both your wordplay and your metaphor offensive, sir," said Vanessa. "If you have a proposition to make to me, kindly do so. If you have merely veiled slurs to offer, I suggest you go join my mother's paper games."

"Very well," said Glimmering. "I am suggesting that you ally yourself to Glimmering rather than Murtagh. I will not fetter you with a husband. I will assume guardianship of your son and his estate, and provide you with a jointure such that you may live in Esmer as fashionably as you please."

It took me a moment to realize Vanessa was laughing at him. Took Glimmering several moments longer.

"It is a solution to your dilemma, Vanessa," said he. "And it has to be more palatable than marriage to a blood-soaked beast like this. Don't be so quick to ridicule it."

"My lord duke," said Vanessa, sobering abruptly, "I don't see how I *can* be a greater fool than you thought possible, for clearly you think I am the greatest fool on the face of the world. I have no fancy to trade Glimmering for Darne, and thus while I thank you for your very *kind* and *selfless* offer, I feel I must decline. And so, Your Grace, good night."

"You're making a mistake," Glimmering said, trying to sound concerned rather than merely angry.

"That's as may be. I still like my mistake, and my blood-soaked beast, better than yours." And from the sound, I guessed that she closed the door in his face.

"What an awful man," said she. "I hope you don't mind if we don't invite him to the wedding."

"Vanessa," said I, "why are you marrying me?"

"Because I have few choices and all of them are bad. If I do nothing, or if I marry again to suit myself, either Darne will swallow Grimglass like a comfit, or he will negotiate with Rodger's brothers—a tax, perhaps some reallocation of currently fallow land. And either way, Richard's inheritance will be lost."

"Do you care so much?"

"I may put it most cogently by pointing out that if Richard is ousted, he and I will have no choice but to come live on my brother's charity like poor Ortenzia, with my mother dripping poison at every turn. And while I am often bored at Grimglass, I don't want to see it, or its people, neglected, nor to see its concerns used as bargaining tokens for political power. Murtagh's proposal actually suits me very well—or it would if you did not hate me."

"I do not *hate* you," I said, although I feared it was a feeble protest.

She snorted. "You would rather be fed to the Yammering than marry me. You've made that much very clear."

Could have said, *And you have been so loving and saintly yourself?* but was not the point and I knew it. "Is not you," I said and went on haltingly. "Is that . . . I became Margrave of Rothmarlin when I was fifteen, and since that time I have followed no man save out of love, and my own sense of duty, and as I chose. But now . . . I am blind, destitute, beholden. I have no choice. What Murtagh appoints for me, I must do."

"Do you think I *wanted* to marry Rodger Pallister?" she said scathingly. "Do you think I don't resent daily, *hourly*, being saddled with his child and his debts and his great ramshackle blot of a house and the *lighthouse*! Sweet blessed Lady, I would rather walk into the sea and have done with it. But I can't. I have to do the best I can with the cards I've been dealt. And if that means marrying you, then marry you I will. And I'm sorry if you don't like it."

"But not very," I said dryly.

"Well, only insofar as that it will make both our lives very unpleasant."

"Well," I said, feeling as if I surrendered again, though I knew not who my enemy was, "maybe we can work on that part."

The scent of lilies and a light touch to the back of my hand. "Maybe," said Vanessa Pallister.

## *Mildmay*

It was close on to the septad-night by the time I got home, and the only reason I wasn't jingling was that Corambins used paper money.

They didn't like me at the Blooming Turtle, especially after what happened to the guy who tried to get in my face about never coming back. I wouldn't go back, though. Not for them, but because I felt dirty. No, not just dirty, that ain't strong enough. *Filthy.* I'd felt dirty back around the first big hand I'd won, but I hadn't stopped until I'd cleaned out the entire table. And even then, you know, if one of them had been stupid enough to pony up, I'd've gone 'round again. And won. Because that's what I did when there was money in the game. When I didn't have to be *careful.*

Powers and saints, I made myself sick.

I climbed the stairs in our apartment building, and by the time I got to the top, Felix was standing in the open doorway, arms folded. I was just as glad he was backlit so I couldn't see his expression.

He waited until I'd heaved myself up onto the landing before he said, "Where have you been?" His voice was kind of tight, but nice and even, so he was upset, but not *really* upset, and he wasn't mad at me. There were a septad and six different ways he sounded when he was mad at me, and none of them had anything to do with "even."

"Stupid," I said, because it was true. "You gonna stand there all night, or can I come in?"

He moved aside and I went in. He followed me, locked the door. Said, "I'll believe many things of Esmer, but not that it actually has a fathom station for stupid. So, a different question: what were you doing?"

"This," I said. I was emptying my coat pockets onto the table. "You think we can give it to the girl hocuses at the Institution or something?"

"Good gracious," Felix said. His eyes weren't bugging out, but he did look more than a little startled, and I could tell he was trying hard to not flip out at me. And I was grateful for it, too. And then he just looked guilty. "Is this because of what I said this morning?"

"Sort of. I mean, yes. But not just that. I'd even talked myself out of it and then Miss Leverick got me all worked up and stupid again."

"You weren't exaggerating when you said you didn't need to cheat," he said. He was looking at the money, not at me. "Miss Leverick? So you went to her society, whatever it's called?"

"The Society for the Advancement of Universal Education," I said. "And hey! I met a cat with blue eyes."

That made him look up, and he actually smiled at me, which made me feel a little less like complete shit.

He said, "Why don't you tell me about your day while we get ready for bed? And tomorrow you can come with me to the Institution. It seems like you might be less likely to get into trouble there."

"Oh, fuck you," I said, but that wasn't what I meant, and he knew it.

## Felix

I had not expected Mildmay *actually* to come with me to the Institution, but the next afternoon when I left the apartment he was right beside me. I used what little common sense I had and held my tongue.

We reached the Institution in amiable silence, and I led the way to my classroom in Venables Hall. It wasn't as pleasant as the Grenouille Salon, but the chairs were comfortable (though mismatched), and there was the option here, as there never was in the Mirador, of opening the windows.

Mildmay looked around carefully. I said, "You do that every time you come into a room. What are you looking for?"

He stared at me blankly for a moment, then quite visibly went back over the last few moments in his head and blushed. And then he gave me the list, ticking the items off on his fingers. "Goons. Doors. Windows. Stuff you could use as a weapon if you had to. Um." His blush got worse, and he was distinctly not meeting my eyes. "You."

"Me?" I wasn't sure whether to be amused or insulted or incredibly flattered. "And which am I, potential threat or potential advantage?"

"Depends what kind of mood you're in."

"Oh marvelous," I said, but I couldn't keep my face straight.

"It's just habit," Mildmay said. "Don't mean nothing."

"On the contrary. It means that if a pack of crazed eteoklides charges the door in the middle of class, you'll be ready for them."

And he'd forgiven me for yesterday, because he said, "What're eteoklides?"

"An ancient warrior cult from what's now Lunness Point. I don't remember most of the tenets of their faith, but they believed that if you died in battle for their god, you would be reborn into the cult. And if you did it enough times, you became a kouraph—not quite a god, but with many of the same benefits. For obvious reasons, the cult went extinct several centuries ago."

"A kouraph, huh? Like an angel?" he said, slyly enough that I knew he was making one of his infrequent and odd jokes. He had told me about Mrs. Weatherby and her theories so, unlike some of his jokes, this one I got.

I smiled back at him. "Blood-drinking angels."

"That's a benefit?"

"To the eteoklides," I said demurely.

"Powers. The things some people think are fun." He retreated into the back of the classroom, and a moment later, the first of my students came in.

They didn't all notice him. Those that did looked at him, looked at me, and showed better discretion than I'd thought them capable of and did not ask. Corbie went and sat beside him, and punched him in the arm at something he said. Cyriack Thrale actually smiled at him and after class—another frustrating hour of trying to teach them something they did not want to believe—went over to say hello. I was trapped at the front of the room by Jowell, the most plodding of my students, so I could not hear Cyriack and Mildmay's conversation, although it seemed lively.

Cyriack was still talking, intensely, earnestly, when they came over to me, and Mildmay jerked his chin. "Just a moment, Jowell. Yes, Mildmay?"

Mildmay said, "Mr. Thrale's got a new bog body, and he wants to—"

"I beg your pardon. A *what*?"

Mildmay looked hopefully at Cyriack, who said, "A bog body. They're what I work on, over at the Mammothium. Ancient people whose bodies were preserved in peat bogs."

I had been told about the Mammothium, so at least that part made sense. "And you're sightseeing?" I said to Mildmay.

"I'm *interested*, okay?" He looked as abashed as I'd ever seen him.

"No, of course, it's fine." I wasn't sure I wanted to see a body that had been buried in peat for hundreds of years, but it couldn't be any worse than Jowell's conversation. I said to Cyriack, "May I come, too?"

"Of course," Cyriack said, almost embarrassingly delighted.

The Mammothium had been a private house, not a public building like most of the rest of the Institution, which made the enormous skeleton in the front hall look even more incongruous. Cyriack was pounced on by another student as soon as we came through the door, and dragged off into another room for what was either an argument or a sexual encounter—nothing else generated that kind of urgency. Most likely an argument. But I didn't mind; I was still staring at the skeleton when Corbie and Mildmay came in.

"That's the mammoth," Mildmay said.

"Rather," I said. "And when were you here before, to be introduced to it?"

He looked at the mammoth instead of looking at me. "Well, that day we moved into the new place?"

"Yes, I remember it vividly, seeing as it was less than a month ago."

"Yeah, well, it was Mr. Thrale that found it for me, because I'd come here looking for—"

"So you've seen these bog bodies before, too?"

"Just one of 'em," he said apologetically.

"You didn't mention it."

He shrugged, still staring at the mammoth. "Didn't think you'd be interested."

"You could have told me anyway. I wouldn't mind."

He gave me a startled glance—trying to decide if I was teasing, I suspected, and I wondered if I deserved that or not.

Corbie straightened up from an examination of the mammoth's toes and said, "And these things lived *thousands* of indictions ago?"

"That's what Mr. Thrale says," said Mildmay.

She was frowning. "How old is the world, anyway?"

A decent answer to that question—which would have taken all afternoon and still would have boiled down to, essentially, *No one knows*—was forestalled by a commotion from the hallway indicating Cyriack's reemergence. "For the last time, Stanhope," he said over his shoulder, "*I can't help you.*" Without waiting for a reply, he said, "I'm so terribly sorry, Mr. Harrowgate. Would you like to come upstairs?"

"What's the matter with Stanhope?" Corbie asked as Cyriack began herding us toward the stairs. I tried not to inquire into Corbie's social life, but I noticed that she was clearly familiar with the denizens of the Mammothium.

Cyriack rolled his eyes. "Those damn sheep in Murrey. He's getting as bad as Jowell and Hutch. He's trying to figure out the cause of death, and he's convinced himself I can help him. Which I *can't*."

"Is that the pesti-whatsit?" Mildmay said.

"Pestilence," I said.

Cyriack said, "Yes. Although now they aren't sure it *is* a pestilence. It's not spreading like one, and the magician-practitioner in Howrack insists the sheep are perfectly healthy—apart from being dead, of course. I keep telling Stanhope the only thing to do is go down there himself, but he acts as if Caloxa were on the other side of the moon. Idiot."

"Well, he's frustrated," Corbie said more charitably.

As we reached the top of the staircase, Cyriack darted ahead to unlock a door halfway down the hall and said over his shoulder, "I don't blame him, but that doesn't make it my problem. Come in, please. There isn't much room, but I don't think we'll be *too* crowded."

The room was dominated by a long table, on which reposed a huddled shape draped by a sheet. "She's not as old as the other one I showed you," Cyriack said to Mildmay. "Maybe a thousand years. And Adept Chellick's trying a new preservation technique," he added, indicating the sheet. Then he twitched it neatly away, and I went lurching backwards, nearly knocking Mildmay over, my whole body going cold.

It was not that the woman was dead, or that her body was twisted and flattened horribly. Or that she stank, of stagnant water and of something sharp and foul that I did not recognize. But the noirance poured off her in waves, so strong I could almost believe it was the foul smell I couldn't identify.

"Whoa," Mildmay said, catching himself with his cane and then steadying me. "You okay?"

"Don't you feel it?" I said to Corbie, to Cyriack—both of whom were staring at me as if I'd lost my mind.

"Feel what?" Cyriack said. He looked at the body critically. "I suppose she's a rather gruesome sight, if you aren't accustomed—"

"Not that," I said. "The noirance. The . . . the darkness."

"The what?" said Corbie.

"Are you talking about her aether?" Cyriack said. "But she doesn't have any. She's dead."

"Preserve me from rationalists," I said under my breath, then, to my students, "No, I am *not* talking about aether. I'm talking about noirance."

"But—" said Cyriack.

"Shut up," I said. "Listen to me while I say it one more time. Our perceptions of magic are filtered through metaphors. Your aether is very useful, as these metaphors go, but it's limited. In this particular case, thinking in terms of aether, which dead creatures do not have, is *preventing* you from seeing that this woman is saturated in magic just as much as she is saturated in bog water. And that the magic in which she is saturated is noirant. Dark. Dangerous."

"Evil?" Corbie said. She didn't entirely look as if she believed me, but she did at least look worried. Although perhaps that was because she thought I was insane.

"No, not evil. Or, not necessarily evil. Noirance is difficult to categorize."

"But she's saturated in it," Cyriack said, skepticism manifest in every syllable.

"Yes." I forced myself to take a step forward; it wasn't nice to keep Mildmay jammed up against the door.

"Show us."

"I beg your pardon." I raised an eyebrow at him, stalling for time. I knew all too well what Cyriack meant. He wanted proof—proof that only problematically existed in the first place, and that under the binding-by-obedience I could not provide. I had avoided direct confrontations during class, but I'd known my luck wouldn't hold forever.

"If there's all this *noirance* floating around, show it to us."

"I can't," I said, and went on before he could fire his next arrow, "but I may be able to teach you to see it if you're willing to try."

"Why wouldn't we be?" Cyriack said, and I knew that pose of careless bravado, knew it from the inside.

"Not 'willing to let my words go in one ear and out the other while you nod politely,' " I said. "Willing to *try*."

That stung him, as I'd known it would, and he agreed on the instant. Corbie was frowning at the bog body; she said, "Sure. It's spooky as shit, though."

"Yes," I said, and reminded myself to go gently with them. I was suddenly—and rather absurdly, all things considered—glad that I'd chosen to bring Ynge's *Influence of the Moon* into exile with me. I'd read it so many times between Mélusine and Esmer that I had the relevant passages essentially memorized. And I knew they would work, if Cyriack and Corbie would let them; they'd worked for me.

I looked around; there was a chair in the corner, and I pointed Mildmay at it. "This may take a while. You might as well sit down."

He gave me the look under his eyebrows he always gave me when I worried about his health, but he sat. Insofar as I could read him, he seemed interested, but not at all alarmed. "All right," I said to Corbie and Cyriack. "Remember you promised to give this an honest effort."

They nodded, Corbie cooperatively, Cyriack scowling with impatience. I said, "I want you to think about the moon. You can close your eyes if it helps, but you don't have to. Think about the moon at the half."

Cyriack opened his mouth to object, caught my eye, and subsided. Corbie had her eyes squinched shut in a look of desperate concentration; I needed to remember to start teaching her basic mental imagery. But cooperation was cooperation; the fine details were a matter for later. "The moon is at the half," I said. "In the night sky, it's half a circle, but you know that in reality, there's a full circle, half-light and half-dark. Yes?"

"Yes," Cyriack said, and Corbie nodded. Cyriack had his eyes closed now.

"Good," I said. "You have a circle, half-light and half-dark. You can see both halves in your mind." Next was the tricky bit; I was careful not to let my voice alter. "Now I want you to imagine this moon, the moon at the half, in a white sky. Where before the dark half was invisible, now the light half is invisible. You have the dark half of the moon hanging in a white sky. Are you still with me?"

Corbie's face had smoothed out; Cyriack was frowning slightly. But they both nodded.

"Good. Now reverse it again: the moon against a black sky. But remember the full circle is always there." I took them through the switch a couple more times, and then said, "Now hold that image of the moon, the full circle, half-light, half-dark, in your head, and open your mind to your magic. Let your magic fill the moon, half-light, half-dark. The moon is your magic, half-light, half-dark. You see both sides at once." I waited a moment, watching their faces, and said, "Now open your eyes and look at this bog body."

Corbie staggered backwards exactly as I had. Cyriack held his ground, but his face went a dreadful color, and his voice cracked when he said, "What is *that*?"

"That," I said, "is noirance. Congratulations."

"But . . . I . . . but it wasn't . . ." He turned to Mildmay. "Do *you* see it?"

"Annemer," Mildmay said, perfectly calmly.

Cyriack turned, like a bear at bay. "Corbie?" Corbie was still staring at the bog body. Cyriack looked wildly at me. "What did you *do* to us?"

I smiled at him. "I taught you a new metaphor."

"But this . . . this isn't . . ."

"I've been telling you for weeks that aether isn't real, any more than noirance is. They're just different ways of looking at something we aren't built to understand."

Corbie announced, "I need a drink."

"Right," said Cyriack. He all but bolted from the room. I didn't entirely expect him to return, but he did, only five minutes later, carrying a bottle and four glasses. He splashed whiskey in the glasses and handed them around. Corbie knocked hers back like a woman taking medicine, and Cyriack poured her more without being asked.

I sipped my whiskey and waited. The next move was clearly theirs.

And they were clearly very uncomfortable with making it. Neither Cyriack nor Corbie would meet my eyes, and I watched the way they both kept glancing at the bog body and then quickly away. Mildmay folded his hands over the head of his cane and observed everything with attentive disinterest. I would have to remember to ask him later whether he'd classed the bog body as a threat or an advantage.

Finally, Corbie couldn't stand it any longer and said, "But if there's all this . . . this noirance, where is it *coming* from?"

"An excellent question," I said, "to which I don't have an answer. Shall we look?"

Corbie looked at me as if I'd suggested biting the heads off babies for fun.

"She's still dead," I said. "Her noirance can't hurt you unless you let it."

"Wait a moment," said Cyriack. "How do you 'let' magic do anything?"

"Don't think of it as a force of nature," I said. "It's not like your elements, fire and water and so on. It's a human force, shaped by human will and human desire. And it holds impressions frighteningly well."

"I don't understand," Corbie started, and Mildmay said, "He means ghosts."

"Well, not ghosts exactly," I said. "Those don't necessarily have anything to do with magic. But necromancy isn't *merely* bringing the dead back to life, and the dead aren't the only nonliving things that can hold, and twist, magic."

Cyriack and Corbie were staring at me now with even greater alarm, and I brought myself sternly back to order. "But my *point* is, unless you are very very stupid and invite it in or otherwise open yourself to it"—as I had done, more than once, but there was no need to tell them I was speaking from personal experience—"it cannot harm you. Most of magic is in your intent, after all."

Not to them, of course, poor lambs. They thought it was all quantifiable, that it had some objective existence apart from their own perceptions. But perhaps they were learning better.

"So," Cyriack said. "You think we should . . . examine the body?"

"It's what you do, ain't it?" Mildmay said.

"Yes, but I didn't . . ." *Know,* he did not say.

"Oh for pity's sake," said Corbie, shaking herself like a dog coming out of the water. "If it hasn't hurt you before, it won't hurt you now. Come on."

She stepped boldly up to the table and there foundered—not so much, I thought, on lack of courage as on lack of experience. She glanced sideways at Cyriack and said, almost shyly, "I don't want to mess up your research."

"Oh," Cyriack said. "Oh. Right. Yes. No, she should be perfectly stable, if Adept Chellick's spell has worked correctly. Which, of course, it may not have." Concern for his specimen got him up beside Corbie, and he said, in a more normal tone of voice, "I haven't really had much of a chance to look at her. I'd better, um . . . Is it all right if I take notes?"

"Why are you asking me?" I said. "It's not *my* bog body."

He said, "Right, right. Back in a minute," and darted away. Corbie continued to stand, both hands pressed palms down on the table, as if she was trying to prevent it from flying away. I looked over at Mildmay, who gave me a flat, green, indecipherable look back and then pushed himself to his feet and came over to the table, where he looked at the body critically.

After a moment, he said, "She don't look very old."

I looked at her face, at her small clutching hands. "You're right. She doesn't."

"And look," he said, bringing his cane up and using it, very very gently, to press her chin up from its position tucked against her chest. "She was strangled."

"How—" Corbie began explosively, and then she saw what Mildmay had seen: brown against brown, there was a rope around her neck, much too tight against her skin to be anything but the instrument of her death.

Cyriack came back then, and Mildmay said, without looking up, "How many of these bog people died of being strangled?"

"I beg your pardon?"

"C'mere," Mildmay said, and Cyriack came and looked.

"Oh," he said, "but that's symbolic. The old word for 'bog' means 'strangling water.' "

"That ain't a symbolic knot," Mildmay said, nudging again with his cane, this time moving aside the flat braided strands of the woman's hair. Then he said, "Oh, shit, that ain't rope, neither."

"Her own hair?" I said after a long moment.

"Still attached to her head," Corbie said. She looked rather sick.

Cyriack reached forward, touching the woman's throat very lightly. From the point of contact with his fingertips, the dark brown dissolved from skin and hair, showing her as tawny as any living Corambin, and the rope around her neck indubitably her own hair. And with the contrast of color returned, it was possible to see the broken hairs where her murderer had knotted her death viciously against her skin.

Gideon died by strangling. I was glad, now, that I had not been allowed to see the body.

"But she doesn't look . . ." Corbie didn't finish that sentence, either. We looked at the woman's twisted, crumpled face.

"She don't look like much of anything," Mildmay said. "And I s'pose we wouldn't, neither, after being in a bog all this time."

"Well, no." Cyriack opened the notebook he'd brought with him and began taking notes in a very small, very precise hand. "To answer your question, not all the bodies have ropes around their necks, of their own hair or otherwise. I'd assumed they'd all drowned, because why strangle someone if you're going to throw them in a bog anyway?"

"Well, it makes it easier to do the throwing," I said and got horrified looks from Corbie and Cyriack. Mildmay just bumped me very gently with his shoulder and changed the subject.

"So, this whole strangling with her hair thing, could it be where the noirance is coming from?"

"Not in and of itself," I said, "although it certainly helps to explain why it has *persisted* all these centuries. Clearly, like the necromancers in Mélusine, they knew the thaumaturgical effects of violent death."

"The thaumaturgical effects of violent death?" Cyriack was staring at me.

"None of them is pleasant," I said.

"Never mind that," Mildmay said, and jabbed toward the table with an impatient finger. "What about her?"

I looked at the noirance wound about the corpse like ribbons. "They must have anchored it somehow . . . I never would have thought of using architectural thaumaturgy on a person."

Mildmay gave me an odd look. "Ain't that what your tattoos are?"

It took me a moment even to understand what he meant, and then I looked down at my hands, feeling as if I'd never seen them before. He was right. The blue eyes tattooed on my palms (*Miss Leverick says sailors think blue eyes are good luck,* Mildmay had said last night), tattooed and then pressed to another Cabaline's palms in the final step of the oath-taking. Tattooed and sworn and unfading, and why had it never occurred to me that architectural thaumaturgy was *exactly* what they were?

"Yes, well," I said, hastily grabbing after my wits. "That's neither here nor there. Cyriack, did the ancient Corambins practice tattooing?"

"Not that I've ever heard," Cyriack said. He looked doubtfully at the bog body. "I suppose we can look."

If she had had clothes, they had not survived with her, except for sandal laces still wrapped around her calves. Cyriack did his small magic on her arms, her thighs; when he touched her left shoulder blade, something that I had taken merely for an effect of her centuries in the bog resolved itself into a series of circles scored into her skin.

Not merely circles. I looked closer, holding my breath against the stench. "A labyrinth," I said. "They marked her with a labyrinth. Mildmay, weren't you telling me that there are labyrinths all over Corambis?"

"That's what the lady said," he agreed.

"Know of any labyrinths associated with your bogs?" I asked Cyriack.

He'd gone back to writing notes. "I, um. I'd have to ask Adept Gower, and *he*'d probably have to ask his friend who's collecting stories for him."

"You mean like all the people who said if you got something evil, you give it to the bog?" Mildmay said.

Cyriack twitched and smudged his notes. I wished I'd been here for that earlier conversation.

"That's certainly what it looks like happened with this poor woman," I said. "They put all their darkness on her."

"And gave her to the bog," Corbie said.

"Yes. And gave her to the bog."

"Sacrifice," Cyriack blurted and then looked as startled as if the bog body herself had spoken.

"Yes?" I prompted.

"When Mr. Brightmore was here"—and there was a story I wanted, but I would ask Kay rather than Cyriack—"he said that the magic these people practiced was probably based on sacrifice, as the Usara's magic still is."

"The Sacrifice of the Caster," Corbie said, almost inaudibly.

"It's a very potent force," I said, as neutrally as I could. "And I told you, the thaumaturgical effects of violent death, while not pleasant, are profound. When they did this, they meant it to stick."

The conversation failed, and we watched silently as Mildmay picked up the sheet from where Cyriack had left it and draped it over the dead woman.

That night, Mildmay read d'Islay to me while I paced around the main room of our apartment. I was not attending very well, and after the third time he'd had to ask me twice for a definition, he put d'Islay aside, very carefully—and one of the reasons I loved him was his gentle reverence for books. I hadn't taught him that; as far as I knew, he'd always had it. He asked, "You wanna tell me what's wrong?"

"No," I said honestly, which amused him. I could hear that in his voice when he said, "You wanna tell me anyway?"

"Violent death."

He understood; I saw it in his eyes when I glanced at him. And then he very visibly braced himself and said, "Could you bring Gideon back? If you wanted to?"

I stopped pacing, staring at him. Finally, I said, "How long have you been sitting on *that* idea?"

He shrugged. "I just wondered."

Which did not answer my question, but I decided to accept his sidestep—decided I really didn't want an answer. I began pacing again. After a while, I said, "I suppose I could. I mean, if I weren't under the binding-by-obedience. I think I know enough of the theory, and I could always consult the Mulkist books in the University library if I needed to. But what I brought back . . . it wouldn't be Gideon."

He said nothing, watching me with those feral green eyes.

"It would be a memory of Gideon," I said. "A pattern of Gideon as he was. Not . . ." I thought of Prince Magnus, trapped forever and eternally at the age of fourteen, and I sat down heavily beside Mildmay on our sway-backed couch. "It wouldn't be Gideon, who rubs your back when your muscles ache from coughing, or Gideon, who writes snippy notes in the margins of books of thaumaturgical theory, or Gideon, who . . ." I swallowed hard.

"Say it," Mildmay said softly.

"Gideon, who kisses me openmouthed," I said in a rush. "Gideon, who butters biscuits for me even when he's mad at me. Gideon, who . . . who . . ."

*"Say it."*

"Who loves me," I said, and it hurt like tearing my heart out through the ribs of my chest. "Gideon loved me and I can't have that back, no matter what I do." I was crying, and I didn't know when I'd started. "I can't have him back and I miss him so much. I miss him so fucking much."

"I know," Mildmay said, and he put his arm around me, letting me hide against his shoulder, knowing, as I did, how dangerous, how fundamentally unsafe it was to confess to love. "I know."

# Chapter 14

## *Felix*

On Venerdy, Mildmay returned to his program of reading to Kay Brightmore; on Domenica, the Institution being closed, I finally gave in to my curiosity and accompanied him.

Kay Brightmore was being kept in the old nursery, where he was incongruous against the pale yellow walls and brightly colored, if shabby, rugs. He was transparently pleased to hear Mildmay's voice, and welcomed me as close to warmly as I imagined he got. I asked after Julian; Kay said, "He is well, although Murtagh is being very foolish. Is not as if Julian can choose whether he will be aethereal or not, so is no sense in punishing him for it. But Murtagh has forbidden him to go to the Mammothium and is talking of withdrawing him from the University."

"That seems . . ."

"Unusually shortsighted in a man as canny as the Dragon of Desperen Field?" Kay was pacing the length of the room as easily and rapidly as any sighted person. "Yes. He seems to consider the matter a personal affront. And I fear my sister Isobel is particularly ill-suited to be either a peacemaker or a comfort. Julian has been coming to me." His tone invited us to share the joke, and I had to admit, he seemed as alien to those roles as he said his sister was.

"And you ain't sent him off with a flea in his ear?" Mildmay said. He crossed the line of Kay's pacing and settled in a battered wing-back chair near the arched windows.

Kay made a noise deep in his throat, exasperation and compassion and amusement all combined. "Is not the boy's fault. And as far as I can tell, he has no one else. His friends seem to be all magicians."

"Cyriack," I said. I followed Mildmay's example and sat on one of the window seats.

"With whom Murtagh has forbidden Julian to have any further contact." Kay sighed. "And I am a little dubious, I confess, as to Thrale's . . ."

"Yes, exactly," I said.

"And in any event, the matter is moot, as Julian is both very obedient and, I think, unwilling to put Thrale's friendship to any sort of real test."

"Poor Julian," said Mildmay.

"Yes," Kay agreed. "But enough! What new witlessness has Mr. Otway in store for us this afternoon?"

"You aren't impressed by Otway?" I said.

"Bah. Has done nothing save sit in a room in Esmer and write a book."

"Scholarship is also a kind of action," I said.

"But is not even scholarship," Kay said. "You would not believe the errors he makes."

"Oh, I dunno," Mildmay said. "Ain't that how history works?"

I twisted to look at him. "What do you mean?"

As always, direct attention discomfited him, and he looked down at the book in his hands. But he said, "Just—I dunno, but it's like storytelling, ain't it?" He glanced up to see if I'd understood him, and interpreted my expression correctly because he looked back at his hands and continued, "You know. One guy tells a story, maybe about something that's really true, and the next guy says it wasn't like that, it was like this. And then a third guy who's been over in Pennycup hearing how *they* tell it comes in and tells it his way. And after a while nobody knows the truth no more, and they just go with what sounds best."

"Well," I said, "history isn't *supposed* to—"

"Oh, come on," Mildmay said. "This all happened, what? A thousand indictions ago? You weren't there. I wasn't there. Otway wasn't there. Nobody knows. So you tell the best story you got and people argue with you. That's how it works."

Kay snorted, clearly unconvinced. "Then he should say he knows not. Should not pretend to be speaking the truth."

"You do that too often, and nobody hears the story," Mildmay said. "I mean, it's all lies anyway. Even if I tell you a story about something that happened to me, I'm not telling the truth."

"You aren't?" I said.

"Course not," he said. "I mean, I ain't *lying*—unless I am, but that's different—but it ain't what really happened."

I wrestled with that for a moment, and he said, "Okay, look. I told you what happened at Nera, right?"

"Mildmay, do we have to—"

"Nera?" Kay said. "You mentioned it once before, but was not time to inquire."

"Okay," Mildmay said and sat up straighter. "Let me tell the story again. And then we can talk about whether it's true or not."

"I don't—"

"Felix, for fuck's sake. I don't come out of this one any better than you do."

I felt myself go scarlet and looked down at my hands. A defensive gesture we shared. Lovely.

"So," Mildmay said, taking my silence as permission, "me and Felix were trying to get to a place called the Gardens of Nephele, because he'd been hurt in his mind, and the wizards there were the only people that could help him. Problem was, the Gardens were farther from Mélusine even than Esmer is, and we didn't really know the geography or nothing. And we had a bunch of other problems, too, but they ain't important. So we were walking, along of not having the money for nothing better, and trying to keep away from the Imperial dragoons, and Felix was . . ." He glanced at me.

"Insane," I said. "You can say it. I was insane."

"You were hurt," Mildmay said. "And besides, the part where you were hearing the ghosts wasn't about you being crazy."

"Hearing ghosts?" Kay said, double-checking—I thought—to be sure he'd understood Mildmay correctly.

"Crying people," Mildmay said, picking the story up again. "He said he heard crying people, and he had to help them. And I didn't know how to stop him without hurting him worse, so I just followed him to where he said his crying people were, and it turned out to be Nera."

"And what *is* Nera?" Kay said.

Mildmay raised his eyebrows at me, inviting me to supply the footnote.

I said, "Nera was the capital of the empire of Lucrèce, which was even older than Cymellune. It was conquered, razed, and annihilated by another civilization. They slaughtered everyone in Nera. Some of them they raped first. The emperor they forced to watch while he bled to death from a spear in his stomach. They burned the bodies like cordwood, giving them neither honor nor peace."

Kay had stopped pacing. "You sound as if you were a witness." He had not turned his head toward me, but I could feel his attention.

"He dreamed it," Mildmay said. "That night. Because his crying people were the ghosts of all the people that got murdered, and they needed us to help them."

"How can one help the dead?"

"Well, it kind of depends."

"Depends? On what?"

"On what they believed when they were alive. These people believed that if they could walk a labyrinth, they could find the way to the White-Eyed Lady, and she'd let them rest."

"The White-Eyed Lady?" Kay said, almost uneasily.

"The Kekropian goddess of death," I said. "Her cult is proscribed but still apparently flourishes. My . . . my lover was a devotee."

"A goddess worshipped with labyrinths? As our Lady is?"

"I dunno," Mildmay said cautiously. "I don't know nothing about your goddess."

"Oh, it matters not," Kay said, shaking his head as if to dislodge whatever was troubling him.

"She ain't a bad goddess," Mildmay said. "I mean, not like the God of the Obscured Sun."

"I pray you," Kay said, beginning to pace again, "continue your story."

Mildmay looked at me. I nodded. I suspected Kay was bothered by the labyrinth under Summerdown, with the murderous engine at its heart, and unless we could offer either comfort or proof, it was better to leave that subject alone.

"Well," said Mildmay, "I told you the ghosts needed a labyrinth, and the nightmare Felix had that night about Nera made it pretty clear that we needed to give 'em one. So we spent that next day making a labyrinth by pulling up grass. Best we could do. And it worked. Because the ghosts used it. But the problem was . . ."

I watched Kay turn toward him.

"The problem was, the ghosts made Felix a promise."

"A promise?" Kay said softly, almost whispering.

"They promised him he could go with them. And if he did, he could find his friend who'd died when he was a kid."

"My only friend," I said. "My . . . my sister in spirit." For surely if there could be spirit-ancestors, there could be spirit-sisters. And that was Joline.

"Hey," said Mildmay, "who's telling this?" But he wasn't angry. "So the ghosts had told him that, and he believed it. And he wanted to go."

"But wouldn't that mean . . ." Kay trailed off uncomfortably.

"Well, that was what I figured," Mildmay said. "So I wouldn't let him. I beat the crap out of him, to be perfectly fucking frank, and pinned him down until the ghosts were gone. I didn't know what else to do." He paused, then sighed and said, "So that's the story."

"All right," Kay said. "But is *not* the truth?"

"Well, I left some shit out," Mildmay said. "Like the rainstorm. And I didn't know about Joline."

"And you still don't know," I said, "whether the ghosts were real or just my delusion."

"Oh, I'm pretty sure they were real. But, here. Here's a thing that means this story can't *ever* be the truth. I don't know why the ghosts made Felix that promise. I don't know if they just wanted somebody else to be dead along with 'em, or if they were trying to do something nice for him, or if it was all lies and they were really, you know, the ghosts of blood-witches or something, and what they wanted all along was to get him in that maze with them."

"That seems rather far-fetched," I said.

He shrugged. "But it could be true. Unless you remember something that says it ain't."

"I don't really remember Nera at all. Except that nightmare. And I remember wanting to go to Joline. I thought you were Keeper, because you wouldn't let me."

"Because I hurt you," he said.

"Because I was insane," I said, and realized too late how sharp my voice had become.

But Mildmay didn't even blink. "So, see, I was there, and I'm telling the story, and I'm trying to tell the truth, but I can't get all of it. Because I only know what *I* saw, and I know I didn't see what really happened, because I can't see ghosts. And it's gotta be a septad times worse when you're talking about something like a battle, where nobody can see all of it, and everybody sees something different, and you know, you gotta feel sorry for the guy who has to try and make sense of it and write it down."

"Maybe," Kay said grumpily. "Is still ridiculous."

"Most human endeavors are," I said.

Kay thought about that, up and back. "I suppose that's true. Are all creatures of folly. Very well, I will be more tolerant of Mr. Otway's idiocies." He pointed, accurately, at Mildmay. "Read."

Mildmay, who had been patiently holding the book open all this time, bent his head and began.

## Kay

"Kay," said Julian on Lunedy morning, coming into the room without knocking, "the man we met at the train station brought a letter for you."

I stopped pacing. "Lucas brought a *letter*?"

"Yes, and he says he has to wait for your answer. He says it's tremendously important."

"Lucas is in the house?" I said, alarmed.

"No. He stopped me on my way back from—well, I was talking to Intended Godolphin. Lucas said he'd wait in the fathom station."

"Thank the Lady," I said and meant it. "Had best read me the letter then."

"Me?"

"Am not going to ask Isobel."

"Right," said Julian, and paper crackled as he unfolded it.

*To Kay Brightmore, the former and true Margrave of Rothmarlin, greetings from your most loyal and devoted servant, Geoffrey Trant.*

"'Sdeath." I found my way to the chair and sat down heavily. Geoffrey Trant was indeed my armsman and had been my father's, but he was also the leader of the Primrose Men, who were the most radical of the various populist groups which had supported Gerrard. The Primrose Men favored not merely independence, but complete separation from Corambis, along with a number of other impracticable ideas. I had always deeply appreciated their loyalty to me—several of them were Rothmarlin men by birth—but also found it somewhat of an embarrassment. And now that I thought about it, I wondered why I hadn't heard from Geoffrey Trant before now.

"Kay?" said Julian, sounding somewhere between doubtful and worried.

"Go on, please," said I.

"All right," said he, still doubtful.

*My lord, I pray you forgive me writing to you in such a fashion and for such a reason. And I pray your forgiveness further that I was not at your side at Summerdown and left you prey to the Corambin jackals.*

"Trant has no love for Corambins," I said in Julian's uncomfortable pause.

*But I could not come to you then, as we were pinned down by the Usara at Cinderfold, and I have not been able to come to you since, as I have been prisoned by the Usara in a place of which I can tell you nothing, save that it was dark and foul and most full of despair, for our captors told us of your fall, and we wept.*

"He was fighting the Usara?" Julian said. "But I thought . . ."

"The great danger of the Insurgence," said I, "aside from our inevitable defeat, was that the Usara would take the opportunity to burn and plunder our lands. So certain of our forces"—those whose hatred for Corambins was so fervent as to make them a liability in battle, but I had not said that to Trant, and I did not say it to Julian—"were ordered to defend against such incursions. Apparently, they, like us, were not successful. I pray you, continue."

*I write to you now, my lord, from Summerdown—*

*"Summerdown?"*

"I'm sure that's the word," Julian said nervously. "Should I go on?"

"Yes, I cry your mercy. Do."

*—from Summerdown, at the behest of the cephar Dothaw. He says that you will remember his name.*

"Keep reading," I said grimly. I did indeed remember Dothaw's name, for he had held me captive for two months the summer I was twenty-four. None of my memories of that time was fond, but I knew that Dothaw was honorable.

*The cephar Dothaw says that he will negotiate our release—that of myself and the five men who were captured with me—but only with you, and that if you will not negotiate, he will have us put to death. I believe that he is interested in further negotiations, but he will not speak of his intentions to me.*

"Dothaw must be mad," I said, getting up again and pacing savagely. "I have no power to negotiate anything, and the Usara may be many things, but they are not *ignorant*. Finish reading, Julian."

*Dothaw permits me to send Vyell and Leadbitter to Barthas Cross to await you. Vyell assures me he can find a way to get this letter to you, despite being unable himself to come to Esmer for reasons I am sure your lordship will remember, and he and Leadbitter will meet every train. My lord, I am sorry to put this imposition upon you, but the cephar Dothaw is unyielding, and while I care not for myself, I cannot wantonly sacrifice these five brave and honest men.*

"And that's it," Julian said. "Kay? What are you going to do?"

I only half heard him. Trant knew not that I was blind; had he known someone would be reading it to me, that letter would have been much more circumspect. And he knew not what he was asking. Was one thing for a sighted man to escape a soft prison like Carey House and make his way to Barthas Cross, but I could not simply . . .

"Kay?" said Julian.

And then I knew.

"Julian," said I, "wilt come with me to Barthas Cross?"

## Mildmay

Lunedy, I went to Carey House only to find out Mr. Brightmore had gone out with Julian. Which, you know, okay, and I suppose he didn't have no way of getting a message to me, but it still kind of stung. Martedy morning, I was watching Felix wander around the apartment the way I'd watched him wander around his suite in the Mirador, with his waistcoat unbuttoned and his tie shoved into one pocket, drinking tea and arguing with the newspapers, his hair hanging in his eyes because he wouldn't use the cream stuff the barbers had recommended, when there was a knock on the door.

Felix raised his eyebrows at me. "Are we expecting anyone?"

"I wasn't," I said, and it wasn't Corbie's knock. So I went and answered the door and it was the fucking Duke of Murtagh, large as life and twice as natural, and behind him was the lady Kay was going to marry.

"Good gracious," said Felix. "Come in, Your Grace, and—I don't believe I know the lady?"

"Vanessa Pallister," she said, and I stood aside because otherwise it looked like she'd just walk straight through me. "Kay Brightmore's fiancée."

"Ah," said Felix, his eyebrows going up even higher. "Charmed to meet you, I'm sure." She was a big lady—taller than me and heavy-built—and she wasn't no looker, with her jaw as heavy as a man's and her eyes too small for her cheekbones, and it didn't help that she wore her hair with these heavy bangs hanging over her forehead. All in all, she really did look like a bear that somebody'd taught to stand up on its back legs and wear a dress.

Which wasn't no nice thing to be thinking, and powers and saints, it wasn't like I had *any* room to talk, so I turned back and said, "Come in, Your Grace," as polite and not mush-mouthed as I could.

The duke came in, and I closed the door. Mrs. Pallister turned to me and said, without wasting no more time, "Have you seen Kay?"

"Um. Not since Domenica."

"He didn't come here? Or say anything about where he might go?"

"Have you misplaced him?" Felix asked, and she gave him a look like bottled poison.

I said, "On Lunedy, they said as how he'd gone out with Julian. But that's all I know."

Felix said, past Mrs. Pallister and me, to the duke, "What's going on?"

The duke said, polite and precise, and oh yeah, he was mad as fuck about it, "Kay left Carey House sometime before twelve yesterday, in company with Julian. Neither one of them has been seen since. Julian left a note, but it is a deplorable example of its kind, being firstly, nearly illegible, and secondly, utterly uninformative. He says, in essence, that he has to go with Kay, but that they'll be back soon, and we aren't to worry. And he adds, very scrupulously, that he has taken a saint from my desk for traveling expenses, but that he will pay me back as soon as he can. Feckless idiot."

"We've already asked at the University and the Institution, and no one's seen them," said Mrs. Pallister. "But I remembered you were reading to him, Mr. Foxe, and he'd told me a little about you, so I thought maybe . . ."

"Sorry," I said.

"If Julian needed traveling expenses," Felix said, "it sounds like they were planning to leave Esmer."

"But that makes even *less* sense," said Mrs. Pallister. "Where would they go?"

"Not to Rothmarlin," Murtagh said. "Kay is not close to his mother, and he loathes his cousin Cecil. And not, I think, to Julian's personal holdings, for Swale has been closed up since he came to live at Carey House, and in any event, there is absolutely nothing there. None of Kay's close friends survived the end of the Insurgence, so . . ."

"Would he return to Summerdown?" Felix said. "I know it preys on his mind."

"It seems unlikely," said Murtagh, frowning. "Although I suppose, if he had a maggot in his head, he might have gone to talk to that magician-practitioner in Barthas Cross, the one who figured out the ritual for Hume. What is the dratted man's name?"

"Don't look at me," said Mrs. Pallister. "He hasn't said a syllable on the subject."

"Oh, I didn't learn about him from Kay," said Murtagh. "Penny! That's it. Anselm Penny. That's a good thought, Mr. Harrowgate. I'll send a message to my agent in Barthas Cross. Vanessa, there's no point in taking any more of these gentlemen's valuable time."

"Oh, you're very welcome," Felix said, and there was a fucking weird note in his voice. Mrs. Pallister didn't seem to notice, and Murtagh just gave him this look that I couldn't make any kind of sense out of, and him and Mrs. Pallister took themselves out.

"What the fuck was that?" I said.

"What was what?" said Felix, but his color was high.

"You gonna tell me what your thing is with the Duke of Murtagh?"

"No," Felix said, and grinned at me. "I have to have *some* secrets from you, darling."

"Drink your tea," I said, because it was no use talking to him when he was in that mood. And I hoped Mr. Brightmore was okay.

## Felix

Mildmay came to my office with me, to sit in the corner and work on d'Islay while I did work of my own in the shape of frantically cramming Grevillian thaumatology so as to be able to keep ahead of my students. Hutch and Ashmead had lent me their personal collections, and I was passionately grateful.

Two hours later, I shoved violently away from my desk and stalked out into the hallway. I wanted someone real to argue with, instead of these dry smug paragraphs, so certain of their truths they were blind to their own fallacies. And I was not going to argue with Mildmay, who followed me patiently.

Hutch wasn't in his office—he was probably off with the Automaton, as he had been most of his waking hours—and I was standing, debating whether I really wanted to pick a fight with John Ashmead, when I realized someone had beaten me to it.

I followed the sound of raised voices and found Ashmead glaring from behind his desk at a blue-veiled intended, like a deerhound brought to bay by a stag.

I wanted an argument, and Ashmead looked like he needed some support. "Virtuer?" I said. "Is everything all right?"

They both turned. The intended was, by Corambin standards, skinny and dark, with a wide, thin-lipped mouth and bulgy, glaring eyes. He looked like a dried-out toad who knew all one's darkest secrets and condemned them.

"Mr. Harrowgate," Ashmead said with audible relief. "This is Intended Marcham, from Our Lady of Marigolds in Howrack. He has a . . ." He wrestled for a moment with a polite phrasing. "A most remarkable story."

"Is not a story," the intended said; his voice was peculiarly strident, even when not raised. "Is truth, and something must be done."

"And what did you have in mind?" I said.

The disapproving eyes raked me from head to toe. "You are the foreign magician all the papers blather about."

"Yes, I suppose I must be."

"And that's your shadow," he said, with a jerk of his chin at Mildmay.

"My brother," I said, less pleasantly.

"Are Mulkist?"

The question was deliberately offensive, and perversely, I felt better. "No, if you're looking for a Mulkist, I'm afraid you're out of luck."

In the moment in which Intended Marcham was bereft of words, Ashmead opened his pocket watch, displayed only slightly exaggerated surprise, and said, "I'm sorry, I really have to run. Felix, if you would . . . ?" and had dodged past Intended Marcham, me, and Mildmay out the door.

Intended Marcham glared at me balefully; I smiled back. "Intended? I would be glad to hear your concerns."

"Have not come all this way to be mocked by heathen foreigners," he grated. "I expect no better from annemer, but I thought magicians would have the motherwit to listen."

"Are you an aethereal?" I said, puzzled.

This look was withering. "I am a magician, bound-by-obedience in the service of the Lady. So don't think you can condescend to me."

"I wouldn't dream of it," I said, trying to conceal my shudder. I might have orchestrated my own binding, as Mildmay had said, but it was a punishment I deserved, not this deliberate, unnecessary sacrifice. And I remembered the anchorite of Our Lady of Fogs. "Really, you might as well tell me. Since I'm a heathen foreigner, I'm actually more likely to believe you than my Grevillian colleagues."

He regarded me narrowly, but in the end, his need for someone to listen won out over his enmity for me. I discovered, as I listened, that I knew much of the story already: the engine beneath Summerdown and Gerrard Hume's folly; the stoppages on the Barthas Cross line, which Hutch bemoaned almost daily; the pestilence among the sheep which Mildmay had read about in the newspaper. But Intended Marcham was much more specific. "Not all sheep," he said. "Not all sheep in Murrey, nor even all sheep belonging to men of Howrack. No. It is the sheep who are grazed on Summerdown that die."

"And what is it you think is happening?"

"Thought at first was a curse," he said. "But I think now is worse than that. Is the engine. It seeks to finish that which Prince Gerrard began and failed in, by drawing vi—'aether,' they call it here—from the sources it can reach."

"The trains," I said, understanding. "The sheep."

"Yes. And now the suicides have begun." He glared at me, daring me to say I didn't see the connection. But I did.

"Sacrifices," I said, my body becoming cold with the truth. "Kay said the engine is at the heart of a labyrinth, and we have just quite recently discovered—"

"The bog body," Mildmay said, and I knew from the horror in his voice that he understood as well. "You mean all them people died on *purpose*?"

I knew what he meant, although he'd said it badly. "It's a sacrifice machine," I said, as certain of that truth as if I'd designed the damned thing myself. "Which means, if Kay *has* gone to Summerdown . . ." I couldn't finish that sentence; one look at Mildmay told me I didn't need to.

"Intended Marcham," I said, giving him the best smile I could muster, "do you happen to have Ottersham handy? And I'm going to have to cancel class. There's a magician-practitioner in Barthas Cross I believe I need to talk to."

## *Mildmay*

We could've gone straight from the Institution to the train station, but it seemed like a dumb idea when we could also take half an hour to go home and pack a bag. And while we were doing that—well, while I was doing that and Felix was pacing around muttering to himself—Corbie knocked on the door.

"Felix? You canceled class? Are you all right?"

"A bit of a crisis," said Felix and gave her this smile that looked perfectly natural, but I knew he had it judged like a barrow wife and a pound of peaches.

"Can I help?" Corbie said, fast as winking.

It was kind of funny watching Felix fall over that—he almost did fall over his own feet.

"C'mon," Corbie said. "You know you can trust me. And if it really is a crisis, you may need someone to do magic."

Felix was frowning, and he opened his mouth. Then he shut it again hard, and after a second, Corbie watching him the whole way, he said, like he hated saying it, "You may be right. We're leaving for Barthas Cross on the fourteen-twenty-five train from Lily-of-Mar. Can you make it?"

"You betcha, guv," Corbie said and disappeared from the doorway so fast you would've thought she'd fallen down a hole.

Felix paced around some more and I finished packing. Then I said, "You really think you might need a hocus?"

"Unfortunately," Felix said, "I really do."

# Part Four

# Chapter 15

## *Felix*

Anselm Penny, the wizard in Barthas Cross, was a magician-practitioner second grade. He was in his forties, his hair mostly gray, his face lined and pinched and chronically unhappy. I was a little appalled that this had been the best Prince Gerrard Hume had been able to do.

He was first surprised to find another wizard on his doorstep, then alarmed—alarmed enough that he would have slammed the door in my face except that somehow Mildmay, who had been leaning on his cane beside me looking utterly harmless, stopped the door (with his foot? his cane? I couldn't tell) and then simply kept going. I remembered him saying once that he didn't want to be somebody's hired muscle; apparently that hadn't been idle speculation on his part.

Anselm Penny looked like he was about to cry.

"You might as well let me in, Mr. Penny," I said. "It'll be much easier than getting him out."

There was really nothing else he could do.

Even when we were seated in his office, though, he remained profoundly unwilling to talk about the engine. But he must finally have realized that we weren't leaving until he did, because he burst out with "I told him not to do it! And I don't know what more I could have done."

"Him?" I said.

"Prince Gerrard." There was no real fight in Anselm Penny; I suspected there never had been. "I told him I couldn't be sure what the engine would do once it was started. I *told* him it was unlikely to be what his childhood stories led him to believe. But I didn't know it would do *that*!"

"Mr. Penny, I'm not trying to lay blame," I said, as patiently as I could. "I just want to know about the engine. How did you figure out how to start it?"

Penny looked suddenly hopeful. "If I give you my notes, will you go away?"

"Your notes?" I said, feeling more hopeful myself.

"I may not be an adept," he said, voice sharp with what was clearly a decades-old resentment, "but that doesn't mean I'm incompetent. Will my notes satisfy you, Mr. Harrowgate? I assure you, I wrote *everything* down."

"That sounds ideal." There was no reason to pretend I was enjoying Penny's company any more than he was pretending to enjoy mine. He turned immediately to the bookcase behind him and pulled down a fat quire bound in blue buckram. He all but threw it at me. I opened it—a neat, slanted hand, far more legible than I had expected and feared: AN INQUIRY INTO THE NATURE OF THE CYMELLUNAR ENGINE SAID TO RESIDE UNDER SUMMERDOWN, UNDERTAKEN BY ANSELM PENNY, MAGICIAN-PRACTITIONER OF BARTHAS CROSS, AT THE BEHEST OF PRINCE GERRARD HUME OF CALOXA.

"If things had turned out differently," said Penny, still resentful, "I could have published."

"Indeed," I said, because I could not think of a better response. "I'll return this to you when my own inquiries are complete."

"See that you do," Penny said and moved pointedly toward the door.

❧

We returned to our hotel room—Corbie, whom I'd sent out to ask at other hotels about Kay, had not yet returned—and I sprawled across the bed with Penny's notes. Penny in the notes was much better company than Penny in person: competent as he had said, meticulous, unexpectedly thorough. He had drawn the engine from several different angles, taken every measurement he could think of, copied down the symbols engraved on its various parts. He had written out Prince Gerrard's stories about the engine; he had also written what the Intended of Howrack had told him, with notes on the etymology of *verlain* and how many generations back the natives of Howrack had been telling their own stories, which were very different from Prince Gerrard's. He'd made detailed bibliographic notes on every book he'd consulted, and equally detailed notes on the three enginists he'd pestered (my word, not his) to get a better grasp on the mechanics involved.

Not that it had done him—or Gerrard Hume—any good, but I couldn't find it in myself to blame him for having failed to imagine the thing's true purpose.

"I don't think I like the ancient Corambins," I said to Mildmay, who was sitting by the window darning one of my socks.

"Um," he said. "Do you think they were really from Cymellune like everyone says?"

"Oh dear. You never ask the easy questions, do you?"

"Sorry. Never mind."

"No, it wasn't a complaint! Just a warning that I don't have a satisfactory answer."

"Oh. Well, okay then." And he gave me a stone-faced look that I knew to accept as a smile. "What do you think?"

I sighed and stretched the cramped muscles in my upper back. "It's obvious that Corambis had contact somehow with Cymellune, and I suppose Agramant the Navigator is as good a candidate as any, since they certainly didn't go overland. But I don't think the Corambins are the lost heirs of Cymellune, either."

"I didn't mean like that."

"What did you mean?"

He concentrated on his darning for a moment, then said, "Well, you been talking about how the ancient Corambins were sacrificing people and stuff, and I was just wondering if that's what they did in Cymellune, too."

"Ow," I said and sat up straight. "That's a very good question. I hadn't thought to turn it around like that."

He gave me a shy flicker of a glance.

"I'm perfectly serious," I said. "We know there were labyrinths in Cymellune—there was one made of mirrors that Ephreal Sand talks about."

"And the one in Nera. Or was that a different empire or something?"

"Um. The relationship between Lucrèce and Cymellune is not, to my knowledge, perfectly understood, although no doubt there's some aged scholar in the Library of Arx who's figured the whole thing out. But let's say you're more right than wrong. Certainly, I don't think we can ignore the possibility that labyrinths and death being connected in Lucrèce—and in Klepsydra, don't forget, which is much later—and labyrinths and death being connected here . . . where was I?"

"Possibility of something."

"Right. Thank you. We can't ignore the possibility that labyrinths and death were connected in Cymellune."

"Fuck," he said. "We know they were connected."

"We do?"

"Heth-Eskaladen. You made me explain it all to you, so don't go telling me you forgot."

"The Trials," I said. I almost had forgotten, but he was right. All of Mélusine's theology was Cymellunar in origin—a fact which made the Corambins' goddess even more of an oddity.

"You have to walk the maze to get to Hell," Mildmay said solemnly. "And that don't seem so far off from dragging someone through the maze to *send* 'em to Hell. It's sort of what the ghosts in Nera wanted, ain't it?"

"How do you mean?"

"A sacrifice," he said, taking care over his consonants.

It took three slow, dull beats of my heart before I comprehended his meaning, and then I ended up with my knuckles pressed against my mouth as if to hold in a scream. Finally, shakily, I said, "Couldn't you have kept that charming notion to yourself?"

"Sorry," he said with a one-shouldered shrug.

"It does make sense, though," I said, so that he wouldn't think I meant for him to stop telling me what he thought. "A sacrifice, a labyrinth, a goddess of death. Their goddess here doesn't *seem* to be the White-Eyed Lady, but I'm a little reluctant to go prying around in their beliefs to find out."

"Well, the White-Eyed Lady ain't always the same, right? I mean, the White-Eyed Lady in Klepsydra—she wasn't the same White-Eyed Lady that Gideon followed."

"It's a good point. But, also, I am beginning to wonder whether modern Corambin beliefs have any great similarity to ancient Corambin beliefs."

"How d'you mean?"

"I haven't seen any significance to labyrinths for *modern* Corambins. The people we've met."

"Only Miss Leverick's crazy friend," he said, and I heard the grin in his voice.

I threw a pillow at him, which he caught without either looking up or dropping his needle. He threw it back, but softly enough that I could catch it.

"So what d'you think happened?" he said. "They just got tired of it?"

"I don't know. But I wonder."

"Yeah?"

"Well, I wonder about the Automaton of Corybant. No one now could build a machine like that, although they're clearly working their way back to it. And I wonder about the lack of records. I wonder how much was lost on *purpose*."

"Huh." He thought about that for a few moments while he finished his darn and turned the sock back right side out. Then he said, "Hey, Felix, what *is* the Doctrine of Labyrinths?"

"How do you mean?"

"Well, it's that book of yours, and the guy went crazy writing it, right? But what *is* it? I mean, is it just that the mazes drove him nuts, or is there something there?"

"Oh. I see what you mean. Well, given that Ephreal Sand was in fact mad—"

"Yeah, yeah, I got that part."

"His theory—his postulated doctrine of labyrinths was that labyrinths act to collect and intensify what he calls manar, which is roughly analogous to what Corambin wizards call aether."

"Anna-what?"

"Analogous. Similar. Can be used as an analogy for. You know what an analogy is."

I knew he did, and he nodded. "Zephyr taught me that. Okay. So he calls it manar and the people here call it aether, and it's really what? Magic?"

"Um. Sort of. But it's also what mikkary is formed out of."

"Oh. *That*. Okay. I get it. So Sand wants to collect magic the same way the ancient Corambin people were collecting badness, right?"

I opened my mouth to say no, but then realized he was exactly correct. Both Sand (in theory) and the ancient Corambins (in practice) had used labyrinths as—I looked wildly at Mildmay's needle and thread—as a spindle. Or, more properly, the labyrinth was the spinning wheel, the person who walked the labyrinth the spindle. Exactly like that poor dead girl in the Mammothium. So the manar, the aether, was drawn into the heart of the labyrinth . . .

"Hold on a moment," I said, diving for Penny's notes. The aether was drawn into the heart and there given to the engine via the sacrifice of seven men. But what did it do with its power then?

"It saves Caloxa," I muttered, flipping back to the stories Gerrard Hume's nurse had told him when he was a little boy. "But *how* does it save Caloxa? It's not a fairy tale. There has to be something that it *does*." The people of Howrack said that the labyrinth under Summerdown was *verlain*, meaning sacred or possibly obscenely, filthily profane. Meaning dangerous. Meaning bad.

*The ancient Corambin people were collecting badness,* Mildmay had said.

It was possible to turn noirant power into clairant, but not in an abattoir, full of blood and pain and the psychic stench of violent death. So they were collecting badness to . . .

To do something bad with it.

I looked at Penny's pictures of the engine again, looked at the way everything focused down on that small oblong plate where (Penny's neat handwriting said) THE CASTER DOTH EXHALE TO MIST THE METAL. Gerrard Hume had done that and died. I remembered what Corbie had said about the Mulkists and the Sacrifice of the Caster, and I crossed out CASTER and wrote above it in my looping scrawl, *sacrifice*.

And then I sat there and thought about sacrifices and about what the people who considered seven men an acceptable sacrifice—who could design and build a machine for the purpose of collecting seven sacrifices—might think "saving Caloxa" meant. I thought about the fact that the engine, improperly and insufficiently primed, was killing sheep and stopping trains and causing suicides.

Mildmay said, "Felix? You okay?"

"How do you save *anything* with noirant power?" I said.

"Um."

"You don't." I couldn't sit still any longer. I got up, paced the inadequate length of the hotel room and back. "Noirance is the magic of death and darkness and twisted things. It doesn't *save*. It *destroys*. So if they were collecting seven men's lives' worth of noirant power, it wasn't going to save anything. It was going to destroy whatever it was aimed at."

"You can aim something like that?"

"I don't know. Penny doesn't know—Penny doesn't have the least idea, and neither did that poor stupid fool who got himself and all his best men killed. Whatever it's aimed at is what its builders aimed it at."

"And it's trying to fire itself, right?" Mildmay said. "That's the big trouble that Intended Whatsisface is so worried about."

"Marcham. Yes. It doesn't have enough power and it's trying to collect power itself."

"And if Kay . . ."

"He's the last part of the sacrifice. The part that didn't work. And if he goes and—"

"Does something stupid."

"Yes, thank you. If he finishes the engine's ritual . . ."

"Well, then what? It fires itself and, what? Like your big green lightning bolts?"

"I don't know. Maybe more like the 'pestilence' that's killing the sheep. Maybe mikkary like a miasma to drive an entire city mad. Maybe the twisting of all Corambis's clairant workings into noirance, which would . . . I don't even know what it would do, but the wizards of this country are utterly unprepared to deal with it."

"Maybe that's what made Nauleverer," Mildmay said. "The last time they set it off, I mean."

"Oh," I said. "Oh *damn*. Of course. It drove the Automaton of Corybant mad. And that's why the Automaton woke again. Because the engine was awake and called to it."

"And the other one? The Clock of Eclipses?"

"No," I said absently. "That was me." And then I sat down hard on the bed.

"Felix?"

"*That*'s what Beckett did. He sacrificed me to the Clock of Eclipses."

Mildmay was looking at me with visible alarm. "But you're alive. Right?"

"Yes, yes. Sorry. Not a ghoul or a ghost. Because he twisted it. He made an analogy. Between sex and magic and death. And because Titan Clocks are, relatively speaking, small engines—not like this monster under Summerdown—it worked. I knew it almost killed me, but I didn't understand *why* any more than Beckett did." I was twisting my fingers together because otherwise I was going to start screaming.

"But what you're saying is, that wouldn't work on the engine under Summerdown, even if somebody knew to try it, which they don't."

"And even if they did, we don't *want* to start that engine again," I said.

"Right. So what it comes down to is, we gotta stop this thing, regardless of whether it helps Kay or not."

The kindness in that *we* nearly undid me. I stopped pacing, ran my hands through my hair. "Yes. I think we'd better leave for Summerdown tonight."

## Kay

I told Julian how to recognize Vyell and Leadbitter, which was fortunately very easy. Vyell was the largest man I had ever met—over six feet tall—and he was almost inhumanly beautiful. "Is his nickname," I told Julian. "Angel Vyell." And when we descended from the third-class carriage at twenty-three-forty on Lunedy night, Julian almost immediately hissed in my ear, "I see him! It has to be him."

"If thinkst it is Vyell, it is," I said.

"And there's another man with him? Shorter, skinnier, big ears?"

"Leadbitter," said I.

"What should we do?"

"Go to meet them. Is why we're here."

"Right," Julian said, though he sounded most uncertain.

"They will not harm you," said I. "Go, Julian! For an you do not, I cannot."

"Right," said Julian again, and this time he did start forward. I kept pace with him, knowing I could trust him to guide me safely.

We had gone maybe fifteen paces when he said, "They've seen us!" He kept walking, and after a few more steps, a voice I recognized as Vyell's said, sounding as uncertain as Julian, "My lord?"

"Am no lord now," said I. "Hello, Angel."

"Strewth," said a hoarse whisper, "what did they do to him?"

"Am *blind*, Leadbitter, not deaf. Vyell, I understand from Trant's letter that thou hast a plan?"

"Who's the young gentleman?" Vyell said warily.

"Julian Carey. He is under my protection, and he may be trusted."

"I hope you are right," said Vyell. "But come. Need not discuss the matter in the middle of the train station."

In fact, there was little need for discussion at all. Vyell and Leadbitter had three horses, as they had assumed it would be the two of them and myself. But since Julian was a stripling still and I was "dwarfish," as the Corambin papers had been calling me for indictions, we could share a horse and not burden the poor beast unduly. Julian was a better horseman than I had expected. "I didn't come to Esmer until I was fourteen," said he when I asked. "I grew up in hunting country—I miss it." He had no difficulty in keeping up with Vyell and Leadbitter, as he might have had afoot; I concentrated on not letting my resentment curdle into hostility that none of my companions deserved. I wondered what Cecil had done with my horses, and knew that I would never be able to bear to ask.

We slept out Lunedy and Martedy, which Julian disliked but did not complain about. Vyell explained apologetically that he was avoiding the main roads and railway lines, meaning that our approach to Summerdown was somewhat circuitous. "But better that than arrested, my lord."

"Angel, I am no lord."

"Say the Corambins," said Vyell.

Martedy night, after Leadbitter and Julian were asleep, I heard Vyell get up and come around the small fire. Was unmistakably Vyell; no matter how silently he moved, he was still an enormous man. "My lord?" he whispered.

"Am awake," I whispered back as he knelt down beside me.

"Wilt come walk with me, my lord?" Angel was violet and cared not who knew it. We had taken pleasure in each other's company more than once; Angel was gentle, willing, and his angel's mouth was as sweet as any jezebel's. But I remembered Gerrard and my love for him that was a burden as heavy as chains, remembered Oliver Carey and Ambrose, whom I had heard at Isser Chase talking to each other with the deep warmth of married persons.

I whispered back, "Why? Why wouldst wish that of me?"

"Why not?"

"Is for pleasure, I am willing. Is for charity"—or hero's worship or love—"I am not."

"An you do not wish it," Angel said, drawing back, "need only say so."

But I could not explain to him what I wished, or did not wish. "Go to sleep, Vyell," I said and rolled over.

"Yes, sir," he said, as sharply as a curse.

❧

We came to Summerdown at midday on Mercoledy. "Is close enough," said Vyell. "Leadbitter, you stay here with the horses."

"But, Vyell—"

"*Don't* argue with me," said Vyell, who had been brusque and impatient all morning.

"Julian, stay here with Leadbitter," said I. "Leadbitter, thou wilt protect him."

"Kay, I don't need—"

"Yes, thou dost, even an thou knowst it not. Leadbitter?"

"Yes, my lord. Will see him safe."

"I thank thee," I said. "Shall we, Angel?"

"Yes, my lord," said Vyell, and the great bulk of him was next to me. I took his arm, and we set forth.

I remembered the approach to the labyrinth of Summerdown distinctly enough, and Vyell had told me that the Usara were camped *in* the labyrinth, to avoid the notice of the locals. Thus, when we came out from among the stand of trees, and Vyell angled slightly to the left, I knew at once and perfectly where we were and how the land lay. In that last week before Gerrard attempted the engine and died, I had spent more than one night putting myself to sleep by designing fortifications to utilize the down's natural advantages. The village of Howrack would be a dead loss, but Summerdown itself could be defended almost indefinitely, given a large enough supply of food and sufficient protection for the spring that rose fifty yards from the labyrinth's entrance.

By my best reckoning, Vyell and I were ten yards from the mouth of the labyrinth when Vyell tugged me to a stop. "Usara," he said. "They have bows."

"How many are there?"

"Is a small band," said he. "The cephar and ten men. More than enough to handle five light-mazed prisoners."

"Is why they do it," I said mildly, hearing the self-reproach in his voice.

"And here's Dothaw," said Vyell.

"Cougar-cephar!" called Dothaw. Once heard, the cephar Dothaw's voice was unforgettable, a great growling bass suited to the crag bear that was his clan's usar. "Will treat with us?"

"Yes, Dothaw," I called in answer. "I will treat with you."

"Vyell comes no farther. We speak only to you, Cougar-cephar."

Lady, keep me strong. "Am blind, Dothaw. Someone must guide me."

There was a mutter of voices, speaking Usaran; I couldn't pick anything out distinctly. "Was the *angverlaint*?" asked Dothaw.

"Yes." *Ang* was the Usaran word simply for "thing," and if anything was an *angverlaint*, a forbidden-thing, it was that cursed engine.

Another mutter. "Aengis will come to guide you," called Dothaw. "Once Vyell has gone back to the trees."

"My lord?" said Vyell.

"Do it," said I. He moved away from me reluctantly, and then I was alone.

The darkness was no worse, I told myself. I was not lost. I was not falling. Were no anchors, but I needed them not. I knew where I was. I was not falling. The ground was solid beneath my feet, solid and safe, and I did not need to go down on my knees, did not need to press my hands to it. Was not going to fall. My nails were digging into my palms, harder and harder, but I was not going to cower down like a rabbit beneath the moon-shadow of an owl. Was not.

And then a voice said, "Cougar-cephar?" and a hand touched my shoulder.

"You are Aengis?" I said.

"Yes, Cougar-cephar."

"Give me your arm," I said, and it took all the strength of will I had not to clutch at it.

I felt the shadow of Summerdown, smelled the cool dampness of the labyrinth, and knew we were within the down.

"Cougar-cephar," said Dothaw, and his hands came to rest heavily on my shoulders. Short as I was, Dothaw was an inch or two shorter, and among the Usara he was a tall man.

"Dothaw," I said. "What are the matters you would treat with me?"

"Is simple, really," said Dothaw, and I felt foreboding like ice across my shoulders and down my spine. "You will give yourself to us, and we will let these men go."

"My lord!" Trant's voice. "Don't! Is not—" Someone hit him.

"I trade myself for them?" I said. "Very well. Then what?"

"Then, Cougar-cephar, I am sorry," Dothaw said, and he sounded sincere, "but you must go to the *angverlaint*, and you must die."

I heard protests—all three of the Caloxans—but I raised a hand and they were silent.

"Is not our wish," said Dothaw. "But the *angverlaint* cannot be stopped in any other way. And it must be stopped, before its sickness spreads. It is only sheep dying now, and the engines of the northermen which can be always brought back to life, but it will not stay that way."

"I understand," I said. "Let my men go. I agree."

"My lord!" cried Trant.

"Get him out of here," I said, and I knew by the sounds that I was obeyed.

"There are necessary rituals," Dothaw said. "Thou knowst the way of sacrifice."

"Of course," I said, and I held out my wrists to be tied.

## *Felix*

Reaching Summerdown turned out to be one of those things that was far easier in theory than in practice. On the map and in Ottersham, it seemed perfectly straightforward. The nearest train station was Pigrin, and the ticket clerk in Barthas Cross assured us we would be able to hire at least a dog cart to take us the rest of the way. Being noted for its chalybeate, Pigrin was better equipped than most Caloxan towns for the needs of visitors. What none of us counted on was not being able to reach Pigrin in the first place.

We traveled third class. Corbie frowned over Practitioner Penny's notes; I took the trumps and sibyls out of the Sibylline, and Mildmay and I played cards, a bastardized version of Long Tiffany that made my abysmal card sense less of an issue.

I was still hopelessly overmatched, though, and the game devolved gradually into Mildmay playing his own hand and advising me how to play mine: more of a private tutorial than an actual card game. I was profiting from my lesson, to the point that Mildmay said something about not being embarrassed to be seen with me. I was about to respond in kind when the train lurched, juddered, and became suddenly silent, although it was some time before it stopped moving. My pile of trumps and sibyls slithered gracefully to the floor.

"Not another machine-monster?" Mildmay said worriedly.

Corbie picked the quire of Penny's notes up off the floor and said, "No, I think is the thing Cyriack and Robin and them have all been beating their brains out over. 'Cause, look—ain't that Summerdown?" She pointed, and Mildmay and I looked at the great hill rising like a cloud bank south of the train.

"Oh," Mildmay said. "So it's that engine stopping this one?" He didn't sound much happier than he had about the prospect of another Automaton, which I supposed was reasonable enough.

"If we've understood Penny's notes correctly," I began, leaning down to collect the fallen cards. My hand froze mid-reach, and I forgot what I had been about to say.

"Felix? You okay?"

"No," I said. Of the twenty-one trumps and four sibyls, three cards had landed faceup: the number I habitually used when reading the cards.

Death, the Spire, and the Prison.

I said, "Corbie, can you go find out how long it'll take to get the train moving again?"

"Sure." She left, and Mildmay said, "Are them cards as bad as I think they are?"

"Yes," I said and picked them up carefully one by one.

"Um," he said unhappily. "What're they trying to tell you?"

"I don't know. Death is obvious and nothing we didn't already know. The Spire is sacrifice—"

"And scapegoats. I remember Mavortian telling me that."

"Yes. And that's fairly obvious, too. So it's down to the Prison, which I'm afraid is not obvious at all."

"Well, what's it mean? You know, generally."

"It's the card of imprisonment." He glowered at me, and I went on: "Bad choices. Dead ends. It's the card for feeling like you have no way out of a bad situation, or that no choice you make will be the right one."

"So." He was frowning. "Why're the cards telling you? What're you s'posed to do?"

"They're probably 'telling' me because it's their nature to respond to patterns in the manar. Or the aether, if you prefer. It doesn't have to mean anything."

"You wanna bet?"

I glared at him. "Well, what do you suggest I do?"

He shrugged. "Whatever I say to do, you won't do it."

"What's that supposed to mean?"

"That you're contrary." He met my eyes, daring me to deny it.

"All right," I said, and even to my own ears I sounded sulky. "I promise I won't reject your idea out of hand. What is it?"

"Well, your cards're already talking to you."

"You want me to do a reading?" But then, he always had been respectful of the Sibylline—oddly so, considering his general attitude toward "hocus stuff."

"It can't hurt," he said, which was both reasonable and true. I shuffled the trumps and sibyls together, leaving the Spire out. It seemed the best candidate for a significator. When the noirance was running clear, I cut the deck and dealt three cards.

Death, the Prison, and the Hermaphrodite.

I was still staring at those four cards when Mildmay said, "Corbie's coming back." I swept the entire pack together and shuffled, more savagely than was perhaps strictly necessary.

Corbie dropped into her seat and said, "The enginists are having a rotten day. They have to start her cold, which takes a while, and something got broken. I can find out what if you really need me to."

"No. Go on. Something's broken?"

"They've sent one of the porters ahead to Pigrin on a handcar, but they don't expect he'll even get back before sundown. And they said that's probably being optimistic anyway. If you ask me, I think we may be here 'til sometime tomorrow."

"Too long," I said.

In another mood, I might have found the wary looks they gave me—nearly identical when one adjusted for individual temperament and physiognomy—amusing. Now, I just said, "We need to get there tonight. If the cards were telling me anything, that was it."

"Cards?" said Corbie.

"How d'you mean?" Mildmay said, and in an explanatory aside to Corbie, "Fortune-telling cards."

"Producing a reading like that, completely at random—there's too much noirant power in the ambient, and it's too active."

"You think the engine's getting ready to do whatever it's gonna?"

"Yes. I don't know if that means Kay's already dead, or that it's stolen enough power from trains and sheep and the two suicides Intended Marcham knew about and whatever else it's found, but . . ."

"Okay," Mildmay said. "What d'you want to do? See if there's another handcar?"

"We could just walk," Corbie said.

"Walk?" I said.

"Summerdown's right there," Corbie said impatiently. "There's no point in going out of our way to Pigrin."

"That's true," I said. I didn't like the idea, but after impressing on them the urgency of the matter, I was in no position to cavil.

"I'd better stay with the train then," Mildmay said.

"What?"

He thumped his right leg lightly. "I'll just slow you down."

"What if I get lost?" I said, and then winced. Foolish and plaintive both.

"You're gonna have a hard time losing track of Summerdown," Mildmay said dryly, which was no more than I deserved.

"I meant," I said with dignity, "in the labyrinth." A lie, but—on the other hand—a cogent point. I had no hope of solving a labyrinth on my own.

"You any good with mazes?" Mildmay said to Corbie.

"Um. I've never been in one."

Mildmay sighed. "Okay then. But no bitching about me not going fast enough."

"I promise," I said, and he gave me a choppy nod and reached for his cane.

## *Kay*

The Usaran rituals preparing a victim for sacrifice were very orderly. I was stripped of my clothing, bathed. A lock of my hair was cut off and burned. The athen who had traveled with Dothaw chanted over me, and I knew enough Usaran to follow most of what he said. He spoke not to the usar, nor to the Lady—in whom the Usara believed, although they did not generally offer her worship—but to a god whom the athen called simply Darkness, the god of the *angverlaint*. It seemed horribly appropriate, and I bent my head and let him trickle water over me, let him prick my finger for blood.

I should, I thought, have died here all those weeks ago. I had had no right to escape. My life should have ended under Summerdown, and I owed it to the Usara, to the people of Caloxa, as much as I owed it to Gerrard and Benallery and the others, to let that error be corrected now.

Someone helped me to my feet again. "We walk the labyrinth now, Cougar-cephar," said the athen. His accent was much thicker than Dothaw's, the running-water lilt of the in-dwellers, the Usara who lived deep in the mountains, who might not bother to seek out the sun from one indiction to the next. "Soon the struggle will end for you."

He understood, I thought. He understood what a struggle it was simply to continue to stand upright from moment to moment. He understood how painful and pointless and lonely it was, and he understood how much I wanted to lay down my burdens, how much I wanted to rest.

His hands, cool with water, took mine, and I followed his urging, first one step, then another, and then there was a terrible commotion, metal and shouting and the stink of wooden torches instead of the Usara's sweet-burning lamps.

"Fear not, my lord!" cried Geoffrey Trant.

Was a folk song Benallery had been fond of, one of those things with interminable verses and a jangling rhyme, about a man who murders his wife and then is driven mad by her cat, which—even after he kills it again and again, in increasingly inventive ways—persists in watching him so that he encounters its balefully staring eyes at every turn.

I understood how that man had felt.

Damn you, Geoffrey Trant, why couldn't you just let me die?

## *Felix*

I kept my promise. Mildmay didn't expect me to; I caught him several times watching me with an expression on his face that I could unfortunately read all too easily. I had seen it in the Mirador so often that I had become aware of its meaning without even noticing. It was the look Mildmay had when he expected me to yell at him. Or deliberately embarrass him. Or send him away. When he expected me to hurt him, and it seemed terrible, walking along a Caloxan dirt road with my shoes rubbing blisters on my heels and along my left instep, that there was a particular and recognizable expression on Mildmay's largely expressionless face that meant that and nothing else. And it seemed even more terrible that I *knew* that, that I'd known it for years and never especially cared.

I dropped back to walk beside him. He tensed visibly, and I thought, Why do you let me do this to you? Why have you let me do this to you from the moment we met?

What I said was "I'm sorry."

It was either gratifying or appalling that that made his jaw drop. After a moment, he collected himself enough to ask, "Sorry for what?"

"For . . ." I made a double-handed gesture, frustrated. There were no good words for this. "For making you expect me to hurt you."

He frowned at me.

"Not physically," I said, before he could ask me what I thought I was talking about. "But . . . you shouldn't *expect* me to be cruel to you."

His eyebrows shot up before he recovered into his stone face.

"You do expect me to be cruel to you."

He bit his lip, making his face briefly hideous, and then opted to tell me the truth. "It's—it's what you do."

"Oh," I said. An inadequate response, but it was all I could muster. I felt as if he'd hit me. No, I would have *preferred* it if he'd hit me. That was simple. That, I could deal with.

"You knew that, right?" he said. "I mean, you do it on purpose."

"I did," I said, the words heavy and crumbling like ashes in my mouth.

"You didn't think I knew?" he said incredulously.

"No, not . . . I . . . Of course you knew."

"You didn't think I'd ever have the guts to call you on it," he said. He sounded almost satisfied.

"Why do you put up with me?" The question burst out; I barely remembered to keep my voice down.

He gave me a wary sideways look, very foxlike.

"Please," I said. "Just . . . you should have left me flat the second you had a chance, and I don't understand."

"Never had a hope of that," he said. "Not from the start." And he bumped me gently with his shoulder.

It would be useless to push him. I walked beside him the rest of the afternoon and on into the dense violet twilight. We didn't say anything at first, but then he gave me another gentle shoulder bump and began telling a story, one I'd never heard before, about a hero named Jenico Sun-Eyes. I listened gratefully; after about half an hour, I realized Corbie had drifted closer to listen.

When it was so dark that we were likely to walk into a ditch if we kept going, I said, "Just a moment, Mildmay. Corbie!"

"Yeah?"

"You wanted to come along in case I needed a magic-user. Well, I need one. Witchlights, if you don't mind."

Her purple witchlight sprang up, and by its light, she made a face at me.

"We'll have to walk on top of each other for that to do us any good," I said. "You can do better."

"How?" she said.

"You're still thinking about the candle, aren't you?"

"Well, yeah," she said.

"You need to change your metaphor."

"But a candle ain't a metaphor."

"*That*," I said, pointing at her witchlight, "isn't a candle."

Corbie stared at me blankly for a moment, and then quite visibly understood what I meant. "Oh! So what metaphor should I be using?"

"Well, it depends on your personal tastes," I said. "I like to think of my witchlights as very small stars, but other wizards imagine them as lanterns or mirrors reflecting sunlight or any number of other things."

"Stars," Corbie said, her face softening, and from one witchlight, there were suddenly ten, and all of them twinkling brightly as stars do.

"Good girl," I said.

"It's all about the metaphors," she said and winked at me, and we started walking again.

Shortly after that, it began to rain.

## *Kay*

It had been foolish of Dothaw to underestimate Vyell's initiative, but many men looked at his size and the beauty of his face and assumed that there could be nothing but witless amiability behind such a façade, an assumption which Vyell was not above fostering. Dothaw had judged Leadbitter correctly—Leadbitter did what he was told—but he should not have trusted Vyell. For Vyell, when he went to Barthas Cross to send Trant's letter to me via its complicated clandestine route, used that opportunity to catch up with the Primrose Men's allies in Barthas Cross and hence to get messages to all of them who had not died or been imprisoned in the end of the Insurgence. And they had all converged on Summerdown, for while I—equally foolishly, I supposed—was assuming that because Dothaw was honorable, he would not lie, Vyell was assuming the worst. Twenty-five Caloxans against ten Usara: no one even died in the fighting, and when Trant suggested executing the prisoners, I said sharply, "No."

"My lord?" he said, sounding both bewildered and hurt.

"*No*. There will be no more death, Trant. Not by my hand nor by my order."

"We can't just let them go, my lord. You know how the Usara are."

"Yes," I agreed. "I know. But we will not kill them. Let me sleep on the problem, and tomorrow I will have an answer."

"Very well, my lord," he said, and although he was dissatisfied, I knew he would obey me. And by morning, I hoped, the problem would be solved. It was a matter of waiting until the camp was asleep. There would be guards—Trant was far too good a soldier to forgo basic precautions—but one would be facing outward into the dark and rainy night and the other would be watching the prisoners, whom Trant had grouped at the labyrinth entrance as well. I needed merely to find the wall and then to turn away from the fresh wet air. Some labyrinths sought to mislead those who walked them, to turn their feet into dead ends. But the labyrinth beneath Summerdown had but one path and it led inexorably to the engine.

Even a blind man could find his way there.

## *Felix*

Summerdown was like a mirage. It got larger but never seemed to get closer. It was only appropriate that as night deepened, the down became indistinguishable from the sky, as if we could walk and walk and neither reach it nor be out from under it.

Thus, it was a surprise to realize that suddenly we were there, that the looming blackness was Summerdown blotting out the stars.

"Huh," Mildmay said. "There's a light."

"Should we talk to them?" Corbie sounded as if she'd rather stay out here in the dark.

"Do we know how to get into the labyrinth?" Mildmay said.

"No." It hadn't occurred to me that there would be any question—but then, I hadn't expected to be arriving in the middle of the night.

"Then we should talk to them." I couldn't tell if the edge in his voice was for Corbie or for me or for something else entirely. " 'Sides, odds are, they're sitting right on top of it."

We followed him like obedient sheep into the radius of lantern light, where two harried men were arguing, and Julian Carey was watching them, white-faced with anxiety. It was not exactly comforting to have my deductions and extrapolations and outright guesses proved correct.

"Wilt not listen to sense?" said one of the men, a great, bulky, beautiful-faced ox nearly as tall as I was.

"I would, an there were sense to be heard," the other retorted. He was older, gray-haired. "But is sheer barking folly to think he'd go in—"

The ox saw us first and rapped out, "Who goes there?" like a sentry in a play. The other man turned: a weather-beaten face and sharp pale eyes. Julian looked around and his eyes got huge. But he didn't say anything.

My cue. "My name is Felix Harrowgate," I said and offered them both a smile. "And if you'll forgive the impertinence, whom have you lost?"

They goggled at me, the pair of them, like indignant frogs. Mildmay said, quite audibly, "Oh for fuck's sake," and stepped in front of me. "Don't mind him. He thinks he's clever. We're looking for the way into the labyrinth, and I'm guessing that's it?" He pointed over the ox's shoulder at an arch of darkness cut into the side of the down.

"Yes," the ox said.

The older man looked from me to Mildmay to Corbie, his face becoming steadily more perplexed. "What's your business with the labyrinth?"

"And in the cereus watch," the ox said.

"Pilgrimage," Mildmay said, daring them to call him a liar.

The ox's face darkened, as if he might take that dare, but another, even younger man emerged from the general darkness and said, "There's no sign of Lord Rothmarlin toward the trees, and Fowler says—"

"Lord Rothmarlin?" I said. "Is that who you've lost?"

"Leadbitter," the ox said, "if I've said it once, I've said it ten thousand times. *Watch your fucking trap.*"

"Shit," Mildmay said. "I got a bad feeling about where it is the guy thinks Lord Rothmarlin didn't go."

It took me a moment to untangle that, but when I did, I felt sickly convinced that he was right. "So you've lost Kay," I said.

*"Kay?"* said the older man.

"We're friends of his. And of Julian's." I gave Julian a smile, and he came very thankfully around the two Caloxans to join Corbie behind me. "His fiancée is very concerned about his disappearance."

"Would be even more concerned if she knew what he was doing, the harebrained son of a—"

"Vyell! Take your own damned advice!"

The ox looked blank for a moment, then stricken.

"I must admit," I said, "I'm a little disappointed that you seem to have lost him."

"We know where he is," the ox—Vyell—said grimly. "Geoff just won't admit it."

"And am telling you—"

Vyell cut him off. "Could not have gotten past Bazley and Polledge, who were not asleep and *aren't blind*."

And they were off again, but Mildmay tugged on my arm and said, "We got to go after him, don't we?" He had no more doubt than I did where Kay had gone.

"Yes," I said. "I'm afraid we do."

"C'mon then," he said and set out toward the entrance, not hurrying but not waiting for questions or arguments, either. I followed him, and Corbie and Julian followed me. The Caloxans stopped arguing, but they didn't try to call us back.

The entrance to the labyrinth was elaborately carved with interlocking quartered circles, a natural opening turned definitively into a doorway. The threshold was marked by a wooden bar on which the same elaborate carvings were still faintly visible, worn almost smooth by centuries of use and weather.

Corbie had doused her witchlight, but she called it back now. The floor was level and very smooth; Mildmay was walking more easily than he had all day. I kept expecting the tunnel to branch, but it didn't, merely coiling back on itself as sinuously as a snake.

"It ain't a maze," Mildmay said after a while, "but it sure does feel like one."

"Are all Corambin labyrinths like this?" I asked Corbie.

"How should I know?"

"Well, at least we don't have to worry about not finding him," Mildmay said.

That hadn't even occurred to me; although I knew that if Kay had been lost, Mildmay would have found him, I still shivered a little, just imagining being blind and lost in a maze. And then it occurred to me that that was not so very different from Kay's day-to-day existence. That was an even less comfortable thought.

I asked Julian what had happened, how he and Kay had come to Summerdown, and he told us the story as we wound and twisted, until we came around one more corner and abruptly found ourselves in the heart of the labyrinth.

It was not as large a room as I had thought it would be. Almost claustrophobic, with the great brooding mass of the engine reflecting dull gleams of Corbie's witchlight off its angles and in the glass globes that clustered at its center—glass globes and arching metal struts and gearwheels, small and large, that were a dull yellow white and did not reflect the light at all.

Bone.

"It's a Titan Clock," I said, the words escaping involuntarily. They echoed vilely. And a clot of shadows on the far side of the room twitched and shifted and revealed itself to be Kay.

He looked as bad as he had when I first met him, ashy sallow, lines of strain and despair etched deep into his face. "Who's there?" he demanded. Corbie's witchlights brightened, and I saw that the darkness on his hands was not a trick of the shadows, but blood.

"It's me," I said. "Felix. You're hurt." I picked my way carefully around the outthrust limbs of the engine.

"Felix?"

"Like a plug centime," I said, forcing my voice to cheerfulness. "Always turn up again when you least want me."

"Or a yellow cat," he muttered; I decided against asking him to explain.

He was trapped in a thicket of metal thorns, his clothes snagged in several places. His hands—palms and backs—were bleeding from several long narrow gashes, and as I knelt carefully beside him, I saw that his forearms were bleeding as well. He had been fortunate, though; none of those knife-edged spines had found his face. Or his throat.

"Hold still," I said. "I'll have you free in a moment."

"I have to find the center," he said. "There's a plate, shining silver. Will you help me? Will not take long for a sighted man."

"And what's your plan after that?" I said, keeping my voice light. "Or are you going to leave me to guess? I must warn you, my guesses are going to be shockingly accurate."

He flinched. "Is the right thing to do," he said, his hand reaching forward and then pulling back again, as if he thought I would not let him touch me. "I should have—"

"No, you should not," I said, knowing how that sentence was going to end: *died with Gerrard*. "Kay, do you know what this thing does?"

"Gerrard said it would save Caloxa."

*"How?"*

He frowned. "I know not. Gerrard . . . Gerrard said to trust him. He knew it would work."

My opinion of Prince Gerrard Hume had not been high to begin with. "Yes, well, I've been to talk to the magician you hired, and I'm not convinced 'save' is the right word."

"What do you mean?" The frown was deepening.

"This engine feeds on death. It is unlikely in the extreme that it gives anything but death in return."

"Am a soldier. I expected nothing else."

That rattled me more than a little, but I pressed on: "Whose death?"

"What?"

"I understand that you're ready to sacrifice yourself—and we can talk later about whether that's noble or just *stupid*—but whose deaths are you buying? Who has to die to save Caloxa—and how many?"

"I—"

"Because if you think this thing can be aimed so that it only kills Corambin soldiers, I'm afraid I have to disabuse you of that idea. As far as I can tell, it can't be aimed at all."

"No, I—"

"And I have the nasty suspicion that, in fact, it's designed to 'save' Caloxa by making it so undesirable that even Corambis wouldn't want it. Like disfiguring your sister—or killing her—to 'save' her honor."

He shuddered hard. "But Gerrard wouldn't . . ."

"Wouldn't he?"

He was silent for a moment, and then his shoulders sagged. "Ah, Lady, have mercy on us all. I know not. We were all half-mad at the end. Perhaps is but fond delusion to think I know what Gerrard would or would not do. He led us all into death from the moment he raised his banner."

"Then stop following him," I said sharply. It was the right thing to say, because Kay lifted his head, and this time when he reached out, he let his hand find me, those blunt fingers closing on my forearm.

"That's right," I said. "I've got you disentangled, but you'll need to move exactly as I tell you, or you'll just get tangled up again. How you got in this situation . . ."

"It trapped me," he said, his voice hard and perfectly certain. "I could hear it moving."

"Mildmay," I said, raising my voice, "Kay says the engine is moving on its own. Will you watch, please?"

"Me and Julian are already on it," Mildmay called back. "And Corbie's taking notes."

"Good," I said, and then to Kay, "We're going to do this slowly, because if you do get caught again, I don't want you getting cut. We don't want to give the engine any more of your vi."

He nodded, then went still, his hand tightening on my arm again. "But, Felix, the Usara said—the only way to stop it stealing vi from everything it can reach—"

"Kay."

He subsided, though his grip was going to leave bruises.

I said, "Something has to be done, yes. But your vi—your death—is not the answer."

"They said—"

Obstinate as a mule. "Are the Usara going to care how many Caloxans it kills?"

"Oh," he said, and his grip on my arm loosened again.

"We're going to think of something," I said. "Which will not involve you dying. Okay?"

His mouth quirked in a smile. "Okay."

---

Much later, we were settled in a curve of the labyrinth, with Caloxan soldiers to both sides. Trant—who'd looked positively ill when we led Kay out into the lantern light—was clearly not taking any more chances. Julian and Corbie had curled up together for warmth, and I had carefully not eavesdropped on their conversation. Mildmay was already asleep, although I knew he'd be wide awake in a second if I needed him. Kay was lying on his back, his bandaged hands resting on his chest, his eyes open.

"Are you all right?" I asked softly.

He sighed. "In truth, I know not. I would have been grateful to be dead." He said it matter-of-factly, without emphasis.

"Why?"

"You need to ask?"

"Yes, actually, I do."

"Shall I give thee the list?" But he could not manage his usual sparking rancor.

"You didn't feel this way in Esmer."

"Perhaps I did, and you saw it not."

But I knew I was right. "You said you're a soldier. Why are you so eager to surrender?"

"Because there is no war. Is neither victory nor defeat, merely an endless series of days to be endured. I am tired of enduring."

"What if things got better?"

"They won't," he said with bleak finality and rolled onto his side, facing away from me. "Should sleep, Felix. Is still the engine to be dealt with."

Rebuff and rejection, and I knew I was far too tired to deal with him without making things worse.

"We'll talk again later," I said and knew by the tense line of his back that he heard me.

I was a little surprised to find myself dreaming of the Khloïdanikos, arriving in it as if I had just stepped through Horn Gate. I took my customary path and found that the perseïd tree had actually put out a single beautifully defiant flower. I sat down, amazed and almost afraid to breathe, and that was how Thamuris found me.

He sat beside me and said simply, "I've missed you."

"Well, there have been some complications." I told him about the binding-by-obedience. "And besides," I said to preempt the outrage I didn't want to deal with, even if it was on my behalf, "I thought you might prefer it if I stayed away." I was careful to keep my gaze on the perseïd tree. "I'm not . . . I don't think I know how to be a decent friend." I didn't deserve outrage on my behalf, not from him.

"That's not true," Thamuris said sharply.

"You're better," I said, to change the subject. "The Khloïdanikos is healing you."

"No. Not healing. But slowing the effects . . . People can live for years and years with consumption, you know. I could have—I could live."

"If you spend all your time asleep."

"You don't understand," Thamuris said urgently. "This isn't sleeping. I can walk here, and it doesn't hurt. And there's always something to study. But it's lonely, if you're not here."

I wasn't sure what to say; fortunately, he didn't wait. "You have to come. Because I don't want to do it without you. It's not worth it if there's no one to talk to."

"You have Khrysogonos. And Diokletian." I wasn't sure why I was arguing, but it made me uncomfortable to think that Thamuris needed me.

"Khrysogonos does his best, but he isn't a scholar at heart. And Diokletian isn't my friend. Not the way you are. I *missed* you."

"You can't depend on me," I said, starting to feel a little frantic. "You must know that."

"Is it so wrong to be needed?"

I would have lied, evaded, distracted, but I was dreaming, not tranced, and my defenses failed me. "Yes. If you depend on me, I will fail you."

He looked at me, not speaking, until I turned back to the perseïd, staring at its black bark. My shoulders hunched tighter and tighter, and when he finally spoke, I startled as violently as if he'd pinched me.

"You believe yourself to be a monster," he said.

"I *am* a monster," I said, not looking at him, not looking at anything but the perseïd.

"Why?"

"What?"

Patiently, he said, "Why do you call yourself a monster?"

"I hurt people for my own pleasure," I said, and there was something darkly satisfying in *saying* it, in admitting something I'd known was true since I was eleven years old.

"Sexually, you mean." His voice was steady, but he was blushing furiously. As far as I knew, Thamuris was a virgin and likely to die that way.

"In part. You've been on the receiving end, so don't pretend you don't know what I'm talking about."

"But that was to defend yourself."

"It's not that simple. Or that excusable."

Another long silence. I didn't mind this one as much; I wasn't trying to hide anything now.

"If you were a monster," Thamuris said, "you wouldn't care."

"If I *wasn't* a monster, I wouldn't do it."

"And you can't stop?"

"I tried," I said. "For two years, I tried to deny it. I failed."

"You're talking about sex again. I meant the other."

"The man whose mind I destroyed. He killed himself. I saw it in my dreams."

"Felix—"

"I don't want to hurt anyone any longer," I said, and I knew it was the truth by how much it hurt to say it. "But, no, I can't stop."

Thamuris did not answer for a moment; then he said simply, "Change takes time. And you have been hurt yourself."

"I deserve it."

He snorted. "Even if that's true, what good is it?"

"What?"

"What *good* is it? What good is your pain doing anyone?"

I was sure there was an answer, but I couldn't find it.

Thamuris said, "You have to understand the difference between an error and a crime. Errors don't make you a monster, Felix, even terrible ones. If they did, I would be every inch as much a monster as you claim you are. Do you think *I'm* a monster?"

"No, of course not."

"Exactly." He stood up. "They're going to want to take me out in the garden soon, so I'd better go. You'll come back, won't you?"

"You really want me to," I said. It wasn't quite a question, but almost.

"I really do," Thamuris said and smiled at me.

"All right," I said. "When I can."

He nodded, said, "Try to forgive yourself," and left, moving slowly. I got up and walked in the opposite direction, trying to decide if what he had said was true, or if it only felt true because I badly wanted it to be.

I could forgive myself for being Malkar's cat's-paw. He had worked a long time to instill the necessary responses in me, and although I wished I had resisted him, I could not truly blame myself for failing. I could forgive myself for Gideon's death. I had not wished it, had done nothing knowingly to cause it. I regretted the way I had treated him, regretted the pain I had inflicted on him. I had been stupid to underestimate the threat posed by Isaac Garamond, but even with hindsight, I was surprised he had committed murder.

As for what I had done to Isaac . . . I wouldn't do it again.

The realization startled me. I stopped by the koi pond, watching the calico fish play hide-and-seek among the water lilies without really seeing them. But it was true. I wouldn't do it again. I wouldn't do it in cold blood. I could not quite bring myself to wish it undone—could not bring myself to wish Isaac Garamond alive and sane—just as I could not deny I had done it knowingly. That, I supposed, made it a crime rather than an error in Thamuris's definition, and the best I could say for myself was I wouldn't do it again.

There, I proved myself a monster, but a monster who perhaps could learn better. And Isaac had been far from innocent himself. If I was a monster, so was he. He *had* acted in cold blood.

And so had I on another occasion. Mildmay might have forgiven me—Mildmay had his own understanding of monsters—but here, truly, was the worst thing I had ever done, and I knew it was a crime.

Here, it was no comfort to know I wouldn't do it again. No excuse of grief or rage. I could claim I had been Mavortian von Heber's cat's-paw, and there was even a sense in which it wasn't a lie, but that didn't exculpate me. I had used the obligation d'âme on Mildmay. I had forced him to murder Vey Coruscant, and I couldn't think of a way to describe my actions that didn't involve the word "rape." What Malkar had done to me, I had turned around and done to Mildmay. That I had thereby delivered him into Malkar's own hands was cruel and unnecessary confirmation of the truth.

"How am I supposed to forgive myself for that?" I said; although my voice was no more than a whisper, I winced.

*Forgiveness is a luxury,* whispered the fantôme from its prison. *Thou needest it not.*

"Yes, well, you *would* say that." I wondered if the noirance of the engine could reach the Khloïdanikos, and then realized that of course it could, that the Khloïdanikos was no more "in" Troia than it was "in" Corambis, and that in any event the fantôme was bound to me, bound in *my* construct, and thus the noirance would affect it through me even if the Khloïdanikos itself were immune. And I knew perfectly well the Khloïdanikos was not immune to noirant power; I'd proved that conclusively.

*Thou wilt yield eventually,* the fantôme said. *And then this foolishness will not trouble thee. I promise.*

"Yes," I said tartly, "because I will have committed suicide. No, tha . . ." My voice died as thoughts of noirance and death and sacrifice and forgiveness lined up in a new way and dumped me abruptly back into the waking world.

## *Mildmay*

I'd woken up around the fourth hour of the morning, and when I sat up, I saw across Felix that Kay was awake, too.

"G'morning," I said, whispering even though Felix was sleeping hard. "I'm getting up. You want to?"

"Yes, please," Kay whispered back. Once we'd worked our way out around Felix, Kay said, "And tell me, please, how you came here. Is most bewildering."

Yeah, I'll bet. So I told him our end, and we came out into the sunlight and there were suddenly Caloxans fucking *everywhere*, falling over themselves to make Kay happy, which mostly seemed to make him embarrassed. But I didn't mind using it to get some breakfast and to find out that Julian was off showing Corbie the horses and, well, I wished him luck.

So me and Kay were eating, with Caloxans kind of hanging around, not exactly with us but where if Kay wanted something, they were right fucking on top of it. And Felix came out with his hair hanging in his face and his eyes all dreamy, and he came up to me and crouched down and said, "I know what to do."

"You know what to do," I said.

"Yes. Come on, take a walk with me. Here, you! Come sit with Kay and make him stop moping." The nearest Caloxan jumped like he'd been bitten.

"Am not—!" Kay said.

"Oh yes you are, darling," Felix said cheerfully. "Come on, Mildmay."

So I hauled myself up and followed him off to where there was nobody else in earshot, and he said, "I know what to do about the engine. But I need your help."

Of course I said, "Okay," because I was never going to be able to say nothing else when he asked me for help. He was kind of wild-eyed and dreamy, and I had to ask him twice before he got around to telling me what he needed me to do. Which was pretty simple, really. Get Kay into the labyrinth, but nobody else.

Simple, but not easy.

All the Caloxans were watching Kay like the world was going to end if they didn't know right where he was every second, and I didn't need to run the conversation through my head but once to give up on the idea of just saying, *I need to borrow Kay for a while if y'all don't mind.* Because they *would* mind, especially when they asked what I wanted him for and I had to say I didn't know.

Yeah, we could just skip that part.

So I went and found Corbie and told her I needed a diversion. And she looked at me funny and said, "What for?" and I said, "Felix says," and powers and saints, that was good enough for her.

I told her to give me a minute to talk to Kay and then draw the Caloxans off any way she could think of that wouldn't actually hurt nobody. I went over to where Kay was standing and glaring at nothing the way he did. I gave the Caloxan watching him a glower and said, "D'you mind?"

Which shouldn't have worked, really, but it got him flustered and he backed off.

Kay turned his head toward me, and his eyes were just about as spooky as Felix's, because I knew he couldn't see me, but it looked like he was staring straight at me and not liking me much, neither. He said, "What is it, Mildmay?"

He just sounded tired, like he figured I was going to lay into him about something. I said, "I need you to cooperate, okay?"

"Cooperate?" Kay most always had about half a frown on, that line between his eyebrows that never really went away, but now he was frowning for real. "Cooperate with what?"

And that was when Corbie—may Kethe bless her wicked heart—spooked the horses. I waited a couple seconds, watched Caloxans heading for the picket as fast as they could go, and said, "Going this way. Please." And I caught Kay's arm and started dragging him toward the entrance to the labyrinth.

He didn't fight me. Kept up with me, even, and said, "What happens?"

"Felix has an idea," I said. "I don't know more'n that."

"An idea about the engine?"

"Yeah. But don't ask me what, because he didn't say and I wouldn't've understood him if he did."

"All right," Kay said, and then we were in the labyrinth, and Felix was saying, "I knew I could count on you," which made me feel warm all over, and fuck, yes, I know how stupid that is.

Felix had a dark lantern, which was better planning than he usually showed, but he went clear around the first bend before he'd open it. I didn't complain, because I opened my mouth to say something, and then thought about Kay, who'd gone the whole distance in pitch blackness that no amount of light was ever going to help with, and I closed my mouth again. I suppose, really, we didn't even need the lantern. It wasn't like we could get lost or take a wrong turn. But I was glad when Felix slid the shutter aside anyway, because it carved out a little circle of light in all that dark and I felt like I could breathe again.

Nobody said nothing for a long while, and then Kay said, "Mildmay says you have an idea."

"Yes," Felix said. "I'm sorry to drag you along, but since I don't fully understand how the engine works, and don't particularly want to experiment, I thought it was better to be safe than sorry."

"You think I . . . affect it, somehow?"

"I think you might. It moved, after all."

"It might have done that for anyone."

"Yes, I know, but that's one of those experiments I don't want to do. I'm not asking you, or Mildmay, to come any farther than the door, but I need it to accept what it's being offered."

"What're you offering?" I said.

"It's complicated," he said.

"You don't want to talk about it," I said, because I could do the math on that one.

"You won't like it. And I don't want to waste time while you try to talk me out of it. I don't think we have much time left. It *moved* last night. And I think it's trying to drive Kay to suicide."

Kay didn't like that, but Felix told him what Intended Marcham had told us about the two men who'd killed themselves for no reason, and that made him think. He said, "Was happening in Bernatha. The suicides."

"Nemesis drove people mad," I said.

"Diadumenian Butler is said to have killed himself by jumping into its gears," Felix said. "Not that that stopped it. But that's not quite the same thing. Nemesis and the Clock of Eclipses—and presumably Juggernaut, although I can't imagine the Bastion would ever admit as much—cause suicides by their working. This engine needs suicides in order to work at all."

"Powers," I said. "Okay. I won't argue with whatever you're gonna do."

"Promise you won't try to stop me."

"You *really* think I ain't gonna like this."

"I know you aren't," he said with a flicker of a smile. "But I promise I have no intention of sacrificing myself."

"Well, you wouldn't. 'Cause that'd make it go off, right?"

"Exactly," he said, and he sounded so pleased with me that I went warm again.

"But what *are* you offering?" Kay said. He'd learned the key thing about any serious conversation with Felix, which was that you couldn't let him distract you.

"Something I think it will accept," Felix said.

"Is no answer."

"No," Felix agreed, perfectly cheerful. "I don't want to waste time arguing with you, either."

"And if I promise not to argue either? Will you tell me then?"

"Are you promising not to argue?"

"How can I make that promise, when I know not what you intend?"

"Impasse," Felix said, still cheerful. "Let me do this, Kay, and I promise I will explain after."

"It sounds as if thou mightst not live to keep thy promise."

Felix stopped. He turned and touched Kay's face gently and said, "I would not be grateful to be dead," and I knew that was part of the conversation him and Kay had had while I'd laid there and pretended to be asleep, but all I could think of was the Road of Corundum in the rain and Felix saying he would've thanked Lord Stephen for sentencing him to death. And something I didn't even know I'd been carrying since then rolled off my shoulders. I practically heard it hit the floor.

"All right," Kay said. "I will not hinder thy knight errantry. Let us, for the Lady's sake, get it over with."

"On we go, then," Felix said, and we followed the turns and twists and ended up back in the heart of the labyrinth with the engine crouching there like a big fucking spider. It knew all it had to do was wait.

I thought it had moved again, since last night, but I wasn't sure enough to say anything.

Felix gave me the lantern. "I want you and Kay to stay here—in fact, move back a few feet. I don't want it to be able to reach you."

"Okay," I said, because I wasn't arguing with that.

"And I want you to *stay* here. I'd use the obligation d'âme if I could. Do you understand?"

"Yeah. I get you. We'll stay put."

"Good," he said. "Remember that, no matter what happens. Don't move." His mouth quirked. "I'd draw you a circle of protection, too, but I haven't any chalk and somehow I don't think using blood is a good idea."

"No," I said, probably a little too hard, and added, "Thank you all the same," which even made him laugh.

Then his head tilted a little, and he said, "I was right. It can feel Kay. It wants its sacrifice."

Kay shivered, and I shivered with him. Felix gave me a weird little nod, which I figured was him trusting me to keep my promise, and trusting me to keep the engine from getting Kay. Which, yeah. I moved us back another three or four feet. I could still see the engine and most of the room around it, but I was pretty sure none of its arms could reach this far. And if I was wrong, we could move further back. Get around the bend, and it couldn't touch us. Which wasn't much of a comfort, but I was hanging onto it as hard as I could. We could get away from this fucking thing if we had to.

On the other hand, Felix couldn't, because when I'd gone backwards, Felix had gone forward.

"What is he doing?" Kay asked, his voice just above a whisper.

"I wish I knew."

"No, I mean—what is he *doing*? What actions is he taking?"

"Oh, right. Sorry. He's walked into the middle of the thing, and now he's just standing there. I'd think he was getting ready to do magic or something, but he can't, so I don't . . ." I knew what him doing magic looked like, and I knew what him in an actual trance looked like, and they weren't all that different, but a little. "He's tranced."

"What means that?" Kay asked, and I realized we were holding hands.

"He's doing something in that world of the spirit thing that he talks about all the time."

"But not magic."

"No. Something else. I'd tell you more if I could."

"I fault thee not," he said. "Is not thy doing that he keeps secrets."

"No," I said, "but—"

In the middle of the room, Felix went stiff, and I heard him say, clear as daylight, "I am yours." And I swear I heard glass breaking.

I clamped my hands down on Kay's, and just in time, because he made a lunge toward the engine.

"He promised," I said. "And he wasn't lying."

"But—" He was fighting me, fighting hard, and I guess it wasn't surprising that he knew what he was doing. Unlike Felix, who was the last person I'd had to wrestle to the ground and sit on. But I could see, and I was bigger than him. I got him down on his stomach, with both his wrists pinned in the small of his back, and then I looked up and Felix was watching us.

Only it wasn't Felix.

I mean, it *was*, tall and skinny and with the hair and the spooky eyes, but I'd never seen Felix stand like that in his life, and, well, the best I can say it is, the person looking at us with Felix's skew eyes was somebody else. Somebody I'd never met and didn't want to.

And somebody who could do magic, because while I just sat there staring, Felix's little green witchlights that I'd never thought I'd miss popped in, one at a time, all around his head like a saint's halo. The person wearing his body like a secondhand coat said, "Thou art the brother." And powers and saints, if Felix had ever given me a smile like that, I'd *still* be running.

Beneath me, Kay quit fighting.

"So who're you?" I said, and I tried to sound like I wasn't scared to death, but I don't know how good I did. Probably not very.

"My name matters not. I am rachenant."

I didn't know that word, but Kay tensed up and said, "A spirit of vengeance. The Mulkists used them."

"Oh," I said. "Oh fuck you're the fantôme."

That threw him. Or her. Or it. Fuck, I don't know. The *thing* in Felix's body. It blinked and kind of shook its head. "He has spoken of me?" And fuck me sideways, it sounded *hopeful*. Like a gal with a crush wanting to know if the guy even knew she existed.

"Not a lot." I'd ask, and he'd say he was handling it, and if I pushed, what I got was a lot of big words and no answers.

"Oh," it said, and it *was* disappointed. I wasn't making that up. And I knew that because Kay said, "But we are annemer, he and I, and Felix does not speak to us of warlocks' matters."

Which was only sort of true, but it was the right thing to say, because the fantôme nodded.

I was going to have some things to say to Felix later, if we all got to "later" and I ever got to talk to Felix again, things like what a stupid stunt this was to pull and had he not considered it might go wrong and could he not have given me at least a fucking *hint* about what he thought he was trying to do so I didn't have to figure it out here with a fantôme watching and the engine getting ready to do Kethe knows what. And okay, what the fuck were you thinking, adding a fantôme into the mix when, according to you, we already had way more noirant magic floating around than we needed? Because there was no way a fantôme wasn't noirant. I might not be real bright, and I might not know fuck all about magic, but I could get that much.

The fantôme took a step toward us, and I wondered how much it knew about close fighting, and then it stopped. Its hands came up and witchlight went out sideways in two arcs and I swear to the powers caught every spur and spine of metal on the entire engine. For a second I was as blind as Kay—nothing but green—and if the fantôme had rushed me, I don't know what would've happened, and that's the truth. But it didn't. I blinked and blinked and finally got to where I could see around all the green, and it was still standing there, head down.

"You said . . . you'd do my bidding." How I knew it was Felix, I can't tell you, but it was.

"I know thy bidding." And that was the fantôme. "The true desire of thy heart. I know it, and thou canst not hide it from me."

Felix's body went to its knees. "No! You do not choose my desire for me. You do not choose what I want."

"Thou knowst not thine own heart," and sweet merciful powers I wanted to be somewhere else, anywhere else, anywhere I didn't have to listen to Felix and the fantôme arguing both in Felix's voice.

"Oh, I assure you, I do." I didn't like the way he said that. "I've tried revenge. If you can see my heart, you can see that. And it isn't what I want."

"Thou canst lie to thyself," the fantôme said, and I liked that tone even less, all soft and patient and almost cooing, like it was trying to jolly a baby out of a temper tantrum. "But thou canst not lie to thy rachenant."

"I forgive them!" Felix howled. "All of them! I forgive their errors and their crimes. I even forgive *you*."

"What meanst thou?" it said, sharp as glass.

My leg couldn't hold no more. I sort of fell sideways off Kay, and he sat up and reached for me, and we ended up huddled together against the wall. Neither Felix nor the fantôme noticed as far as I could tell.

"I mean," Felix was saying, and it was his silky voice, the one that sounded like Strych and always meant trouble, "I forgive you. I forgive you for the people you killed. I forgive you for deceiving and entrapping me. I forgive you for the rape you are trying to commit. I forgive you—"

"Stop it!" cried the fantôme.

"I forgive you," Felix said, his voice rising, "for being a mockery of the person you once were. *I forgive you.*"

I couldn't tell who was controlling Felix's body because the scream it made was, powers, it was like metal. It got to its feet like a puppet being worked by a drunk. It wobbled in a sort of circle, and it was the fantôme whimpering, "This is not thy desire, cannot be thy desire. Thou dost not want this," while Felix's body lurched two steps forward and one step sideways and grabbed onto the upright bar of metal in the middle of the engine like you'd have to break all its fingers—again—to make it let go.

"This is my bidding." Felix's voice, through his teeth. "And you will do it."

I couldn't see what happened exactly, but the next second Felix threw himself flat and five of the engine's arms swung through the empty air where he'd been standing.

Except it seemed like it wasn't empty. I didn't exactly see anybody there, but I didn't exactly not, either, and the engine's arms pulled back and up into a shape sort of like the ugliest flower you can imagine, and you didn't have to be a hocus to know it was getting ready, gathering itself like a cat about to pounce, and if I was thinking anything at all, it was, Kethe love us, we are fucked.

And then it was almost like the engine hiccupped. Its arms jerked, and jerked again, and from somewhere in the middle of it I heard something shatter, like the tiniest glass ball a glassblower could possibly make.

I shouted at Felix, "Keep your fucking head down," even as I was rolling me and Kay over, pressing us up against the wall, protecting my neck and the back of my skull with my hands as best I could. And my instincts were right, because the next thing that happened was the engine exploded.

# Chapter 16

## *Mildmay*

So the whole fucking world showed up in Howrack. Hocuses came from Esmer and from Bernatha where they were studying that clock. There was a whole swarm of intendeds. The Margrave of Murrey, which was where we were, showed up and picked fights with everybody. And the Duke of Murtagh came swanning into the middle of it, too. Like a fucking carny ring.

Even that complete asshole Edwin Beckett showed up, but wouldn't nobody give him the time of day, and I heard that Murtagh sent a couple guys around to lean on him, so he left pretty quick. I would've liked to break his nose first, just for starters, but Felix wouldn't let me. He said it would just make Beckett feel persecuted and like he was being martyred for his beliefs, and, well, I guess so.

Felix had to explain everything to the hocuses, and then he had to explain it again. And again. And he had to explain about the fantôme and how come his magic was working again, and then about the Automaton of Corybant, and then he had to explain about the Clock of Eclipses and just exactly how it was that Mr. Beckett had got *it* going, which I thought was going to kill him, but powers and saints, he stood up and did it. And the hocuses listened and took notes and their eyes got big as bell-wheels and none of them could really look him in the face after, except that Virtuer Ashmead got up and came over and said, "I will resign before I put the choke-binding on you again."

"Me, too," said Virtuer Hutchence.

"It wasn't that bad," Felix said uncomfortably.

"I watched you suffer under it," said Virtuer Ashmead. "Yes, it was."

"Maybe you should anyway," Felix said. He wasn't looking at either of them. "Surely this proves once and for all that I cannot be trusted."

"That's an interesting interpretation," said Virtuer Ashmead. "When I think of all the things you *could* have done, I would say that it proves exactly the opposite. Don't think I don't understand the temptation you were faced with in the rachenant."

Felix kind of glanced at him. "I couldn't have."

"I know," said Virtuer Ashmead. "And that's how I know you can be trusted. We do, however, have a problem, although please believe me when I say it isn't your fault."

"I make them nervous," Felix said softly. He was looking at the other hocuses: two other virtuers and three adepts from Esmer, and a virtuer and four adepts from Bernatha. "It's the Mirador all over again."

Virtuer Hutchence said, and not like he was happy about it, "People—such as for example my esteemed colleague Virtuer Wooller—are going to start saying that you're unfit to teach our innocent young men."

"Hutch," said Virtuer Ashmead.

"Oh, come on, John! Tell me he won't."

"No, I know he will. And I'm afraid most of the Circle—certainly the majority of the Congress—will agree with him."

"I'll be fired," Felix translated, and his shoulders hunched just a notch tighter.

"Unless we find you another position first," Virtuer Hutchence said, and got another startled glance from Felix.

"You seem to be under the impression," Virtuer Ashmead said, sharp as lemon, "that we don't understand what it was you saved us from. I assure you, we do. And we are not simply going to *abandon* you as a reward."

"I thought," said Virtuer Hutchence, "that perhaps you would accept the lighthouse keeper's position at Grimglass."

"Grimglass? Isn't that out at the back of beyond?"

"It is," Virtuer Hutchence said and made an apologetic face. "But we need a virtuer out there, and—"

"I'm not a virtuer," Felix said.

"You will be," said Virtuer Ashmead. "That much even Wooller can't argue with." And then he sighed. "Especially if you're safely out of sight at Grimglass."

Felix shoved his fingers through his hair. "I must be the only person in the history of the world to be exiled from exile."

"I think you'll find the lighthouse itself very interesting," Virtuer Hutchence said, kind of hopefully, "and there are several centuries' worth of records.

Nobody's ever catalogued Virtuer Grice's papers, for one thing, and he's the one who did the initial workings."

"You have pinpointed my weaknesses with uncanny accuracy," Felix said, but he looked like he was fighting a smile.

"Was that a yes?" said Virtuer Ashmead.

"Yes," said Felix, and his shoulders finally relaxed.

## *Kay*

Was excessively odd, how people kept asking for my opinion on matters. I had no authority of any kind, and yet Murrey wanted me to tell him what he should do about the Usara, and the Reeve of Howrack wanted me to tell him what he should do about the Primrose Men, and Murtagh wanted my opinion on a thousand things, and no matter how many times I said, "I know not," they kept asking. I would have thought it a conspiracy, save that Murrey was the most contrary man in Caloxa and one could no more successfully conspire with him than one could teach a pig to preach.

And finally, for they would not leave me alone, I told Murrey to let the Usara go with their sworn promise to return to their clan halls, the reeve to bid the Primrose Men return to their homes and families. "No more death," I said. "Please, for the love of the Lady, let there be no more death."

Was even more surprising that I was obeyed. Dothaw insisted on coming to swear to me personally, as if were more binding to swear to me than to Murrey. Trant and Vyell also came to bid me farewell, though they were both unhappy with me. "Gerrard is dead," I said to them. "The Insurgence is over."

"Nothing has changed," Vyell said.

"And if you keep fighting, nothing will change except that sooner or later, you will be dead."

"We would die for you, my lord," said Trant.

"I know that," said I. "And I want it not. Would rather that you live, not for me but for yourselves. Go home, raise your families. Fight when you must rather than merely when you can."

Vyell came closer; I felt him kneel down beside my chair. "Would stay with thee, my lord," he said very softly, "an thou wouldst let me."

I knew not for certain what he offered—most likely Vyell knew not, either—but I knew I could not accept it. An it was fealty, I was no longer his lord, nor any man's lord, and could give him nothing in return. An it was love, I loved him not. "Go home, Angel," said I. "Leave the war behind you."

"Is not that simple," he said.

"I know. But wilt thou try? For if no one tries, then it will never end."

"I hear you, my lord," he said, and he kissed my forehead. "Very well." I knew that most of the Primrose Men would return not to their families, but to their hidden dens, to their scheming and skirmishing. But I had done all that I could, and at least, after they left, the reeve let me be.

Murtagh was the worst, though, insisting on discussing the magicians' inquiries with me, asking if I was content to have Felix Harrowgate as the Virtuer of Grimglass. Finally, I could bear it no longer. "What does it matter if I am content? Is not my decision, neither my responsibility nor my concern."

"Have you not been listening?" Murtagh said. "I'm sure I've said distinctly at least three times that when you marry Vanessa, you will be Warden of Grimglass."

"Is but words," said I. "I will be a blind man pacing a nursery in Whallan instead of a blind man pacing a nursery in Esmer. Is all."

"Will you stop that?" he said, so sharply and so suddenly close, that I startled back in my chair.

"Stop what?"

His hands closed on my shoulders, pinning me in place. "You think you're useless, but you're *not*. Do you know how long the Pallisters have been mismanaging Grimglass? It's at least ten indictions, since the death of Rodger Pallister's father, and in truth, I'm willing to bet it's more like fifty, since no one ever said of Everard Pallister that he could count to twenty with his boots on. Vanessa is a shrewd woman and a better politician than most of the Convocation, but she doesn't know how to deal with an estate the size of Grimglass. She doesn't have the training. It's nearly the same population as Rothmarlin, you know, and although there aren't Usara raiding every summer, it has its own problems, some of them fairly dire. Kay, for once in your mule-headed life, *listen* to me and try to believe what I am telling you. I am not *giving* you Grimglass, either as a gift or as an excuse to be rid of you. I am *saddling* you with Grimglass because I know that you will not merely take responsibility for it, but you will *care* for it, that you will be the same good steward for Grimglass that you were for Rothmarlin, and that you will fight Darne tooth and nail to protect it. Because you don't know any other way to be. So stop assuming that I pity you or hold you in contempt or *whatever* it is you imagine my motives are. For I tell you now and tell you plainly, I do not."

"I hear you," I said.

"Do you believe me?"

"I . . . I will try to."

"Good," said Murtagh, and let me go. "Because I'm thinking of sending Julian out there with you."

"Julian?"

"You deal with the boy far better than I do. And you can teach him much that he needs to know. He's too frightened of me to learn."

"Is your own fault," I said.

"I know that," Murtagh snapped. "But I cannot . . . I had an elder brother as well as a younger, you know."

"No," I said. "I knew not."

"I did. Clovis should have been duke, but when he was Julian's age, he started seeing things, going into trances in public, having screaming fits in the middle of our father's receptions."

"An aethereal."

"Yes. And he could not or would not control it. He just *gave up*. He is an anchorite somewhere in eastern Corambis now. I don't even know where. And I cannot bear to have Julian . . . Never mind. The point is, I want Julian to learn from you. And he's quite excited at the thought of going to Grimglass with you. I think he is not as happy at the University—"

"Now that everyone looks at him as he were a plague carrier," I said.

"Quite," said Murtagh. "But he will be an excellent secretary for you, and you certainly need not fear that I have sent *him* to do your job."

"Murtagh," said I, "that was unkind."

"I have my moments," said the Dragon Duke.

Julian, when he came to see me, was indeed excited, nearly incoherent with assurances that he would not fail me and he would work extremely hard and he was already practicing to improve his penmanship.

"Good," said I, "for I have a letter I wish you to write."

"A letter? Me? Now?"

"Unless you need more time to practice."

"Oh no," he said. "I'd be happy to . . . Who are you writing to?"

"Have you pen and ink?"

"Just a moment!" he said, and there was a tremendous flurry, as I had asked him to build an engine to take us to the moon. "All right. I'm ready."

"Good," said I and rose to pace. "To Richard Pallister of Grimglass from Kay Brightmore. Although we do not know each other . . ."

## Felix

I had my magic back, and the feeling was both like joy and like the cessation of pain. In its profound relief, I could admit that Mildmay was right. I had let the Circle cast the choke-binding on me, and perhaps it was because I deserved the punishment and perhaps it was because of what had been done to me in Bernatha. Either way, now I understood why Mildmay had been so angry with me, why he had fought so hard against something I had considered both right and inevitable.

It was another thing I wouldn't do again; eventually, I might be able to tell him that.

In the meantime, it was a pity the Duke of Murtagh was so carefully avoiding being alone with me.

And there were other considerations. I owed it to Kay to talk to him before I accepted the position of Virtuer of Grimglass, even if I didn't know what I'd do if I didn't take it. I left Mildmay with Corbie and Julian because I didn't particularly want witnesses for this, even a witness who already knew what I was going to say.

Howrack had no hotels, so Kay and the duke were established in the reeve's house, and the reeve's nervous wife led me to the front parlor, where Kay was sitting by the front window, enjoying the sun as unabashedly as a cat.

"It's me," I said. "Felix."

"I am not surprised," said Kay.

"I thought, before I accepted the position, I should give you the chance to . . . I should let you know what you're getting. And if you say no, I won't take it. You shouldn't have to be saddled with me."

"*Saddled* with you?" he said, his eyebrows going up. "How would that be?"

"I, um. I'm developing quite a reputation in Corambis, and I'm afraid it's well earned."

"A reputation?"

"As a monster." Which wasn't what I'd meant to say, but once the words were spoken, I couldn't deny their truth.

Kay considered for a long moment; my heart was beating painfully in my chest.

"Do you consider yourself a monster, Felix Harrowgate?"

"I . . ." I took a deep, shuddering breath. "Yes."

"Why?"

So I told him. I told him everything, starting with the fantôme and the Clock of Eclipses, continuing to Malkar and the Virtu, to Mildmay and the obligation d'âme, and ending, finally, with Gideon and Isaac Garamond. Somewhere in the middle, the reeve's nervous wife brought lemonade; without it, my voice would probably have dried to a husk before I finished. And Kay listened; he listened as intently and patiently as Mildmay, and he did not interrupt.

"And you consider yourself a monster because of this?"

"Yes. Because of what I did."

"To the man who murdered your lover." His voice seemed to catch a little in the middle of the phrase, but I might have imagined it.

"And to my brother."

"Why did you do it?"

"What?"

He sighed impatiently. "Sit. Here." And when I sat, he reached and found my hands, and held them firmly, his gaze as steady on my face as if he could see me. "When you sent your brother into danger against his will, why did you do it?"

Hindsight made the reasons all cruelly specious. "I thought I could . . . I wanted to make Malkar show himself, so I could . . ." I swallowed hard. "So I could kill him."

"And the other? The man who murdered your lover?"

"I wanted to hurt him," I said flatly. "That's all I wanted."

"And when Malkar hurt you, when he raped you with his magic, what did he hope to accomplish?" Kay's hands on mine were like anchors, and I needed them, for I felt otherwise as if I might simply fly apart.

"He broke the Virtu," I said. "I told you what—"

"Exactly," Kay said. "When he hurt you, he did it for gain. When you . . . The things you did, you did from your own hurt. Not to profit from them."

"And that makes it *better*?"

"Does not make it worse. And if what you have done is wrong, surely is better to have done it for the right reasons."

"Revenge is a right reason?"

"Love," he said. "Grief. Rage. They are better reasons than envy and malice and pleasure in destruction."

"You describe Malkar as accurately as if you knew him."

"I listened to you," he said and let me go. "You knew him very well."

"When you live with a beast, you learn its habits. You have to."

"A beast, you call him?"

"He was brutal. And . . . he was very very old. Brinvillier Strych must have been more than a hundred years old when I finally killed him, and I don't know—no one knows—if Brinvillier Strych was the name he was born with, or if that, too, was a name he chose and assumed after some other name wore out. He was not Mélusinien, you see."

"Are sure?"

"Oh yes. If he had been in Mélusine all along, there would be stories, as there are stories about Brinvillier Strych."

"You think him older than the name Strych, then."

"'Think' may be too strong a word. I *believe* him to be older because it explains so much about him."

"How so?"

"How bored he seemed sometimes. Power interested him. Pain interested him. Nothing else seemed to. He wasn't interested in magic for its own sake, and he's the only wizard I've ever met who wasn't. Conversely, though, he knew a *tremendous* amount, especially for someone who wasn't particularly interested. And . . . Mildmay said once he was like an evil wizard in a story, and it's probably the truest thing anyone's ever said about him. Because he was. He was more like an evil wizard in a story than he was like a real person, and I think it's because he had been a blood-wizard for so long, and because he used blood-wizardry to extend his life. Considering the stories told about her, I suspect his pupil Vey Coruscant was starting to go the same way."

"You mean he traded his humanity for his magic?"

"No. That would almost be forgivable. Honestly, I think all wizards do that to a certain extent."

"Then what?"

"Blood-wizardry is based on pain—on human blood, and not that of the caster. So Malkar chose to extend his life by those means, and he extended his life so that he could continue his practice of blood-wizardry. He traded his humanity, very broadly speaking, for the opportunity to continue hurting people for power."

"Had not much humanity to begin with, then."

"Maybe not."

"Did you love him?" he said, very gently.

"Loved him, hated him, feared him, worshipped him. And then, of course, I killed him."

Kay seemed to consider me, although I knew it was an illusion. "You say that as if killing him should free you from your love and fear."

"Shouldn't it?" But there was no conviction in my voice.

"Why would it?" Kay said. "My father has been dead these twenty indictions, and I love him still. And resent him still for the love he would not show me. Killing Malkar freed you from *him*, right enough, but you cannot kill your own monsters by killing another man."

"Oh," I said—stupidly, because of course I knew that.

"You are not a monster like your master, whatever else you may be." He reached out, laying one blunt hand on my chest. "Your heart is not made of gears."

"Like clockwork?" I asked, trying to follow the logic of his imagery.

He leaned back again. "Is an old story about the Automaton of Corybant. It was a magician who made himself a heart of gears, and then a body to go around it, and then, as he had forgotten love, he destroyed that which he had loved the most." The sunlight made his eyes very clear. "You have not forgotten love."

"No," I said, almost inaudibly.

"Moreover, I have no right to judge you. I am as much a monster as you are."

"You . . . What?"

"Know you how many men I've killed?"

"You were a soldier."

"And that serves as excuse and exculpation all in one?" His tone was sardonic, and I flinched a little. "The Corambins call me a beast and a butcher, and I have earned those titles seven times over. *My* heart, I fear, is more gears than flesh."

I started to protest, but he cut me off. "We are both monsters, Felix. But I would not slay you, and you, I think, would not slay me, either."

"No," I agreed, feeling something knotted in my chest relax. "I would not."

"And as your brother is as much a monster as I, or as you, then I think we may be fairly said to suit."

"My brother? You've—"

"We have traded tales of monsters," he said. "Felix. I admire your bravery, and I appreciate your honesty, but your concerns are groundless." He tilted his head, seeming to appraise me. "Will you come to my wedding?"

"Of course," I said, and he finally smiled.

---

The wedding of Vanessa Carey Pallister and Kay Brightmore was held at Our Lady of Mirrors, the largest and most beautiful cathedral in all Corambis—or so Julian Carey earnestly assured me. Mildmay and Corbie and I all dressed up to the occasion. I slicked my hair back, and as I was straightening my tie in our crooked mirror, taking a childlike delight in illuminating my efforts with my witchlights, Mildmay came in and put an oilskin package down on the table in front of me. It clicked sharply.

"What in the world?" I said.

He caught my gaze and held it. "Your rings," he said, slowly and as distinctly as was possible for him.

"My . . ."

"Your rings that I've carried all the way from Mélusine. They're *yours*. And you're a virtuer now, and you ain't in disgrace, and will you please put them on?"

I looked at him. He was going red. "You miss them."

"Fuck me sideways," he muttered. "Yeah, I miss them, okay? You don't look right without 'em. And"—a sharp flick of eyes green as sin—"I wanna see everybody's eyes bug out."

"You are an evil, evil man, Mildmay Foxe," I said, which pleased him. "Well, all right." I opened the package. Ten massive rings, gold and garnet, strung together on a narrow gold chain. After a moment's puzzlement, I recognized the delicate flower-shaped links of the chain and had to blink hard. It was Shannon's, the only thing he had of his mother's. He never wore it; as far as I knew, he'd never shown it to anyone but me.

I unfastened it, drew it through the rings. Mildmay raised his eyebrows at me.

"It belonged to Gloria Aestia," I said. "Shannon . . ."

"He understood," Mildmay said.

"Yes." I slid the chain into my inner waistcoat pocket, where it would be safe. And then, one by one, I put on my rings. I had missed the weight of them without even knowing, half the time, what it was I missed, and they blazed across my hands like fire. I raised my hands, backs outward, and looked at the effect in the mirror against my sober, dark, Corambin suit.

"Yeah," said Mildmay, and when I glanced at him, he shrugged. "A peacock ain't a peacock without the feathers."

"Oh shut up," I said, but I was grinning too hard even to pretend I meant it.

---

In the carriage—provided by the Duke of Murtagh, naturally—Mildmay watched the streets of Esmer, and Corbie fidgeted with the drape of her skirt, the cuffs of her coat. Her hands kept moving toward her elaborately braided hair and then jerking back. Finally, I said, "Corbie. Spit it out already."

She jumped as if I'd stuck a pin in her. "Spit what out?"

"Whatever it is that's bothering you." Mildmay gave me a look, but I shook my head. I was fairly sure this was my problem to deal with.

"Oh. Well"—she jerked her hands back down to her lap again—"I know I pestered you and pestered you to be my teacher, and I know I said I'd do anything if I didn't have to deal with the Women's College, and that's *true*, and it's not like I can't—"

"Corbie."

"Right. Shut up. Fuck, I hate this." She made a noise that was half sigh and half laugh, and then very visibly braced herself to meet my eyes. "I don't want to go to Grimglass."

"You don't have to," I said.

"I want to be a virtuer," she said, the words bursting out as if she had been struggling to keep them unsaid for days. "I want to be a virtuer, and fuck the Women's College and what women can't do or shouldn't do and all the rest of it."

"Good for you," I said.

She gave me a wide-eyed, mistrustful look.

"We've had this discussion. There's no reason you can't become a virtuer, and I think you should make the Institution *eat* every single reason they think they have to stop you."

As she believed that I meant it, she began to smile. Then her face fell. "But you're my teacher. I shouldn't—"

"Oh, don't *start*," I said. "I promise you, my feelings aren't hurt. If you'd wanted to come, I would've been glad to keep teaching you, but this isn't a test of your loyalty, and you aren't betraying me."

"Even if I ask Hutch . . ."

"*Even* if you ask Hutch," I said firmly.

And Mildmay said, "Hey, I think we're here."

The wedding was lovely, if mostly incomprehensible. Vanessa Pallister would never be beautiful, but the obviously antique fashion of her wedding dress suited her and someone had persuaded her to wear her hair off her face. While it was not that she was elated or radiant or any of the other adjectives traditionally associated with brides, it was clear that a tremendous strain had been lifted from her, and she looked *pleased*, like a cat who has found a way into the creamery. Kay looked somber as ever, but he was not actually scowling.

After the wedding, when in Mélusine all the attendees returned to their own bedrooms to celebrate the marriage in the best and most private way, Corambins apparently threw a party. Murtagh had finagled St. Nath's Tower, which was magnificent with flowers and crystal. Mildmay stuck to my side like glue.

"Are you *trying* to make people think you're still under the binding-by-forms?"

"Hey, if it'll keep them from talking to me. Look alive, here comes the duke."

Murtagh looked very nearly as pleased as Vanessa, but I felt revenged, even if only slightly, by the double take he did at my rings. He recovered quickly, said smooth as silk, "Virtuer Harrowgate, there are some gentlemen who would be very pleased to meet you."

"Of course," I said. I followed him, being sure to smile brilliantly at anyone I noticed staring, and found that his "gentlemen" were two wizards and an annemer, all wearing sharply tailored uniforms in green and gold. The annemer was missing his right arm below the elbow, and I was not surprised when he was introduced as Captain Glew of the Convocate Navy, and his companions as Magician-Lieutenant Rastell and Second Magician-Lieutenant Edey.

From my exposure to the Bastion's methods—and results—I was inclined to be wary of wizards with military titles, but I quickly found that the Corambin navy was quite different from anything I'd encountered. While Rastell was clearly Edey's superior, there was nothing in Edey's bearing or occasional withering comment to suggest that he was being exploited and preyed upon in the way Kekropian wizards were.

The reminder of Gideon hurt, but not crushingly, and then Edey made a dry comment that made both Rastell and Glew roar with laughter, and I jerked myself back to the conversation.

They wanted to know about Mélusine, of course. I was glad to oblige, and all three of them pelted me with eager questions until I said in self-defense, "But what about Ygres? Surely it's every bit as exotic as Marathat?"

They stared at me as if the idea had never occurred to them. Glew and Rastell were both embarrassed enough to become incoherent. It was Edey who managed to say, "I'm afraid you've fallen afoul of our national infatuation with Cymellune."

"As has happened to me many times before," I said, smiling to take the sting out of it.

"You must curse the name of Agramant the Navigator," said Rastell.

"Sometimes," I said lightly.

"Oh, don't lay it on Agramant," said Edey. "The myths that have built up around him aren't his fault."

"Myths?" protested Captain Glew.

Edey startled, and I suspected Rastell had just kicked him. "Sorry, sir," said Edey. "I just don't see how Agramant could have ended up here, when the prevailing current is toward Ygres."

"And we've had this argument so many times I swear sometimes I *do* have it in my sleep," Rastell said. "Besides, I'm afraid most of my memories of Ygres are unpleasant rather than romantic. But truly, Virtuer, is your city as beautiful as Challoner says?"

"More so," I said promptly, and described the great cathedrals to them. Then Glew had a question about the Sim, and I was trying to explain the river's course to men who knew far more about water and its ways than I ever would, when Murtagh returned and bore me off to be introduced to someone else—a plethora of someone elses—until I began to wonder if the best cure for homesickness was to talk the thing to death. Mildmay continued to shadow me until I finally said, "Look, why don't you go talk to Kay? It's got to be more interesting than this."

"You sure?"

"I don't *actually* need a bodyguard," I said.

"The way them ladies are looking at you, I wouldn't count on it."

"Darling, please. I've dealt with worse than them. Go on."

He went, and I thought it was not coincidental that the next time Murtagh extracted me from a conversation, he said, "Let's take a turn in the gardens, shall we? The rose garden in particular is worth a look."

"All right," I said. I knew an excuse when I heard one.

The roses were beautiful, though, and I got a little distracted from Murtagh's agenda until he said, "Virtuer Harrowgate."

"You *could* call me Felix," I said, straightening from my inspection of a richly red rose named, according to the neat plaque in front of it, Glory of Cassander.

Murtagh actually blushed. "I, ah, I wanted to apologize."

"For what?" I said; I honestly couldn't think of anything.

"In Bernatha," he said.

"You want to apologize to a prostitute for hiring him?" I said blankly. "Shall I tell you how badly I needed the money?"

If anything, that disconcerted him further. "I shouldn't have . . ."

"Your Grace," I said, "please believe me when I say you have nothing to apologize for. You were . . ." And then I suddenly realized what this was about. "You were *nothing* like Edwin Beckett and his . . . his *cult*. You did nothing to me that I didn't agree to. Honestly, you did nothing to me that I didn't want. I *am* a martyr. A shadow." And this time, the admission didn't hurt; it was just the truth, like the rings on my fingers were the truth.

"I am glad," Murtagh said, staring fixedly at a yellow rose named Gartrett Aggas. I'd have to remember to get Corbie out here and show it to her. "I didn't want to think that . . ."

"No," I said firmly. Movement near the doors of the tower caught my eye. "I think your duchess is looking for you."

I saw the moment's painful conflict on his face—he loved her, although she was bitter and barren and although there was so much about himself he could not show her—and then he smoothed it away and said, "Thank you for your indulgence." And then he gave me a smile, a tarquin's smile. "Felix." And he strode off.

I returned to the party and this time searched determinedly until I found Kay. He was sitting in a corner, Mildmay beside him. They were, of course, not even talking to each other. I rolled my eyes and set to work. Within a few minutes—and with some judicious nudging—I had Kay involved with Edey and a nobleman whose name I'd forgotten, arguing amiably about whether the eastern or southern Perblanches had the higher peaks, with a good deal of ancillary discussion of waterfalls and caves and suchlike, leading the conversation eventually to the Usara.

Here the argument became rather less amiable, as Kay and the nobleman had radically differing views of the Usara and even more radically differing opinions over what ought to be done about them. Kay seemed to see them as honorable enemies. He'd fought them, from what he said, all his life, and what he wanted was for the far south of Caloxa and the far east of Corambis (he distinguished scrupulously between the two) to be properly defended. The nobleman thought that hostilities should be stopped and the Usara be given help.

"Help? They neither want nor need your help—nor will thank you for offering." Kay's tone was derisive and supremely confident; I couldn't even blame the nobleman for being offended, as he very clearly was.

I intervened, playing the Ignorant Foreigner card. "So who *are* the Usara, exactly? I know they live in the mountains, but—"

I was inundated with people trying to explain. The Usara were the elder people according to one informant, savages according to another. They lived in great halls beneath the Perblanches, or in squalid camps in "any cave they can drive the bears out of." They had their own language—"crude" said some, "ancient" said others—and their social system was a complete mystery to outsiders. "They're all up there marrying their sisters," one woman said with a comprehensive shudder.

"And why are you fighting them?" I said politely.

"Mineral rights," said Lieutenant Edey and looked immediately abashed.

"Pastureland," Kay said gloomily.

"We must secure the passes," said a choleric gentleman.

Kay sighed and actually leaned back in his chair. "The Usara don't harass travelers," he said, in the tones of a man who had said this so many times he was sick of the sound of his own voice. "The problem is the cattle raids. And slave raids."

"Slave raids?" I said, appalled.

"Oh, yes," Kay said. "Children between six and fourteen and any young woman who isn't visibly pregnant or nursing. We do not fight them for the joy of it."

"Where I come from," Edey said somberly, "they don't take slaves. They just kill the miners."

"Thieves," Kay said in explanation. "My great-grandfather hanged thieves, too."

"But the copper mines aren't stealing from the Usara," the choleric gentleman said.

"By our reckoning," Kay said. "By theirs, the wealth of the mountains belongs to the usar, the . . . We haven't a word that means anything similar. 'Descent' is close, but wrong." He added after a moment, "They work in copper. Quite magnificently."

"Greedy beggars," said the choleric gentleman.

"Yes," Kay said. "Of course, so are we."

I bit down on a crow of laughter as the group, after a stunned pause, exploded in protests and justifications. Kay refrained from smirking, but I could see his satisfaction, and he did not lose it even when Vanessa approached.

"Is time?" he said before she'd even spoken. Of course, I realized: the scent of her perfume was almost as good as being able to see her.

"I think it is," she said. He rose and took her arm. I didn't think they were more than friends, but at least they had that much.

"Felix," he said. "Mildmay. Will welcome you at Grimglass with great happiness. Now—and I ask it as a personal favor—if you would *not* participate in the traditional farewell to the newlywed couple . . ."

"What *is* the traditional farewell to the newlywed couple?" I asked Vanessa while Mildmay leaned over and said something in Kay's ear that actually made him laugh.

"A gauntlet of rose petals," she said. "It offends his dignity." Then she tugged on Kay's arm. "Come on, bonehead. Let's get it over with."

Mildmay and I didn't participate. But we did watch.

❧

One sunny Savato morning, a very few days before we started west for Grimglass, I took the rubies out of their hiding place beneath a floorboard in the closet, and walked to the Institution. The rubies were a lump of mikkary and unease in my pocket; I felt as if ruby bees were crawling very slowly up and down my spine.

The Experimental Nullity was housed in the basements of Venables Hall. As I started down the basement stairs, my magic was gone, as sudden as a snuffed candle. I stopped and clutched at the bannister—it wasn't that I hadn't believed Hutch about what the Nullity did, but I hadn't . . . Well, I didn't know what I *hadn't*, and I very nearly turned around, but then I realized I couldn't feel the rubies, either.

The basements were brick, high-vaulted, dry and clean and very well lit. There was a student, clearly on duty as a sort of porter, and when I asked, he blinked owlishly up from his books and told me that the Automaton had had to be put in the subbasements, it being too large for the Nullity's area of the basements. He pointed me at an iron hatch, standing open, and a ladder leading down into the darkness. "Hutch went down there an hour and a half ago, and I don't think he'll come up before dinnertime."

I wished, with painful acuity, to be able to call witchlights—the Nullity was an ugly reminder of the choke-binding—and started down.

Gripping the rungs of the ladder was difficult and uncomfortable, but I spoke firmly to myself about how much more uncomfortable falling would be and persevered. Ten rungs, twenty rungs, twenty-eight, thirty-five, forty-two, and just as I realized I'd fallen into the old childhood habit of counting by septads, I reached the bottom of the ladder and the positively miraculous light of a phalanx of lanterns, standing about the sprawled bulk of the Automaton like funeral candles and illuminating the brick vault of a tunnel similar to those of the fathom.

"Felix!" Hutch said cheerfully, looking up from where he was patiently cleaning some of the more delicate mechanisms of the Automaton. "That's right, you said you had something you wanted to talk about."

I had dredged up all my courage and mentioned it to him at the wedding reception, both of us half-drunk. "Um. Sort of a favor I wanted to ask, actually."

"Well, ask," he said, raising his eyebrows at me.

"The, um. The Nullity. It's working now, yes?"

"You know it is," he said, sitting back on his heels to regard me more attentively. "Whatever made this thing wake up, it can't happen again."

"Good," I said, realized I was wringing my hands nervously, and made myself quit. "I, um. I wondered if . . ."

"Lady love you," said Hutch, frowning. He straightened and came around the Automaton toward me. "You look like you're about to be sick. What is it?"

I took a step back, for if he touched me, I knew I'd bolt. Except of course that there was nowhere to bolt to. I had to say it. I took a deep breath, although I couldn't make my voice stay steady: "I wondered if I could put something down here."

"Well, certainly," Hutch said. "But why would you want to?"

My face went immediately burning red. "I, um . . ."

"You don't have to tell me," Hutch said quickly. He stepped back, palms raised. "It's all right."

"No, I should," I said. "I just . . ." And then a horrible thought struck me. "What about when you end the Nullity? What happens then?"

"Everything goes back to normal?" Hutch said slowly, as if he wasn't sure what he should say. "But we've no intention of closing the Nullity. Certainly not until we understand the Automaton. I've no desire to reenact the destruction of Corybant, thank you very much."

"But then it would be down here with them . . . Oh, I can't do this. It's just the Khloïdanikos all over again, and I can't—"

"Felix." Hutch caught my arm, and I jerked back. He was staring at me, his eyes—dark for a Corambin's—deeply worried. "I don't know what you're talking about, but whatever it is, it can't be as bad as . . . well, as bad as you look like it is. Tell me about it. Please?"

"I *can't*," I said. Had I thought I could be rid of Malkar? More fool, I. I would never be free of him. Killing him hadn't done it. The *katharsis* hadn't done it. Reflecting what he had done to me onto Isaac Garamond certainly hadn't done it. Trying to leave his rubies in the Khloïdanikos had made it worse, and now I was trying to make the same mistake again. The same stupid selfish mistake. "I'm sorry. I was stupid. I should just—" But my fingers skidded off the rung; I pounded the flat of my hand against the wall. "*Damn.*"

"It sounds to me," said Hutch, "like you need to tell *someone*. Have you talked to your brother?"

That was almost funny. "He knows," I said. "But it is a peculiarly thaumaturgical problem."

"Well, it must be, if it's something you want to put in the Nullity."

"It's these," I said, in a sudden savage access of fury. I pulled the wash-leather bag out of my pocket, spilled the rubies out across my palm.

"What are they?" said Hutch.

"Rubies," I said. "The rubies from the rings that were worn by my master Malkar Gennadion. And they . . ." There was no word for this, not in Ynge, not in all the Mirador's treatises about architectural thaumaturgy, certainly not in Grevillian thinking. "They're haunted."

"Haunted," said Hutch.

"Not literally," I said. "But the magic that was done with them has left a . . . call it a residue. Or a curse, if you like."

Hutch looked as if he would like nothing less.

"Poison?" I said. "Can you believe that something can be thaumaturgically poisonous?"

"I . . . I'm not sure," he said, and I saw his gaze slide to the Automaton. He felt some of its noirance, then, even though he didn't know what it was. "But I believe that you are serious about what you're trying to tell me. And, yes, you may put the rubies here."

"But—"

"We have documentation," Hutch said patiently. "Even if I'm not here when this nullity is closed—*if* this nullity is closed—it will be in the documentation that these rubies are to be put in another nullity, or kept separate from the Automaton, or whatever instructions you want to leave. And they'll be followed. I know you don't think much of our imaginations," and he smiled crookedly, "but I promise you, Corambins are very good at following instructions. And maybe by then, you will have figured out a better answer."

I poured the rubies back into their bag. "Are you sure?"

"Absolutely." He moved one lantern out of a niche in the wall. "Put them here." And when I hesitated, he said, "Felix. Whatever magic they have, poison or curse or whatever it is, I swear to you, it is completely inert down here. It's like . . . like trying to kindle a fire underwater. You *can't*."

"All right," I said. "All right." And I put the bag in the niche.

# Conclusion

## *Mildmay*

This is the best story I know about hocuses, and it's true.

Late in the summer, me and Felix went out to Grimglass. Instead of the train we took a boat called a paddle-steamer, and I got to say, the *Lilibet Sawyer* is the neatest fucking thing I've ever seen. It was slower than the train, but we weren't in no hurry.

We'd finally finished with d'Islay, and although I thought he was a fuckhead about a lot of things, I agreed with what he was really trying to say down at the bottom of it, that bravery wasn't about killing people or dying for a great cause or whatever it is the stories make it out to be. D'Islay said it was two things. One was doing what you knew was right, and the second was figuring out what "right" meant. Most of his book was about that, actually, about how you judged what was right and wrong and about facing yourself down when you'd done something that you'd thought was right but now you were kind of thinking was wrong. Or, Felix said, how you dealt with yourself when you'd done something you *knew* was wrong and whether you could ever honestly do something right after that. And I knew he was thinking about Isaac Garamond, but also about what he'd done to me. And I couldn't lift that off him, but I did finally tell him about Bartimus Cawley and the fuckload of wrong stuff I'd done in my life.

"How did you figure it out?" he said. We were standing at the rail of the *Lilibet Sawyer*, watching the long, slow Corambin countryside go by. It was kind of like Kekropia to look at, but greener. "How did you figure out it was wrong?"

"I dunno. How'd you figure out that what Malkar taught you was wrong?"

"I don't know," he said. "Sometimes I don't think I ever really did figure it out until he broke me in half and abandoned the pieces. I know I'm still a terrible person, but I'm better than I used to be."

"You ain't that bad," I said.

He gave me a sidelong look that called me a liar clear as daylight. Then he shrugged and looked back at the shore, where there was a herd of something-or-other watching the boat go by. "At least now I *care* that it's wrong. For a long time, I didn't."

"I did some awful things," I said. "I mean, really awful. Worse'n what you done."

"I think we should avoid turning that into a competition," he said, real dry.

"Yeah, well. But what I mean is, I figured out finally that it was something wrong with me."

"There's nothing wrong with you," he said, sharp like I'd insulted him.

"The fuck there ain't," I said. "I mean, I don't do it no more, but that ain't because I *can't*."

"You would have killed the virtuers for hurting me," he said. He was looking down at the Crawcour now, brown and fast and nothing like the Sim.

"Yeah," I said. "I would've. And I wouldn't've been sorry. I mean, I know it's wrong, killing people, and I ain't gonna do it, but that's because I worked it out. I ain't proud of what I was, but I ain't . . ."

"You don't feel guilty?" he said.

"Not the way I do about Ginevra."

"Ah," he said, and we watched the river for a while longer before he said, "But you don't want to be that anymore."

"No," I said. "I really don't."

"Good enough to get by on," he said, and grinned at me sidelong.

So we'd finished d'Islay, and Felix hadn't even really asked if I wanted to start another one. Now we were reading a book Miss Leverick had given me along with a letter to the President of the Society chapter in Whallan. This was a book about Corambin religion, and we were going kind of carefully, along of not being quite sure what we might run into. And Felix was reading three different books on Mulkist magic that Corbie'd dug out of the University library for him.

"You think she's gonna be okay?" I asked him on a different day. We were in a hillier part of Corambis now.

"I had very long discussions with both her and Hutch," Felix said. "I think Hutch wants her to succeed almost as badly as she does."

I remembered Virtuer Hutchence sitting on the Circle's table and grinning at me. "He said something—I think maybe they gave him a hard time about becoming a virtuer. So maybe he understands."

"Yes," Felix said. "I think he does. And anyway, you heard her. She doesn't want to live at Grimglass."

"Not even for you," I said and bumped him real soft.

He gave me a look. "I thought she'd be more upset at your leaving."

"Me?"

His eyebrows went up. "You mean you *weren't* sleeping with her?"

Which was what I got for needling him. "Once or twice," I said. "But it was just for fun. And, you know, I think she was only fucking me because she couldn't fuck you."

He went bright red, and I figured I won that round.

And I went and hung out with the enginists some, and they explained how the *Lilibet Sawyer* worked, and Felix flirted with the ship's captain, whose eyes had just about fallen out of his head when we came on board. And we stayed up too late at night, reading and talking with Felix's little green witchlights everywhere around the bed.

And when the countryside leveled out again, I saw something standing up like a spike on the horizon. "Look," I said to Felix and pointed. "You think that's Grimglass?"

He squinted, and if he couldn't make it out, he wasn't going to admit it. "Well, really, what else could it be?"

"D'you think it's gonna work out?" I said. "I mean, do you think you're gonna be happy?"

"I *hope*," he said, giving me a stern look, "that *we* will be happy. But I don't know. All we can do is try." And then he smiled at me, the real smile, the rarest one, and said, "But I'm glad we're trying together."

And all I could say back was "Yeah. Me, too."

# Acknowledgments

The writer of a four-book series inevitably accumulates more debts than she can count, but I want to say thank you especially to Jim Frenkel, who gave me some of the most valuable advice I've ever received, and to Jack Byrne, Anne Sowards, Judy York, Judith Lagerman, and everyone else involved in the arduous process of turning my airy nothing into an actual series of actual, and beautiful, books. Thank you all very much.

Thanks are also due to Allen Monette and Sarah Wishnevsky for bearing with me, and bearing me up, through some very ugly months of angst and fraughtness. And special shiny thanks to my friend Tisha Turk, who let me invade her house for a three-week DIY writer's retreat, without which this series might never have been finished at all.

And I couldn't have done it without Earl the Writing Frog.